THE RAGING FIRE

He had gripped her hand in his. In the half
light she could see his eyes on her and then
unexpectedly he had taken her in his arms.
What was meant as a light kiss became
something deeper and it proved to her without
a shadow of doubt that five years had not
killed the passion that had once existed
between them. It shook them both before he
released her, pressed her hands and was gone
quickly not trusting himself. She stood there
shaking, her hands pressed against the mouth
he had kissed. She had lived these five years
without love, devoting herself to her child, and
now was frightened at her hunger for it. Her
body had come tinglingly to life. She had a
mad desire to race after him, bring him back.
It made her realize she had been right. It would
be impossible for them to work side by side
and not yield to it. When he came back she
knew he would do his utmost to persuade her
and she wondered if she would be strong
enough to resist the pressure when the very
thought of it made her dizzy with longing ...

About the author

Constance Heaven is a well-known writer of historical novels, including THE HOUSE OF KURAGIN, THE ASTROV INHERITANCE, LORD OF RAVENSLEY, HEIR TO KURAGIN and CASTLE OF DOVES.

The Raging Fire

Constance Heaven

CORONET BOOKS
Hodder and Stoughton

Copyright © Constance Heaven
1987

First published in Great Britain
in 1987 by William Heinemann
Ltd.

Coronet edition 1989

Printed and bound in Great Britain
for Hodder and Stoughton
Paperbacks, a division of Hodder
and Stoughton Ltd., Mill Road,
Dunton Green, Sevenoaks, Kent
TN13 2YA (Editorial Office: 47
Bedford Square London WC1B
3DP) by Richard Clay Ltd.,
Bungay, Suffolk.

British Library C.I.P.

Heaven, Constance, *1911–*
   The raging fire.
   I. Title
   823'.914[F]
   ISBN 0-340-49744-0

FOR
EVE KELLY
with great affection

Oh Love, that fire and darkness should be mixt
Or to thy Triumphs so strange torments fixt!
Is't because thou thyself art blind, that we
Thy Martyrs must no more each other see?
Or tak'st thou pride to break us on the wheel,
And view old Chaos in the pains we feel?

Elegy XII: 'His Parting from Her',
John Donne

Part One

1

There were few people about in the quiet street off the Nevsky Prospect and those who passed buried their noses deep into their fur hoods and hurried home not sparing a thought for the two who hesitated, lit by the darting flame of the night watchman's brazier at the corner. A casual observer might have taken them disapprovingly for lovers, the boy's arm around the girl's neck, hers closely twined around his waist, except that every now and then as they walked slowly on she looked furtively behind her and the dark stain spreading ominously on the boy's jacket looked uncommonly like blood. He stumbled and she jerked him impatiently to his feet. The young face under the sheepskin cap shone greenish-white in the fitful light.

In February the snow in St Petersburg still lay thick on the pavements and shrouded the rooftops. For a few magical moments the fiery glow from the dying sun had tinged with pink the spire and crenellated walls of the dreaded Peter and Paul Prison turning it into the pinnacles of a fairytale castle, but now the light had faded. It was intensely cold, a freezing wind whipped around corners and grey shadows of mist rolled across the frozen waste of the Neva.

The couple had paused at last in front of a tall, well-kept apartment house and the girl scanned the list of names on the plate outside before she tentatively pushed the door. It swung open and she slipped through pulling her companion with her. She propped him against the wall and listened anxiously, finger on lips, but the housekeeper dozing in front of her wood-burning stove in the basement did not stir.

The boy's head had fallen forward on his chest as if all strength were spent. The girl shook him a little.

"Come," she whispered. "We are there now. In a moment you will be safe."

He made a strong effort to pull himself upright mumbling something and letting her lead him across the hall to the door of the ground floor apartment. She knocked very gently and waited. If the man she sought was not there or if he rejected her she did not know what she would do, all this time wasted, all this effort for nothing. She felt stifled suddenly remembering the danger that every passing second brought closer.

The door opened. She saw the tall figure outlined against the yellow lamplight but she could not distinguish the face.

"Dr Aylsham?" she breathed.

"Yes. What do you want?" was the brusque answer. "Who are you?"

"You must help us," she went on in an urgent whisper. "Please, please help us. He may die if you don't."

"I'm not a practising doctor . . ."

"I know. That's why I have come to you."

He still hesitated and then the boy settled the matter by giving a sighing gasp and lurching forward. The girl tried to hold him but he slipped through her hands and was caught and held by the tall Englishman. He helped him through the door guiding him firmly to the sofa. The boy fell back against the cushions, a little groan escaping through tightly shut lips. Simon Aylsham looked at him dispassionately for an instant, then turned to the girl.

"What happened to him?"

"It was at the demonstration this afternoon."

"I thought I heard the shots coming from somewhere near the Mikhailovsky Gardens. Whom were you trying to assassinate this time?" he said drily.

"No one," she answered fiercely. "It was not like that at all. It was just the students. A peaceful demonstration to show what we felt about the injustice. Three of us have been imprisoned simply because we had been distributing books from Europe, harmless books we had spent night after night copying out and then passing around among us. What is there wrong

2

in that? And because we didn't turn and run like cowards, they fired on us."

"And your friend was shot?"

"They were brutes. He was trying to protect me."

He watched her for a moment and she stared back at him seeing the tall figure, the thin features with the long nose and finely moulded mouth, the crisply curling brown hair and cool grey eyes beneath straight dark brows. Simon Aylsham was twenty-seven and carried himself well. There was power in the shoulders beneath the white ruffled shirt. She glanced around her. It was a man's room but handsomely furnished showing taste and wealth. The black evening coat lay across one chair and she felt suddenly nervous, aware of how little she really knew about him.

She said slowly, "I'm sorry . . . I've spoiled your evening . . ."

"Never mind that. It was not important." He frowned. "Haven't I seen you before?"

She raised her head. "You won't have noticed me. I am Galina Panova. I've been attending your lectures. That's why I came . . ."

"Because if you had gone to a Russian doctor, he would have had to report it to the police. Am I right?"

"Yes."

"How do you know I won't do just that?"

"Will you?" she caught her breath in sudden fear.

"No." He smiled grimly. "A sick man is a sick man whatever crime he may have committed. Were you being followed?"

"I don't think so. I hope I gave them the slip."

"So do I. However we'll cross that bridge when we come to it. First we had better take a look at our patient. I may need your help or are you one of those who faint at the sight of a little blood?"

She sighed with relief. "I'm not afraid."

"Good. Come, my friend."

He bent down and with a powerful heave lifted the boy in his arms and carried him into the adjoining room. In contrast to the sitting room it had a spartan simplicity with no more than bare necessities. As she turned back the coverlet on the bed, he put the boy down gently pushing a pillow under his head.

"Now let's look at the damage."

Together they stripped off the boy's outer garments so that his hurts could be examined. Simon Alysham might not be practising as a doctor in Petersburg but he had brought his instruments and drugs with him. He rolled up his shirt sleeves, opened the case and set to work.

There was a blow on the back of the head where the blood had congealed and matted the hair. Galina poured water into the handbasin and watched the strong capable hands cut and cleanse, fixing the gauze and lint before he turned to the bullet wound in the chest. The boy struggled to sit up and was thrust gently but firmly back against the pillow.

"Now lie still, my friend. I am going to hurt you but I promise I'll be as quick as I can."

Scraps of cloth had been driven into the wound. He regretted having no ether or chloroform. He was forced to probe deeply for the bullet and mercifully after a moment saw his patient succumb to the pain and was able to work swiftly and easily. He swabbed and cleansed while the girl stood silent beside him handing him what he asked for, almost as white as the boy but never flinching. When all was done and the bandages fixed, he felt the pulse, then picked up the blankets and wrapped them warmly around the patient.

Shivering a little she poured the bloodstained water into the slop pail.

"Will he live?" she whispered.

"Why not? He is young and healthy. Nothing vital is damaged. There could be a little fever of course." He poured fresh water into the basin to wash his hands. "You did well, Galina Panova."

"I would like to be a doctor one day."

"Would you indeed? That's an ambition that won't be easy to achieve."

"Nothing worthwhile is easy."

"You've found that out already, have you? Who is he? Your brother or your lover?"

"Neither."

"Who then? Come," he went on as she hesitated. "I must know his name if I am to help him."

"He is Prince Nicolai Malinsky," she said reluctantly.

"What!" She had taken him by surprise. He swung round, the towel in his hands. "He's the grandson of General

4

Malinsky, the hero of the Crimea, a pillar of the constitution?"

"Yes. You know him?"

"Very slightly. What the devil is *his* grandson doing playing at being a revolutionary?"

"He believes in our cause," she said stiffly, "just as you do, Dr Aylsham, or why should you give up your time to give us lectures in science and medicine when the authorities frown on them?"

"Why indeed?" He smiled. "I don't believe in causes, my dear. They create too much trouble and involve too many innocent people. I do it because I'm bored and it amuses me."

She flashed him a glance. "Even if it is dangerous?"

"That merely gives it added spice."

"I don't believe you."

"Then you should. Never trust to appearances. They can be very deceptive."

"You won't . . .?"

"Betray you and young Malinsky? Oh no," he said lightly. "Far be it from me to tangle with the police in Russia of all places!"

He studied her for a moment while he rolled down his shirtsleeves and replaced the gold cufflinks. It was an unusual face, not beautiful in any accepted sense and yet undeniably striking with its high cheekbones and large eyes that flashed sometimes green, sometimes tawny. The face of a saint, he thought, a Joan of Arc with a goodly touch of the devil. Nineteen or twenty he guessed, not his type, but attractive all the same and he wondered if that stern young mouth had ever softened and blossomed into passion. Then his doctor's eye observed how pale and taut she was.

He said quickly, "You had better come into the other room and sit down or I could well have two patients on my hands."

He put an arm around her shoulders feeling her tremble and then relax wearily against him. In the next room he put her on the sofa then poured a little water into a glass, dropped a powder into it, stirred it and put it into her hand.

"What is it?" she said doubtfully.

"I'm not drugging you. Drink it and try to relax. It will help to steady you. Then perhaps you had better tell me everything so that we can decide on the next step. He'll do well enough for the time being."

He picked up the decanter to pour brandy for himself when they heard the hammering on the door. Momentarily they froze.

"Merciful God, the *Okhrana*," she whispered. The dreaded secret police who hunted down ruthlessly all those who rebelled in however small a degree against the authority of the state. She started to her feet. "I had better go."

"No. It's too late for that." He listened for a moment and then came to a decision. "We must make it appear that we are spending the evening together. Do you understand? They have no cause to suspect me."

He slopped brandy carelessly into the glass so that the fumes spread through the room, undid the buttons of his shirt and ran his fingers through the thick brown hair. Nicolai called out something in a feeble voice and he went to the door of the bedroom.

"Listen to me, young man. If they do come in, you're drunk, very very drunk, remember that, but I'll head them off if I can."

He shut the door and turned back to the girl. She had grasped his meaning, had loosened the high neck of her blouse and pulled the pins from her hair so that it fell in a shining mantle of chestnut silk around her shoulders. He turned the lamp down so that the room was full of shadows and threw himself on the sofa. She pulled up a footstool, dropping down on it and leaning back against him. His arm went around her shoulders pulling the blouse aside, his fingers just touching the curve of her breast. They were only just in time. When the housekeeper knocked and opened the door, the policeman smelled the slopped brandy and saw with strong disapproval a young foreigner already half drunk amusing himself with a woman of the people who ought to know better.

Simon raised his head deliberately slurring his speech. "What the devil is the meaning of this? Who the hell are you?"

The policeman stood his ground. "We're hunting a terrorist who was seen to enter this street and may have taken refuge in one of these houses."

"Well, he didn't come here. We've not seen any little revolutionary, have we, darling, we had something better to do," and with a tipsy giggle he bent his head nuzzling into the silky hair.

The policeman scanned them from head to foot. "Never-theless," he persisted with painstaking zeal and obvious disgust, "I am afraid I must ask to see your papers."

"Oh lord, you Russians, how you love your bits of paper with stamps and signatures on them!" Lazily Simon got to his feet, hunted through the coat on the chair and threw a package on the table. "There you are, quite in order I assure you. Really if you're going to make a habit of this kind of a thing, I shall have a word with our embassy."

"Are you acquainted with the Ambassador?"

"I have close friends on his staff."

The officer examined the papers closely one by one and then put them down.

"You speak very good Russian for an Englishman."

"Is there any reason why I shouldn't?" said Simon insolently.

"None at all," said the man woodenly but he did not move, his eyes moving carefully around the room.

"Damnation!" exclaimed Simon with a burst of temper. "Have you taken root? Search the room if you wish. Perhaps he is hiding under the table or in the cupboard."

"I don't think that will be necessary," said the officer austerely. "Thank you for your co-operation."

Neither of them moved till they heard the retreating footsteps and the shutting of the front door. Then Simon crossed to the window.

"He's gone and his henchmen with him," he said and laughed, a carefree laugh as if it had been no more than a boyish escapade. "First round to us, I think," he went on and stretched out a hand to Galina pulling her to her feet. He waltzed her around the room, both of them laughing in relief, and then he kissed her hard on the lips, aware of the instant response, the softening of her mouth under his before she thrust him away from her.

"Don't do that."

"Don't you approve of kissing?" he said teasingly.

"This is serious," she said rebukingly, pushing back the heavy hair and rebuttoning the neck of her blouse. "It's not a game. It's bad enough that he took me for your mistress."

"It worked though, didn't it? Did anyone tell you what a good actress you are, Galina?"

She shot him a swift glance. "That has nothing to do with it."

"No, you're right," he said more soberly. "It's no laughing matter. I'd better take another look at our patient, then you and I will get down to discussing ways and means."

She followed him into the bedroom. The young man had struggled up in the bed, his face flushed.

"What has happened? What were you doing out there?" He gripped the hand of the girl who had come to the side of the bed, his eyes on the loosened hair and disordered dress. "What has he done to you?"

"Nothing. It's all right," she said soothingly. "The police have gone."

"I mustn't stay here any longer. I must go." He pushed back the blankets and tried to get up.

"You'll do nothing of the kind," said Simon firmly taking him by the shoulders. "You must lie back and keep quiet unless you want to undo all my good work."

"I don't trust you. I never wanted to come here."

"Now listen to me, Prince Malinsky . . ."

"You know who I am?"

"I know you for a hot-headed young fool who is not going to put me or Galina Panova into any more danger than you have done already – at least not if I can help it. Understand? So lie still and be quiet. They'll not come back so you're safe enough here for the present. The important thing is that you should rest and gain some strength. You've lost quite a fair amount of blood. Now I'm going to give you a drug which will help you to sleep. After that we shall see."

"I don't want it," said the boy rebelliously. "I won't take it."

"You will if I have to pour it down your throat," said Simon measuring the laudanum into a glass. He put an arm around Nicolai's shoulders and raised him up. "Now no nonsense please. You'll drink this at once."

The stronger will prevailed and after a short struggle the boy swallowed the draught, his eyes still on Galina as he lay back.

"You won't let him harm you."

"Now why on earth should I?" exclaimed the doctor in exasperation tucking the blankets around his reluctant patient. "Go to sleep, you young idiot. We'll talk in the morning." He stood up. "Come, Galina, we'll leave him to his dreams."

"Perhaps Niki is right," she whispered as he shepherded her out of the room. "He shouldn't stay here."

"And where do you propose to take him even supposing he could walk?" he said shutting the door behind them.

"I have a place of my own. It's not much but it's in a poor part of the city. He could hide there . . ."

"And die there too probably. Is that what you want?" asked Simon brusquely. "Don't you realize that with that chest wound he needs constant care and should not be moved for at least two or three days?"

"I had not thought of that."

"Why didn't you tell me that the boy is in love with you?" She looked quickly away. "Why do you say that?"

"My dear girl, it is obvious. Is that why you risked so much to save him?"

"No." She moved away from him impatiently. "Oh he only thinks he is in love with me. The truth is he's not really one of us. He believes that to be a revolutionary is to be a hero, that it's rushing into the forefront of the battle, waving a banner and shouting about an ideal Russia."

"And isn't it?"

She looked at him scornfully. "Of course it isn't. We want to teach people. We hold classes for peasants and factory workers. We want to educate them, help them to improve themselves, to understand, so that they will act spontaneously when the time comes and we break through."

"It sounds uphill work to me," he commented ironically. "Most people hate to be educated and have no desire to be forced to think, and I still don't understand why you took so much trouble for this foolish young princeling who sounds more of a liability than an asset."

"The village where I grew up is on his grandfather's estate," she said reluctantly. "I was once maid to his sister Nina. The General was kind to me. But for him I would never have reached the university."

"I see." Childhood memories are persistent. Perhaps a fair-haired Niki had once played kiss-in-the-ring with a merry little girl at village festivals. "Well, Galina," he went on, "I've been thinking. Leave him here for the time being. When he is fit to travel I'll see he goes back to his grandfather if I have to take him myself and concoct some tale to account for his hurts."

"He won't go."

"I'll make sure that he does. He needs a few months in the country till the hunt has died down. I'll read him the riot act."

She frowned. "I don't understand."

"Never mind. I can be very persuasive when I put my mind to it. You'd be surprised. Tell me your address and I'll contrive to let you know."

"You're being very kind."

"It's not kindness." He put out a hand and turned her face towards him. "You don't know very much about men, do you, Galina Panova?"

She jerked away. "I know enough."

He laughed. "Now you really had better go or who knows what may happen."

She picked up her heavy woollen shawl and wrapped it around her head and shoulders.

"You had better tell me where you live," he said as she moved to the door.

"I have a room on Vassilievsky Island but it is better if you don't come there. It's a poor place. They'd begin to ask questions about a gentleman like you, an Englishman."

He grinned. "I could always disguise myself."

"No," she said decisively. "I will see you at the university."

"Not for some weeks."

"That will be soon enough."

She slipped away from him down the passage and he followed after her.

"Wait – not so fast. I'll make sure the coast is clear. Those police busybodies could be keeping watch."

He looked cautiously up and down the street, dark and cold now with drifting snow. Then she had gone past him walking jauntily with head flung up, pride in every line of her.

He closed the door quietly and went back to his room. There was still a faint reek from the spilled brandy. With a gesture of distaste he replaced the stopper in the decanter and picked up the fallen cushions. Then he went into the bedroom. The drug had taken effect. The boy was sleeping uneasily, his face, pale and drawn, looked touchingly innocent and young.

He came back to the sitting room, picked up his black coat and then impatiently tossed it aside again. The night with friends he had promised himself had suddenly lost its charm. He knew only too well how it would finish up, the endless arguments, setting the world to rights with owlish solemnity, nobody could beat the Russians at baring their souls over innumerable glasses of vodka. He had outgrown that kind of thing years ago. So why indulge in it now?

Damn the girl! She had disturbed him, forced him to look at himself and dislike intensely what he saw. He had been like that once, with one shining aim before him to be the greatest surgeon in the world, better even than the man who had been his mentor and guide, the uncle he had admired more than anyone and whose last scalding words he could not entirely forget.

"Go if you must, boy, take the coward's way out but don't think you will escape yourself. You'll still have to live with the fact that a young woman died under your knife and until you come to terms with it, you'll never be of any use to man or beast."

He was right of course but then he didn't know everything. He didn't know the secret fear that haunted him – the dreadful moment when he had looked down at her on the operating table and had wanted her to die, the bitter anger that had welled up in him so that afterwards he had wondered – was it deliberate or wasn't it? Had his hands betrayed him? Had he murdered the thing he had loved so passionately or hadn't he?

For weeks and weeks afterwards he could not enter the operating theatre without those clever hands shaking and the sweat breaking out on his forehead, until at last he knew he could not trust himself, until the day he had feigned sudden sickness and let his colleague take over and after that in self-disgust he had quit. He had come away as far as he could to the Russia where he had spent two years of his boyhood, where no one knew him, where letters took weeks to reach him and realized that his uncle had spoken the truth. He had not escaped anything. You can spend nights with girls, you can drink yourself into a stupor, but it is still there when you crawl out of bed in the morning, you still have to face up to your own gnawing conscience.

He would have to do something about that fool of a boy in there. Years before he was born, his father had known General Malinksy as a young man in London. It would give him an excuse to introduce himself. He could keep the boy here until he was strong enough to face the drive into the country. He was aware as any intelligent person must be that there was considerable unrest even here in Petersburg in this year of 1904. Russia was like some enormous sluggish animal beginning

11

to stir after centuries of torpor but he had no wish to embroil himself in any of the political disturbances. It would simmer down as it nearly always did. He poured a glass of brandy and then left it untouched. Abruptly he crossed to his desk and took out a couple of unopened packets. His uncle had given him letters of introduction and still painstakingly sent him the latest medical and scientific papers. He stared at them for a long moment, then slit them open with the paper knife, went back to the armchair and settled down to read.

It was late by the time Galina stumbled up the stone stairs of the tall shabby lodging house in the dingy street. There was the usual dank smell of dirty rooms and faulty drainage coupled with the greasy reek of innumerable meals cooked on tiny stoves behind half-closed doors. Cold and hungry her stomach heaved against it. She climbed wearily to the top floor and was putting the key in the lock when the door opposite burst open and a man loomed up in the darkness.

"Is that you, Galina?"

She stiffened. "Who else would it be?"

"You're very late. Where have you been?"

"That's my business."

The tall thin young man came up behind her. He gripped her shoulder roughly swinging her round to face him.

"What happened to the boy?"

"He's safe enough."

"They didn't get him then?"

"No."

"That's a mercy. Damned fool! He would have wrecked us all."

"You've no right to say that. He was the one who was shot."

"You're too soft, Galina. I suppose you think you owe him something because of his grandfather. You don't, you know. It won't be long before it'll be we who will be calling the tune and then all those bastards will have to dance to our measure."

"Oh for God's sake, stop preaching at me. I've had enough for one day and I'm tired."

Angrily she pulled herself away from him, went into her room and slammed the door in his face, leaning back against it wearily. He hammered on it but she made no move and after a second heard the retreating footsteps and the shutting of his door. She sighed with relief.

Ever since Igor Livinov had joined their small group he had singled her out for his attentions and there was something about the long bony face, the shaved head, the blazing fanatical eyes, that frightened her. They all knew he had served a prison sentence and was intensely proud of it. Sometimes she wondered if his work in the medical department was only a blind and he was one of the agitators who all this past year had been infiltrating the student groups inflaming the youngsters to wild acts of riot and disturbance.

She shivered in the icy cold and then moved to light the lamp. The room was clean enough but very bare and formed a vivid contrast to the luxurious apartment she had just left. Was that why she had refused to give him her address? Was she ashamed that he should see how she lived? She had always been fiercely proud of her independence, scornful of those who hankered after trifles such as fine clothes and rich food, very sure of her own stern resolve to forge her way to the top unaided and without any kind of emotional entanglement. She was not like her mother – she was *not*! She had sworn that to herself long ago and yet . . .

She took out the loaf of black bread and then paused, knife in hand, staring in front of her, remembering unwillingly the moment when his fingers had touched her bare flesh, his laughter, the feel of his arms around her and his mouth hard on hers.

She cut through the bread savagely and pulled the cheese towards her. Simon Aylsham with his dandified air, his charm and his careless indifference to all that she thought of as important, was not for her, despite his brilliance in his own subject which had kept a class of students, men and women, hanging on his every word and held her enthralled for the last two months. One part of her rejected him utterly and all he stood for, and another part, a small unreliable part, was obstinately pleased at the tiny link that had been forged between them.

2

On that late afternoon in June, it was very warm and when Galina came into the bedroom and saw Nina seated at the dressing table in her white petticoats staring absorbedly into the mirror, a wave of mingled affection, exasperation and envy flooded through her as it had done so often before. She gazed around at what had once been so familiar and which she had firmly put behind her, the rich untidy room with the muslin curtains blowing in the light breeze, lacy underwear tossed across a chair, bronze slippers kicked carelessly aside, a satin dressing gown dropped to the floor where it had fallen from slim shoulders, gowns laid out on the embroidered bed cover ready for their owner to make her choice. Then Nina caught sight of the face in the mirror and swung around on the dressing stool with a squeal of surprise and pleasure.

"Galina! I had no idea! Where have you sprung from? How long are you staying? Is it for Grandfather's name day? You should have been here this morning. There was such a crowd all bringing him gifts. I thought you were in Petersburg studying hard and forgetting all about us. Niki says you're so much cleverer than he is and leave all the boys behind which makes them madly jealous." She lowered her voice to a dramatic whisper. "You know all about what happened to him, don't you?"

Galina laughed. "So many questions all at once! I'm here to see my mother and wish the General long life and happiness and I did happen to hear something about your brother."

"Oh Galina, you don't have to pretend with me. Niki told me everything though the English doctor who brought him back here spun some tale to my grandfather about an accident when they were practising at the shooting ranges."

"And did the General believe him?"

"I don't know. He said he did but Grandfather is clever at hiding what he really thinks. Father was absolutely furious.

He raged at Niki for wasting his time, but then he never wanted him to go to the university but into the Guards as he did as a young man and they are always at loggerheads over everything. Mamma cried all over him because he looked so thin and pale but it was you who really saved him, wasn't it?" she went on, all on one long breath.

"Well, it was in a way," admitted Galina and came to perch herself on the side of the bed shifting the silk and lace evening gowns out of the way.

"How I envy you! Nothing ever happens to me. It is all so dull down here. It must have been *thrilling*!"

"I wouldn't have called it exactly that, more terrifying," remarked Galina drily. "If we had been arrested, it could have meant prison, perhaps exile – for both of us."

"I know. That's what Niki told me," went on Nina more soberly, "and if that had happened Father would have suffered an apoplexy and poor Mamma would have died of shame." She glanced up at Galina slyly from under fringed lashes. "What made you decide to go to the English doctor for help?"

"I'd heard him lecture. The English are different. They believe in freedom of ideas. I thought he might be sympathetic towards our cause."

"And he was. I think that's *so* romantic," sighed the young girl, "especially when he's so handsome too."

"I don't see what that's got to do with it," objected Galina, "and he's not nearly as handsome as all those young men who were swarming around you when I was here last summer."

"Oh them! They're all so young, only boys really."

"They're older than you *and* very rich. I seem to remember you were violently in love with one of them – what was his name? Valentin, was it?"

"Valentin Skorsky – but that was over a year ago," said Nina loftily. "I'm different now. I've grown up." She picked up a comb and turned back to the mirror. "You know he's coming here today – the English doctor I mean – Grandfather quite took to him. He knew his father years and years ago in London and he has invited him to stay with us for as long as he wishes."

Galina had not expected it and her heart beat a little faster before she had time to discipline it. She had seen Simon only once since that first meeting. He had stopped her one day as she left the lecture hall and told her guardedly that Nicolai had made a good recovery and was safely back at the family home.

"There's to be dancing tonight and I've been trying to decide what to wear," went on Nina. "Come and help me choose. Do you remember what fun we used to have in the old days and I was only in the schoolroom then?"

And now she was grown up, nearly eighteen, and ravishingly pretty with her fair hair falling in clusters on the white neck and her large blue eyes. Galina had a vivid memory of the first day she had come to Dannskoye, a shy awkward twelve-year-old to act as maid to the ten-year-old Nina and unexpectedly they had become firm friends to the strong disapproval of the aristocratic Princess Malinskaya who had once been lady-in-waiting to the dowager Tsarina Maria Feodorovna and greatly preferred all servants to be kept in their place.

"What do you think?" went on Nina holding up an exquisite creation of cream silk draped with fine lace. "Will this do? Mamma had it made for me in the spring when I was presented to the Tsar or do you think it is too elaborate for a summer ball?"

"It's beautiful and you will look enchanting," said Galina loyally.

"I've just had an idea," said Nina impulsively. "Why don't you come and join us? Come to the terrace after we have supped."

"Nina, are you out of your senses? I can just see your Mamma's face when the daughter of one of her serfs comes waltzing into the ballroom."

"There are no serfs any longer and anyway you're now a young lady from Petersburg. Niki will be over the moon if you do," she added wickedly.

"Maybe but your Papa won't be – nor the General."

"They probably won't even notice. They'll be too busy playing cards and talking politics. Do come, Galina, it will be such a lark. I'll give you a dress if that is what is worrying you. We were always much of a size and there is one in a deep yellow. I've never worn it. It doesn't suit me, makes me look sallow, but it will look wonderful with your chestnut hair." She was rummaging in the wardrobe and pulled out a rich silk the colour of a golden harvest field and held it up against

16

Galina. "There you are. You look in the glass. It might have been made for you."

"No," she protested but Nina laughing pushed her towards the mirror and against her will she caught a glimpse of herself, cheeks a little flushed, hair loosened, the rich gold bringing a warm glow to the ivory cheeks. Then abruptly she thrust the gown away from her.

"No, I couldn't. It wouldn't be right. Your Mamma would be angry with you. I don't think she really approves of what the General has already done for me."

"It's *my* dress. I can do what I like with it," pouted Nina.

They stood for a moment, Galina shaking her head and Nina frowning at the rebuff to her generous gesture, when the door opened quietly and a girl stood there, small, plain, her mousy hair hanging around her face in two long plaits.

"What is it, Marta?" said Nina irritably. "Can't you knock before you come in?"

The girl's eyes roved around the room and settled on Galina before she said tonelessly, "The Princess wishes to see you before you go down to the drawing room to welcome the guests."

"Very well. Tell her I'll come in a few minutes."

She grimaced at the door as the girl shut it behind her.

"That's Marta, my new maid."

"Isn't she the daughter of the overseer at the hemp factory?"

"Yes, she is. Her mother died and she has younger brothers and sisters so Mamma took her into service, but I don't like her. She's a sneak and she spies on me."

"Oh Nina, that's nonsense surely."

"No, it isn't. She listens all the time. I've caught her at it more than once. Oh heavens," she exclaimed in sudden dismay, "just look at the time and I'm not nearly ready. Come and help me with my hair, will you? Mamma will be so cross if I keep her waiting."

It was a familiar cry and Galina obediently came to stand behind her twisting up the curls with deft fingers and putting in the little pearl-studded combs to the best effect. Then she held the cream gown for Nina to step into and hooked it around the narrow waist. When she was ready the young girl pirouetted around the room.

"How do I look?"

17

"Ravishing."

"Will *he* think so?"

"Who?"

"As if you didn't know!" she replied teasingly on her way to the door.

"No, I don't know and you've forgotten your gloves *and* your fan."

"Oh dear, I shall leave my head behind one of these days." Nina came back to take them and then turned at the door, her eyes alive with mischief. "Don't forget. On the terrace after supper." Then she was gone, the door slamming behind her.

Galina stood quite still for an instant, then just as she had done so many times before she began to pick up the fallen garments one by one, tidying them into drawers and cupboards or putting them ready for the laundress to collect. Last of all she took up the yellow dress and was about to hang it in the wardrobe when she abruptly changed her mind. She folded it neatly, put it over her arm and ran down the back stairs and through the kitchens calling a greeting to the cook and other servants on her way to the gardens.

She hurried across the stone-paved courtyard in case anyone should stop her and ask questions, not that she intended to do as Nina had suggested. The very idea was ridiculous – a village girl who had once been in service in the great house daring to show her face among the aristocratic guests decked out in one of her mistress's cast-offs – it was unheard of and yet the small rebellious devil that lurked within her was sorely tempted. She knew it was stupid, unworthy of the high aims she had set herself, but just for once how would it feel to be on equal terms with Nina, so pretty, so spoiled, whose every idle whim was gratified by indulgent parents?

The village lay at a considerable distance south of the great white house and all around her was the sweet scent of the grass newly cut to emerald velvet. She went through the flower garden and past the pond with its fountain and the small stone summer house where the family had taken tea that very afternoon. One of the footmen was clearing away the chairs and called out to her but she did not stop. At the edge of the formal gardens was what the children used to call the wilderness where Nina and Niki with the sons and daughters of neighbours had brought their dogs and played all kinds of games through the long hot summers, games in which as a privilege Galina was occasionally allowed to take part even if it was only to run errands. Afterwards the wilderness had become her refuge, a place where she could be alone when things went wrong.

She reached the copse of birch trees standing sentinel like slim silver wands and then she could see the blue onion dome of the tiny village church while beyond lay her mother's house, a little apart from the others, a little isolated. Still further off, far enough away to be safely concealed from the house, lay the ugly black buildings of the hemp factory set up fifty years before when the extravagance of the old General's grandfather had brought the family to the verge of ruin. She had been frightened of it as a child, frightened by the barrack-like living quarters and the wild ragged dirty urchins who stared and shouted at her in a lingo she did not understand.

"How many times have I told you not to go near there?" her mother had scolded when she ran home, white-faced and shocked. "They're none of them from these parts. Savages from some distant place only brought here to work the hemp. The factory is not for the likes of you."

She had seen far worse places now in parts of Petersburg and heard stories of others which filled her with indignant and helpless rage that such conditions should exist, but it was not of these things that she was thinking today.

Her mother's house was sturdily built and had two rooms instead of the usual one as well as a tiny loft where she had slept as a child. The small garden plot had been well dug and boasted green vegetables and even a flower or two and she wondered cynically what man in the village had been persuaded to work in it for the sake of a smile from the handsome Vera Panova who called herself a widow. When was it she had first realized who the men were who came and went usually by night, who pinched her cheek or gave her a sugar pig and a coloured egg at Easter and occasionally stole a sly kiss till slapped down by her mother?

She must have been nearly ten before she fully understood, when the taunts of the other children told her what she was, a bastard, a nobody, and she fiercely demanded which of all that raffish crew was her father. Her mother had only laughed.

"Only God knows the answer to that, my little pigeon,"

but all the same she did know, Galina was quite certain of that, and also that with it had come the privileges that she enjoyed.

She had tried to put it away from her, told herself she didn't care ever since the day the old General found her reading his granddaughter's school books and sharing her lessons. He had consulted Nina's English governess and then questioned her closely himself, telling her that one day he intended to start a medical clinic here in Dannskoye to serve the village and the factory and if she worked hard and passed her examinations in pharmacy, she could come back and play a part in it. It had seemed a breathlessly exciting dream then but now after the time at the university her outlook had widened. What was one small factory in the country compared with the vast ills that needed a revolution to right, or so Igor preached?

Her mother was sitting on a low stool leaning back against the wall enjoying the evening sunshine and for a moment Galina paused looking at her, handsome still though she was over forty, a scarlet handkerchief bound about her dark hair, an embroidered blouse and striped skirt showing off the fine figure. She had a lazy sensual grace that Galina both resented and secretly envied.

She opened her eyes as her daughter came towards her. "What have you got there?"

"Nothing important. Some old gown Nina no longer cares for. I wouldn't have taken it but she was so pressing. It might cut up into something."

Her mother leaned forward fingering the skirt. "That's pure silk, my girl, and new from the dressmaker. Hold it up, let me see it." Reluctantly Galina shook it out. "Mother of God, it's just your style and colour. What made the Princess so ready to part with it?"

"She is a madcap, always was. Told me I ought to put it on and join the dancing up at the house this evening."

"And why don't you?"

"Are you as crazy as she is? What kind of a fool would I look in front of all that grand company?"

"Think yourself a beauty, my girl, then others will believe it. The trouble with you is that you don't make enough of yourself. You don't seize the chances when they come to you and it's worse since you went off to the city. What's the use of all that book learning when you look like you do? Where do

20

you want to end up, eh? A dried up spinster like that English governess up at Dannskoye? That's no life for a woman, believe me."

"Maybe it's better than becoming a whore with a score of lovers," retorted Galina bitingly.

With one swift movement her mother had risen and slapped her daughter hard across the cheek.

"Shut your dirty mouth! I've lived as I chose and caused harm to no one least of all to you, you little fool."

Galina's hand flew to her face. For a moment she was tempted to retaliate and then let her hand drop. It was true in a way. Her mother was not liked but neither was she hated. The women might look at her askance but most of them were secretly envious. She knew too many useful things, how to keep a husband from straying, how to prevent too many babies coming when the harvest failed and starvation threatened. She had a lazy good nature and had sometimes proved a good friend in sickness or taken pity on a girl in distress whose lover had deserted her.

Somewhere beyond the village there was a sudden babble of voices and the sound of music. She knew what it was. It was St John's Eve, midsummer night. The country people still kept to the old ways and soon they would be lighting the bonfires and dancing around them.

"The fools down there will be keeping it up till dawn," said her mother. "Are you going to join them?"

"No."

"I suppose you think yourself too grand nowadays, is that it?"

"Not grand, just not a child any longer, that's all."

She brushed past her mother and climbed the rickety ladder to the upper floor, a mere shelf under the roof. It was maddening that on these rare visits to her home she lost all the self-confidence, all the independence she had painfully learned in the rough and tumble of student life and was once more the nameless village brat who had fought the other children like a wild cat when they called her filthy names, and who had afterwards engaged in a more deadly battle with her mother until she had obtained her freedom. Better to go away, she thought tossing the silk gown on the truckle bed, return to the stuffy room in the summer heat of Petersburg than endure this feeling of frustration.

She unbuttoned the high-necked blouse and slipped off the cotton skirt with the intention of dipping face and hands in the bowl of water she had fetched that morning and which stood on the low table under the tiny window. For an instant she stood in the plain white chemise and then with sudden resolution she picked up the yellow dress and stepped into it. She shivered as the smooth rich silk touched her skin. She was an inch or two taller than Nina and fuller breasted so that it fitted her snugly as she hooked the narrow wasit.

It was impossible to see more than a very small part of herself in the tiny mirror balanced beside the washbasin. She was bending down turning from side to side when she heard her mother call.

"What are you doing up there?" She was standing at the foot of the ladder. "Come on down, girl, and show yourself."

Common sense kept reminding her to do no such thing but something stronger and more primitive urged her on. She gathered up the full silken skirt, climbed slowly down and came to stand in the mellow gold of the evening light.

Her mother walked around her looking her over critically, adjusting the dress here and there so that the low-cut neck revealed the slim shoulders and the curve of the young breasts. Then she pulled the pins from her hair, ran a comb through it, swiftly plaited it and wound it into a coronet on the small shapely head while Galina let her do it. It was as if she had become a child again, standing obediently and a little breathless as she had done years ago when her mother had decked her out for some village festival.

"I'm not going up there," she said suddenly, defiantly, but her mother paid no heed. Instead she lifted the hem of the skirt and looked down at the bare feet thrust into the bark sandals worn by all the village girls during the summer.

"Certainly you're not, not in those shoes," and she went away to rummage in the carved wooden chest tucked away in a corner of the living room. She came back with a pair of black dancing pumps and a silk fringed shawl that must once have been cream but had turned parchment yellow with age.

"Where did those come from?" she asked wonderingly.

"They were a gift."

"From my father?"

Vera raised heavy slumbrous black eyes. "Maybe. From him or another what does it matter? Put them on."

They must have come from that hidden period in her mother's life about which Galina knew nothing except what others had told her. Vera Panova had been seventeen when she ran away from the village and it was five years before she returned heavily pregnant but apparently widowed and flaunting a gold band on her finger in which no one quite believed.

Galina hesitated, then slipped her feet into the fine kid. They were a little tight but fitted well enough.

"Just one more thing."

Her mother darted out into the garden and returned with a newly opened rose in a deep apricot with a blush of pink. She tucked it into the bosom of the dress so that Galina felt the cool damp and the thorns that pricked her bare flesh.

"Now off you go."

"I don't know which of us is the more crazy."

"Go on. Show yourself," she went on tauntingly. "You've talked often enough about the future when the peasant will be as good as his master. Let's see you prove it."

For a moment Galina stared deep into the inscrutable black pools of her mother's eyes, then with something of that inherited grace, she threw the silk shawl around her shoulders, turned her back on the village and walked through the birch trees, through the scented garden, past the sparkling water of the fountain until she could hear the violins and see the light streaming from the great windows that opened on to the stone terrace.

When Simon Aylsham came into the drawing room that evening, a little apologetically as he was later than he had intended, he had no notion that it was to prove so momentous and eventually change the whole course of his life. He had accepted the General's invitation lightheartedly. Now that summer was here it would be pleasant to escape from the city for a few days, give himself time to think, perhaps make an end of the aimless life he had been leading for the past year. Time had dulled his first passionate rejection and his hands itched to return to the work he knew best. He had already delivered some of the letters of introduction that his uncle had given him and had been received kindly if a little cautiously into high medical circles. What might come out of it he was not yet sure except that he was still reluctant to return to

England and take up the career on which he had so wilfully turned his back.

He had liked General Malinsky from the first. When he had brought Niki back and told his story of a shooting accident he was well aware that he was not believed. The lean white-haired man who still maintained an upright soldierly bearing though he had lost an arm at the Crimea listened to him gravely; but Simon guessed that he knew perfectly well what his grandson had been up to, but was also prepared to shield him from the wrath of his father until the boy had grown up and learned better sense.

Simon looked across to where Prince Paul Malinsky was talking with his wife beside him, both of them handsome still but stiffly self-righteous, convinced of their own importance and resolute against any change that might infringe upon their dignity or their place in society. Little wonder that brother and sister were in active rebellion against their parents and worshipped their grandfather.

They came hurrying across the room hand in hand to greet him and it struck him how alike they were with their fair hair and blue eyes and how very young, two beautiful children rushing headlong into life with a joy that took no heed of the pitfalls that lay ahead. It made him feel old, he thought ruefully, as he bowed over Nina's outstretched hand.

"You're late," she said reproachfully, "we thought you had forgotten us."

"How could I possibly forget when I've been dreaming for weeks of the pleasure of dancing with you?"

"You're teasing me, Dr Simon, you know perfectly well you've never given it one single thought."

"Am I then a liar?" he said in mock despair.

"Isn't that true of all men?"

"I deny it absolutely."

"Then you must prove it." She put her fingertips on his arm possessively. "I shall hold you to your promise. You must come and dance with me this very minute."

"It will be my greatest pleasure."

Niki said warningly, "Take care, sir. Nina has as many beaux as she has fingers on both hands so look out for squalls. You could be heading for trouble."

"Are you doubting my courage?"

"Depends on how straight you can shoot."

"Why? Am I likely to be called out?"

"They're not in the Guards for nothing."

"Niki, don't be such an idiot," said his sister crushingly putting an end to the banter.

Her brother laughed and they each took an arm drawing Simon with them into the drawing room and introducing him to their particular friends and to their cousin Sonia, a quiet dark-haired girl, almost completely eclipsed by the bubbling vivacious Nina but whose eyes, he noted, followed Niki wherever he went.

Presently when the musicians began to play again he swept Nina into a waltz to the fury of some half a dozen young men who eyed him with a strong sense of grievance and turned indignantly on Niki.

"Who the devil is this damned Englishman?" demanded Valentin Skorsky who liked to think himself prime favourite.

"A great deal above your touch, my dear fellow," he replied loftily, "one of my new acquaintances in Petersburg."

Later Simon seeking an opportunity to greet his host and hostess had a strong feeling that the invitation extended to him owed very little to his professional status but a great deal to his family connections. He was after all the Honourable Simon Aylsham and his father sat in the English House of Lords.

The Princess extended her hand to him graciously. "We expected you earlier," she said tapping him with her fan in playful rebuke. "Are the children looking after you?"

"Thank you. I have been made very welcome."

"We shall be sitting down to cards presently. Join us if you wish," boomed the Prince, "though I know how my little Nina loves to dance."

From one or two casual questions when he brought Niki back he had a faint suspicion that he was being carefully looked over as a possible son-in-law. It amused him but all the same he would need to be very careful if he didn't wish to become involved.

It was some time afterwards that he excused himself to his partner and walked through the long windows and out on to the terrace. He drew out one of the brown Russian cigarettes and was about to light it when he glimpsed the solitary figure sitting rather forlornly on the stone parapet. A beam of light lit up the face half turned away from him and he thought,

25

"By God, I was right. That girl's a beauty if she wants to be but what the devil is she doing here at this time and in that dress?" Then he threw away the cigarette and strolled towards her.

Galina started as she heard the footsteps and got hurriedly to her feet. She did not know how long she had been there but it must have been a considerable time, and she had grown more and more angry with herself. It was obvious that Nina had forgotten all about her impulsive gesture and the urgency that had carried her there, the fierce reaction to her mother's taunts, had died when she had reached the house and could see into the drawing room with its magnificent crystal chandeliers, the white and gold walls, the elegantly dressed men and women. If she had caught a glimpse of Niki, if she could have entered the room on his arm, it might have been different, she would have braved them all, but alone her courage had failed her.

Simon has reached her by now. "Galina, isn't it? This is a very unexpected pleasure." He captured her cold hand and raised it to his lips. She snatched it back from him.

"Don't do that please. There is no need. I'm just going."

"Not yet surely. The night is still young and you're looking far too lovely to waste it."

"Don't make pretty speeches. I know I shouldn't be here. It was nothing but a silly joke. It was Nina's idea. I'm wearing her dress and I'm playing the fool. The sooner I go home to where I belong the better."

He sensed the angry tears in her voice and caught at her arm as she brushed past him.

"Not until you have at least had one dance with me. That would be too unkind."

She swung round on him, eyes flashing. "Don't be sorry for me and don't pretend. Go back in there where you belong."

"Isn't that a mazurka they are playing?" he went on ignoring her. "I'm not very expert but I'll promise to do my best. Come now, you'll not desert me."

With a tiny sob of mingled laughter and tears she let him slip an arm around her waist and take the first tentative steps. Then driven by the rhythm of the lively music, she flung up her head and they danced up and down the terrace so intent on one another that neither of them noticed the slight figure with the long plaits who watched from the far end and then slipped purposefully into the house.

If it had not been for Niki nothing might have come of it. The music stopped and she looked up at Simon a little breathlessly.

"That was good of you. You've given me back my self-respect. Now I can go away and laugh at myself."

"Is it far? Shall I walk with you?"

She shook her head. "The lamps have been lit and I know the path well."

She picked up her shawl and would have gone if Niki had not come through the long window at that very moment, looking anxiously about him. He came to her at once seizing both her hands and drawing her into the light.

"I knew nothing about it. Nina has only just told me," he said impetuously. "How beautiful you look, Galina. You must come in with me. You must meet our friends."

"No, Niki, no, not now. It wouldn't be right."

She was trying to pull away from him when the Princess Malinskaya came through the door looking regally magnificent in her grey satin dress embroidered with pearls, diamonds glittering on her neck and in the piled hair.

She said sharply, "Come away from that wretched girl, Niki, and come here to me."

"No, Mamma."

"Go please, Niki, it will be best," whispered Galina.

He allowed her to withdraw her hands but still stayed defiantly where he was.

The Princess turned on Galina.

"Now girl, what do you mean by coming here and flaunting yourself in one of my daugher's gowns?"

"I gave it to her, Mamma, and it was I who asked her to come."

Nina had come to her mother's side and the Princess raised a quelling hand.

"Be silent, child. I will speak to you later. As for you, Galina, all this is no doubt due to the General's misguided generosity. I shall make sure he knows of this outrageous behaviour. You will go back at once to your mother's house and restore that dress tomorrow morning. Don't let me see you inside Dannskoye again, not now, not at any time."

"That's not fair," exclaimed Nina indignantly. "It was my fault and I know who has sneaked on me. It was Marta, wasn't it? She's a liar and she listens at doors. She's a hateful spy . . ."

"Control yourself, Nina. I've heard quite enough," interrupted her mother icily. "You will return to your guests immediately – now don't argue with me, I won't have it, do you hear? Niki, you will go with your sister – at once."

The boy would still have defied her if Galina had not given him a little push.

"Go, Niki, please, please go."

The Princess's eyes rested on Simon for a moment disapprovingly.

"Dr Aylsham may do as he pleases," she went on coldly, "but neither my husband nor myself would expect one of our guests to encourage a servant's impudence."

She turned away with a magnificent gesture shepherding brother and sister helplessly before her into the drawing room and the little crowd that had gathered at the windows opened to let her through, some shocked, some secretly smiling and all of them intensely curious.

"Phew! That's put me in my place!" said Simon humorously. "I've never felt so put down since my grandmother scolded me for bringing my dogs into her drawing room teaparty. Have I made it worse for you, Galina?"

"No, it was my fault," she said ruefully. "I've learned my lesson. If you try to leap a gulf and miss your footing, you've only yourself to blame."

She turned and walked quickly away from him and he followed after her, stirred to a quick sympathy. Although it was late it was not yet dark. The air was warm and scented. Lamps glowed here and there among the trees like golden fruit and the tiny sparkling gleam of fireflies flitting from bush to bush added to the magic of the pearly light.

When they reached the edge of the birch copse they could hear the shouts of laughter and the strident beat of the balalaikas strummed by unsteady hands. Simon had come up beside her.

He said curiously, "What is going on?"

"Don't you know? It's midsummer eve. It's always like this on the General's name day, an opportunity for the villagers to enjoy themselves."

"Shall we join them?"

She looked up at him, her face ivory pale in the half light. "Why not? It's where I belong, isn't it?"

He touched her cheek with one long finger. "You belong to

yourself, Galina, remember that. Now come on. I'm curious to take a look."

He drew her arm through his and they walked briskly to where they could see the flare of the bonfires. It was a large open clearing and there were a great number of men, women and even children, all in their finery, dancing, laughing and drinking. In the centre couples were lining up in front of one of the fires, a very special one it seemed, that every now and then burned with a blue flame as if some powder had been thrown on it. The air was thick with the smell of the burning wood and some sweet musky scent.

"What are they waiting for?" he whispered.

"In a moment they will be leaping across the fire. If they can clear it together and still remain hand in hand, then they are what they call hand-fasted and will be married before the year is out."

"And does it always work out like that?" he asked amused.

"More often than not. You don't leap the fire unless you are sure of what you want."

"I wonder how many centuries this goes back."

"Hundreds of years long before Christianity. The priest doesn't like it. That's why they wait until he has gone to his bed. You see it's magic, old country magic, which the church doesn't approve of or understand."

"And you? Do you believe in this magic?" he asked smiling down at her.

"No, of course not, but I have grown up with it."

Other people had begun to notice them by now, staring at Galina's borrowed finery and Simon's elegant black evening dress. Then the music took a new haunting rhythm and the couples began to leap, the shifting firelight flickering across their faces, some solemnly intent, some laughing, some landing still hand in hand, some falling apart to handclapping and jeering laughter.

Galina caught sight of her mother watching them and tried to nudge Simon away but she was too late. Vera had drawn near. She was looking at her challengingly.

"Well, daughter, are you going to take the leap into the future?"

"Don't be absurd. You know it's all nonsense."

She would have pulled Simon away but he was stubborn.

The flames, the eddying woodsmoke, gave the scene a touch

of eerie fantasy. So that was Galina's mother, eyes like black sloes under her gypsy red scarf, a handsome woman who knew her power and how to use it if he were any judge.

"Nonsense or not we'll take our chance," he said recklessly. "God forbid that I should spoil the fun by refusing to play my part."

Galina would still have drawn back but he had tight hold of her hand. They jumped together. For one terrifying moment she felt the heat and the flames leap up and engulf her seeming to seize upon her silken skirts, then they were safely over still hand in hand. Simon kissed her lightly on the lips and the watching crowd clapped their hands and stamped their feet.

The colour flamed into her cheeks. She felt as if they were all laughing at her, the village girl decked out in her mistress's cast-off gown. She pulled herself away and ran up the path out of the circle of light and Simon went after her.

"What's wrong? Are you angry with me? It's only a game."

"That's where you're wrong. They take it seriously."

"Rubbish. It is you who take things too seriously. Enjoy yourself, Galina, have a little fun."

"Lying together under the bushes or tumbling one another in the hayloft – is that what you mean by fun?" she said savagely.

"You know I don't," he replied quietly. "Stop fighting me and yourself."

"I'm sorry. I shouldn't have said that. I can't seem to stop making a fool of myself tonight. I think it's time I went home."

"And it's time I returned to the drawing room or Lord knows what they will be thinking," he said lightly.

They walked together in silence for a few minutes and when they reached the wooden house, she stopped turning to him.

"Goodnight, Dr Aylsham."

"Galina," he said reaching for her hand, "those studies you told me about. If you find them difficult, I have books, I would be very willing to help."

She paused looking at him uncertainly but tempted.

"I don't know . . ."

"I'm only staying here for a few days. Come and see me in Petersburg. We will talk about what is best for you."

"Perhaps. It is good of you but . . . I don't know . . . I don't know. I can't seem to think clearly tonight."

He pressed her hand, then impulsively kissed it. She drew it away quickly and ran into the house. He looked after her for a moment, wondering if he had done right or was behaving like a fool. Then he shrugged his shoulders and thoughtfully retraced his steps through the park.

When he reached the terrace the musicians were still playing, the couples were still circling the floor. He stood in the doorway bringing with him a breath of the night and the magic of the midsummer fires. When the music ended, Nina came dancing up to him.

"Where have you been all this time?"

"In another world."

"I don't understand."

"Never mind."

"Wasn't it dreadful about Galina?" she confessed in a whisper.

"Dreadful. You ought to be ashamed of yourself."

"Are you reproaching me?"

"Don't you think you deserve it?"

"Oh that's unjust. I meant well."

"People who mean well are usually the most dangerous," he went on sternly.

She glanced up at him, saw the smile that lurked about the firm mouth and felt thrillingly grown up and on the verge of some intriguing mystery.

"Too dangerous to dance with?"

"Maybe I'll risk it this time."

He slid an arm around the slender waist and took her other hand and as they glided on to the floor she leaned against him giving herself up to the heady joy of the dancing and the music.

The house was empty when Galina entered it. Her mother must have seen them leave together and said nothing. Heaven knows what she was thinking. She climbed wearily up the steep ladder and slowly stripped off the silk dress. She looked at it for a moment in all its rich magnificence, then took up a pair of scissors and fiercely hacked it into ribbons.

She bundled it together, dipped her face in the cool water and began to pack her few possessions in the old carpet bag. Early tomorrow morning before her mother was up she would leave the bundle at the servants' entrance and tramp the five miles to the railway station to take the first train into Petersburg.

It was not until she was lying on the hard bed staring sleeplessly into the warm stuffy darkness that she thought again of what Simon had said. Did he mean it or was it idle pity and was she going to take advantage of his offer? It would help her immeasurably, she was well aware of that, but all the same ... she could still smell the fire, still feel the tremor of fear when the flames shot up and the taste of Simon's quick kiss on her mouth. It was all foolish superstition of course, and yet somehow that small incident seemed to have done something, set a kind of seal on their relationship. Then she told herself angrily she was a fool even to imagine such a thing. It was no more than an evening's amusement to him, something to laugh over with his men friends when they next sat drinking together. She buried her hot face in the pillow. She would try not to think of it again, but the plain fact remained that he had opened a door and left the decision to her.

At five o'clock in the morning she got up and without disturbing her mother dressed quickly, took up the torn dress and the carpet bag and set out on her long walk still undecided.

3

Despite her late night Nina was awake early and scrambling out of bed before Marta brought her morning tea. She knew that Niki had arranged to ride before breakfast with the English doctor and was determined to go with them.

"You can put out my riding clothes and then go," she said more sharply than usual because the girl's sullen face made her feel a little ashamed of herself.

Before she had retired to bed she had been called to her mother's room and severely scolded for her irresponsible action and Marta's satisfied smirk when she came back to her own room had so enraged her that she lost her temper, calling her sneak and spy before slapping her hard across the cheek. It was not the kind of behaviour encouraged at Dannskoye and she knew that if her grandfather heard of it, he would be gravely displeased but she was not going to apologize, not to that hateful girl, not for anything in the world. She stared fixedly into the mirror while Marta moved around the room and waited until she had gone before she started to dress. She was gathering the fair hair into a net under the small tricorne hat when Marta came back again.

"This was left for you at the servants' entrance, Princess," she said contemptuously and dropped the torn yellow dress in front of her. "That girl brought it."

"Very well, leave it," said Nina coldly taking care not to look at it until Marta had gone and then receiving a shock.

There was something disturbing about the anger that had hacked the expensive silk into jagged pieces. She looked at it uncertainly, then picked it up and ran along the passsage and up the stairs to the next floor where she knocked impatiently at a door and then burst in without waiting for any reply.

"Really, child, do you have to come rushing in like a hurricane at this hour of the morning," said her governess mildly. "It's not at all good for my nerves."

"I don't believe you have any," retorted Nina. "I wanted to ask you what I should do about this," and she spread out on the bed the ripped yellow silk gown.

"Oh dear," said Miss Hutton gravely, "oh dear, I see what you mean. What a pity, it was a lovely gown too, but we really mustn't let your mother see it, must we?"

"That's what I thought. It will make her even more angry and – and she might try to stop Grandfather paying for Galina in Petersburg and that would make me feel *terrible*."

"And so it ought," said her governess sternly. "Leave it with me. I'll dispose of it somehow but you know, Nina, it was really very thoughtless of you to do what you did."

"Oh don't you start. Mamma went on and on and on and it was only a joke. I never thought Galina would really do it."

"That's what surprised me," said Miss Hutton thoughtfully. "She is such a sensible girl as a rule, but then I suppose we all indulge in an impossible dream now and then."

"It was horrible out there on the terrace, I felt so guilty but the English doctor went off with her and was gone for ages so perhaps he consoled her a little," remarked Nina with an airiness that did not quite deceive her governess.

"Do I detect a note of jealousy?"

"No, of course not, don't be silly. Why on earth should I be jealous?"

"Why indeed? Only I did happen to notice how many times you danced with him last night and I wasn't the only one."

"Well, he *is* a guest," she said defensively, "and Niki's friend."

"And what about all those other young men who spend their time mooning after you?"

"Oh they don't mean anything. I seem to have known them since they were babies," she said scornfully. She bent to look in the mirror pushing in a straying curl. "You know Niki is in love with Galina, don't you?"

"I've guessed at it," said her governess crisply, "and I never heard of anything so foolish. I hope you don't encourage him."

"Why is it so foolish?"

"My dear child, you know perfectly well that she is not at all the kind of wife your father would wish for his only son, so for heaven's sake be sensible about it."

"Why should Niki listen to me?"

"Don't put on those airs with me. You're very close, the pair of you, and I don't like to see Sonia so unhappy."

"Oh Sonia makes me angry. She doesn't even *try*, she just moons after him like a sick puppy. You won't forget about the dress, will you? I must fly or the others won't wait for me."

"Take care now. Don't go losing your heart to the young Englishman."

"You don't have to worry about me. I'm not Sonia." She bestowed a hasty kiss on her governess's cheek. "You really are a darling. I shall miss you terribly when you leave us in the autumn."

"And I shall miss you too," sighed Miss Hutton as the door slammed behind her headstrong volatile charge. "More than I would ever have believed possible."

Miss Emily Hutton, affectionately known as Missy, had come to Dannskoye when Nina was six and though she had grown to love the child dearly she had few illusions about her. Nina had grown into a lovely young woman with an elusive fragile charm that already threatened to send young men crazy about her but she was also as changeable as a weathercock, given to wild excitements and sudden passions that could end in equally frantic tears and despairs.

34

Miss Hutton was of the opinion that she would have benefited from a spell in boarding school, at the Smolny Convent perhaps where a stern regime endeavoured to teach the daughters of the aristocracy how to become responsible wives and mothers, but the General who idolized his granddaughter refused to allow it and at Dannskoye his word was still law. So Nina, spoiled and indulged, was educated at home, and it was left to Missy to find the right answer when, at eleven, she climbed out of her bedroom window and ran away, to escape well deserved punishment, and, at fourteen, fell in love with her French singing master and went on hunger strike after he was summarily dismissed.

Miss Hutton shook her head over the ripped silk. It was she who had been principally responsible for the General's interest in Galina. Struck with the girl's intelligence and filled with the typical English zeal for self-improvement, she had drawn his attention to the waste of what was potentially good material. Now she felt attacked with sudden doubt as to whether she had done right.

She stood in thought for a minute or two, then folded the dress into a tight bundle, wrapped it in a large sheet of paper and took it down to the stableyard. Vassily, the head coachman, was a grave middle-aged man who had come to the rescue once or twice before. He nodded discreetly, promising to make sure it was destroyed in the furnace that heated the water and no one any the wiser.

She stood looking around her before returning to the house. It was early still but the yard was filled with bustle, fresh straw being laid down, boys washing the carriages and polishing the brass till it shone like gold. Horses were being led out for exercise, carriage horses, riding horses, all housed in stables far better built and a great deal larger than the huts provided for the farm workers and the black crowded barracks where the factory hands lived and bred and died.

It reminded her of her youth in her father's vicarage in Devon. How she had envied the young ladies up at the manor house, how she had longed to be riding out with them when they trotted past the garden gate on their splendid horses! She had never achieved that dream and now after forty years in other people's rich houses she had no desire to return to that quiet country village. Her father was dead, her mother living in modest poverty, her brother a retired naval lieutenant who had never quite achieved the success he had hoped. In the autumn she would retire to a tiny flat in Petersburg. With her savings, a small pension and the occasional teaching of a backward pupil, she had no doubt she would be able to live very comfortably. Russia, that vast country that had once seemed so terrifying to a shy girl of twenty who knew not a word of the language and only spoke schoolgirl French, had in some strange way become home and the youngsters she had taught, some of them married now with babies of their own, had become dearer than her own family.

She picked her way very carefully in her sensible shoes through the straw and muck of the stableyard and hoped that Nina was behaving herself. The child could be so very impulsive. It would have been easier if she had been more like Sonia, she sometimes thought. Sonia was a distant cousin whose parents had died in a smallpox epidemic when she was ten years old, an heiress too with large estates in her own right, which was perhaps why the Malinskys had not been sorry to bring her up with their own children. A quiet girl with more depth than was apparent on the surface, and, poor child, quite desperately in love with Niki who treated her with careless good nature and still thought of her as the shy girl who had trailed after Nina and himself.

She paused as she entered the house. Young people nowadays were very self-willed and all the good advice in the world would not stop them making foolish mistakes so why worry over them, but stupidly she still did, far too much. She sighed as she went upstairs.

Niki and Simon had been joined by Sonia and Valentin Skorsky who was a near neighbour. They were waiting impatiently in front of the house when Nina came running down the steps.

"You're late," said her brother crisply. "Why can't you be more like Sonia? We've been waiting for hours while you've been prinking in front of the mirror."

"I haven't been doing anything of the sort," she retorted and made a face at Sonia. "If you must know I had to arrange something important with Missy."

"Speaking for myself, I'd willingly wait a lifetime for such a charming result," said Valentin with a glance at her that sent the blood running up into her cheeks.

What's come over him, she thought, he's usually such a dull old stick. It must be the competition.

"Heavens, Val, where did *you* learn to turn a pretty compliment?" said Niki ironically. "If you're ready, Nina, let's go."

The two borzois and the English setter belonging to the General went bounding ahead. Valentin moved his horse beside Nina and Simon allowed them to ride ahead, bringing up the rear as they followed the path that wound through the park. It was still deliciously cool and fresh though the sun was breaking through an early morning mist. Very soon they had left the gardens behind and were making their way through the birch forest where the pale trees gleamed like silvery ghosts hung with fantastic loops of glittering spiders' webs. The air smelled sweetly of the rich black earth and the green moss under the horses' hooves. This was where the children came to pick wild strawberries and later gather baskets of early mushrooms. Then they emerged into the open fields where men were already harvesting the wheat and called a respectful greeting to Niki.

Something about the immensity of Russia stretching on either side of him to a limitless horizon with no other house in sight reminded Simon of his home on the Fens, the broad expanse of the marshes where as a boy his father had taught him to shoot wild duck with the salty smell of the sea wind icy cold on his face.

He was roused from his thoughts by Nina who, not a little piqued at his neglect of her, had hung back and was riding beside him.

"You're very silent," she said challengingly.

"Am I?"

"What are you thinking about?"

"What a mysterious country Russia is, so huge and magnificent, and yet this morning not so very unlike where I come from."

"Tell me about it."

"What is there to tell?"

"Is it like this?"

"Only because there too it is flat and you seem to look into distances and the light has a strange pearly glow as it does here in the dawn and the sun goes down in a splendour of gold and crimson. There are great dykes with giant windmills churning out floods of brown water. In the winter it is all ice and you can skate for miles. In the old days it used to be said that the people of the Fens were born with webbed feet like ducks."

Nina gurgled with laughter. "Go on. Tell me about your family."

"I have an elder brother who is married with three small daughters and who farms the land and a sister who is a little older than you."

"Will you ever go back there?"

"What a question! Perhaps. I don't know yet."

"Niki said you gave wonderful lectures at the university."

"You shouldn't believe everything your brother tells you."

"Are you a good doctor?"

"I used to think I was."

"And now?"

He smiled. "You ask too many questions."

"Do I? But then I like to *know* about people."

"You might be bitterly disappointed if you did."

She shook her head. "No, I wouldn't, not about you."

There was something about him that intrigued her. Beside him the boys with whom she had played childish games, who danced with her in their handsome uniforms and skin-tight breeches and who stole a chaste kiss whenever they could, seemed callow and without charm. She knew everything about them and was quickly bored, but the tall grave Englishman was different. She bestowed a Byronic glamour on him, a mysterious sadness, and thought with sudden panic – what is happening to me? Am I falling in love? Is this what it feels like? And was thrilled and a little frightened.

Niki was talking with Sonia pointing something out to her. Nina glanced from Valentin to the Englishman and was possessed by a devil of mischief. The bridle path stretched straight before them.

"I'll race you," she said suddenly, "both of you. Catch me if you can," and before they could protest she had whipped up her mare and shot ahead riding so dangerously fast that her hat flew off, the long fair hair streaming out behind her.

Both young men went after her, Simon with a very real fear that such madcap behaviour was bound to lead to disaster. He outdistanced Valentin but had still not reached her when he caught his breath and shouted a warning.

A pile of brushwood loomed up on the path ahead. Nina pulled the horse's head round but it took the jump and the girl flew from the saddle rolling over and over in the soft ploughed earth and then lay still.

Simon reined in, leaped from his horse and went on his knees beside her. She lay with closed eyes and looking down on the pale creamy face, the tumbled fair hair he was struck by the likeness to the girl he had once loved and lost so disastrously. He gathered her gently into his arms and she let herself lean against him feeling an inexplicable sweetness and warmth as he drew her closer and passed a hand lightly down her body.

"Are you hurt?"

She had won his interest, heard the anxiety in his voice and for an instant lay still enjoying her triumph.

"Nina, answer me. Are you in pain?"

She opened her eyes looking up at him with a hint of laughter. "Not in the least. Only a bruise or two."

"You imp! You're shamming," he exclaimed, half annoyed, half amused.

By this time Valentin had reached them followed by Niki with Sonia urging on her quiet old hack.

"You'll do that once too often," said Niki sharply. "Get up, Nina, you're making a show of yourself."

She sat up indignantly. "Don't be such a pig, Niki. I fell off, didn't I?"

"Oh you fell off all right. I must tell you, doctor, that Nina has been doing these circus tricks ever since she learned to ride. She taught herself to fall off without hurting herself and loves frightening everyone to death. One of these days I swear she'll break her neck."

"My heart was in my mouth but you rode magnificently. I was proud of you."

Valentin was holding out the hat she had lost and the admiration in his eyes gave her a little tremor of excitement on this thrilling morning. Then Simon was helping her to her feet, torn between a certain indignation at having been made a fool of and an unwilling respect for her reckless courage.

Sonia said rebukingly, "You shouldn't do that, Nina. I've told you over and over again. If your mother hears of it, she would be very angry and upset."

"Oh for goodness sake, Sonia. I know my Rusalka. She

would never let me down," and she put an arm around the horse's neck and kissed the soft nose. "You wouldn't, would you, darling?" She grinned up at her cousin. "I'm not an old slow coach like you."

"Thank goodness she is. One of you is quite enough to worry about," said Niki tartly. "Come on, do, and stop playing the heroine. It's time to turn back. I want my breakfast."

They were taking a different path riding a good deal more sedately when Simon saw some way off a cluster of black huts and buildings and asked curiously what they were.

"It's the hemp factory and the workers' living quarters," said Niki shortly. "We don't need to go through them."

He knew the wretched conditions in which the men and their families lived and worked. It was something he was powerless to change so he had shut his eyes to it but it made him feel both angry and ashamed.

As they drew a little nearer it was obvious that something was causing a commotion. They could see people milling about and hear a sound of shouting.

"Something must have happened," exclaimed Nina. "Shouldn't we go and find out what it is?"

It was the last thing he wanted especially with his English guest and Valentin would probably think him off his head if he interfered in some peasant dispute.

"No," he said decidedly, "it's not our concern."

"Yes, it is. They work for us and Grandfather says we should take an interest in the men and women we employ. I'm going to see for myself," and Nina spurred Rusalka forward cantering off in the direction of the factory.

"Oh Lord," said Niki resignedly, "I'll have to go after her or heaven knows what she'll get up to. Val, will you take Sonia back to Dannskoye?"

"No, I'm coming with you," she said firmly.

"Well, if you must, you must," he went on with an angry impatience, "but don't do anything silly. Yakov is the overseer and he runs the place in his own way. He doesn't like interference even from Father."

Simon already a little ahead saw that Nina had reined in and sat motionless and when he reached her, he realized why. A man was being brutally flogged. He had been stripped naked except for a rag around his loins and was tied to a wooden pillar. The lash was falling again and again on the

40

quivering flesh which slowly crimsoned. Nina, white as a sheet, was staring in a sick fascinated horror. She put a trembling hand up to her face.

"Oh God, I never thought . . . I never realized . . ."

Simon stretched out a hand and pulled her horse round.

"Don't look. Come away."

Then Niki had reached them. "Stay with Sonia," he said commandingly, "and keep away, both of you. I'm going to find out what has happened."

He spurred forward and Simon went after him. The crowd parted to let them through. The miserable victim had sagged against the whipping post and Simon drew a quick breath. In places the cruel lash had cut to the very bone.

"Stop!" Niki was yelling. "Do you want to kill him?"

He flung himself from his horse and boldly confronted the overseer.

Yakov was a big man, over six feet tall, towering above those around him but it was not just brute strength, judged Simon shrewdly. There was a powerful intelligence in the dark eyes under the bushy eyebrows.

"Wretches of his kind don't die so easily, your honour," he said calmly. "He stole from his comrades, not once but many times. It's a just punishment."

"I don't care what he has done. There are other ways," said Niki fiercely. "I understood that my father had forbidden flogging with the knout."

"His excellency leaves the running of the factory in my hands and trusts to my discretion in matters of this kind," went on Yakov with a touch of irony. "If you will forgive me for saying so, Nicolai Pavlovich, you are rarely here and have never shown a great deal of interest in those who work on your father's estates."

Niki flushed at the implied rebuke. "That may have been true once but not any longer. Have that man released and his hurts attended to."

Yakov shrugged his shoulders. "As your honour pleases."

He made a gesture and a man stepped forward. He cut the rope binding the hands and with a groan the unfortunate victim fell in a crumpled bloody heap.

"Take him to the hospital."

Another man came forward and callously threw a bucket of water over him. Then the two of them began to drag him to his feet. All Simon's instincts to help and heal rose in a strong rebellion.

"Take care. That back needs treatment and a doctor."

Yakov's dark eyes studied him from head to foot before he said sarcastically, "Your honour must be joking. A great man like Dr Antonov doesn't soil his hands with the likes of us."

He knew it was foolish. It was not his concern and the poor wretch would probably die in any case but he could not allow a fellow creature to suffer in agony if there was anything he could do to alleviate the pain. He slid from the saddle.

"I am a doctor and I have no fear of soiling my hands."

Niki said doubtfully, "Simon, I don't know whether it would be wise . . ."

"I'd not abandon a dog in that condition," he said brusquely. "It may not be much but I'll do what I can. Show me the way."

The long low hut to which they led him was some distance from the main barracks. He was not unaccustomed to tending sickness in conditions of poverty and squalor since he had often worked in the clinic run by his uncle in the worst slums of London's East End, but he had never encountered anything quite like this. The gloom in the windowless hut, the hot fetid air, the terrible stench, hit him like a blow and nearly drove him backwards, but only momentarily. He shut his mouth firmly against it and strode forward.

The men and women who had been watching the flogging crowded into the doorway after him staring curiously and nudging one another.

"Clear that lot out of here," he said abruptly to Yakov who had come in with him. "I only want one to assist me."

The overseer spoke a few harsh words and the peasants backed away from him, all except Niki staring down at the bloodstained back with a sick disgust that he tried hard to conceal.

"I'll help," he whispered.

"No, not you, Niki. Stay outside and for God's sake make sure the girls are kept away."

"Valentin has taken them back to the house."

"Good. Wait for me outside."

Ashamed but grateful for the respite he pushed his way out.

Simon's eyes had grown accustomed to the gloom by now and he could see that more than half the beds were occupied with patients, some lying flat as if already half dead, but others propped up on their elbows staring at the unexpected sight of the handsomely dressed stranger.

He stripped off his coat and rolled up his shirtsleeves before kneeling down beside the low truckle bed. He was considering how best to treat the mangled lacerated back without the help of the medicaments any competent surgery would have been able to provide when he realized that a woman had come and knelt on the other side. She was carrying a bowl of clean water and had brought with her a supply of white rags.

He looked up and to his surprise saw that it was Galina's mother.

"Do you work here?"

"Not regularly."

"But you have come prepared."

"I know him," she replied briefly. "Show me what I must do, doctor."

Together they worked over the injured man, bathing and cleansing, then applying some herbal ointment she had brought and laying clean linen lightly over the lacerations.

When they had finished, she said dispassionately, "Will he recover?"

"Perhaps. I wish I knew. If shock and loss of blood don't take their toll he has a chance, but I doubt if he will ever be the same man. He is going to need constant care."

"I'll come."

"Is he a relative of yours?"

"No, a friend, a good friend. Yakov lied. He is no thief."

Simon looked into the unfathomable black eyes and thought he is her lover perhaps and Yakov furiously jealous that another should enjoy what he has been denied, but it was not for him to question.

He rinsed his hands and wiped them on the rough towel she handed to him.

"Is Galina still with you?"

"She went back to the city very early this morning."

He frowned. "For what reason?"

"Need you ask, doctor?" said her mother ironically.

"I'm leaving here shortly myself but I'll come again before I go."

"I'll be here."

"Very well."

He picked up his coat and went out of the hut thankful to stand still for a moment and take deep breaths of the clean air. Niki was waiting for him.

"It was tremendously good of you but there was no need . . ."

"There was every need," he said, a flood of anger rushing unexpectedly through him. "That place in there is a disgrace. You allow your people to be housed worse than your pigs."

"I didn't realize . . . I had no idea," said Niki unhappily.

"That's an easy excuse. Wouldn't it be better to clean up your own backyard before you devote your energy to useless demonstrations and plotting the assassination of blundering politicians?"

"I never thought of it that way."

"Well, start thinking now. If you don't, you will find others who will do it for you and they will be likely to set light to such a bloody fire that neither you nor anyone else will know how to put it out."

"I never heard you speak like that before."

"No, you haven't. Perhaps that's what has been wrong with me."

One of the men had brought their horses and they took the reins from him silently.

It had been a small incident, one man flogged unjustly. It must happen in a dozen ways all over the country and no one cared a straw about it but it had done something to him personally. For too long he had been brooding over his own troubles and he was ashamed of his absorption in one personal tragedy when a world of suffering waited for his own special skills. He had the power to heal and was spending his strength and energy in idle dissipation.

He realized suddenly that he had been making Niki suffer for his own dissatisfaction and he turned to him with a wry smile.

"I'm not blaming you. You've seen ugliness, injustice, for the first time with your own eyes and it's not pleasant, is it? But at least it is something you can put right."

"I can try but my father and I have never seen eye to eye. Grandfather understands but he is not here very much. He has a house down south on the Black Sea and now he is old it suits him better to live there for the greater part of the year. I used to talk about it with Galina. Between us we wanted to make a new Russia, or our part of it at least. We had all kinds of wonderful plans," he confessed boyishly, "but when she went to Petersburg she changed."

"Maybe she simply grew up," said Simon gently. "She has seen a wider horizon than this small part of it and has realized there is more needed than childish dreams."

"I used to think she cared for me but all this year ever since Igor Livinov joined our group she has been different."

"Who is he, this Igor? Why don't you like him?"

"I don't know. Sometimes I do when he talks to us, when he says that we must destroy Russia before we can rebuild it, that the tree of freedom must be watered with blood if its roots are to flourish and to inspire terror is the only way to prove our strength, but is he right, Simon? He is a marvellous speaker and he carries us all with him but afterwards – I don't know. You know he was sentenced to Siberia for his political ideals and he glories in it but somehow I don't trust him."

Simon guessed that a little of Niki's dislike sprang from a natural jealousy but all the same when he returned to Petersburg he would make it his business to find out a little more about this fiery hothead. He did not want to see that young girl with her gallant courage tempted into some crazy action that could damn her for the rest of her life.

The ugly scene of the morning, the brutality, the filthy hospital with its spectral patients, seemed to be part of some other world when they rode through the sunlit flower garden where a boy was on his hands and knees weeding the paths and the Princess Malinskaya in a wide shady hat was cutting roses, followed by Marta with the basket. The dogs were stretched on the terrace raising lazy heads to greet them and a young man came running to take the bridles of the horses.

In the hall Nina came down the stairs. In her white muslin dress, ribbons in the fair hair, she looked to him like a lovely eager child.

"What happened?" she asked breathlessly. "That poor man! Did you save him? Sonia said she was sure you would. I wished I could have helped but I'm not brave as she is. Valentin made us leave and brought us home."

"He was quite right. Don't distress yourself, dear child. That poor man is being cared for."

"And it was all because of you. I know it was," and carried

away by an emotion she scarcely understood, she shyly stood on tiptoe and kissed his cheek.

Automatically he put his arm round her as he had done so often before when his young sister had run to him with her childish troubles. He touched her hair lightly.

"Believe me I did very little. It was Niki who was the hero bravely standing up to the formidable Yakov."

"That brute!" she exclaimed drawing away from him and blushing a little. "I don't know why Papa employs him."

"He is no doubt very good at his job."

"Pooh! That's not everything," she said disdainfully. She took his hand. "Now you must come and breakfast. I shall pour your coffee for you myself."

He allowed her to lead him into the dining room where she began to pile his plate with spiced ham, and eggs devilled with cream and green peppers until he protested and Niki laughed.

"You're honoured. She doesn't fuss over me like that."

And he smiled and thought of her as scarcely out of the schoolroom still subject to fits of hero-worship for any older man who was different from her usual companions.

He had not intended to stay at Dannskoye for more than a few days but a week passed, then another, and he admitted to himself that the leisured life in the great white house had a kind of dreamy charm of its own. In the summer heat they seemed to live almost completely out of doors. Early morning rides, picnics, carriage drives to nearby places of interest and a constant flow of young people, laughing, irresponsible, seemingly without a care in the world. There were long evenings when he lightly flirted with Nina in the flower-scented garden, listening to the nightingales in the birch wood or taking the carriage down to the river to watch the gypsies sing and dance on the opposite bank. Sometimes the General would join them for cards. The old man was shortly travelling south and intended taking Niki with him. Simon guessed that, disappointed in his own son, he was putting all his hopes for the future in his grandson.

Always beneath the charm there was that strange split between the two worlds though they lived side by side. He was strongly aware of it when he visited the barracks hospital where the flogged man was making a slow painful recovery.

There could not have been a greater contrast to his own well-ordered home in the Fens where his father kept a strict eye on the state of his cottages and his mother and aunts seemed perpetually concerned with the welfare of sick villagers and the children of the deserving poor, and yet, God knows, England had its share of disastrous slums of which he had seen more than most.

He thought Niki was beginning to grow conscious of what was needed but Nina went her happy heedless way and opened her blue eyes very wide when he mentioned it to her. It was one morning when they were in the stableyard and he saw the filthy ragged children carrying tins of wild strawberries, snatching eagerly at the few coins paid to them at the kitchen door, watching him warily through their tangled dirty hair, fighting one another like wild animals when unwisely he threw them a handful of kopecks.

"Shouldn't something be done about those children?" he asked while Vassily brought out their horses.

"For goodness sake why? They love doing things for us and they are paid for what they do."

"Has your father never thought of setting up a school for them?"

"A school! Why ever should they want to go to school? I *hated* my lessons."

Yet she could weep bitterly over an injury to a dog. One day that week he came down early to find her sitting on the lawn with Shani's head on her lap. The borzoi bitch was her own particular pet and she was whispering loving words and tenderly stroking the long aristocratic head.

"What's the trouble?" he asked squatting beside her.

"I don't know. It's her front paw. She is limping badly and she won't let anyone touch it, not even me. Vassily tried and she bit him."

"Let me take a look."

"Careful. She could be savage."

"Not with me."

Simon had grown up with animals, and dogs have a queer instinct for those who know and love them. He spoke gently and soothingly while he examined the swollen paw and the big dog let him handle it, except for an occasional whimper of pain.

Nina was watching him anxiously. "What do you think?"

47

"She has trodden on something and it has driven through her pad and is setting up an infection. That's why she is in such pain. I'm afraid I shall have to use the knife to cut it out."

"Oh no!" she was biting her lip. "I don't think I can bear it." She was looking at him piteously and he smiled.

"We'll find Sonia, shall we? She will help."

So it was Sonia who held Shani firmly when he made a quick clean cut and found the piece of glass embedded deep and causing a festering wound. He washed away the pus, cleansed the paw thoroughly and then fixed the lint and gauze bandages.

"Leave it on for a few days, then it can come off. She will keep it clean herself. Animals have their own healing powers."

It was a routine little operation he had performed a dozen times on animals and children but Nina was gazing up at him with wonder and admiration which both amused and touched him.

On his last evening they danced together on the terrace while Missy at the piano played old country melodies.

Nina said, "I wish you would stay with us all the summer. Why don't you?"

"My dear child, I've idled enough time away. I must work."

"Does that mean you are going back to England?"

"Not yet. There are sick people everywhere and I would like to work here if I am permitted to do so."

"Papa says we are not going to Petersburg until later in the year. You will come and visit us."

"Of course I will. I shall look forward to it."

She and Niki came with him to the railway station and saw him on to the train. There were tears sparkling on her lashes when she said goodbye to him.

"It's been such a lovely lovely summer and now it's all finished."

"There will be many more lovely summers for you," he said pressing her hand before he kissed it. "Many many more."

"You promise?"

"I promise," he said lightly.

He waved to her as the train drew out of the station and then sat back on the seat and forgot her. He was not a vain man and, regarding himself as almost middle-aged to her seventeen, he did not guess that Nina in her own wild tempestuous fashion was already tumbling into the dangerous headiness of first love, something that he had unwittingly inspired and that was to bedevil both their lives.

4

The summer heat in Galina's small room under the roof was appalling. She spent as much time as possible out of it but the nights tossing and sweating on the narrow mattress seemed endless. Fortunately Igor was away on some secret mission he divulged to nobody so she could leave the door ajar to catch as much air as possible without fear of him invading her privacy. Unlike the mansions of the rich the lodging house had no cellar packed with ice where food could be kept cool. The milk went sour, the butter was rancid and flies buzzed on the spiced ham so that she turned away from it sickened. She found herself living on slices of black bread, a grating of cheese and an occasional egg whipped up with slices of cucumber. The allowance paid to her by General Malinsky however carefully managed did not allow for many meals eaten in even the cheapest of restaurants.

Last year she had spent the hottest weeks of the summer at Dannksoye with her mother, going for long walks, picking mushrooms with the children, helping the other women bring in the harvest and had been very content glorying in the possession of her books and her independence when the autumn came and it was time to go back to the city. But now she was restless, unhappy, furiously angry with herself and all because of that stupid incident over the borrowed dress. But was it only that? Wasn't it because she knew now that whatever she did, however hard she studied, she could never be on the same level as Nina, lively irresponsible Nina with not an idea in her pretty head, dreaming only of her new gowns, the fun she was going to have now she was grown up, the man she would one day marry, the rich household she would rule as her mother did. Or even more to the point was it because she knew only too well that Dr Simon Aylsham, son of an English Lord, would never think of her except as that poor silly girl dressed up in someone else's finery, making a fool of herself and suffering a horrible humiliation?

Tormentedly she would push aside the books she was trying to read and storm out into the streets walking at random but always ending up among the fashionable shops gazing at the silks, the velvets, the costly furs, sable and lynx and white fox. Sometimes in the early evening she would stand on one of the bridges over the Neva and watch the pleasure boats lined with velvet, gay with many coloured striped canopies, the boatmen in cherry-coloured liveries with embroidered jackets and feathered hats, taking their carefree passengers to picnic on Koestevsky Island or to eat at the Samarkand where the Tsigane sang and danced till dawn.

She had never envied them before, had even poured scorn on their idle wasted lives, but now that small rebellious fire that had begun to grow in her kindled a bitter resentment and in that same wild mood she spent nearly all the money she had on a blouse of finest muslin beautifully embroidered and tried it on one night, loosening her hair into curls around her neck, gazing at herself in the flyblown mirror until in a fit of revulsion she tore it off because she had no one to show it to, no one to laugh with her and tell her she was beautiful even though she knew he lied.

That was the night she went out and walked along the canal banks till dawn. These wonderful Petersburg nights when it never grew really dark, the pearly light had a glamour and a mystery that seemed made for pleasure and love and the years of hard work, the passing of examinations, the skills she aimed at seemed barren and without real purpose. Once in the early evening she walked past that tall brown house where she had taken Niki that freezing night in February wondering if Simon had returned. Should she knock and ask? But the linen blind was drawn and the house seemed to shut itself against her. Would he welcome her if she took him at his word or would he treat her kindly and at the same time make her feel as if she had presumed on a casual invitation never meant to be taken seriously?

At the end of the month she had an unpleasant shock. Her allowance had always been paid to her by the Malinsky lawyer. When she made her way to his austere office on the appointed day she was always received by his clerk, a small mean-faced man who reminded her of a large grey rat and who always handed over the money with a look of contempt and some grudging remark.

"Take care of it, my girl, and don't squander it. Roubles don't grow on trees, you know. I wonder if you realize how fortunate you are."

She had often been tempted to give him a saucy answer but knew that he would inevitably report it and she had too much respect for the old General who had shown her kindness.

This time he did not even look up from the ledger he was bent over. He went on writing keeping her standing for a full quarter of an hour in the stuffy office before he sat up, pulled out a white silk handkerchief, mopped the sweat from his bald head and eyed her up and down before he spoke.

"And what are you doing here, Galina Panova?"

"You know why."

"Haven't they told you yet?"

"Told me what?"

"There's no more money from that source, none at all."

She stared at him. "No money . . . but I don't understand. Why?"

He sat back in his chair, one hand beating an impatient little tattoo on the desk.

"You've cooked your goose, my girl, that's why. These great people like a proper gratitude, they want you on your knees calling down a blessing on their charity, not the kind of impudence you like to show. Haven't you learned that yet?"

She couldn't believe it. Surely it wasn't possible. The General, that wise far-seeking kind man, would never have taken offence at such a silly escapade.

"There must be some mistake," she muttered.

"Oh no, there's no mistake. Do you take me for a fool? I know my orders and they're plain as daylight. No more queening it at the university. You'll have to take your chance like the rest of us poor mortals." He leaned across the desk, piggy eyes leering up at her. "What have you been doing, eh? Playing around with the young master? That won't do. You want to mind your step, young lady."

She nerved herself to say, "I suppose you mean it is just a punishment – for this month?"

51

"Not this month, nor next month, nor next year," he said flippantly and she thought he sounded pleased. "You'll have to go back home and think again, Galina Panova. It shouldn't be difficult, not for a fine girl like you." He gave her a sly glance. "I could be in the market myself. What do you say, eh?"

"I'd starve first!"

She gave him a withering look and with head held high marched out of the office, down the stairs and into the street, too bitterly resentful at the injustice to realize yet what it was going to mean or how she was going to cope with such a sudden and unexpected blow.

Presently she found herself in the Summer Gardens without quite knowing how she got there and sat on one of the benches watching the nursemaids in their gold embroidered *sarafans* and headdresses of blue velvet wheeling the handsome prams, the governesses with their pampered charges, small boys in English sailor suits, girls in frilled muslin and beribboned bonnets, chasing one another across the velvet lawns with their overfed little dogs, falling into flowerbeds and being scolded, all of them facing a life of ease and plenty while she stared into a bleak future where hope and ambition had been abruptly killed.

That hateful grey rat of a man had been right. There would be no more university, no more lectures, no possibility of the degree in pharmacy which she had so passionately wanted to achieve. What opening was there for a young woman like herself abandoned in Petersburg, half educated, belonging to neither one world nor the other? For the past year she had helped out voluntarily at the hospital but the only paid work open to her there would be in the laundry standing over boiling tubs pounding soiled bed linen for twelve hours a day and scarce enough money to keep body and soul together. There must be something else she could do, there had to be. She got up and began to walk quickly avoiding the sly glances of lounging men always on the look-out for a pick-up and unaccustomed to seeing a decent young woman walking alone in a public park.

Her thoughts were rudely interrupted by the thunder of cannon. She stopped dead bewildered while the volley went on and on. All around her were people looking at one another and then breaking into smiles and excited chatter. A three-hundred gun salute from the Peter and Paul Fortress could mean only one thing – the birth of an heir to the thone. After four daughters the Tsarina had paid her debt to Russia at last. Someone yelled "Long Live the Tsar!" and they all began to run towards the Winter Palace, shouting and cheering.

Galina walked on. The future of the Romanov dynasty might be secured but her own immediate prospects were not so certain.

On one thing she was determined. She was not going to return to Dannskoye, not after the Princess Malinskaya's biting words. So for week after week she scoured the city in search of work, any kind of work that would keep hunger at bay, starting at the top and working down lower and lower until in despair she was walking from one to the other of the small factories that had sprung up on the outskirts of the city and that employed women, drawing back in disgust from some of the worst places where the workers were herded together in huge grey barracks, sleeping in bunks one above the other, airless, filthy, stinking in the summer heat, no privacy, men, women and children, eating, breeding and dying. She learned about horrors she never knew existed.

She regretted bitterly the money she had squandered on the expensive blouse. The tiny savings she had accumulated melted away with alarming speed and she took to avoiding her comrades at the university and never attending the secret meetings of the Liberal Labour Group in case they might think she was begging something from them.

By the end of August she had become close to desperation. She was drinking a glass of tea at one of the poorest teashops in the artists' quarter when another girl sitting at a different table eyed her for a few minutes, then crossed over and put down one of the *blinis* from her own plate squarely in front of her.

"Go on, eat it," she said, "you look as if you could do with it."

Galina stared down at the pancake filled with hot spicy meat and her mouth watered. Then she looked up.

"Oh no, I couldn't. You see, I can't . . ."

"Pay for it, I know. Never mind about that. Eat it. I know what it is like to be down on your luck." She sat down on one of the chairs. "You don't remember me, do you, but we met at one of the meetings of the Lib Lab Group."

53

"Did we?" Galina smiled faintly through the first grateful bite of the *blini*. She frowned trying to think back. "Did you come with Igor Livinov?"

"That's right. I'm Luba Mastova." The girl was blonde, plump and coarsely pretty. She grinned showing her strong white teeth. "Proper gasbag, isn't he? Talk the hind legs off a donkey, that one, given half a chance. He's a friend of my gentleman."

"Your gentleman?"

Galina was eating slowly trying to make the tasty *blini* last as long as possible.

"Oh not what you're thinking. I model for the artists, not the great ones of course, they're above my touch. There's not much cash in it, but plenty of food if you're lucky, and there are other things to be picked up if you know what I mean," and she winked and giggled. "When I saw you at those meetings, I thought you were clean above me, studying at the university an' all. She's too proud to look at the likes of me, I said to myself."

"Oh no, I never felt like that, never," exclaimed Galina earnestly.

And because she had not spoken to anyone for weeks and because Luba was so sympathetic, ordering more tea for both of them and sitting with her pretty face propped between her two hands ready to listen, Galina found herself pouring out the whole story only omitting any reference to Simon Aylsham.

"If you ask me," remarked Luba thoughtfully, "it's not the old General who is punishing you, it's that Princess Malinskaya. She sounds a proper spiteful old cow." She gave a little giggle. "I'd like to have seen her face when she saw that dress cut to ribbons. You did rather ask for it, you know, but what a spirit. I can't help admiring it."

"Yes, I know," sighed Galina ruefully. "It felt good at the time but look where it has landed me."

"Never say die. And you can't sit down under it forever, now can you? Something like it happened to me once. A kiss and a cuddle from the son and heir *and* I never even asked for it. He would never have been my choice, not in a hundred years, fat and slobbering with hot hands that never knew their place. But it was all the same to his mother. I was out on my ear and in winter too. I thumbed my nose at her and got myself here but you'd better not ask how."

"You're a lot braver than I am."

"Not brave, just know my way about a bit. Had to, see, no kind old General in my life." She looked Galina up and down critically. "You've a decent figure, good bones, that's what they look for. Why don't you try your luck at the modelling?"

"Would I have to take my clothes off?"

Luba roared with laughter. "Is that what you are afraid of? It's not so bad, you know. They look at you mostly as if you were a joint of meat and that's what you look like sometimes in winter, pale blue with goose pimples, but I'd say *you* needn't worry. You're not the type. Not enough flesh on your bones. You could sit for one of those saints on the icons, you know – St Catherine on the wheel or St Ursula dying a thousand deaths in boiling oil rather than lose her virginity."

Galina smiled. "Is that what I remind you of?"

"That or one of those martyrs letting herself be tortured to death rather than yield up her faith, poor bitch. I wouldn't do it, you know, I'd give in at the first tweak of pain. What do you say? I could take you along with me. I know Sergei is looking for someone new to model for him. You might be just right."

"I don't know . . ." said Galina hesitantly drawing back from venturing into a world of which she knew nothing.

"At least you'll eat," said Luba practically, "and believe me, that's quite a lot. I know. I've done the other thing and after a few weeks I was willing to sell anything – my very soul let alone my body – for a piece of bread and a morsel of sausage."

And that was how Galina became an artists' model for a few weeks and in a way she had never expected, she enjoyed it. Sergei was a young wild-haired boy, half Polish, and passionate about only two things, his art and the coming revolution. They would argue about it when she had her rest and boiled up the samovar for endless cups of weak tea.

"If I were to be the chosen one," he said once very earnestly, "I would kill if I had to and afterwards destroy myself. No murderer should be allowed to live," and she thought with a shiver he really meant it. He was the kind of fanatic who would not care if he died in the act of assassination, yet ordinarily he would not hurt a fly. He put down food for the mice that nibbled his canvases and befriended with loving care an old mangy cat that had wandered into the studio one day, soaked, filthy and starving.

Unfortunately he was almost as poor as she was and it was a very bare living. If he failed to sell the little sketches he drew and peddled in the market, they did not eat. She grew very thin and pale as the days wore on and ended up with one of those malarial fevers that were endemic in Petersburg when the cold wet mists of early autumn came creeping up from the marshes and bogs upon which Peter the Great had built his city.

She had always had such excellent health that at the start she could not believe it. Sergei sickened first and she willingly nursed him through it until, spectre-thin, he was up again and painting hard at what he confidently believed was to be his masterpiece, and he simply did not realize that his saint whose delicate bones he was transferring to his canvas was slowly wasting away to a ghost before his very eyes.

Day after day after hours of alternately shivering and burning she dragged herself to the studio until a morning came when she got out of bed and collapsed on the floor, when her head throbbed and her bones ached and she could do no more than crawl back into the bed and lie there until the spasm should pass. And it was there towards evening on the following day that Simon Aylsham came knocking at her door.

In her sick and fevered state it seemed to Galina that it was Igor battering at her door and she called out, "Go away! Leave me alone!"

She believed that she shouted but the feeble trembling voice that reached Simon alarmed him. He tried the door and then grimly put his shoulder to it. It held firm and he had drawn back ready for another assault on it when the lodging-house keeper came lumbering up the stairs in considerable agitation.

"Now you, stop that at once, young man. If you break the door down, then who is going to pay for a new one? You tell me that!"

"I'll pay, don't worry," said Simon impatiently. "Have you a key?"

By this time the small, fat, grey-haired woman had arrived on the landing beside him.

"And why?" she said belligerently. "What's going on? What's the trouble? Maybe she don't want young men pushing their way into her room. She's not that kind let me tell you."

"For God's sake, woman, I'm a friend of hers. She answered me but she sounded sick. Don't argue with me. Open the door."

Somewhat impressed by his appearance and manner, she said grudgingly, "It's true enough I've not seen Galina Panova go in and out for a day or two now. I thought she'd gone off with that friend of hers – a flashy sort she is, dressed up like a dog's dinner." Still muttering to herself she inserted the key in the lock and opened the door.

The linen blind had been drawn and the room was stuffy and filled with shadows.

Galina said feebly, "Go away, Stasia Ivanovna, I'm all right. I'll be better soon."

"You certainly will if I have anything to do with it," said Simon striding in and letting up the blind. He took in Galina and the miserable state of the room with one comprehensive glance and then turned to the old woman.

"She'll not die, will she?" She was quavering. "It's not infectious, is it? I couldn't be doing with anything like that in this house. If it is, then out she goes, never mind the rent she owes."

"She's not going to die," said Simon brusquely, "I'm a doctor. I'll take responsibility for her. Now get out, old woman, leave her to me."

He took her firmly by the shoulders and thrust her, still protesting volubly, through the door, then shut and locked it before coming back to the bed.

"You shouldn't have done that to Stasia Ivanovna," muttered Galina in a thread of a voice. "She won't like it and she'll take it out on me."

"She won't get the chance. My dear girl, what on earth have you been doing with yourself to get into this state?"

"It's nothing, only a summer fever. Why have you come here?" But her small stock of strength was already ebbing. She closed her eyes and seemed to slip away from him.

He very soon realized that she must have passed a crisis of fever during the day. Her forehead burned, her pulse was irregular and the cotton nightdress and the sheet were soaked in sweat. The first essential was to get her warm, dry and comfortable. He looked around him, opening a drawer or two and found a fresh nightgown and a clean sheet, both of them pathetically patched and darned. He lifted her in his arms and began gently to pull the gown over her head. She protested, shaking her head and trying to draw away from him, but he persisted.

For a moment as he looked down at the lovely length of her, the full breasts, the flat stomach, the long beautiful legs, he was reminded of that other body that had been stretched on the operating table and for an instant sweat broke out on his face and his hands trembled. Then he pushed the memory away from him, dressed her in the fresh garment, wrapped the sheet around her and lifted her into the old rocking chair that in happier days she had bought in the flea market. He remade the bed with an expert hand, lifted her back into it, warmly tucked a blanket around her, rolled the soiled linen into a bundle and moved towards the door.

"Where are you going?"

Despite the valiant bid for independence he heard the quaver in her voice.

"Don't be anxious. I'll be back in a minute."

He went out, found his way down to the basement and gave the bundle to Stasia Ivanovna with the brisk order to get it washed and dried as soon as possible.

"Are you going to send her to the fever hospital?" she asked.

"There's no need."

She was not going there even if it meant taking her back to his own lodging. In those crowded wards packed with all the varying sicknesses of the poor and the outcast she would surely die.

"Is there someone who can go to the chemist for me?" he demanded.

"There is my grandson," said the old woman doubtfully.

"Go and fetch him." He wrote rapidly on a sheet torn from his notebook and when the boy appeared he said curtly, "Now fetch that as quickly as you can and on the way buy some oranges, as many as you can carry, never mind the cost, also bread, fresh butter and eggs." He put the money into the grimy hand held out to him. "There will be more for you if you do it in double quick time."

The boy nodded and sped off like an arrow while Simon returned to Galina. He found a jug of water, filled a basin and brought it to the bedside table. Gently he began to wash her face and hands and brush back the sweat-soaked hair.

She accepted his ministrations with a kind of wonderment leaning back against the pillows he had put behind her, too weak to ask many questions.

"You shouldn't be doing all this for me."

"I'm a doctor. My job is to cure the sick when I can. Now don't argue with me. You'll exhaust yourself. When the boy comes back I'm going to give you some medicine which will help the fever. Then I'm going home to eat and change before I come back."

She shook her head. "There's no need for you . . ."

"There's every need. These malarial fevers go in cycles. I'm not sure you've got through it yet. Later when you feel stronger, you shall tell me all about it."

He did exactly as he had said. The mixture of quinine he gave her was unbelievably bitter but she swallowed it obediently. Then he squeezed the oranges and gave her a long cool drink.

"No food yet. We'll see about that tomorrow. I'm going now but I'll be back," he promised and she found the quiet assurance in his voice infinitely comforting. The tension left her aching body and when an hour or so later he returned she had fallen asleep.

He lit the lamp and stood looking down at her. Maybe he was worrying unnecessarily, maybe he need not have stayed with her, but he felt in some curious way deeply responsible. She seemed so alone, so friendless in a city teeming with people who cared nothing. To abandon her now was impossible. He had taken the precaution of bringing a travelling rug with him. He took off his jacket, loosened his necktie and sat down in the rocking chair. He pulled the rug over his knees regretting bitterly that he had not come in search of her earlier.

He had returned to Petersburg with the firm resolution that he was not going to involve himself in any kind of political agitation. That was not his purpose. He was a doctor. He had sworn to heal the sick as far as he was able and with that thought in mind he took pains to follow up the introductions given him by his distinguished uncle.

Dr Deverenko, chief physician to the Tsar's family, had been courteous if doubtful of this young Englishman who came from Britain apparently loaded with honours. However, as soon as he realized that Simon possessed an income of his own, had no intention of poaching on their privileges and expressed a gratifying interest in treating patients from the poorest districts of the city – a duty some of them shirked whenever possible – his attitude changed. Simon found himself admitted to the highest circles and was already being offered an honorary visiting physician's post at the hospital.

It was not until the university term re-opened that he began to think seriously about Galina and wondered why she had not come to him as he had suggested. He was surprised not to see her at the course of lectures he was asked to give, particularly when all the students of the previous year came crowding in. He made enquiries among them but no one seemed to know what had happened to her. Then someone mentioned one day that he believed she had a room in the same house as Igor Livinov.

"Igor Livinov?" he repeated remembering what Niki had said after the flogging. "Is he a fellow student?"

The boy tapped his nose significantly. "He's a sly one, excellency, he comes and goes as he likes."

He supplied the name of the street but no number so it had meant an hour or two of patiently going from house to house until he had finally tracked her down. But why on earth was she reduced to such dire poverty? . . . At this point he drowsed off into a half sleep from which he was awakened by an insistent tapping at the door.

He looked at his watch, saw that surprisingly it was past seven and glanced at Galina. She looked very pale and thin but her forehead was cool and she was sleeping lightly but peacefully so he went to the door and opened it quietly. Outside there stood a remarkable vision in a pink and green striped gown with a flower-strewn hat perched on a mass of blonde curls.

"Who the devil are you?" she demanded staring at him belligerently.

"Ssh, she is asleep and I don't want her disturbed." He pulled the door to behind him. "I might as well ask who you are. I'm her doctor."

"Doctor?" Luba's eyes scanned his unbuttoned shirt, the unshaven cheeks, the ruffled hair. "Come off it. No doctor I know ever looked like you. Well, if Galina isn't the dark horse! She never said a word to me about you."

"Very likely not. However my appearance belies me," he remarked drily. "I *am* her doctor and she has been very ill but is now recovering."

"I thought she might be sick," said the girl, "seeing that she hasn't turned up at the studio for days and Sergei is

60

practically foaming at the mouth because he can't finish his masterpiece."

Simon frowned. "Who is Sergei and what is this about a masterpiece?"

"Don't you know? He is an artist – not all that good yet of course but he might be one day – and Galina has been modelling for him."

"Modelling?" he repeated.

"Yes and don't say it like that. It's better than starving any day in the week and it's not at all what you think. He's painting her as St Helen or St Margaret or some such. He has his head full of saints and martyrs, that one, not like my fellow, nymphs and satyrs are more his mark. Didn't she tell you?"

"No, she didn't."

"Maybe she thought you'd be jealous though Lord knows you don't need to be. Sergei is not that kind at all. Anyway I can't stay. Tell her, will you, that Luba called and Sergei wants her back badly." She gave him a saucy look. "You can tell her too that I approve her taste in doctors," and her rich laughter floated up to him as she ran down the stairs.

Galina was awake when he came back into the room. The fact that he was there, had come to her rescue, had handled her so intimately the night before, had a strange, dream-like quality as if the long hours she had spent lying on this very bed trying to put him out of her mind and helplessly failing had suddenly become reality. It warmed and frightened her at the same time.

He came back to the bed, one cool hand taking hold of her wrist as he smiled down at her.

"How do you feel?"

"Better but as if I wasn't really here, as if I were floating somewhere in space. Does that sound silly?"

"No, it's quite usual in these cases. It will pass as you grow stronger."

"Who was that at the door?"

"A young woman who calls herself Luba and says Sergei needs you to complete his masterpiece," he said drily.

"Oh heavens, Sergei! I had forgotten him. He'll be in despair. I ought to go to him now."

She started up in the bed and he pushed her firmly back.

"You'll do no such thing, not today, nor tomorrow, unless he wants his saint to turn into a martyr in the cause of art. In a few minutes you can tell me the reason why a serious student of medicine is cavorting with a bunch of disreputable artists but first things first. I'm going to give you some breakfast."

"I'm afraid there is no food," she said weakly, giving in.

"There is now. I've taken the liberty of supplying some. I may not be a *chef de cuisine* but in my student days I could scramble an egg with the best of them. It's food you need right now. When did you eat last?"

"I don't remember. I haven't felt hungry."

"And how long has that been going on? A great deal too long from what I saw last night," he said busying himself neatly and practically with the spirit stove, some butter and a couple of eggs. "I could count every rib. What you need and badly is some flesh on your bones."

In a very short time he turned triumphantly, plate in hand, and she turned away from him blushing furiously at the thought of the way he had stripped her nightgown from her and had held her naked in his arms.

"What's wrong now?" he said lightly. "Do you think it's the first time I've seen a young woman's body?"

"No, but . . ." She felt confused. How could she explain that to her it was different. Try as she would she could not separate the man from the doctor.

Then he was helping her to sit up, putting the plate on her knees, telling her briskly to eat up while he occupied himself with the samovar. Presently he brought her a glass of tea.

"No sugar, I'm afraid."

"I prefer it like that."

"Good."

She could not eat very much and he did not press her. He took the plate away, drew the chair close beside the bed and took her hand in his.

"Now tell me," he said gently, "why did your friend Luba say you were starving and if that was true, why didn't you come to me?"

"I couldn't. I couldn't take advantage of your generosity."

"Do you think I would have seen it like that? Surely you know me better."

Bit by bit he got the whole story out of her and leaned back in the chair angry at the heartless cruelty that had left an innocent girl of nineteen alone and penniless in a great city.

"At first I thought it must be because Nina had shown that wretched dress to her grandfather," she said painfully.

"That child would never have done that."

"I didn't want to believe it of her and afterwards I guessed it must have been Marta. She has always hated me even when we were children."

"And what will you do now?" he asked. "Go back to Dannskoye?"

"No, never, never!" she pushed herself up in the bed, two spots of colour flaming in her cheeks. "That would be to lose everything I've fought for. I know I can never hope to become a doctor now, but I can still work, I can study and pass my examinations."

"And support yourself by modelling for threadbare artists at starvation wages, I suppose?" he said ironically.

"If I must," she flashed at him, "and what's wrong with that? It is better than running home with everyone in the village laughing at the girl who had the stupidity to think herself so much better than anyone else."

"But then you are, aren't you?"

"Don't laugh at me." She turned away from him and he put a hand quickly on hers, recognizing the touchy pride with which she strove to keep her independence.

"Believe me, I'm very far from laughing."

An idea had sprung into his mind but he would not speak of it yet. He got to his feet.

"I have to go now, Galina. Tell me about that woman downstairs – what's her name? Stasia Ivanovna is it? Will she bring you food if I speak to her, will she take care of you?"

"I'm sure she will," she said eagerly. "She is really very kind. You don't need to worry about me any longer."

"We'll see about that." He pulled on his coat, then paused to say firmly, "Now take care of yourself. No leaping out of bed and running off to this artist of yours. I'll be back tomorrow to make sure you're behaving yourself."

He patted her cheek as he might have done to a sick child and she caught hold of his hand.

"I don't know how to thank you," she murmured and pressed her lips against it.

"No need," he said gruffly.

For a moment he looked down at her, in his mind a fleeting memory of the fire they had leaped together hand in hand.

He had a feeling he was committing himself to something he had never intended. Then he drew his hand away, picked up his hat and went quickly out of the room.

Presently old Stasia came bustling up the stairs putting everything to rights, promising to make fresh tea and suggesting various dainty dishes she could prepare to tempt an invalid's capricious appetite, partly because of a natural kindness of heart when it was to her advantage and partly to the plain fact that she had been greatly impressed by the well-dressed foreigner who spoke Russian so fluently and not only paid up all the overdue rent but put down a generous sum to cover the next few weeks and any expensive food she might be obliged to buy for Galina. It was going to be something to boast about to her cronies when they dropped in to chat in the evening and would show that Igor Livinov for whom she had the greatest contempt that this was a decent respectable house and not a nest of good-for-nothing revolutionary layabouts.

Having rested all day and tried valiantly to eat the tasty dishes Stasia brought her Galina felt so much better the next morning that she made up her mind to get up and go to the studio. After all she owed it to Sergei. He had willingly shared all he had with her and she knew the picture was intended for an exhibition, not a very important one it was true, but it meant a good deal to him.

Once out of bed she felt far more shaky than she had expected but at last she was dressed and cautiously creeping down the stairs before Stasia could hear and try to stop her. The cool damp air revived her but the walk along the canal bank and over the bridge seemed longer than she remembered and by the time she reached the house her small stock of strength was very nearly exhausted.

The studio was part of a group of tall buildings built around a large courtyard and occupied by a great variety of tenants, artists, musicians, poets, even singers from the operatic chorus, bound loosely by the fact that they were all to a greater and lesser extent active members of what Luba called irreverently 'the Lib Lab lot'.

Sergei was far too delighted that she had come back to notice her pallor. He threw his arms around her, hugging her exuberantly and bursting into a flood of his native Polish which he was liable to do in moments of stress. Then she was changing into the long clinging white robe he considered suitable for his martyred saint who had withstood the assault of wild beasts (these were represented by a rather mangy lion and a snarling wolf borrowed from a friendly taxidermist) rather than give up her Christian faith. She took up the awkward pose he insisted upon and Sergei began to paint furiously while one or two of the other inhabitants of neighbouring flats dropped in to watch as they often did.

That was the picture that met Simon's eyes when he crossed the courtyard and bounded up the stairs in search of her. He had arrived at Galina's room far later than he had intended having been detained at the hospital and found to his surprise and considerable annoyance that his patient had flatly defied him. He berated Stasia Ivanovna severely for allowing her to leave the house.

"I was at the market, your excellency," she wailed, "only for a few minutes and she was lying so quiet in her bed, pale as a lily she was. I never dreamed of any such madness. Look for good fresh food, you told me, excellency, good country butter and fish straight from the sea and that was what I was doing . . ."

"Yes, yes, I know," abruptly he cut her short. "Where is this damned studio?"

She repeated the direction she had already given to Igor Livinov who had returned early that morning from one of his mysterious journeys and had enquired after Galina.

Simon took a cab. Maybe it was not all that important but his mind was full of what Nigel had told him when they had met by chance at the English Club on the previous night. Nigel Drew and he had been at Harrow together, losing touch for a while when he studied medicine at Edinburgh and Nigel went on to Oxford and the diplomatic, but now he was at the embassy in Petersburg the old friendship had revived although they were so different. Nigel was calm, well balanced, outward-looking. He spoke fluent Russian, French and German, was shrewd and intelligent but without Simon's occasional flashes of genius and he had never brooded over anything in his life. He was also happily married.

"Do you happen to know anything about a fellow called Igor Livinov?" Simon asked casually over drinks and delicious Russian hors-d'œuvres.

"Why?"

"He happens to lodge in the same house as a young woman student of mine."

Nigel shot him a glance. "In that case you'd better advise her to keep very clear of him. There are some nasty rumours flying about."

"What kind of rumours?"

Nigel shrugged. "Nothing specific, nothing you could put your finger on and it doesn't really concern us, but any kind of student riot and he's in the thick of it, only when the police show up, he has melted into thin air."

Simon frowned. "You mean he plans it and then betrays it to the *Okhrana*?"

"Something like that. There may be no truth in it of course. Petersburg is full of such rumours these days. You'd do well not to get mixed up in them, Simon," went on Nigel more seriously. "There's something brewing. We don't know yet what it is but ever since the Minister of the Interior was assassinated a couple of months ago, the secret police have been jumpy. It's natural enough. It was Sipyagin two years ago and now Plehve and both murdered by student fanatics, but these boys are only the instruments. There's a powerful organization working behind them, that's for sure, and we're pretty certain the police know. There's a hotbed of them over in the artists' quarter, poets, writers, artists, all damned fools fired with a mistaken heroism, but they can be dangerous."

"There's not much the *Okhrana* can do to me," said Simon shrugging it off carelessly.

"Even a British passport might not save you from trouble. I should hate to have to haul you out of some dungeon in the Peter and Paul Prison," said Nigel half jestingly, "so you keep your nose clean."

"I can take care of myself," he said, but what about Galina – little fool – landing herself right in the midst of them?

So that was why he was there standing in the doorway, his eyes on her. She was transparently pale, sickness and hunger had refined her features giving them an austere beauty. The light caught the chestnut glow of the loosened hair falling around her shoulders. Something deep within him that he had believed dead and buried began to stir. Like the saint she represented she was alone and friendless in the midst of a herd of ravening wild beasts and it was his eyes who saw what the others had not even noticed.

"For God's sake!" he exclaimed suddenly and crossed the studio kicking aside the moth-eaten lion and the bare-fanged wolf to catch her in his arms before she fainted. "Are you blind, all of you? Couldn't you see she was ready to collapse?"

Sergei stopped painting looking bewildered, the others all began to talk at once as Simon carried her to the dilapidated studio couch and laid her gently down.

"Is she all right?"

The artist was at his elbow, his brush still in his hand, a smudge of paint on his cheek.

"No thanks to you if she is. She should never have come here. Stand back, all of you. Someone fetch me a glass of water."

"I'll go," said Luba.

When she came back Galina was already sitting up and asking what all the fuss was about.

"I just felt horribly dizzy for a minute, that's all." She pushed the heavy hair out of her eyes. "Dr Simon, what are you doing here?"

"Get dressed," he said briefly. "I'm taking you out of this place here and now."

"And supposing I won't go?"

"You will if I have to carry you out just as you are."

"You can't force me. I promised Sergei . . ."

"No, no, you mustn't stay, not if you're really sick, Galina," began the artist, "I wouldn't want that," and he was rudely elbowed aside by Igor Livinov.

Tall and lean he confronted Simon. There was something formidable about the shorn head, the harsh angular lines of his face, and he knew immediately that this was the man Nigel had warned him of.

"By what right do you come here? Are you her protector, her guardian," he said bitingly, "that you think you can command Galina Panova, saying what she must do or not do?"

"I have every right as her doctor. Don't you understand? She is sick. She needs the care she obviously won't receive here."

"Why not let her decide? It could be that she prefers our company to yours, Englishman."

He fixed those brilliant eyes of his on Galina and she trembled. She felt almost as if he were mesmorizing her into

67

agreement with him, as if the two of them were battling for possession of her, soul, mind and body. He moved towards her and Simon stood in his way.

They faced one another in a compelling silence, the others bunched together staring at them, and suddenly Galina couldn't endure it a moment longer.

"Stop it!" she cried out. "Stop it, both of you! Why can't you leave me alone?"

But it was Luba who brought them back to earth, who said sturdily, "What nonsense all this is. Why should Galina have to decide anything? She has been ill and she came back too soon, that's all. Let her go home and get well. After that she can do as she pleases."

"Yes, do that," said Sergei eagerly, getting behind his easel to avoid the icy glare Igor gave him.

"Come with me," went on Luba cheerfully, "I'll help you to dress."

"I'll wait for you downstairs," said Simon, thankful for her plain common sense in this overheated atmosphere.

It was there that a few minutes later Luba joined him with a protective arm around Galina.

"You properly set the cat among the pigeons, didn't you?" she said gleefully to Simon. "Igor doesn't like anyone to stand up to him. Most of them run like frightened mice if he so much as frowns at them. You'd better watch out."

Simon shrugged his shoulders. "I should worry."

He took Galina by the arm to help her into the waiting cab but she resisted him.

"Tell Sergei I shall be back," she said defiantly to Luba before he picked her up bodily, put her into the carriage and followed after her.

They sat in an unfriendly silence until they reached her lodging. From her basement window Stasia Ivanovna peered up at them as they alighted from the cab and approved the masterful way Simon took her firmly by the arm and propelled her up the stairs.

"That's what these independent young women need," she muttered to herself, "a strong man to show them what's what!"

When they were safely inside the room and the door was shut, Galina turned on him, white and trembling with anger at the high-handed manner with which he had marched into her life.

"Those people were friends of mine and you shamed me in front of them. I'm grateful for what you've done for me but I don't need your help any longer." There were tears of sheer frustration in her eyes. "How can I ever go back there and if I don't, how can I find the money to repay you?"

"Oh for heaven's sake," he said impatiently, "you owe me nothing. I'd have done the same for anyone."

"I suppose that's how you think of me," she went on stormily, "a miserable beggar, a stray dog on which you have taken pity. Don't let the poor bitch die in the gutter! Isn't that how you see it? Well, I won't be like that. I won't, I tell you. I'll find a way to fight my way back. I don't want anyone's pity or their charity either."

"Galina, listen to me . . ."

"No, no, no! Go, please go, leave me alone!" and she turned her back on him.

He paused a moment and then she heard him move towards the door, heard it open and shut before she fell face downwards on the bed, weakness and misery overwhelming her. Everything had gone wrong. This was not how she had wanted him to come to her. She buried her face in the pillow trying to stifle the tears that came welling up in spite of herself.

A few minutes later with a mighty effort she pulled herself together and sat up, her breath still catching in her throat, and looked around her helplessly for a handkerchief.

"Here – try this. It's quite clean."

She saw the outstretched hand. Infuriatingly he was still standing there, his face grave, but a faint glint of amusement in the grey eyes.

"Oh," she exclaimed with a gasp of exasperation, "why when I'm with you do I always make such a fool of myself?"

"It's a calamity we're all subject to at the most inconvenient times," he said kindly. "I'm no more immune from it than you are."

"I doubt that, I doubt it very much." She had taken the handkerchief and mopped at her face with it. "I thought I asked you to go."

"I know you did but I do have something to say to you, something quite important, if you are willing to listen."

She still avoided looking at him, sitting hunched up on the bed.

"I suppose I must. What is it?"

"Would you care to take on the job of my assistant?"

"What!" She stared up at him, her eyes enormous in her white face. "I don't understand."

"I have been discussing with the Director of the State Hospitals an idea which my uncle in England suggested to me. He would like me to carry out a survey of all the state institutions – the foundling hospital, the poor hospital, the isolation wards, the medical facilities provided at some of the larger factories and so on. It will be a mammoth task and I'm going to need someone to assist me, to take notes, to transcribe them afterwards, to run about for me, and I must have someone who knows what I'm talking about. It won't be all that pleasant and I shall work you extremely hard, also the fee paid for the work will be pitiful, but you will learn a great deal about how the poor, the wretched and the sick are treated and it might be a stepping stone to something better, who knows? It's not work usually undertaken by a woman and I've had a hard fight to get you accepted but I have the advantage of being a foreigner and am therefore permitted to be somewhat eccentric. What do you say?"

She was looking at him with glowing eyes. "I couldn't do it. I don't know enough."

"You will very soon learn. I'll make sure of that. Don't decide now," he went on coolly, "think about it. In any case it won't start for a week or two, maybe longer, knowing how slowly the Russian mind works. When you have made up your mind, come and tell me."

"This isn't – isn't just because you're – you're sorry for me?"

"Certainly not. Where my work is concerned, I'm ruthless. You will soon find that out."

He was being deliberately cold and formal so that she looked up at him almost shyly.

"I must go back to the studio, you do understand that. I couldn't let Sergei down."

"You must do as you think right, Galina, but I would strongly advise you not to go there till you are really fit and not to have too much to do with Igor Livinov, especially as I understand he lodges here."

For one flying moment she wondered if he were jealous and then dismissed it as an idle fancy.

"Why should I? I don't much like him in any case, I never have."

"Good. I'm going now. Don't take too long before you make up your mind."

He went out closing the door and then paused on the landing outside not quite sure what he had let himself in for. She had not realized how nebulous the whole plan was. It was true that the idea had been discussed and his part in it welcomed. It was certainly going ahead but the question of an assistant was still quite undecided. He could see the frown on the face of authority at the very mention of a young woman, no matter how clever, being used in such a manner. Oh to hell with it! He squared his shoulders and ran down the stairs. No one could stop him employing her and if it was necessary he would pay the salary himself. He did not stop to analyse his reasons for making the proposal to her. The whole project would probably take months. It was something that deeply interested him and the thought of an intelligent young mind which he could train gave him pleasure. He strode up the street happier than he had been for a very long time and did not spare a thought as to what the outcome might be. The future could take care of itself.

5

In the Foundling Hospital the cast-iron beds stretched in long depressing rows against the gaunt grey walls and Galina shivered despite the black Dutch stoves battling with the damp November cold. Not even the carbolic with which the floors had been washed could dispel the stale sickening smell of poverty and sickness. Some of the babies were crying lustily and the wet nurses, country girls who had abandoned their own infants for the money and plentiful food, ran to pick them up and put them to the breast. Most of them, hardly more than a few days old, lay still under the coarse blankets, tiny, wizened, staring up at her with huge imploring eyes. They came in at the rate of eighty to a hundred each day, many of them sick, filthy, half dead from hunger and cold. They were given a number, registered, stripped of their rags and bathed, like so much flotsam, unwanted wreckage cast up on the sea of life. Where had they sprung from? A moment of self-indulgence, an hour of so-called love? How could a woman who had carried that tiny creature inside her for nine long months abandon it into this cold unfeeling world? She could never do that, she thought, never, never – somehow she would have to find the means to keep her child. Had her own mother felt tempted when she found herself pregnant, alone and deserted? She felt an unexpected wave of affection and gratitude that Vera Panova had possessed the courage to bring her baby up, give it a healthy start in the rough comfort of village life.

These babies were only kept here for at the most four weeks, the young doctor had told them, and were then sent away into the vastness of the Russian countryside, two or three hundred miles perhaps, arriving cold and exhausted to share the life of the peasants, so many of them that the foster mothers often had no beds for them to sleep in and they were hung like helpless baby birds in baskets suspended from the ceiling. Was it any wonder that more than half of these waifs died in the first few weeks? She put a finger down to touch one pale cheek and a tiny hand gripped it as if it were a lifeline to hope. She would have liked to pick it up, hold it against her for a moment, but knew she must not. Any contact was strictly forbidden.

"Galina!" Simon who had been talking to the doctor in charge was calling and she hurried across to them. "I think we've about done here. Have you got everything down?"

"Yes, I think so."

"Good."

He thanked the doctor for his time and trouble in showing them around the hospital and then they were hurrying down the immensely long corridor and out into the street. The pavements were wet with recent snow and an icy grey mist was creeping up from the Neva but it felt good to be out of that huge ugly building and she was grateful even for the keen bite of the flying sleet in her face.

"I don't know about you," said Simon suddenly, "but I need something to take the taste of that place out of my mouth. I think hell must be something like that, not a fiery furnace but grey, depressing, hopeless and smelling like a sewer. I need wine, food, music. What do you say? Shall we go and dine somewhere?"

She looked down at her shabby coat where the fur was worn and scuffed, the black boots that were long past their best and knew she couldn't bear to shame him in some fashionable restaurant.

"Perhaps it would be better if I went home. I have all these notes to write up and they're going to take quite a long time."

"Damn it, girl, they can wait, can't they?" he said impatiently. "There's no hurry. Come on, we'll go to Leiters," and he waved down a passing cab and bundled her into it.

Leiters was where the artists went, the actors from the theatre, the ballet dancers from the Maryinsky, talking and arguing over caviare and Black Sea oysters. The restaurant sprinkled sawdust on the floor and had the look of a country tavern but boasted the finest delicatessen and the most intellectual society in Petersburg and its proprietor, accustomed to artistic vagaries, cared not a rap how you were dressed. She wondered if Simon had guessed at the reason for her hesitation and chosen it deliberately.

She had been working with him now for over two months. The investigation had taken them into terrible places and she had seen sights she would never forget but somehow they had all been grown men and women who still had a fighting chance. She had never felt quite such a feeling of despair, such utter helplessness as in that home of abandoned childhood.

During these weeks she had seen a Simon she had only guessed at, no longer the rich aristocrat playing at life she had thought him at first, but a man dedicated to his work of healing, an inquiring mind, ruthless in its search for knowledge and quite unflinching in the face of appalling conditions. He would not permit her to follow him into the fever hospitals with their isolation wards though he explored them himself and came out looking shaken and disturbed. But there were other places where he expected her to accompany him and she would have died rather than let him see her draw back or reveal her sick revulsion. Among the worst had been the medical centres in some of the smaller factories and workshops dedicated to producing the articles of luxury, the costly trifles seized upon by the rich and the fashionable.

In one of them the workers slept on the floor or on looms covered with planks and since heat and moisture were needed to the processing of the fibres, the walls were cracked and eaten away by brownish mould, the ceiling dripped, a grey film covered the windows and at each step Galina's feet sank into the black mud on the floor. There were children there too, crawling between the machines and a woman sat on an upturned bucket suckling her baby. These were the places where the only medical help was provided by an overworked young doctor in a tiny room, dirty and inadequately supplied with drugs and medicines. He attended patients one day a week and was concerned only with getting them back to work as soon as possible or be in mortal danger of losing his job.

Simon demanded a great deal from her, expecting her to take careful notes and transcribe them afterwards, impatient when she was slow in understanding but often willing to explain afterwards. She learned about symptoms and how to detect them, about the use of drugs and how to alleviate pain and because she was so receptive and eager to learn he worked her extremely hard but she did not mind. The personal contact, the growing friendship between them, meant everything to her. These were wonderful weeks and she asked nothing more than to go on working with him.

Leiters was crowded when they arrived there. A waiter found them a table tucked away in a corner and it felt marvellous to be there with her handsome companion. She slipped off her shabby coat and forgot the plain white blouse and serge skirt when he smiled across at her and asked what she would like to eat and drink.

"You choose," she said happily, "I'm not used to anything like this."

"Very well. Do you know this is the first time we have eaten together? I think we should celebrate."

He ordered champagne and oysters and partridges à la crême and followed with a rhumbaba dripping with cream, laughing at her childish delight in the delicious sweet. The wine made her eyes sparkle and helped her shyness. They talked about themselves instead of their work and unwittingly she revealed more of her hopes and fears than she realized, her childish struggles, the determination to rise above her condition, the humiliations and the pleasures. He sat back sipping the wine and watching the play of the light across her face and felt he had at last come in from the wilderness and was beginning to live again, to live and even to love.

They were finishing the black Turkish coffee when a couple

who had risen from a nearby table paused on their way to the door.

"What have you been doing with yourself, my dear fellow," said Nigel slapping Simon on the shoulder. "We dined with the Malinskys yesterday and they were all asking after you, particularly the Princess Nina. Very indignant she was at your neglect. They have been a month in Petersburg and you've not even taken the trouble to call."

"I've been so busy, I never realized they had come up from Dannskoye," said Simon a little guiltily. "I didn't know you were on visiting terms."

"H.E. is an old friend of the General." He glanced across at Galina. "Won't you introduce us?"

"Yes, of course, forgive me. Galina, this is Nigel Drew, one of the pillars of our embassy and his wife Lydia – Galina Panova is one of my students at the university and is now assisting me in a kind of survey of hospitals, institutions, medical centres and so on."

"Heavens," exclaimed Lydia smiling at Galina, "you must be terribly clever."

"It is the doctor who is clever. I just follow around after him," said Galina, a little overawed by this elegant English couple and envious of the sleek fur coat carelessly draped around Lydia's shoulders, the fashionable gown of dark blue silk, the light brown hair cut with the latest curled fringe and piled high on the shapely head.

"Don't let him work you too hard. We know Simon, don't we, Nigel? When he is set on something he has no mercy on himself or on anyone working with him."

"That's a lie," he exclaimed indignantly. "I'm the most considerate of men."

Lydia made a face at him. "That's what you think."

"What about dining with us one evening?" said Nigel. "Just *en famille* and bring your friend with you."

"I'd like that."

"Make it next week," went on Lydia. "What about Wednesday and come early then you can say goodnight to the children. You've not seen them since the summer."

"All right, I will. Make a note of it, Galina, don't let me forget."

"Good. We'll look forward to seeing you both. Goodnight."

Lydia took her husband's arm, they smiled their goodbyes

and went on their way while Galina looked at Simon in dismay.

"They can't really want me to go with you."

"Of course they do. They wouldn't have invited you if they didn't." Simon was summoning the waiter for the bill.

"But they don't know about me. I mean – the Princess Malinskaya may have said something . . ."

"I don't think either Nigel or Lydia would be in the least impressed if she had." He dropped the roubles on the plate deferentially held out to him and then stretched a hand across the table and put it on hers. "Listen, Galina, you are yourself, not the past, not what your mother may be, not maid to the Princess Nina – forget all about that. Nigel and Lydia and everyone else will value you for what you are now and are capable of in the future just as I do. Now I'm going to take you home. It's late and we've had a very long day."

He picked up her shabby coat and held it for her as if it were a sable cloak and she a princess and as she slipped her arms into the sleeves, he pulled her back against him and gave her a little hug.

"If I am working you too hard as Lydia says, then you must tell me."

"Oh no," she said fervently, "oh no, I love it, every minute of it."

But in spite of what Simon had said she *did* worry of course about such stupid things as whether grand people from the embassy dressed for dinner even if it was *en famille* and, if so, what on earth was she going to wear?

Her wardrobe was scanty. She had never worried about it before but now it seemed desperately important not to let Simon down. She even consulted Luba about it. The painting was long since finished and she had not been back to the studio since nor had she attended any further meetings of the Social Revolutionaries as they now rather grandly called themselves, but Luba had the habit of looking in to see her occasionally, bringing her the latest news. On the Saturday after the night at Leiters she came knocking at the door. The first really heavy snows of winter had fallen in the previous couple of days and she came in laughing and shaking the loose flakes from her coat and shaggy fur hut.

"The river is freezing over," she said gaily, "we shall be skating soon."

Over glasses of tea and a supper of pickled herring with

little patties of meat and cabbage, Galina confided her dilemma and Luba eyed her quizzically.

"Won't your beloved doctor help you? Give him one of your big-eyed helpless looks and he'll take you down the Morskaya and buy you the prettiest gown there."

"Luba, don't make fun! It's not like that at all. I'm his assistant not his fancy woman."

"You know, my pet, you don't manage things very well, do you? In your place I'd have that big handsome Englishman eating out of my hand by now, but oh no! You just let him walk all over you and when this wonderful survey or whatever it is you're doing is over and done with, off he'll go and pouf!" she snapped her fingers, "you'll be back where you started."

In one way it put into words the dread that had haunted her more than once and it made her angry.

"You don't understand. What I do or don't do is my own affair and it's got nothing to do with this anyway."

"All right, all right, I'm ignorant, I don't know anything, but don't take it out on me. I'd lend you one of mine except that you are so much slimmer and ..."

"And they're not at all my style. What looks ravishing on you would make me seem like a popinjay at a fair."

"Thank *you*!" said Luba ruefully. "Now I know what you think of me."

"I didn't mean ... " Then they were both laughing together over it.

"In any case," went on Luba more soberly as the laughter died, "I won't be able to get into them much longer myself and what I'm going to do about that, the Lord only knows."

"What do you mean?"

"Haven't you noticed? I've let myself in for it like any fool of a girl up from the country with no more sense than a rabbit caught in a trap. I'm pregnant."

"Oh Luba, no, I thought ..."

"That I had more sense and so did I." She got up and walked away from Galina and stared out of the narrow window into the night of drifting snow.

"What does Conn say?"

Constantine was the artist with a passion for nymphs and satyrs for whom Luba had been modelling and whose bed she had shared all this last year as Galina knew very well.

"He doesn't know yet."

"Will he marry you?"

"Heavens, no! That's never been in our minds. Anyway it's not his child."

"Oh Luba!" Galina looked at her in dismay. "Then whose is it?"

"Igor Livinov's."

"What!"

For a moment she felt out of her depth and the other girl turned to her.

"I know it sounds unbelievable expecially after all I've said about him and I know what you're thinking. I've said it to myself a thousand times – don't get your fingers burned and here I am, properly caught in the fire."

"But how? Why?"

"God knows when I don't even like him!" She let herself drop into the rocking chair with a helpless gesture. "I don't really understand it myself but I must tell someone about it or burst. It was that night at the studio after your doctor carried you off. Igor was flaming mad about it, anyone could see that. Later that night there was a meeting, the usual, you know, a lot of hot air most of it, but for some reason he was transformed. He was like someone possessed. I can't remember all he said now but he had everyone roaring with enthusiasm. From somewhere there were bottles of vodka being passed around, cheap stuff but fiery as hell, and for two pins we'd all have rushed out and set fire to the Winter Palace if he had said the word. Actually all that happened was some windows smashed and a few broken heads but for a little it felt glorious, even I thought so – too much vodka on an empty stomach, I suppose," she went on ironically. "It got a bit out of hand and we ended up being chased by the police. Igor grabbed me and we ran together like lunatics and took refuge in a cellar where from being the Archangel Michael with a flaming sword, he turned into something more terrifying than old Nick himself and here I am, not at all sure what it is in my belly except that it is a gift from him."

The flippant tone did not deceive Galina in the least. She guessed at the underlying panic.

"Are you sure?"

"Oh yes, absolutely sure. You see Conn is a darling but he can't father a child. He told me once."

"What about Igor?"

"Can you imagine me telling *him*? He would laugh in my face. I'd as soon think of marrying a snake!"

"What are you going to do?"

"I don't know. I did try once to get rid of it – some filthy concoction one of the girls told me about but it didn't work, only made me sick." She paused and looked across at Galina "I suppose your doctor wouldn't . . ."

"No," she said firmly, "no. I couldn't ask him."

"No, of course you couldn't. Oh well," she went on with a faint attempt at her usual cheerfulness, "something will crop up, I expect. I'll manage somehow. I don't know what made me pour it all out like that. I never meant to say a word."

"I'm glad you did." The memory of that hateful hospital, the rows of patient abandoned babies flashed through her mind and she leaned forward clasping Luba's icy cold hand. "If you should need any help – at any time, no matter what it is, you would come to me, wouldn't you?"

For a moment Luba said nothing then she turned away her head. "Don't make me cry," she said huskily.

"Do if you want to – if it would help."

"No. Tears are a fool's game. I learnt that very early. All they do is to make you sorry for yourself and that never helped anyone." She brushed a hand across her eyes. "That's enough about me. Now let's talk about you. What about that dress? We must be able to think of something."

In the end they pooled their resources and when Simon came to collect Galina on the following Wednesday, she was waiting for him in a cream blouse of finely tucked wool edged with cheap lace, a skirt belonging to Luba in a deep wine colour nipped into her slim waist with a broad belt. She had brushed her hair till it shone, tried it in a dozen different ways and in the end chose the simplest, plaiting it loosely and piling it on top of her head. She saw with thankfulness that though he was dressed formally he was not in elaborate evening dress. Then he had handed her into the waiting cab and they were off.

The Drews lived in a large apartment in the diplomatic quarter, comfortably but not luxuriously furnished. Embassy staff were not overpaid and Nigel's father, an army man of distinction, was not as wealthy as Lord Aylsham, but their friendly unpretentious manner soon put Galina at her ease and she enjoyed the evening more than she had expected.

79

Just before they sat down to eat, the elderly English nanny appeared in the drawing room and Lydia got up.

"Will you excuse me for a few minutes? I must tuck the children up. Will you come, Simon?"

He rose at once and Galina with him.

"May I come too?"

"My dear, of course if you wish. They can be little fiends but they love to see visitors," and Lydia put a friendly hand on her arm as she led the way upstairs to the nursery.

Edward, aged two and a half, and Selina, just four, in their long white nightdresses looked at her shyly but made a concerted rush on Simon.

He laughed as he picked them up in turn, Edward trying to look very manly as he was tossed in the air while Selina slid her arms round his neck and whispered in his ear.

"I know what you are after, puss, and I haven't forgotten."

He whipped out of a pocket a gaily coloured bag tied with gold ribbon. "Now whose is it going to be?" he said and tossed it in the air. Both children made a dive for it and it was neatly fielded by Nanny.

"You shouldn't, Dr Alysham, you really shouldn't. You spoil them. No, Master Edward, you're not having any at bedtime, not even one. Tomorrow morning after breakfast, if you are good and eat up your porridge first."

"It's rank bribery," laughed Lydia. "They worship anyone who indulges them so shamefully. By the way Nanny is a great friend of Miss Hutton who used to be Nina's governess. Did you know she's come to live in Petersburg now that she's retired?"

"Missy has? Oh where?" exclaimed Galina before she could stop herself. "I'd so much like to see her again."

Lydia looked at her in surprise. "Do you know her then?"

"Galina grew up at Dannskoye," said Simon quickly while Galina still hesitated.

"Oh I see. In that case I'm sure Nanny will be happy to give you the address, won't you, Nanny?"

"Certainly, Madam. I'll write it down for the young lady."

Nanny had seen at once like any experienced English servant that Galina was not from the same stable as her employers or Dr Aylsham but far be it from her to make any comment. All the same it would be something interesting to talk over when she next took tea with Miss Emily Hutton.

Nigel spoke fluent Russian and Lydia understood a great deal more than she could find words for so they managed very well over dinner with Simon translating where necessary. They discussed the survey he was engaged in and Galina acquitted herself so well on the subject that Lydia smiled at her across the table.

"You're so young and so knowledgeable. You put all us embassy wives to shame."

Galina blushed. "You're laughing at me. There are a thousand things about which I'm so woefully ignorant."

When the servants came to clear the table Lydia rose.

"We'll have coffee served in the drawing room and don't keep Simon talking too long, Nigel."

"I won't, darling," promised her husband.

He opened the door for them and then came back to rejoin Simon at the table pushing the decanter across to him.

"Can't get any decent port, but the brandy is not too bad." He poured a measure for himself and sipped it before he went on. "There's something I'd like to ask you, Simon, something you may have heard in medical circles. There's a rumour that the baby Tsarevich is a haemophiliac. Any truth in it?"

"If he is, it's a very closely guarded secret and they're not very likely to confide in me, a foreigner, but Dr Deverenko was called in recently and afterwards he did happen to ask me in a roundabout kind of way about treatments undertaken in England. You probably know it's in our own royal family. The Tsarina is a granddaughter of Queen Victoria and the disease is conveyed through the mother."

"Poor woman! Four daughters before the longed-for son and this is what happens. Is it a killer?"

"It could be. There are treatments and alleviations but if it's true – and the baby is only very young and diagnosis could be wrong – he will never be able to lead a normal life."

"What a piece of damnable luck! At the very moment when the country needs stability above everything, we've a Tsar who suffers from a hopeless inability to make up his mind except disastrously and an heir who may not live beyond babyhood."

"Have you met the other children? Perhaps Russia is destined for another Empress Catherine."

"Olga, the eldest, is a shy pretty girl of ten but no autocrat, I fear."

"What is going to happen, Nigel?"

"Your guess is as good as mine. There is unrest certainly. The war with Japan is going badly and there is something brewing among the factory workers that could break pretty soon, but cloistered in our diplomatic circle we don't hear much, you know." He finished the brandy thoughtfully. "When are you going home, Simon?"

"I've not made any plans at the moment."

"But when this job you've set yourself to do is finished, what then? You can't go on living from day to day."

"Why can't I?"

"Oh for heaven's sake, man, you're wasting yourself. Forgive me for asking but is there any reason why you can't return to London?"

"No. Uncle Jethro writes that my old post at the hospital would still be open to me."

"Then why, for God's sake?"

"I don't know." He fiddled with his glass then looked up, smiling wryly. "Cowardice perhaps."

"That's rubbish," said his friend flatly. "If you're not intending to leave Russia, are you going to set up in practice here?"

"I might even do that."

"With that young woman you've brought here as your assistant I suppose," he said ironically.

"Perhaps. She is extremely intelligent, hard-working and personable, don't you think?"

"And is that all?"

"What more do you want? Don't nag at me, Nigel."

"Well, you shouldn't be such a damned awkward fellow," exploded Nigel well aware that he was being kept firmly at a distance. "Let me know if you do. You'll have the embassy staff queuing up on your doorstep." He pushed aside his glass. "We'd better join the girls or Lydia will have my blood."

In the drawing room Lydia said, "Come and sit near the stove. It's warmer here. How I long for a lovely English fire! In my old home we used to burn huge logs from the forest. They smouldered day and night in the great hall."

Galina, who had understood only about half, smiled but said nothing.

The servant brought the tray of coffee and Lydia poured a cup and brought it to her.

"How long have you known Simon?"

"Nearly a year. I attended his lectures at the university."

"Were they good?"

"We all thought them wonderful." She hesitated then went on boldly. "He helped me when I was being hunted by the police."

"Police?"

"Yes. It wasn't for – for stealing or anything like that," she said defiantly.

Lydia smiled. "I didn't suppose it was."

"It was a student demonstration that went wrong."

"That would be just like Simon. Nigel told me that he never cared a great deal for authority even at school."

She had fetched her own coffee and dropped down on the fur rug as close as she could to the porcelain tiled stove, her casual informal manner astonishing Galina who still sat rather primly on the edge of the sofa.

"You know it's a great relief to Nigel and me to see him looking so much more like himself. When he came here about eighteen months ago now, we were really very worried about him."

"Why?"

"Well, he'd thrown up a successful career in London and would not tell us the reason. He had been spoken of as one of the most promising young surgeons at Barts – that's a famous hospital – and yet here he was looking dreadful, wasting his time, drinking too much . . ."

"Why? Why should he do that?"

"God knows. He has never said a word, but Nigel did hear from someone else that there was trouble over a woman and some sort of scandal. He has never spoken of it to you, has he?"

"Oh no. He would not talk to me about something so – so very private to him."

"I think it might be a lot better for him if he did. Confession is good for the soul, isn't that what they say?"

"Yes perhaps," said Galina doubtfully.

Then Nigel and Simon came in together and conversation became general.

By the time they left the snow had become very thick but Nigel's manservant had a cab waiting for them and when it pulled up outside the shabby apartment house, Simon got out with her.

"Enjoy yourself tonight?"

"Oh yes. I never thought grand people like that would be so – so friendly."

"Lydia would laugh to hear herself called grand."

"They are to me."

"They're nothing of the sort. You know what you are, Galina, you're an inverted snob."

He used the English word for lack of a Russian equivalent and she repeated it frowning.

"Inverted snob? What is that?"

"Someone who pretends to be humble and believes herself a great deal better than anyone else."

"I'm not at all like that," she replied in high indignation.

"Oh yes, you are, and there is no need. You are as good as you believe yourself to be and don't you forget it."

The faint light from the carriage lamps lit her upturned face and he knew he wanted very much to kiss it, feel that firm defiant mouth soften under his, strip off the worn coat and feel the slim body in its pathetically pretty blouse warm and tremble and yield to him. But in a way, as Nigel had hinted, she had become his responsibility and some innate feeling of decency and honesty held him back. Instead he took her hand and pressed it warmly.

"Goodnight and sleep well. We've a long day tomorrow."

He went back to the cab and she walked up the stairs with a kind of singing happiness deep inside her because the evening had given her a new picture of Simon, a deeper sympathy, and tomorrow she would see him again and the day after that and she did not guess that Igor Livinov watched them from an upper window.

The incident at the studio still rankled. He saw the intimacy between them and burned with an angry jealousy for all those privileged by rank, or money, or intellectual brilliance, a passionate desire to see them torn down, ground into the dust, thrown into the holocaust that he firmly believed would surely come sooner than anyone expected.

At much the same time Lydia was brushing her hair before going to bed when her husband came in from his dressing room.

"Nigel," she said thoughtfully putting down the brush and beginning to tie back the long fair hair, "do you think that young woman is Simon's mistress?"

"What a question! As a matter of fact I don't. I doubt if he would have brought her here if she was."

"In case I might be corrupted? Oh darling, don't be silly. If I started being prudish I'd have to turn my nose up at quite a number of young women I meet every day."

"Lydia, what *are* you saying?"

"Don't pretend you don't know. I could name quite a few but I won't. Look at the Tsar, goody-goody though he always seems. Everyone knows that the ballerina Mathilde Kschessinska is his mistress."

"Not since his marriage I'm told."

"Are you sure of that? Anyway nobody cares. They all flock around her like bees round a honeypot. Still maybe you're right about Simon but she's in love with him, that's certain."

"How can you possibly know that?" objected Nigel discarding his dressing gown and climbing into bed.

"Woman's instinct. The way she looks at him. He's God-come-down-to-earth for her at the moment so he had better look out. He couldn't marry her."

"Why couldn't he?" said her husband lazily. "He's not the eldest son and England is a long way from Petersburg."

"They'd never accept her."

"Times are changing, Lydia. In ten years' time nobody will care about things like that," and he had no notion how true his half laughing words would prove.

"She's prickly, not quite sure of herself, but I liked her," went on Lydia. "Shift over, you brute, you're taking more than your half." She got into bed and pulled up the coverlet. "She's been good for him too, captured his interest, got him working again."

"Oh be blowed to Simon! He's quite capable of managing his own life."

"Nina Malinsky would be a good match for him. Her father is rich and she's really delightfully pretty."

"And an empty-headed little noodle," said Nigel sleepily. "Don't wish her on him and stop trying to run other people's lives for them. They won't thank you for it," and he pulled her against him. "Think about your husband instead."

"Don't I always?"

"Not as much as I would like."

"Don't be greedy."

She settled herself into the curve of his body and made up

her mind to have a little chat with Nanny. All these English servants enjoyed a good gossip when they met on their days off. She would find out if there was anything interesting to know about Galina Panova.

6

On Sunday afternoon with the December day already drawing in, the frozen Neva was crowded with skaters; young women in costly furs escorted by army officers in brilliant uniforms, working folk bundled up in padded coats and long scarves, students flying across the ice in parties of three or four, arms linked, and shrieking children everywhere darting in and out of the more stately skaters and threatening to overturn them. Lamps had been lighted, casting great pools of golden light across the ice, fires burned in giant braziers at the river edge and there were stalls peddling glasses of scalding tea and hot savouries of all kinds wrapped in white paper and eaten in the fingers. The artists, writers and actors from the studios on the island were there in force and Luba had dragged a reluctant Galina from her attic room.

"I've work to do," she protested.

"Not on a Sunday you haven't! What is he, this doctor of yours, some kind of a slave driver or what?"

"No, of course he isn't but – the truth is I haven't any skates."

"You can borrow mine. Conn says I'm not to risk falling flat on my face or on this," and she patted her stomach with a rueful grin.

"Have you told him?"

Luba nodded. "Yes, I have and the poor darling believes he's achieved the impossible. I know it's wicked of me to let him think the baby is his, but the look on his face when I was only half-way through so took my breath away that I hadn't the heart to go on and tell him the truth."

"Is that wise?"

"What *is* wise? I don't know – I never did. So don't let's go on about it. Are you coming or aren't you?"

"I'll get my coat."

At the river bank the artists crowded around her asking questions about what she had been doing and not listening to her replies in their eagerness to tell of their own triumphs. Sergei had sold his picture and was in funds for once, Conn had a commission from a rich German merchant for a couple of paintings to adorn his mistress's bedroom ("Naked nymphs," giggled Luba, "but not me this time, thank goodness!") and someone else had had a poem accepted in a high-class literary magazine and was jubilant. It was only afterwards that she glimpsed Igor, a solitary figure, keeping himself aloof from the others and yet somehow it was as if he still had power over them all and she shivered a little not just from the cold.

She was lacing up Luba's boots when she saw Simon. He was hand in hand with Nina who looked radiant, white fox trimming her scarlet coat and framing the laughing face upturned to him. Half a dozen students from the music academy broke into a Strauss waltz and the other skaters drew aside as the couple glided on to the ice. He was spinning her round and reversing, turning her under his arm, letting her go, then pulling her back to him with a skill that brought a round of applause from those who had paused to watch.

"Heavens," he gasped when they stopped at last, "it's such a long time since I tried anything like that, I didn't know whether I could still pull it off."

"I never thought the English could skate," said Nina breathlessly.

"Neither can they, most of them. We haven't your opportunities. I used to be what they call a 'Fen Tiger'. We competed in races, four or five miles at a stretch, but that was a very long time ago."

She hung on to his hand teasing him to try again but he shook his head.

"It's tempting fate – only someone very foolhardy does that."

He put an arm around her leading her back to the others and Niki clapped him on the back.

"Well done! You and Nina make quite a pair!"

That was when Galina knew for the first time a sudden and

overwhelming jealousy. She was quite aware it was absurd. He had told her casually that he was paying a duty call on the Malinskys. No doubt they had urged him to join their skating party and why shouldn't he? She had no claim on him and yet she experienced a deep burning pain to see him dancing so gaily and intimately with Nina. She suddenly hated the borrowed boots, the ugly worn coat, the red woollen scarf she had wound around her head and shoulders. The others pressed around her and she felt stifled in the midst of their laughing chatter. She pulled herself away skating alone down the ice longing only to get away.

Simon knew she was there but thought her happy to be with her friends. Half listening to Nina he saw how Igor caught up with Galina and was angrily thrown off. He excused himself quickly and went after her. She was skating fast, the red scarf streaming out behind her, and by the time he reached her they were well away from the lamplight and winter dark was creeping in full of shadows. He came up behind her slipping an arm around her waist.

"I told you to leave me alone," she said fiercely and tried to pull away.

He tightened his grip. "It's all right. It's only me."

"Oh," she said on a long breath. "I thought it was Igor. Why aren't you with the Malinskys?"

"I was. Why didn't you come across and join us?"

"How could I? It would only embarrass Nina in front of her fine friends."

"Nothing of the sort."

She dragged herself free but he caught at her hand and pulled her back to him.

"What's wrong? Are you angry with me?"

"Why should I be?"

"That's what I want to know. You're shaking."

"I'm cold."

"Well, that's soon remedied. Come on, Galina, stop this foolishness. Doctor's orders. I'm going to make sure you drink something hot."

She gave in and let him skate her back. He bought her tea and a *blini* so burning hot that it fell through her fingers. He tried to catch it and missed so that they began to laugh helplessly and it was Nina's turn to feel the quick prick of anger. He had been happy with her till he had seen that girl. She had meant to speak to Galina, tell her she was sorry for all that had happened but now in a fit of pique that Simon had abandoned her so cavalierly, she turned her back on the others. She and her brother had skated since they were hardly more than babies, sliding and falling on the frozen lake at Dannskoye. She let the impetus carry her away spinning round on one foot and then on the other in graceful pirouettes until unexpectedly she missed her balance and sat down with a bump. Two strong arms lifted her up and set her on her feet. An unfamiliar voice spoke close to her ear.

"That wasn't very clever, was it, Princess? Are you hurt?"

"No."

A little breathless she was looking into the face of Igor, lean, bony, arresting.

She frowned. "I don't know you, do I?"

"Your brother does," he said carelessly. "Ask Niki who I am."

In her sheltered life she had never met anyone quite like him before at such close quarters; the cultured voice, the faintly insolent manner, the workman's clothes, the student cap worn at a rakish angle. She was intrigued and at the same time a little afraid.

"Do you mean you are one of the revolutionaries Niki used to tell me about?"

"Childish stuff," he said off-handedly, "we dig a little deeper than that now."

"How?"

"Tell Niki to bring you to one of our meetings and you'll find out."

"I don't think he would. Niki has changed. He has promised my father to spend more time running our estates."

"But that still leaves you."

"I don't understand anything like that."

"I could teach you." He reached for her hand deliberately pulling off the fur gloves and playing with her fingers. "What do you say?"

She shivered. "Perhaps," then abruptly she shook her head suddenly scared by what she was doing, by the peculiar glitter in his eyes, "and perhaps not."

She drew back her hand and glided quickly away from him.

He was left standing, the glove still in his hand. He looked after her thinking nothing of the encounter except that it might be amusing to pursue that pampered fair-haired doll, find out what, if anything, lay behind the spoiled pretty face. Women meant little in the solitary life to which he had dedicated himself, no more than an hour's physical release as it had been that night with Luba when he was intoxicated with his own sense of power. He had wanted Galina, and still did, partly because in her he had sensed a quality he might use one day and partly because she had so vehemently rejected him from the very first. One of these days he would bring her to her knees, he would make her repent her easy contempt, acknowledge him as master.

He had been only sixteen when his elder brother, a shy diffident boy of nineteen, had been arrested for an act of terrorism in which he had in fact played only a very small part. Despite desperate pleas for mercy from his mother, he was hanged along with the three others concerned. The shame and shock had killed their schoolmaster father. Burning for revenge Igor had taken part in a foolish noisy demonstration and with the other law students had been thrown into prison, but instead of the usual punishment and release, he had been judged more harshly because of his brother and banished to Siberia for three long years during which his mother, overcome with grief and poverty, had died. He returned a confirmed revolutionary dedicated to revenge against the injustice. He was clever and had not wasted his three years in exile. He could speak French and German, he could mix with people when necessary and was already proving himself useful. He knew so well how to play upon young idealistic minds urging them to perform deeds of violence in which he took care not to involve himself. He had a burning conviction that he was destined for great things when the day came at last. He watched Galina with that damned Englishman and knew in his bones that the opportunity would come. He had only to wait. Then he skated across to where the Malinskys were preparing to leave.

"Your glove, Princess," he said smoothly and contrived to press the fingers she stretched out to him.

"Thank you," she faltered.

He gave her a sketchy salute and skated away.

Niki was frowning. "Where the devil did that fellow spring from? He's not been pestering you, has he?"

"No, of course not. I dropped my glove, that's all, and he returned it. Do you know him, Niki?"

"His name is Igor Livinov and you keep away from him."

"Why? Because he is a revolutionary?"

"So he *has* been speaking to you."

"No, not really. I just guessed at it when he said he knew you."

"Well, don't go encouraging him."

"As if I would! Really, darling, don't be silly. He's not in our set at all."

But all the same her brother's disapproval had added to her interest rather than diminished it. A little devil of mischief rose up in rebellion. Not that she meant to do anything about it of course, but all the same there *had* been something rather fascinating about him.

It was a few days before Christmas when Galina called one afternoon on Miss Hutton in her tiny flat. She had brought a gift, a pretty Chinese lacquered box of tea which she knew Missy particularly enjoyed.

"My dear child," exclaimed the governess when she unwrapped it, "how very kind of you and how clever to remember my favourite Lapsang. Now sit down and tell me all about yourself. I was very worried after that wretched business in the summer and very glad to hear that you had succeeded in finding a post for yourself. I want to hear all about it."

Galina began to tell her about the work with Simon, omitting the weeks of misery and near starvation, and watching the way her eyes glowed with enthusiasm when she spoke of the hours they were spending together, Miss Hutton inwardly uttered a little prayer that the child was not being deceived and riding for a fall.

"And now he has brought one of these new typewriting machines for me and I've been teaching myself to use it so that when it is all finished, I can type it all out ready for printing. There is not really enough room in my attic so he has taken an extra room adjoining his apartment and I work there with him sometimes."

"It certainly sounds fascinating but when it is finished, what then? What are your plans, Galina?"

"I don't know," she confessed. "I've not looked beyond that. Perhaps I could find work of a similar kind. It has been wonderful experience." She glanced up at the clock guiltily. "Just look at the time. I've been talking for hours all about myself. I really ought not to be taking up so much of your time."

"I have plenty to spare nowadays and I'm certainly not going to let you go without a cup of this delicious tea."

"Can I help?"

"No. It won't take a few minutes."

As she rose the bell rang again and she went to let in another visitor. Nina came hurrying in, her coat and hat of sealskin sprnkled with snow, her face rosy from the cold.

She greeted Galina effusively. "I've been meaning to come and see you but you know how it is when we are in Petersburg. There never seems to be a minute. Mamma expects me to go shopping with her and what with that and receiving visitors and making return calls, to say nothing of evening engagements, the days simply fly by."

Galina smiled but said nothing and Nina prattled on.

"I've brought you a little present, Missy darling. I hope you like it," and she put down a box elaborately wrapped in striped paper.

"What is it?"

"Open it and see."

It was a cashmere shawl in a deep rich violet. She shook it out and draped it around her governess's shoulders.

"It will keep you warm in this bitter weather."

Miss Hutton shook her head disapprovingly. "It's much too expensive. You're an extravagant puss, but it's very kind of you." She leaned forward to kiss Nina's cheek. "I was just going to make some tea. You'll stay and take a cup?"

"Oh yes please. I'd love some."

"Very well. You talk to Galina while I fetch it."

Left alone the two girls eyed one another a little warily.

Nina said casually, "Niki told me that you have been working with Dr Aylsham."

"Yes. I've been very fortunate. It's a hospital survey he is engaged on and he needed someone to go around with him and transcribe his notes afterwards."

"Do you enjoy it?"

"Oh yes, very much. I'm learning a good deal too."

"I'm sure you are. I hear he actually took you to dinner with his embassy friends."

"Yes, he did. We met them by chance after a day's work together so they included me in the invitation."

"You *were* lucky. What were they like?"

"Charming. Lydia has two children, a boy and a girl. You should have seen how they adored Simon."

"Lydia and Simon! My word, you *are* on friendly terms, aren't you?"

Nina was restlessly wandering around the room picking up books and putting them down again and it struck Galina for the first time that she was jealous – Princess Nina with all her advantages jealous of one of her father's serfs – the very idea was ridiculous enough to make her laugh. Then the other girl swung round suddenly and faced her.

"You know why he asked you to act as his assistant, don't you?"

"I hoped it was because he thought I was suitable."

"Oh no, it wasn't that at all," said Nina carelessly, "it was because he was so sorry for you. You see the hospital director would not hear of a girl student being employed in such a way so of course he had to pay you himself and only pretend that you had been engaged by them."

Galina stared at her. "That's not true."

"Didn't you know? Ask him if you don't believe me. He told Niki and they had a good laugh over it. 'Heaven knows what they're thinking,' he said, 'but I had to do something for the poor girl!'" – all of which was not strictly true. Niki had heard a garbled story from quite another source. Simon had mentioned it to nobody.

She ought to feel grateful but instead a deep burning anger surged through her. He had made her feel she was important to him, that she was a person in her own right, able to pull her weight in the work they had been doing together, and all the time it had been simply out of pity, a crust thrown to a starving dog, something to laugh over with Niki and his other friends.

It boiled up inside her so that it was difficult to sit quietly drinking tea and chatting lightly while Nina talked on about her new gowns, the visits to the Maryinsky to see the new ballet, the parties she had attended and the ball her father had promised to hold for her eighteenth birthday in a month or so's time. As soon as she decently could Galina excused herself, kissing Missy warmly and promising to come again soon.

Outside it was dark already and the street lamps sent shafts of light across the newly fallen snow. She would have liked to go to Simon now, face him with it while it still seethed inside her but she knew he was spending the evening with friends and she must wait patiently through the night until the following morning.

That was the worst part. Hours and hours when she lay awake, that fierce prickly pride of hers rising up in rebellion. She should have seen through it at the very start. Luba was right. She had let herself fall under his spell, had followed where he had led like any silly moon-struck girl because stupidly, idiotically, she had fallen in love with him, something she had sworn never to do, never – she despised herself for that. How could she have been such a fool! And he had laughed about it, about the simple girl who ran after him like a little dog! She sat up in bed and beat her fist angrily on the pillow – it was so hatefully humiliating.

It was a fine bright morning but bitterly cold. She was up early and dressed with special care. She needed all her dignity, all her pride in herself. She would tell him exactly what she thought and then walk out with a grand gesture. Let him find someone else on whom to bestow his pity and run his errands for him.

She walked quickly across the frozen Neva and through the streets to the tall brown house that had become so familiar to her only to find that he was not there. Instead a folded note lay on the table.

"Called away but back this evening," and beside it lay a pile of notes corrected and annotated in his neat script ready for her to type again. It was an infuriating setback. She doggedly worked through the day not even stopping to eat while the first flush of high indignation slowly ebbed away leaving her feeling tired, deflated and utterly miserable.

About five o'clock she heard the outer door slam. There was a quick step in the adjoining room, then he was there looking unusually bulky in his thick winter coat with the astrakhan collar, the shaggy fur cap cocked over one eye. He banged the flakes of snow from his gloves bringing a breath of the fresh icy air into the stuffy room.

"Sorry I wasn't here," he said breezily, "did you find the sheets I left for you?"

"Yes, they're almost finished."

"Good." He glanced down at the neatly typed pile. "It looks as if you've done enough for one day. Put your hat on, we're going out to eat and then we're off to the opera. I've got a couple of seats for *Boris Gudunov*. Chaliapin is singing. They say he's tremendous. They were all sold out but Nigel had two he can't use so he let me have them." He was pulling off his cap and unbuttoning his coat as he spoke.

"I'm not coming," she said quietly.

He paused on his way out. "Don't be silly. Of course you're coming and no nonsense about not being dressed suitably. We're not sitting in the royal box."

"Perhaps you'd rather be there – with Nina."

"Is that meant to be a joke?"

She had risen to her feet, very pale and determined. "No, it isn't and didn't you hear what I said? I'm not coming."

He was frowning at her now. "What's wrong? Aren't you well? You've been working too hard, that's what it is. You shouldn't neglect yourself. You'll feel quite different with some food inside you."

"I don't want your food. I can buy my own."

"What the devil are you talking about?"

"It's quite simple. I don't wish to go on living on your charity. I never did. I thought I made that quite clear. You never really wanted me at all, did you? You only took me on out of pity."

"Where did you hear all this?"

"From Nina if you really want to know. She and Niki thought it a grand joke. You must have enjoyed telling them about it and how easily I swallowed it all."

"I never spoke of it to anyone."

"But it *is* true, isn't it?"

"Yes, it's true but not in the way you mean."

"In what way then? Did you want to buy me? Have a hold over me so that I was under an obligation to you for the rest of my life? Was that it?"

"For God's sake, Galina, don't you know me better than that by now? Do you imagine I would have taken you into my confidence, discussed the work with you, spent so much time with you if I didn't believe in your intelligence, in your ability, your good sense – if I hadn't thought it worth while for both of us?"

"Why didn't you tell me right at the start?"

"Because if I had you would have curled up like the little hedgehog you are, all bristling prickles and died rather than accept it from me. Isn't that true?"

"I don't know," she said unhappily. "I only know I can't go on as it is."

"My dear girl, can't you learn to accept as well as give? Isn't that part of the relationship between friends? And we are friends, aren't we?" She didn't answer and in exasperation he crossed to her, taking her by the shoulders and giving her a little shake. "Don't just stand there. Answer me. Are we friends or aren't we?"

Abruptly at his touch all her defences crumbled. It had been a long wretched day and she gave a strangled sob and collapsed against him. His arms went around her and after a moment he tilted up the tear-stained face.

"You little fool, don't you understand anything?"

He kissed her lightly and quite suddenly it was not kissing away his young sister's troubles or petting the spoiled pretty Nina but something utterly different. He felt it in the very fibre of his being and so did she. He pulled her roughly to him and kissed her hard and long. They were shaken by the violence of the emotion that raced through them. It was like a river bursting its dam, a flood that had been rigorously held back for weeks had suddenly swept them together and they were helplessly caught up in it.

The storm had taken them both by surprise and he was the first to pull himself together. He drew away from her.

"Go and wash your face and get dressed. We're going out," he said huskily.

Dazed she watched him walk away from her and then quietly did what he had asked. Her hands shook as she tidied her hair staring at her face in the mirror. Was it possible that he really cared? She must not dwell on it. She must not hope.

It was a strange evening when they hardly dared to touch one another in case restraint should suddenly snap and they would fly into one another's arms. In the small quiet restaurant to which he took her she never afterwards remembered what she ate or even what they talked about, only that when he filled her wine glass and his fingers touched hers, she trembled, and when they rose to go and he put her coat around her shoulders holding her close to him for an instant a thrill ran through her whole body. All through the opera sitting in the crowded stalls pressed close against him, the glorious singing of the chorus, the great procession surging across the stage in all the majesty of old Russia, seemed part of the wonder, the rich bass voice of the great singer full of power and torment and grief becoming part of her feeling for the man beside her.

Afterwards in the foyer with people crowding them on every side, he said, "Are you hungry? Would you care for some supper?" She shook her head. It was not food she craved. But all the same the practical side of life had to go on.

"I left papers and notes I shall need for tomorrow," she whispered.

"We'll pick them up and then I'll take you home."

The cabs had already changed their wheels for sleigh runners. The driver almost as broad as he was tall in his enormous padded coat drew up with a flourish of his whip, then they were off flying across the frozen snow. At the house he grinned slyly at them as Simon put the money in his hand and followed her through the door.

A lamp had been lit and the soft glow suffused the room. He stood for the moment looking at her as she gathered notebooks and papers putting them into a portfolio. The fur hood had fallen back and her face was ivory white. He knew every expression by now, how laughter would lighten her eyes at some childish joke, the radiant wonder when she listened to him explaining some knotty point, the stubborn pride. He had not realized how dear it had become to him. He had loved once and it had ended cruelly and disastrously. He wanted this girl, had wanted badly to make love to her for weeks now, but she was alone and defenceless. It must be her decision, not his.

He suddenly made up his mind. He crossed to her, taking the portfolio out of her hand and putting it aside. She looked up at him a little startled, the chestnut hair dampened by the snow curled around her ears and neck. He touched her cheek gently.

"Galina," he said huskily, "do you want to stay with me?"

She had known what was coming. It had become inevitable all during the evening and she had hoped for it with so fierce a longing that it frightened her. She nodded, unable to speak and he cupped her face between his two hands.

97

"You are sure? It's not because you feel you owe me something because you don't, nothing at all, and if that is in your mind, then I am sending you away from me this very instant."

She shook her head finding the right words at last.

"Do you remember the very first time I came here and we played a game for that policeman? I loved you then and didn't know it. I've been waiting for this moment ever since."

The honesty, the simplicity, enchanted him. He held out his arms and she walked into them.

At some time during that night when she lay wakeful and he drowsed, his head close to hers on the pillow, his hand, that shapely surgeon's hand, on her breast, she thought, "Maybe I *am* like my mother after all. Maybe she felt like this when she loved my father for the first time."

She thought she would remember it for ever, his tenderness, the touch of his lips on her breast, the blush of shame when she remembered the darned white petticoat, the plain cotton chemise, forgotten when he carred her to the bed, the laughter when they remembered that other time when he had stripped off her nightgown and tended her with such care, and afterwards the passion, the pain and the ecstasy. Above all the companionship, to know that she was needed, that she belonged, that she was no longer alone. What the future held did not concern her yet. She held the joy within her like something infinitely precious and was content.

7

"What's happened to you?" asked Luba eyeing Galina curiously one evening a few weeks later when she called in for a chat and a bite of supper. "You're different somehow."

"How do you mean – different?"

"I'm not sure but for one thing you're not listening to me. I don't think you've heard a single word I've been saying."

"Yes, I have," protested Galina guiltily only too well aware how true it was. Ever since that night she seemed to have lived in a dream so that nothing that happened in the outside world had any real importance for her.

"*And* I believe I know why," went on Luba triumphantly, "it's your English doctor, isn't it? He has come up to scratch. Good for you."

"I don't know what you're talking about."

"Oh yes, you do, and you're over the moon about it, but do be careful, darling, don't get trapped like me."

"Oh Luba, please . . ."

"All right, all right, if you don't want to talk about it . . ."

"No, I don't." It was still a secret joy which she didn't wish to share with anyone, not even Luba. She refilled their glasses with tea and pushed the sugar across the table. "Go on with your story. Weren't you telling me something about Igor?"

"Only that he's cock-a-hoop too but for *quite* a different reason. Has anyone told you about this enormous rally fixed for next Sunday?"

"What kind of rally?"

"A demonstration really. It seems it all began at the Putilov steelworks."

"Oh I do know something about that. Hasn't there been a strike? Simon was to visit their medical centre and it was postponed at the last minute. Has Igor organized it?"

"Not exactly, but he's part of it. Can't see him being left out, can you? It has grown and grown. Conn and I went to a mass meeting and this priest got up, Father Gapon, he calls himself, quite a heart-throb, my dear," she went on with a giggle, "one of those with a foot in either camp if you ask me but a marvellous speaker. He had them all hanging on his every word. There's going to be a united advance of workers from all over the city to the Winter Palace and a petition of their grievances presented to the Tsar though heaven knows what they expect *him* to do."

"You're not intending to join it, are you?"

"Yes, we are, both of us. I think it's tremendous. It's not just the men on strike who are marching, it's everyone, women and children too."

She spoke of it as if it were a gigantic picnic but Simon took a much more cautious view when Galina told him about it.

"It's a day to keep off the streets in my opinion. Heaven knows what is likely to come of it."

That morning they had both been accidentally caught up in the crowd gathered to watch the time-old ceremony of the Blessing of the Waters, an ancient rite going back to antiquity and based on the baptism of Christ in the River Jordan. So many people had packed on to the river bank that they couldn't move and were obliged to stand there while the square hole was cut through the Neva's thick ice amidst a stately procession of priests from the cathedral, robed in golden vestments hung with pearls and precious stones. The Tsar, looking small and insignificant beside their magnificence, sipped from the glass of water handed to him and the water was solemnly blessed.

"Let's hope he doesn't contract dysentery or typhoid," whispered Simon wickedly into her ear. "That water must be crawling with germs!"

The guns standing among the ranged troops fired a salute and suddenly there were screams of panic as a wall splintered and one of the police close to the Tsar gave a strangled cry and collapsed. Simon grasped her firmly against him holding her up against the stampede of people trying to get away. Afterwards rumours ran all around the city that the guns had been loaded with live ammunition instead of blanks in an attempt to assassinate the Tsar.

Some of the embassy staff curious to see the outcome of the Sunday demonstration hired a room above a confectioner just where the Nevsky Prospect led into the square and Nigel asked Simon to join them. He was not all that eager but gave in to Galina's urging. No one anticipated any real trouble. Despite the intense cold and a bitter wind bringing flurries of snow, the crowds began to gather from all the workers' districts very early, marching together, men carrying icons and banners, women with prams, children riding on their fathers' shoulders, dogs barking and getting under everyone's feet, all of them singing hymns and scheduled to reach the square in front of the Winter Palace by two o'clock when the long elaborately written petition would be handed to the Tsar.

In that upper room it was like a party. Coffee was brought up from the shop below and someone had thought to bring vodka. From the windows they could see the wide street packed from side to side with a good-natured happy mob still with a devout trust in their Tsar, their 'Little Father', a distant, glorious God-like figure whom most of them had never even seen. Bystanders, pressed back against shop fronts, bowed and crossed themselves as the icons swayed by. Galina caught a glimpse of Luba arm in arm with Conn and Sergei laughing and happy. She waved but doubted if they could see her. In front of the palace presumably to keep order was a long line of Cossacks motionless on their black horses. They raised their rifles threateningly but the crowd happy and still good-tempered took little heed. They linked arms and surged forward. The singing rose to a crescendo and then the un-believable happened.

The soldiers fired, not above their heads in an effort to disperse them, but straight into the heart of that laughing cheerful crowd. The bullets ripped through them, killing and wounding, tearing icons and banners to shreds. For one moment they stood as if stunned and then turned and fled in panic, stumbling over fallen comrades, screaming in terror and pain, in disillusionment and baffled anger.

Aghast Galina was staring out at a scene of carnage, then Simon beside her stirred and moved to the door.

"I'm going down there."

Nigel tried to stop him. "Don't be a fool, man. What can you do?"

"I don't know but there are friends of ours among them. Even if they're unhurt, they could be trampled to death."

Nothing the others could say would dissuade him and after a moment's hesitation Galina went with him, but once in the street there was very little that could be done.

People were running in fear and bewilderment trying to escape the hooves of the rearing horses as the Cossacks advanced slowly but relentlessly, unsheathed sabres in their hands. She could not find Luba or Conn or any of her friends from the studios and could only hope they had been able to find refuge somewhere. Simon with blood on his hands and staining his coat was trying to drag the wounded out of the way of the trampling feet of those who fled in terrified mindless confusion.

The horror of the day seemed to go on and on. Not one of those thousands ever reached the Winter Palace or presented the petition. The Tsar in any case was out of the city and it seemed that the government had panicked. As the five con-verging columns advanced they were met at bridges and road ends by contingents of troops who did not hesitate to shoot down the leaders. How many died and how many were wounded it was impossible to tell and it was late afternoon when at last ambulances fought their way over the blood-stained snow picking up the dead and the dying. Every hospital was crowded to the doors. Simon offered his services which were gratefully received. All throughout the rest of the day and far into the night they worked. Galina distressed and sickened would not stir from his side, doing any job that came to hand.

It was four o'clock in the morning when he took her home to her attic room where she still insisted on maintaining her independence.

"A baptism of fire, my darling," he said touching her cheek gently. "Now you know what it means to have a surgeon for a lover."

He kissed her and for a moment they clung together before he climbed wearily back into the cab.

She went slowly up the stairs. Igor's door was shut and she wondered if he had been amongst the leaders and with his usual gift of self-preservation had fled before the worst had happened.

She fell exhausted on her bed without doing more than dip her face and hands in clean water and was awakened a few hours later by a furious hammering at the door. She struggled off the bed, the nightmare of the day still part of her uneasy dreams. Outside was Conn, his thick coat bundled on anyhow, a woollen cap pulled down to his eyes, looking so distraught that she cried out in alarm.

"What is it? What is wrong?"

"It's Luba," he blurted out. "She's in agony."

"How? Why? Have you fetched a doctor?"

"We've never had occasion to use one and the hospital can't help. I went there first. There are patients lying on the floors and in the passages. I had to step over them."

"What happened to her, Conn?"

"It was the demonstration. When they began to fire at us, I tried to get her away quickly but she slipped on the ice and fell in the snow. The rush knocked me off my feet, it was a minute before I could get back to her and by then she had been badly kicked. She swore it was nothing, only bruises, but now there's so much blood. I don't know what to do." He reached out seizing Galina's hands. "She's not going to die, is she?"

"No, of course she isn't," she tried to sound reassuring.

There was only one man she could go to for help but would he come? He was even more exhausted than she was after that appalling day.

She said, "Go back to her, Conn. Cover her up and keep her warm. Have plenty of hot water ready, we may need it. I'll try and persuade Dr Aylsham to come."

"Oh God, Galina, I'm so frightened for her."

"Try not to worry. Whatever happens I will come. Now go back quickly. Don't leave her alone too long."

It was seven o'clock already but still very dark before she managed to stop a cruising cab and reached the house. Simon wakened by the knocking on the door got groggily to his feet still in the shirt and trousers he had been too weary to take off the night before. The door was usually answered by the house-keeper but either she had not heard it or had gone out early to the market. He staggered along the passage and exclaimed when he saw Galina.

"What are you doing here at this ungodly hour?"

"It's Luba," she said. "She's terribly ill. Conn can't get a doctor and the hospital won't help."

"What's wrong with her?"

"She is pregnant and today in that crowd she fell and was hurt before Conn could get her away. She's in great pain and bleeding, he says. He didn't know what to do. Oh Simon, I know it's a great deal to ask but please, please come."

She was asking more than she realized but he tried to think clearly, shake the weariness from him. A life was a life and he must do what he could to save it.

"I'll have to put things together. I'll be as quick as I can."

"Oh Simon, thank you," she breathed. "I have a cab waiting."

"Good. You'd better come inside."

"No. I'll stay in the cab."

He went back to his room, dipped his face in ice-cold water to wake himself up and dressed quickly. He looked through his instruments and drugs. Since he had been helping out at the hospital he had obtained new supplies for his medicine chest. As a last thought and knowing the conditions most of the artists lived in, he took the sheets from the bed and rolled them into a bundle. He might need them.

In the cab he asked a few pertinent questions.

"How long has she been pregnant?"

"I'm not sure. About five months I think."

"Is it Conn's child?"

Galina hesitated. She would not betray Luba's secret. "I presume so. I never asked."

"She hasn't been trying to get rid of it."

"No, never."

Conn almost fell upon his neck with gratitude when they climbed the steep stairs to the studio apartment. Doors opened and heads peered out at them as they passed. There had been a police round-up after the events of the Sunday and everyone was on the alert for trouble.

Conn had recklessly piled wood into the stove and the small room where Luba lay was stiflingly hot.

Simon threw off his heavy coat and moved to the bed.

"Dr Simon himself – I'm honoured," whispered Luba with a ghost of her old cheery smile, but he saw the panic in her eyes and the way she braced herself against the pain.

He put a hand on her forehead. "Try and be brave, my dear. We'll soon have you feeling a lot better."

He turned back the bed clothes to make his examination. It was worse than he had anticipated. The bruising had been heavy and extensive. He knew he must act quickly and it might be necessary to use the knife. For an instant his mind clouded. He was back once again in that operating theatre. He felt the sweat cold on his body and his hands shook. He raised his head fighting his weakness and saw Galina watching him, her eyes luminous with an absolute trust that he knew he could not betray. He drew a deep breath and miraculously the spasm passed. He knew this time he would not fail. He was suddenly cool and steady.

He took off his coat, rolled up his shirt sleeves and looked across at Conn.

"Lift her up," he said crisply, "so that Galina and I can put a clean sheet on the bed and then fetch me boiling water."

Conn did as he was told, only too glad to be of use, while Simon scrubbed his hands and sterilized his instruments.

He took a bottle from his medicine chest. "I'm going to give her a whiff of chloroform. Not too much and I haven't a proper mask so you must hold the pad over her face, Conn, and do exactly as I tell you. Galina, you will have to help me."

"Yes, of course."

She was determined not to flinch, to be ready at his nod to hand him what he needed and found very soon her fear that she might fail him was swallowed up by fascination as she watched those clever hands at work, so calm and precise and skilful, seeming not to hurry and yet working with speed and deftness and an infinite pity for the tiny dead creature, a perfect baby in miniature that they quickly wrapped in a clean sheet.

In what seemed to her an incredibly short time he had finished and straightened up knowing the work well done before he turned away to wash his hands. Then he busied himself with making Luba as comfortable as possible while she still lay very still under the influence of the drug.

Conn was looking at him anxiously as he bent over her carefully feeling her pulse.

"You won't go, doctor, you won't desert us."

"Not until she comes round which should be fairly soon."

He stood up stretching himself wearily and it was only then that Galina noticed how pale he was. The room reeked of blood and the heavy fumes of the chloroform. He took out a handkerchief and wiped the sweat from his face.

"It is stiflingly hot in here. I need a breath of air. Stay with her, Conn. I'll be back in a moment."

He went out of the small bedroom into the huge gaunt studio. It was icy cold and reflection from the white world outside filled it with light. He walked a little unsteadily towards the window. He drew a deep breath looking out on to rooftops mantled with freshly fallen snow.

Galina had followed him. She said anxiously, "Are you all right?"

"Yes."

"Will Luba recover?"

"There's no reason why she shouldn't. She's a strong healthy girl."

"Should she go into the hospital?"

He knew only too well the danger of infection in the crowded hospitals of the poor, and had learned to fight it in the London slums.

"She'll be better off here but I'll have to report the birth or there may be trouble."

He sighed leaning his forehead against the icy window pane, one hand gripping the back of a wooden chair.

"Two years ago I swore I'd never touch a case of this kind again."

"Why?"

"The last patient died on the operating table and I blamed myself."

"Wasn't that foolish? There must always be danger."

"This one was different."

She drew closer to him hardly daring to question and yet remembering what Lydia had told her about him.

"Why was it different?"

"Because I was in love with her."

He was not looking at her. It was almost as if he was talking to himself, as if once started he could not stop.

"She had been my delight and my torment for more than a year."

"Did she love you?" She murmured and was afraid of the answer.

"Sometimes I believed it and sometimes I knew I was deceiving myself. She went to Paris to study music for a few months. 'When I come back we'll be married,' she said, and I lived with that promise."

He stopped, still staring unseeingly out of the window and after a moment she said, "What happened?"

"I don't know, I shall never know, but one day when I was on night duty she was brought into the hospital." His hand on the back of the chair clenched till the knuckles whitened. "She was pregnant and some back street abortionist had done his worst. To me she had denied everything and then given herself to a man who cared nothing. I was shaken by pity and by a furious anger but her case was desperate and I was the only surgeon there. Did I want to save her or did I want her to die? Did my hands betray me? I've never been sure. It has haunted me ever since."

"I don't believe it," she whispered, "I won't believe it. Your first thought has always been to save, never to destroy."

"Perhaps." He looked down at his hands. "Perhaps you're right. For the first time tonight I felt certain of myself again. You can't know what that means."

She had looked up to him as a sort of God, always sure of himself, skilled, confident, and in this fraught moment he had become vulnerable, needing comfort. She wanted to put her arms around him, offer him her own trust and belief, but knew instantly she must not. This was a battle he had to fight and win alone. The most she dared to do was to slide a hand across the chair back and after a moment felt his fingers close over hers with a painful pressure.

He said briskly, "I must go and see how our patient is progressing," and was forestalled by Conn who appeared in the doorway.

"I think she is coming round."

"Splendid. I'll take a look at her."

Luba still hazy managed a smile as he came to the bedside and took her hand.

"I'm sorry, my dear," he said gently, "but I could not save your baby."

"I know. Conn told me."

"Give yourself six to nine months before you try again."

"Oh I will, believe me."

"I'm not sending you into the hospital but you must take great care," he said warningly. "I'll come and see you tomorrow."

"I'm causing you a lot of trouble, aren't I? I was so sure I could manage it on my own."

"You're a brave lass and you'll do very well."

Galina helped him to repack his bag. "I'm going to stay with her for a few days. Conn is kind but she shouldn't be here alone. You don't mind, do you?"

"The present emergency has put a stop to everything for the time being. I promised to go back to the hospital. They will be run off their feet."

He gave her some instructions and she went with him to the courtyard. The events of the day and the night had brought them so close in spirit that she hardly even needed his reassuring kiss. His arm went around her, holding her close against him for a moment, then he hailed a passing cab and she went back up the stairs.

Later that day when she had made fresh tea and prepared a simple meal for the three of them, Conn went back to painting in the studio and she came to sit beside Luba.

The girl was staring in front of her looking small and frail against the banked up pillow.

"I couldn't say it to Conn and I know it is wicked," she

said slowly, "but I'm glad this has happened. The baby might have grown up into a second Igor."

"You would still have loved it."

"Would I? I'm glad I haven't to try, and yet . . ." she turned away her face. "It's so silly now of all times and yet I can't help crying."

Galina said nothing only pressed the small rough hand with its bitten nails that lay helplessly on the blanket. Presently Luba turned back to her, tears still in her eyes, but her voice steady.

"I envy you, Galina. He's a good man. How lucky you are."

"Yes. I think perhaps I am."

"Is he going to marry you?"

"Oh Luba, don't be foolish. Marry me – a bastard whose father could be one of her mother's dozen lovers when he is the son of an English lord!"

"Does that about your mother make you feel bitter?"

"It did once but not any more."

"Supposing Simon goes back to England? What will you do then?"

The very thought made her tremble inwardly but she would not admit it, not even to herself.

"I don't know," she said simply, "I only know that I love him and that to be together gives us both a wonderful joy and that's enough. I'm not counting on a future."

It was late in the evening of that tragic day that Igor stirred painfully in his cramped hiding place. The cold was intense and he shivered as he struggled to his feet. He had been amongst the leaders of that pitiful procession striding beside Father Gapon, that handsome glib-tongued charlatan, whom he had never really trusted and who had been among the first to turn and run when the bullets ripped through them thrusting aside ruthlessly the men and women he had tempted into marching on that fatal day. He might have known how it would turn out, thought Igor bitterly, but there had been something magnetic about that damned priest's oratory and even he, with his utter contempt for the government, had never imagined that what had been planned as a peaceful demonstration would have turned into a massacre.

In the midst of the panic he had stooped to lift a child out of the way of a rampaging horse and had himself been thrown under the trampling hooves, his thigh and leg so badly kicked and bruised that he could do no more than crawl dragging himself agonizingly through the snow and slush though he knew the hunt was up and arrests being made. He cursed his folly in appearing openly at so many of the priest's fiery meetings. There had been something so compelling about his oratory that for once he had forgotten his usual caution. He could so easily be denounced by some poor wretch only too anxious to curry favour with the *Okhrana* and save his own life.

He had made slow progress during that long afternoon with danger lurking at every step until at last as the winter day drew in he had found himself in a street of fine houses belonging to the aristocracy. At the back there were courtyards with outhouses and stables where they kept their carriages and horses, most of them locked and barred against the thieving rabble who are always ready to take advantage of any city disturbance. Frozen, his boots soaked through and in great pain he could go no further. He was near to despair when he saw that one gate was still open. He pushed it cautiously and crept into the yard. All was dark except for a lantern hung outside a back door. He listened carefully but no sound came from the kitchen quarters. He heard the clink of horses' feet as they shifted munching at their feed but one stall appeared to be empty. He limped quietly through the door and was greeted by a low growl. As his eyes grew accustomed to the darkness he saw that a large dog was lying on a nest of straw and hay with half a dozen puppies squealing sleepily and tumbling over one another as they tried to suckle. He gave them a wide berth, dragging himself to the back of the stall where he found a heap of sacking with a pile of half-rotten fodder and sank down thankfully to wait until it was fully dark before he made his difficult way back to the island. Somehow he had to get help in escaping from the city until the hunt had died down.

The hours dragged slowly by until he guessed it must be about nine or ten and time to make a move. He felt sick and faint with cold and hunger but thankfully the pain had lessened a little and he had satisfied himself that at least no bone was broken. He stood upright with an effort and was trying out a few tentative steps when he heard voices and shrank back quickly as far as he could into the shadows.

"For heaven's sake, can't you leave those wretched mongrels to the servants?" said a voice he was almost sure that he recognized.

"No, I can't and Shani isn't a mongrel," was the sharp reply. "Vassily forgot her yesterday and she has all those puppies to feed. I'm going out to make sure."

"If you must, but be quick about it. It's late and the gates should be locked. There's been enough disturbance today already."

The stable door creaked open and a shaft of light slanting across the courtyard showed Igor a slight figure in a long fur cloak, a scarf tied over her hair, who came in carrying a jug in one hand and a bowl piled with food in the other.

She paused as if uncertain and he glimpsed her face in the faint light. Then she crossed to where the bitch lay with her puppies. She knelt down speaking gently to the dog as she picked up one of the babies, cuddling it against her. Involuntarily Igor shifted his wounded leg and something clattered on the stone floor. She froze at the sound but before she could cry out in alarm, an arm had come around her neck and a hand was clapped across her mouth.

"Don't scream, Princess, and you won't be hurt. What have you got in the jug?"

"Milk," Nina whispered through chattering teeth. She twisted round a little and gasped as the light caught the bony features, lighting the face into queer frightening angles. "You!" she breathed. "It's you!"

"Quiet!" he hissed.

"Were you with *them*?"

"Yes. Are you going to shout for help?"

She shook her head still frightened but at the same time thrilled and excited. She had been forbidden to stir out of the house all day but the servants had brought garbled stories, each one more horrific than the other, so that her fevered imagination had seen the city streets running with blood.

"Are you hurt?" she asked trembling.

"Don't move," he said harshly and then took up the jug and drank half of its contents thirstily. "What food have you got in that bowl?"

"What was left from the servants' supper. It's for Shani."

"Shani must go begging. My need is greater than hers."

He took a hunk of the bread with a chunk of the meat,

slapped it together and put it in his pocket.

"Have they locked the outer gate?"

"Not yet. Vassily will wait until I've finished in here."

"Good. Stay talking to the dog until I get away."

"Are the police hunting you?"

"They could be."

"Where will you go?"

He shrugged his shoulders. "Out of the city – anywhere."

"You could go to Dannskoye. You'd be safe there. No one would ever suspect a Malinsky."

He grinned at the unconscious arrogance of these aristocrats, the blind belief in their untouchability. One day they would find out what it felt like to be at the mercy of a ruthless police.

"I might even do that, Princess."

She saw the gleam of his teeth in the half light, then he had bent down suddenly, taken her by the shoulders and kissed her hard on the lips before he limped painfully to the door. He took one swift glance around the yard and then seemed to melt silently into the darkness.

She sank back on her heels. No one had ever kissed her like that before. A tingling excitement raced through her and she did not know whether she was furiously angry at his impudence, terrified or thrilled. Then she heard Niki calling her and hurriedly poured the rest of the milk into the dog's water bowl and put the meat and bread close beside her.

"Nina, what on earth are you doing out there?"

A moment later Niki appeared in the doorway.

"Only looking at the puppies. They're so sweet. Do you see? They have their eyes open already."

"Was someone here? I thought I heard voices."

"I was talking to Shani," she said breathlessly.

"Go in, Nina, before Mamma hears about it. I'm going to make sure the gates are properly locked."

She bestowed a kiss on Shani's silky head. The highly bred borzoi had been guilty of a *mésalliance* and if it had not been for Nina's stormy intervention, the six illegitimate puppies would have been drowned by Vassily so she had a special affection for them.

"God, what a day!" said Niki coming back and putting an arm round his sister. "I shan't be sorry to go back to Dannskoye."

"Not until after my birthday."

"If Papa doesn't cancel the ball he's been planning."

"Oh no, he wouldn't, would he?" she exclaimed in dismay, "not just because of what happened today. It doesn't really concern us, does it?"

"I suppose not. What a child you are, Nina, always thinking about balls and having fun."

"Isn't that what growing up is all about?" she retorted and then had a twinge of guilt because a few minutes before she had seemed to touch a grim reality and was deliberately hiding it from Niki, something she had never done before. She shivered suddenly and her brother's arm tightened around her.

"You've taken cold and I'm not surprised playing nurse to those confounded puppies. What the devil are we going to do with them anyway?"

"Take them to Dannskoye. Oh don't fuss, Niki. I'm freezing. Let's go and bully cook into making a hot drink for us."

They went in together happily reunited in the old childish companionship so that she could forget that disturbing little encounter and her rash promise of providing shelter at Dannskoye.

8

The ballroom in the Malinsky house looked very handsome on the night of Nina's eighteenth birthday. Everything had been cleaned and polished to the highest degree by a host of servants under her mother's eagle eye. The walls were panelled in red silk damask outlined in gold, the crystal chandeliers blazed with light and pillars of hothouse flowers rushed up from the south at huge expense stood at each corner of the great room.

Nina herself standing beside her parents was radiant in white satin. The bodice was embroidered in silver and cut discreetly low enough to reveal the slender neck and white shoulders and she wore her first real jewels, a collarette in pearls and diamonds, a gift from her father.

"Looks good enough to eat, doesn't she? A peach ready for plucking," murmured Nigel wickedly to Simon as they moved slowly up the curving staircase. "How about it, old boy?"

"Ssh," whispered his wife warningly on his other side. "You shouldn't say such things. Someone might hear you."

"It won't be news to them. It's pretty obvious her father is putting her up for auction to the highest bidder."

"Do be quiet, Nigel, it's not decent," hissed Lydia and then dissolved into a giggle behind her black lace fan.

Simon said nothing. He felt curiously detached from the whole glittering scene. Only three weeks since that day that had already begun to be called 'Bloody Sunday' and yet not a ripple had appeared on the brilliant surface of society. The season was in full swing with the same balls, the same flushed faces bent over card tables where rivers of gold were won and lost, the same perfumed guards officers pursuing illicit love affairs, the same frantic rush after every new trend, every new craze.

Ever since that night when he had treated Luba he had felt released, a weight had been lifted from his spirit. He felt a tremendous expansion of energy, a fierce longing to get back to what meant more to him than anything, the craft of medicine, the mending of sick and broken bodies. It was beginning to crystallize into new plans and he had almost made up his mind to refuse this invitation if Galina had not persuaded him.

"You must go. Nina will be very disappointed if you don't."

"She won't even notice me among that crowd of admirers."

She gave him a quick look wondering how he could be so blind as to how women looked at him.

"Oh yes, she will and in any case Niki will be hurt."

"I believe you're still a little in love with him," he said teasingly. "Why don't you come with me?"

"I tried that once and look what came of it."

"I fell in love with you."

"Did you – honestly – on that night?"

"I must have done. The fire gripped me with its magic without me recognizing it."

"You're laughing at me."

"Never!"

He had his arm around her and she had hold of his hand playing with the strong capable fingers. There was not the smallest part of him that she did not know and love.

He had consulted her as to what kind of gift would be suitable for him to send.

"Not jewellery," she said judiciously, "too intimate," and they settled on a bouquet of white gardenias at a fabulous cost and a tiny Chinese dog carved in pink jade.

"I would far rather be buying these things for you," he grumbled when they went shopping together.

"I don't need them. I have you," she replied simply.

'His Puritan', he called her because she stubbornly rejected the gifts he would have lavished on her.

He came out of his abstraction to see they had reached the top of the staircase. He shook hands with the Prince, bowed to his wife and kissed the small hand Nina stretched out to him. He saw that a cluster of the gardenias he had sent her were fastened in the blonde hair with a diamond clasp. She thanked him prettily for his gift.

"The little dog reminded me of Shani," he said lightly and was surprised to see the delicate colour run up into her cheeks unaware of that encounter with Igor in the stable about which she still felt guilty.

"She has had six puppies," she whispered. "You can have one of them if you will come and choose it."

He smiled an acknowledgement and she looked after him as he walked away. The most attractive man there in her opinion and yet quite the most unattainable. It was so unjust. There were so many others only too eager to come running at her lightest gesture, all except him, so kind always and yet so distant. For a moment in the warm scented air she felt quite stifled with frustration until her mother's whisper brought her back to her duties.

"Remember your guests!" she said sharply and Nina turned to find Valentin Skorsky holding her hand far longer than he should and murmuring compliments she did not want to hear.

It was an evening like so many others and Simon found himself quickly bored. He had never been particularly attracted by the frivolities of high society even back in England. He danced with Lydia who talked exclusively of Edward since she feared he was developing a worrying tendency to asthma.

Funny how even the best of one's friends expected a doctor to hand out help and advice on everything under the sun, he thought humorously.

"What does your own physician say?"

"He's a Russian and I don't trust him an inch. Besides Edward doesn't like him. Last time he bit him when the poor man wanted to examine his throat. Do come and take a look at him for me, Simon."

"My dear girl, I'm not an expert on respiratory diseases."

"Don't slip out of it that way. Nigel says you can diagnose anything just by looking at a person. You once said, 'That man doesn't realize it but he is suffering from a serious heart ailment and will be dead in six months', and he *was*."

He laughed aloud. "I'm sure I was never so arrogant. I'm not a witch doctor, Lydia, nor, I hope, so dire a prophet of doom, but if it will comfort you, I will come round and we'll find out if Edward bites me. If you're worried about the boy, why don't you take him and Selina down south for a few weeks away from this raw Petersburg winter."

"I might do that but Nigel does hate me to leave him."

"Dr Deverenko told me he is obliged to accompany the Tsar when he takes the family to Livadia in March and suggested I might like to go too. I think he wants to show off the sanatoriums and hospitals established there for tuberculosis and chest patients. I have to admit in this instance they are one up on Britain."

"Will you go?"

"Perhaps. The thought of sunshine and warmth is rather tempting."

She longed to ask him if he would be taking Galina with him but didn't dare. There were unexpected reserves in Simon and one could come up against a stone wall. She would have to prod Nigel into finding out.

He took her back to her husband and stood talking with them for a while before he went in search of Nina. He had some difficulty in tracking her down and when he did, she turned on him with an angry flick of her fan.

"I made sure you had abandoned me."

"Now why on earth should you think so badly of me?"

"Oh I don't know. Everything is going wrong this evening and on my birthday too. It's so unfair."

She sounded so much like a petulant child that he only

smiled and led her among the dancers. They circled the floor for a few minutes in silence. The scent from the gardenias in her hair floated up to him and he saw that angry tears sparkled on her lashes.

He said gently, "What's gone wrong? You're like a little cat arching its back ready to spit and scratch."

"What a horrid thing to say."

"Not necessarily. A kitten in a temper can be very attractive."

She looked up at him and then smiled reluctantly. "You make me sound so silly."

"I don't mean to. Tell me now what is spoiling your evening."

"It's Valentin," she confessed. "Without saying a word to me he has approached Papa for permission to pay his addresses to me. That's how he puts it. Doesn't it sound *stupid*?"

"I think it is probably meant as a great compliment."

"But I don't even *like* him."

"What will your father say about it?"

"Oh it's not Papa who worries me. I can usually get around him but I know exactly what Mamma will say. He's an excellent match because his lands run alongside ours and he is the only son and a Guards officer like Papa was and he is very rich."

"He seems to have all the right attributes," he said lightly. "What more could you ask?"

"A great deal more. For one thing I don't love him, he doesn't know how to laugh, and his house is hateful, so gloomy and dark, *and* he has a horrible mother. She rules him with a rod of iron and she would rule me if I married him. I couldn't bear that. We would fight all the time." She gave an angry little laugh. "When we were children, Niki and I used to invent all kinds of excuses, even made ourselves ill sometimes, so that we didn't have to accept her invitations to visit there."

"My dear child, aren't you making a mountain out of a very tiny molehill? No one can force you into anything. You're eighteen and very beautiful with all your life in front of you and half Petersburg at your feet."

The music had come to an end and left them standing by one of the pillars of flowers. Nina was looking at him provocatively.

"That's so easy to say. Do *you* think I'm beautiful?"

"Of course I do. Aren't I one of your most devoted admirers?"

"If that's true, then prove it," she whispered.

"Tell me how," he said lightly, still humouring her.

"Like this."

She suddenly flung both her arms around his neck, pressing herself against him, kissing him with such abandon that taken by surprise he was still holding her in his arms when a furious Valentin confronted them.

"Is this man forcing his attentions on you, Princess?" he asked angrily.

She did not at once draw away but still stood close beside him.

"Certainly not," she said flippantly. "If you want to know, *I* was kissing *him*. Have you any objection?"

"I have every objection."

"Then you can forget it. I'm not your fiancée yet and I hope I never shall be."

Valentin flushed at the rebuff, then turned to Simon. "And you, sir, what have you to say?"

Simon furious with embarrassment at the false position he had been forced into said coolly, "You have heard what the lady said."

"I've a damned good mind to call you out for this," said the young man threateningly.

"I hope you will do nothing so foolish. Nina was merely thanking me for my birthday gift in her own charmingly impulsive manner. Do you wish to create scandal out of such a childish gesture?"

Baffled Valentin bit his lip, then he offered his arm to Nina.

"Your mother was asking for you," he went on stiffly, "will you permit me to escort you to her?"

Nina was about to refuse then caught Simon's almost imperceptible nod. She gave him a defiant look, then deliberately snapped off a camellia from the flowers beside her and held it out to him. He took it and bowed.

"Thank you, Princess, I am honoured."

She smiled radiantly at him ignoring the scandalized look on Valentin's face, then placed her fingertips on his arm and allowed him to lead her away.

Simon was left standing, uneasily aware of one or two interested spectators of the awkward little scene. He looked down at the flower in his hand and then carefully replaced it among the others. He should never have permitted himself to become involved but he had always found it difficult to think of Nina as more than a pretty impulsive child. Now he realized how wrong he was and knew he must be careful if he didn't wish to cause trouble. There was a certain wildness in Nina, a lack of balance, something no doctor could put a name to but did exist in certain societies, overbred, bored, seeking for sensation even danger to satisfy their craving for excitement. He saw it all around him in this crowded ballroom and felt suffocated by it. He wanted only to escape. To avoid causing comment he made up his mind to disappear quietly without speaking to anyone, not even Nigel and Lydia. They knew him well enough to understand. He slipped around the ballroom nodding to acquaintances without pausing. The guests were already moving into the supper room when he collected coat, hat and gloves from the surprised footman. The hall porter hailed a cab for him.

"Where to, sir?" he asked and looked astonished when Simon gave the direction.

Galina had spent a quiet evening surrounded by books, many of them loaned by Simon. In what spare time she had she was trying to continue her studies. Even though she was not at the university it was still possible to take outside examinations and to be a qualified student of pharmacy could be a stake for the future.

Later in the evening she washed her hair, drying it by the wood-burning stove while she ate a frugal supper. She went to bed still with a book in her hands but she did not read. Instead she thought of Simon, imagining him in that grand company, wondering how it would feel to enter that ballroom on his arm, acknowledged and accepted, but as what? Certainly not his wife, she could never aspire to that despite all Luba liked to say. As his mistress, his *chère amie*? It was easy to imagine the horror on the Princess Malinskaya's face at such a confrontation even though society was riddled with such *affaires de coeur*. She thought of him dancing with Nina, with other women, beautiful, scented, richly dressed and readily available. Was that all *she* meant to him? She shivered refusing to let herself think of such a thing, put down her book and resolutely turned out the lamp.

The quiet but insistent knocking roused her from a half sleep. She sat up and listened. She knew that Stasia Ivanovna went to bed early but sometimes there was an emergency. She could not ignore it. She pulled a shawl around her shoulders and crossed to the door.

"Who is it?" she whispered.

"It's me – Simon – may I come in?"

She drew back the bolt and opened the door cautiously. He slipped quickly into the room and she stared at him, her eyes wide with surprise. It was as if her thoughts had somehow materialized him in all the panoply of his evening dress, caped coat, top hat, white gloves, white silk scarf.

"It must be midnight," she said at last. "What are you doing here? You should be at Nina's ball."

"I know I should but I was desperately bored. If you had been there we could have laughed together at it all but alone I couldn't stand it another minute." He was shedding coat, hat, gloves and looking for somewhere to put them. "I do wish you would let me take a better apartment for you. This place is like a rabbit hutch."

"It suits me." She took the clothes from him, hung them up and relit the lamp before turning back to him. Hair ruffled, eyes bright, he looked quite unlike himself. "Simon, are you drunk?"

"Certainly not," he said indignantly. "A few glasses of champagne that's all but I *am* hungry."

"Haven't you eaten already?"

"Didn't wait for it. Have you any food?"

"Not very much," she said ruefully. "Eggs, spiced ham, a little caviare, bread."

"That'll do. You get back into bed, you're shivering. I'm going to cook supper for both of us."

"Not dressed like that," she exclaimed. "I'll do it."

"No, you won't." He peeled off his evening coat and rolled up his cuffs. "I've done it before. Don't you remember?"

She protested but he picked her up and dumped her on the bed so she gave in, sitting up with the blankets pulled around her watching him work with the same skilful efficiency with which he had dealt with Luba and the medical emergencies at the hospital.

Presently he brought her a plate piled with scrambled egg topped with ham and a spoonful of caviare. Then he sat down in the old rocking chair with his own plate on his knees.

"All we need now is a bottle of wine but we can't have everything," he mumbled with his mouth full.

It was ridiculous and wonderful she thought that he should abandon that rich and fashionable society to come and picnic with her in this squalid room.

Presently as they ate, she said tentatively, "Did Nina look very pretty this evening?"

"Yes, she did, quite lovely. She is growing up, Galina. Valentin Skorsky wants to marry her."

"He always did or at least his mother planned it that way. That's what Missy used to say."

"But Nina does not want *him*, it seems."

"No, it's you she wants," the words slipped out before she could bite them back.

He looked up quickly and she was ashamed of the thrill of pleasure that ran through her to know that she had succeeded when the spoiled Princess so far above her had failed.

"That's utter nonsense," he said sharply. "The trouble with Nina is that she doesn't know what she wants," and he began to collect the plates and put them aside.

"Simon, what made you come here to me tonight?"

He was standing looking down at her in his white evening shirt, the hair falling across his forehead, the soft glow of the lamp lighting the long nose, the firmly cut mouth.

"I don't know how to tell you," he said slowly. "I suddenly felt that nothing around me was real any longer, as if all those people there, so rich, so well bred, had no real aim in life. They were all looking for pleasure, for the gratification of the senses – maybe I was being unjust, they are not all like that, Nigel and Lydia aren't – but I knew I wanted none of it. There was nothing they could give me – I wanted reality, I wanted you."

All the doubts that had plagued her earlier that evening seemed to melt away. She could not speak, only held out her hand and he took it in both his.

"Is that how you feel, Galina?"

But he did not wait for her answer. He sat on the edge of the bed and pulled her into his arms. Her hair was still slightly damp and smelled of the herbs she had used, her skin was fresh and sweet, free from paint or powder or perfume. Her lips were open to his kisses.

"Move over," he said huskily, "I'm coming in with you."

"It's very narrow . . ."

"All the better."

The desire between them was quick and urgent and when he made love to her he marvelled again at the way she responded to him. He would tease her sometimes because she would not accept anything from him, because she occasionally held aloof holding back some secret part of herself even from him and yet in his arms she became a creature of fire and passion exciting and delighting him.

As for Galina she thought that perhaps that night for the first time she really believed in his love.

9

The Malinskys returned to Dannskoye when the season ended at the start of Lent for which Simon was profoundly grateful. Nina's sudden and unexpected visit to his rooms a week or so after the ball had put him in something of a dilemma. For a young girl of her class to call on a man in his bachelor apartment without a suitable chaperon was unheard of and very heavily frowned upon. Even worse, she had caught him unawares. He was still struggling into his jacket when the housekeeper showed her in with an infuriatingly sly smirk on her round peasant face. Heaven knows what kind of a tale she would be spreading around among her cronies.

"My dear Nina," he said as he moved to greet her, "I'm delighted to see you of course but surely you shouldn't be calling here alone like this."

"Why ever not?" she replied brightly. "You didn't come to fetch your puppy as you promised so I have brought him to you. This is Ranji, the best of the litter," and she thrust the puppy into his arms.

"I don't think your Mamma would be very pleased if she hears of it."

"She won't know. She thinks I'm calling on Missy but I dismissed the carriage, told Vassily to come back in about an hour, took a cab all by myself and here I am. Don't you think that was very clever of me? I wanted to see how you live and what you do and where you work."

"For that, I'm afraid, you would have to come to the hospital."

She was wandering all around the sitting room and into his bedroom with him following after her still holding the puppy who licked his face and tried to chew his ear but he had not grown up in a country household for nothing. He controlled its exuberance firmly.

Nina peeped into the small cupboard-like office.

"Is this where Galina works?"

"Yes, when she is here."

She turned over the piled papers curiously, struck a few keys on the typewriter, picked up the books and frowned at their titles.

"Is she good at it?"

"Very good indeed. I rely on her absolutely."

She came back into the sitting room. "If she comes here whenever she likes, then why can't I?"

"My dear child, it's quite different. You know it is. You are the Princess Malinskaya . . ."

"And she was one of Papa's serfs, but I don't see why that makes any difference. I'm still me and I'm eighteen and grown up." She sat down in one of the armchairs and looked defiant. "I think I'd like some tea."

It was the last thing he wanted. He put down the puppy and looked around him rather helplessly.

"I suppose Galina usually makes it for you."

"Sometimes when we are working together. I will ring for the housekeeper."

"No, don't trouble. It doesn't matter. You *will* come to us at Dannskoye during the summer, won't you?"

"If I'm invited, of course I will."

"You know that Niki is going to marry Sonia."

"I did hear something about it," he said cautiously. "I'm sure he will be very happy."

"Well, I'm not but he has really made up his mind. Niki's changed. He has become so *ordinary*."

Simon smiled. "He's grown up, that's all."

"But we've known Sonia since we were children. It's so tame. There's nothing exciting about it."

"Maybe excitement is not quite what one looks for in marriage," he replied with some amusement.

"Well, it ought to be. That's what they say in books, don't they?"

"Not always. After all in *War and Peace* Natasha plumps for dull old Pierre in the end, doesn't she?"

"That's what made me so furious. Anna Karenina left her dreary husband and ran away with Vronsky – I remember Missy telling me about it. She disapproved of course, just like Mamma."

"She did end up under a train," he objected.

"But that was only afterwards."

He had no intention of embarking on a literary discussion and was searching for some polite reason to get rid of her when the puppy diverted them by worrying fiercely at his silk scarf which had been left lying across a chair. They were both on their knees laughing as they tried to get it away from him when Galina came in, her hands full of hot rolls which she had been out to buy. She took in the situation at a glance, picked up the little dog and was very polite indeed to Nina while Simon was never so thankful to see her in his life. He put Nina into a cab and saw her safely on her way back to Missy's flat.

"Whatever was she doing here?" asked Galina coolly when he came back from seeing her off.

"Not at my invitation you may be sure of that. Thank heaven you came in when you did. She brought me the dog. You'll have to look after Ranji for me."

"He is rather a pet, isn't he?" and she laughed, the faint jealousy vanishing at the look of relief on his face.

"I'm glad you're here. I have something very particular to tell you."

"What?"

"All in good time." He collapsed into a chair. "I've had no breakfast and I'm exhausted. Be a good girl. Make me some tea and butter the rolls. Then we'll talk about it."

Luba bursting into Galina's room one evening a week later found her on her knees brushing and combing the two-month old puppy.

"Where on earth did that come from?" she demanded going down beside her. "Is it a stray?"

"Certainly not. Nina gave it to Simon and he handed it on to me."

"Heavens, isn't she the Malinsky girl? Does she still fancy him?"

"Luba, what a thing to say!" Galina went on combing the little dog who wriggled and squealed trying to nibble her fingers. "I suppose she does in a kind of way."

"You look out, my girl. She's rich and her father may be a stiff old stick but he is fearfully well-connected. Men think a lot of such things. Your Doctor Simon could do a great deal worse for himself."

"I'm not afraid of Nina," said Galina confidently. She picked up the puppy and hugged it. "Isn't he a darling? He has a very high-born Mamma and a much shadier Papa, a bastard like me, aren't you, Ranji?"

"Oh Galina, you *are* a fool. As if anything of that kind really matters." Luba sat back on her heels. "What's happened? You're looking almighty pleased with yourself."

"We're going away."

"Where?"

"Down south, to the Crimea. Simon is to visit all the sanatoriums and hospitals so it will be a kind of working holiday and I'm going with him."

"As what may I ask?"

"As his assistant, his secretary," went on Galina airily.

"*And* what else?"

"I can't think what you mean."

"As if you didn't know!" and they both of them burst out laughing. "Anyone has only to look at you two together to know exactly what's going on. Oh dear," went on Luba, "that's really taken the wind out of my sails. I was going to surprise you with some news of my own."

"What news? Oh go on, Luba, don't sulk. Surprise me with it now."

"Well, if you must know, Conn and I are going to be married."

"What! Oh darling, I'm so glad for you." Galina gave her a quick hug and then drew back looking at her anxiously. "It *is* what you want, isn't it?"

"I suppose it must be. I didn't once – I thought how marvellous it was to be free to pick and choose, but when things are not going so well, it's such a comfort, isn't it, to have someone of your own, and Conn may not be the greatest genius in the world and he is certainly not a romantic hero like your doctor, but he's so kind, so reliable."

"Do you love him?"

"I suppose I must do – not *la grande passion* – I don't know if that exists anyway outside poetry and nonsense of that kind but in a funny sort of way I am very fond of him." She gave a little giggle. "He says he wants to make an honest woman of me – a bit late in the day, but there it is. He has got a good commission from a publisher to design illustrations for some children's books so we're celebrating it by getting married, all very nice and proper. Will you come?"

"Of course I will and Simon too if there is time before we leave."

Luba lowered her voice and looked mysterious. "Have you seen anything of Igor? I saw his door was shut when I came up the stairs."

"He's not been back since that awful Sunday but Stasia Ivanovna told me someone had sent enough money to cover the rent for months ahead."

"Keeps it as a bolthole, I expect. He's a sly one. He must be hiding out somewhere till it's safe to show himself again. We had the police asking questions for weeks, not that I saw anything of them, Conn guarded me like a dragon, but some of the others were taken in for questioning and you know what that can mean."

Both of them were silent for a moment as if the shadows around that dark enigmatic figure still hung over them, then Galina shook it away from her.

"I'm going to make us some tea."

She looked so radiantly happy as she busied herself with the samovar that Luba felt afraid for her. She was a realist and had suffered enough hard knocks in her short life to know how easily fate can catch up with you when you least expect it. But she was not going to act the wet blanket now. In a funny kind of way they had both got what they wanted. In her philosophy it was just as well to make the most of it while it lasted.

The next morning when she arrived early ready for the day's work, Simon said, "By the way Lydia wants you to lunch with her."

"Why?"

"Don't ask me, some feminine whim. Take the afternoon off. You work much too hard." He touched her cheek caressingly before he hurried away.

She was surprised but Lydia had the gift of making her feel welcome and they had a pleasant light lunch with the children.

Afterwards over their coffee she said, "Would you like to come shopping with me? I'm longing for something new after being bundled up all the winter and you might see something you'd like to buy for yourself. It will be very warm down south. I know because Nigel and I spent some time there a couple of years ago."

"I don't think I can afford to buy very much," she confessed a little diffidently.

"Never mind about that. If you find something you can always pay me back later."

She knew nothing of the conversation Lydia had had with Simon when he called to examine Edward's chest and afterwards asked for her help.

"Advise Galina on the right things to buy. I can't do it. She won't let me buy her so much as a handkerchief, but you can do it tactfully and send the bills to me."

"Simon, are you going to marry this girl?"

"Perhaps."

"She's madly in love with you. You do know that."

"I am very fond of *her*."

"Is she your mistress?" she asked bluntly.

"You don't really expect me to answer that, do you, Lydia?"

"I don't see why not," she said in exasperation, "I'm not exactly a child. I only hope you know what you are doing."

"Believe me, I do," he said very seriously. "Everything went wrong for me once. I don't want it to happen again. I want to be very sure. So be a good girl and don't ask too many questions. And incidentally don't worry too much about Edward. My witch doctor diagnosis tells me that cough of his is not asthmatical but slightly bronchial. Be careful of him in cold damp weather and with any luck he should grow out of it quite soon."

So in gratitude she did as he asked and found to her surprise that Galina had an innate good taste which made her task a great deal easier.

Let loose in the shops Lydia was inclined to buy lavishly and Galina rashly allowed herself to be carried along with her and it was only afterwards when exhausted they were sipping glasses of tea that she looked down at the dress boxes beside her and felt horribly guilty.

"I must have been crazy to buy so much," she admitted shyly. "I don't know when I shall be able to pay you back for all these."

"I shouldn't worry too much about that," said Lydia helping herself to another cream cake, "it's all settled anyway."

"What is settled? What do you mean?"

"Oh nothing really," Lydia was annoyed with herself for letting the words slip out without thinking. "I have an account. The bills don't come in for ages."

Galina was frowning. "I think you meant something quite different. Is Simon paying for all these?"

"Well, as a matter of fact he did say something about it," she said reluctantly.

"I see. I didn't know."

Galina said nothing more but there was a set look about her mouth and inwardly Lydia sighed. After all she had done her part. Why couldn't the girl accept her lover's generosity and leave it at that?

But that was something that Galina found very hard to do. She went straight from the teashop to Simon's apartment still carrying the boxes with her and aware that more would be sent to her in the next few days.

He was not there which was maddening until she remembered it was the day he usually helped out at the hospital in one of the poorest quarters of the city. So she waited and was still there in coat and hat and long woollen scarf when he came in, cold, hungry and very tired because it had been a long wearying day when it seemed nothing he could do would alleviate the grim effects of ignorance, neglect, malnutrition and dire poverty.

"Hallo," he said surprised to see her, "I thought you would be spending the day with Lydia."

"So I was." She was standing very still and straight. "Why didn't you tell me you were ashamed of me?"

He had begun to take off his coat and stopped to stare at her. "What the devil are you talking about?"

"It's true, isn't it? You asked your friend to take me out and buy me some decent clothes because it offended your pride to be seen by your elegant friends with someone like me, a peasant, one of the people, a girl who doesn't even have the right to a name of her own."

"Will you tell me what all this is about for heaven's sake?" he said in some annoyance.

"Don't pretend you don't know. 'Clean her up, dress her nicely and I'll foot the bills!' Is that what you said to Lydia? If that's how you feel about me then it's Nina you should be taking away with you, not me."

"Perhaps it's a pity I'm not if you're going to throw back in my face everything I try to do for you," he said in exasperation.

"I saw her here with you that day. She'd be only too delighted to go with you. She's part of your world, isn't she? The Princess Nina, not like me."

"Oh Galina, for God's sake stop acting like some stupid little shopgirl. Most young women would be only too pleased to be let loose in the shops to buy whatever takes their fancy."

"But I'm not most women, I'm me. Why didn't you tell me honestly? I'm not your kept woman."

"My God, and don't I know it! I try to please you and this is all the thanks I get for it," he said, fatigue and irritation getting the better of him. "If you don't want them, then take the whole damned lot and throw them in the river!"

"That's just exactly what I'm going to do."

"Very well then, get on with it. Do as you please and let that be the end of it," and he stormed into the bedroom and slammed the door.

She stood for a moment horrified at what she had done, too shaken to move. Then she snatched up the boxes and stalked out of the room, but when she reached the riverbank she did nothing of the kind. The Neva was still frozen over for one thing and in any case it seemed a futile gesture. She was standing there, utterly miserable, knowing she had behaved abominably and had let her stupid pride offend him deeply when the sound of hurried footsteps made her turn away her head to hide her distress.

"Shall I throw them in for you?" said the voice behind her, and she swung round looking up at him through a mist of tears.

"I'm sorry, Simon, it was hateful of me. I know you meant to be kind. I don't know what makes me do it . . ."

"Because you're my prickly little hedgehog with a pride like a mountain but for my sins I love you for it." He kissed her cold nose and offered his handkerchief. "Come back with me, put on one of these new falderols and we'll dine in style at Donons so that I can show off my kept woman."

"Oh darling, don't make me laugh."

But that is exactly what they did. She pulled out of its wrapping a jacket and skirt in a fine sage green velvet with a ruffled blouse in silk and lace and had the exquisite satisfaction of seeing one or two heads turn to look at her when she entered the fashionable restaurant on his arm.

They set out for the south at the end of March, just after the imperial train heavily guarded had drawn out of Petersburg station. The assassination in Moscow of the Tsar's uncle, the Grand Duke Sergei who was also the husband of his wife's elder sister, had cast a gloom over the whole royal family and Simon thought that the poor man must have been only too glad to leave the capital where he had been plagued by strikes, civil disturbances and stormy arguments with his ministers.

The train journey to the Crimea meant two days and nights jolting over the interminable vastness of Russia, miles and miles across the gaunt brown stretches of the Ukraine with occasional stops when they could get out and stretch their legs until at last they reached Sevastopol and took the steamer for the four-hour sea trip round the Black Sea coast.

To Galina it was the beginning of the greatest adventure of her life. Long afterwards when she looked back at that time she thought she had been too happy. Maybe God, that all powerful divinity who lived behind the iconostasis in the great cathedrals, only permitted each person a limited allotment of pure happiness, of unadulterated joy in living, and she used up her whole ration in these few months before Simon went to England and her life fell to pieces.

"Take what you want," her mother had said once when she was still a child, "but remember nothing is free. You must be prepared to pay for it." She would remember that later but no thought of that kind spoiled the sheer delight of those first few weeks.

They had left cold gloomy Petersburg still caught up in the

throes of winter and emerged into the magical beauty of a southern spring. After the hours and hours of travelling, sometimes freezing, sometimes stiflingly hot, their faces smudged with grime, clothes sticking to them, longing for a bath, they suddenly found themselves in a vast perfumed garden.

Wisteria hung in great mauve clusters over the white walls of the hotel just outside Yalta where they stayed. The gardens were fragrant with jasmine and lilac and white acacias. Everywhere they looked were drifts of white and pink blossom in orchards of apple, peach and cherry. The air was warm but spicily fresh from the sea breezes. Rugged peaks still tipped with snow rose from blue and emerald water covered with forests of pine, with vineyards and groves of cypresses. To Galina who had never seen mountains before it was breathtakingly dramatic.

They bathed in the sea, running from the hot sunshine into the shock of icy water and Simon taught her to swim amid a great deal of laughter and teasing with Ranji barking madly and plunging in after them. They hired horses and though she had never ridden except bareback on the old farm horses she jogged along beside him contentedly spending long days in the whitewashed villages with the fretted minarets of mosques gracefully outlined against a cobalt blue sky. The people of the Crimea were mainly Tartars, the men lean and sombre in their short embroidered jackets and tight white trousers, their women, handsome dark-eyed creatures, who wore floating veils to hide their faces from strangers.

In this holiday place society was more liberal than it was in the capital. No one questioned them or looked askance at Galina, not that they mixed with anyone very much or needed any other company but their own. Every day they seemed to be discovering new things about one another. They read books together and Simon was surprised to realize how much Galina had devoured in the library at Dannskoye, stealing books to read overnight and putting them back secretly in the morning. Missy's lectures on Pushkin, Dostoevsky and Tolstoy – who still lived, a grumpy difficult old genius, at Yasnaya Polyana – had gone clean over Nina's head but taken root in Galina. In between times she still studied. Simon laughed at finding a textbook under her pillow and then took it seriously, discussing knotty points with her.

"If you insist on taking this examination, then I'm determined you shall do me credit," he said.

Once calling on Dr Deverenko he met the royal family and reported on them to Galina when he came back.

"What are they like?" she asked wide-eyed, her view of them still much that of the peasant who saw them as stiff unreal figures in robes encrusted with jewels.

"Very ordinary," he told her, "just like any other family. The four little girls were romping with their father on the beach and the baby Alexis was being watched over by the Tsarina like any other anxious mother."

He had guessed from the royal physician's guarded comments that the boy was almost certainly a haemophiliac, a tragedy for any family and disastrous for the heir to all the Russias, and felt an infinite pity for the Tsarina from whom that fatal taint must have come.

They visited together some of the sanatoriums and hospitals scattered on the mountain slopes where the patients had the most advanced treatment known, lying out on balconies shaded from the brilliant sun and they were greatly impressed by their cleanliness and efficiency.

"The only sad thing about it is," said Simon as they drove away, "that the poor devils who really need this cure would never be allowed to receive it. It will need a revolution to accomplish that and I can't see it happening in our lifetime."

They sometimes argued quite fiercely about the evils that beset Russia and how to cure them. Galina, still remembering the passionate debates of the student unions, was all in favour of immediate action while Simon was infuriatingly level-headed about it.

"My dear girl, if you blow up society," he said patiently, "you will probably put something worse in its place. Remember your Bible – cast out one devil and seven far worse come to fill the empty space. A true reformer must allow for the past, be cautious with changes, pave the way for the future."

"Is that what you would do?"

"I'm not a politician, thank God. I'm only a doctor. I try to mend broken bodies, and minds too, if I can, and that is work enough for any man."

She would listen to him and think there was nothing she wanted more than to share that work with him.

But she never thought of the future when they made joyous love in the cool delicious nights or sometimes when they woke in the morning with the breeze blowing through the opened windows. If what she was doing was wicked, she didn't care. For the time being she was utterly content.

The events that went on outside their charmed world never really impinged on them until they called on General Malinsky at his small elegant villa some way from Yalta in the foothills of the mountains. He received them very kindly and if he was surprised to see her with Simon and so fashionably dressed he made no comment.

They were served glasses of tea with delicious cherry jam and afterwards while Galina was shown over the villa by the General's housekeeper, the old man strolled in the garden with Simon and asked him about his future plans.

"I've been making up my mind during these last weeks. I intend to stay here in Russia and set up in practice. I have been fortunate in many of my medical contacts thanks to my uncle and I do not think I shall be made unwelcome."

"You may not find it too easy. Even here in this retreat of mine I hear a great deal that deeply distresses me. I'm beginning to believe that this country of mine is in a state of dangerous disruption and those who should know better remain complacently blind to it. It saddens me to hear of so much violence. I am told that even the Navy, always before the most loyal of our armed forces, are now rioting in the streets of Odessa and as always it is the innocent who suffer. The Tsar, well-meaning man though he is, seems quite incapable of grasping the reins of power as his father did."

"This is a vast country that is slowly beginning to find itself," said Simon thoughtfully, "it is that which interests me. I'm not one of those who preach total destruction before it can find its new way but I'd like to be part of it as far as my own profession will allow."

The old man paused for a moment. Beside him a camellia had burst into snowy bloom. He touched one with a gentle finger.

"Beauty is but a flower," he said, "and it can grow on graveyard or dungheap." He smiled at Simon. "You are a young man and you believe you see your way very clearly before you but I would like to give you a word of advice. You speak Russian well but you are still not one of us and I think perhaps you do not entirely understand my people. They are obedient, they can almost be sheeplike after years of tyranny and servitude, but there comes a time when they explode.

Then they will kill and kill in a mindless fury that cannot be halted even though it is their own brother who stands in their path."

They began to walk slowly on again.

"You probably think me an old man and that you know better but I would beg you to remember it if such a time should come. Now let us talk of happier things. I had thought once that you might have chosen my little Nina to share your life with you but you have decided otherwise. I worry about her. She is like a wild bird that needs a strong but gentle hand to tame her."

"Nina is a very lovely child," said Simon a trifle awkwardly. "I am sure she will soon find the right man with whom to spend her life."

"I know that Valentin Skorsky is anxious to marry her but I have not encouraged his suit. My daughter-in-law is strongly in favour of the match and she has a will of her own, I'm afraid. It does not always lead to family harmony."

Then Galina came to join them and they spoke of other things. Nothing was said about the cutting off of her allowance and she had a feeling that he regretted it but was obliged to maintain family loyalty. There was a sadness about their parting. The old man was close to ninety and very frail.

"God willing I shall see you later in the year when Niki marries Sonia," were his parting words.

There were so many wonderful moments to be treasured. Sometimes when she lay awake at night she would count them over and think she would remember them for ever. They attended the Easter mass in the tiny village church that somehow made it so much more real and intimate than in the Cathedral of St Alexander Nevsky in Petersburg. She stood beside Simon, lighted candles in their hands, and listened to the chant of the priest rising and falling in rich harmony, saw him come through the iconostasis at the head of the procession, the magnificent copes a little worn but the colours still glowing, the swinging censers sending up clouds of incense, heard the joyful cry, "Christ is risen" and the heartfelt answer, "He is risen indeed", when husbands embraced wives and children hugged their parents. Maybe it was blasphemous, she thought with a stab of conscience but Simon's kiss was like a seal on their love.

The honeyed days raced by and it was the end of May and the last week of their stay. The heat had increased. With it came an influx of holiday visitors and a little of the magic departed.

Their hotel was invaded by a group of young officers of the Imperial Guard on leave. Galina was uneasily aware of their eyes on her when she sat on the terrace or came to meals. For the first time their bold stares made her conscious of who and what she was and she resented it.

One night there was informal dancing. Carpets were rolled up, chairs pushed back against the walls and a small orchestra gathered to play.

Simon had been unusually silent during dinner. Afterwards he looked with distaste at the improvised ballroom.

"Do you want to dance?"

"I don't think I do."

"It's a lovely evening. Let's walk a little."

The night air was delicious but cool and she shivered in her silk dress. "I'd better get a shawl."

"I'll fetch it for you."

She waited for him in the doorway looking idly at the dancers, the young officers with the demure daughters of the local gentry and a sprinkling of girls from the town. One of the soldiers, magnificent in his green and gold uniform, approached her.

He clicked his heels. "Captain Ratov at your service. Will you do me the honour, Mademoiselle?"

"Thank you but I'm not dancing."

"Oh come, one turn on the floor. What harm is there in that?"

He was young and in his way good-looking, black eyes scanned her from head to foot. A little nervously she made the mistake of smiling at him and before she realized what was happening, he had pulled her into his arms and swept her among the dancers. They circled the room, his arm around her waist holding her too tightly, his hand burning through the thin silk of her dress. She saw Simon come to the doorway, her shawl over his arm, and tried to break away.

"Please, Captain, my friend is waiting for me."

"Let him wait. He is not your husband, is he? He doesn't own you."

She guessed that he was a little flown with wine and tried again to extricate herself.

"Please let me go."

But he laughed and held her tighter, looking provocatively at Simon as they danced past and then quite deliberately he bent his head and kissed her full on the lips. The next moment he had been jerked away and was faced by an angry young man, grey eyes blazing.

"What the devil do you think you are doing?"

"Amusing myself."

"Not with this lady you're not!"

"Why? What's so special about her?" he said insolently. "Can't she choose for herself? Maybe she prefers someone a little more lively."

Unexpectedly Simon hit him so hard that he staggered backwards.

"The lady whom you have just insulted happens to be my fiancée, my future wife."

The soldier had gone white. He dabbed at his bruised mouth with his handkerchief.

"I'll dispute that with you any time you like with swords or pistols. Take your choice," he said thickly.

"If you're challenging me to a duel then you can forget it," said Simon contemptuously. "I'm a doctor. I save life, I don't destroy it, not even drunken idiots like you."

He took Galina's arm and swept her through the door, rushing her through a garden filled with the scent of flowers and cool from the water the gardeners had painstakingly sprinkled earlier in the evening.

Galina torn between a wondering surprise at what he had said and a terrible fear that the fiery young man might follow after them and shoot Simon dead hurried beside him breathlessly. When they were clear away and the music was only a thread of sound behind them, he slowed down.

"Damn the fellow!" he said explosively. "He ruined my plan."

"What plan?"

He paused looking down at her. The pale moonlight had whitened her face and her eyes, large and dark, gazed up at him anxiously.

"Haven't you guessed?" he said quietly. "In all we've spoken of, all we've shared these last weeks?"

"I don't know . . . I'm not sure . . ."

"You're going to marry me, aren't you? We're going to do together all these things we've talked about and planned."

"Marry you?" She had dreamed of such a thing but never expected it would come and now she was face to face with it. "But Simon, I can't . . . it would not be possible."

"Why wouldn't it be possible?"

"You know why," she said distressed. "You know who I am."

"Yes, I know who you are," he took her face between his two hands, "you're the woman I love. I've known for a long time but I had to be sure. Can you forgive me for that? Have you doubted my good faith?"

"Never, never!" she said passionately. "I have never in all my life been so happy but, Simon, there is so much to be thought of, your father, your family in England."

"They will understand," he said confidently, "but it does mean I may have to go home for a time. There are matters to be attended to if I'm to make my life here in Russia with you."

"Do you really want that?"

"Now listen to me," he said firmly, "there are to be no objections this time, no prickles, no proud rejection, no throwing it back in my face. I want a plain answer – yes or no."

"Oh yes, yes, a thousand times yes."

"Thank God for that."

He was just about to kiss her when there was an interruption and a strong arm thrust them apart.

"If you won't fight like a gentleman, then we'll settle it this way," said Captain Ratov and he gave Simon an uppercut that sent him reeling back against the rustic bridge that spanned a little stream. But he had not gone through the mill of Harrow and university without learning the art of self defence. He launched himself at the young soldier so quickly that he went staggering clean into a very large and very prickly shrub, looking so surprised that Galina found it hard not to laugh.

Simon dusted off his hands and said coolly, "If you care to come back to the hotel, I'll treat that split lip for you and those rather nasty scratches."

For an instant the soldier looked black as thunder, then unexpectedly he burst out laughing.

"One up to you, doctor, there's more in you than I thought. Maybe I'll take advantage of your offer if your lady permits."

136

Simon pulled him to his feet and the three of them walked back to the hotel where he efficiently dabbed lotion on the various cuts and bruises and they parted on surprisingly friendly terms.

"My felicitations, Mademoiselle," said the Captain correctly, "and good wishes for your future happiness."

She smiled and gave him her hand. He kissed it gallantly.

"Now you know what it will be like married to a doctor," said Simon humorously as they went up the stairs together. "The most important moments of one's life irretrievably ruined. Called out at all hours of day or night because someone inconsiderately chooses to have a baby or falls from the top of a tree or decides it is time to die."

10

Nina came down the steps of Dannskoye and stood waiting impatiently for Vassily to bring her horse. Shani rose to her feet and came to greet her but for once Nina did not respond with her usual loving caress. She flicked her riding crop discontentedly against her boot and decided that "growing up" and "coming out" had not proved the unalloyed pleasure she had been led to believe. Summer in the country had always been a delightful time when she and Niki had run free and done more or less whatever they pleased but now she seemed to be hedged in with all kinds of restrictions. Niki had changed too during this past year. He and Sonia were for ever going into huddles together from which she was excluded or he was riding around their farms with the estate manager or conferring with Yakov at the factory where there had been serious discontent and angry demands for higher wages and better housing.

"We can't afford to give in to them," his father had said obstinately.

"If we don't do something we could have the place burned down over our heads."

"You're rushing your fences, my boy. Because I've allowed

you to have your way about certain matters, it doesn't mean you have a free hand. I've been at this game far longer than you. They grumble, they make a great fuss and then it is all over for another year."

His father's comfortable assumption that all would be well had not impressed his son.

"Not this time, I think. Have you ever *looked* at the place, Papa?" he said in exasperation, "I wouldn't house a pig in it!"

He never seemed to have time for dancing or picnics or anything in the least amusing these days and Nina felt aggrieved. To make things worse she had just come from a scorching few minutes with her mother.

"You're eighteen, Nina, not a child any longer, and I wish you would remember it. For heaven's sake behave responsibly and I don't like you riding around the countryside unattended. If Niki is too busy to go with you, then you should take Sonia or let Vassily ride with you."

"Grandfather never minded and neither does Papa," muttered Nina rebelliously.

"Your grandfather and your father have always been far too indulgent," went on her mother repressively. "The Countess Skorsky does not approve at all. She hinted as much to me the other day and I did not know what to answer."

"I don't see what it has to do with her," objected Nina. "I have no intention of marrying Valentin. I've told you already, Mamma."

"That remains to be seen. You won't receive many such offers, believe me. He is a charming sensible young man and will make you an excellent husband."

"He's also rich," murmured Nina disparagingly.

"I would have thought that a distinct advantage," replied her mother crisply. "There's many a young girl who would be only too happy to receive his attentions."

"They can *all* have them as far as I'm concerned."

"That is no way to speak to me. I don't know what has come over you this past year. You would be very foolish indeed if you refuse him without careful thought and when he comes here for Niki's engagement, I hope you will make him welcome."

"If I must," said Nina sulkily edging towards the door. "May I go now?"

"Not yet. There is just one other thing. If you are still hankering after Doctor Aylsham . . ."

"I have never done that."

"Oh yes, you have, Nina, and shown it too openly. I'm not blind and I tell you now that you can put it right out of your mind once and for all. He is behaving quite outrageously – travelling to the Crimea and taking Galina Panova with him! I could scarcely believe my ears when I heard about it."

"Why shouldn't he? She has been acting as his assistant."

"Is that what they call it nowadays?" said her mother sarcastically.

"I know what you're hinting at," said Nina defiantly, "and I don't care. Lots of men have mistresses and it doesn't mean anything. The Tsar did before he was married and so did Papa."

"And who told you that, Nina?"

The stony look on her mother's face frightened her.

"People talk."

"You should know better than to listen to such wicked scandal. To speak like that of His Majesty and of your father – you should be ashamed!"

"Why? You keep telling me I've grown up. Isn't that what it means? Knowing what the real world is all about and whatever you say about Simon, Niki intends to ask him to his engagement party because he told me so," and she flung out of the room slamming the door before her mother could make any further protest.

"Hell!" she said aloud standing in the corridor for a moment because despite her bold defiance she had tried to put the thought of Simon and Galina out of her mind and there it was staring her in the face.

"Hell!" she said again and stormed down the stairs.

Vassily had come up from the stables bringing Rusalka with a boy leading another horse.

"I don't want you with me, Vassily."

"The mistress has ordered that you should not ride out alone, Princess," he said with a hint of reproof.

He had been with the Malinskys for most of his life and knew a great deal about family tensions.

"I'm only going through the park. Mamma doesn't understand."

She started away from him before he could reply and Shani went bounding after her. Vassily was about to follow and then changed his mind. The young mistress was proving something of a handful but there was nothing new in that. Hadn't he known her since childhood? He shrugged his shoulders and told the boy to take his horse back to the stable.

Nina had no intention of keeping to the parkland around the house. It was a beautiful morning, not yet too hot, the dew still wet on the grass. There were long open stretches where she could gallop Rusalka. She took the same path they had followed last summer and she smiled remembering the way she had engineeered the fall from her horse, how she had lain in Simon's arms, felt the gentleness of his hands on her body. He couldn't really be in love with Galina, it wasn't possible, not with a girl from the village with no father and a scandalous mother, a girl who had been her own maid. Men had these fancies, everyone knew that, but they didn't marry them. There was old Count Leo of course who lived a few miles away and had married his cook, but he was nearly eighty and wildly eccentric, not a handsome young man, son of an English Lord, with a distinguished future in front of him.

A feeling of enormous frustration surged through her. Why had everything suddenly become so disappointing? She gave Rusalka her head and raced furiously along the open path, only slowing down when she approached the belt of trees and could hear the sound of the sawmills. The sharp scent of the resinous wood was carried to her on the wind. There were a number of men working, they touched their caps to her respectfully, all except one who was piling logs at the further end of the clearing. It piqued her curiosity and she trotted Rusalka towards him.

"Are you new here?" she asked.

He carefully placed the length of timber before turning round. Despite the slouch hat to keep off the sun, the stubble of a new reddish beard, it was Igor's lean sardonic face looking up at her and it gave her a shock. She had tried to forget that evening in the stable and her rash suggestion that he might take refuge in Dannskoye.

"Good morning, Princess. I took your advice, you see," he said coolly. "How are Shani's pups?" He put out a hand as if to pat the dog and the borzoi backed away from him with a low growl.

"How did you get here?" she whispered breathlessly.

"I walked. I was lucky. Your father's overseer was taking on extra hands."

"And you were not followed?"

"Not as far as I know."

"How long will you stay?"

"No longer than I have to, Princess, you may be sure of that."

"I could tell Niki that you are here."

"Will you?"

For a moment silence hung between them, then she shook her head.

Some of the men had begun to eye her curiously. She called the dog and rode on quickly, disturbed, wondering what her father or her brother would say if they guessed she was harbouring a dangerous revolutionary. Something about him made her tremble but how could she betray him? Even among her privileged circle rumours had reached her of the brutal punishments inflicted by the *Okhrana*, floggings so savage that death became merciful. The sight she had witnessed last year had given her nightmares for weeks. After all what could one man do in the comfortable well-ordered home of her childhood? She did not realize till afterwards how wrong she was and how it only needed a very small spark to set dry timber alight.

Igor smiled to himself as he turned back to his work ignoring the coarse jibes of his fellow labourers.

The revolutionary is a dedicated man. He has no personal inclinations, no emotions, no attachments, no property, no name. That was the creed preached by the secret group with whom he had identified himself and he believed in it utterly, but all the same he was still human and it had amused him to see the light of interest in the Princess's eyes. She'd not give him away, he was sure of that.

He had been very careful these past weeks cultivating a silent sullen manner, his astute mind had already guessed at the discontent among the factory workers that was slowly spreading to the peasants who worked on the land. As yet it was no more than talk but he had wormed his way in amongst the younger and more fiery rebels. A bitter restless spirit was spreading through the whole of Russia and when the right moment came even in this peaceful countryside it would be in his power to strike a savage blow for freedom.

The invitation to Niki's engagement party came at the beginning of June. Galina opened it with other mail and handed it to Simon.

"It's from Dannskoye. You must go of course but not me."

He glanced at the card and then met her eyes across the table. "Why not you?"

"You know why. Have you forgotten that last year the Princess Malinskaya forbade me ever to enter the house again."

"It's you who are forgetting, my darling." He leaned across and lifted the hand on which he had put the sapphire and diamond ring. "You are my affianced wife. When I come back from England in the autumn we shall be married. In future you stand by my side."

"But . . .," she said doubtfully.

"No buts. It is settled. I would be glad to wish Niki and Sonia future happiness and we must both of us visit your mother. I would have done so before but there has been so much to be settled."

She still found it hard to believe that it had really happened, that her whole life had changed so dramatically. Ever since they had returned from the Crimea they had lived in a whirl of activity. There was the long review of hospitals and health centres which they had worked on all the winter to be concluded. They talked about where they should live and even went to visit some suitable houses. Nigel held a party for them, and Lydia taking Galina up to see the children kissed her warmly.

"I guessed it from the start," she said, "and I'm very glad. It's wonderful to see Simon looking so happy."

"You don't think he may regret it?"

"My dear, why ever should he?"

"Sometimes it worries me. I'm such a nobody. I'm so afraid it may be held against him."

"If he were Russian, perhaps it might," said Lydia frankly, "but the English are allowed to be eccentric and he's such a very good doctor. It will be what we call a 'nine days' wonder' and then they will all be flocking to him."

"I'm going to work hard to pass my examinations while he is away, than I shall be a qualified pharmacist and I shall be able to work along with him."

"You're such a glutton for punishment," said Lydia a little amused. "Why not just enjoy yourself?"

"Oh no," said Galina shocked. "I would be ashamed to do that. You must work to make a better world and be able to help others."

She was still apprehensive when they took the early afternoon train to Dannskoye and thought she had successfully hidden it, but in the carriage driving them from the station, Simon drew her arm through his.

"Don't worry. You are looking very beautiful and I love you," he whispered.

It comforted her so much that she was able to enter the house proudly on his arm and ignore the curious eyes that turned to stare at the newcomer into their select ranks.

She saw the frozen look of outrage in the Princess Malinskaya's eyes, she saw her open her mouth to express her anger but before she could brace herself to face it, the General had come forward to greet them with outstretched hand.

"My dear Simon, it seems we must celebrate two engagements today. My congratulations and to Galina also," and he leaned forward to kiss her on the cheek.

There was a momentary silence but he was still master in the house. The Princess muttered a few frosty words, there was a kinder greeting from her good-natured husband, then Galina could turn with relief to Niki and Sonia. Nina was standing at one side, quite rigid with shock, her face as white as her muslin gown, her hands clenching and unclenching. Then she suddenly turned her back on them and ran from the room.

Galina said anxiously, "Is she ill? Shall I go after her?"

Simon stopped her. "No, best to leave it. She will be all right."

In the bustle of guests greeting the happy couple no one appeared to have noticed. Nina raced up the stairs, along the corridor and into her own room. Marta was there tidying away scattered garments. She looked up in surprise.

"Is there anything wrong, Princess?"

"No, it's just the heat. I think there is going to be a storm," she said distractedly. "If anyone asks where I am, say I'm lying down." Then as the girl went on calmly with her work, she suddenly screamed at her. "Go, go, leave me alone."

Offended, Marta dropped the garment she was folding and stalked from the room. When the door shut Nina flung herself on the bed, beating her hand against the pillow. It couldn't be true, it couldn't. He couldn't do such a thing to her. All along she had been quite sure that in the end he would be hers. All last summer, all the winter she had dreamed of it, never realizing how unreasonable it was, how he had never given her cause to believe him any more than a kind and attentive friend. She had lived in a fantasy world of her own creating and had now been brutally awoken from it.

She got up walking about the room until she felt she could not stay in the house a moment longer, could not endure to go down to the drawing room watching them together, Galina so proudly in possession of the man who by rights should have been hers. Presently she tore off her summer gown, pulled on her riding skirt, tied a scarf over her hair and went out down the back stairs and through the kitchen quarters. This was a day when all the servants were celebrating with their masters and food and drink had been provided for them. There was no one in the stableyard so she brought Rusalka out of her stall and saddled her, working with trembling hands that fumbled over the heavy straps and buckles. Then she had scrambled on to the mare's back and gone trotting down the path oblivious of the yellowing sky that was beginning to obscure the sun and the intense heat growing more and more oppressive every minute.

It was early evening when Galina slipped away to see her mother.

"I will follow you," said Simon. "I think we're going to have a devil of a thunderstorm. I'd like to get away before it breaks. Niki is pressing us to stay for a few days but I think not. What do you say?"

"Oh heavens, no, much better not," she exclaimed and they exchanged a smile.

Everything had gone off well, much to her relief, but she did not relish more than a few hours under the old Princess's disapproving eyes.

She crossed the paved terrace and went through the flower garden past the fountain. A year ago and she had run down this path with very different feelings and a faint sense of un-reality still persisted though now there surely could be nothing that could affect the security of their love.

Dark clouds had begun to mass overhead and she thought Simon might well be held up if the storm came sooner than they expected.

Vera was standing in the doorway of her hut, looking so exactly the same in her red scarf and striped skirt that Galina felt again the old childish rebellion as she faced up to her.

"Well, Mother."

"Well, daughter."

The black eyes scanned Galina's champagne-coloured silk gown with its draped skirt and matching jacket, the fashionable hat, one elegant rose weighing down the drooping brim.

"You're looking very fine."

"I'm glad you like it."

"Not quite so handsome as the Princess's yellow ballgown, but perhaps that's just as well," and they both laughed and moved together under the low doorway.

"So the midsummer fires worked their magic spell and your doctor was captured."

"That's all nonsense, Mother."

"Is it? And he is really going to marry you?"

Galina held out her hand so that the ring sparkled on her finger. "There's proof of it."

"There's many a slip . . ."

It irritated her because it echoed her own thoughts. "Oh Mother really – do you have to say that?"

Vera was standing back against the stove where no wood burned because of the heavy heat.

"Are you lovers?"

"Why do you ask?"

"That means you are. I can usually tell. There's something about a woman who has been loved, a satisfaction, a fulfilment."

"Yes, it's true," she said with a touch of defiance, "and I'm not ashamed of it."

There was a sudden lurid flash of lightning that lit the room. Her mother moved towards the window.

"It will rain soon. Did I ever tell you?" she went on almost casually. "Your father was a doctor."

Galina had been taking off her hat. She dropped it on the table. "No, you didn't. I thought that . . ."

"That it might have been Prince Malinsky? Oh no, he came here once or twice, poor man, looking for escape from that frigid wife of his but that was all."

So that was the source of the small luxuries she had always enjoyed.

Galina was staring at her. "Did you love him – this doctor?"

Vera smiled faintly. "With all my heart but he didn't love me. He was young then, working in the Petersburg lying-in hospital for a special course and I used to launder his shirts and his linen. I was beautiful in those days and he was lonely – that's all it was. Ridiculous, isn't it? At the end of his year's course he gave me that silk shawl I once lent to you as a parting gift and went away."

"Did he know?"

"No. Fool that I was I was too proud to beg from him *and* too unhappy so I came back here. Men, I thought, are all the same, they look only for pleasure and never beyond it, so after you were born . . ."

"You took lovers."

"Sometimes when it pleased me, not so often as you believed. There were times when they just wanted to talk and I could be a good listener."

"What was his name?"

"Is that important?"

"It is to me. I've always felt so – so alone, so without roots."

"You won't believe me if I tell you."

"Why won't I?"

Her mother shrugged her shoulders. "Sometimes I scarcely believe it myself. It is Basil Makarov."

"But he is famous – a gynaecologist. He is at the hospital in Kiev but is constantly consulted here and in Moscow."

"So they tell me."

She still found it hard to believe.

"Is this really true?"

"Why should I lie?"

"It seems so – so utterly impossible. I've heard him spoken of so many times with praise, with admiration, almost with reverence and he is *my* father!"

"Don't go claiming kinship. Men, even great ones, scatter their seed and take no heed where it takes root. He would laugh at you," said Vera ironically, "and yet when you are angry, you have a look of him. That was how he appeared when despite all his care, a patient of his died," she went on almost dreamily probing back into the past. "He was a handsome man and his hair was of your colour."

146

"You don't know what you have done for me," she exclaimed with a rare show of affection. "I always thought . . ."

"Your father was one of a dozen – tinker, tailor, beggarman, thief," said her mother drily.

"I'm sorry," she said remorsefully, "I should have known."

"Why should you? Will you tell your doctor?"

"No, not yet. He has never questioned. I'll hug it to myself, my secret. Tell me more about Makarov."

"There's nothing to tell." Inside the hut the day had darkened so much with the impending storm that she lit a couple of candles. "Shall I make some tea?"

"Please."

When it was made they sat sipping it closer than they had ever been, not saying much but drawn together because in their different ways they had both loved deeply. Outside a restless little wind had blown up shaking the leaves of the trees. Huge drops of rain spattered on the roof and on the dusty beaten earth and still Simon did not come.

Within the hour the storm broke. The lightning lit up the threatening sky followed by a clap of thunder so loud that it startled Rusalka. She shied badly and Nina momentarily lost her stirrup but she clung to the mare's mane and within seconds had righted herself. She had been riding fast and furiously trying to escape her own angry frustration and had not realized how far she had come. She was country bred and not scared of storms but she had never been out alone in one like this before and she shivered. It was going to be a long ride home. Each side of her stretched limitless fields empty of any kind of shelter except the occasional copse and to take refuge under trees might well be disastrous. There was another long rumble of thunder and she spoke soothingly to the nervous horse as she forced her head round towards Dannskoye. Within minutes the rain came down in blinding sheets turning the dusty path to liquid mud and she was forced to go very slowly.

It was not late but the storm had darkened the sky to a sulphurous yellow. The heavy rain beat into her face, soaking through her thin jacket and her hands kept slipping on the reins. Surely she couldn't have come so far, she thought despairingly, and she was beginning to wonder if she had missed her way when she glimpsed the dark buildings ahead and

realized she must have come round by way of the hemp factory. Ever since the trouble had started, Niki had warned her
to keep away from the place so she pulled up looking around
her. It was then she saw the long thatched hut built of roughly
hewn logs lying to the side of the track, a desolate place sometimes used as a storehouse, more often as a kind of prison
where men could be chained up for a day without food or
drink until they had sweated out their punishment for
drunkenness, or robbing a comrade or fighting murderously
over a woman. Rashly she thought she might take refuge there
for a few minutes waiting for the first violent downpour to
abate a little.

As she trotted towards it she saw one or two men come out
pulling sacks over their heads, looking neither to right or left
as they hurried away. She hesitated but after all she was the
Princess Nina accustomed to instant respect so she went boldly
forward, dismounted and led Rusalka through the half-open
door. Very little light came through the one unglazed window
and she blinked in the semi-darkness. The place smelled horrible but she would not be there long and she pulled the soaked
scarf from her head and shook out the long wet strands of
blonde hair.

She had begun to wring the water from her dripping skirt
when Rusalka gave a frightened whinney. Two hands had
seized her by the shoulders and swung her round, a dark
bearded face loomed above hers, she was being crushed against
a rough jacket that stank vilely of sweat and filth. She struggled violently but the arms tightened around her and a greedy
mouth closed down on hers bruisingly. Rusalka butted into
them and her attacker swung a brutal arm hitting the mare
across the nose so that she screamed and reared. Her ravisher's
hand was locked in her hair dragging her head back as he
tore at her blouse, his hand grabbing at her breast so that she
cried out in pain and outrage. The next moment the heavy
door had been swung back, someone had plucked her attacker
away from her and sent him reeling against the bales of straw.

With a volley of oaths he scrambled to his feet but her
rescuer was ready for him. He seized him by the shoulders
and hurled him through the door to fall heavily on his face in
the churned up mud.

Nina had sunk to her knees trembling with shock and
disgust. The blood from her split lip was trickling down her

chin, the sour taste of that vile kiss was still in her mouth, she buried her face in her hands shaken by long shuddering sobs. She shrank back in fear when she was raised to her feet.

"You and I do appear to meet in the most extraordinary places, Princess," said a quiet voice and she opened her eyes to see Igor looking down at her in his rough workman's dress with his reddish beard and close-cropped hair.

She was trembling so violently she could scarcely speak.

"Who was that man?"

"An animal. Don't think of him."

His eyes ran over her loosened hair, her dishevelled appearance, then he bent to pick up his cap lost in the struggle.

"Why aren't you at Dannskoye celebrating your brother's engagement?"

She was dabbing at the blood when suddenly the shame, her anger and her humiliation all seemed to come together.

"It is Galina," she sobbed, "all this — everything — it is because of Galina."

"Galina?" he frowned. "What has Galina Panova to do with you?"

"She is going to marry the doctor — my doctor. She has stolen him from me."

"What are you saying — is this true?"

The fierceness of his reaction had taken her by surprise, he had seized her by the shoulders, shaking her, his eyes blazing. So he too had been captured by Galina and the angry jealousy grew and swelled until she could not longer hold it back, it poured out in a bitter stream.

"Oh yes, it is true, I swear it is. She was there this afternoon glorying in it and Mamma was angry, terribly angry, because he had brought her, brazening it out in front of everyone when she has been his mistress for months."

He had dropped his hands and was staring at her, those brilliant eyes that seemed to penetrate to her very soul and made her shiver.

"What are you saying?"

"It is true. Didn't you know? He took her with him to the Crimea," she went on wildly, "Galina, one of Papa's serfs, a maidservant, a nobody, a peasant who does not even know her own father . . ."

Her voice was rising into hysteria and he slapped her cheek hard.

"Be quiet, you little fool. You don't know what you are talking about. What do you and those like you know about the people, the real people? Galina is worth a dozen of you and she could have been – she could have achieved so much if only . . .," his voice choked and then went on with a quiet deadly fury. "She has sold herself for a rich living, for money, for fine clothes."

He spat out the words, his bitter anger, his utter contempt all the more telling for its quietness.

"When?" he said turning on her. "When do they marry?"

"I don't know," she was stammering now, shock and exhaustion taking their toll. "Niki says he must return to England first so it will be when he comes back to Russia."

For one moment the look on his face terrified her. That, she thought, in her dazed mind must be how the devil looked when he defied his creator's damnation. Then it had vanished.

"Come," he said practically, "the rain has stopped. They will be searching for you. It's time you returned to Dannskoye."

Calmly he led Rusalka outside and lifted her into the saddle leading her through the living quarters of the barracks and past the factory on her way home.

"You'll be safe enough now," he said, "and say nothing of what happened to you, do you understand? If you do, it could harm not only you but your whole family, and you wouldn't want that, would you?"

She stared at him, frightened by she hardly knew what and then slowly nodded. He watched her go slowly and dejectedly up the bridle path. Then he squelched his way through the black mud to the long filthy dormitory which he shared with a dozen others. Methodically he packed his few possessions into a canvas bag, slung it across his shoulder and slipped out. His mind was made up.

It was Valentin who first raised the alarm. It was shortly after Galina had gone to visit her mother. He had arrived rather later than the other guests and asking for Nina was told she had a headache and was lying down; but as the time went by and she did not appear he became anxious. Marta closely questioned confessed she had not seen her mistress since early afternoon and when she went up to her room to prepare for the evening, she had found the dress Nina had been wearing discarded on the bed. It was Vassily who clinched it, reporting rather shamefacedly that Rusalka had disappeared when the stables had been temporarily deserted.

"What the devil is she up to?" exclaimed Niki more annoyed than worried at this stage. "What sort of madcap trick is this?"

Sonia, more aware of Nina's restless moods than her brother, said, "She may have felt she needed some air. It has been terribly hot and stuffy all the afternoon."

"But to ride out on a day like this! What *can* she be thinking of?"

Valentin said, "Shall I go out and look for her?"

"We've no idea where she has gone," objected Niki. "Better not make too much fuss about it. It will only upset Mamma."

"There's going to be a storm so she's bound to be back soon. Let's wait for a little," pleaded Sonia.

But an hour passed and anxiety grew. Several guests had left already wishing to drive home before the rain came down. However, the Countess Skorsky, forbiddingly disapproving, was still there with her son. Nina's mother had to be told and was very angry indeed with her daughter for behaving so irresponsibly. Her father, more easily upset, promptly lost his temper, severely rated the servants and sent Vassily off at once to search for her.

"I should have gone with him," said Simon uneasily.

"Why you? Oh God, I hope she's not tried one of her foolish tricks and been thrown." Niki was pacing up and down, a great deal more upset than he was willing to admit. They might quarrel and argue but he and his sister had always been very close. He gave Simon a quick glance. "I think your engagement may have hit her rather hard," he said wryly, "you did rather spring it on us."

"I'm sorry but it happened like that and I promise you that I never gave Nina any reason to think . . ."

"That you cared for her beyond ordinary friendship, I know that," said Niki. "I'm not blaming you but you know what young girls are . . . they do get the silliest notions in their heads."

"Damn it!" exclaimed Simon. "I can't sit here waiting. Anything could have happened. I'm going out after her."

"I'll come with you."

But before the two young men had done anything more than pull on boots and arrange for horses to be saddled, they saw the bedraggled figure come trotting slowly and wearily up the long garden path. The rain had stopped and the sky was beginning to clear. A watery sun gleamed fitfully on dripping trees, on huge puddles and rain-soaked flowers.

Simon raced down the steps and caught hold of Rusalka's bridle.

"Thank God you're back safely," he exclaimed.

He reached up to her and she gave a little sighing gasp and collapsed into his arms as he lifted her from the saddle.

He carried her back into the house closely followed by Niki and a few interested guests. He had taken in at a glance the blood on her bruised face, the torn blouse, the tangled hair and was afraid.

"Keep them away," he said hurriedly to Niki, "and ask Sonia to show me her room."

"You don't think . . .?"

"I don't know yet."

By that time Sonia was with him and leading the way. Upstairs in the bedroom he was brisk and efficient.

"Undress her and fetch warmed blankets. Bring something hot to put at her feet. She is soaking wet and chilled through."

He had laid her on the bed and she clung to him pitifully.

"Don't leave me, please don't leave me." .

"I'm not leaving you," he said reassuringly, "but first of all we're going to make you warm and comfortable. Then you can tell us all about it."

He left Sonia and Marta to undress her, wash the mud and blood from her face and hands and wrap the blankets around her.

When he came back to the bed, she was lying very white and still.

"Now let me take a look at you," he said gently. "You've got some very nasty bruises. How did that happen?"

She shook her head and he read shock and bewilderment and something very like fear in the dilated eyes, in the way she clutched at his hand as if it were a kind of sheet anchor in a distraught world.

He noted the bruises on her breast and drew his own conclusions but there appeared to be no other damage, thank God.

Niki had come in followed by one of the servants with a tray of hot tea. Simon joined him while Sonia helped Nina to sit up and held the cup while she sipped from it.

"How is she?" asked her brother.

"She won't talk yet but I think that possibly she has been attacked."

"Not . . .?"

"No, not raped, but enough to leave her shocked and very distressed."

"Thank God it's no worse. If she won't tell us who it was, I don't know how we can find out without creating a tremendous scandal. Mamma's holding them all at bay downstairs. We don't want any unpleasant rumours for Nina's sake. By the way Galina has come back. She was worried because you didn't turn up."

"Good. Ask her to fetch my bag for me, will you?"

Like many doctors Simon usually carried his medical bag with him. Emergencies could occur at any time and he liked always to be prepared.

When Galina came in a few minutes later he was sitting beside the bed talking soothingly to Nina. She still refused to answer any of his questions and he guessed that the experience had been so frightening that she wanted only to blot it out of her mind, and thought it inadvisable to press her too hard in her present state.

He went to meet Galina as she put the bag on the table and opened it. She had•heard a garbled story from the servants downstairs and looked at him questioningly.

"What happened to her?"

"I'll tell you later. I'm going to give her an injection to calm her down. Get it ready for me, will you?"

He went back to Nina and Galina prepared the syringe and brought it to him. Nina's violent reaction shocked her. She sat up in the bed, her eyes huge in her pale face.

"Go away," she screamed, "go away. It is because of you, it's all happened because of you. Tell her to go away," sobbing wildly she threw herself into Simon's arms and he held her shaking body very closely.

"Ssh," he said soothingly, "don't distress yourself like this. It's all right. Now listen to me. I'm going to give you something that will make you feel a lot better and Galina is helping me with it, that's all."

She quietened then and lay passive while Galina prepared her arm and Simon put in the injection as gently as he could.

"You'll stay," she whispered imploringly as he tucked the blankets around her.

"Yes, until you fall asleep. Don't be afraid."

Nina's unexpected attack had shaken Galina. She felt guilty as she repacked the medical bag and yet why should she feel like that? What had she done after all? She had not taken Simon from Nina, he had never been hers; and yet the feeling persisted, accentuated because he was going away from her so very soon.

When Nina had fallen asleep and Sonia offered to stay with her, Simon had a last few words with Niki.

"She will soon get over it, there's no serious hurt, but I think you should send for your own doctor in the morning just as a precaution. Your mother will be happier about that," he added wryly, "I don't think she has much trust in me."

He insisted on them leaving that same evening, late though it was. Nina's dependence upon him was far too dangerous. He had treated patients like that before, hysterical young women clinging to their doctor. It was better that she should not see him again. When he came back in the autumn and was safely married, it would be different.

"I'm not sorry that's over," he said thankfully to Galina when they were in the train, "Has it been hard for you, my darling?"

She shook her head. "Not really, except for Nina. Why should she be so jealous of me?"

"Because you have many advantages which she would like to possess."

"Including you."

"I never gave her cause," he said ruefully.

"I know." She sought for his hand and gripped it tightly. "I'm so happy that sometimes it makes me afraid."

"Of what? Some jealous God that might snatch it away from you? That's very pagan, my love." He smiled down at her indulgently, putting his arm around her waist and drawing her close to him. "What possible harm can come so long as we love one another? We will defy the dark hand of fate together."

154

11

It so happened that Simon left Petersburg sooner than he had intended. Only a day after they came back from Dannskoye a cablegram from his brother reached him via the embassy. Lord Aylsham had suffered a stroke and was seriously ill.

"I must go," he said, "though God knows if I will reach Ravensley in time to see Father alive. I can't leave Robert and my sister to face it alone. I've been away from them too long."

She realized then how strong was the pull of his distant family and she was suddenly afraid. If his father died, what would happen? Would they persuade him to stay in England? She would be so far away from him, in another existence, in another world. She tried hard not to let herself dwell on it. She packed for him while he made hurried financial arrangements leaving an account at his bank on which she could draw, paying advanced rent for his apartment, thinking of her constantly even in the anxiety for his father.

"I wish you'd give up that wretched attic and come to live here," he said once during those busy hours. "I can't think why you like it there so much."

She found it hard to explain even to herself except that it made her feel less like a kept woman and more like a person in her own right.

"Perhaps I will now," she said. "After you have gone, I'll go there, settle it all up, give some of the odds and ends to Luba, and then Ranji and I will wait for you here."

Please God don't let it be too long, she prayed, but would not say it aloud. She must not let him know how much she dreaded his leaving her, how desperately lonely she was going to be, how insecure she still felt.

The hours flew by only too quickly. He was to leave very early on the following morning and after a hectic day, he took her to supper at Leiters. The restaurant was crowded as usual despite the late June heat. Artists, actors, writers, poets, all talking noisily and she remembered vividly the first time they had gone there when she had been so desperately ashamed of her shabby coat and worn boots. How different it was now. Hands were waved, greetings exchanged. She had been accepted into this easygoing raffish society far more quickly than among the aristocratic circle of Dannskoye.

They walked home together through the magical beauty of the summer night when it never seemed to grow completely dark. The giant statue of Peter the Great on his leaping horse was etched against a sky of pearl, the river flowed by, darkly gleaming and mysterious, and the air was scented by the flowers in great baskets which the gypsies had spread out for their early morning customers.

Simon stopped to buy her a great cluster of roses, creamy white and velvety crimson, and she buried her face in the cool damp blooms. The black eyes of the old woman twinkled up at them from a brown face seamed with a hundred wrinkles.

"The night is for joy and laughter, isn't that so, excellency?" and she chuckled.

How right she was, thought Galina later, when she lay in Simon's arms. They had never loved so deeply with such passionate intensity, the edge of their desire sharpened by the imminent parting, never had she given herself to him so completely, so without any reserve. The joy of it stayed with her and afterwards it seemed foolish to sleep when the time together was so very short. Dawn was brightening the window when he half sat up.

"I must dress."

"Not yet, it's still early." She reached up to him laughing a little. "I've just discovered something new about you, a little brown mole just behind your left shoulder."

"It's my devil's mark."

"Your what?"

He was smiling down at her. "You didn't know what a dangerous man you've been entertaining in your bed, did you? You see when I was about three years old we had an under-nurse who came from the Fens. It's wild and strange country, Galina, full of superstitions and ghostly legends. She told me that it was the mark of the devil and the big black dog that haunts the marshes with red gleaming eyes and slavering jaws would come one day and claim me as his own."

"She said that to a child?"

"She'd grown up with it, I expect, just another tale to her but needless to say a night or so later I woke screaming my head off and sobbed out the whole story to my mother when she came to comfort me. 'Rubbish,' she said, 'that little brown mark means you are my farthing baby. When the doctor brought you to me in his black bag, that is what I had to pay, just one farthing,' and that, my love, is the smallest British coin."

"A farthing baby," she repeated and smiled up at him in delight. "I shall remember that always."

Then quite suddenly the laughter, the gaiety, had vanished. It was as if a black shadow had risen up between them terrifying her and she sat up clinging to him, her face pressed against his chest, her arms holding him as if she could never let him go.

"Here, here," he said gently, "what's all this? I'm not going to war, you know. I'm coming back."

"I know, I know," she said breathlessly, "just for a moment I couldn't bear it. I'm sorry."

"Foolish one." He tilted up her chin and kissed her lips. "All better? Now I really must dress if I'm going to catch that train."

He was right. She was behaving idiotically. She had so much to do, the time would soon pass and he would be there in her arms again. That was what she said firmly in her mind when she watched him vanish as the train drew out of the station and she refused to allow the desolation to invade her heart.

The examinations were to be held in a month's time. Simon had taught her a great deal and she was determined to do brilliantly, as much for his sake as for her own; so she must settle down to a few weeks of close revision. It would be far more comfortable to work in his spacious apartment than in the stuffy room at the top of the house so on the very next day she decided to go there, collect her books with the few items she valued, pay the housekeeper anything that was owing and shut the door for ever on that part of her life.

It was late afternoon when she crossed the bridge and made her way down the narrow street. Stasia Ivanovna greeted her effusively eyeing curiously the summer costume of dark blue linen with the crisp white blouse and shady hat. Her former lodger was obviously going up in the world.

The last thing Galina wanted was to stay and gossip. "I'm getting married," she said briefly, "so I shall be leaving here. I've only come to fetch a few personal things. You must let me know how much I owe you."

"Married, eh? And who is he, the lucky man?" exclaimed Stasia, "am I allowed to know? Not one of those beggarly artists from the island?"

"No, he's a doctor," said Galina trying to edge away.

"Not that Englishman who came here when you were so sick?" She gave a little shriek. "Who'd have thought it? A proper gentleman, that one was, and no mistake. Married, you say!" Stasia Ivanovna obviously found it very hard to believe. "Well, you're one of the fortunate ones, I must say."

"Yes, I am, aren't I?" said Galina. "Now I must really get down to work."

"One of those friends of yours from the island was here, asking for you," shouted Stasia after her as she ran up the stairs but she didn't listen. It was probably only Luba and she would be seeing her soon.

The house was very quiet, all the inmates out in the sunshine or hard at work. The door to Igor's apartment was firmly shut and she did not give him a thought.

Her attic was unbearably hot and stuffy and she opened the window to let in what air there was. Except for one brief visit she had spent no time there since before Simon took her to the Crimea and she looked around her in something like dismay. The room was thick with dust and looked as if a hurricane had blown through it. She had taken the precaution of bringing a little food with her, some bread, cheese and fruit so that she would not have to waste time going out to eat. She took off her fashionable costume and fresh white blouse, hung them up, put on her old cotton dressing gown and set to work. By the time she had sorted everything out, placed on one side the books and personal items she wanted to keep, piled together the oddments she had bought herself, a chair, a small cabinet and a bookshelf that she thought Luba might be glad to have, it was quite late and she suddenly decided to stay the night there and arrange for a cab to collect everything in the morning.

She ate some of the food she had brought, brewed some tea on the old stove and laughed at herself because not expecting to stay she had brought no nightgown. The room under the roof seemed to hold the heat of the day so presently she stripped off her undergarments, slipped on her lawn petticoat, put on the dressing gown again and lay down on the bed happily content.

The room was filled with so many memories, some of them painful, many of them filled with joy. She lay thinking of the first time she had come there, so proud of her independence, the dangerous excitement of those illegal meetings of the students' unions, the fiery speakers, the inspiring feeling of working for some wonderful new future. It was there she first saw Igor whose speeches had thrilled her and it was only afterwards that she grew frightened of the ruthlessness that seemed only to corrupt and brutalize their ideals.

Then of course there had been Simon. Dreamily she let her mind run back to when she had taken Niki to him, the night they had jumped across the fire, those terrible despairing weeks from which he had rescued her with such gentleness, the magical night when he had abandoned Nina's party to come to this very room and she knew that he truly loved her and whatever he should demand from her she would willingly give.

She was drowsing into sleep when she heard someone come running up the stairs but thought nothing of it. Then a door banged noisily and she sat up. The house had seemed so empty when she entered it that foolishly she had not thought to lock her door. She had no real fear, still it might be wise to do it now. She was half off the bed when it was flung open and Igor was standing there framed in the doorway, Igor in his rough workman's blouse, looking the same as he always did except for the reddish beard. It was so unexpected that for a moment she stared at him stupidly, then she hurriedly got to her feet clutching her dressing gown around her.

"What are you doing here? Can't you see that I'm going to bed? Please go at once."

"You didn't expect to see me again, did you? I want to talk to you."

"I've nothing to say to you now or at any time. Please go, Igor, and leave me alone."

"Oh no, here I am and here I stay," and he came further into the room slamming the door behind him.

"If you don't go immediately, I shall scream, I shall call for help."

"Oh no, you won't do that," he said mockingly. "A man in your room – you wouldn't want a scandal. That wouldn't suit your handsome English lover, would it?"

Quite calmly he locked the door. She made a rush to snatch the key from him but he flung her roughly back.

"No, my dear, that stays with me," and he dropped it in his pocket.

Up to that moment she had not been seriously alarmed. He was behaving as he had always done, deliberately provocative, sure of his own power; now suddenly she guessed at his purpose. The room had become stiflingly hot. She felt the sweat break out on her forehead as she frantically tried to think of a way of escape. Those brilliant eyes were fixed on her, probing into her, paralysing her.

Love had increased her beauty, he thought, softened the austere lines of her face, given her a glow, a radiance, that filled him with an impotent fury because she had gone beyond his reach.

"You whore! You worthless bitch! You once had something I was fool enough to admire, a strength, an integrity, a capacity for something beyond the ordinary, and you betrayed us. You sold yourself for fine clothes, for rich food, for all those things that are without importance or value."

His voice, low and intense, had a corrosive bitterness that cut deeply and she resented it furiously.

"It's not true, it's never been true. He is a doctor, he is dedicated to life, not to your creed of murder and death, and I love him, I tell you, I love him . . ."

"Love!" he repeated with a searing contempt. "What is love?" and he snapped his fingers. "I'll prove to you what love is – no more than a lusting after one another like animals."

"You're mad," she cried out but he had brooded over it too long. A raging fury took possession of him and now she was in his power.

He made a lunge to grab hold of her but she evaded him and raced to the door. She shook the handle violently but it was firmly locked. She banged on it shouting for help only there was no one to hear.

He seized her by the shoulders swinging her back into the room. She resisted strongly and it inflamed him further. The thin cotton of her dressing gown split and he tore it from her.

She fought him then, but the room was small and there was no escape. A chair crashed over, a cup and glass smashed and rolled across the floor. She snatched at a knife from the table but he bent her arm back so cruelly that it dropped from her fingers and he kicked it aside.

It was terrifying, hideous, grotesque, but could have only one end. Igor was tall and thin but immensely strong. She stumbled against the carpet bag she had filled with books and he caught hold of her, lifting her easily and flinging her on the bed. She struggled to get away from him but he held her pinned down by the shoulder while his other hand tore the flimsy lawn petticoat from neck to hem. She brought up her knee trying to throw him off her and he hit her bruisingly across the jaw. She was fighting him every inch of the way, clawing, biting, her nails ripping down his cheek and bringing blood. She saw his face looming over her, then his mouth had clamped down, his tongue forcing open her lips. She tried desperately to roll away from him but his weight held her under him. She shut her eyes against the appalling inevitability.

He took her so brutally that she cried out at the pain and outrage. It was so vile, so agonizing, that she wanted to die under it but that would be far too easy. It seemed to go on for ever, then it was over. He raised himself a little staring into her face.

"Now you know what it means to mate with a real man, a man of the people," he said hoarsely.

She lifted her head and spat full in his face. The blood and spittle trickled down his cheek.

"Get out," she whispered, "get out! GET OUT!"

He stood up staring down at her, the lustrous hair tumbled about her white face, the beautiful naked body he had so viciously ravaged, the long lovely legs, and suddenly deep within him though he would never have admitted it, there was shame. It boiled up in him like bile, it filled his mouth with bitterness, a fierce unreasoning anger so that he wanted to smash things, to burn and destroy and kill because he knew no other way to assuage that shame.

He crossed to the door, unlocked it and flung the key at her.

"Go to hell any way you choose, but don't think I've done with you. You won't escape me, you'll never escape!"

He went out slamming the door behind him. For a long moment she could not move, her body racked and aching, but worse than that was the shame, the revulsion, the despair. Then she dragged herself off the bed, picked up the key and locked the door. She poured water into the basin and frantically washed every part of her body as if somehow she could wipe away the horror and the stain.

She could not bear to stay there late though it was. She was filled with a terrible fear that he might come back. Igor was a fanatic. He would not give up easily. The hideous thing that had quivered between them could only end in his death or hers.

She began to dress hurriedly, bundling up the torn petticoat, pulling on her clothes anyhow. She would leave everything to be fetched another day. Now all she wanted to do was to escape.

When she was ready she crept out of her room and listened. No sound came from behind Igor's closed door. She went down the staircase as quietly as she could and out into the warm sweetness of the summer night. A few hours before she had come there so happily, now she was running away from it like a beaten animal, shamed, unclean.

It was a bitter kind of relief to find herself back in the apartment so full of Simon, the faint scent of the cigars he smoked, the toilet water he used, a shirt he had discarded lying across the bed, books he had left behind on the table. Distractedly she picked one of them up, an English poet she had been trying to read with him. It fell open and she read the lines he had marked.

> Our two Souls therefore, which are one
> Though I must go, endure not yet
> A breach, but an expansion
> Like gold to airy thinness beat.

Like gold the love between them was stretched but indestructible. She clung to that thought in her wretchedness. The body that had belonged solely to him for his love and delight had been cruelly violated but somehow she must learn to live with it. She crumpled up on the bed burying her face in the pillow that still smelled faintly of him and wept, hard dry sobs that tore her apart and brought no relief.

*

The only way to stop herself thinking about it was to work. She set herself down to it doggedly, studying hard for long hours every day and going to bed tired out in the hope of escaping from the nightmares that plagued her during the next few weeks, horrible dreams from which she would wake sweating and distraught. Sometimes she wondered what she would have done if Simon had not gone away. Would she have poured it all out to him or would she have remained silent in case the very fact of her body being violated by another man would fill him with revulsion? To write about such a thing was an impossibility. By the time he came back it would have been mercifully buried in oblivion and need no longer be agonized over, or would it? The only thing she knew with certainty was that she could not bear to speak of it to anyone, not even to Luba when she went over to the studio, taking the items she had put aside for her.

The room was in its usual state of comfortable squalor. Luba was no housewife. She never at any time caught up with the everyday chores, but there was always a flowering branch or two stuck in a jar, she would share her last kopeck with someone in need and no starving animal was turned away without a crust. There was a warmth about her welcome that comforted Galina.

"I'm not going to say no to them," panted Luba when the chair, cabinet and bookshelf had been lugged up the stairs. "They give us a bit of class if I can only stop Conn from putting a wet paint-brush on the polished surface." She gave the cabinet a flick with a stained rag doing service as a duster before she eyed Galina. "You're looking peaky," she went on, "working yourself into a frenzy over those examinations, I don't doubt."

"Well, they are important," said Galina defensively. "A diploma in pharmacy means I can always earn my own living."

"I thought you were going to have a husband who will do all that for you," objected Luba.

"Of course he will but I still want to be able to play my part in his work. He gives me so much I want to repay it in the only way I can."

"I'd say there were other ways a lot more pleasant," murmured Luba, "but I see your point. If I had any sense I'd be doing something like that except that you need brains and

163

I'm short on those." She sighed. "Conn finished his work with the children's books and that source has dried up. I'm back to the modelling again – oh don't look shocked, not in the altogether. He's suddenly gone respectable and won't allow his wife to show off her charms and the other is not so profitable so I'm doing a turn for one of the student unions."

"Doing what?"

"Distributing leaflets. Ever since that frightful Sunday the printing presses have been rattling them off till they're red hot, breathing fire and slaughter against the government, the Tsar and anyone else who wears decent clothes and washes regularly."

"Oh Luba, that can't be true."

"Not in so many words but that's what it comes to. It's only a pittance but it helps pay the rent."

"You shouldn't be doing it," said Galina earnestly, "it's against the law and it's dangerous. If they catch you with them, it could mean prison or worse."

"They won't nab me. I know their faces, most of 'em, sly devils they are, but you get an instinct for them."

"What about the press?"

"It's in a cellar and the owner of the house believes we're printing banknotes and turns a blind eye, poor fool." Luba giggled and then was suddenly serious. "Igor has turned up again. Did you know?"

Galina went cold all over and felt her flesh creep at the very mention of his name.

"No, I didn't know."

"In dead secret and disguised of course. He's grown a beard, makes him look like a professor gone motheaten at the edges. He's up to something but didn't give anything away, vicious too as if something had caught him on the raw. He was ready to hit out at anyone who dared to argue with him."

"Don't have anything to do with him, Luba. He's dangerous, I tell you. Look at what he did to you."

"Oh that." Luba shrugged her shoulders. "I hated him for it but in some ways I'd only myself to blame. I didn't exactly fight him off."

Now it was all over and the burden lifted from her Luba could look back and laugh and Galina wondered if she would ever be able to do the same. She was filled with an irrational fear of what Igor could still do to her and to Simon.

*

The examinations took place at the end of July and were always undertaken by a great many young women candidates, many of them like herself sprung from the working classes. It was one of the few degrees granted by the university to women who were only allowed to attend lectures on sufferance and could not gain the same academic distinction as the men. The day before she had received her first letter from Simon. It told her that his father was still alive but very gravely ill, that he had told his sister all about her and Margaret was looking forward to meeting her.

The familiar handwriting, the very feel of the paper his hands had touched gave her comfort. She put it in her pocket, a talisman against what she might have to face in the examinaton hall.

In actual fact she was so well prepared that it did not prove as forbidding as she had anticipated. She thought she had done moderately well until the final day which was an oral test before a board of distinguished doctors and pharmacists.

She woke that morning feeling horribly ill. She was seized with giddiness when she got out of bed and felt far too nauseated to eat or drink anything. She must have driven herself too hard, she thought, but she was not going to fall down on it at this stage. Somehow she dressed and got to the examination room but she looked so white when she stood up before them gathering all her strength to find the right answers that one of the examiners more kindly than the rest asked her if she would like to sit down. She gave him a blurred look of gratitude when a chair was brought. It helped to steady her and when at last she rose to leave the room, the same kindly man gave her a smile and a nod as if he admired her tenacity. She took note of him then, a man about fifty, thick dark brown hair greying at the temples, a strong face with a forceful chin, not one to suffer incompetence lightly, she thought, and felt encouraged.

It did not strike her at first what was wrong with her. The heat in Petersburg in early August was intense, the examination rooms had been stiflingly airless and she knew she had been overdoing it with long hours of study when she had often forgotten to eat. Her usual monthly period was late but stress sometimes had that effect and she did not let it worry her. It was only when the malaise continued into the next week and the week after that she guessed at the cause. She had lived too close to the life of the villagers and their animals not to know that she was almost certainly pregnant. For a few dizzying minutes she was both wildly happy and scared. To bear Simon's child would be a joy even though it would undoubtedly create problems for both of them.

She lay in bed one morning thinking about it when suddenly out of the blue it hit her. She felt as if she had fallen from a great height and was now lying on the hard unfeeling earth winded and terrified. Supposing it was not Simon's child but belonged to Igor?

A burning flush of heat raced through her body, then fled leaving her icy cold. The more she thought of it, the more likely it became. She and Simon had been together for six months. They had loved often and passionately but she had never conceived, now after that one violent assault from Igor she had become pregnant just as Luba had done all those months ago.

She went over and over it in her mind. Those last hours with Simon before he went away to be followed the very next night by Igor's brutal rape. What potent force did he possess? How could she ever know whose seed had been planted in her womb? How could she live through nine long months in agonizing doubt? How could she possibly marry Simon and not tell him that the child she was carrying was maybe not his but a bastard forced upon her by a man he despised?

The next few weeks were the most difficult, the most tormenting she was ever to experience. Once the first realization was over, she tried hard to consider it dispassionately, to hunt for a soluton that increasingly became impossible to find.

At first she prayed as unhappy young women have done the world over that by some miracle it would vanish, it would be all over and she could breathe again, but when her next period was missed, she knew she was not to be saved so easily. She visited a doctor in an outer suburb of the city and he confirmed her fears. He was a morose elderly man. He examined her efficiently but perfunctorily and pronounced her fit enough.

"A little too thin but that will soon be remedied," he grunted. "The baby is due early in April." His cynical eyes summed her up gloomily. "There is always the foundling hospital for young women in your trouble," he said and pocketed the fee she had laid down.

She felt the colour flood into her cheeks and fled. Never, she thought, never, even if it proved to be Igor's child, could she condemn a living creature to that hideous comfortless hell.

Simon had written that he would be obliged to stay longer than he wished since his father was close to death and he could not abandon his brother at such a painful time. He was full of loving reproaches that her letters to him had been so short and so uninformative. She knew he was right. She could not write joyously and freely of their future together when there might be no future.

The examination results came through. She had passed with the highest honours in her class and the success was dust and ashes in her mouth. She would have been so proud to stand at his side, fully qualified, and now . . . if only there had been someone in whom she could confide. There was her mother, there was Luba, but she knew exactly what they would say, "Brazen it out. Tell Simon it is his child."

But she could not do that. She could not live with him in deceit and lies and she shrank from the truth. Would he believe it? Sometimes when she had been so insistent on keeping her room and preserving her independence, he had said jestingly, "I believe it's that fellow Igor that keeps you there," and had laughed at her strong indignation. But now . . . oh God how would it seem to him now? She could hear all those friends and acquaintances who had been so doubtful of their liaison, so scornful of their engagement, perhaps even Lydia and Nigel . . . "What do you expect from a girl of that class? He leaves her for a few months and she is pregnant and by whom — I ask you!" How could she endure to put such shame on him?

She thought of abortion and shrank from it. There were men and women who would do it at a price and even if she could bring herself to submit to something so hateful and so dangerous, how could she ever hide it from him? The man she would marry was a doctor, one who knew every intimate detail of the body. Besides it *could* be his child and the very thought of deliberately destroying something that would be so precious to her was unthinkable.

Backwards and forwards scurried her thoughts during those September days when mists began to creep up from the river and the first cold winds blew from the east. Last year at about this time he had lifted her from despair into life. She had had one glorious year with him. Perhaps that was all the jealous gods allowed. Something of the fatalistic acceptance of the peasant still clung to her. Then quite suddenly there was no more time left. She must decide and quickly. The last letter from England told her that Lord Aylsham had died and in a month or six weeks Simon would be returning, bringing his young sister with him. Suddenly Galina was frantic. It was that fact that brought her to a decision quicker than anything. His young innocent sister eager to attend her brother's wedding and the bride-to-be pregnant in the most doubtful, the most horribly indecent manner.

Then there was Nina. It was a day or two later with the ultimate decision still lying heavily on her mind when she came in one morning from walking Ranji in the English Gardens and was astonished to find Nina waiting for her.

"It's such a long time since we've seen you I thought I would call while we are in town and find out how you are," she said with a bright insincerity. "The doorkeeper said you were out with Ranji and wouldn't be long."

"I see. It's very kind of you."

Galina unclipped the dog's leash and he trotted across to Nina sniffing at her skirts.

"I expect he smells Shani. He has grown quite splendidly, hasn't he, almost completely borzoi. No one would guess he is really only a mongrel."

Galina guessed what was in Nina's mind. It was not the dog she was thinking of. She took off her light coat and laid it carefully over the chair.

"I'm sure you didn't come here to talk about Ranji," she said evenly, "so why are you here, Nina?"

"I told you. We're in Petersburg for dress fittings. You know Niki is to be married at the end of December. Sonia wants the wedding to be at Dannskoye. She thinks it would please our people there. Stupid really. It would be so much more exciting at the Cathedral and a great deal more convenient for all our friends but she won't be budged. Is Simon still in England?"

So that's what she really wants to know, thought Galina. "Yes, he is," she replied calmly. "His father died and he has been obliged to stay much longer than he intended. There is a great deal to be settled."

"Perhaps there are other reasons why he is not hurrying to return."

"And what exactly do you mean by that?" asked Galina coldly.

"Well, after all if anything should happen to his brother he would be Lord Aylsham, wouldn't he, and *you* would be Lady Aylsham. Have you thought of that?"

"It's a very long chance. His brother could have a son."

"Yes, of course. You don't mind me speaking like this, do you, Galina? We're such old friends," went on Nina airily, "but as Mamma says, if Simon is really intending to set up as a fashionable physician, it won't exactly help him when he marries his mistress, will it, but I expect you've already realized that."

She had thought of it over and over again but to hear it spoken of so glibly was more than she could endure.

"I have realized it and so has Simon," she said as coolly as she could and at the same time longing to slap Nina's pretty face. "He is a doctor, a real doctor, not a fashionable quack and his choice of wife won't affect the kind of work he intends to do."

"Heavens, you're not going to turn him into one of those Social Revolutionaries, are you? I imagine that will damn him completely before he even starts."

"Is that all you came here to say because if it is you're wasting your breath?"

"No, it isn't actually." Nina was fiddling with one of her fine suede gloves smoothing out the fingers before she looked up, an edge of malice in the light pretty voice. "Do tell me – was Igor Livinov ever your lover?"

It was so unexpected that try as she would she could not prevent the hot colour surging up in her cheeks and quickly turned her head away.

"What posssible reason can you have for saying such a thing?" she said in a stifled voice. "What do you know of Igor?"

"Only what Niki told me. You were all together in the same group at the university, weren't you? Did you know that he took refuge at Dannskoye after that terrible Sunday?"

"No, I didn't." Galina looked at her searchingly. "Was it he who attacked you on the day of Niki's engagement party?"

Nina bit her lip. She had admitted more than she had intended. "No, of course, it wasn't. I fell from my horse because of the storm and he helped me, that's all."

"Did you tell Niki about it?"

"No, I didn't dare."

"What do you mean – you didn't dare?"

"Oh do stop questioning me," she said pettishly. "Anyone would think I'd done something dreadful. It was because of that Sunday night in Petersburg. He hid in the stables. He was hurt and desperate. I had to do something . . ."

"And so you told him to go to Dannskoye. Oh Nina, how could you be so foolish? Don't you realize that Igor is dangerous? If he went there it was for some purpose of his own. Wherever he goes he leaves a trail of destruction behind him."

"You sound just like Mamma. Anyone would think we are all to be murdered in our beds."

"You might very well be."

"You seem to know a great deal about him."

"I certainly know more than you do. I'm serious about this, Nina. Warn Niki, warn your father."

"It doesn't matter now. He's gone away."

"How can you be certain of that?"

She shrugged her shoulders. "If you must know I told him about you and Simon. He was dreadfully angry and afterwards he disappeared."

So that was it. Deliberately or not Nina had precipitated something of which she had never dreamed but it had served her purpose only too well. Galina suddenly felt so weary she could scarcely stand. She put out a hand to the table to steady herself.

Nina was staring at her curiously. "What's the matter? Are you ill?"

"It's nothing, I'm all right."

"Does Simon know him?"

"They have met." She said with an effort, "Perhaps you'd better go. You must have a great deal to do."

And Nina having dropped her poison was quite ready to leave. "I have actually. You see Sonia having no parents it all falls on Mamma's shoulders. You'll come of course, won't you?"

"Oh yes," she said dully, "I'll come if Simon returns in time."

After she had gone Galina sank into a chair feeling sick. She had an irrational feeling that Nina had guessed her secret though she knew it was impossible. The friendship that had once been between them lay in ruins. All that day the same arguments churned endlessly through her mind. If she told

Simon what would happen? He would be kind, she knew him well enough to be sure of that, but she remembered how deeply he had felt the betrayal of the girl he had once loved and if she were to read rejection in his eyes she would not want to live. Even if he kept his promise and they were married, the knowledge could in some subtle way destroy the love between them. She was haunted by fear of Igor. What harm might he not do to Simon? What was there to prevent him coming to their house, boasting of what he had done, turning her into a willing partner who was now bearing his child while she stood between them shamed and shivering. Fantasies that left her weary and sick.

At last the stark truth faced her. There was only one thing to be done. She must go away, hide herself somewhere until the child was born, until the agonizing doubt was settled one way or the other. After that if it should be Simon's child, then she would come back. It was a fantasy that had little basis in reality but a dream to which she clung during that last week when she was making final preparations, during the wakeful nights when she stared into a bleak future. Simon had become part of her life, to cut him out of it would be like cutting away some vital part, but she had become obsessed with the one overpowering desire to leave him free, under no obligation to her, untouched by any shame or dishonour.

Letter after letter she wrote to him during those days, tearing them up in despair because it was so impossible to put it into words that had any real meaning. Better to go and write nothing, bury herself in some distant city where she could be lost among a multitude because he would search, no doubt about that, he would ask everyone so no one must know where she had gone.

Afterwards she was never quite sure when she decided to go to Kiev. It was an ancient city deep in the Ukraine on the River Dnieper, once many centuries ago the chief city in all Russia. There was a university, there were many hospitals where she might find work and there was one other fact. On that last day at Dannskoye her mother had told her that the unknown father was a doctor in Kiev. Now she suddenly found that she clung to it. She had no claim on him, she would probably never meet him or even recognize him if she did, but it formed a kind of link. In some queer way it was not quite going into the unknown.

The die was cast, the decision was made, and there was to be no going back on it. She packed her clothes and books, she had spent very little since he had been away and she took from the bank account he had left for her no more than her fare to Kiev and enough to cover the first few weeks. She looked for a long time at the ring he had put on her finger and knew she could not part with it. That at least must go with her. Then there was Ranji. At first she thought she might leave him with Luba but that would involve long explanation and she had grown too fond of him. He was nine months old now, nearly fully grown. He watched her pack with anxiety in his golden eyes and she could not abandon him, unwanted and unloved.

While the cab waited to take her to the station she stood in the apartment that held all she had ever known of love and happiness. She walked around the room touching the familiar objects, the table where they had sat together over books, laughing and happy, the samovar where she had sometimes brewed tea late in the night, the neatly stacked typescript of the long report which had brought them together, the chair where he sat so often reading to her and smiling at her clumsy attempts to translate the English she was striving to learn.

The book of poetry was still lying close by. She picked it up and opened it.

> I wonder, by my troth, what thou and I
> Did till we loved . . .

What indeed? Her throat ached with unshed tears. She slipped the book into the small handbag she was carrying, took up Ranji's leash and went down to the waiting cab.

Part Two

INTERLUDE
DANNSKOYE–KIEV
1905–1906

12

Simon returned to a Petersburg in the throes of a general strike. In fact the train in which he was travelling was stopped by a belligerent group of strikers massed across the line in a small station about ten miles from the city and after a great deal of shouting and argument engine driver, firemen and guards obstinately refused to move it any further despite vehement protest from infuriated passengers left stranded in a dismal village in the pouring rain, miles from anywhere and with no reasonable accommodation.

Fortunately for Simon he had brought Jake Starling with him. Starlings had worked for Aylshams for generations and Jake had begun as a sturdy five-year-old pulling up weeds in the garden and had developed into an extremely reliable, intelligent and useful member of the outside staff. Simon and he were roughly of an age and had shared many an illegal adventure, lying heroically to save each other punishment until Simon had been packed off to Harrow. Having recently been turned down by the pretty but flighty daughter of a local farmer he was only too ready to accept the young master's invitation to accompany him to Russia and take up a post in his new household.

He had an extremely low opinion of any country outside Britain so was not altogether surprised at being turned off a train. It was just the kind of thing these jabbering foreigners were likely to do but he was nothing if not resourceful. They were not going to spend the night in this Godforsaken hole, not if he could prevent it.

173

"You leave it to me, sir," he said.

He jammed his hat down, turned up his coat collar and trudged off through the mud. Anyone born in the Fen country was impervious to a little rain. Simon remained, keeping an eye on their luggage and thankful that his young sister had not come with him. At the last moment his three small nieces had developed chicken pox and she felt obliged to stay and help her sister-in-law through the crisis.

"I might even be infectious," she had said to him bravely facing up to the disappointment. "It would be too awful if your Galina came out in spots on the wedding day, but don't think you have got rid of me. I shall come and visit you in the spring."

In a remarkably short time Jake returned with a very dilapidated carriage driven by a sturdy if elderly horse whose peasant owner was willing to drive them to Petersburg for a price. How he had managed to persuade him with only half a dozen words of basic Russian was a miracle, but there it was.

Half the passengers would have clambered on to it if he had not been firm. As it was, the ancient vehicle was grossly overloaded but it didn't break down and they trundled into the city long after midnight to find a state of utter chaos, no gas, no electricity, no water, no transport.

They groped their way to the apartment in pitch darkness and were obliged to hammer on the door to rouse the house-keeper. She came to open it in fear and trembling. There had been riots and disturbances since the strike had begun and she nearly fell on Simon's neck in thankfulness when she saw who it was.

"What the devil is going on and where is Galina Panova?" he demanded. "Isn't she here? Didn't she tell you I would be returning?"

"Not a word, excellency, not one single word. She left about a fortnight ago," she quavered, "and took the dog with her."

"Why? Where did she go? Didn't she leave word?"

"Not with me, she didn't," she babbled still so agitated there was no getting any sense out of her.

"Oh very well," he said impatiently, "find us some light for God's sake."

For the moment he was surprised but not alarmed. In these

wretched circumstances she might have gone to stay with Luba or even with her mother.

Jake busied himself bringing in the luggage and it was not until candles had been found and lit that Simon saw his last cablegram telling her the time of his arrival lying unopened on the table and began to wonder what had happened. But it was the middle of the night and nothing could be done. In the morning it was very different.

During the first few days he hurtled from surprise to disbelief to anger and finally into something like despair. She had disappeared, vanished without trace, with no letter explaining what had happened or where she had gone. It simply could *not* be true. He was groping through a fog of doubt and uncertainty while the strike continued and spread throughout Russia.

Factories closed down, shops were shut, even the *corps de ballet* from the Maryinsky joyfully joined the strikers and paraded through the streets. With no trains running, food supplies began to run out and what there were became very expensive. There were protest marches and counter marches, demonstrations demanding better pay, better working conditions, the transference of power to the masses, the foundation of a democratic government. The Tsar marooned with his family at the Peterhof Palace well away from the civil riots battled with his ministers, none of which events mattered a straw to Simon as he searched hopelessly for the girl he loved.

He went first to the attic room on Vassilievsky Island and bounding up the stairs flung open the door to be faced by an indignant stranger. He stormed down to the basement and Stasia Ivanovna, confronted by this distraught and angry young man, took refuge in voluble excuses.

"It was months ago, your honour, early in July. She came one day and took all her possessions and I swear to God I've never seen her from that day to this."

What she failed to tell him was that the appearance and disappearance of Igor Livinov had occurred on that same day. After all what young women got up to when their lovers were away was not her business and he would not be the first man to be played false.

From there he went to the studio and Luba looked at him apologetically.

"I've not seen Galina since she brought us the bits of furniture. I meant to go because I knew she would be missing you dreadfully but it's not been easy these last few months."

He noticed then how thin and pale she was and how bare and cold the studio. In times like these who was going to commission a portrait or a new set of illustrations for a book?

"If it's a question of money," he said taking out his notecase, "let me help."

She turned away. "No, I couldn't. I couldn't take from you. Galina wouldn't like it."

"What is money between friends?" he said gently. "We'll call it a loan. When I'm settled, I may be able to put something in Conn's way."

"A loan then and only enough to stop them turning us into the street." She pushed the rest back at him. "And I'll pay you back I swear. I only wish I could help you with Galina."

He went to Dannskoye and spoke to Vera. She looked at him steadily, offering no explanation except to say, "Galina loved you heart and soul, that I do know. If she has gone away, then it is for your sake, not for her own."

"But in God's name, *why*? What possible reason could there be?"

"There is a great gulf between you – have you never thought of that?"

"I believed we had bridged it."

He returned to Petersburg without seeing the Malinskys. He could not face the pity on their faces, the shrugged shoulders, the implied comment that he had stepped out of line and must face the consequences.

He questioned Lydia but they had spent the summer months with Nigel's parents in Europe and could give no help.

Afterwards Nigel said wrathfully, "Whatever can have induced the wretched girl to vanish like that? My God, what more could she want? She had him on a string. I've never seen a man so much in love."

"Something happened to her," said Lydia thoughtfully, "something which made her feel she was letting him down. She was always uncertain of herself."

"She couldn't have let him down more drastically than she has done."

"I know." She looked concerned. "You don't think he will do something silly?"

"Like what?"

"Like throwing himself in the Neva one dark night?"

"No, that's not Simon. He has far too much sense of duty to do that."

"He was terribly upset before."

"That was different. He blamed himself for that. He'll weather it but I'm damned sure of one thing. He'll not be the same man when he comes out of it."

Reluctantly Simon went to the police but they had their hands full in a desperate attempt to keep order in the city and were distinctly unhelpful. With the country seemingly trembling on the edge of revolution, the disappearance of one young woman was a very small matter. No doubt she had found a wealthier lover, thought the police chief cynically, let this angry and disturbed foreigner take his troubles elsewhere.

He had discovered that she had withdrawn an amount from his bank which while not large was certainly more than she would have needed to cover a few days so it must have been planned and not a sudden impulse. The frustration, the unanswered questions hammered at his mind and nearly drove him crazy. Two things saved him from utter despair. After disbelief, a shattering grief, an aching physical loss, he took refuge in anger. How could she have abandoned him when he had done so much for her? How dare she subject him to so much pain and humiliation and wretchedness? Did all the plans they had made for their future mean nothing to her? Almost it would have been easier to endure if she had died instead of this appalling doubt, this nagging worry that she had not gone willingly, that some other factor had driven her away from him. But it still did not drive him away from Russia as Nigel had at first believed. Beneath the rage of anger there was still the hope that she would come back, that it was only some horrible mistake, a temporary testing time which he must live through. The second fact was more grim: a wave of cholera that swept through the more crowded parts of the city like a raging fire as a direct result of the strikers abandoning all work in the water supplies.

It was the kind of epidemic that periodically ravaged the poorest quarters and was not usually considered a major catastrophe but at this difficult time with so much disturbance, with reports coming in every day of violence, of burnings and murders all over the country, the government was in disarray and doctors able and willing to serve in the fever hospitals were in short supply. Simon, with a feeling that he no longer cared whether he lived or died, offered his services.

All through November and December he worked selflessly day after day scrupulously battling against neglect, pollution and ignorance. He kept himself away from all his friends and saw no one but Jake who showed himself as capable of working as a personal servant as he had been in the gardens and stables. In his endless and more often than not useless fight against death Simon somehow learned to conquer his own extreme unhappiness and disillusion. In some as yet unformed way he was beginning to move towards what would be his lifework.

It was the end of December by the time the worst was over and he could start to look around him and take stock of his life.

Action was being taken against the strikers. Very gradually services were renewed. The city slowly creaked into life again. It seemed that the Tsar's new Prime Minister, Count Sergei Yulevich Witte, had begun to realize reluctantly that savage reprisals were not the right answer. He persuaded his master to issue a Manifesto turning him into a constitutional monarch with a further promise that a parliament of people's representatives, a *Duma*, would be called together in the very near future.

"It won't last," prophesied Nigel gloomily, "not even Witte believes in it and the Tsar has always had a blind belief in himself as an all-powerful monarch divinely appointed by God, and so has his wife. However, so long as it gets the city back on its feet again, that's something."

Sporadic bursts of violence still broke out all through the country, but it is difficult to maintain revolutionary fervour at fever pitch for longer than a few weeks and slowly these began to die down.

One cold morning near the end of the month Simon sat at the breakfast table running through the mail that had accumulated during the previous weeks when he had been too occupied and too exhausted to deal with it. There was a long letter from his sister with all the news of home and asking for the date of his wedding. Somehow he must reply to it though he had shrunk from telling his family what had happened. There were notes inviting him to various functions which he tossed aside and a gilt-edged card announcing Niki's wedding at Dannskoye on New Year's Eve.

He did not want to go. Dannskoye was filled with memories of Galina. He had no desire to face the sympathy in Niki's eyes, the icy "I told you so" glare from the Princess Malinskaya, the pitying looks of the guests he would be obliged to meet but it was in three days' time, a reply was long overdue and simply to ignore it would be churlish. He would go just for the ceremony, remain to wish Niki and Sonia future happiness and then leave immediately.

He looked up as Jake came in to clear the table.

"There's a wedding I must attend at Dannskoye. Will you find out a train that will get us there in time for the ceremony at one o'clock? It's about five miles from the station so we'll need a cab to take us to the church."

"Am I to accompany you, sir?"

"I thought it would give you an opportunity to see a little more of Russia. I have no intention of staying there but pack a bag with a few necessities. At the present moment it's as well to be prepared for anything."

"Very good, sir."

Jake had not yet said a word to his master about the altered circumstances but he knew perfectly well that the bride-to-be had unaccountably vanished. Privately he considered that any girl who turned Master Simon down must be a fool or worse so maybe it was for the best and he would now get himself hitched to some decent English young woman who would appreciate him, not that he intended saying a word about it even to his closest intimates.

Simon had walked across to the window watching the clouds of huge feathery flakes throwing a mantle of purity over roofs and trees and dirty pavements. It had been snowing like that the first night Galina had come to him. He had watched her slim upright figure disappear into the night never dreaming how she would grip his imagination and his love. He thrust the painful memories behind him.

"You must have guessed that my plans have necessarily changed," he said curtly. "I'm not now getting married but I still intend to set up in practice here in Petersburg. If you would rather return to Ravensley I shall understand."

"I'd much prefer to stay, sir, if it's all right with you."

Simon swung round. "I would be immensely grateful, if you're quite sure it won't be too lonely a life for you here."

"Not a bit of it," said Jake cheerfully, "I've always been

179

one for change and there's quite a community of us down at the English Club." He piled plates on a tray and grinned at his master. "I'll see about those trains and make sure your wedding gear is pressed and ready."

They arrived at the church in good time but it was already almost filled. The usher, recognizing Simon, led him to a place in the front among close family friends who smiled and nodded while Jake found a spot discreetly at the back. Despite the bitter cold the roads outside had been crowded with villagers since early morning in their thick padded coats and felt boots, most of them looking forward to the abundant wedding feast already prepared for them.

Simon, absorbed in his own thoughts had noticed little, but Jake's sharp eyes had detected small sullen groups of dirty ragged men and women among the cheering smiling villagers. Already accustomed to the enormous gulfs existing in Russian society he thought very little of it.

Simon watched the long ceremony with mingled bitterness and pain, Niki in the uniform of the nobility, a black coat with lapels and collar embroidered in gold, Sonia mistily radiant in her cream satin gown and gossamer veil, the chanting of the priests in their jewel-encrusted copes, the crowns held above the heads of the bride and groom, the moment when they both drank from the silver cup and the priest bound their wrists with the white silk scarf, leading them three times around the altar, symbolizing that in future they would walk hand in hand through life.

Galina and he had not decided how they would be married, whether in the austere English church or using the ancient orthodox ceremony. Though brought up a Protestant he had been quite willing to marry in the Russian church if she had wished it.

He was thankful when it was over and the procession streamed down the church with the guests following after. Outside, the first carriage waited for Niki and Sonia. The crowd pressed forward and raised a cheer as they drove away. He glimpsed Nina amongst the bridesmaids looking enchanting in her lace gown with flowers in the blonde hair. She gave him a flashing smile of recognition and he smiled back. Then the second carriage moved on and there was the General leaning heavily on his son's arm, the gold braid on their uniforms catching the last rays of the sinking sun. The old man had taken his seat in the carriage with his son opposite him and his daughter-in-law beside him when it happened.

A dark figure thrust his way through the crowd and hurled something. A second later the explosion ripped through the air. The terrified horses reared in a tangle of harness, the carriage seemed to split apart, women were screaming, there was chaos and pandemonium and blood everywhere.

Simon forced his way through the confusion. It was a small bomb but it had done its fatal damage. It was very quickly obvious that nothing could be done for the General. He was dead from the violent shock as much as from the terrible wound that had torn across his chest. They had lifted the Prince from the shattered carriage. Simon knelt beside him. He was still alive but only just. The extraordinary part was that the Princess Malinskaya was covered in blood but still unharmed. She was standing rigid with shock and horror. The woman who was on her knees beside her husband with his head on her lap was Vera Panova.

She bent over him to hear his agonized whisper. "Niki . . ., my wife . . .?"

"They are safe," she murmured gently, "quite safe."

"Thank God." His eyes closed.

She looked at Simon. "Is he dead?"

"Not yet. Can we carry him somewhere?"

"There's my house."

While they cleared the debris the General and his son were carried into Vera Panova's small dark room where she knelt beside the Prince while his wife stood by, her face a frozen mask of grief and anger.

The carriages that had gone ahead had pulled up. Niki came racing back and with him came Nina stumbling through the snow in her thin satin shoes and bridesmaid's finery. Tears were pouring down her face as she fell on her knees beside her grandfather, trying to raise his head, frantically stroking his face.

"I did it," she was saying, "it's my fault. I knew he was here and I didn't warn them. Help him," she said wildly to Simon, "please please help him!"

"He's dead," he said gently, "there is nothing anyone can do."

"There must be, there must be!" She was beating her hands against his chest. He caught hold of them gripping them hard.

"Try to be calm. There are others needing my help."

By this time Valentin Skorsky who had been acting as best man had reached them. Simon put the distraught girl into his arms.

"Take care of her," he said, "she is in shock. She doesn't know what she is saying."

Gradually the confusion sorted itself out. The driver of the carriage and one of the horses had been killed. The horrified guests began to depart. Tearful bridesmaids were gathered up by distracted parents. Another carriage was brought up. They lifted the General and his son into it. Dr Antonov who was almost of an age with the General went with them. Shocked and distressed at his old friend's terrible death he still seemed able and willing to give what assistance was necessary. The Princess, wrapped in her fur mantle but still preserving a marble dignity, followed after with Niki's Uncle Kolya, his father's younger brother. Nina was huddled into a corner of the same carriage looking so white and pitiful that Simon leaned across to press the small cold hand. The tears started again to her eyes, then the carriage jolted forward.

It was only then that Simon saw the assassin and recognized him as the man who had been flogged in what seemed now like another world. Had he nursed revenge all this past year? He had been extremely roughly handled. Blood was running freely from his mouth as he sagged helplessly between Yakov and another of the factory workers. Simon wondered fleetingly if someone was going to make absolutely sure that in his last agony, he would not give away the names of those who had devised this brutal outrage.

Several people had been badly cut and bruised by flying glass and debris from the smashed carriage. Vera's cottage became a temporary dressing station. She found towels and old soft linen. Jake materialized with their bags which had been left in the cab still waiting to whisk them back to the railway station. Simon began to do what little he could to help the injured.

It was a good deal later and the day had already closed in by the time he and Jake reached Dannskoye. To leave now without offering to do anything he could to help would have been heartless. It was a tragic end to what should have been a happy family occasion. The festive meal had been abandoned, the servants distressed and bewildered, had done nothing yet to clear the tables. The young couple's wedding trip which should have taken them to Petersburg and then into Europe had been cancelled. Dr Antonov, feeling the weight of his years, was only too glad to lean upon his younger colleague's strength.

Niki met him at the door of his father's room. He was white and drawn but still master of himself and Simon admired the courage that at twenty-two could face the loss of grandfather and father without complete breakdown. Only the slight shake in his voice betrayed the inner tension.

"Thank God, you're here," he said. "Dr Antonov is a good old man but this has hit him hard and he is out of his depth. I must know, Simon, can Father survive? Mother frightens me. She just sits there beside him holding his hand as if she is willing him to live."

"Is he conscious?"

"Now and again but he is in terrible pain."

"Let me see him."

A second examination only confirmed the first. Outwardly there was little blood but the power of the explosion that had hurled him up and then brought him down with crashing force had smashed his spine and damaged his lungs beyond any possible repair. He knew with absolute certainty that it could only be a matter of hours.

He drew Niki aside. "I could give him an injection of morphine. It may shorten the few hours left to him but it will put him out of pain."

"Give it to him. Anything is better than to see him suffer such agony."

But when he approached the bed, syringe in hand, he met the Princess's stony glare and she motioned him back imperiously.

"Do you want to kill him?"

"No, Princess, only ease his pain."

"My husband has been a soldier. I know he would prefer to meet death in his right mind."

"Mamma please," urged Niki, "please let him die in peace."

"You're not master here, Niki, not yet. I faced life with him and I'll face death. You'd be far better occupied hunting down his murderer and punishing those responsible. All this year you have opposed your father. 'Give them what they ask', you said, 'show yourself generous and they will respond generously', and this is the result, this brutal murder. They are worse than animals. If it were I in command I would willingly see them all hanged."

Her icy anger appalled them both. To persist in face of such opposition seemed impossible. Simon replaced the hypodermic and followed Niki out of the room. The Princess's voice pursued them.

"Where is Nina? Her place is here with me."

"She was with Grandfather," said Niki briefly. "I must go now, Mamma. The local police are here already."

But Nina was not with the General, not in her own room, not anywhere in the house.

"Oh God," exclaimed Niki. "Aren't things bad enough without Nina running off and hiding somewhere."

It was Sonia who said calmly, "Don't worry, Niki. Leave it to me. I'll find her. Uncle Kolya is with the local police. They are waiting for you. It will be morning before anyone can reach here from Petersburg."

Simon looked at her and marvelled. This quiet girl who had lived nearly all her life under the shadow of the turbulent Nina cherishing her secret love for Niki, had at last come into her own. She had changed from her wedding gown into a simple dark dress and in the absence of the Princess Malinskaya had taken quiet control of the household. This day that should have been the happiest of her life, marriage to the man she loved, surely the fulfilment of every young girl's dream, had been brutally wrecked; the wedding night, the honeymoon, all denied to her and yet she remained serene, a rock on which Niki could lean, an inner strength that would be there when he needed it most.

"Where do you think Nina has hidden herself?" he urged when Niki had gone to the library where the police chief waited for him.

"I've known Nina since she was ten, Dr Simon. She has always run away from trouble, it frightens her. Whenever it threatened she would take refuge somewhere, in the attics or even out with the dogs and horses, and she would stay there until whatever it was had blown over and everyone was so worried about her that they had forgotten that she probably deserved punishment."

"Aren't you being a little hard on her?"

"Perhaps." She smiled wryly. "But then I've grown used to her. You're quite right though. We must find her before she harms herself."

"I'll go outside if you'll search the house," he offered.

"Very well. There are boots and coats in the garden room if you need them."

Outside the snow, frozen hard, crisped under his feet. The gardens appeared to be empty and the stableyard when he reached it was bathed in brilliant moonlight. It was very quiet, no sound but the occasional stir of a restless horse, the jingle of harness as they munched their evening feed. He stood quite still listening and then he heard it, a catch of breath, a choked sob like a child who has wept to exhaustion. He pushed open one of the stable doors and saw her. She was crouched on a bale of straw, her arms tightly clasped around Shani, her face buried in the dog's silky fur, while Rusalka disturbed stamped her feet uneasily and then peered round as Simon came in.

"My dear child," he knelt beside her, "whatever are you doing here in this bitter cold?"

"I couldn't remain in the house with Grandfather and Papa, I couldn't – I couldn't –"

"Niki and Sonia are very worried about you. You must come in."

He lifted her to her feet and she leaned wearily against him. The bridesmaid's dress was thick with mud and the white fur wrap soiled by the muck of the stable floor.

"They would hate me if they knew what I had done," she murmured pitifully.

"And what is this terrible thing you have done?" he said humouring her. It seemed quite clear to him that shock and exhaustion were playing tricks with her. "Come now," he went on bracingly, "we're going inside. It's late and you need food and warmth."

Her thin shoes slipped and skidded on the icy path and at last he picked her up and carried her. She leaned her head with its tousled blonde curls against his shoulder like a tired child.

At the house he delivered her over to Sonia and Marta.

"Put her to bed and keep her warm," he said briefly. "I'll give you a sleeping draught for her."

The wretched night wore on. The assassin was brought to the house and sternly interrogated, but he insisted over and over again that the attack had been planned and carried out by himself alone with no other persons involved.

"He is lying," said Niki afterwards to Simon when they sat together over a sketchy meal that neither of them felt like eating. Uncle Kolya was keeping vigil by the side of his dying brother and they were alone. "I know how these Social Revolutionaries work. After all I was one of them myself once. They form a cell somewhere and then they act, no matter how useless or unjustified the murder. The point is that it proves their power. It was that which I found I could not swallow and neither could Galina. You must know that. Someone has been working against us here and found a response among our workers but who?" He pressed a hand wearily against his forehead. "Oh God, Simon, how am I to care for Mamma and Nina and Sonia with this weight on my mind? How shall I ever feel at ease with our people again?"

"I think that these revolutionaries having, as you say, once proved their point will move on. If the new Prime Minister's plans prove workable, and they appear to be an answer to some part of the demands made, they will begin to lose support among the workers," said Simon trying to sound reassuring.

"That's what Uncle Kolya says but he has lived in the south of France for years. He is out of touch. We can only pray that you're both right."

It was long past midnight before Simon went up to the room prepared for him. Jake had opened the overnight bag and laid out the few articles they had brought with them. The wood-burning stove had been lighted and the room had a faint warmth. A lamp glowed on the table. He did not undress, simply kicked off his boots, discarded coat and waistcoat and loosened the neck of his shirt. Then he threw himself on the bed and drew the heavy down quilt over him.

It seemed a century since he had watched the wedding ceremony, his mind filled with Galina until events had banished her from his mind. Now unwillingly the memories came rushing back, the first time he had danced with her on the terrace, the midsummer fire and her hair smelling muskily of the smoke when he kissed her. He was tormented by a physical ache for her that was almost unbearable. The old unanswered questions rampaged again through his mind – why had she gone from him? Was she ever coming back? And for the first time hope died and left him feeling empty and desolate.

How long he lay wakeful he did not know but he was roused from a light doze by the opening of his door. For a fleeting second he thought the figure in the long white nightgown was Galina and then almost immediately knew he was wrong.

He was off the bed in a moment.

"Nina, what is it? What are you doing here?"

"I thought I heard Mamma cry out. It frightened me. Does it mean that Papa is dead?"

She was speaking slowly and thickly and he guessed that she was still partly under the influence of the opiate he had given her.

She began to cry helplessly and he went to her putting an arm around her shoulders.

"Come. I'll take you back to bed."

She resisted him. "No, there is something I must tell you. I must tell someone."

"Tell me what?" She started to shiver violently and he picked up the down coverlet and wrapped it around her. Then he drew her to sit beside him on the bed. "Now what is this you must tell me?"

"I saw him only two days ago. He had come back, you see, and I didn't warn Niki. Galina told me I should but I didn't. I thought I knew him better."

"Saw who and what has Galina to do with it?"

"She knew him, you know, she knew him very well."

"Knew whom? For God's sake, Nina, pull yourself together. Who was it she knew?"

"Igor Livinov."

"Igor!" he exclaimed. "Do you mean that Igor was here at Dannskoye?"

"Yes, and the dreadful part of it is that I brought him here."

Stumbling, disjointedly, she told him about the first meeting, about telling him to take refuge here, about meeting him again when Niki was engaged.

"I was sure then that he had gone, that it was all over but he came back and then all this happened and Galina was right, you see, she said he was a destroyer but I didn't believe her and now Grandfather and Papa are dead and it is all my fault. If only I had said something . . ."

She had still not told him everything but he thought he could see it very clearly. This foolish blundering child had been dipping her fingers in things she did not understand, had seen herself as the great lady compassionte towards the unfortunate victim of the law, and Igor had no doubt manipulated her to suit himself. Even if she *had* warned Niki and her father he doubted if it would have altered anything. That slippery devil after setting everything in motion would have quietly disappeared. He had always known how to make good his own escape.

Pouring out her tangled story seemed to have lifted a weight from Nina's mind. She gave a little sigh and leaned against him closing her eyes.

He picked her up in his arms, thick coverlet and all, and carried her back to her room putting her in the bed and tucking the blankets firmly around her.

"Now go to sleep," he said, "you will feel better about it in the morning."

"Will I?"

"You must. Niki and Sonia are going to need all the support they can get."

"I know – I do know."

"Good. Then remember it."

He straightened up and she caught at his hand. "Kiss me goodnight," she whispered.

He hesitated a little exasperated. Then he bent to kiss her forehead but she stretched up her arms pulling him down to her and kissing him full on the mouth.

He pulled himself away and said brusquely, "Go to sleep, Nina," and strode to the door remembering to shut it very quietly in this silent house, and quite unaware that a pair of sharp eyes had seen him stand for a moment and then go swiftly and silently back to his own room.

Marta had been coming up the stairs. She stopped when she saw him, storing the incident away in her mind. It might form a useful weapon one day which she could use against the young mistress she both envied and disliked. Then she went to knock at Simon's door.

"The Princess asks if you will come," she said when he opened it. "She fears her husband is dying."

The room, when he reached it, seemed filled with shadows and crowded with people, the priest, Niki, Sonia, Dr Antonov, Uncle Kolya. He joined his colleague beside the bed but one glance was sufficient. They exchanged a look and then withdrew, letting the priest take their place.

It had occurred to him that now the end had come, the Princess's marble composure might break down but he was wrong. She bowed her head in prayer but he sensed an iron will while beside her Niki and Sonia seemed like weeping children. Dannskoye might be Niki's inheritance but he would have to share it with his formidable mother.

It was several days before he returned to Petersburg, his resolve to remain in Russia strengthened rather than weakened by the tragedy. To run away now would seem like weakness and he would never yield to that again. He might be a foreigner but he felt he could contribute something sane and clearheaded towards the badly needed reforms even in his own medical world. A nagging doubt planted by Nina lay at the back of his mind. He had thought he knew everything about Galina, but did he? How close had she been with Igor Livinov? He strove to dismiss it but again and again it returned, until in some strange way that enigmatic figure became the embodiment of the violence against which he would battle and in the end must either win or lose.

13

About ten days before Simon returned to Petersburg Galina arrived in Kiev after a long and bone-shaking journey of over thirty hours. The strike had already begun to bite throughout the country. There had been long inexplicable delays, stations were hopelessly disorganized and it was impossible to buy a glass of tea or even beg a bowl of water for Ranji. If she had not thought to take a little food with her they might well have both starved.

Guiltily aware that she was using Simon's money and anxious not to spend more than was necessary she had unwisely bought a third class ticket and it was not until she reached the station that she realized her terrible mistake. The long green coach with its bare wooden benches was crammed with peasants surrounded by their baskets and packages, men, women and children, dirty, ragged, some of them no doubt verminous, all huddled together in a reeking squalid mass of humanity. They turned to stare at her in open-mouthed disbelief, the elegant young woman in her long fur-collared coat with her handsome luggage and aristocratic dog.

It was a long way from the first class coach which she had shared with Simon on their trip to the Crimea and her first frantic thought was to find a railway official and try to change her ticket. Then the decision was taken out of her hands. One of the *moujiks*, an old man with long greasy hair under his shaggy hat and the grey beard of the patriarch, rose to his considerable height shoving a couple of young louts roughly off the wooden bench.

"Make room, you oafs," he boomed, "if the *Barina* is to travel with us, then let us give her a seat."

He bowed and flicked a dirty red handkerchief over the place he had vacated and after that she felt she had no choice. These were her people, the people that she had once made up her mind to work for, still, despite revolution and riot, innately generous and respectful. She could not refuse the courtesy but all the same the journey was a penance hard to endure and she was not sorry when at one of the stops and with many expressions of gratitude she was able to move up the train and find a seat in a second class compartment.

More than eight hundred miles south of Petersburg, deep in the Ukraine, autumn lingered in the giant chestnut trees lining the streets outside the station and the air still held traces of summer warmth. The cabs were lined up along the pavement. The drivers were always very knowledgeable and she approached one of them to ask if he could recommend a quiet district where she might find lodging. A pair of small black eyes looked her up and down critically. This one was not a "woman of joy" bound for the red light district, more like one of those cursed students who were causing such trouble throughout the city with their demonstrations and riots.

"There are streets near the university," he growled, "but you'll be lucky if you get anywhere near them today."

"Why? What is so special about today?"

He gave her a pitying look. "You'll soon see," he remarked laconically and waited for her to climb into the dusty carriage with the stale straw underfoot and a reek of cheap perfume from some previous occupant.

He was only too right. As they drew near the Khreshchatik which runs through the centre of Kiev, they heard shots and could already see people running distractedly towards them. He pulled up abruptly.

"This is where I stop. I'm not having *my* head blown off and neither will you if you have any sense. You go back to where you came from."

"You can't just leave me here," she said indignantly.

He shrugged his shoulders. "Go that way," he said pointing with his whip, "those alleys lead through to the university and may God go with you. I'm not risking my neck."

He snatched the fare she held out to him, dumped her luggage on the road beside her, whipped up his horse and trotted back down the road.

She was tired, hungry and very angry. If he liked to play the coward, then she was not going to do the same. She stubbornly picked up the bag which seemed to grow heavier at every step and still holding firmly to Ranji's leash set off up the narrow road he had pointed out to her.

Perhaps she took the wrong direction, she was never sure, but at the end of it she was suddenly caught up in the opposing forces. A vast crowd who had been demonstrating outside the Town Hall in the Khreshchatik was surging down what she was later to know as the Shevchenko Boulevard. They were driven by a long line of Cossacks on their black horses only to meet an opposing group of students from the university, a great mob of young men, shouting, gesticulating, yelling abuse, and before she could extricate herself she was in the midst of them.

The next few minutes were terrifying and she would never have contrived to hang on to her bag and to the dog if it had not been for a tall lanky young man with a shock of black hair who grabbed hold of her and took her along with him.

"What the devil are you doing in this lot?" he gasped.

"What is happening?"

"Someone said the Tsar had published a manifesto granting us all we've asked for and now it has been denied and the Cossacks are firing on us, God rot them!"

His white face was alive with some kind of wild excitement.

She was desperately afraid of losing her footing, only too well aware that if she were once to fall she could be trampled to death before any help could reach her. There were one or two shops along this side of the street with doors shut and bolted and shutters closed. She pressed herself against them edging along step by step. There was another volley of shots, women were screaming and the pressure suddenly became much heavier. She was breathing in great gasps when suddenly the door against which she was leaning opened behind her, the lanky student pushed her through it and then the door slammed shut again. The sudden change from light to semi-darkness confused her. She stumbled down a couple of steps, she heard Ranji growl, put out a groping hand, felt somebody take it in a firm grip and then fell forward into blackness.

The next thing she knew she was lying back in a chair, sharp acrid smelling salts held firmly under her nose.

She choked, sneezed and tried to sit up but a hand pushed her back.

"Easy now. That was a nasty experience. You'll feel better in a minute. I'll get you something to drink."

After a few seconds, the faintness ebbed and she could look around her. She was in a chemist's shop, a large one by the look of it. All around her was the usual paraphernalia, huge porcelain jars with their gold lettering, green glass bottles, rows of small phials, scales, mortars and pestles for the grinding of drugs and the sharp aromatic scent of the medicinal herbs, familiar and somehow comforting.

The owner came back with a glass filled with a white cloudy mixture.

"Sip it," he said, "it's quite harmless but it will revive you."

She eyed him cautiously over the rim. He was small, very dark and really rather ugly, bushy eyebrows, a hooked nose, a jutting chin with bristling grey beard. His brown coat was liberally sprinkled with dust from the pills he must have been compounding but the small dark eyes behind the pince-nez perched crookedly on his nose were looking at her kindly. She felt a little reassured.

"Feeling better?" he asked after a moment.

"Much much better."

"Good. Now let's see to the needs of your dog. Water, old fellow, that's what you want, isn't it?"

He fetched a bowl and Ranji lapped at it greedily.

"I was watching through a crack in the shutter and it was the dog that first caught my eye," he went on conversationally. "'Who has been fool enough to bring an animal into this muddle?' I said to myself, then I saw that Mordecai was holding you up, he waved to me and here you are."

"Is he the young man who helped me?"

"That's right. I know him, He comes here sometimes for prescriptions."

"I'm tremendously grateful to you but now I think I ought to go."

She struggled to rise and again he stopped her.

"It'll be a few hours yet before that crowd out there is cleared even with the help of the Cossacks," he said ironically. "You had far better stay here for the time being. Maybe I'd best introduce myself – Ivan Alexandrovich Zubov," and he gave her an awkward little bow.

"Galina Panova," she said. With the tension eased she suddenly felt limp with exhaustion.

Her pallor was not lost on her rescuer but he only said cheerfully, "Now we are officially acquainted, may I ask if you have recently arrived in our city?"

"Very recently, only an hour or so ago," she said ruefully and went on to tell him about being abandoned by the cab driver.

"So you're looking for a decent lodging," said Zubov, looking at her thoughtfully. "I might be able to help you there. If you care to share my humble luncheon, my dear young lady, I'll take you to see the *dvornik* who looks after the students' apartments. I understand one of them is free just now."

"Why are you being so kind to me?" she asked curiously.

"It's a poor world if one can't extend a helping hand from time to time," he said drily. "Besides I happen to have taken a fancy to your dog and I think he likes me."

It was true. Ranji, usually fastidious in his choice of friends, had come to lay his head on the chemist's knee while one brown hand, the fingers stained by the innumerable drugs they handled, scratched soothingly at that tender spot behind the big dog's ears.

There was a surprisingly large room at the back of the shop, sparsely furnished but clean, and they ate off the corner of a table piled with books, pamphlets and newspapers, dog-eared and obviously very well read, and in danger of toppling to the floor when he pushed them aside to make room for the food. It was a frugal meal, a pasty filled with chopped fish and mushrooms, an apple or two, glasses of tea, but it was reviving to Galina who had eaten nothing since six o'clock that morning on the train when she had shared her last piece of bread and sausage with Ranji.

"Are you intending to study at the university?" he asked putting slices of lemon into her tea and pushing across the sugar.

"On the contrary, I shall be looking for work of some kind," she replied anxious not to give away too much or even mention where she had come from and he did not press her.

Later that day she was to bless that cab driver who had left her so cavalierly since it had meant meeting Ivan Zubov and finding herself settled in a decent room in one of the old houses grouped around a tiny square of garden immediately behind the chemist shop. Her window looked out on to the patch of dusty grass and the huge lime tree in the middle that next spring would fill it with its fragrance.

The long journey, the fatigue, the exertions of the day had brought on the start of a migraine and the pharmacist, skilled at recognizing the signs, offered a powder to relieve the pain. She accepted it gratefully and lay on her bed, her eyes closed in relief.

Since leaving Petersburg the hours had been so crowded, so full of stress, that they had in some measure blunted the edge of her unhappiness. Now with the strain lifted, it all came flooding back.

She ached for Simon, for his love, his laughter, his comradeship. How was she to exist without him? How face up to the birth of her baby, to the rearing of a child who would be her sole responsibility, a baby who might so easily bear the hateful taint of Igor in his veins? Had she done right or was it an act of unparalleled folly? Again and again the agonizing doubts beat through her mind until at last the drug that Zubov had given her began to take slow effect, easing the tension, soothing her into acceptance and ultimately into sleep. Tomorrow must take care of itself.

The slow weeks went by shot with pain and loneliness but also full of surprises. She learned to appreciate Ivan Zubov. He had a dry wit and he could be candid to the point of rudeness having no patience at all with a weak yielding to self-pity but he could also be a true friend on whom you could rely and she soon found that she was not the only one to benefit from his generosity. He was a chemist of considerable skill and learning who had studied at the university and might have gone on to greater things if he had not chosen to live this quiet bachelor existence in Kiev.

The shop was a large and important one. Eminent doctors, surgeons and consultants sent their prescriptions to him or sometimes called in person to discuss the uses of some recently discovered drug. But she also found out quite by accident that he had another and more hidden clientele, a small side door to which there came one or two evenings a week the poor, the humble and the sick who could never afford the glossy physician in his splendid carriage, but who were genuinely in need of help or advice or comfort and he would in his brusque way give them what he could and charge nothing, though he had a sharp eye for the impostor, the malingerer, the cheat. He had an assistant who helped in the shop, a boy of about sixteen, son of some distant relative and who drove him wild with his careless slipshod ways.

"Supposed to be learning the trade," he remarked caustically to Galina once on her way through the shop, "one of these days he'll poison someone important and then he and I will hang for it!"

"Why don't you get rid of him?" she said.

"You may well ask! But his mother is a widow and Mitya is the apple of her eye – oh damn it, what is one to do? Tell her the son she adores is a nitwit, a ne'er-do-well – can't be done."

Christmas and the New Year had come and gone but she had not yet found any work. Her small stock of money had all but vanished. Her pregnancy was obvious by now and was proving a further hindrance to finding a suitable post. Then one afternoon Zubov asked her if she would be good enough to take over the shop since he was called to the hospital and Mitya had chosen not to turn up.

It was simple enough. Prescriptions already packaged and clearly marked, a few remedies which she knew how to dispense to suitable buyers. The time slipped by and at seven o'clock she shut and bolted the door and was going to her own room when she saw the long queue gathered hopefully at the side door. She hesitated and then went across to them explaining that Zubov was not there and they must return another day. But they begged and pleaded, some of them mothers with babies who had trudged a long way, and at last, greatly daring, she promised to do what she could. After all she was familiar with so many of these remedies, she had studied their uses, she had helped Simon treat a great number of similar cases in the poor hospitals, so she worked away, only dealing with those about which she was certain and giving comfort and encouragement to those she advised to come back later. It was long after nine when the last had gone and Zubov returned.

He blew up into a towering rage when she told him what she had been doing.

"Don't you realize that you could have me disqualified? If any of these poor devils suffers ill effects and if the police find out what has been going on, they could be on us before we can turn round and it will be no answer to say that someone I left in charge had the impudence to set herself up as a physician and believe she can dispense remedies with the best. God in heaven, woman, were you out of your mind?"

On and on he stormed in a long tirade until when he paused for breath she at last contrived to interrupt.

"If you'd only just stop long enough to listen to me for a moment," she said icily, "I can tell you I have a first class diploma in pharmacy from Petersburg University and in addition I have been assistant for the past year to an eminent English doctor working in the very highest circles in the city."

He stared at her so completely dumbfounded that she was tempted to laugh.

"Is that so?" he muttered.

"I'm sorry," she said a little shamefaced, "I've never blown my own trumpet before but you made me angry."

"Why in God's name didn't you tell me all this?" he exclaimed in exasperation.

"You never asked."

He thumped his forehead. "That's my fault. I might have guessed something of the sort. All this time wasted."

"What do you mean – wasted?"

"Isn't it obvious? There's work for you here and you'd be a great deal more useful to me than that fool of a boy – that is, if you'd consider it. With your qualifications you could get something better than assistant to an old codger like myself except that . . ." his eye ran over her swelling figure.

He had never referred to her pregnancy, never made any inquiry as to her status, had simply accepted it and she had been grateful for his reticence. Now she finished his sentence for him.

"Except that no one is likely to employ me until the baby is born," she said bluntly. "That's what you mean, isn't it? But haven't you forgotten Mitya?"

"That fly-by-night!" he said sarcastically. "I never know from one day to the next whether he will deign to turn up. I'll not throw him to the wolves. He can still make himself useful running errands."

She looked at him for a moment. It was salvation. She couldn't ask for anything better, but that independence, that hedgehog pride of hers as Simon had loved to call it, was still active.

"I can manage, you know. I didn't treat those poor people in order to curry favour with you."

"God Almighty, woman," he exploded, "do you take me for an idiot who can't see beyond the end of his nose? If I'd thought that, you'd never set foot inside my shop and that's as certain as I'm standing here. I'll not be paying you a fortune and I'll work you hard but the job is there if you want it and let's not have any more nonsense."

So it was agreed and whether Mitya resented her or whether he grudged the long journey on his bicycle from the outer suburbs through the bitter cold of January, she never knew, but one morning Zubov waved a letter under her nose when she was opening up the shutters.

"His mother writes – in tears, poor soul – that Mitya has gone for a soldier. No doubt he's decided to kill his fellow men by shooting 'em instead of poisoning 'em," he said ironically. "Well, there it is. He may have broken his mother's heart but he has certainly not broken mine."

So that was that and instead of long hours tramping the streets or brooding alone in her room she had work to do, difficult exacting work which she knew and enjoyed, and with a man who was willing to impart his knowledge to a receptive mind. They argued sometimes, he snapped at her and his temper could be uncertain, but she respected his learning and in one way at least she was almost content.

She had guessed for some time that Zubov was a passionate radical, in theory if not in practice. The books and pamphlets heaped in his room had told her that and she knew too that once a week students from the university and the polytechnic piled into that large room talking, arguing about literature, spouting poetry, their own or that of someone else. There were passionate enthusiasts for Tolstoy and critics of Turgenev who had deserted Russia for Europe; addicts of Tchehov who had seen *The Cherry Orchard* in Moscow, that poignant study of decadent nobility and the rising merchant class, fought bitterly with comrades who boasted of meeting Gorky, that boy from the slums whose play *The Lower Depths* had shocked society by exposing the horror of prison life among the dregs of humanity. Once or twice she joined them but she never stayed long, only too conscious of her pregnancy, and she never dreamed that literary discussion was only a mask for the Social Revolutionaries, that when the books had been put away and the shutters closed, there were other arguments more relevant to the forces that were splitting Russia apart, never, that is to say, until late one evening in March when she had come back to the shop to fetch a headache powder and had run full tilt into Igor Livinov.

He was changed of course. A thick mat of reddish hair now covered the shaved head. He had discarded the student cap and workman's blouse for the sober black of a clerk in the Civil Service and glasses partly hid the diamond-bright eyes, but never, never so long as she lived would she ever forget that bony face with its prominent cheekbones, that unmistakable look of arrogance, that frightening feeling of menace.

With him was the lanky young man who had saved her from the mob all those months ago. She shrank back hoping that they had not seen her but it was too late.

Igor whispered something, his companion went on to the back room and they were alone in the shadowy shop.

For a moment he said nothing but she felt as if his eyes were on her stripping her clothing from her, leaving her shamed and helpless.

"So he deserted you," he said at last in a harsh whisper, "your handsome doctor with all his fine ways, left you alone and pregnant."

"No, no," she said fiercely, "you're wrong."

His face changed suddenly. "Or is the child mine?" He came across to her swiftly and silently seizing her by the shoulders. "Is it mine? Answer me. Is it?"

She stared him full in the face. "If it were," she said in a low voice vibrant with loathing, "if it were I swear to you I'd have torn it out of myself. I'd have killed it long ago."

He was so close she heard his quick intake of breath, felt his fingers digging painfully into her flesh.

It maddened him that her pregnancy only seemed to have made her more beautiful and he knew he still wanted her. A revolutionary should have no feelings, no passion except for the cause – and God knows he had tried to live like that and now he had work to do, important work, but he did not immediately release her. He gripped her close against him, his breath hot on her cheek.

"You don't know me, you've never seen me before, do you understand, never. Remember that if you don't want to ruin everyone here."

Then he dropped his hands and strode away from her towards the back room.

She was so shocked she could not even move for a moment. What was he doing here? What devilry was he plotting? He was obviously in disguise. He had always been clever at escaping the notice of the police and leaving others to bear the brunt. She must watch carefully, be ready to warn if necessary, and an immense weariness swept through her. At this time it seemed almost too much to bear.

She was always inclined to think that Igor's sudden appearance and the shock it gave her precipitated the birth of the baby but of course it was not so. The fact that it was a week earlier than expected was only miscalculation or simply that babies obey other rules than mathematical ones but nevertheless it happened and it did upset all her carefully made plans.

This apartment house mainly occupied by noisy young men was scarcely a suitable place for bearing a baby so she had arranged to go to the lying-in hospital where with equal impartiality unmarried mothers were accepted along with the wives of working men. But in the event she never got there.

The first pains struck in the middle of the night. By dawn they had become a great deal worse. She managed to drag herself down the stairs to rouse the *dvornik* who had been prepared to drive her to the hospital but it was his wife who came to the door in answer to her knocking. Fanta was a big bouncing good-natured countrywoman who had seen a great number of babies come into the world.

"Fedya will be gone for most of the day," she said practically "and you're in no state to go in one of those cabs, the way they drive the poor little creature would be born before you ever get there. You leave it to me, Galina Panova. I know how to look after matters of this kind. Didn't my mother have ten little ones after me and six of them still hale and hearty?"

Talking all the time she hustled Galina back up the stairs and began to make preparations by which time her patient was in too much pain to make any protest.

She lay all day in a state of intermittent agony, roused now and again to drink glasses of boiling tea. The sweat ran down her face and was wiped away. Towards evening she knew Zubov was there in the doorway whispering with Fanta but when she questioned them, they only said soothingly that these things take time and she must be patient.

Something was wrong, she knew it was. She began to be afraid, to be haunted by terrible nightmares. She remembered Simon operating on Luba. Was it going to happen to her like that? Was she going to lose the baby so that all the anguish would have been for nothing? Then the pain was so intense she thought she would surely die and the child would be sent to one of those hideous foundling hospitals where it would never know either love or comfort. She could not allow that to happen, she could not. She must fight, fight for her child.

"Help me!" she cried aloud. "Help me!"

"That is what I'm here for."

She opened her eyes with no notion of how many hours had passed except that a lamp had been lit so it must be night. A man was smiling down at her. He was in evening dress which seemed to her extraordinary. Then he began to take off his coat, the light fell on his face and she thought she must be dreaming because it was the face of the doctor who had been kind to her that day in the examination hall.

His hand was on her forehead. He said something reassuring but she could not reply because pain again overwhelmed her.

"It's all right," he said gently, "now try to breathe deeply."

The sweet heavy smell of chloroform was all around her. Her senses began to swim. "I'm dying," she thought, "I'm dying and the baby will die too and Simon will never know. Simon!" she cried in a stifled voice. "Simon!" and then went down and down into a velvety darkness.

She came back to consciousness through veils of heavy mist

still nauseated by the sickly drug but miraculously alive and out of pain. She felt weak as a kitten but relaxed and oddly peaceful. Someone wiped her face with a cool damp towel. Then the doctor was there again.

"You have a son," he said, "a fine bouncing boy."

"May I see him?"

So it had come at last, the moment she had longed for and dreaded.

Fanta brought the baby wrapped in a blanket, a little screwed up face, button nose, round blue eyes, a fuzz of reddish hair on the tiny head, no noticeable features.

"As fine a child as I've seen," said Fanta, "and I've known a few in my time. Not a blemish save just one tiny mark."

"Mark? Where?" said Galina. "What mark is that? Where?"

"It's nothing at all, nothing to worry about, There – see – on the right shoulder blade."

The blanket had been pushed aside and she saw it, a round brown mark smaller than her thumbnail but quite unmistakable. It must be proof, it had to be proof.

"My farthing baby!" she exclaimed in English, "my farthing baby!" and began to laugh and cry at the same time.

"Nothing to cry over," said Fanta heartily, "a mark like that is a sign of good luck. Didn't they ever tell you that? He'll never lack for friends or fortune, you take my word for it. Isn't that so, doctor?"

She glanced up a little shyly at the great man who was standing there smiling at the vagaries of young women while he rolled down his shirt sleeves and put on his fine black coat.

It was a day later when she learned the truth about that night when Zubov came to visit her, looking a little awkward and carrying a great bunch of sweet-scented lilies of the valley. He dropped them on the bed all dripping from the flower seller's basket and Fanta clicked her tongue disapprovingly and carried them off to put them in a bowl.

It seemed that the baby had been wrongly placed for an easy birth and as the hours went by Fanta had become increasingly afraid. She had run to consult him. It was then that he had thought of the eminent doctor whom he had known since university days and who still sometimes dropped in at the pharmacy to talk over old times, and he had run through the muddy streets to his fashionable house in the tree-lined avenue and found him just risen from a dinner party. It was her good fortune, Zubov told her impressively, that not only was he a fine doctor but also a man with a great feeling for suffering humanity. He abandoned his guests and came to her rescue.

"I thought I knew his face," she said thoughtfully, "I believe he was one of the doctors on the examination board at my oral test but I never knew his name."

"Makarov," said Zubov, "Basil Romanovich Makarov."

Her eyes widened. It could not be possible. She wanted to laugh aloud at the absurdity of it, the ridiculousness of life's accidents that the doctor who had saved her life should be the one who had fathered her carelessly in a moment of self-indulgence on his pretty laundrymaid.

He came to see her again the following day to make sure his work was well done and advise her to go slowly, to rest and not exert herself because he had been obliged to use the knife and she must allow time for complete healing. She lay and watched him, a handsome man still, the thick brown hair only lightly silvered. What would he say, she wondered, if she were to tell him that it was his grandson he had lifted from the cradle and was handling so expertly? Would he laugh or deny it or be shocked that his illegitimate daughter had just borne him an illegitimate grandchild? Only of course she was not going to say anything of the sort.

"Nothing to worry about here," he said smiling, "mother and baby doing well." She held out her arms and he put the boy into them. "It's been puzzling me," he went on, "haven't you and I met before?"

Was it himself he was seeing in her face? Vera had said she had a look of him.

"It was in the examination room in Petersburg last summer."

"That's it of course. I remember now. I thought you were going to faint. It does happen, you know, with young girls sometimes. They panic and forget everything, though you had no need to be worried, God knows. If I remember rightly, you did very well."

"Yes, I was fortunate."

He glanced around the room, neat and clean but lacking all luxury. How many times had he seen this happen? A really promising candidate with everything before her wrecked by a disastrous love affair.

He said, "I could arrange for the baby to be adopted if you wish."

"No, never. He's my son. I could never let him go."

Her vehemence surprised him. He said gently, "And his father?"

"His father has nothing to do with it."

"I see. Well, it is your affair." He took up his hat and gloves. "A few more days in bed and then take it very easy for a month or so. Zubov tells me you've been acting as his assistant. He's a good fellow, but don't let him tempt you into listening to his politics. It is one of the points upon which he and I agree to differ. Good day to you, Galina Panova."

All that month after the baby was born and while she slowly recovered her strength Galina was strangely content. It was as if the burden of doubt and indecision and unhappiness had suddenly been lifted and the relief was like a blessing. For that short space of time she did not dare to think beyond the present except to revel in her freedom. She was no longer tied to the wheel of uncertainty. She could return to Petersburg whenever she wished and every day it seemed to her that the baby grew more like the man she loved. She had thought long about what name she should give him. Simon was still too precious but he had a second name – she had seen it once on his passport – Andrew, after some long distant ancestor he had told her. So Andrei it was and Zubov was his godfather.

April merged into May and spring seemed exceptionally delightful here in the Ukraine, lacking the damp cold winds that blew across the Neva from the Gulf of Finland. One or two days were so warm that she took a chair out on to the patch of grass, the baby in a basket cradle beside her and the sweet scent of the lime all around her. Outside in the tree-lined avenues the young leaves of the chestnuts were a translucent green in the sun and soon their candles would be lit, great masses of cream and pink blossom.

She was sitting there one morning when Zubov brought her a letter. It was the first she had received and she stared at it in surprise. Who could have written to her when none of her former friends knew where she was? It was a Swiss postmark which puzzled her for a moment and then left her feeling cold. Switzerland where so many of the revolutionaries took refuge when the *Okhrana* was hot on their trail, Geneva from which came the forbidden *Iskra*, the *Spark*, the paper illegally imported and eagerly passed from hand to hand until it was threadbare. It gave her a shock to realize that the letter could only be from Igor.

Zubov was bending over the baby making ridiculous cooing sounds. He was the most unhandy of men and held the boy as if he might break in two and yet strangely enough the baby took no offence at the dark face bent over him, only blew little bubbles of pleasure.

She slit open the thin foreign envelope. There was no letter only the cutting from a newspaper with an announcement heavily outlined in red ink. She stared at it stupidly.

"A marriage will shortly take place at St Isaac's Cathedral between Doctor the honourable Simon Aylsham, younger son of Lord Aylsham of Ravensley, England, and the Princess Nina Pavlova Malinskaya, daughter of the late . . ."

The words blurred and then slowly righted themselves.

It was impossible. She could not believe it. It couldn't be true. A hot flood of anger raced through her and her cheeks burned. So she had captured him at last. Nina had made up her mind from the first and she had always got what she wanted, always. How could he have done it? He was married . . . all her castles in the air fell crashing to the ground. The flush in her cheeks subsided leaving her very pale.

Zubov was looking at her oddly.

"Is there anything wrong?"

"No, nothing, nothing at all. It's just a . . . just a circular. The sun has gone, it's growing cold. I think I'll go in." She was talking at random.

"I'll carry the basket for you."

"No, no, I can do it. I'm quite strong now." She was frantic to get away from him.

She got up hastily and the paper fell to the ground. He picked it up. His eye took it in swiftly, a marriage announcement and the name. So that was it. The man who had given her a child and then abandoned her. If he ever had him here, he'd let him know what he thought of him, but now he said nothing, simply put the paper in the basket she was carrying and watched her go from him before he went back to the shop fuming with impotent rage against that damned English seducer.

Upstairs in her room the baby uttered a loud wail of protest. She picked him out of the cradle and walked up and down while the anger vanished leaving her desolate and bereft, seeing it with a cold remorseless clarity. It was she who was to blame. She had left him without explanation so what did she expect him to do? Wait for ever in a hope that might never be fulfilled? He had always had a fondness for Nina, an indulgence for her wilful ways.

Oh God, how she hated her and what a fool she had been and yet, what else could she have done? She sat on the bed hugging the baby so tightly that his wails grew louder. Automatically she began to rock him to and fro. She could never go back now, never. She saw it all so clearly – just married, returning from a wedding trip and his mistress on his doorstep with his bastard son in her arms. It would blast him in the eyes of society before ever he was established. All her pride rose up in rebellion. She had chosen her lot and so she must abide by it.

"Take your pleasure and pay for it," her mother had said and it seemed she must go on paying, and yet she was more fortunate than some. She had somewhere to live; work which she could do and a son to make it worthwhile so why was she weeping? Why were the tears running helplessly down her face? The answer to that lay locked in her heart and must stay there. It was something on which she must turn the key if she was to go on living.

Part Three

SIMON AND NINA
1911

14

The heat in Petersburg in that August of 1911 was particularly oppressive and after they had dined together Simon suggested to Nigel that they might take their coffee and brandy out into the small terraced garden behind the big old house in the Morskaya. Both of them were temporarily alone. Lydia had taken the children to the country and Nina was spending a couple of months with Sonia at her late grandfather's villa in the Crimea. It was a little cooler now and the faint breeze smelled sweetly of grass cut that afternoon.

Nigel looked across at his friend lying back in the long chair, a brandy glass held between his two fine hands. He had come a long way in the last five years. At thirty-three and married to the Princess Nina, with his lean good looks, the slight touch of arrogance and a faint aura of mystery linked to the past, he had become an instant success not only with the English community but with fashionable society, which was always feverishly hunting for something different. The very fact that he treated their largely imaginary ills with a brusque impatience only made him more intriguing particularly to the women, old as well as young. He attended two of the hospitals and as Nigel knew, though many others didn't, he had established a clinic in one of the poorest quarters of the city and somehow found time to visit regularly. His wife had given him a daughter and a nine-month old son. He ought to have been the happiest of men and yet Nigel wondered.

After the first months he had never mentioned Galina.

Lydia was of the opinion that he nursed a hidden wound which her husband was inclined to dismiss as romantic fancy but all the same at times when he was not on guard his eyes had a haunted look as if he stared into a void which held no comfort for him.

Nigel drained his glass and said lazily, "You work too hard, Simon. Why don't you take a holiday? Go down to the Crimea, spend a week or two there and bring Nina home."

Simon came back from wherever his thoughts had strayed. "I may do just that. As you probably know the Tsar is going to Kiev in a week or so. He is unveiling a statue erected to his father and making one or two official visits to schools and so on. I've been invited to go with his entourage. I've never visited Kiev. It could be interesting and I can go on from there to Sevastopol and Yalta."

"Excellent idea. I must say I miss Lydia like the devil when she is away and the children too."

"Do you? Speaking for myself I rather welcome the opportunity to do a little serious research." He smiled briefly and slapped at his face. "The mosquitoes are flying in. We'd better go in or we'll be bitten to hell."

For about the hundredth time Nigel wondered what had induced him to marry Nina. Once or twice he had approached the question in a roundabout sort of way only to meet with stubborn resistance. Where it affected him personally Simon took refuge behind a wall of silence.

Nigel left before midnight since his host pleaded an early call at the hospital but all the same Simon did not go immediately to bed. He came back through the silent house to the small study that adjoined his consulting room. The table was littered with books, manuscripts, closely written pages of notes. He was engaged in a detailed research into haemophilia. An impenetrable blanket of secrecy was maintained about the health of the Tsarevich but though all questions were met with absolute silence he was pretty certain in his own mind that this was the disease that threatened the five-year-old Alexis. It had sparked his interest and helped him to combat the pain that time had blunted but was still there like a scar that never completely ceases to ache.

Haemophilia was as old as man and had come down through the centuries misted in legend, shrouded with the fearful taint of a hereditary curse, known and dreaded in the

Egypt of the Pharaohs and mentioned in the most ancient books of the Bible. It was an inherited blood-clotting deficiency handed down through the mother only to her sons and no one as far as he could discover had as yet been able to trace exactly where the faulty gene sprang from or how to cure it.

He sat down at his desk and drew the books towards him. The house was very quiet. The servants were in bed. Nina had taken her personal maid and the children's nurse with her and Simon had insisted on Jake travelling with them. He could be trusted to make sure they were cared for and had every comfort that could be obtained on the journey. He read for a while and then pushed the books aside impatiently. He had intended working for a couple of hours but tonight he was restless.

He had been quite unable to explain to Nigel that nothing would persuade him to go down to the Crimea. He had refused time and time again during the last five years inventing all kinds of excuses which he was quite sure Nina did not believe. He could not tell her that he would be haunted by Galina at every step.

The study was stuffily warm and after a while he got up, went into the room where he saw his patients and pushed open the long window opening on to the garden. A certain freshness flowed in fragrant with late roses and he went out into it walking up and down and thinking what a crashing mistake it had been to marry Nina and yet what else could he have done? He did not often allow himself to think back. What was done was done and it was useless to cry over it but tonight Galina was so alive in his mind that he could not help remembering the crass folly of those few months of bitter unhappiness.

After the tragedy that hit the Malinskys he had seen a good deal of Niki and Sonia, his sympathy going out to them, so young and struggling with a burden almost too heavy for them. And because Niki was worried about his sister who seemed to hurtle from nightmares to fits of despairing weeping he had become to some extent involved with her also. He had been aware of the Princess Malinskaya as an implacable figure immensely dignified in her sombre mourning trying to thwart her son's attempts to bridge the gulf that had arisen between him and his estate workers and utterly dedicated to raising the family's status to its former importance by marrying off her daughter to the rich and influential Skorskys.

But he did not realize how deep was the split between mother and daughter until one evening in March when he had come home very late to his apartment and found Nina ensconced in his armchair with a bulging suitcase and Shani lying beside her.

"I've run away," she announced calmly. "I've told Mamma that I would and that I was coming here. I'm going to stay all night and I'm going to make sure that everyone knows. After that Valentin's mother will never let me come anywhere near her precious son."

He was appalled but tried to tell himself it was some stupid childish defiance.

He said sternly, "Nina, this is ridiculous. Of course you can't stay here. Now be a good girl and get up. I'm going to take you home immediately and we'll concoct some story to account for your coming here."

But she did not stir.

"If you do, I'll tell her that you invited me here, that you're my lover and we've been meeting in secret for weeks."

"Don't be absurd. She would never believe such rubbish."

"Oh yes, she would. She doesn't like you, you know. She thinks you're a bad influence on Niki and that you're only nice to us because you think the Malinsky name will help you when you set up in practice."

He frowned. "Nina, that is absolute nonsense. She knows that and so do you. For heaven's sake pull yourself together. Tell your mother once and for all that you are not going to be forced into a marriage you dislike and that will be an end of it."

"No, it won't, it won't. You don't understand what it has been like." Her voice began to tremble. "I think she has become a little mad ever since Papa was killed. Grandfather was the only one she ever listened to and he is not there any longer."

She was crying now, great heaving sobs that shook her painfully.

He said a little desperately, "What about Niki? Won't he help?"

"Niki *wants* me to marry Valentin. He likes him, so does Sonia. They think I'm being obstinate for no reason but I'm not, I'm not." Her voice rose. "If I marry him, I shall die. I know I will. I shall kill myself."

"Nina, stop this, stop it at once. You'll make yourself ill."

He caught hold of her by the shoulders trying to quieten her and she flung her arms around his neck.

"You must help me, dear dear Simon. You are my only friend. Please, please help me."

She was pressing herself against him, reaching up to kiss him wildly, passionately. He could feel her tears on his face and just for a second and partly in an attempt to soothe her hysteria he made the great mistake of responding to her kiss.

Then he had put her firmly away from him but she was staring at him in triumph.

"You kissed me! I knew I was right, I knew it. Oh Simon, please, please. I love you so much, so very much. I've never wanted anyone else from the very first moment that you came to Dannskoye."

"No," he said, "no, Nina, it's quite impossible. Now do be sensible. I'll come with you. I'll speak to your mother, I will speak to Niki."

And quite suddenly she was quiet, standing very still, childishly forlorn in her black dress, the blonde hair falling around her neck.

"If you say so," she murmured, "if that's what you really want. Doesn't it matter to you at all that you're breaking my heart?"

"Don't be melodramatic," he said in exasperation, "hearts don't break so easily."

"I can't go home looking like this," she said pitifully lifting tear-filled eyes to his. "What would they think?"

"Very well. Go into the other room and wash your face but be quick. It's very late and we must go."

He might have guessed what would happen but he didn't. It was only when some minutes had passed that he went to the bedroom and knocked on the door only to find it locked against him.

"Nina, don't be a little fool. Open the door. Come out of there."

"No, I'm staying here till the morning."

He argued, begged, pleaded, but she wouldn't listen and apart from breaking down the door, and what a scandal that would cause, what could he do but let her stay there?

He spent an uncomfortable and sleepless night in the armchair with a disturbed Shani who whined piteously and ended up lying across the bedroom door. At a reasonably early hour he got up resolutely and knocked on the door. Presently she came out looking fragile and very pale but outwardly calm and resigned.

"I'd like some tea," she said in a small voice.

"No time," he said brusquely and went into the bedroom to plunge his face into cold water and make himself as presentable as possible. The rumpled bed, the faint odour of perfume, reminded him painfully of Galina and he shut his mind against it. The sooner this distasteful business was over the better. He came back into the room determined to treat the whole episode as if it were no more than a foolish schoolgirl prank.

"Now listen to me," he said firmly, "this is our story. You ran away to Missy but finding that she was not there and the flat closed up you took refuge here. I was out all night only returning this morning and immediately decided to take you home."

It was decidedly thin but for want of anything better would have to serve.

"If you insist," she said meekly. He put her coat around her shoulders and she twisted to look up into his face. "Do you hate me so very much?"

The tears were trembling on her lashes again and made him feel he was behaving like a brute. He touched her cheek with a gentle caress.

"Of course I don't, you silly child. Now let's go."

But it was no childish prank as he very soon found out. Nina had burned her boats behind her. She had let Vassily drive her openly to his apartment and leave her there. She had left notes for her mother and for Niki to be delivered in the early morning so that when they arrived at the house they were faced with the Princess Malinskaya's icy anger and Niki's look of pained disbelief.

He stumbled over an explanation that sounded not only remarkably unconvincing but had the unpleasant sound of a man old enough to know better shifting responsibility on to the shoulders of an innocent young girl. She had thrust him into a dilemma from which he found it increasingly difficult to extricate himself honourably. In these disgracefully lax times the

Princess hinted an escapade such as this between two people already secretly engaged might just be accepted but a young girl spending the night with a man who rejected her openly on the following morning could not only blast her own reputation but his also.

To add to the confusion on that morning Nina suddenly gave a little choked cry and collapsed against him. He caught her before she fell and carried her to the sofa. It was genuine enough, lack of food and an intensity of emotion had exhausted her. As he looked down at the white face, the tumbled hair, an unwanted memory dredged up of that first love of his. He had thought the guilt purged for ever but perhaps he was still being asked to pay. To abandon her in her plight called for a ruthlessness he did not possess. Missy when she heard about it afterwards warned him that pity was never enough but he did not heed her advice.

In the end in weariness and disillusionment and with the strong conviction that so far as personal happiness was concerned his life was over anyway he gave in to the inevitable and inevitably it had not worked. Nina, a radiant bride, ecstatic at getting her own way, had gradually been obliged to face the truth. He was kind, he did his best to please her, he adored his small daughter, but he did not love her. At the core of their marriage was an emptiness she could not bridge and as the years passed she resented it more and more deeply. Nina had always wanted all or nothing. She could not accept what he was prepared to give and it worried him. To escape into his work was his only remedy and even that became the subject of friction.

Knowing that he would not sleep he walked in the garden till dawn and then went in to bathe and dress. If he were to take a few weeks of holiday then he must begin to arrange for his colleagues to take on his more urgent cases.

For security reasons and to minimize the danger of a bomb attack two identical Imperial trains set out a few hours apart so that no one could be certain in which the Tsar and his family would be travelling. Simon was in the second train, not part of the official retinue but simply because friendship with Nigel had given him an entry into high diplomatic circles.

The talk among them was mostly political, to which he listened but made little comment. He had no wish to embroil himself with any party, his interests and his work lay else-where. Peter Arkadyevich Stolypin who had succeeded Witte as Prime Minister was also on the train. A few years previously a bomb had been thrown through the drawing room window of his country villa bringing down part of the house and cruelly maiming his two young children as well as many of his servants. Simon had admired the courage with which he had faced the tragedy. He was a man of the right, a conservative, a passionate patriot, and he had developed a wide network of spies and informers who were ruthlessly employed in ferreting out every hint of revolutionary violence. It had made him severely unpopular with those who leaned towards greater powers being granted to the people's representatives in the *Duma*.

"He's cooked his goose with the Empress. He's obliged the Tsar to banish the abominable Rasputin from the palace, much to her fury," said a young man attached to Stolypin's staff and Simon pricked up his ears.

It was over a year ago since Nina had come home from a party of her young friends, starry-eyed and describing in glowing terms a man who had been present, a miracle-working peasant, from all accounts, who could cure almost anything simply by the laying-on of hands.

He had been seriously disturbed. It was not the first time he had heard of Gregory Rasputin. He was what was called a *starets*, a holy man, a phenomenon which could only occur in a country like Russia with its millions of illiterate and superstitious peasants. Almost every country estate and village had one of these holy pilgrims attached to them, wandering through the countryside, living lives of poverty and asceticism, their purpose to guide other souls through times of anguish and turmoil. Only Rasputin was different. Arriving in Petersburg, huge, uncouth, barbaric in speech and manner, he had been welcomed into the society of young aristocrats bored with orthodoxy, avid for excitement and dabbling in the occult; a society which Simon despised, rich and dissipated, living in an atmosphere of decadence, too much champagne, dancing all night, staking fortunes on the card tables or at the race track, gathering around them mediums in darkened drawing rooms and seeking to communicate with the spirit world.

There had been some ugly stories circulating about Rasputin, about his wild success with fashionable princesses and wives of army officers, women tired of their dull husbands, to whom making love with a peasant with grimy hands and filthy verminous hair was a new and thrilling experience.

"I'm thinking of consulting him myself," said Nina airily, "you know I've not been feeling really well for months now."

It was true that her second pregnancy had proved troublesome. She had suffered sickness and minor ills and was irritated because he could not provide an instant cure.

"You'll do nothing of the sort, Nina. I absolutely forbid you to have anything to do with this man." He had spoken so forcibly, so unlike his usual gentleness, that though she pouted rebelliously she did not dare to disobey him.

"I don't see why," she grumbled. "He has been introduced into the palace. The Tsarina thinks very highly of him."

"Maybe but that has nothing to do with you."

When the baby was born, though he was frail and needed constant care, she quickly recovered her usual health and he had thankfully seen her off to the south with the sensible Sonia.

"What do *you* think of this laying-on of hands, doctor?" asked the man who had first brought up the subject. "Can anyone be cured by such a method?"

"It's possible," he said cautiously, "simply through the patient's faith in the healer especially if he possesses hypnotic powers. I once knew a dentist who could extract teeth from a hypnotized patient without any ill effects, which would be a great advantage to someone suffering from excessive bleeding."

He could say no more but the hint was enough. The others exchanged glances.

"Maybe that's the influence he has gained over that sick child *and* his mother."

"I'm not saying it is so, only that there is a strong possibility."

Even in the privacy of the railway carriage mention of the disease afflicting the Tsarevich could not be pursued with any safety.

It was a conversation he was to remember a few days later when he watched the procession go rattling by with a wildly cheering crowd who waved to the two elder daughters of the Tsar riding with their governess. As Stolypin's coach rolled

215

along, there was a momentary hush and in it a loud voice cried out dramatically, "Death is pursuing him! Death is riding at his heels!"

He looked over the heads of the crowd and saw Rasputin for the first time, a giant of a man, long dirty hair falling to his shoulders, a matted beard, but wearing a Russian blouse of scarlet silk bound with a silver tasselled sash, black velvet trousers tucked into fine kid boots, a gold cross and chain around his neck. So that was the *starets*, that was the miracle worker! For a few seconds he felt the weight of that mesmerizing black stare, then the people pushed forward and he had vanished.

He spent part of the day walking around Kiev, a city about which he knew very little and ended up close to the golden domes of St Sophia. The original church went back to the eleventh century, built in a barely Christian Russia, but though the exterior had been largely rebuilt, inside the magnificent Byzantine frescoes were still intact. He gazed up at the calm face of the Virgin and wondered if it was blasphemy because it reminded him of Galina when they lay together in the peaceful aftermath of love.

He spent an hour or so there and it was a golden September afternoon when he came out, strolled up to Shevchenko Boulevard, saw a chemist's shop and remembered that a member of their party had asked him for help for a disordered stomach. Too much rich food of course but he could provide him easily enough with a simple soothing mixture.

It was a large and well stocked pharmacy, he noted, looking around him as he waited while the assistant struggled with a large self-important customer who obviously thought she knew better than her doctor or the pharmacist. After a good deal of argument she slapped down the money, snatched the package held out to her and went out.

For a moment he was totally bereft of words. It was as if the fresco at which he had been gazing had suddenly come to life. It was Galina. The face framed by the high-necked blouse above the long white coat was older but even more beautiful than he remembered.

She had seen him. She was as speechless as he was, their eyes devouring one another until he broke the spell.

"It is you, isn't it? I can't believe it. I've waited so long for this."

"Simon!" she breathed and then her throat seemed to close up.

He was aware of the door opening, of people coming in, but he took no heed.

"There's so much I want to know, so much I must know. Please, Galina, you must tell me."

"Yes, but not now, Simon. I can't talk now. I'm in charge here this afternoon. There are customers waiting, prescriptions to be made up."

It was as if she were fighting for time and he wanted to damn them all to hell.

"When then?"

"This evening."

"What time do you close?"

"Seven o'clock."

"I'll be here." His grip on her wrist tightened. "You won't vanish again. Promise me."

She shook her head, dangerously close to tears.

He took out a notebook, tore off a leaf and wrote quickly. Behind him people were moving impatiently. He had been speaking in whispers, now he raised his voice.

"Can you prepare this for me? I'll call back for it."

"Certainly, doctor, it will be ready for you."

He moved away but still could not take his eyes off her. He had a feeling that if he let her out of his sight, she would be gone again. It would be like one of those futile dreams that had haunted him for so long when he seemed to hold her in his arms and woke up to find them empty.

She gave him a faint smile and he took heart from it. He went out of the shop scarcely knowing how he was to get through the hours till he could return.

Listening to customers explaining their symptoms, giving helpful advice and making up prescriptions, it was a wonder that Galina didn't poison someone that afternoon, she was so distracted. She knew it had to happen one day, they were bound to meet and yet when she had seen him it had taken her breath away. It was as if the years had rolled away, that nothing stood between them and it had frightened her. She would have liked longer to prepare herself and yet the hours dragged and she was filled with fear in case he might think better of it and not come back. She didn't even know why he was in Kiev or where he was staying.

Zubov had gone to visit his sister and would not be back till very late. She shut the shop and went to fetch Andrei and Ranji from Fanta, who looked after him on those days when she had work to do.

Andrei was tall for his age, a slim wiry child with abundant bright brown hair, large grey eyes and his father's straight nose. He came running to greet her, full of the small events of his day and for once she cut him short.

"We must hurry. It's time for supper," she said and marched him off to their own apartment, a better one now, three small rooms on the ground floor. This was the time he usually shared with his mother when she talked to him, played games, read him stories, and he felt aggrieved. She set out his supper, told him to get on with it and contented herself with a single cup of tea looking abstractedly out of the window while he told a long exciting story of chasing a big rat with Ranji and the boy from across the garden, how it had run into the flat belonging to that horrid old lady, Maria Useva, and she had come at them with a big stick because she was so frightened ... he looked across at her reproachfully.

"You're not listening," he said accusingly.

"Yes, I am, darling," she started guiltily, "but I don't really like you to go rat hunting with Ranji and you shouldn't scare old ladies even if you don't like them, it's unkind. I've told you before, haven't I? Now finish up your supper, it's high time you were in bed."

"It's not seven yet," he protested with his mouth full.

"I know but Mamma has to – has to see someone."

"Who is it?"

"Oh just someone connected with Uncle Ivan and the shop but it is rather important. Now come along, do."

In a spirit of pure mischief he was deliberately naughty, running off giggling when she tried to wash him, wriggling away from her after she had undressed him capering, all round the room mother-naked until exasperated she grabbed hold of him and gave him a slap on his small bottom.

He gazed up at her resentfully.

"I don't think I like this man you've got to see."

She suddenly hugged him to her wanting to say that this man was the most wonderful person in the world *and* his father, and then doubting if she ever would.

218

When he was in bed and she was bending over him to kiss him he suddenly clutched hold of her.

"You're not going away, Mamma, are you?"

"No, of course I'm not going away, Andrushka, whatever made you say that?"

But he couldn't explain. It was just a feeling that somehow life had become different and it frightened him.

She tucked him in and he lay watching the red light burning in front of the icon she had hung beside the truckle bed. It was one he had chosen himself, a saint on a blue horse killing a fiery red dragon and it was what he was going to do when he grew up. He was going to kill the dragons that Uncle Ivan had told him about, the wicked dragons who still lived in Russia eating up all the food so that poor people and children who were not lucky like he was starved and died.

Galina looked at herself in the mirror, tidying her hair with nervous fingers, wondering how much she had changed and what she was going to say to him, reminding herself that he was married now, he was not hers any longer, could never be hers again. It was past seven by the time she went into the darkened shop and saw the shadow through the glass panelled door.

She crossed swiftly and unbolted it. "I'm sorry," she said breathlessly, "have you been waiting long? There were things I had to do."

"I thought you might have changed your mind," he said wryly, and followed her through the big back room across the patch of grass and into her small apartment. Then she shut the door and they were alone.

He put down hat and gloves and she looked at him hungrily, noting the new lines etched on his face, the cheekbones more accentuated. He was thinner, a certain tenseness about him. Amazingly, though there were so many unanswered questions lying between them, they spoke first of trivial things, exchanging news as when old friends meet, almost as if they were afraid to touch upon the past as yet. He told her about the clinic and about Luba.

"She has qualified as a nurse and has become my right hand," he said. "She is so downright. She doesn't mince her words when she is dealing with malingerers and layabouts but she is a wonder with those who really need help. She makes them laugh and they feel better at once. God knows what I would do without her."

"And Conn?" she asked.

"He has a job in a publisher's office. Nothing much in his line, I'm afraid, but he still paints in his spare time."

He told her about the death of the old General and Prince Malinsky without mentioning Nina and in return she talked about Zubov, how good he had been to her, how he had employed her as assistant and how she did a good deal of his dispensing and even visited the hospitals.

"They told me you passed your examinations with first class honours," he said drily.

"Thanks to you."

Then they were silent for a moment. There was a constraint between them that neither seemed able to break. The room was darkening and she busied herself with lighting the lamp.

"Shall I make you some tea or would you prefer coffee?"

How often she had said that in the old days after they had spent hours working together. He was standing with his back against the window and his face was in shadow.

He said quietly, "Galina, why did you go away from me? Was it someone else? Was it Igor? Nina told me once that you and he had been very close."

"No," she said fiercely, "no, never. If she told you that then it was a lie. How could you think such a thing?"

"What did you expect me to think?"

She dropped down on one of the chairs burying her face in her hands. He wanted to go to her, put his arms around her but first he had to know.

"Is it so hard to tell?"

"It shouldn't be, not now. It's so long ago." She raised her head staring in front of her. "It was like this. The day after you left I went to my room to pick up what was mine and settle everything and while I was there, Igor came back. It was so long since I'd seen him, I had never given him a thought so the door of my room was unlocked and he came in . . . quite unexpectedly . . . when I was already in bed . . ."

She told it simply and without detail but he saw it clearly in his mind's eye, the revulsion, the struggle, the violation, so that the anger rose and nearly choked him.

"Did you think I wouldn't have understood what you went through? Why couldn't you have trusted me?"

"That wasn't the end of it. If only it had been!" She looked away from him. "I was pregnant and I didn't know – I couldn't know – was it by you or was it Igor?"

"Oh my God, my poor love!"

"What was I to do?"

She tried to keep her voice steady but the misery of those weeks of uncertainty flooded back to her.

"If only I had been there!" he said despairingly.

She was staring in front of her with haunted eyes.

"Perhaps I did wrong. Perhaps I should have stayed and faced it out with you but at the time I was so afraid. I thought it would kill everything between us – the child of another man, a man you had despised – it would have destroyed all the plans we had made together."

He saw her so young and friendless battling with something too big for her and cursed the fate that had kept him away from her at that crucial time.

"And so you ran away to Kiev?"

"Yes." She smiled faintly. "It was something my mother said to me once about the man who was my father. He had come from here and I had to go somewhere."

There was something so desolate, so heartbreaking about that lonely admission that his self-control slipped. He went across to kneel beside the chair and take both her hands in his, wanting to know and almost fearing to ask.

"And the baby?"

"Andrei is your son." She gave a little laugh that ended in a sob. "He even has your devil's mark."

It brought back their last night together so vividly that his arms went around her. He could not endure to think of what she must have gone through bearing his child alone in a strange city.

"Why didn't you come to me then?" he whispered. "If you knew how I waited and hoped, how I prayed for the miracle that would bring you back to me."

"I thought of it but for a while I could not travel and afterwards it was too late. I knew you were married."

"Oh God what a fool I was, what a damnable fool! I should have known, I should have waited."

"How could you, and you always had such a fondness for Nina."

"A fondness, yes." He got to his feet. He could not bring

himself to tell her how she had tricked him into marriage, the weakness that had made him yield. She was his wife and he owed her his loyalty at least. He could blame only himself which made it all the more bitter to know he was committed. He could not escape without doing more harm.

"How is Nina?"

She was striving to sound normal, to bring down the highly charged feeling between them into something more ordinary.

"Well enough. We have two children, Tanya who is four and the baby Paul."

"They must make you very happy."

"Yes, of course," but this other one was different, this was a child born of their love. He swung round on her. "May I see my son?"

But she was not prepared for that yet.

"He's in bed and asleep. It will only upset him and if we go into the room Ranji will become excited and it will wake him."

"You still have Ranji?"

"Yes," but she didn't tell him how bringing the dog had been like carrying a little of the old life with her.

"I'll come again," he said impetuously, "I'll come tomorrow," then he paused. "Damnation, it can't be tomorrow. I'm committed to a luncheon with the doctors at the hospital and in the evening there is the gala performance at the Opera House. I travelled with the Tsar's retinue, I can't get out of it."

She smiled. "In any case I shall be at the opera too. Zubov has asked me to accompany him. We shan't be anywhere near your grand party but we shall be seeing it together."

"It will have to be the next day." He began to make plans. "You can come back to Petersburg. I will take a flat for you. You must let me provide for you and the boy. We might even be able to work together again."

"No, Simon, no." She stopped him in full flight. "No, it would be impossible. It wouldn't be fair to Nina. Far better that I stay here."

"I can't lose you again, not after I've found you at last. I can't, Galina, you can't ask it of me. I can't go on living and know you are here so far away from me."

"You must. It's the only way."

"No, Galina. I refuse to accept it. The boy is mine. I have a right to share him with you."

"Maybe but you have no right to command my life, Simon. Suppose I should wish to marry, what then?" she said quietly and smiled a little at the look of shock on his face before he controlled it.

"Do you? Is there someone?"

"Not immediately."

He frowned and would have questioned further but she stopped him with a gesture.

"It's very late. I think you should go. I'm a respectable woman, you know. I don't usually entertain gentleman visitors."

He gave in then thinking he could come again, he could persuade her to listen to him. There must be some way, there had to be some way in which he could see her and yet still not hurt Nina.

She went with him to the door. There was a light in the room at the back of the shop and she knew Zubov must have returned. He would have to know, but not yet. There would be time enough later.

"There's another way out," she said. "I will show you. You don't need to go through the shop."

It was a narrow passage between the pharmacy and the next house. She led him along it.

"It leads into Shevchenko Boulevard," she said, "you can get a cab there to your hotel."

He had gripped her hand in his. In the half light she could see his eyes on her and then unexpectedly he had taken her in his arms. What was meant as a light kiss became something deeper and it proved to her without a shadow of doubt that five years had not killed the passion that had once existed between them. It shook them both before he released her, pressed her hands and was gone quickly not trusting himself. She stood there shaking, her hands pressed against the mouth he had kissed. She had lived these five years without love, devoting herself to her child, and now was frightened at her hunger for it. Her body had come tinglingly to life. She had a mad desire to race after him, bring him back. It made her realize she had been right. It would be impossible for them to work side by side and not yield to it. When he came back she knew he would do his utmost to persuade her and she wondered if she would be strong enough to resist the pressure when the very thought of it made her dizzy with longing.

It was some minutes before she could compose herself and go quietly back to the apartment. She looked in on Andrei. He lay spread-eagled, the blankets kicked off, one arm flung up above his head. She covered him up again and he stirred but did not waken.

"Did I have a Papa like Sasha?" he had asked one day coming in from playing with the boy opposite.

She didn't know how to answer him. "Of course you did, darling, but he had to go away from us," she had said at last.

"Is he in prison?"

There had been some arrests during the last year among the young men who gathered in Zubov's house and he must have heard the talk about them.

"No, not in prison. He is a doctor and he had his work."

"Shall I ever see him?"

"One day."

Now that day was here and she wondered how the child would react or whether it would be wiser to keep him in ignorance. He was a boy of strong likes and dislikes who even at only five years old was not always easy to control. She touched the tumbled hair gently and then went out of the room.

It was while she was undressing that she heard the sound of voices outside. Whispers only but it was unusual when it was so late. Early September was very warm so the shutters were not completely closed and she peered through the crack. Two men were standing close together at a little distance and the lamp above their heads shed a kind of ghostly radiance around them. One she recognized at once. It was that same lanky young man who had rescued her from the mob and whose name she knew was Bogrov. Mordecai had been in the nature of a good-natured nickname because he was a Jew though sometimes she thought he had resented it. He came to some of Zubov's meetings and though she was always friendly with him, she did not really trust him. There was something unpleasantly secretive, something almost sinister, about the blazing fanatical eyes, the lean white features under the black hair. Then the other man shifted his position, the light fell full on the face under the peaked cap and she saw it was Igor.

She had not seen him since before Andrei was born and instinctively she drew back though it was impossible that he should have seen her. She had believed him in Switzerland with the other revolutionaries but something must have brought him back and she was instantly aware of danger, which was stupid since the security of the Tsar's visit had been exceptionally strict, not a mouse could get through the guards surrounding him. She was overwrought, she told herself as she pulled her nightgown over her head. Seeing Simon had put her on edge. She peeped out again and the two figures had vanished, the grass plot was empty and all was quiet.

If she lay wakeful that night it was not the thought of Igor that kept her sleepless.

15

Changing into evening dress for the gala performance at the Opera, it seemed to Simon that the day had been one of the longest he had ever experienced. Normally he enjoyed meeting doctor colleagues, discussing cases and treatments, exchanging ideas with some of the younger and more adventurous spirits like himself. But the meeting with Galina had disturbed him. He was impatient for the next day when he would see her again and together they could somehow plan a future.

The Opera House when he reached it was crammed with a largely fashionable audience. Jewels glittered under the giant chandeliers, gold-braided uniforms, red sashes and diamond stars were scattered among the tiaras and feathers of the ladies. In the gallery parties of boys and girls from the high schools were wild with excitement at this special treat. He looked for Galina but it was impossible to find anyone in that crowded house. Prime Minister Stolypin and the other ministers were in the front row of the stalls, his own seat a few rows behind. Police appeared to be everywhere. The Tsar came into his flower-decorated box with his two elder daughters, the audience rose and the orchestra burst into the national anthem.

Rimsky-Korsakov's *Tsar Saltan*, based on Pushkin's romantic poem, was a colourful fairytale with magnificent sets and brilliant costumes.

In the first interval Simon strolled up the aisle and caught sight of Galina. She waved and smiled. It seemed ironic that the last time they had seen the opera had been at the Alexandrovsky in Petersburg. The small dark man sitting beside her looked at him sharply and frowned. It was stiflingly hot. He went through the foyer for a breath of air. Outside in the street people still eddied to and fro hoping for glimpses of some of the great ones.

At the next intermission he remained in his seat. Stolypin was standing up, his back against the orchestra rail. Simon looked up idly as a young man in full evening dress walked down the aisle towards the Prime Minister, his face oddly white against the jet black of his hair. Stolypin was smiling at him enquiringly as the assassin whipped a pistol from under his evening cape, fired twice, then calmly turned his back and walked away.

It was so totally unexpected that for an instant no one stirred. The Tsar came hurrying back into the box. Stolypin raised a bloodstained hand and tremulously gestured to him. Simon leaped over the row in front of him and reached his side. Professor Chernov, the surgeon he had met at lunch that day, came hurriedly across the aisle. Blood had begun to soak through Stolypin's uniform. The theatre was in an uproar. Women were screaming, people were trying to force their way through the doors before they were slammed shut. An officer had leaped to the floor from one of the first tier of boxes and seized the assassin. A crowd immediately surrounded them. Police surged up from all quarters; they fought off his attackers, but he was in a terrible condition, his clothes ripped, blood streaming from his mouth. They dragged the man away for immediate questioning.

An ambulance came galloping up outside and a stretcher was brought down the aisle but Stolypin shook his head. Supported by friends he walked slowly from the theatre, his courage earning him a tremendous ovation. Simon saw him lifted into the ambulance and a police escort immediately formed up around it. When he came back the curtain had been raised and the actors were singing the national anthem. The Tsar standing at the front of the box was very pale but showed no sign of fear. He left afterwards and the audience began to stream out of the theatre. Simon looked for Galina but she and her escort had disappeared. They had probably thought it wise to leave before the doors were closed.

*

The moment Galina had seen that lanky young man walk so purposefully down the aisle she knew what was in his mind though she could not guess at his victim. She had known something was going to happen when she had seen him with Igor but had shut her mind against it. She would have started after him with some vague idea of preventing it if Zubov had not gripped her arm.

"Let's get out of here."

The shots rang through the theatre and in the hushed silence she turned on him.

"Did you know about this? Did you?"

But Zubov only shook his head. He was pulling her away urging her out of the theatre and they squeezed through the doors with a number of others before they were shut and locked. The square outside was empty. Mounted police were dispersing the crowd and pushing them up side streets. Zubov had hold of her arm and was hurrying her away towards Shevchenko Boulevard and safety.

"You haven't answered my question," she said breathlessly, shocked and distressed that Ivan Zubov, one of the kindest of men, should be linked with such an outrageous attack on Stolypin who was a good man, an honest statesman.

In the safety of the shop, doors shut, shutters closed, she turned on him again.

"Did you know about this? And if so, why, Ivan, why?"

"I knew and yet I didn't know," he said wretchedly. "You must have always realized what our meetings here have meant. You came to some of them. I've never wanted anything more than to open their young minds, teach them to think constructively of the future, awaken them to dreams of freedom, of liberation of thought and ideas. That was how this group started but it has changed. There are some who want only destruction, kill first and rebuild afterwards, is their creed. They forget that violence breeds violence, that the destroyer also destroys himself. In the last few years I've learned that there is what they call a 'combat' section of the Social Revolutionaries and it is they who are taking over all the country. I've fought against it but there are terrorists moving from group to group inciting them to murder but taking care not to involve themselves."

And Igor is one of those, she thought, one of many who blaze a trail of violence and conveniently vanish.

"What will happen now?" she whispered.

"I'm not sure. I have never entirely trusted Bogrov. There is something twisted in his mind, a bitter resentment because he is a Jew and at times they have suffered badly in Kiev. The police will begin to make enquiries, they will be ready to follow any lead." He glanced at her and then away. "It might be best if I were to take a little holiday, close the shop for a month or two. I could go to my sister. You too, my dear, is there anywhere you could go?"

"But why should I run away? I have done nothing."

"The *Okhrana* doesn't always stop to ask questions. I wouldn't like to think I had put you under suspicion. If it would be of any help you could come with me. My sister is a good woman, she would not refuse to give shelter. We could take the early morning train out of the city."

"I couldn't leave, not now, not immediately. There are reasons . . ."

He gave her a quick glance. "Is it that man in the theatre, the man you recognized? Is he one of the reasons?"

"Yes."

"I have never asked, it is your life after all, but is it possible that he is the father of your son? The man who abandoned you?"

"You're wrong, Ivan. It was I who abandoned him. I cannot do it a second time, I cannot, and surely we are exaggerating the danger."

"I hope to God we are but in the meantime it is only sensible to be prepared and since you won't come with me, I could leave you in charge of the shop."

"If I can help I would be only too glad." She put a hand on his arm. "You pack your bag with what you need and I'll run across to speak to Fanta. She is looking after Andrei for me but I'll be back. Make haste. Don't risk anything."

Zubov went up the stairs to his flat above the shop and Galina crossed the grass and tapped quietly on Fanta's door. She opened it a few inches, looking scared.

"What has happened? Fedya came in saying something about a shooting."

"The Prime Minister was assassinated in the theatre tonight," sad Galina briefly. "Can I leave Andrei for a little while longer? Zubov has to leave the city in a hurry and I'm helping him."

"Lord protect us!" exclaimed Fanta crossing herself fervently. "What do they want with shooting people? What good does it do except make trouble for decent folk who've never lifted a finger? I knew he would be in trouble sooner or later carrying on with those hotheads night after night."

"It's just a precaution," she whispered. "He may not be in any danger at all."

"God go with the poor man and don't you worry about the boy. He's sleeping sound enough and I'll not let any of them busybodies come poking their noses in here. You can be sure of that."

Galina went back to the shop and she and Zubov were together in the back room when they heard the sound of running feet and then the hammering commenced. He had been giving her last minute instructions about the pharmacy and they paused looking at one another before he shrugged his shoulders resignedly.

"It seems they've lost no time. It's sooner than I hoped but it had to come," he said wryly. "Luck has a damnable way of running out."

"No," she urged, "no, you mustn't give up so easily, not yet. There is still time. We can go through the garden. You can hide in my apartment till they've gone away, then you can slip through the passageway and make for the station."

But they were already too late. Someone in deadly fear of the *Okhrana*'s rigorous questioning had babbled of the meetings in the backroom of the pharmacy on Shevchenko Boulevard. The first light of dawn was paling the sky when Galina hustled Zubov into her apartment pushing him into the child's empty bedroom. By the time she had reached the door again the police had come swarming down the passage and across the grass plot, knocking on doors, pulling young men out of their beds, bundling them together into police vans. Enraged at the cynical flouting of their strict security precautions they were taking no chances.

She met the lieutenant of police calmly at the door of her apartment. Yes, she had accompanied Ivan Zubov to the Opera but she had no idea where he was now, asleep in his bed more than likely.

"Is he deaf as a post then that he declines to open up when required?"

"How should I know how deeply he sleeps?"

"I beg leave to doubt that," said the policeman insolently, still smarting from his chief's scalding rebukes for negligence. He summoned two of his men. "Search the rooms."

"There is a child asleep," said Galina desperately trying to bar their way.

"Asleep or not we have our duty to the state."

"You have no right to search . . ."

"Out of the way, woman," he thrust her roughly against the wall and was immediately confronted by Zubov himself coming from the inner room.

"If you are looking for Ivan Zubov, then you have found him," he said calmly, "and you can take your filthy hands off the lady. She is innocent of anything except a desire to give refuge to an old friend."

"Innocent is she?" he answered. "We'll see about that. Arrest them both."

"I have a child. How can I leave him?" she said frantically.

"You should have thought of that before, shouldn't you?" said the lieutenant and gripped her arm painfully.

Fanta put her head out of the door and withdrew it quickly while Galina and Zubov were hustled through the narrow passage and into the waiting police van. She fell bruisingly to her knees and was helped to her feet by willing hands. She saw in the semi-darkness that there were others, men and women, all crowded in together.

"They say it's just for questioning," said a voice cheerfully, "if we're lucky, we'll get away with it."

She would need more than luck, thought Galina wretchedly. They could prove nothing against her but what did the *Okhrana* care about proof if they wanted to make an example? It had all happened so suddenly, she felt bewildered and horribly afraid. She was still wearing the thin dress she had put on for the Opera with only a shawl around her shoulders and she shivered. What was going to happen to Andrei . . . and what of Simon? He would come to the shop and find it abandoned. Why, oh why had she been such a fool as to let herself become involved? She was suddenly filled with despair that this should have happened now at this very moment when she had found Simon again. Someone had taken her hand and was holding it firmly clasped in his.

"I'm sorry," whispered Zubov, "God knows I'm sorry."

She returned the pressure ashamed of her anger with him. It seemed that fate, destiny, or was it perhaps the God who controlled her life, had not yet done with her.

*

By morning the city was in a ferment. Somehow the news had spread that the assassin was a Jew and a centuries-old hatred stirred and sprang to life. Simon came out from his hotel to see the streets crowded with refugees. Outside the hospital where Stolypin lay slowly dying straw had been laid down in the road and the traffic diverted but elsewhere every available vehicle had been commandeered by Jews terrified of massacre and fleeing with their wives, children and as much baggage as they could take with them.

Orders had been sent out bringing in the Cossacks to keep charge, long lines of them had come riding in since dawn, their naked sabres gleaming in the early morning light.

Nobody had slept in the hotel that night, there were too many rumours flying about from one to the other. Already it was hinted that Bogrov had led a double life, a revolutionary *and* a police informer. One thing was certain he had led the police on a false trail of an assassination plot and by the time they discovered their mistake he had calmly entered the Opera House on his official pass. Bruised and bleeding he faced his interrogators with an arrogant contempt saying nothing and prepared to meet death without flinching.

Unable to find a cab, Simon pushed his way through the thronged streets to Shevchenko Boulevard and stood aghast at the sight that met his eyes. The looters, the vandals, had already done their worst. They had ravaged the pharmacy amusing themselves by smashing the porcelain jars, the green glass bottles, the precious pots of sweet smelling salves and ointments. The senseless destruction disgusted him as he picked his way through the debris to the back room, saw the books ripped from the shelves, the torn leaflets, the scattered pamphlets, and more and more afraid of what he would find went across the grass and knocked on the door of Galina's apartment. Receiving no answer he knocked again louder.

A window flew up and Fanta looked out.

"You can knock till doomsday, young man, but you'll get no answer, she's gone."

"Gone? Gone where? What do you mean? Why?"

"So many questions." She looked him up and down. "Who are you? What do you want with Galina Panova?"

"I'm a friend, a very old friend, I was here the night before last."

She stared at him for a long moment, decided that he was what he said he was and opened her door.

"You'd better come in. There are too many sharp eyes and long ears about here."

He followed her into the tiny lobby and she took a closer look at him, a gentleman obviously, and rich too more than likely.

"It was the police," she said, "coming here early this morning, tearing the place to pieces. They've arrested her and Ivan Zubov. For questioning they said," she sniffed, "we all know what that means."

"But why for God's sake? She had nothing to do with this wretched affair surely."

"Not she. Galina Panova wouldn't harm as much as a mouse, but that Zubov, he's a different kettle of fish. A kind man, mind you, but wrong in the head, always saying that if only the people were in power, then we'd all be living in some kind of a paradise, not that I could ever see that happening, not with some of them going around shooting people but you see he had been good to her when she had no one so she thought she owed him something and when they came hunting him down, she hid him in her apartment. After that they arrested them both."

Out of all this he got a fair grasp of what must have happened. "And her child?" he asked. "Have they taken the child too?"

"Not they. I took care of that. He's happy enough. He's used to me, see. Told him his Mamma had to go off for a day or two but what I'm going to say to him if she doesn't come back, that's something else."

The first thing to be done was to find out how serious the charge was and whether it could be made to stick.

"Will you continue to care for him for a day or so until I can find out what the police are likely to do with them? If it's a question of payment . . ." he took out his wallet.

She pushed his hand away indignantly. "I don't want your money. Didn't I help to bring him into the world? He's been like my own ever since. But he'll begin to fret, mind you, he's close to his Mamma never having had no father if you know what I mean."

"Yes, I do know. Let's hope it won't be for long. I'll come back, I promise you."

"If anything should happen to her which God forbid, I'd keep him for my own but Fedya, he wouldn't like it. Not that he's an unkind man but he's never taken to children specially since we've none of our own. It would break my heart but I'd have to let him go."

His son, Galina's child, alone, friendless, thrust into some orphanage! Never! He would have liked to have taken him now but first he must break through the police barrier, see her, discover how much she had been involved. Oh God, to find her and then lose her again. It was unbearable. He could not let it happen, not a second time.

During the next few days while the city gradually calmed down and the Tsar against all advice continued his round of official visits, Simon battled with the police and met with a stubborn opposition. Bogrov of course would hang, there was no doubt about that at all, but the Kiev Chief of Police still suffering under strong accusations of negligence was determined to prove his zeal by making a clean sweep of all revolutionary elements in his city once and for all. He was not inclined to grant any favours to this importunate foreigner however distinguished. In the end it was one of Simon's new medical acquaintances who pointed out how he might at least be allowed a few minutes with her.

"Make a plea on grounds of health – a heart condition – something of that nature. If they think she is likely to fall sick or die on them, they might agree. The *Okhrana* don't care to be accused of unnecessary brutality whatever happens behind closed doors."

"I never thought of that," said Simon gratefully.

Dr Makarov looked at him keenly. "Galina Panova, you say, an old pupil of yours in Petersburg, was she? I believe I delivered her child a few years ago now. So she's mixed up with Ivan Zubov, is she? I did warn her. Good chap, excellent pharmacist too, but got a bee in his bonnet, tied himself up with politics. I'm sorry to hear it has caught up with him, waste of a fine brain. If I can be of any help, don't hesitate to call upon me."

To Simon's surprise the scheme worked. He was grudgingly granted a short interview and she was brought under police escort to a separate small room where he waited for her. Conditions in the crowded prison had not been pleasant and in the five days she had already lost weight and there were dark shadows under her eyes. He wanted to sweep her into his arms and take her away from this vile place but was obliged to hide his feelings under his most professional manner. He ordered the guard to wait outside. No decent young woman, he pointed out icily, could be expected to strip before anyone but her own doctor.

"Simon," she breathed when the door shut behind him, "how did you manage it? No one else has been allowed visitors."

"You're sick, didn't you know? Begin to unbutton your blouse – I must appear to be examining you at least. We haven't much time. As a matter of fact it was a certain Dr Makarov who put the idea into my head."

"Makarov? Basil Makarov?" and she began to laugh helplessly as she fumbled with the hooks of her high-necked blouse.

"What's so funny about that?"

He pushed her hands aside and completed the work himself.

"You don't know, you just don't know, I'll tell you sometime." She leaned against him weak with reaction and just for a moment it was as if the years had vanished and they were back to what they had been before, sharing each other's thoughts, their laughter and their tears.

"Steady," he whispered into her hair, "steady in case someone is watching."

She gulped and drew away from him and he began to sound her chest.

"Now listen to me," he said brusquely, "this is important. Stolypin died this morning so it has altered the circumstances. Attempted assassination has become murder. You and the rest of the suspects are to be taken to Petersburg for trial. I'll hire the best lawyer there is. I swear I'll get you out of this if it is humanly possible."

"You mustn't put yourself into danger, Simon, you mustn't, not just for me."

"Oh God," he said, "Why did you do it? Why now of all times?"

"It just happened. There wasn't much time to think. He had done so much for me. I'd never have forgiven myself if I hadn't at least tried."

"And was that the only reason?"

"What other reason could there be?"

"How do I know?" he said tormentedly. "For five years we have been apart, it's been as if I didn't exist for you."

"Are you asking me if Zubov is my lover?"

"He or another – how can I know?"

"Are you jealous?"

"Yes, I am, jealous of every hour you have lived away from me."

"And how am I supposed to feel about you and Nina?" He looked away from her fiddling with the stethoscope in his hand and after a moment she went on drily. "If it will comfort you there has been no lover."

"I'm sorry, Galina, I'm sorry. God knows I have no right to question. What is done, is done, and we must face it. Now to be practical. I've prepared some pills for you to keep up the pretence. If they do nothing else they will help to calm you. Your neighbour Fanta – is that her name? – she has packed a bag of necessities for you and will care for the rest till I can send for them."

"And Andrei?" she asked her voice trembling, "Andrei and Ranji? I've been thinking of them every minute of the day. She is a good soul but she has little money and she can't go on caring for them."

"I'll take charge of them. Don't be afraid."

"Nina will not welcome a child of mine in her home."

"Nina doesn't enter into this. In any case she is away just now. She'll not be returning from the Crimea till the end of the month."

"He's only a baby still, Simon, he will need a lot of care."

"Aren't you forgetting? He is my son too and it won't be for long. Keep that hope always in your mind."

There were a hundred things she wanted to tell him, trivial things – that he didn't like drinking milk, that he suffered from nightmares and sometimes woke screaming, that he loved to be independent and could fly into a temper when crossed, that he needed a great deal of love and understanding, but the guard had opened the door and was waiting impatiently. The few minutes allowed to them had fled all too quickly.

"Take the medicine three times a day," he said professionally "and try to rest as much as you can."

"I'll do my best, doctor," she said meekly and gave him her hand.

The guard was watching them closely and he could do no more than press her fingers.

"I will see you in Petersburg."

"If you're lucky," growled the policeman. "They're not so lenient as us at the Fortress."

The Fortress, the Peter and Paul Prison, the place people sometimes called the Russian Bastille where prisoners had been known to disappear and never be heard of again. It struck cold to his heart. Surely they were not already condemned. He watched her walk away with a feeling close to despair. He had achieved one small step but another much more formidable loomed before him. He was filled with a futile rage at the injustice. She was being treated as a criminal, being made to suffer for one simple act of kindness towards a friend.

He had been in Kiev for barely a fortnight and yet his whole life had been turned upside down. As yet he could not see clearly the way ahead only that he had found Galina and could not endure to lose her again no matter how much it cost him. The prisoners had already been despatched to Petersburg herded together in what was little better than a cattle truck but there was nothing he could do about that. Now he must make preparations to return himself. He sent a cable to Nina telling her that he was prevented from coming to the Crimea and then faced the next problem. How could he win the trust of a small child so suddenly bereft of his mother, a boy who was his own son? Better to say nothing about that relationship for the time being, it would only confuse him further.

Apart from taking the little Andrei back to Petersburg with him he had not yet made any plan for the future. When Nina was away he led a kind of bachelor existence in the big house. He could guess at the speculation among the servants if he arrived with a small boy and no credible explanation. It would be grossly unfair to Nina. When the time came he would tell her the truth himself but by then, by some hopeful miracle, it would all be over and Galina would be free. Meanwhile he was pretty sure Missy could come up with some solution, or there was always Luba.

Occupied with his efforts on Galina's behalf he had put off actually meeting the little boy himself simply leaving word with Fanta to have him ready and his clothes packed on the morning they were to leave. Galina had been so certain that the child was his and yet there had been a tiny lingering doubt which vanished abruptly when Fanta pushed forward the small boy and he saw oddly enough not himself but a sudden unmistakable likeness to his brother Robert. So this was his son, the child born from their last night of loving and parting. Unexpectedly it moved him so deeply that for a moment he could not speak.

Andrei was standing very straight, one hand firmly holding on to Ranji's collar.

"Fanta says I must go with you," he said in a small voice.

"Yes."

For all his determination to be brave Andrei's voice had trembled a little. He was used to the students who laughed and joked, played games with him and pulled his hair, but this tall, well-dressed man looking down at him so gravely scared him. This must be the stranger Mamma had had to meet that night when his childish world had so alarmingly fallen to pieces. He clung to the dog as the one stable element in this shifting life.

"Fanta says you will not want to take Ranji with us."

The stranger smiled and the future suddenly looked a little less black.

"Fanta is mistaken. Of course Ranji will go with us. Now say goodbye to her and thank her for looking after you so well."

Fanta hugged him and cried over him and came out to the waiting cab.

"May God go with you, doctor, and with Galina Panova too. You'll not forget. It's a lot to ask, I know, of a gentleman like you but you will write me a line . . ."

"I will. I promise you."

His offer of money had been firmly rejected but she was a good soul. He knew Galina would want it and he was grateful.

He had expected tears and was prepared to deal with them. To have suddenly lost his mother and be taken away by a total stranger from everything that was familiar was a traumatic experience for any child, but there were no tears, only a stubborn silence. To any attempt at conversation Andrei turned on him those large dark-fringed eyes that reminded him so painfully of Galina and only answered yes or no or simply shook his head.

237

At the station he very nearly lost him. Simon had engaged a first class compartment in the northbound express. The enormous blue, yellow and green coaches snaked along the crowded platform. He let go of Andrei's hand for a moment while he dealt with the luggage and the porter made heavy weather of piling it into the compartment. Simon turned to lift in the boy and the dog and they were both gone, lost amid the huge jostling crowd of men and women, Russians, Cossacks, Kurds, Tartars, a motley crew in every kind of costume and speaking every sort of language. Where to find one small boy and one large dog in that throng? Could he possibly have run out of the station and tried to find his way back to Fanta?

The first bell sounded. That meant he had only ten minutes before the train left. He raced along the platform looking for Ranji rather than the boy and he had nearly given up hope when he saw them at the far end on the very edge of the runway in earnest conversation with the driver perched on the footplate of the engine. Thank God for the eternal fascination of trains for small boys! It was the first time Andrei had seen anything like this towering monster.

Sheer relief made Simon speak far more sharply than he intended.

"Now listen to me, Andrei. Never run away like that again, do you hear? Never. You could have been lost and the train gone without us."

Startled at the stern rebuke the boy looked up at him with something like defiance.

"No, it wouldn't. The driver promised that he'd wait for me. He says we're going to Petersburg and it will take a whole day and a night. Do we have to sleep on the train?"

"Yes, we do. Now in you go."

Thankfully Simon lifted the boy into the carriage, pushed Ranji in after him and got in himself just as the second bell clanged and the doors began to slam.

And that was almost the last word he got out of the boy for the rest of that very long day. He leafed through the coloured picture papers Simon had bought for him. He dutifully looked out of the window when his attention was drawn to something of interest but he stubbornly refused to eat anything, not even when they stopped at a large station and the steaming samovars drew up outside and waiters came hurrying through the first class with trays of all kinds of delicacies. All he could be persuaded to take was a little sweetened tea and a biscuit which he gave to Ranji. Simon shrugged it off. When he was hungry he would eat.

Andrei had made up his mind that this stern stranger was the cause of all the trouble. He had spirited away his mother and was now taking him thousands of miles away from everything he had ever known and he was not going to yield an inch except for the most pressing human needs.

In the evening when the lights came on in the carriage and Simon saw the boy's eyelids begin to droop, he lifted out the back of the seat and it turned into a comfortable couchette, took off Andrei's shoes and his jacket, bedded him down and covered him with the light travelling rug. When he thought him sleeping he opened the door quietly into the corridor with the intention of smoking a cigar when the boy suddenly shot up.

"Are you going away?"

He heard the note of panic and answered reassuringly. "Only just outside. You can see me through the glass panel."

When he came back he saw that the boy had taken Ranji up on to the couch beside him and lay asleep with his face buried in the dog's silky fur.

He pulled out his own seat, then took off his coat and lay down not with much hope of sleeping, his mind was too occupied with the problems that lay ahead. At some time between drowsing and waking he heard the stifled weeping and longed to take the boy into his arms and cradle him into sleep as he had done once when Tanya had earache and he had walked the nursery with her all night.

In the early morning he got up, stretching cramped limbs and longing for the pleasure of a bath. The attendant brought hot water and he stripped off his shirt and began to take out his shaving kit when Ranji landed on the floor with a bump and he turned round to see Andrei standing bolt upright on the bed and pointing his finger at something.

"I've got one like that," he said in high excitement.

"One like what?"

"A big brown spot – it's on *my* back too and I can't see it properly because my head won't go round far enough but Mamma showed me in a mirror. She calls me her farthing baby – what's a farthing?"

"A very small coin, why?"

"Mamma told me that I should be proud of it because my Papa had one too and you have, I can see it. Does that mean that you are my Papa?"

So the recognition had come and in the strangest way. Standing up on the couchette and swaying a little as the train raced on Andrei was almost on the level with Simon. They were looking into each other's eyes.

"Would you like it if I were to say yes?" said Simon slowly.

"I asked Mamma if you were in prison like Sasha's Papa but she said no but that you had work to do and one day you would come back."

"And now I have."

"Are you going to live with us now?"

"Perhaps. I'm going to look after you from now on."

"And Mamma too?"

"And Mamma too."

For a moment the boy just stared, assimilating this new and startling idea, this stranger who had become the father he had often wondered about. A sudden jerk tumbled him forward. Simon caught him and for a moment held him very close against him.

Then he said briskly, "Let's get washed and dressed and after that we'll look for some breakfast. Are you hungry?"

The boy nodded, his eyes alight. "Starving."

"Good. That's what I like to hear."

In some totally unexpected way the ice had been broken. The child asked no awkward questions. He was prepared to accept a god-like father who had suddenly and miraculously appeared at exactly the right moment. They still had a very long way to go but by the time the train drew into Petersburg station and ground to a halt they were already on cautiously friendly terms.

16

The train was several hours late due to an unaccountable hold-up. There were rumours that a bomb had blown up part of the line, but whatever the reason it was past midnight by the time Simon's cab drew up outside his house on the Morskaya, far too late to take the boy to Luba as he had first intended. He lifted out a sleepy Andrei whose dazed eyes took in the tall dark house with the pillared portico and handsome brass lamp shedding a ghostly light on the flight of steps. He clung tightly to his father's hand.

The door was bolted so that Simon could not enter quietly with his own key and it annoyed him that it was Marta in her plain woollen dressing gown, her plaits hanging almost to her knees, who opened up to his knocking. He had not wanted her in his household but the Princess Malinskaya had insisted and Nina had weakly given in. He had a strong feeling that she spied on them, reporting back every word that passed between him and his wife.

He said irritably, "Where is everybody?"

"Gone to bed, doctor. We had not expected you to arrive so late." Marta was eyeing curiously the small boy and the large dog who might have been brother to Shani. "Will you be requiring supper?"

"No, we ate on the train. As you see we have a visitor. You had better prepare a bed in the nursery."

"Very good, doctor. I'll see to it myself. Shall I take charge of the little boy for you?"

She stretched out a hand but Andrei had taken one of his inexplicable dislikes. He turned his back on her and buried his face in his father's coat.

"He's tired out. I'll see to him myself if you'll get the bed ready. Prepare some tea and a few biscuits and then you can go back to bed."

"As you wish, doctor."

But Marta's sharp eyes had noted the way the child clung to him and the gentleness of the hand that caressed the tousled brown hair.

In the large comfortable nursery on the second floor, they drank their tea and nibbled a biscuit. Then Simon opened the boy's small valise. He pulled out a nightgown and with it came a rag doll who wore baggy red pants, a spotted shirt, a wide white frill and a clown's cap.

"What on earth is this?" he exclaimed holding it up.

"It's Gobbo," said Andrei sitting up on the bed and holding out his arms. "I thought Fanta had forgotten him."

"And who is Gobbo?"

"Don't you know? He's the most famous clown in the world. Mamma took me to the circus and afterwards she made Gobbo for me." The small face suddenly puckered. "When am I going to see Mamma?"

"Very soon, I hope."

"Tomorrow?"

"Perhaps."

Simon avoided the awkward question. He pulled the nightgown over the boy's head and tucked him into what was usually Tanya's bed, the clown with its painted face lying on the same pillow.

"Now go to sleep. Ranji is here with you quite close to the bed. You're not frightened, are you?"

Andrei shook his head. He would have died rather than confess that he hated to be left in the dark because of the hungry-eyed monsters who crept out of cupboards and from under the bed and then by a miracle this stranger whom he still only half-believed to be his Papa seemed to guess at his fear without being told. He lit the little red lamp beneath the icon that hung on the opposite wall and though it was not his own icon with the blue horse and the scarlet dragon, it was still very comforting. He fixed his eyes on the glowing star in the shadowy darkness and within a few minutes was fast asleep.

When he woke he could not think where he was. The room seemed so large and though it was light already, the closely drawn curtains still shrouded it in semi-darkness. He lay quietly for what seemed hours and was actually about ten minutes and then decided to explore. He climbed out of the bed, hushed Ranji who stood up and gave a mighty shake and crept towards the door. He had no idea where his slippers or dressing gown were but the carpet was thick under his bare feet and inspired by a spirit of adventure he opened the door, pushed Ranji back into the room and proceeded boldly down the passage to where he could see the curving rail of the staircase. He went down cautiously step by step and came to another landing where there were a number of doors. He had paused uncertain which one to open first when Marta appeared at the far end and he stood still clutching Gobbo under one arm as she came purposefully towards him.

"And what do you think you're doing walking around the house at this time in the morning?"

Her tone was sharp and he reacted with his only weapon, a stubborn silence.

She knelt down, her face close to his and he backed away.

"What's your name, boy? Where do you come from? Where's your Mamma, eh? Tell me that."

But he stood there shaking his head until she lost patience, grabbing him by the shoulders and giving him a violent shake.

"The doctor – is he your Papa? Is he? Drop that silly doll and answer me!" and she snatched the rag doll away and threw it on the floor.

But that was too much. He kicked out at her, not very effectively since his feet were bare, but it jerked her away and he picked up Gobbo and ran down the landing opening the first door he came to. By pure luck it turned out to be the right one.

It was the biggest room he had ever seen with a huge bed that was all shining brass and draped with muslin curtains but there was his new Papa in the very act of pulling his shirt on and he was so relieved that he very nearly burst into tears.

Simon's head emerging from the shirt caught sight of him and he smiled in surprise.

"Good God, where have you sprung from so early?" Then he caught the hint of tears and with one swift movement caught the boy up in his arms. "Never mind, we'll get you dressed and then we'll have breakfast together. How about that, young man, eh? Just wait till I'm ready."

He sat the boy on the bed and went back to the mirror to adjust shirt, collar and cufflinks while Andrei gazed around him. He had never seen anything so luxurious, silver-backed brushes on the dressing table with gold-topped jars, an enormous mirror swinging on a stand, lace curtains and draped velvet with silk fringes and a bed so big it could easily have held six of him.

It was so far removed from the cosy three rooms he had shared with his mother that he was not at all sure that he liked it, not even when half an hour later, washed, dressed, his hair well brushed, he was perched up on a chair at a table big enough for an army, eating a boiled egg. He wrinkled his nose at the milk offered to him but accepted tea with lemon and watched his father pour coffee from a tall silver jug now and again giving him an absent-minded smile as he skimmed through a pile of mail. But it was by no means the end of that day's surprises.

As soon as breakfast was over and though it was not much after eight o'clock he was whisked off in another cab with Ranji and his valise driving through unfamiliar streets, past towering buildings and a church whose domes sparkled red and blue and gold like gigantic pineapples in the September sunshine and across a river which ran smooth and dark. When they alighted it was almost like Kiev again, tall houses grouped around a square of grass, though there was no sweet-smelling lime and in one corner a bonfire of debris slowly smouldered with acrid smoke that tickled his throat and made him cough.

They toiled up and up a staircase so steep that his small legs ached and then they were in another huge room but not at all like where he had spent the night. There was no carpet on the floor only a bright coloured rug and it was terribly untidy. His mother would never have let him leave things lying about like that, a jumble of books, clothes, magazines, dirty cups, half-empty glasses, picture frames and canvases and a basket of kittens that made Ranji bristle. There was a huge easel with a painting of what appeared to be naked ladies though they weren't like any ladies he had ever seen, all angles and lopsided faces and a man in a smock covered in paint who waved a greeting, brush in hand and dropped a huge green splash on the floor which no one appeared to mind at all. Then there was a lady who came hurrying from an inner room, her hair tied up in a bright scarf gypsy fashion who reminded him of Fanta only she was much younger and much prettier.

244

"Doctor Simon," she was exclaiming, "how dare you come so early? You've caught us on the hop, Conn and me. It's not fair. I thought you were still in Kiev."

"Luba, my dear, I want you to meet Andrei."

She gave him a quick inquiring glance and then squatted down in front of the boy.

"Andrei, is it? That's a lovely name. I'm Luba," and she shook hands solemnly.

"Andrei Simonovich Panov," he repeated carefully as he had once been taught, "and this is Gobbo."

"How do you do, Master Gobbo?" said Luba and shook the limp sawdust-filled arm. "And now you'd better come and meet Conn."

She took him across to the man who was painting and who looked rather like a kindly bear with a thick brown beard and a great bush of red hair. He paused long enough to extend a paint-smeared hand.

"Ask him to tell you all about what he's painting," said Luba and went back to Simon.

"Well, well," she said in a half whisper, "what is all this? Has your murky past come home to roost, Doctor Simon? He is yours, isn't he? That's as certain as the nose on your face."

"Do you think so? I think he's more like my brother Robert."

She was looking up at him, her head on one side. "So I am right and you a pillar of society too. Who would have thought it?"

He smiled. These two, so different in every way, had been good friends for quite a time now.

"Luba, I have a great favour to ask of you."

"I guessed it might be something like that." She gave him a rueful grin. "God knows we owe you one, in fact more than one, a good half dozen, Conn and me."

"You know whose child he is, don't you?"

Her eyes widened incredulously. "Galina's? No, it can't be. It's impossible."

"It's true. I have found her, Luba, working in a pharmacy in Kiev."

"Oh my God! With the boy – alone – is that why she did what she did?"

"Not exactly."

"Then what was it?"

Very briefly he sketched in the details.

"But why, why?" she exclaimed when he came to an end. "Why didn't she come to me? Why didn't she trust you?"

"You know Galina. Always so damnably independent. She bore her trouble alone."

"But this! I could kill Igor," she said suddenly with a fierceness that surprised him.

"If I could meet up with him I'd save you the trouble," he said grimly. "But that's not the worst. She is in the Fortress."

"In prison? For heaven's sake, why?"

"For trying to save a man who had been good to her."

"The Stolypin affair?"

"You know about it."

"Something. How like Galina to do that. She used to warn me not to get mixed up with the revolutionaries and yet all this time the *Okhrana* have never touched Conn and me. She does nothing and is thrown into prison for it. How desperately unfair life is."

"I'm going to get her released if it's the last thing I do but until then will you care for Andrei for me?"

She was looking up at him oddly. "And if you do succeed, what then?"

"I don't know, Luba. It happened so quickly we had no time . . ."

"Once the *Okhrana* get their teeth into someone, they don't give up easily. What will you do then?"

"I refuse to accept it. I have just found her, Luba, I can't let her go. I won't lose her again."

Luba looked across at the boy. Conn had given him an old brush and a sheet of paper. He was kneeling on the floor drawing great swathes of colour across it and glanced up at them, a blue streak across one cheek.

"Poor baby," she said softly. "How much he must miss her!"

"It's a terrible experience for a small child. That's why I've come to you. Nina is away with the children and their nurse. I can't leave him in the hands of servants. He needs love."

"He needs *you*, Simon. You will come."

"As often as I can. I still have a week or two before I take up work again."

"God help you," she said gently, "it's not going to be easy."

She was right. It was not easy at all, in fact it was impossible. This was Russia, not England as he ought to have known. There was no such thing as "innocent till proved guilty". If it was expedient the administration could sentence suspects without any form of trial, and that was what happened to the group who had been arrested in Kiev. It was necessary to get rid of them as soon as possible before there could be too much public sympathy for their plight. So it was three years in Siberia, regardless of how little or how deeply they had been involved and there was nothing that Simon could do about it. He argued, pleaded, used every tiny scrap of influence he possessed and got absolutely nowhere.

It was Nigel who said, "For God's sake, Simon, give it up. You've lived here long enough to realize you're battering your head against a stone wall. You'll end up by coming under suspicion yourself, British or not. You'll have the secret police camping out on your doorstep if you're not careful and that would be very unfair to Nina."

Simon was standing with his back to him staring unseeingly out of the window.

"It's such a damnable place they are sending her to, plagued by mosquitoes and every kind of filthy fly in summer and sixty degrees under in winter. I heard something about it from a medical team who went out there a few years ago. If the climate doesn't kill you, then typhus, malaria and a dozen other ghastly illnesses will have a good try and she has done nothing," he brought his fist down on the sill with bruising force, "absolutely nothing!"

"Are you so sure of that?" argued Nigel with some impatience. "If I remember rightly Galina was mixed up with some very unsavoury types over on the island, that fellow Igor Livinov for instance. Wasn't she thick with him at one time? Couldn't he be at the back of this assassination?"

"What the devil are you implying?"

"Well, you must face up to it, old man. It's only what *she* tells you after all. She walked out on you five years ago without a word of explanation and quite a lot can happen in five years in more ways than one. She could be far more deeply involved than you think."

"Even if she was I would still owe her a great deal. She is the mother of my son."

"That's easy to say. She knows you well enough to be very

247

sure of winning your sympathy with a tale of that kind, you must realize that. Meeting her in Kiev so suddenly is bound to have knocked you sideways. She's a clever young woman and she always had you properly hooked, didn't she? She would naturally take advantage of that and who could blame her after all?"

"Are you quite finished?" Simon turned round and Nigel thought he had never seen anyone's face have so bleak a look. "If I didn't know you meant well," he went on evenly, "I might feel inclined to cram those lies down your throat. If you imagine for one moment that Galina was a mistress to be picked up and tossed aside without a second thought, then you're wrong. We had become part of one another. When I knew she was gone, it was as if I had lost part of myself. Nina is unhappy because I give her so little and I know it and it makes me feel guilty. I loved Galina and I still love her and there's nothing I can do about it. To find her again and then lose her is like chopping off part of myself for the second time. So now you know."

It wasn't a boy's outburst of passion. It was something so deeply felt that Nigel was appalled. He said tentatively, "In that case what *are* you going to do?"

"I don't know, not yet. I have obtained one concession. I am allowed to see her, ostensibly to decide about the boy. Prisoners are allowed to take their children with them and what that could mean to a five-year-old child is something that doesn't bear thinking of but she must decide."

"And then what?"

Simon shrugged his shoulders but before he could reply a door slammed, there was a burst of childish voices and Lydia appeared in the doorway with Selina and Edward. They rushed across the room hurling themselves on Simon.

"Papa said you had come back from Kiev."

Selina at nine was tall and slim, a living picture of her mother. Edward, a sturdy seven-year-old, had outgrown his baby weakness. He swung on Simon's hand, his eyes bright.

"Papa said you were in the theatre when there was all that shooting. Did you really see it?"

"You shouldn't ask things like that," said Selina reprovingly.

"Why not? It's interesting. Was there lots and lots of blood?"

248

"Not as much as you'd think."

He gave a huge sigh. "It must have been so thrilling. Nothing like that ever happens to us."

"I should hope not." Across their heads Lydia exchanged a smile with Simon. "Forgive my bloodthirsty brats. That's quite enough from you two. Be off with you now. Nanny will have your tea ready."

"Goody, I'm starving," announced Edward. "Will you come too, Uncle Simon? Cook makes scrumptious cakes."

"Not this time."

"Go on, both of you," said Lydia, "and don't keep Nanny waiting." As the door slammed behind them, she turned to Simon. "Are you sure you won't stay and dine with us? We're on our own, no guests."

"No, Lydia, thank you. I've a great deal of work to catch up on after the last week or so and Nina comes home very soon."

"We'll have a party when she does. We've seen nobody all the summer. It will be like old times."

"Nina will enjoy that."

Lydia went with him to the door of the apartment and reached up to kiss his cheek.

"I'm sorry about all this, Simon, really I am. I liked Galina so much. If there is anything I can do . . ."

"There's nothing, but bless you for thinking of it."

He pressed her hand and went quickly.

Galina was sitting on the narrow iron bed trying hard to be calm and marshal her thoughts into some kind of order. She had been told she was to see Simon that afternoon and the very thought of it was both wild happiness and pain. Everything had happened so quickly that she was still overwhelmed by it. The meeting with Simon that had shaken them so profoundly, the attempt to save Zubov which had ended so disastrously.

She had been in the Peter and Paul Prison for two weeks and the first night had been by far the worst. The train from Kiev had been hours late. Exhausted after the two-day journey in cramped uncomfortable conditions they had been conveyed in closed carriages through the dark streets, informed curtly by the prison governor that they would be detained until sentence had been passed and then were marched along dark stone corridors and down green slimy steps before being turned into solitary cells. The doors clanged dismally one after the other. When it came to her turn she was thrust through so roughly that she stumbled to her knees on the rough stone floor. The guard's lantern flashed over the iron bed, the small table, the wooden stool, and then was taken away. She was shut into darkness till morning with walls five feet thick and no sound except the squeaking of the sentry's boots as he paced up and down outside, and the tolling of the cathedral clock at each quarter of an hour, ticking away one's life minute by minute.

She was in the Fortress, a name that had created terror since childhood, the place where Peter the First had strangled his son with his own hands, where the Empress Catherine had imprisoned the Princess Tarakanova for daring to raise her eyes to the throne, the rats climbing over her when the Neva flooded her cell with black filthy water. Good men and bad, statesmen, poets and revolutionaries, saints and martyrs, had been tortured, murdered, buried alive, chained to walls, condemned to a long slow death or driven to insanity in the loneliness and despair of dark deep dungeons.

She went through hours of nightmare till morning crept through the long slit of window high above her head and in desperation she dragged the stool over and clambered on to it even though all she could see was a grey outer wall and a tiny scrap of blue sky. Then a bird flew across it and she told herself that if she could survive a night like that, then she could survive anything.

At first she thought the deadly monotony would drive her mad. The sour prison smell that no amount of carbolic could kill turned her sick, the thick walls seemed to close in on her so that she could not breathe. In the humid heat of September the walls ran with moisture and she felt stifled though at night she shivered under the one thin blanket.

After the first few days the prisoners were allowed half an hour's daily exercise in the prison courtyard and though they were forbidden to speak to one another, it was wonderful how much could be communicated in whispers and by gestures. At first the others shunned her. She had never been one of them and afterwards she learned that they suspected she was a police informer put in the prison to spy on them. The men were exercised at a different time from the women so she did not see Zubov and it was not until the end of the first week that she made any kind of contact. One of the prisoners was a young girl hardly more than a child and during that daily march around the courtyard she suddenly gave a sigh, sank to her knees and collapsed on the rough dirty cobbles. The sentry would have jerked her to her feet if Galina had not stopped him while the others crowded around.

"Can't you see she is sick? She needs medical help not punishment," she said sharply.

He was only a country boy and overawed by the voice of authority. He fetched his sergeant and she was taken away to the infirmary. When she returned a few days later she drew Galina aside.

"I have to thank you," she whispered.

"How do you feel? Are you better?"

The childish lips trembled. "The doctor tells me I'm pregnant. What am I going to do?"

"Is your husband one of the prisoners?"

She blushed. "Stefan is not my husband, not yet. We were to have been married in the New Year."

"You could plead your pregnancy. They might let you stay here."

"Oh no, I couldn't. I couldn't let him go without me. One of the prisoners in the hospital said that if you are married they sometimes let you stay together. Do you think that will happen to us?"

"Perhaps. We can only hope."

There wasn't much Galina could do for her but after that the girl continued to walk as close to her as she could and in trying to give comfort she somehow found a certain relief from her own torturing thoughts.

When the guard came to fetch her she was trembling. She had not been able to eat anything and the bowl of thin soup and the slice of black bread lay untasted on the table. Her heart thudded so thickly as she followed the soldier along the dark corridor that she could scarcely breathe. Then they had climbed up from the dank stone walls of the old prison and were in a much newer part of the fortress. A door was opened, she was thrust inside and blinked in the sudden blaze of light. Not only Simon was there but Luba in a gay red scarf and a small boy who stared and then screamed "Mamma!" and came running towards her. They met half-way and she was hugging him and he was burrowing his head into her while the other two looked on saying nothing.

He was trying to tell her everything that had happened to him so that the words tumbled over one another.

"We were a day and a night on the train, Mamma, and then we went to the hugest house I'd ever seen and Ranji was there and Gobbo and now I'm staying with Luba and Conn is showing me how to paint pictures. Look, I've brought one for you," and he pushed a grubby sheet of paper into her hand.

"Thank you, darling, that's beautiful."

"Papa is going to buy me a box of real paints and then I can draw lots and lots of pictures."

"Papa?"

"He has come back. You said he would but I didn't know at first. I found it all out by myself on the train. He has a brown spot on his back just like me and he says he was a farthing baby too . . ."

It brought so many memories flooding back. She glanced up at Simon and then back again at the boy.

"And does that make you happy?"

"Oh yes. I *like* him." He paused looking up into her face anxiously. "You like him too, don't you, Mamma?"

"Yes, darling, I like him very much."

"Is he going to live with us now?"

"I don't know yet."

But the happiness of reunion was necessarily very short-lived.

Simon said quietly, "I'm sorry but we are not being allowed very much time and there are things we have to discuss."

"Yes, I understand." She got to her feet looking across at Luba. "It's wonderful to see you and I'm so grateful to you for looking after him."

"Oh Galina, you idiot! You know I'd do anything." Luba came running throwing her arms around her, hugging her tightly. Then she scrubbed at her eyes and grabbed the boy by the hand.

"Come along now, Andrushka."

"No," he said defiantly, "I don't want to go."

"I'm afraid you must for a little while." There was a note of authority in Simon's voice and the boy looked up at him, lips trembling.

"I want to stay with Mamma."

"Go with Luba, darling," whispered Galina and gave him a little push.

"Will you come?"

"Very soon."

Reluctantly he let Luba lead him out of the room and Galina turned away ashamed of the helpless tears running down her face.

After a moment Simon said, "Take this," and she groped for the handkerchief he was holding out to her.

"I'm sorry. I didn't mean to behave so foolishly." She mopped at her face and turned resolutely towards him. "I meant to be so sensible, so calm and strong."

"I tried, Galina, believe me I tried every way I could to get you released."

"I know." She was twisting the handkerchief between her hands. "I've been trying to think clearly ever since I knew where we were to be sent. It's not a place to take a child, is it?" There was a catch in her voice. She controlled it with difficulty. "And yet what can I do? It's not fair to burden Luba. There's my mother. She would care for him if you were to take him to Dannskoye."

"My God, Galina," he burst out, "do you imagine I would let anyone bring up my son but myself?"

"You have children, Simon, Nina's children. You can't expect her to welcome your mistress's bastard in her home."

"Nina is my wife. She will do as I say and that's an end of it."

There was a hardening in him she had never expected. If Nina had got her way with him once, she would not succeed again.

"But will he be happy?"

"He will learn to be happy. It's all any of us can hope for." He paused and then said quietly, "I too have been thinking. There is an alternative. I could come with you."

"Come with me?" she whispered.

"Why not? It's not unknown and there is a crying need for doctors where you are going. I'd be doing far more useful work than I do here in Petersburg dealing with the imaginary ailments of the over-indulgent rich."

For a few seconds the thought was so dazzling, it gave her such a lift of the heart that she could only stare at him, then sanity returned with a rush. She knew Simon and she knew herself. They could never live happily at the expense of someone else. It would end by destroying their love – better to keep it as it was, better to endure the pain of parting.

"No, Simon, no. Nina is your wife, you can't abandon her."

"Our marriage is little more than a sham. I'm not blaming Nina. The fault is as much mine as hers. She is unhappy because I can't give her what she wants."

"I know Nina better than that. She loves you, Simon, she needs you. She must have a prop to cling to, she always did, and if you were to leave her, she would go to pieces. How could you live with that? How could I? And there are your children, the little Tanya, your baby son – what would happen to them? I'd give anything in the world for it not to be like this, but we must face reality."

"You don't understand, Galina." He turned round to face her. "You don't know what this means to me. I had just about come to the end of the rope when I met you in Kiev. It seemed like a door opening, giving me renewed hope, renewed life, and now the door is slammed shut again and I am left outside it with nothing."

"Simon, dearest Simon," she said earnestly, "you have your work and it is valuable, you know it is, and even if you were to come with me, they would never let us be together. I've spoken to some of the people here. They have more experience of exile than I have. Unless you are married, there is no certainty of even being sent to the same place. We could be hundreds of miles apart and you would have sacrificed everything that makes your life worth living for nothing. How would I feel then?"

She was right. He had known it from the start but some inner need had compelled him to make the gesture he knew was impossible. They were silent for a little, the width of the room between them that would soon stretch to more than a thousand miles.

She said quietly, "There is something you could do for me."

"What is that?"

"It's going to be hell on earth if I cannot work. Medicines are always needed and I do have skill. It may be possible to start a dispensary. If you could pack a box for me. You would know better than I what would be most useful and if Zubov is sent to the same place, perhaps we could build it together."

He felt a sudden rage of anger that someone would be working beside her and he would know nothing of it, have no right to know anything. She had her life as he had his. He watched her face. It had grown thinner in the prison, the cheekbones more sharply defined, shadows under her eyes. It reminded him of the first time he had seen her, the face of a saint or martyr he had thought then, a Joan of Arc but filled with fire and passion and it tormented him that she had somehow gone beyond his reach.

"Yes, I can do that," he said at last. "I'll make sure it goes with you and some money too."

"I shan't need that."

"You will take it and be glad of it. Money can buy comfort wherever you are even in the hell of Siberia."

The guard knocked and they knew their time was up.

"I'll see you again before you leave," he said quickly, "I'll come to the station. I will bring the boy."

"No, don't, much better not. Explain to him afterwards. Love him for me, Simon, please please love him for me."

The guard knocked again more impatiently this time and she hesitated and then flew across the room putting her arms around his neck. He felt her tears on his face, her lips warm and clinging to his, then she had pushed him away and run from the room, stumbling in her haste. The door slammed behind her.

He returned home to find the house swarming with children, nurses and servants amid all the bustle of sudden arrival. Jake was in the hall busily superintending the luggage.

"It was the mistress," he explained, "who suddenly took it into her head to come home so the Princess Sonia decided to come with her." He grinned. "It was a fair old picnic on the train I can tell you but we managed."

Simon frowned. It was the last thing he wanted at this moment but there was no help for it now.

"Where are they all?"

"With the children in the nursery."

"Is everything all right, Jake?"

"Aye, doctor, right as ninepence so far as I could see. Here, take care of that box," he called out to the boy bouncing one of the trunks up the steps, "it's got breakables in it."

Simon had not expected Nina for at least another week and he wondered what had brought her back so abruptly. He went on up to the second floor and collided with Tanya careering along the corridor in her usual headlong manner.

"Papa!" she shrieked and he picked her up in his arms.

"Well, my pet, glad to be home again?"

Tanya looked like a blonde angel but could be an imp of mischief. Even Sonia's twin boys though they were six months older stood in awe of Tanya in a rage. She put her arms around his neck and planted a cold wet kiss on his cheek.

"I can swim," she announced grandly, "ever so far, miles and miles."

"That's my clever girl."

He carried her into the nursery where the two nurses and Sonia were busily unpacking essential luggage and the servants were carrying in nursery supper. The two boys, fair-haired like Niki and as like as two peas, galloped joyously up to Simon, both talking at once.

"QUIET!" yelled Sonia, well accustomed to topping them. "Do you want to deafen Uncle Simon? For heaven's sake sit down, both of you, and let Nurse give you some supper. Tanya too. No nonsense now."

They gave in to authority and peace restored, she came across to Simon taking his arm.

"Sorry for the invasion," she said. "We'll have to stay the night I'm afraid. Our house is shut up for the summer and Nina decided to come home in such a hurry, there was no time to wire Niki. He'll be here tomorrow to take us back to Dannskoye."

"What made her come back suddenly like that? I thought she intended staying till the end of the month."

"That's what we had decided." She glanced across at the children squabbling happily over their supper and drew him away towards the window. "It was Baby Paul really. He was taken ill about a month ago and though he is better now she really is terribly worried."

"Why? What's wrong with him?"

"We don't know. No one seems to know. He is just beginning to walk and he fell over. Nobody thought anything of it. It seemed just a little bruise but it got much worse, very dark and discoloured, and he was in such dreadful pain, he screamed and screamed. We called the doctor. He wouldn't say anything, didn't give any real explanation, only gave him something to soothe the pain and make him sleep. Then it faded gradually and he seemed quite well again."

"The doctor may have been right. It could be nothing. I'll take a look at him."

"He's asleep now." Sonia put a hand on his. 'Be gentle with her, Simon. She is very upset and she has such faith in you. Nothing would satisfy her but that we should come back at once so that he could be in your care. She was terribly disappointed when you did not come as you had promised."

"I had to stay. Something has come up. Thank you for telling me, Sonia. Where is she by the way?"

"Getting settled in, I expect. I said I'd look after the children."

"I'll go and find her."

It so happened that there was no opportunity to talk about anything serious that evening. Niki turned up unexpectedly and over supper they talked of a thousand things as people do who have not seen one another for three months. Simon gave them a guarded account of the assassination but didn't mention Galina. Niki had news of the estate to which he was devoting so much of his time and the progress of Sonia's particular favourites among the animals and humans and they both went to bed soon after ten since he was anxious to make an early start in the morning.

Simon took the opportunity to pay a short visit to the nursery. The excitement of coming home had been too much for Tanya and she was still awake when he bent over her. She put up her arms to pull him down to her.

"I missed you, Papa."

"Did you, darling? I missed you too."

"Why didn't you come when you said you would?"

"Papa has to work to pay for things like this," he said pulling the ear of the white fur rabbit tucked in beside her. "Now go to sleep like a good girl. You can tell me all about it in the morning."

He tweaked her nose, making her squeal with pleasure and then went across to the cot where his baby son lay asleep. Paul was now a year old and looked brown and well, much fatter and stronger than when they had gone away. He lifted the light covering and saw the plump legs quite unblemished under the long nightgown and yet he was worried. What Sonia had told him had an ominous sound but on the other hand babies fell and bruised themselves with no harm done and he would not let himself believe his little son was suffering from anything worse, not yet, not until it was proved without a shadow of doubt.

One thing struck him forcibly as he went down the stairs. Galina had been right. Even if his crazy notion of going with her had even been remotely possible he could not have deserted Nina and still lived with himself.

When he came into their bedroom she was already in her dressing gown and brushing the long fair hair.

"Where have you been?" she asked.

"Saying goodnight to the children. Tanya, little monkey, was still awake."

"And Paul?"

"Sound asleep. He looks a great deal better than he did. He's put on weight."

"Did Sonia tell you about what happened?"

"Yes, she did."

"It was dreadful, Simon. He was in such pain and there was nothing we could do to ease him. I thought he was going to die. And the doctor was so strange. He kept asking me questions – had my brother or my father ever suffered in the same way? Well, Niki certainly hasn't and neither had Papa. Two of Mamma's brothers died young, I believe, but what has that to do with Paul? It can't mean anything, can it?"

It could mean a great deal but he was not going to say anything about that yet.

"Don't fret about it. Now you're home we will watch over him carefully. There's no point in worrying yourself sick over something that may never happen again."

She put up a hand and clasped his. "It makes such a difference knowing that you're there. I feel safe. When your wire came, I knew I couldn't stay any longer. As soon as Paul was fit to travel, I urged Sonia to come back."

She had risen and taken off her dressing gown. "It feels so good to be home again. Aren't you coming to bed?"

"Not yet."

After the long absence she would expect him to share her bed, make love to her and he couldn't, not after that afternoon, not when his mind was still filled with Galina and their inevitable parting. He felt empty of feeling, drained of emotion. To take her in his arms and simulate a false passion revolted him.

"You must be very tired after days and nights of travelling and I am terribly behind with my work. Better if I leave you to sleep undisturbed tonight."

It was a lame excuse and he knew that she was aware of it. She climbed into bed and pulled up the fine linen sheets but when he bent over to kiss her goodnight she turned away her face.

"Who was the little boy you brought here while I was away?" she asked.

"Who told you about that?"

"Marta said something."

He might have known she would and now he was faced with either lying or making the long explanation when of all times he would have avoided it. And yet to deceive her would only make it worse in the end.

"I was intending to tell you but there has hardly been time, has there, with Sonia and the children and Niki?"

"Who was it, Simon? Was it the child of one of your doctor friends whom you had been asked to bring back to Petersburg?"

Almost it seemed as if she was begging him to lie to her, concoct some tale that she could believe and then put it out of her mind and he could not do it. He could not allow his son, Galina's son, to grow up in secret as if he were ashamed of him, not even to spare Nina's feelings.

"No, it was not quite like that," he said at last, "but it's very late. Let's leave it till morning. I'll tell you the whole story then."

So it could be true after all, she thought. What was it that Marta had said in that sly voice of hers? "The boy was so like the master, so very like, it quite struck me." She had told her sharply not to be silly and dismissed it from her mind but now – perhaps she was right after all.

"I'd rather you told me, Simon. You know how lightly I sleep. It will nag at me all night if you don't."

"Very well, if you insist." He took the plunge into deep waters and prayed they wouldn't drown, both of them. "If you must know, Andrei is Galina's son."

She looked up quickly. "And yours?"

"And mine."

The simple admission nearly took her breath away. "But how? Why? All these years I thought . . ."

"It's not at all what you're thinking. I had not seen her since the day I left for England till a few weeks ago when I walked into a pharmacy in Kiev and there she was."

"And the child too?"

"And the child."

"Is that why she went away, because she was pregnant?"

"No, not entirely."

"Why then?" And when he did not reply immediately she sat up in the bed beating one hand on the coverlet. "I must know, Simon, I must know."

He told her briefly, unemotionally, his voice dry and controlled, about their parting, the rape and the agony of doubt that had driven her away.

"And you believed her?"

"Yes, I believed her."

"You fool!" She began to laugh. "You blind fool! Of course that wasn't the reason. She went off with Igor. It's obvious, isn't it? And then of course he deserted her, left her high and dry when it suited him. It would be just the kind of thing he would do. What a godsend it must have been to her when you turned up."

"Be quiet, Nina, don't say such stupid things when you know they are not true."

"Of course they are true. And you swallowed it all whole. I can just see you, on your knees to her, swearing to care for the boy, to bring up Igor's brat as if he were your son."

The laughter was becoming wilder and he swung round on her.

"Stop it, Nina, do you hear me? Stop it at once."

But she couldn't stop. She was shaken by a mingling of laughter and tears that was rising into hysteria and he slapped her cheek hard, stunning her into silence.

She stared at him, one hand flying to her face, her eyes filled with surprise and indignation.

"You hit me."

"I'm sorry. It was the only way to bring you to your senses. Do you want the whole household to hear you?"

She leaned back against the pillows, white and shaking, and knew he was right. It had been a battle against something she had always feared and now it had happened and she could do nothing about it.

"What are you going to do?" she asked hopelessly.

"There's nothing I can do. In a few days time she will be banished to Siberia, three thousand miles away. That should make you very happy."

Galina could be ten thousand miles away but it still wouldn't bring Simon back to her.

After a moment she said, 'Where is the boy now?"

"Luba is taking care of him."

"Since he means so much to you, I wonder you have left him with people like that."

His friendship with Luba and Conn had always been a bone of contention between them.

"She happens to be a trained nurse, she understands a child's needs and above all she will give him love," he said coldly.

"Oh, of course, she is Galina's friend so she can do no wrong, I suppose. Well, one thing is sure, I won't have him here. Do you understand, Simon? I won't have him sharing a nursery with Tanya and Paul. What would people say if I did? What would Mamma think?"

"I'm not in the least concerned with what your mother may think or any of your so-called friends. He is my son and this is his father's house. Whether or not I bring him here to share our life is my decision and you will abide by it."

"And supposing I refuse?"

"There is an alternative. We can live apart."

"You can't mean that."

"Only if you drive me to it. My mind is made up, Nina. You won't change it by threats or tantrums or fits of childish hysteria. We're beyond that now."

She moved restlessly against the pillows, the fair hair tumbled about her face.

"Oh God, I was so happy to be home and now you have spoiled it all."

"I'm sorry. I wanted to wait and break it to you more gently but you couldn't do that, could you?"

"Would it have made it any better?"

"Perhaps not." He sighed looking down at her for a moment. "I'm going to fetch you something to help you to sleep."

"I don't want it."

"You're going to take it whether you like it or not. I'm your doctor as well as your husband."

When he returned with the mixture in a glass she pushed his hand away pettishly but he insisted, putting his arm around her and raising her up, the glass held firmly to her lips as if she were a child again.

"Come along now, drink it or you'll be fit for nothing in the morning."

"Will that matter?"

"Certainly it will. You've been away for three months. The household needs the mistress's hand."

She swallowed it with a grimace and caught at his hand as he took the glass from her.

"Do you still love her, Simon?"

He did not reply immediately, putting the glass carefully down on the table before turning back to her.

"Do you want me to answer honestly?"

She turned away her head. "That means you do."

"There is more than one kind of love, Nina," he said quietly then bent over to kiss her cheek. She moved her head quickly so that his lips brushed against hers and he drew back.

"Try to sleep, my dear. You need the rest."

When he had gone she buried her head in the pillow too unhappy and too spent even to weep. She had not lost him because she had never possessed him, she thought wretchedly. There might be other kinds of love but she had only wanted one and that had been given to Galina long ago and now she had reclaimed it. It was a bitter truth she found hard to accept and her tempestuous spirit rose up in rebellion against it. Somehow, though God knows it would be difficult, she was going to fight against it.

A few days later when she was lunching with her brother, Nina put down her knife and fork and said casually, "Will you go with me to the railway station this afternoon?"

Niki had taken his family back to Dannskoye and come up to the city again on a legal matter connected with the estate. He looked across at his sister frowning.

"What do you want to go to the station for?"

"Isn't it the day the prisoners leave for Siberia?"

"How the devil do you know that?"

"Valentin told me. Part of the guard are called out." She glanced at him suspiciously. "Simon has told you about it, hasn't he? You knew all the time. You came up specially."

"No, not specially, but after all Galina grew up with us, didn't she? I felt — I don't know — kind of responsible."

The servants came in with fresh plates and a dish of fruit. She waited till they had gone.

"I suppose you know that Simon is going to bring her son here"

"I thought perhaps he would. As the boy is his, he can't really put him in an orphanage, can he?"

"Oh you men! You all stick together. Nobody thinks about me. Why should I be forced to put up with my husband's bastard in my house? If the child *is* his?"

"Here, steady on, Nina. Of course he is."

"And what are people going to say about it if I do?"

"What they damned well please." Niki had an aristocratic contempt for what he thought of as middle-class morality. He grinned suddenly. "Don't you remember Great Uncle Gaev? He had three boys all by different mothers living together in his house in Moscow and Great Aunt Nadia never turned a hair. Did pretty well for themselves too. Sonia would have him like a shot but I expect Simon would prefer to keep him under his own eye."

Nina irritably pushed away her plate and stood up. "Well, if we're going, I suppose we'd better get ready."

"If you must but I don't know what you expect to gain from it."

He looked at his sister as she stepped into the carriage and thought she had dressed more for a fashionable garden party than the departure of a bunch of convicts. The long sable stole Simon had given her on her last birthday hung gracefully over an elegant pearl grey costume and ostrich feathers curled in her black hat. The nurse brought Tanya down the steps in her white coat and straw bonnet with its pink ribbons.

"Look here," he protested, "we can't take the baby with us. It's not the thing at all"

"Tanya is not a baby and one is never too young to know about those less fortunate than oneself — at least that is what my husband says."

"Have it your own way," grunted Niki, "but Simon won't like it."

He lifted the child into the carriage and nodded to the coachman. She's showing off, he told himself, she wants to make sure that Galina is fully aware of how much she has missed and I don't much care for being mixed up in it.

At the station the prisoners were crowded together surrounded by guards. Niki pushed his way forward with Nina close behind him holding Tanya by the hand and with his air of authority and a judicious handful of roubles was allowed to pass through the barrier.

It was Tanya who saw her father first. She screamed "Papa!" and went racing down the uneven platform. She tripped and would have fallen if Simon had not caught her up in his arms and it angered him deeply that Nina should be determined to spoil even these last few moments with Galina.

"Are we going on the train?" demanded Tanya.

"No, we are saying goodbye to someone who is."

"Why, Papa, why?"

"Because she is going a very long way away."

He put her down and she stared up at Galina. "Is it you?"

Galina smiled at the little girl. "How pretty your daughter is, Simon, and how like her mother."

Then Nina was there with Niki close behind and she put her hand possessively on her husband's arm.

"I thought I'd find you here, dearest. They telephoned from the hospital, something about one of your patients." She turned to Galina, smiling brilliantly. "Simon is always being run off his feet, you know. He's so popular. What a long time it has been, hasn't it, Galina?"

"A very long time. No need to ask how you are, Nina, you look wonderful."

There could not have been a greater contrast between the two women, Nina so elegant, so fashionably chic, and Galina in a long dark coat, a scarf tied peasant fashion over her bright hair, and yet her face had an austere beauty, a strength, a calm acceptance that Nina against her will found herself envying.

The guards had begun to hustle the prisoners into the train, a long third class coach with its bare wooden benches attached to the Siberian express. There was hardly time for Galina to smile at Niki and for him to take her hand warmly in his.

"You wouldn't know me these days. I'm what Nina calls a country bumpkin only interested in my horses, my cattle, my timber crop and the factory output, not forgetting our two boys. Sonia sends her love."

"Tell her I think of you all very often."

The guard had taken her by the shoulder and was pushing

her away. Simon had both her hands in his, only time for one last long look between them before he kissed them one after the other and she turned quickly to climb the steps and vanish from his sight.

The train slowly drew out with a long drawn-out scream, a lot of clanking and clouds of white steam.

Tanya said, "Who was that lady, Papa?" and when he did not answer, she plucked imperiously at his sleeve. "Where is the train going?"

"Don't ask so many questions, pet," said Niki detaching the little girl and firmly taking her hand. "Where would *you* like to go? Shall I take you and Mamma to Yelisavetev for a special tea?"

"With cream cakes?"

"As many as you like."

"Are you coming with us, Simon?" asked Nina.

He turned around then. "No, my dear, I'm going to the hospital. If they telephoned it must be something serious. Niki will see you and Tanya home. Enjoy your tea."

He gave the child a fleeting smile and walked quickly away.

For a moment it seemed as if Nina would go after him, then she shrugged her shoulders and took Tanya's other hand.

"Come along, darling, let's forget about Papa and find that special tea Uncle Niki has promised us."

17

A week after Galina had gone, Andrei and Ranji were installed in the nursery. To do him justice Simon tried to be scupulously fair but as a reaction against the emotional disturbance of Galina's sudden return to his life, he plunged into work early and late so that his visits to the children's quarters were not so frequent as they had been. Tanya with a child's acute perception was aware that this rather silent little boy who inexplicably called her own beloved father "Papa" occupied a large part of his heart.

She was a child who took everything hard just as Nina had done and she had been spoiled not only by her mother but by her Russian nurse. Simon would have preferred an English Nanny like the starched Miss Roberts who had ruled his own growing up, but Nina had insisted even before Tanya was born that her own beloved Nianya should join the household. Marina was a peasant, almost illiterate, but warm-hearted, generous, loving. In all her baby troubles Nina had fled to her for comfort and Tanya had done the same.

There was friction almost from the start. If Andrei so much as touched one of her toys, Tanya flew at him like a small wild cat, backed up by Marina for whom she could do no wrong. Andrei retreated into a stubborn resentful silence but as the weeks passed there was worse to come.

"Silly old rag doll," Tanya said scornfully one day when he had sat Gobbo on a chair beside him. "Only babies have rag dolls."

"He's not a rag doll, he is a clown."

"He's dirty. My Mamma says he ought to be burnt."

She tried to snatch Gobbo from him and in the struggle one arm was torn off. Andrei looked down at the beloved doll, the bright yellow shirt split, a trickle of sawdust oozing out of the battered body. He gave a howl of rage and flew at Tanya. They fell to the floor, fighting, biting, kicking, till a horrified Marina tore them apart. Nina was called in. Andrei was sent to bed supperless and the rag doll taken away and hidden on the top shelf of the toy cupboard. It was one of the last links with his mother now hopelessly lost to him. He did not cry then but waking up in the night Tanya heard stifled sobs coming from the bed over on the further side of the room and was guiltily triumphant.

The day disaster struck was about a fortnight later. November was doing its worst. Outside snow and rain swept along the streets blown by the icy winds and a thick wet mist crawled up from the black waters of the Neva.

The morning began badly at breakfast time when Andrei said suddenly, "When I lived with Mamma we used to have honey on our bread."

"Your Mamma is wicked," said Tanya thickly through her creamy porridge.

"No, she isn't."

"Yes, she is. That's why she has been sent away."

"No, it's not."

"I saw her go. You didn't. She went by train, thousands and thousands of miles away. Papa told me. She didn't want you any more so she left you behind."

"That's not true."

"Why didn't she take you with her then?"

Tanya waved her spoon triumphantly and Andrei unable to think of an answer gave her a push. Porridge slopped all over the table.

Marina coming in with the baby in her arms clicked her tongue disapprovingly. She frowned at Andrei.

"You ought to know better than to hit your little sister, a big boy like you. Now finish your breakfast, both of you."

The long day dragged on. The weather was too bad for them to be taken for their usual morning walk and tempers began to fray. In the afternoon they were left alone for a while. Andrei had become very fond of Paul and in some strange way the baby responded to him with delight, crowing and laughing at his antics as he never did with Tanya.

He was learning to walk even if rather unsteadily and Andrei was playing with him urging him to take a few steps and then taking care to catch him before he sat down with a bump. Tanya watched them with a growing jealousy.

"Let me have him," she said trying to push Andrei away.

"No, you might let him fall."

"No, I won't. Paul is *my* brother."

"Papa said he was mine too and I must help to take care of him."

"No, he didn't."

"Yes, he *did*. Go *away*, Tanya. Paul doesn't want you."

"Yes, he does." Resentment boiled over. "You've no right to be here at all. You're only a – a – a bastard. I heard Marina say so."

Neither of them had the slightest idea what the word meant only that it was something dreadful.

"I'm not," he shouted at her, "I'm not, I'm not."

"Yes, you are, and your mother is too, a horrid wicked bastard!" screamed Tanya triumphantly and gave him a tremendous push.

Taken by surprise he fell backwards cannoning into the baby. Paul stumbled across the floor and hit the huge porcelain stove that warmed the nursery. There was a stunned silence and then he began to scream with fright. A moment later Marina rushed in followed by Nina.

Tanya terrified at what she had done was pointing at Andrei.

"He pushed him," she sobbed, "he did. I saw him, I saw him!"

"I didn't, I didn't." Andrei was on the floor, his arms around the baby trying to comfort him.

Marina snatched Paul from him and Nina white with fear turned on Andrei, the bitter angry words pouring out.

"You wicked, wicked child. Do you know what you have done? You've killed him. Wait till your father comes home. When he hears of it he will send you away."

Scarcely knowing what she was doing she picked up the first thing that came to hand which happened to be Ranji's leash lying on the table and slashed Andrei across the face over and over again. Then she threw it away from her and followed Marina into the night nursery. With one horrified look at the wheals slowly crimsoning across the boy's cheeks Tanya ran after her.

It was the culmination of weeks and weeks of silent misery. Andrei went straight to the toy cupboard, clambered on a stool, found the mutilated form of Gobbo, listened for a moment to the voices in the other room and then went out of the door. It was late afternoon, the servants busy in the kitchens. He crept down the two flights of stairs to find the hall empty. He could not unfasten the front door, the lock was too high, but he knew there was a small door which he had gone through once with Jake to see the horses in the stables. He opened it quietly and went into the courtyard. Ranji who had been taken out earlier and was drying off in one of the stalls came to peer out of the door. Andrei called him softly, then grasped his collar and led him out into the street at the back of the house. The snow and rain hit him in the face as he turned the corner lashed by a raw wind. He shivered and then walked boldly forward through the grey cheerless afternoon.

Simon had had a long hard day at the hospital and he returned home late and very tired. Nina met him in the hall looking distraught.

"Thank God you're here at last. We tried to contact you but they said you could not be disturbed."

"I was probably in the operating theatre. There has been

an accident at the steelworks and some appalling injuries." She was helping him off with his heavy coat and shaking off the rain and snow. "What did you want me for?"

"It wasn't my fault, truly it wasn't," said Nina defensively afraid now of what she had to tell him.

"What wasn't your fault?" There had been crises before which usually turned out to be trivial. He put an arm around her shoulders and took her with him into the dining room. "It's freezing outside and I'm perished. What about pouring me a drink, then you can tell me all about it."

"Brandy?"

"Please."

Her hand shook so much that she half filled the glass. He laughed as she handed it to him.

"I've eaten nothing all day, my dear. What do you want to do? Make me drunk? Now what's all this about?"

"Andrei has disappeared," she said bleakly.

"Disappeared? What on earth do you mean?"

"What I say. He's just not here. We've searched everywhere, the house, the attics, the stables, everywhere we could think of. He must have run away."

"But he can't have done." He put down the glass almost untasted. "He's hardly more than a baby still. Where on earth could he run to?"

"I don't know," she said wretchedly, "I don't know, Simon. The servants have been out searching, Jake, Vassily, all of them. I didn't know what else to do."

"When was this? You'd better tell me what happened."

"The children were playing together in the nursery. Marina came to speak to me about something. Then we heard terrible screams. We rushed upstairs. It seems Andrei had been teaching Paul to walk and because he wouldn't do what he wanted, he hit him and flung him away from him. The baby crashed into the stove, Simon, he's not only badly bruised but his face is scorched all down one cheek. I've been half out of my mind with worrying about him."

Simon was frowning. "Andrei would never do a thing like that."

"Oh of course you would say that about your favourite but you don't see as much of the children as I do. He's jealous, Simon, jealous of Tanya and Paul. Marina has mentioned it more than once."

"I still can't believe it." He looked at her keenly. "What did you do to him?"

She turned away her head. "I was terribly upset naturally *and* angry. I might have spoken sharply to him, that's all."

"And what part did Tanya play in all this?"

"It was she who told us what had happened, sobbing as if her heart would break, poor child. You know how fond she is of Paul. We've had quite a difficulty in quietening her."

"And when was all this?"

"Oh I don't know. I suppose it was about four o'clock when we knew he had disappeared."

"Good God, over three hours ago. Do you realize that anything could have happened to him, a child alone out in the streets on a night like this?"

"Jake says that Ranji has gone too. He must have taken him from the stables."

"We'd better get on to the police. He might have been picked up somewhere."

She clutched at his arm. "Please, Simon, come and examine Paul first. I've been desperately anxious about him."

"I'll telephone, then I'll come."

He had already guessed that there was more beneath the story than appeared on the surface and cursed himself because in his preoccupation he had not probed too deeply, simply assumed that the children would shake down together. He was overwhelmed by a wave of guilt. He had failed Galina. He had promised to cherish their son and this was the result.

The police had no information of any child found wandering and he went up the stairs to the nursery, his mind filled with the picture of a distracted boy walking through those crowded streets, frightened, desperately lonely, looking for what? – his mother? Where was he likely to go? How does one begin to search?

The baby was sleeping uneasily, soothed by one of Marina's own herbal remedies which against his will he had been forced to accept as sometimes proving very effective. He examined him carefully. The contusions were of a dark purplish colour, there was some swelling and Paul stirred at even the slightest touch. Though Simon spoke reassuringly, Nina knew by the look on his face that he was unhappy about it. But for the moment there was nothing he could do to ease the child further and he went down again to question Jake and the other servants.

He was putting on his heavy coat when Nina came running down the stairs.

"Are you going out yourself?"

"I can't just sit here waiting for news which may never come. God knows where I can look for him first."

He was on his way to the door when the telephone rang in his consulting room. Nina answered it and came back.

"It's for you. A woman."

"Damnation! Probably the hospital."

But it was Luba's voice which answered him.

"Thank goodness you're there, Simon. Andrei is here."

A huge wave of relief surged through him. "How? Why?"

"I can't talk now. The telephone belongs to a neighbour and she doesn't like me using it. I think you had better come."

"Yes, of course, at once. He is not hurt, not injured in any way?"

"No, but he needs you badly."

"I'll get there as soon as I can."

Nina was watching him anxiously. "Is it Andrei?"

"Yes. Luba has him."

"Luba?" Resentment flared in her at once. "Why her? How did he get there?"

"God knows. I'm on my way now."

"Why must you go? Now you know he is safe she can bring him back. Why not stay and eat first?"

"For heaven's sake, Nina! I don't like to think what the boy must have gone through . . ." He shouted to Jake to call him a cab.

"You won't stay there?"

"I don't know. It depends what I find."

He brushed past her leaving her looking after him, resentful and yet half-ashamed of what she had done.

The rain had turned into a blinding sleet and it was very cold. When he reached the studio, he paid off the driver and bounded up the stairs two at a time. Luba met him at the top.

"Where is he?" he demanded. "What happened?"

She restrained him with a hand on his arm. "Wait a moment. He's in bed wrapped up warmly. Conn is with him."

"How, in God's name, did he find his way here?"

"That I don't know. He's only been here once since that first time."

"When was it?"

"About an hour ago." She was helping him out of his coat. "Conn and I had been out. When we came back up the stairs we heard Ranji growl. Then we saw him. He was crouched against the door, soaked through to the skin, with his arms around the dog."

"He must have been wandering about the streets since four o'clock."

"We rubbed him down and wrapped him in a warm blanket but he won't speak, Simon. He just looks at me and shakes his head and he won't eat either, not a mouthful. And there is something else you should know. He's got great red wheals across his face. Someone has hit him and savagely."

"God Almighty, what could she have been thinking of?"

"Nina?"

"I don't know, Luba, I don't know. I'd better see him."

In the little bedroom off the gaunt studio Conn got up from beside the bed and Simon took his place. A damp Ranji lifted his head and then lay down under the caressing hand. The boy looked tiny and defenceless in the big bed. He still clutched a sodden Gobbo who had been wrapped in a piece of clean flannel.

Simon put his hand gently on the flushed forehead. "Well, son, what's all this about then?"

To begin with he had no more success than Luba. Andrei turned away his head and Simon could see the cruel marks of the leather strap on the pale cheeks and he burned with anger. He went on speaking gently, soothingly and after a while the large eyes so like Galina's were turned towards him.

"Is he dead?" he asked in a tiny whisper. "Is Paul dead?"

"No, he's not dead, far from it. He's only bruised."

"She said I'd killed him."

"Who did?"

"She did. Tanya's Mamma."

"And then she hit you?"

"She was angry. She said you would send me away."

"And that was when you ran off."

"I was frightened. I wanted to find Luba."

"Thank God, you did."

272

"Are you going to send me away?"

"No, of course I'm not. We're farthing babies, don't you remember? We stick together."

The boy stared at him and then with a gulp buried his head against his father's coat. Simon's arms went round him. Over the tousled head he met Luba's eyes and nodded. Presently she came in with two steaming bowls of soup.

"Now, you two great babies," she said cheerfully, "you are going to eat something, the pair of you. It's no use you shaking your head, young Andrei, you're going to eat it all up and so is your Papa. He has spent all day making people feel better and so he needs to keep his strength up."

She gave Simon the plates to hold while she sat the boy up against the pillows. Then she put the plate on his knees and held up the spoon threateningly.

"Now am I to feed you like a baby or are you going to eat it up like the big boy you are? Your Papa too. I'm not going away till it's all gone, every single drop."

Out of the corner of his eye Andrei watched his father take a mouthful and then tentatively he dipped in the spoon. The soup was hot, thick and very tasty. He suddenly discovered he was starving.

"That's my brave boy," said Luba when it had all gone. She picked up the rag doll. "Poor Gobbo looks as if he could do with some feeding up too. If you let me have him, I'll make him as good as new while you have a little sleep. Would you like that?"

"You won't burn him?"

"Burn him? Certainly I won't. He'll be there up to all his tricks when you wake up. Don't be afraid."

She took the plates away and left them alone together. Relieved of fear and guilt the boy relaxed and bit by bit Simon wormed most of the story out of him until he had a pretty clear picture of what had happened. He stayed with him until he had drowsed into sleep, then he tucked him up and went to join Luba and Conn.

"I can't tell you how grateful I am. I tremble to think what could have happened if he'd not found his way here."

"Poor little beggar," said Conn. "It must have seemed like the end of the world. What are you going to do about it, Simon?"

"I blame myself. I should have realized what was happening.

273

Marina is a good kind soul but the children need someone calm and sensible and unprejudiced in charge of them and I think I know just the right person if I can persuade her to come."

"Who is that?"

"Nina's old governess, Miss Emily Hutton. She's retired now of course but she might do it. I'll go and see her tomorrow."

"What about Nina? What is she going to feel about it?"

"I'll deal with Nina myself. Luba, will you keep him for a few days with you? Let the heat go out of it. Let them all calm down. I'll come each day just in case that soaking brings on a fever."

"Would you like to stay the night here? We're not very grand but we could manage."

"No, better not. Nina worries about the baby. It's easier for both of us if I'm there."

"Well, you know where to come if you want a refuge and to take care of yourself," said Luba going to the door with him. "Galina left you both in my charge, you know."

He smiled and kissed her cheek. "Sometimes I don't know what I'd do without you."

It was past midnight by the time he reached home and found Nina waiting up for him. She was curled up on the drawing room sofa and she looked up when he came in.

"I thought you'd never come."

"You look worn out, my dear. You should have been in bed hours ago."

"I couldn't have slept. Did you bring him with you?"

"No. Luba had put him to bed. He was wet through and very chilled."

"Will he be all right?"

"I hope so. I pray so."

"Shall I ring? Do you want some food?"

"No, Luba gave me something." He suddenly turned to face her. "Nina, why did you tell the child that he had killed the baby?"

"I told you. I was so upset I didn't know what I was saying."

"Is that why you hit him across the face with a leather strap?"

"Is that what he told you?"

"He didn't need to. It was obvious. You wouldn't treat one of the dogs so brutally. Is it because he is Galina's child? Do you hate him so much? You knew we were lovers before you married me. It didn't matter to you then."

"Oh but it did, it mattered very much but I thought it was all over." She got up and moved restlessly around the room. "Now it's different. How do I know you've not been lovers since?"

"My dear girl, I met her in Kiev for a few hours one evening. We did not spend them in bed and His Imperial Majesty's prisons do not permit intimacy of that kind," he said ironically.

"Oh you can think up very clever answers but what would have happened if she had not been arrested? What would you have done then?"

It was late and they were both of them tired and strung up. He knew it was the wrong moment and yet he had to answer truthfully.

"I don't know, Nina, I honestly don't know but I can tell you one thing. When I knew it was to be Siberia, when for one very brief moment I thought I might go with her, it was Galina who rejected me, Galina who reminded me that I had a wife and children who depended on me."

"Of course *she* is your saint, *she* can do nothing wrong! Well, I'm different. This is *my* home and I won't have her child here, I won't I tell you."

And suddenly he was angry, too angry to be kind, too angry to compromise. "You will, Nina. I've let you have your own way about almost everything but in this instance you will obey me and no threats will change my mind. You will accept him here and you will treat him just as you treat Tanya and Paul."

She faced him, wild-eyed and rebellious. "All you think about is Andrei. Even Tanya feels it and as for Paul, you've never cared about him. He could be sick, he could die, and you wouldn't grieve. He doesn't matter to you any longer, does he, because you have another son, *her* son?"

"Nina, that's not true. You're talking nonsense."

"Am I? You wouldn't come to the Crimea when he was so sick . . ."

"I didn't even know . . ."

But she was not listening, she swept on without pausing.

"And now he might be dying upstairs after what happened today and all you can think of is Andrei and whether he has taken a fever. I hate you for that, I hate you! I'll go to Dannskoye, I'll take the children. Niki will care for us and you can stay here alone with your bastard . . ."

"Nina, this is crazy. Listen to me . . ."

He took her arm but she jerked herself away from him.

"Let me be. Don't come near me, don't touch me . . ."

She flung open the door and stormed out of the room, running up the stairs and into their bedroom. He followed her only to find the door slammed in his face and the key turned in the lock.

He stood there for a moment uncertain what to do for the best. There had been storms before and in some measure he had grown accustomed to them but never one quite so serious. After a little he knocked gently but there was no response and he went slowly down the stairs and through the consulting room into the study which so often before had been his refuge.

He sank into the armchair utterly weary realizing he had handled it badly, and yet not knowing how else he could have behaved and yet be honest with himself and with Nina. And it wasn't true that he did not care about Paul. These past three months he had watched the baby carefully, had discussed similar cases with other doctors, had tried to make up his mind as to the best treatment and faced alone the tragic possibility that the child might be condemned to an early death.

He sat there for a long time, his head in his hands, too tired even to make the effort to go up to the room where he slept occasionally when he was on call at the hospital.

It must have been a couple of hours later when he told himself he was being ridiculous. He had a long day in front of him and at this rate he would be fit for nothing. He was just about to get up and turn out the lamp when the door slowly opened and Nina stood there, looking like a ghost in her long white nightgown, her fair hair tumbled about her shoulders. For an instant she stared at him, then she ran across the room to fall on her knees beside his chair stretching up her arms to him, her face wet with tears.

"I'm sorry, Simon, I'm sorry, I'm sorry."

"My dear girl, what on earth are you doing wandering around the house like this and with bare feet? You'll catch your death of cold."

"I don't care. I had to come to you."

"Well, I *do* care. I'm going to carry you straight back to bed."

"Not yet. I want to talk to you."

"We'll talk upstairs," he said firmly. "I'm not having another patient on my hands." She put her arms around his neck as he lifted her up. "Gently now," he whispered as they went up the stairs. "We don't want to wake up the entire household."

He put her on the bed and pulled up the blankets but she caught tight hold of his hand.

"Don't go, Simon, please don't go. I didn't mean any of those hateful things I said. It's only because I love you so much and I can't bear to know that you . . .," she choked a little over the words, "that you don't love me in the same way. You do understand."

"Yes, I understand. You're shivering. Are you sure you're warm enough? Shall I fetch you something? I daresay I can rustle up a hot drink quite as efficiently as Cook."

"Oh darling," she smiled tremulously, "I'm sure you can but I don't want it, really I don't. There is something I must tell you. I've thought and thought about it and now I must say it."

"What is it?"

"It's about Paul." She looked up into his face. "You know what is wrong with him, don't you? You've known all along and you've been keeping it from me."

That startled him. "What do you know?"

"I was in your study one day. I know you don't like the servants touching your papers. I looked at the books on your desk. I read what you had been writing. It's haemophilia, isn't it? That dreadful blood disease. That's what the doctor in the Crimea suspected, it's what he was trying to tell me and it means that he is going to die."

"My dear, we can't be certain, no doctor can. Many children grow up and live to a good age. We will have to watch him carefully, guard against falls and accidents. We'll fight it together. There's no need to despair."

"And there's something else," she went on, "I know now why you have kept away from me. You don't want me to have another baby, do you, because if it's a boy he could be like Paul and it all comes from me. I read that too. It made me feel sick with myself. It's not right, it's not fair to you. Mamma should have told me why my two uncles died so very young."

She was shaking now but there were no more tears. For perhaps the first time in her life she was trying to face a crisis bravely and not run away from it.

"You mustn't think that, Nina," he said gently. "It does not always happen. There are so many things we don't know. We are still only groping in the dark. Think of Niki. He is strong and well and so are his two boys."

"But Sonia comes from Papa's side of the family, not from Mamma. She doesn't carry that dreadful taint."

"Oh my darling," he said moved to an infinite pity. "Don't call it that. You're not a leper. Such a thing was never once in my mind." He drew her towards him. "You've been tormenting yourself with it all these weeks and never told me."

"I suppose I was afraid. I thought if I didn't speak of it, it would somehow miraculously go away. That's being silly, isn't it?"

"Not silly. We all do that sometimes."

She leaned her head against his shoulder staring in front of her. "It's so unfair," she whispered, "so cruelly unfair. Why should this happen to me? When I was young, I used to think how wonderful to be grown up, to be married, to have babies of my own and now . . ."

"Real life has not measured up to the dream. Poor Nina."

She was nearly twenty-five but sometimes she still seemed the tempestuous girl of seventeen he had first known. He pushed back the heavy hair and kissed her forehead.

"What about those sleeping pills I gave you? Shall I fetch one?"

"No."

"You should get some rest and so should I for that matter," he smiled ruefully. "I'm operating tomorrow. My patient won't thank me if my hand shakes."

She looked up into his face. "Simon, will you stay with me tonight, please darling? Then I'll know you forgive me for Andrei, for everything."

"I think maybe we need to forgive each other."

He got up and began to take off his jacket. Presently the lamp extinguished, he slid into the bed beside her and she lay curled up against him too spent for love or passion. Galina might hold his mind in thrall but alone in the wastes of Siberia she did not have the warm living body, the strength, the gentleness and the comfort, she told herself, she still had the best of it and for the time being at any rate she knew a measure of content.

"My dear Simon, are you really asking me to give up my comfortable life and my dear little flat and go back to teaching two no doubt quite abominable children?" said Miss Emily Hutton looking across at him seated in her best armchair, a cup of her finest China tea in his hand.

He had outlined the situation quite frankly. It was never any use beating about the bush with Miss Hutton. She had a quiet way of probing to the heart of a problem in no time at all.

"You needn't leave here if you don't wish it. Jake can fetch you in the carriage in the morning and bring you back at night."

"Do you realize that I'm sixty-eight, much too old to begin again with babies. What about one of those nice girls who come over from England quite regularly? There are one or two I could recommend."

"They are not babies. You know Tanya, and Andrei is a bright child. He can read already, Galina saw to that." He set down his cup and leaned forward. "If I engage one of these English girls, Nina would be at loggerheads with her in a week but she knows you. You are her dear Missy, she respects you, she will listen to you. Just for a year or two, that's all I'm asking," he went on persuasively, "till Andrei is old enough to go to school."

She looked at him quizzically. "I warned you about Nina, didn't I? But like all men you thought you knew best. You do like to make trouble for yourself, Simon. Is it wise to bring up Galina's son with Nina's children?"

"I don't know whether it is wise or not but that is what I intend to do," he said flatly. "I promised Galina and I intend to keep my promise."

"And she still matters to you so much?"

He got up and moved away from her. "If you must know, she does, but that has nothing to do with this." He turned round to face her. "Will you come?"

"And what about the arthritis in my left hip? I'm not as agile as I was."

He smiled. "I promise you shall have the very best treatment I or any of my colleagues can give you."

"Bribery now, is it? Very well, I will come, God help me, and God help you too, you may need it."

"Bless you." Impulsively he bent down, taking her hand and kissing it. "I can't tell you what a weight you've taken off my mind."

"Oh well, I was always a fool where a handsome man was concerned," she said lightly, "and I'm fond of Nina and of Galina too. She's got more 'bottom' as my old father used to say of his hunting friends than any of you. When do you want me to start?"

"In a few days' time if that will suit you. Luba is taking care of Andrei but I shall fetch him home soon."

"That will do very well. It will give me time to get back into harness as they say of an old carthorse."

"You're a fraud," he said affectionately, "in your heart you're younger than any of us. Don't get up. I'll see myself out."

So it was settled. Missy came to preside over the nursery, only insisting on spending her Sundays in her own little flat and Simon heaved a sigh of relief. Tanya was still wary of Andrei though dear Papa had explained very carefully that she must be specially friendly towards him because he didn't have a Mamma like she had. She also discovered that though Missy could be very kind she was not in the least impressed by tears and when in a fit of pure rage at not getting her own way, she threw herself on the floor and refused to move, no one ran to pick her up with hugs and kisses. Instead they let her lie there carefully stepping over her and it all became so boring that she gave it up. So the next few weeks passed peacefully enough before they went to spend Christmas and New Year at Dannskoye.

At the beginning of December the snow came falling in great thick feathery flakes and the countryside was transformed. Gone were the grey mists, the drenching sleet, the damp biting cold that ate into your very bones and instead the snow lay white and sparkling in the sunshine and crackled under foot. Frost edged trees and shrubs and Andrei who had never lived in real country before was entranced by the huge house, the gardens that seemed to stretch into infinity where he could run and run, the slender birches black and silver skeletons against the blue sky.

The servants had built a snow mountain for the children, a tall wooden construction with a long flight of steps to reach the top and great chunks of ice formed into a long chute. For days water had been thrown over it freezing hard and then smoothed into a long slippery slide. On Christmas Eve the children were all out in the garden, only Paul left behind in the nursery. Selina and Edward were already there with their Nanny; Lydia and Nigel would be coming later with Simon when he was free from the hospital. Valentin Skorsky had ridden over and he was sportingly taking the younger children down the slide on the improvised sledges that looked rather like big tea trays. They shouted and screamed as they fought and squabbled over their turns. Shani, growing elderly now, refused to leave her warm corner by the stove but Ranji with the other dogs as excited as the children tore madly from one to the other barking hysterically.

The short winter's day was already beginning to draw in when Niki said firmly, "One more turn everybody and that's the lot. It's growing too cold out here."

"We can't go in yet," objected Tanya. "Papa isn't here."

"He will be very soon."

"I want more slides down the mountain," she insisted.

"Very well. But only one more turn each then in we go. Come on now, no nonsense."

He had begun to shepherd them all together when they heard the distant roar.

"There he is," yelled Tanya and they all stood still to listen, but instead of the clip clop of horses' hooves on the icy road there came the steady purr of an engine and out of the faint mist came the shining black monster, two enormous yellow eyes turned full on them. There was a blast on a motor horn and the sleek Mercedes rolled to a standstill with Simon at the wheel, Jake beside him and Lydia and Nigel in the back, all in goggles and veils and long motoring coats like creatures from some other planet.

Tanya screamed "Papa!" and the children swarmed around the car. They were still comparatively rare even in Petersburg so excitement rose to fever pitch.

"My God, cutting up the rich must pay well!" exclaimed

Niki admiringly to his brother-in-law. "So you bought one after all."

Simon grinned. "Delivered just in time. It's Nina's present. Where is she?"

"In the house with Sonia."

"I'll fetch her," said Selina and darted up the steps.

"I want to ride in it, Papa," said Tanya hanging on to his hand.

"And me, and me!" came in a chorus from Andrei and the twins and even Edward who had been trying hard to be very grown up.

"Wait till Mamma comes, then we'll all go."

Nina and Sonia appeared together in the doorway bundled up in furs and gaping at the black monster with its handsome brass fittings.

"Your motor car, Madame, complete with chauffeur," said Simon with a grand gesture towards Jake looking rather bashful in his elegant uniform, black to match the car.

"For me?" Nina came running down the steps. "Oh Simon, it looks marvellous."

"Now you can show it off to all your smart Petersburg acquaintances. Want to try it?"

"May I?"

"Come on, the lot of you."

He helped her into the front seat. Tanya and Andrei fought over who should sit with her which he promptly settled by dumping the little girl on her lap and Andrei between them. The other children with Sonia piled into the back and they set off on a stately drive round the estate at a thrilling twenty-five miles an hour.

"Did you really buy it for me?" asked Nina when the car had been taken away by Jake to be housed in the stables and the children had been packed off to the nurseries.

"Of course I did. I'm not all that enthusiastic myself. I still prefer horses. Are you pleased?"

"I've wanted a motor car for ages and didn't dare to mention it. Thank you, darling," and she reached up to kiss him.

In the drawing room a giant spruce had been installed and Sonia had decorated it with long strands of silver looped in and out the branches.

"How lovely that tree looks. We never had one before."

"I suggested it to Niki. We always had a tree when I was a

boy. I thought the children would enjoy it," Simon replied.

If that was a little touch of England, Russia also had its ancient customs and, modern and sophisticated as the young people were nowadays, they still formed part of the Christmas feast.

There was the traditional *kutya*, boiled wheat sweetened with honey and sprinkled with poppy seeds and never served till the first stars glimmered in the sky. No one did more than taste it of course but it was there and up in the nursery the hay was spread on a table under the icon with a pot of *kutya* and a candle stuck in it to remind them of the Christ Child in the manger.

Niki remembered his father telling him that *his* great grandfather always threw part of it into the winter fields saying at the same time, "Grandfather Frost, here is a spoonful for you, please do not touch our crops!"

The morning after Christmas Day Nina was down early to ride with her brother. Sonia was pregnant again and feeling the effects of it and so preferred to lie late in bed.

"Where's Simon?" asked Niki giving her a hand into the saddle. "Enjoying a well-earned rest?"

"Heavens, no. That's not like him at all. He has taken Andrei to see Galina's mother."

"Has he, by Jove? Well, she *is* the boy's grandmother after all. In actual fact I asked her if she would like to join us for part of the festivities."

"Niki, you didn't!"

"Well, since Mamma decided to go off to Uncle Gaev in Moscow, I thought why not? But she refused." He gave his sister a sidelong look. "Is it all settled between you?"

"If you mean about Andrei, yes, it is, more or less." She was silent for a moment before she turned to him.

"Niki, will you do something for me?"

"If I can."

"Will you try and persuade Simon to give up that wretched clinic of his? He wears himself out with it in addition to all his other work and I know he pays for it himself. It's not good enough. He is far too busy and too tired to go anywhere nowadays. We hardly go into society and if you and Sonia are not in Petersburg, it means I either have to go alone and make excuses for him or not go at all."

"My dear girl, do you think he would listen to me for a single minute? Simon is a man dedicated to his work. You should know that by now."

"Oh I do, I do, and I'm tremendously proud of him, but sometimes it is not so easy."

"You married the wrong man, my love. You should have done as Mamma always wanted and taken Valentin Skorsky."

"Don't be silly," said Nina scornfully, "as if I could ever have married anyone as dull as that. I would have been crazy with boredom in a week."

"You'd be surprised. Val has blossomed since his mother died. He's quite the man-about-town these days, puts me to shame *and* he's still a bachelor. Eating his heart out for you, I shouldn't wonder."

"What utter nonsense."

"It's sober truth." Niki paused and then went on more seriously than usual. "You wanted Simon, Nina, and went all out to capture him but you never stopped to think what you were taking on, did you? He's not really one of us. He is a radical-thinking, liberal-minded Englishman with a strong sense of duty. That's what Galina understood so well."

"I don't want to talk about Galina."

"Of course you don't but it's true all the same. You didn't bargain for that, did you, or that though he spoils you . . ."

"He doesn't do anything of the sort."

"Oh yes, he does. Sonia hasn't half the gowns or luxuries you take for granted, but all the same in anything important you can't change him, try as you may. Now Valentin would have been like putty in your hands."

Nina stirred uncomfortably at her brother's shrewd analysis. "You don't know what you're talking about. I love Simon."

"I know you do and that makes it all the worse, doesn't it?" He smiled and leaned across to pat her hand comfortingly. "Anyway that's enough brotherly preaching for one morning. Val's coming tonight and bringing his house party with him. I thought we might have some dancing. I daresay Missy will tinkle the ivories for us and I'm sending for two fiddlers from the gypsy camp on the other bank of the river."

Nina's eyes lit up. "What fun. It'll be like the old days."

"You can flirt with Val and make your husband jealous," said Niki lightly.

"I wish I could but you forget. I'm an old married woman with two babies."

"What's that got to do with it? Come on, I'll race you to the next copse."

Niki smiled and spurred his horse forward.

"Wait for me, you beast."

Laughing she caught up with him and as the horses galloped side by side for a brief moment they were boy and girl again putting behind them the frustrations of marriage and the endless problems of a great estate in these troubled times.

That evening despite what she had said to her brother Nina dressed with a very special care. Her evening gown of peach coloured silk was fashionably draped and dazzlingly embroidered with golden beads.

Simon coming in said teasingly, "You look grand enough for a ball at the Winter Palace. Is it new?"

"Yes, it is. I haven't had anything to dress up for lately, have I?"

"No, you haven't and that's my fault. Sorry, my dear," and he dropped a kiss on the fair hair. "You look enchanting."

It was a family party of mostly close friends and without the presence of the Princess Malinskaya presiding over them like a figure of doom in her rigid mourning black, they ate and drank and danced till long after midnight. With one eye on her husband Nina flirted outrageously with Valentin who, at first taken by surprise, ended by playing up to her and enjoying himself immensely.

After the more formal dances the fiddlers began to play lively gypsy airs and she whirled about the room moving from one man to the other, skirts flying, and ending flushed and triumphant to a burst of applause.

She looked across to where Simon was standing beside Sonia's chair applauding as loudly as anyone. Her husband, she thought bitterly, the most distinguished man in the room and the most indifferent, not in the least disturbed by her antics with Valentin.

She moved purposefully across to him. "I suppose you realize you haven't danced with me the whole evening."

"I thought you had more exciting partners."

"Last waltz," announced Niki taking Sonia by the hand and the fiddlers broke into a sweet slow melody giving it a sensuous yet stirring quality as only they could.

Simon put his arm around her and they glided on to the floor. In actual fact he had not been so indifferent as she believed. He had been thinking how young she still was and how difficult these last few months had been for her. It made him feel guilty and he drew her close feeling her press herself against him, warm, clinging, vibrant. The new perfume from Paris that he had given her was subtly provocative.

It was nearly four o'clock before the party broke up. The guests began to depart, shouting goodbyes as the stars paled in the sky. The horses snorted and stamped, their breath like mist in the icy air as the sleighs slid over the packed frozen snow.

Missy yawned. "I'm off to bed. I'm too old for these junketings."

The servants were gathering up glasses and extinguishing lamps and candles. Niki and Sonia went up the stairs hand in hand.

Simon said, "You go on to bed, Nina. I'll just take a quick look at the children."

He undressed quickly in the small dressing room, put on a gown and went along to the nursery wing of the big house.

Andrei lay spread out, his arms flung above his head, Gobbo on the pillow beside him, his new toys piled on a chair beside the bed, content for perhaps the first time since his mother had been lost to him. Simon touched his cheek gently and pulled the covers over him.

Tanya had her nose buried in the pillow, the new doll nearly as big as she was half pushing her out of the bed. He turned her over. She stirred sleepily but did not waken. The baby Paul, recovered, thank heaven, was sleeping peacefully.

They still used lamps at Dannskóye and the huge bedroom was full of shadows when he returned to it.

Nina said, "You've been a long time."

"Just wanted to make sure they were all right. They've all been over-excited as well as over-eating these last few days."

He slipped off his dressing gown, moved to the bed and then stopped. There was a childish wantonness about the naked body bathed in the golden light that caught him by the throat.

"What are you trying to do?" he said huskily. "Seduce me?"

He saw the colour flood up into her face. She made a grab for the sheet and he stopped her.

"No, don't."

Then he turned out the lamp and took her in his arms.

Their loving that night was fierce and passionate and afterwards when blissfully contented she lay sleeping, his arms still around her, her head pillowed against his shoulder, he lay wakeful despising himself for satisfying his hunger for another woman on the body of his wife.

Where was Galina now, he wondered? Did she ache for him as he did for her or had she found someone else to give her love and comfort? He was ashamed because the very thought still gave him pain. It was long past dawn and the house was already stirring before he slept.

Part Four

LEON
1913–1917

18

The Municipal Dispensary in Kirensk was a low wooden building of two rooms, one where the drugs and medicines were compounded and dispensed and one behind which served as living quarters where Galina lived alone. The rooms were divided by a huge brick stove which heated up when lit and needed to be fed constantly with chunks of pine, heavy to carry and difficult to chop for a woman alone. Ice formed in corners of the rooms and never melted during the long winter so that sometimes despairingly she thought she would never grow used to the intense cold.

One evening in the February of 1913 she was unpacking a large wooden chest of medical supplies which often took as long as five months to reach them so that essential items had always run out long before the next consignment arrived.

"Good evening. May I come in?"

The courteous voice was so unexpected that she looked up startled. The stranger in the doorway bulked enormous in thick padded coat, scarlet muffler and felt boots and she wondered if he belonged to the geological team who had lately arrived in Kirensk on their way east exploring this inhospitable and barren region for valuable minerals.

"What can I do for you?" she said briskly.

He pulled off his shaggy fur cap as he came in and ran his fingers through the thick black hair.

"Have you anything to cure a confounded headache?" he muttered almost as if ashamed to confess to anything so puerile.

She looked at him more closely. A hangover after a night of illicit drinking would have received short shrift but she had learned to observe and diagnose and was fairly sure that it was not that which was troubling him.

"A throbbing pain behind the eyes, distorted vision, a feeling of nausea?" she asked.

"Yes," he said in surprise. "How the devil do *you* know that?"

"It's my business to know. You are suffering from a bad migraine, my friend."

"Oh no," he exclaimed in disgust. "That's a sickness for grandmothers and pregnant females!"

His strong indignation made her laugh and he thought he had never seen anything more attractive in this frightful place to which an unjust fate had banished him. He liked the broad brow, the large eyes smiling back at him. He was not sure what he had expected in a female pharmacist but it was certainly not this.

"Pain is no respecter of persons," she was saying. "It can strike even the strongest. Do you have frequent attacks?"

"Pretty seldom, thank God, but I'm fit for nothing when I do. Can you give me anything for it?"

"Certainly I can. I'll give you some powders. They should help but whatever you do, don't wash them down with vodka."

"Not much chance of that," he replied drily.

"Are you with the new batch of exiles?" she asked as she handed him the medicine.

"Yes, Leonid Pavlov at your service," and he gave her a sketchy little bow. "I am a geologist or I was until they booted me out of my job."

"And now?"

"I'm in charge of the team under Sergeant Rodinsky of His Imperial Majesty's police force."

"I gather you don't like him."

He shrugged his shoulders. "Does anyone like their gaoler? Also he is a bully and as ignorant as a pig."

"Pigs are very intelligent creatures."

"So they are," he returned her smile. "I beg their pardon. What do I owe you for this?"

He put down some money on the table and she took it, giving him some change.

"Take the powders sparingly and if they don't work, come back again."

"I most certainly will." He gave her a flashing smile revealing very white teeth in a face tanned by sun and wind, replaced his cap and went out.

She looked after him with the first spark of interest she had felt for many weary months. He had brought a freshness, a touch of life and vigour into the hut with him and she regretted that he would soon be moving on and the deadly monotony would seem all the more unbearable because of it.

She went back to finish her unpacking, putting the drugs carefully on the shelves and checking them off her list.

Sometimes it was almost impossible to believe that she had been in Siberia for over a year though God knows there were times when the days seemed interminable, especially in the winter when they were shut into icy darkness for most of the twenty-four hours.

Parting from her son had left a gaping wound that time had done no more than skin over. The meeting with Simon, the few hours they had spent together, had brought to vivid passionate life all the love and longing she had fought so hard to conquer. It had hit her so hard that wrapped in her own misery she had scarcely noticed her companions on that interminable train journey taking her further and further away from everything she had known and loved. It was not until they reached Irkutsk on the edge of Siberia that she woke from her frozen apathy and it was Zubov who roused her, deliberately harsh, deliberately provocative, forcing her to feel ashamed of giving way to self-pity.

"If you're going to live then you've got to fight," he castigated her. "Forget your son, forget your lover, there's work to be done here and to work is to worry about others, to think about them, to help them, no matter how maddening or difficult they may be. It's anger that keeps one alive."

So she began to look around her. The group from Kiev had contrived to remain together, shepherded by Zubov. They were nearly all of her own age or younger, earnest, intelligent and mostly with a brave acceptance of the injustice that had sent them there coupled with a burning conviction that one day they would win through and return triumphant.

In Irkutsk Olga, the pregnant girl from the Fortress, was married to her Stefan in a pathetic ceremony to which everyone

291

tried to contribute something, if it was only a pretty handker-chief or a pinch of carefully hoarded tea. It was there that Galina opened the box that Simon had packed for her and which incredibly had arrived intact since he had made sure to label it medical supplies. He had chosen with care, drugs and remedies of every kind which she might need and would know how to use with a medical dictionary which could provide further instruction. There was money too in an oilskin wrap-ping and she drew out a little of it to buy a wedding veil for Olga and then hid the rest away, not that she didn't trust her companions but some of the guards, poorly paid and brutal, would think nothing of robbing a female prisoner.

From Irkutsk it was the task of the governor to allot the prisoners to various destinations scattered among the small towns and villages and it was Zubov who fought to get himself appointed official pharmacist and Galina as his assistant. The governor was a humane man and prepared to listen to an intelligent and educated man who promised to provide a useful service in the wilderness to which he was obliged to send so many hapless human beings.

In the spring when the ice melted and the River Lena was navigable they moved up to Kirensk. They travelled by *pausok*, heavy flat-bottomed boats moving with the current and in the very first week a child was swept overboard and lost in the swirling river water among the enormous chunks of floating ice, and during that fearful journey with poor food and no drinking water but the river itself they all suffered from fever and sickness. The delicate Olga fell ill at once and in caring for her Galina found something with which to combat the deadly apathy that had engulfed her at first, not that she was an easy patient or a rewarding one. She grumbled continuously at the hard fate that had condemned them to this misery.

The appalling loneliness began when Zubov died. He had succeeded in his aim and a government controlled dispensary had been set up. In their spare time he had organized evenings as he had done in Kiev, when they not only fought out political battles but also discussed literature and poetry. The few books they had with them were read and reread until they fell apart and the worn pages had to be carefully mended.

Then in the early January after that first winter when the cold was like icy hands gripping every part of your body,

Zubov caught a severe chill. He had always been careless about his health. He refused to take to his bed. It turned to pneumonia and despite everything Galina could do, he died. It had been a shattering blow. All that winter he had been a rock to which she could cling, his courage, his quirky sense of humour, his stubborn refusal to lie down under tyranny were a constant source of strength. He had been both father and friend and everyone in their little community mourned his loss.

She sighed as she locked the medicine cupboard. It was not only Zubov's companionship she missed but his skill. No one had been found to fill his place so she battled on alone praying that what she prescribed would not prove disastrous. "If completely at a loss," Simon had advised her, "then give the patient something harmless that tastes disgusting. He will believe it is doing him good and faith is a wonderful thing."

Later that night she took some medicine to the hut which Olga shared with another couple. Her baby girl was nearly a year old now and had been down with a bronchial cough.

"Have you heard?" wailed Olga the moment she came through the door. "That beast of a Sergeant has been here. He says that Stefan is to go with the team – Stefan whose health is so delicate. It will kill him, I know it will. I told the Sergeant so and he laughed, said he couldn't go on eating the bread supplied by the State without working for it. When do we ever get bread," she went on wildly, "or even the flour to make it with?"

Privately Galina thought that a spell of hard physical work might be the making of Stefan but she only said soothingly, "It probably sounds worse than it is. Their foreman seems a decent man. He'll probably make sure he is not put to something too hard for him."

"Oh you've met him already, have you? He's quite a dish, isn't he?" said Maria who was older than either of them and respectably married but still had an eye for a good-looking man. "I saw him go up to the dispensary. What did you make of him?"

"I'm afraid I didn't take much notice except that he was rather better spoken than the rest of them," she said evasively. The fact that she lived alone and kept herself a little aloof from the others always aroused speculation.

The arrival of the geological team had been received with

mixed feelings in their little community. They were a rough crowd, mostly peasants who would be required to undertake the heavy digging and she knew that the Sergeant had been gathering recruits to increase their number. At least they were not forced to march in chains like the convicts sent to the salt mines. They had passed through just before the New Year and she had seen the black despair in their eyes and the bleeding wounds on ankles and wrists. All the same, thirty extra mouths to be fed when supply was already short had caused anger and resentment while Sergeant Rodinsky had already made himself very unpopular. It wasn't long before she had an opportunity to see him for herself.

He came swaggering into the dispensary demanding instant attention for a knife slash running down his arm and across his hand. She wondered which husband or brother had been responsible for that.

She unbound the filthy rag he had tied around it, cleansed it and rebandaged it telling him briefly to return in a couple of days for her to look at again.

"It'll be before then," he said lounging on the table watching her as she put the gauze and lint together. "What's a good-looking woman like you doing in this hell-hole? Handing out pills and potions like some damned quack?"

"It's work and it's needed," she replied coldly.

He leaned forward as she passed him and caught her round the waist pulling her against him.

"I can think of better ways of passing the time."

She jerked herself away and got the table between them as she returned the medical supplies to the cupboard and locked it.

"I've already told you, Sergeant," she said levelly, "come back in a couple of days and I'll re-dress it for you."

"Like that, is it, *doctor*?" and he laid an ugly emphasis on the word grinning unpleasantly. "I'll be back. You can be dead sure about that."

She was afraid then. Once before on the boat from Irkutsk there had been a guard who had done his best to catch her unawares until one night when Zubov lay in wait and tripped him up so that he fell overboard into the river. She remembered vividly his spluttering rage when he was hauled out to the jeering laughter of the prisoners; but now she had no one to protect her.

294

He came back as she knew he would just as she was closing the door one evening, demanding instant attention which she dared not refuse. The bandage was filthy again and she unwrapped it treating the wound with a strong disinfectant that made him jump and swear. Then she rebandaged it while he watched her with narrowed eyes. His breath was offensive and she guessed that he was already partly drunk. This life could be as stultifying for guards as for prisoners except that they had an easy access to liquor.

"It's partly healed," she said crisply, fixing it firmly with a clip. "You can leave it now for a few days untouched. Goodnight Sergeant."

But he did not stir.

"You fancy yourself, don't you, Galina Panova? I've been hearing something about you. A rich lover, isn't that true? *And* a nice little fortune in roubles tucked away. Don't you know that prisoners are not allowed to own more than the state permits them to earn?"

Someone obviously must have been talking, perhaps out of jealousy.

"I don't know what rubbish you've been listening to but I have no money except what is here in the cash box," she said as coolly as she could and wondering at the same time if she could somehow edge round him and out of the door.

"I could report it," he went on swinging one booted foot idly and giving her a sly look, "but that would be a pity, wouldn't it? What about a fair exchange? A few kisses and I won't say a word."

"I dispense medicine not kisses, Sergeant," she replied with a boldness she was very far from feeling. "Now if you would please leave. I'm closing the dispensary."

But he did not shift. Instead he shot out a long arm and swept her against him in a bear-like hug. She tried to twist herself away but he was a powerful man and before she could avoid it, his mouth had come crushingly down on hers. She could taste the liquor on his breath and smell the sour reek of sweat and cheap tobacco. She fought gamely to free herself. A bottle she had been using crashed to the floor and smashed. She kicked savagely at his shins and he swore but only gripped her more firmly.

"Fight me, would you, you hell-cat? If that's what you want, then I'm your man!"

295

She was frightened then, horribly frightened. His powerful fingers dug into her flesh. It couldn't happen to her again, it couldn't. She wanted to scream and her throat tightened. He was laughing sure of his victory when a cool hard voice seemed to cut across it.

"Sergeant Rodinsky, may I have a word with you?"

A black shadow had appeared in the doorway.

Still gripping her Rodinsky said thickly, "Get to hell out of here whoever you are!"

"Come now, that's no way to treat a lady."

"Lady!" repeated the Sergeant and followed it with a string of obscenities.

"*And* I don't like dirty talk!"

Without a pause Leon had grabbed hold of him, swung him away and hit him hard on the jaw. Taken by surprise, he staggered back, but he was by no means defeated. He recovered himself with lightning speed and then they were fighting in grim earnest while Galina watched helplessly, her back against the wall, wondering whether it was possible to dodge around them and shout for help.

The room was small and they bounced from table to wall to cupboard and dangerously near the stove. A stool crashed to the floor. They were well matched in height and strength. Round and round the battle raged until to her horror she saw Leon trip over the fallen stool. The Sergeant was on him at the instant, his hands on his neck, his thumbs gouging into his throat remorselessly while Leon struggled desperately to free himself from their brutal pressure.

She could not let it happen, she had to do something. She looked about her desperately for a weapon and saw the rifle the Sergeant had leaned up against the wall when he came in. She grabbed it and swung it with all her strength. It hit him on the temple. He stood for a moment as if stunned and then went crashing to the floor. His opponent was leaning up against the wall, his hands on his bruised throat, gasping for breath. He stared at her for a moment then fell on his knees beside the fallen man.

"I had to do something," she whispered helplessly.

"Thank God you did. I can still feel his hands on my throat."

She watched, terror growing inside her as she saw him look into the eyes, rip open the tunic and put a hand inside to feel the heart of their enemy.

"Is he – is he – ?"

"He's dead," he said briefly.

Horror engulfed her. "He can't be."

"He is, stone dead like the filthy rat he is."

She fought down the rising nausea. "What are we going to do?"

He looked from the dead man to her and then got to his feet.

"The first thing is to get him out of here. Then you can shut the door, lock it and go to bed. Behave normally as you always do. Leave the rest to me."

"How can I? It is I who am to blame. I can't let you suffer for it."

"No one is going to suffer on account of this carrion, not if I can help it. Do as I say and no one will be any the wiser. Do you have any vodka or brandy?"

"Only a small amount for medicinal use."

"Give it to me."

She fetched the brandy with shaking fingers. He stuffed it inside his padded coat and took the dead man by the shoulders. "Open the door. Tell me if the coast is clear."

Outside the darkness was thick, no stars yet and the intense cold hit her in the face arousing every sense to quivering life. She looked around her. It was silent as the grave, not a soul stirring. He had dragged the body to the door.

"Now help me hoist him up," he ordered.

Somehow between them they got the helpless body up so that with its arms around Leon's neck he was being dragged along. She watched the grotesque couple, the living and the dead, stagger into the velvet darkness like two drunken revellers after an evening's orgy.

She did as he had told her, locked and bolted the door, but she could not go to bed. She sat huddled under a blanket shivering, appalled at what she had done. She had killed a man, one who, however degraded, was still the authority, and what the consequences would be for herself and for the man who had rescued her she dare not think.

The night passed desperately slowly. In the morning the whole village buzzed with rumours. Sergeant Rodinsky had disappeared. The team were to have moved on that day and were left stranded, until Leon Pavlov suggested a search party should go out and offered to lead it himself.

They found his body fallen down a deep cleft in the ice where he had obviously stumbled, his head striking a piece of projecting rock and knocking him senseless. In that intense cold he would have been dead in a few hours. Drunk of course – the empty bottle smashed by his fall, the brandy soaked tunic were proof of that. An inquiry produced nothing. Nobody had seen him leave the village but then everyone was shut inside as soon as the sun went down. Apart from punishing the whole community nothing could be done. So, after a few days of confusion, the geological team were ordered to pack the sleighs with their equipment and the ice still holding, they were instructed to move forward under a new guard and with them went Galina Panova and the wives and children of the men recruited from the village.

Minor accidents were frequent and in the absence of any regular doctor Galina was ordered to deal with such emergencies as best she could. Whether they suspected what had happened and this was a way of punishing her she never knew, but it was the beginning of her friendship with Leon Pavlov.

Conditions in the place to which they were sent were so harsh that she did not know how she would have survived if it had not been for his help. The hut allocated to the dispensary was not only small but disgustingly dirty. It took two days of scrubbing to make it even partly habitable in a cold so extreme that you dare not expose even the smallest part of your body for longer than a few minutes. The native tribes who lived in the forest clearings outside shared their tents of hide and tree bark with their animals, the only window a thick chunk of ice stuck into a hole through which filtered a dim light.

When the spring came and the ice melted, water trickled through a dozen different places until Leon patched the roof, and during the short hot summer they were plagued with clouds of vicious flies rising from the stagnant pools. Yet they survived, even the fragile Olga and her baby daughter, clinging to life with a tenacity that astonished her.

Petersburg seemed as far away as the moon. Was there ever a time when she had hot baths, dressed in fine silk, went to opera and ballet, danced, read books, played with her little son? It was like a dream world. News filtered through very slowly. That year of 1913 the Romanov dynasty celebrated its tercentenary with balls and receptions and a grand mass at the Cathedral of Our Lady of Kazan. Rumours ran round among the exiles that an amnesty might be granted to some of the political prisoners but nothing materialized and hope began to die.

"It was far too good to become reality," said Leon cynically. "I wonder if anyone has ever told the Tsar or his German wife how some hundreds of his subjects with some of the most potential brains hang on to their existence by the skin of their teeth. I don't suppose they would believe it, either of them."

She had grown to know and like him during these months. She still had occasional nightmares when she remembered that terrible night and his strong undemanding friendship strengthened her against despair. There could not have been a greater contrast to Simon. She doubted if he ever read a book except those connected with his work. She once lent him their precious copy of *Anna Karenina* and he returned it two days later with the comment that he could not think why the silly bitch made such a song and dance about leaving her dull husband. She laughed at him but still found his strong outgoing vigorous temperament refreshing in these almost intolerable conditions.

He told her once that his father was a priest in a tiny village in the Caucasus and his mother was his peasant housekeeper. They had both wanted him to become like his father but at quite an early age he knew that their simple orthodox faith was not for him.

"I was always fascinated by the earth and its riches. I wanted something I could grasp in my hand, to be explored and developed. This country of ours is so enormously rich, Galina, gold, platinum, iron, all kinds of minerals and still mainly unexploited and will be until we have a government that can look beyond the capital, spend money on real expansion."

On his own subject he could be eloquent and she listened with interest.

"What happened to send you here?"

"I was a fool. I had a good job with a mining company. They were even considering sending me to Europe to study developments in other countries but like most of the younger staff I joined a group of Social Revolutionaries. I don't know why, I was not all that politically minded, but it seemed the thing to do. They ran a printing press so old that it broke down every second day. They all had brains bulging with wonderful theories but no one knew how to mend a simple machine. The day the *Okhrana* raided the cellar where it was kept, I was trying to make the damned thing work so I was arrested with the rest of 'em. Perhaps I'm lucky in one way. At least they recognized I knew something about the land and though the equipment given to us is out of date and the men hopelessly inadequate to deal with it, I am still learning something. One of these days I intend to put it to good use."

The short summer vanished and winter was on them again though now they were a little better equipped to deal with it. One afternoon she stood on the edge of the forest from where she could see the glory of the sunset. It was the one magical moment in this bleak and hostile country where it was a fight to live. It was so bitterly cold that she had wound a thick scarf around her neck and face so that only her eyes were visible for the few minutes she stood there. Though it was barely three o'clock, the brief splendour was soon gone. The fiery red ball disappeared and was succeeded by a grey twilight. Reluctant to return to the hut where so many hours had to be passed she still lingered until two hands in thick woollen gloves closed over her eyes.

"Guess who?" said a familiar voice.

"Leon!" she exclaimed and swung around. "You're back very early. Has something happened?"

"Yes, it has. What are you standing here for? It's perishing."

"I know but it's beautiful too."

"Oh you!" he said affectionately, "you'd find beauty in a rubbish tip. Come on, let's go inside. I've something to tell you."

Inside the hut he pulled a white snow hare out of the leather bag he had slung across his shoulder.

"A present for you."

She took the still warm body into her hands.

"Where did you get it?"

"I put snares down when I can. They don't always work. It breaks the neck, you know. It's very quick."

She touched the white fur gently. An hour or so ago it had run free and without care but it was useless to think like that. It was fresh meat and that was a rarity not to be wasted.

"I'll skin it for you," he went on, "if you'll invite me to share it."

"Willingly. We'll have a feast."

"That's the good news," he said taking out his knife. "Now for the bad. There's been an accident. Part of the trench fell in."

"Was anyone hurt?"

"I'm afraid so. It was Stefan. It buried him. He had to be dug out."

"Is he badly injured?"

"He is dead."

"Oh no, not that!"

"Suffocated." He moved impatiently. "The boy had no feeling for the work. Anyone else would have got out in time. He should never have been sent out with us."

"Do they ever think of that?" she said bitterly. "How are we going to tell Olga?"

"I thought it would come better from you. They'll be bringing him back soon. I came on ahead."

"She'll take it very badly and she is not well. She's been sick for days now and nothing I can give her seems to help."

"I know. Stefan was worried about her. It's damned bad luck. Will you do it? She thinks so highly of you."

"I'll have to, won't I?"

"Good girl."

With a few swift movements he skinned the hare and dismembered it.

"I'd better go and meet the team. I'll see you later," he said and left quickly.

The men would be returning slowly so she still had a little time before she need brace herself to her distressing task. She began to wash the hare in the snow water she had brought in earlier and boiled. They had very few vegetables and what they had were small and wizened but she put it all together in the iron pot and sprinkled in some of the precious salt and pepper. She lit the kerosene stove and put the pot to cook slowly, then wrapped her thickest shawl around her and went along to the hut Olga still shared with Maria and her husband. Rumours had already spread. The girl rushed to meet her seizing hold of her in frantic disbelief.

"They're saying Stefan has been hurt. It's not true, is it, it can't be true."

"I'm afraid it is," she said as gently as she could. "You're going to have to be very brave."

"You don't mean – you can't mean – "

"Yes, he's dead. Leon said they dug him out as quickly as they could but it was too late. He had been suffocated."

"Oh, no, no, no!"

For a moment she stared in anguish at Galina, eyes wide, face as white as the snow outside, then with a gasp she collapsed to the floor.

They had some difficulty in reviving her and when they did, she broke into a storm of wild weeping and it was a long time before Galina could leave her in Maria's charge and return to her own hut.

A savoury smell of the cooking hare pervaded the room so much more appetizing than the tasteless stew made from the chunks of frozen meat which had been all their ration for most of the winter. She made what simple preparations she could. It was only on rare occasions that Leon shared a meal with her.

"They'll talk if I come more often," he said once with a wry grin. "In this place what else is there to do?"

"I don't think I care."

"Well, I do," he said surprisingly and left it at that.

He was washed and clean when he came in later that day, bringing with him a breath of the snow outside.

"That smells good," he said throwing aside his cap and rubbing his hands in anticipation.

"I feel guilty keeping it just for ourselves."

"My dear girl, shared with that mob it wouldn't be a mouthful each. Forget your tender conscience for once and let's enjoy it."

And enjoy it they did, every tasty mouthful, mopping up the gravy with hard black bread and carefully putting some aside for the next day. Afterwards she spared a little of the precious tea Simon had sent and they sipped the amber liquid without sugar or milk but still something of a luxury.

The box had taken many months to reach her, battered out of shape, opened and searched, no doubt some of its contents stolen, but still wonderful. A letter from Simon, brief, practical, written in the knowledge that it would be opened and censored, and with it a photograph of Andrei, seven years old now, grown taller, his eyes looking straight out at her. "For my Mamma", he had written across it in large capitals. She had propped it on the wooden chest that was all she had to hold her few possessions and it was there that Leon saw it leaning across to pick it up.

"Who is the small boy?"

No use denying it now when she had been foolish enough to leave it there.

"My son."

"And you left him behind?"

"Would you bring a child to this place? He is with his father."

"His father?"

He had never probed before, never asked questions sensing her reserve, but now his eyes fell on her hand and she realized she had said more than she had intended.

"He is married."

"And this – this man left someone like you to be sent out here, alone and unprotected, and did nothing about it?"

"Please, Leon, I don't want to talk about it."

"That's as you wish but you can't change what I think."

"You don't understand."

"I understand enough." He paused staring down at his hands, the powerful fingers stained by his work though he had scrubbed them. "May I ask one question?"

She smiled at him. "Of course you can."

"Do you still care for this man who fathered your child?"

"Why do you want to know?"

"I thought you might have guessed by now." He got to his feet replacing the photograph carefully and then turning to face her. "It's been in my mind for months now. Galina, you must know what I think of you."

"I like to believe we are good friends."

"More than that, far more. Galina, will you marry me?"

"Marry you?"

She had not expected it. He had never groped after her or tried to kiss her. He had in fact been more like the brother she had never had though she had been aware of a warmth in his manner, a care for her well being, a gentleness reserved for her alone, and suddenly the thought swept through her – why not marry him? Why not take the chance offered? She liked him, admired his courage, his steady purpose, his vigorous intellect, and there were times when she hungered for the strength of a man's arms around her, to be loved and to love in return, was she never to feel those simple pleasures again? And yet – she felt suddenly confused and uncertain.

"How can we be married up here, so far from everywhere?"

"It could be arranged," he said eagerly encouraged because she had not rejected him immediately. He took her hands and pulled her to her feet. "We're letting life slip by but together we might be able to make something of it."

"I don't know – I had never thought of such a thing. When this is all over perhaps – "

"And when will it be over? This year, next year, sometime, maybe never."

"In another year or if the amnesty comes through and we go home . . .", but what home did she have to go to? She was suddenly overwhelmed with the thought of Simon. She had loved once deeply and it could never come again, she was sure of that.

But now he was insistent. "Don't say no, not yet. Think about it. Promise me you will."

He took her in his arms and kissed her then, not savagely, but with a gentleness that gradually deepened and it was sweet and satisfying. She felt something melt a little inside her and without consciously intending it was responding to him, and he was exultant. He had been patient but now he held this rare creature close against him and felt confident that, given time, victory would be his. He drew her to sit beside him.

"If you know how long I have dreamed of this," he whispered into the softness of her hair.

She leaned against his shoulder, closing her eyes for a moment of shared warmth and intimacy. It was the loud knocking at the door that drove them apart.

"Let them knock," he said.

"No, Leon, I can't do that. Someone may have been taken ill."

It was Maria standing outside when she opened the door huddled into a thick shawl.

"It's Olga," she quavered. "She's terribly sick."

"How do you mean? Is she hysterical? What's wrong with her?"

"I don't know but she's in terrible pain. Please come, Galina, please."

"Very well. You go back to her. I'll look out one or two things which may help and follow after you."

"You won't be long?"

"No, I promise you."

Maria hurried away and Galina went to the medicine cupboard.

"I'll come with you," offered Leon. "There may be something I can do."

She looked her gratitude, then wrapped herself in the thickest garment she had and went quickly through the freezing night.

Olga was tossing on the pallet bed moaning softly – her forehead burning with fever.

"She keeps asking for water but when I gave her some she couldn't keep it down," said Maria anxiously.

"Is it the same pain that she has had all along?"

"Yes, only it's worse, much worse. She has never been like this before."

Galina tried to summon all her medical training to her aid, all she had learned with Simon as she went around the hospitals with him. She located the pain to the right side of the abdomen and was almost sure that this was something for which she could provide no remedy.

"What do you think it is?" asked Leon who was waiting in the outer room.

"I can't be absolutely sure but I think it is an inflamed appendix," and when he looked puzzled, she went on hurriedly. "I saw a case once and a surgeon I know operated. This is something for which we need a skilled doctor and there is no one within miles."

"There is," he said slowly, "I heard of it only yesterday. A medical team from Petersburg who have been sent here to observe and diagnose some kind of epidemic among the tribesmen. They have been afraid of it spreading. They should still be at Yakutsk. I could go there, ask one of them to come."

She looked doubtful. "But will they listen to you?"

"I don't know but we could try. We owe it to Stefan. That poor devil was killed in the service of the damned State, the least they can do is to help his widow."

"Could you go? Would they let you leave here?"

"I won't ask. I'll take one of the team's sleighs. Across the ice I could do it in five or six hours. It's only nine now. If he will come we'll be back before morning."

He was strong and determined, partly out of a genuine sympathy, and partly because he longed to prove himself capable in a crisis. Her heart warmed to him.

"It would be wonderful if you could."

"You do what you can for her," he said, "I'll bring one of those doctors back with me if I have to do it by force."

She watched him disappear into the night, confident that if a way could be found then Leon was the man to find it. Then she went back into the hut. Olga seemed a little easier, the pain not so intense. She thought she might risk giving her a mild sedative.

"You go to bed, Maria, and take the baby with you. I'll sit up with Olga."

"Are you sure? I don't mind taking a turn."

"No, your husband needs his rest. I'll be all right. I don't think I could sleep anyway."

She wrapped herself in a rug and sat near to the stove praying that a doctor would come and shoulder the awful responsibility. Her experience told her that without expert help Olga would surely die in agonizing pain while she would be forced to stand by helpless. It was an appalling thought.

She was tired and her mind strayed from one thing to another. Leon must have got away safely or else he would have returned. In this remote settlement their guards had become lax, chiefly because escape across the frozen wastes and through the dense forest was a practical impossibility. Minutes crept by like hours. Once she started up at hearing the distant keening of the wolves. In the winter hunger drove them from the forest as far as the villages in search of food. She had seen them herself at night, long grey shapes running like shadows from hut to hut.

It must have been about six when she heard movement outside, the crunch of snow under booted feet and a gentle tapping at the door. She ran to open it. It was still pitch dark but the light fell on Leon and behind him a tall man in a heavy padded coat.

"Here we are," he said cheerfully. "We made it quicker than I had thought possible."

"Thank God," she breathed. "Come in, come in."

She stood back as they brushed past her. She bolted the door and turned. The stranger was unwinding the thick muffler that hid his face. Then they were staring at one another, the shock of recognition keeping them silent, oblivious of everything around them.

Simon was the first to stir, putting down the woollen scarf and unfastening his coat.

"Now I am here, I had better see my patient. Where is she?"

"She is in here, doctor."

Galina took up the lamp and led the way into the inner room. Olga was awake and moving restlessly. She bent over her.

"We've brought a doctor to you. Don't worry. He will know what to do."

Leon stood at the door and watched them. They had not flown into each other's arms, they had scarcely spoken a word and yet he was certain of it. This man, this doctor, it was he who had been her lover, the father of her child, and he cursed because it had to be he who had brought him there on this night of all nights when what he had wanted for so long had seemed to be within his grasp. He saw how they worked together, how she obeyed his slightest gesture as he made a long and detailed examination, saw too unwillingly how his manner, firm but kind, calmed and reassured the sick girl.

As Simon drew the blankets over her again, Olga clutched at his hand.

"Am I going to die, doctor?"

"You mustn't talk like that. Don't be afraid, my dear, we are going to find a way to make you better."

He straightened up and glanced across at Galina. She took the lamp and he followed her into the outer room.

"Is it what I think it is?" she whispered.

"It's the appendix right enough and, I would judge, badly inflamed. It must be removed as soon as reasonably possible."

"Can you operate?"

"I can, but not here, not in these conditions."

"Why? What's wrong with you? Do you have to have the comfort of your Petersburg hospital, your team of pretty nurses, before you can make an attempt to save a life?"

There was contempt and anger in Leon's voice, though at first he had been impressed by the stranger who had been the only one of the five doctors who had listened sympathetically and volunteered to come with him.

"I don't think you understand," said Simon quietly. "It's not the cutting out operation, that is simple, it's the infections that can creep in, it's the possible complications and the after-nursing. Galina knows very well what I mean."

"Then what *are* you going to do?" went on Leon brusquely. "Say 'I'm sorry' and leave her to die."

"Certainly not. We can take her to Yakutsk. God knows conditions there are crude enough but at least I can secure a modicum of efficiency and care."

"How can we do that?" exclaimed Galina. "We're prisoners, Simon. Leon has already risked a great deal in coming to fetch you."

"I'm aware of that but I've been thinking. Who is in charge here?"

"Lieutenant Rylov is with the geological team. This is a very small community linked with it and he only has two other guards under him."

"Take me to the Lieutenant."

"What good will that do?" objected Leon frowning. "He will be out at the mining camp by now and wondering where the hell I am."

"All the better. I'll take the responsibility. We had better go there now, the sooner the better." He turned to Galina. "Keep her as warm as you can. Nothing to eat. A little tea or milk if she asks for it."

His brisk efficiency took Leon by surprise as it did Lieutenant Rylov when they reached the camp. He was a man in his early thirties who had once had a flourishing career in a good regiment until the day he got drunk and foolishly opened his mouth too wide about the alleged scandalous relations between the Tsarina and that abominable mystic Rasputin. An envious colleague reported him. He was demoted from Captain to Lieutenant and sent to cool his heels in this remote community. His bitter resentment at his harsh treatment made him sympathetically inclined towards the exiles.

He was impressed by this distinguished foreigner who spoke such excellent Russian, rolled out a lot of impressive names and showed him the paper authorizing him to inquire into, report on and use any conditions necessary in this region of Siberia.

"You must understand, doctor," he protested, "that it is forbidden for any prisoner to move more than a very short distance from his allotted village."

"My dear Lieutenant, surely you would not allow such a trifling regulation to stand in the way of saving a life? If you forbid this removal and allow this young woman to die miserably, I am strongly of the opinion that you could have serious disaffection on your hands and they won't like that when it

308

gets back to Petersburg. I regret to say that I would be forced to report on what I had witnessed and believe me I carry a lot of weight amongst the hospital authorities."

It was perfectly true, he thought unhappily. The fate of Sergeant Rodinsky had never been properly accounted for and he had no wish to end up like him with a split skull in a freezing ditch. It was a damnably awkward situation. Whatever he did was bound to be condemned but all the same he was here on the spot while Petersburg was three thousand miles away. He hesitated to commit himself and Simon took advantage of it.

"I will make absolutely sure that these two prisoners, Leon Pavlov and Galina Panova, who will be accompanying me are returned here when the matter is concluded."

"May I have that in writing?"

"With pleasure if it will satisfy your scruples."

So Simon signed for them as if they were bales of goods instead of human beings and they went back to the village to make preparations.

Maria had prepared a hasty meal and they choked down the tasteless stew and drank a cup of boiling tea before they set out. Olga, swaddled like a cocoon in blankets, was made as comfortable as possible in the sleigh with Galina to watch over her during the difficult bumpy journey. Simon had given her a light injection to keep her drowsy till they reached Yakutsk and the whole little community turned out to see them leave.

The track followed the river for a while and the Siberian pony kept up a good steady pace. Simon sat beside Leon while Galina was in the body of the sleigh, holding on firmly to Olga. The sick girl now and again stirred fretfully. Very soon they had entered a long stretch of forest. The pines, tall and straight and black, towered above them with no undergrowth.

Maybe it was the lantern they carried that attracted them, maybe the scent of man, but it was Galina who saw them first. They came slinking through the trees in the eerie green gloom, the leader first, then another and another, until there were more than a dozen silently padding behind them, their eyes now and again gleaming green as glass.

"Wolves!" she whispered and then again more urgently, "Wolves!"

Leon looked over his shoulder. "How near?"

"A good way off but they are gaining."

"Hell and we have no gun."

"I have," said Simon. "I've made sure of carrying a pistol since I've been up here. I'll move to the back of the sleigh. If they draw near I'll shoot. That will hold them up."

Leon looked at him doubtfully. "How good a shot are you?"

"Fair."

"You'd better let me take it on. They're fiendish to see in this gloom."

"No. You drive as fast as you can and leave it to me. How far off are we?"

"Another hour at least."

"Right. Drive like the devil!"

He groped his way to the back of the sleigh pausing only long enough to grip Galina's shoulder reassuringly. Up to now they had said nothing that might not have passed between strangers but they were intensely aware of one another. It was both pain and a glowing joy to feel him close beside her as he leaned across the back of the sleigh, pistol in hand.

They came swiftly, grey menacing shadows. Now and again one of them would raise his head and howl, a fearful uncanny sound that sent shivers down the spine. Leon was right. This was nothing like going out at dawn to shoot wild duck across the Fens. The leader, head down, muzzle pointed, ran ahead of the others. Simon concentrated his vision, waiting with narrowed eyes till he was sure, until he could see the green glitter in the darkness, then he fired. The wolf made one gigantic leap into the air and then fell, shot clean through the head. The others pounced upon it tearing at it savagely with fierce yelps and snarls. The pony, scenting the wolves and frightened by the shot, went into a tearing gallop. It was all that Leon could do to hold it steady while the sleigh rocked wildly from side to side. Olga cried out in alarm and Galina crouched beside her, held her in her arms whispering words of comfort.

Some half a dozen of the wolves were tearing at their dead leader but the others came on relentlessly and were beginning to gain. Simon fired again and again; each time an animal fell and temporarily held them back, but he could not shoot them all.

Galina crept up beside him.

"Is there anything I can do?"

"Keep down," he said fiercely, "keep down and hold on."

At this rocketing pace with the sleigh going from side to side she could be thrown out and torn to pieces before he could save her. He tried to remember how many shots he had fired and how many were left, possibly two, no more. It would not be easy to reload with numbed fingers in this swaying sleigh. For a moment his concentration wavered and it was then that it happened. They bounced over a deep rut, the sleigh tipped and almost went over and at the same time a monstrous beast made an enormous leap. Its front feet clawed down Simon's arm knocking the pistol out of his hand. Galina could see the jaws slavering with froth and blood. Wild with terror she seized the pistol and fired. It fell back in a hideous tangle of blood and fur and Simon recovered himself, grabbed the gun from her and fired once more.

Then miraculously they were out of the forest, the track opened out before them. The impetus of that first attack began to die away and the wolves gradually fell back.

The sleeve of his coat was bloody, slashed from shoulder to wrist.

"Are you hurt?" she gasped.

"No, it's not my blood. Thank God for the padding."

"Are you all right back there?" shouted Leon over his shoulder.

"Yes, we're fine."

Then they were hugging one another laughing helplessly in sheer reaction.

"What's so funny?" grumbled Leon still breathlessly hanging on to the racing pony.

"Nothing, nothing at all."

For a few seconds they clung together tightly. She felt his icy lips touch hers, then he had put her from him and clambered back to the front.

"You did well, doctor," said Leon in grudging admiration.

"It's not an experience I'd care to live through again. How near are we?"

"Almost there."

Half an hour later, with the pony at full gallop and every sense still alert for danger, they were racing through the gates of Yakutsk.

*

The doctors who had made up the medical team had already left on their homeward journey but Jake who had accompanied Simon was still there and considerably relieved to see him return safely. He eyed Galina curiously but was far too well trained to make any comment.

The infirmary at Yakutsk was badly run, its attendants slovenly and dirty, the one doctor in charge more often drunk, than sober, but somehow Simon had it galvanized into efficiency. The wooden table which served all kinds of uses as well as operations was scrubbed till it was white, every instrument was newly sterilized and the floors were washed with carbolic. The attendants, accustomed to carrying on in their usual slipshod manner, were rushed off their feet, hardly realizing what had hit them and Galina working alongside them was amused. They didn't know Simon as she did.

Leon, after making sure that the pony was housed and fed found himself roped in and to his own surprise obeying orders meekly like everyone else, even to swabbing out the long room that served as a ward and carrying out all kinds of disgusting rubbish with strict instructions to make sure it was burned and not left lying about to accumulate and spread germs.

When it was all done, when everything was as spotless as good elbow grease could make it and Olga had been suitably prepared, they were alone for a few minutes while Galina shook out the hospital gown which she had washed herself.

"What do you think?" she asked. "Will it be successful?"

"It has to be, hasn't it?" he said wryly. "I have stuck my neck out so far I have simply got to bring it off."

As she knew very well operations for appendicitis were still fraught with danger. It was only a few years since King Edward VII had been stricken with it and nearly missed his coronation while all England held its breath. But when it came to the point Simon was cool and steady, fatigue forgotten in concentration on the work before him and she felt she had never admired him so much.

Afterwards when it was all over and he was stripping off the gown, she saw the sweat on his face.

"It was a near thing, wasn't it?" she ventured.

"Very near. It was touch and go. Another few hours and the abscess could have burst and after that nothing I could do would have saved her."

"And now?"

"We shall know in a day or so but all the signs are good."
He sighed and stretched. "Perhaps now we can have a little
time to ourselves."

Later that same day, having made sure that Olga was reasonably comfortable, she was left in the care of the superintendent
of the infirmary, a respectable middle-aged woman considerably in awe of Simon. In the room allocated to the doctors
during their brief stay in Yakutsk Jake had rustled up some
kind of a meal and afterwards they sat together. So much to
be said, so many questions to be asked, and yet for a little
they were simply happy to be together in a companionable
silence.

"Did you know about me when Leon asked you to come?"
she asked.

"No. He mentioned no names but I'd seen a great deal that
sickened me since I had been out here. The others thought I was
being hopelessly quixotic – after all what is one exile more or less
– but it went through my mind that this sick young woman
could have been you and then how would I have felt?"

"Tell me about yourself, Simon, tell me about Andrei?"

"He started school this autumn. At eight years old Missy
felt he was ready for it. She's been a tower of strength in the
nursery. Even my harum scarum Tanya is in awe of her."

"And Nina?"

"I think there is a kind of armed truce between her and
Andrei, young as he is. He is as wary of her as she is of him.
It's not the best kind of situation but it's all I can do. He sees
a lot of Luba and Conn and he is happy with them."

"And you, Simon?"

"Do you need to ask? He is the boy of my heart, Galina,
but I mustn't show too much favour, I have to try to be fair.
Oddly enough I think he realizes that."

"And you yourself, Simon, what about you?"

He shrugged his shoulders. "I work. The clinic has grown.
I have taken on an assistant. It's an uphill task and sometimes
it seems to me I do little good. What's the use of curing
someone when they are forced to return to the frightful conditions that have caused the sickness and yet you still have to
do what you can. Nina hates it. She would prefer me to increase my private practice." He smiled wryly. "It's one of the
things we argue about. She would like me to be in constant
demand among the rich and the famous."

"And are you?"

"Quite sufficiently for my liking. I don't always care for the friends she makes, then I tell myself I must be fair. Parties, balls, glittering social occasions are her way of combating the anxiety about our little son."

She looked across at him. "Why, Simon? Is he sick?"

He rarely spoke of the boy's condition to anyone except one or two of his closest colleagues but although they had been so much apart, Galina still seemed part of himself; with her there had never been any barriers.

"Paul suffers from haemophilia. He is four now and a bright happy child except for the constant fear. A fall, bruising, even a cut finger, and he can be in agony. Nina has an obsession about it, Galina, she watches over him too closely which is not good for the boy and she blames herself greatly."

"You mean she knows it is hereditary?"

"Yes. I tried to keep it from her but she read some of my notes and it is as if she can't forgive herself."

He got up and began to pace up and down the room, hesitating to burden her with what had worried him for over a year now and yet here in this remote place so far removed from his everyday life it was easier to speak of it.

"A year or so ago she became pregnant again." It had been after that passionate night at Dannskoye which he still despised himself for, but he could not tell her that. "At first she was happy about it and then she began to be afraid. She was convinced that the child would be like Paul. I tried to reason her out of it. It does not always follow, in fact only very rarely, and in any case there was no certainty that the baby would be a boy. She called me callous and unfeeling because I would not give her an abortion."

And Galina, watching his face, found pity for them both. Poor Nina, she thought, she had always expected so much from life and had come up against tragedy.

"That wasn't the worst of it," he went on. "I had bought a car for her that Christmas. She had longed for one passionately and I wanted to make her happy. Nothing would satisfy her but that she should learn to drive it. I agreed on the understanding that she was never to take it out except with me or Jake beside her."

"That won't have pleased Nina."

"No, it didn't," he confessed, "but I insisted. One day after one of our futile arguments she flung out of the house saying that she was going to Dannskoye, something she often did when things became too much for her. Niki and she are very close still and Sonia always has a calming effect. I never dreamed she would go alone. Somewhere on the road the car went out of control. It bounced across a shallow ditch and hit a tree. By some miracle she was not seriously hurt, mostly cuts and severe bruising, but she lost the baby and she could never afterwards explain how it happened. It has haunted me ever since. Was it really an accident or did she do it deliberately?"

Galina could see it all so clearly. It was the kind of wild crazy thing that Nina would do, trying desperately to escape reality and never really counting the cost to herself or to her husband.

Simon had come to stand beside her. "I never meant to speak of that to anyone but when I am with you, it's as if I were talking to my other self."

What was it about her that stirred him so greatly? She had grown thinner during these hard years but she had always had fine bones, the kind of beauty that age would never spoil or diminish. She had taken off the peasant scarf and her hair, loosely knotted, still had its bright sheen. He knew then that he badly wanted to make love to her, not with the wild passion that had once been theirs but with gentleness and warmth that would bring tranquillity and the richness of fulfilment, but not now, not greedily, later perhaps as they grew closer in thought and spirit. He sat down again leaning forward to take her hand in his.

"That's enough about me. Tell me about yourself. You know when I accepted the offer to come on this trip, I thought now I shall know a little of what she is going through. I did not think that I should be lucky enough to meet up with you."

"There's so little worth telling," she said smiling, "mostly a grinding monotony and a perpetual battle to keep alive."

She began to tell him of the journey, of Zubov's death, playing down the loneliness, the humiliations, the death of the Sergeant, but laughing with him over some of her cases at the pharmacy.

"I tried so hard to remember all I had learnt, all you had taught me. I think I've ended up with becoming a sort of wise woman. It's rather daunting to be thought infallible when you know how inadequate you really are. I sometimes wonder if I am killing as much as I'm curing!"

And while he listened the idea was born and began to grow in his mind.

"Galina," he said suddenly, "have you ever thought of escape?"

"Escape?" she looked at him in surprise. "No, never. When I was first out here some of the exiles talked of nothing else, but it was just a dream and they all knew it. The only tracks are along the river and through the scattered villages. You must have realized that already. You need sleighs, ponies or dogs, money, food and even then some of the tribesmen are hostile. They are desperately poor and if one of the escaped prisoners is murdered for the sake of what he carries with him, who would care?"

"Alone of course it would be impossible, I see that, but I am here, I have money, I have a certain influence." He was like a boy in his eagerness. "Listen to me, Galina, supposing when it is time for you to return to the mining camp, we set out together seemingly going our different ways. We arrange a meeting place well away from Yakutsk and there you join me and Jake. We could then travel on together through to Kirensk and finally to Irkutsk where we can take the train."

It sounded like a fairytale, an adventure story, and had about as much reality.

"How *can* we do such a thing? You know as well as I do that you can't travel anywhere in Russia without passport and papers and I have none except those which state exactly who I am and why I am here."

"Surely among these exiles there is someone who can forge fresh papers for you," he said obstinately. "You could travel as my assistant. I could vouch for you. Once near Petersburg I know there could be problems but I am sure they can be overcome. Nigel would help me obtain a passage through to England. My brother and his wife would welcome you. Think, Galina, think what it would mean – freedom to live again, to study if you wish, it was one of the things you always wanted to do, and Robert would arrange all that for you if I were to ask him."

For a few seconds the very thought was compelling. To be free of this hateful place, free to live a normal existence, to know warmth and comfort once again. She was only twenty-eight and sometimes lately it had felt as if her life was ended, but away from here she could make a new beginning. Then, like a douche of cold water, realization hit her. She was just like all the others indulging in a ridiculously impossible dream. There were so many insuperable problems which he didn't understand. She began to point them out to him.

"Even if we could escape from here, we would be bound to be taken up somewhere along the route, and then it is you who would suffer. Anyone who helps a prisoner to escape, no matter who it is, is subject to the harshest penalties. Not even your standing, not even your British passport, could save you. If you were imprisoned or deported out of the country, what would happen to Nina and your children? And as for me it could mean another and even longer sentence. I would far rather die."

He would not accept her objections even though in his secret heart he knew she was right, that what he had suggested had too many flaws to be feasible.

"These are difficulties that could be overcome."

"You can't ignore them and they are not the only ones," she went on earnestly. "What about Lieutenant Rylov? You gave your promise, he trusted you, how will he act if Leon returns alone? He will sentence him to *katorga* – do you know what that is? Twelve years of hard labour in a penal settlement. I couldn't let that happen to Leon. He has suffered for me once already, I couldn't let it happen again."

Simon had got up and was pacing around the room. "So it's this fellow Leon, is it? It's he who is the stumbling block. He's in love with you, isn't he?"

"Why should you say that?"

"It's obvious from the way he looks at you, from the plain fact that he dislikes me. It's true, isn't it?"

"I suppose it is," she admitted unwillingly. "He wants me to marry him."

"Marry? Good God, that's absurd. The man is nothing but a peasant."

"You seem to forget, Simon, that I am a peasant too. Leon is a geologist, he is expert in his own field. Without him I doubt if I would have survived this past year."

He stopped still, looking down at her. "You like him, don't you?"

"Yes, I do," she said firmly. "He has been a very good friend. I couldn't let him suffer any penalty on my account."

"Is he your lover?" he asked abruptly.

"Why? Are you jealous?"

"I have no right to be but I am. Is he?"

"He has asked me to be his wife not his mistress," she said coldly.

"I'm sorry, Galina, I'm sorry, I shouldn't have asked that. Are you going to marry him?"

"I don't know – perhaps. Why shouldn't I?" she turned on him suddenly. "Must I live all my life with nothing, no home, no husband, no child? Must I live a barren empty existence because once I had the bad luck to fall in love with you?"

"Galina, don't say that," he said struck to the heart, "don't ever say that."

"Isn't it true?" she went on fiercely. "What is there for me when this exile is over, if it ever is?"

"We will find some way to be together, I swear we will."

"No, Simon, I'm not coming back to Petersburg to be your mistress, your plaything, your cushion against Nina's tantrums," she went on recklessly. "I have paid and paid all these years but not any more. I want to live my own life and if that means marrying Leon, then it will be my decision and mine alone."

"Oh God, what a selfish bastard you make me feel."

Torn by conflicting emotions, her mind fogged by fatigue, she got to her feet. With him standing there so close to her, no longer a shadow from the past but alive and demanding, she could not think straight. She had to escape, she had to be alone. She moved towards the door.

"I think it is time I went to see how Olga is getting on."

"Not yet, please not yet. Call me everything you like, Galina, but don't hate me for it."

"Hate you?" she said wearily, "Sometimes I wish to God I could."

He had come up behind her, his hands on her shoulders, and she knew with an awful certainty that he had only to touch her for all her defiance, all her brave resolution to crumble away.

"Let me go, Simon," she whispered, "please let me go."

"No," he said huskily, "not now, not ever. The fire bound us together, don't you remember?"

"Oh God, why should loving one another create such a hell for both of us?" she said despairingly.

"I wish I knew."

He turned her round to face him and she shivered as his lips met hers, every bone in her body seemed to melt with a hopeless longing as his arms went around her, and it was at that precise moment that Leon knocked and receiving no answer opened the door.

She broke away feeling oddly guilty and Simon spoke brusquely.

"What is it? What do you want?"

"Sorry to break it up," said Leon ironically, "but Florence Nightingale downstairs thinks you should take a look at your patient."

"Very well. I'll come at once."

He glanced from Leon to Galina and then went quickly from the room. Leon would have followed him but Galina stopped him.

"I've not had an opportunity to ask you. Have you found somewhere to eat and sleep?"

"Oh yes. Don't concern yourself about me. One of the women exiles here has offered me bed and board."

"I'm glad."

"Are you? It gets rid of me, doesn't it? You can share your lover's bed with an easy conscience."

"Why should you say that?"

"It's obvious, isn't it? He's the one, the rich Englishman, the handsome doctor, who gave you a child, abandoned you when you most needed help and has only to appear for you to fall into his arms. I thought you would have had more pride."

What had pride to do with the ache and torment of loving someone?

"You've got it all wrong," she said wearily.

"Have I? Seems clear as daylight to me."

"If you must know, it was I who wronged him."

He looked at her uncertainly and then shrugged his shoulders. "Well, whatever it was, it has put paid to us, hasn't it?"

"Must I lose your friendship as well as everything else?"

"It isn't friendship I want, Galina, you know that. I thought . . . oh hell, what does it matter what I thought?"

"I'm sorry, Leon. How could I know this was going to happen?"

"Perhaps it's better this way. At least we know where we

stand." He made a move towards the door and then came back. "There's a small party travelling part of the way back to the mining camp tomorrow. I thought I might go with them."

"Then I must come with you."

"Isn't he working a miracle and whisking you away with him?" said Leon drily.

"Are you crazy? We live in a real world not a fairytale and I was taught to pay my debts."

He looked at her oddly. "You owe me nothing."

"When do you leave?"

"In the morning some time."

"I'll be ready."

When he had gone she stood still for a moment. It seemed that whatever she did, she was always the loser. An immense weariness of body and spirit washed over her. It took a few minutes before she could pull herself together and go resolutely down to the hospital ward.

Simon was still there and he looked up as she came to the other side of the bed.

"How is she? Is anything wrong?"

"A slight fever but her pulse is strong. I don't think there is anything to worry about but I shall stay within call," he said to the elderly nurse.

"Thank you, doctor, I should be grateful. We haven't had many operation cases."

"Would you like me to share part of the nursing with you?" asked Galina.

"No, my dear, you've done enough. There is a bed made up for you in my room at the end of the corridor if that will suit you."

"Thank you, that will be wonderful."

Outside in the dark passage she turned to Simon.

"Leon tells me there is a party leaving for the mining camp tomorrow. I shall go with them."

"You must do whatever you think best."

It was as if a glass wall had risen between them and they could not break through. Too much had been said, too many nerves exposed. An hour or so ago and he could have swept her off to his bed but now he did not dare even to touch her hand.

"I'll see you in the morning," she went on. "Maria will want to know the latest news of Olga."

"Of course. She will have to stay here for a week or two but I will make sure all is going well before I leave."

"Goodnight, Simon."

"Goodnight."

And then because these few minutes in this sour smelling passage were all that were left to them, she could not leave it like that.

She said chokingly, "Simon . . ."

He turned then, had caught her in his arms holding her so suffocatingly close that she could feel his heart beating, feel his breath on her cheek, his hand tangled in her hair, his mouth on hers urgent and demanding, before she broke away, running down the corridor into the cold little room at the end to throw herself breathlessly on the bed.

Why, why did this have to happen to her and yet despite the pain, the frustration, she could not regret Simon's coming. It might have lost her Leon but it had brought her tinglingly to life again and that was what was important. To suffer pain is to live, Zubov used to say, when a patient feels nothing, then is the time to worry because despair is the death of the spirit. She had never felt that, not even at the worst moments. Always deep inside her there was a certainty that some day, some time, they would be together. Lying there, huddled beneath the thin blankets, facing cold, hunger and loneliness once again, she would not let herself be defeated. She could not escape as Nina did but faced it with that inner strength that Simon knew so well and Leon had already sensed. Staring into the thick darkness she thought how strange it was that Simon, the aristocrat, so concerned with the sick and the poor, and Leon who wanted the good things of the earth to hold in his strong hands, had more in common than they believed.

19

In the hot July of 1914 Tanya was sitting cross-legged on the big bed watching her mother dress. She loved the pretty, lavish room with its pink silk hangings, the deep rose carpet like velvet under her feet, the fabulous dressing table with the triple mirror and gold-topped bottles, the huge wardrobe crammed with row upon row of gowns in silk and satin and velvet. That was the kind of room she was going to have when she was grown up, only it seemed a very long way off when she was still only eight years old.

Marta was arranging Nina's hair in a new, fascinating style with a soft fringe of curls on the forehead. There was her gown of sea-green silk with crystal embroidery that shimmered as she stepped into it and the collarette of pearls and rubies clasped around the slim white neck. Tanya sighed with envy and thought Mamma looked like one of the Rusalki that Marina had told them about, the water sprites who lived in the bottom of lonely lakes with emerald eyes and skin the colour of moonlight. They lured young men with their siren songs until they went willingly to their death in the black waters. It had made her shiver deliciously though she had never quite been able to imagine it happening to Papa.

It must be a very grand party for Mamma to dress so carefully but then ever since the spring and all during this gloriously hot summer the whole of Petersburg seemed to be in festive mood. Balls to welcome Admiral Beatty with the magnificent British Fleet which she and Andrei had watched sailing majestically down the Baltic, the arrival of the French President and a state banquet at Peterhof where Mamma had gone with Uncle Niki wearing the Malinsky jewels in diamonds and sapphires that Nurse said would be hers one day. There had been a review of thousands of troops with Uncle Val looking splendid on his black horse. No one had seemed to be at all concerned about the assassination of the heir to

322

the Austrian throne at some obscure place called Sarajevo and if it ever reached the ears of the children they had soon forgotten it, but it did seem the greatest pity that Papa should have missed all these wonderful events. He had been away for months and months ever since January caring for sick people in Siberia, Missy had told them.

She suddenly thought of it now and raised her head to ask: "When *is* Papa coming home, Mamma?" and then regretted it because Nina turned round at once frowning at her.

"Whatever are you doing there, Tanya, and don't sit like that. It is not at all nice in a little girl. Just look what you're doing to your frock. Isn't it time for supper?"

"That's just what I told the Princess. It's past six o'clock," said Marta virtuously picking up discarded garments and tidying them away.

Tanya stuck her tongue out at her and then slipped off the bed straightening her sadly crumpled skirts.

"Where is the party tonight, Mamma?" she asked loitering on her way to the door.

"It's on Kamenny Island," said Nina absently.

"Will there be gypsies?"

"Probably. Don't ask so many questions. Run away, Tanya, and don't bother me. If I don't hurry I shall be late and Uncle Val doesn't like to be kept waiting."

It was never safe not to obey Mamma but Tanya did not go straight back to the nursery. She hung about on the landing and was presently joined by Andrei who had just been fetched from school and had come up by the servants' staircase.

"What are you doing there?" he asked dumping his satchel and crouching down beside her.

"I thought I'd watch Mamma leave. She's wearing the most gorgeous gown," she whispered.

Below them in the hall, Valentin in full dress uniform was waiting with a small bouquet of white gardenias in his hand. Presently Nina passed them in a cloud of silk and perfume. They watched silently as Valentin picked up the velvet wrap, then bent his head to kiss the nape of her neck before he put it around her shoulders. Tanya gave a wriggle. She didn't know why but it made her feel vaguely uncomfortable.

"I don't like Uncle Val much, do you?" she whispered to Andrei.

He shook his head, "Not much," which was ungrateful

because Valentin brought them chocolates and had even been known to offer them a ride in his sleek grey Rolls which they obstinately compared unfavourably with their own Mercedes.

"Come on," said Andrei pulling Tanya to her feet, "let's see what's for supper. I'm starving."

The early jealousy between them had faded. Tanya, high-spirited, volatile, changeable as a weathercock, had found something comforting in Andrei's practical, more reliable temperament. On certain matters they presented an united front in a hearty detestation of Marta, for instance, who could always be relied on to make trouble for them; in a kind of awe mingled with dislike of Tanya's grandmother, the formidable Princess Malinskaya who persisted in refer-ring to Andrei as "that peasant boy", in a spirited defence of a mongrel puppy rescued starving and filthy on one of their walks. Nina had insisted that it should be destroyed and was faced with a storm of tears and an impassioned appeal to Simon so that she was obliged to give in. Washed, deloused and brushed by Jake it turned out to be quite pre-sentable and was now attached to the nursery under the benevolent if autocratic rule of Ranji.

On these long summer nights when it never grew really dark it was almost impossible to get the children to bed. After supper all three of them crowded on to the window seat watch-ing the busy traffic below them, elegant motor cars with be-jewelled ladies and opulent looking gentlemen, troikas, their bells ringing madly driven by dashing guardsmen, a band of students singing as they marched arm in arm, hurrying pedes-trians, all bent on an evening's pleasure. Presently a cab drew up outside their own house, a man jumped out and opened the door, a tall familiar figure in a broad-brimmed hat stepped out and paused to pay the driver.

"It's Papa!" yelled Tanya.

"No, it isn't."

"Yes, it is and Jake too. Can't you see, stupid?"

"Papa's come home," they all shouted in unison to Missy who had come in to see what all the commotion was about, and they tore past her out of the room and down the stairs followed by both dogs.

"Wait for me," wailed Paul unable to run as fast as the other two, and it was Andrei who came back to take the little boy by the hand, so that by the time he reached the hall

Simon was already there with Tanya dancing up and down and firing questions at him, both dogs barking their heads off and Jake carrying in the luggage and smiling all over his face at being back in civilization once again.

"Was it terribly cold in Siberia? Were there wolves there – tigers – and bears?"

"Hundreds of them."

"Did you shoot any?"

"A dozen or so."

"Oh!" the children looked at him awestruck. "Were they chasing you?"

"They were indeed." Simon laughed and picked up Paul who was clinging to his hand. "How's my baby then?"

The little boy cuddled against his neck. He was a shy but very loving child.

"And where's your Mamma?" he asked looking around at them.

"She's gone to a party with Uncle Val," volunteered Tanya, "and she looked gorgeous. He gave her some flowers and then he kissed her ...", she stopped suddenly in full flight, "he comes quite often," she ended lamely.

"Does he now?"

Then Missy had come down the stairs. "For heaven's sake, let your poor Papa get his breath," she said sharply. "I never heard such an uproar. Back to the nursery, all three of you. If you're good he'll come and talk to you when you're in bed."

'Will you, Papa?"

"Certainly I will."

"Promise?"

"Off with you," commanded Missy firmly.

They went reluctantly, taking Paul with them. Simon looked after them for a moment before he turned to her.

"Didn't Nina get my wire?"

"Oh yes, but she was promised to this party and felt she couldn't get out of it."

"Where is it being held?"

"On Kamenny Island, a very grand affair indeed with the Grand Duke Dmitri and Felix Yussoupov."

"I see," Simon frowned.

"Don't be hard on her, Simon. She had a worrying time in the spring after you left. Paul fell and badly bruised his ankle. It was over a month before he could walk again."

"Why should I be hard on her as you put it? In fact I may go along and pick her up."

"Valentin Skorsky is with her."

"So Tanya told me."

"Won't you eat first? You must be tired after travelling all day."

"A bite of food and a glass of wine is all I want. I'll get washed and changed, then I will go."

Missy guessed at his disapproval and though to some extent she shared it, she hoped it wouldn't cause too much trouble between them.

The Grand Duke Dmitri, first cousin to the Tsar, was dazzlingly good-looking, with wit and elegance and the morals of an alley cat. He and his friend, Prince Felix Yussoupov, who was heir to more splendid palaces and many more millions than his Emperor, were famous for their wild parties where they gambled all night and dabbled in dangerous drugs, where the younger members of society rubbed shoulders with actors and singers, with gypsies and prostitutes, with anyone at all who could think up some sensational amusement guaranteed to stir a jaded appetite. It was hardly the kind of affair which the young wife of a distinguished physician should be attending without even the protection of her husband.

Maybe he had only himself to blame, he thought, washing off the fatigue of the journey and taking up the clean evening shirt laid out for him. He had never intended to be away so long, but the delay caused by his treatment of Olga and the fact that by the time he was ready to leave the ice on the river had begun to break up, had made his homeward journey twice as along as it should have been.

Bathed and dressed he went along to the night nursery. There was pleasure in Tanya's arms stretched up sleepily to pull him down to her and a pang of anxiety at the frailty of his little son when he tucked him into his bed. Then he went to where Andrei now slept on his own. The boy was sitting up waiting for him with the question he was burning to ask.

"Did you see my Mamma?"

"Yes, I did."

The room was shadowy except for the light under the icon. The boy's eyes watched him anxiously.

"Will she ever come back?"

"Maybe sooner than you think."

"Shall I see her then?"

"Of course you will."

"Where will she live, Papa?"

"We shall have to see about that when the time comes, won't we?" He ruffled the boy's hair. "I've brought some presents for you all. You shall have them tomorrow."

He sighed when he left the room. The boy's innocent question had carried him back to those last few hours together, to so much that lay unanswered between them.

It was late by the time he reached the island but it was not yet entirely dark. The moon had risen and the Neva was a sheet of silver, the long ripples widening out behind them as the boat crossed the water. The sky above them was a shimmering pearl grey streaked with opal. The gardens around the house were starred with golden lamps and the wild strains of the gypsy orchestra flowed out to greet him with the intoxicating perfume of night-scented flowers.

There seemed to be people everywhere as he walked up the path, sitting close together, lying in each other's arms, chasing one another through the shrubberies with whispers and laughter. He caught glimpses of silken gowns blanched by the pale moonlight, of the white, scarlet and gold of uniforms. A sudden thrilling note of gypsy song piercing the air with a long drawn out wail halted him for a moment and then was abruptly silenced.

He reached the terrace where long tables had been laid out with every imaginable kind of food, abandoned now, some of it spilling over on to the ground, the costly Sèvres plates smashed. Crystal glass mingled with upturned bottles, champagne, vodka and wine, the colour of blood staining the damask tablecloths. Fresh from the experience of Siberia, the harsh bare living scratched from the earth, the unbearable conditions in which the exiles were forced to live, the contrast filled him with a sharp anger. Was this the way they lived when the government tottered on the brink of ruin and all Europe seemed to be moving inexorably towards a disastrous war?

He stood for a moment looking around him and a figure in a flowing gown with slanted eyebrows and painted face, floated up to him.

"Where did *you* spring from, darling?"

An arm slid around his neck with a waft of heady perfume

and he saw with disgust that it was not a woman but a young man and guessed that he was not the only one. These were the kind of tricks they had always indulged in. He thrust him away and the boy gave a tipsy giggle. He felt his gorge rise at the thought of Nina among these creatures.

No one spoke to him or even took much notice as he stepped across the patio, avoiding fallen food and broken glasses, and went through the long windows into the drawing room. The room smelled of some exotic perfume and it took a moment to adjust his eyes to the shifting light of the candles. Then he saw Nina.

She was surrounded by a little group of young men among whom he recognized Dmitri.

"Sing for us, darling," he was saying, "sing for us, Nina."

She shook her head and Simon thought, "My God, she's drunk! and they're making fun of her, the innocent, helplessly lost among this vicious decadent society."

Before he could reach her strong arms had lifted her on to the table and they stood around, jeering, mocking. She swayed there for a moment, the green dress shimmering in the candle-light, staring glassily in front of her and it went through his mind, "She's not drunk, she's drugged!"

He started forward as she began to sing in her small sweet voice, a little childish ballad he had heard her sing a dozen times at Dannskoye and sometimes in the nursery when the children begged it from her. It struck him to the heart.

They were laughing and clapping by now and he strode through them roughly thrusting them aside, lifting her down and holding her close against him.

"Simon," she said uncertainly trying to focus on him, "Is it Simon?"

"Who the hell!" exclaimed Dmitri, then with a grin of recognition, "Who'd have thought it? The worthy doctor himself!"

He had once treated the young man for an injury received in some midnight brawl.

"I think you know me well enough," he said curtly. "I've come to take my wife home."

"By all means, my dear fellow," Dmitri waved a negligent hand, "take her. She's all yours."

He had his arm firmly around her and urged her away.

"I can't go," she protested weakly, "not without Valentin, he brought me."

328

"Valentin can look after himself. You're coming with me."

He took her across the gardens to where the boats waited at the little landing stage. He lifted her in and took a seat beside her. The boatman pulled out into midstream and she shivered as the night breeze blew up the river. He took off his coat and wrapped it around her shoulders. Her face was chalk-white and she stared in front of her, only half-conscious.

There were always cabs plying for hire on these summer nights so they were very soon back at the house. He opened the door with his own key, disturbing no one. He knew Marta's tattling tongue and was not going to have the servants gossiping about the mistress being brought home drunk and incapable. In the hall Nina swayed suddenly and he caught her up in his arms carrying her up the stairs and into their bedroom.

She protested feebly as he began to undress her but he took no notice, fumbling a little over unfamiliar fastenings but managing pretty well. He pulled her nightdress over her head as he might have done for Tanya, took the pins from her hair so that it hung loose around her shoulders and then lifted her into the bed. She lay back against the pillows, eyes closed, looking very frail and young and vulnerable.

"Are you angry with me?" she whispered.

"Yes, very angry, but that can wait until tomorrow."

"I feel dreadful," she said fretfully.

"I'm not surprised. How much did you have to drink?"

"Only a few glasses of champagne."

"What else did they give you?"

"I don't remember . . ."

"Try. I want to know. It's important."

She stirred uneasily rubbing a hand across her face.

"It must have been the cigarettes. They were all smoking them. Dmitri and Felix were laughing and urging me to try them. At first it felt wonderful," she went on dreamily, "as if I were floating high up on a cloud, so happy that nothing mattered any more, no anxieties, no worries, just absolute bliss . . ."

What the devil was it? Opium probably, or even cocaine, some foul concoction to give them a kick, the damned fools! They could go to hell any way they chose but they weren't going to take Nina with them, not if he had anything to do with it.

"My head," she moaned suddenly, "it feels dreadful. I think it's going to burst."

He didn't dare to give her a sleeping draught without knowing exactly how much of the drug she had smoked. A mild pain killer might do the trick and then he could stay with her till she fell asleep naturally. Any inquest could be left till the morning.

He mixed a powder in a glass but had some difficulty in persuading her to take it. Afterwards he fetched a cool damp towel and wiped the sweat from her face.

"Don't go," she whispered suddenly, her eyes wide, dark and frightened. "Don't leave me alone."

"I'm not going. Try to sleep. I'll be here if you want me," he said gently as he might have said to one of the children when they woke from nightmare.

He had settled himself in an armchair close to the bed when there was a light tap at the door and he opened it quietly to see Missy outside in her neat dark blue dressing gown and lace nightcap, looking so like his own old Nanny that he smiled involuntarily.

"I couldn't sleep," she said, "so I heard you come in. Is Nina all right?"

"Quite all right and I've not beaten her yet nor do I have any intention of doing so."

"I didn't think you would but you know, Simon, she does miss you so dreadfully when you are away."

"Does she? She has a very odd way of showing it," he said drily.

"But that's why," she went on seriously. "She feels she has to keep proving to herself that she is pretty and desirable and that people like her, because she is so unsure of you."

He looked at her, knowing there was truth in it but feeling too utterly weary to think of any solution.

"She is sleeping now," he said at last. "You go back to bed, Missy. I'm staying with her."

In the morning, bathed, shaved and dressed he met Marta carrying Nina's tea tray along the passage and took it from her. He put it down beside the bed and then mercilessly pulled back the curtains so that brilliant summer sunshine flooded into the room.

Nina putting a hand up to shield her eyes said resentfully, "Did you have to do that?"

"Yes. It's time to wake up and take a fresh hold on yourself. How do you feel?"

"Ghastly."

"I thought you might." He poured a cup of tea and brought it to her with two pills. "Take these and you'll feel a lot better."

"I don't want anything."

"Yes, you do. Drink it now at once and then we'll have a little talk."

"I shall be sick."

"No, you won't. Come along now, no argument."

He thought for a moment that she might throw the cup at him but she didn't and after a minute she sipped the tea and swallowed the pills he handed to her, one by one.

"That's better. What about another cup and some toast?"

"No . . . thank you."

"Very well." He took the cup, set it down and then stood looking down at her dispassionately. "Will you answer a straight question?"

"If I must," she said wearily.

"Did you urge Valentin to take you to this disreputable orgy because you were aware that I'd disapprove and because you knew very well that I would be coming home last night?"

"Yes, if you must know, I did," she said defiantly.

"I thought so. Why, Nina, why?"

"Isn't it obvious?"

"I'm thick-headed this morning. Explain it to me."

She stirred impatiently and the movement painfully jarred her aching head.

"Does it have to be now?"

"Yes, it does. I want to know."

She suddenly turned on him. "This trip of yours to Siberia was to last three months, wasn't it? That's what you told me last December. It would be three months and was very important for you and for your work, but it was not three months, it was seven and I know why. I think I knew from the start. Oh I daresay you did all you had set yourself to do and more, I know you well enough for that, but that wasn't the *real* reason, was it? It was Galina you were determined to meet. I know you write to her and it was so very convenient, wasn't it, so far away, no one would know, no hint of scandal for you or for her, so very discreet. You and she together for

331

weeks and weeks while I was left alone here with a sick child . . ."

"You could have called in Dr Deverenko. I made sure of that before I left."

"Oh I knew I could and he was very kind but when the other doctors returned without you, they were whispering behind my back while you and she indulged in your secret love affair. Did you think I wouldn't care? Did you expect me to sit here waiting to welcome you, no questions asked, no word said? All this summer with all these important events and I was alone, my friends pitying me, 'Where is your husband?' they asked *so* sweetly, 'Isn't he back *yet*?' I felt so wretched, so angry."

It poured out in a long flood of bitter reproaches and the contrast between her wild imaginings of some love nest where Galina and he had rioted together and what really happened in that barren land of freezing cold was so absurd that he had a crazy desire to laugh, except that it was more serious than that and somehow he had to make her understand.

"You're quite wrong, Nina," he said at last. "It was not in the least like that."

"Oh I knew you would say that, I knew you would deny it and I don't want to hear."

"You're going to listen whether you like it or not." His voice hardened, suddenly becoming so stern, so formidable, that she looked up at him startled. "Have I ever lied to you, have I?"

"I don't know – "

"You do know. Sometimes I think it might have been better if I had." He looked away from her for a moment letting his mind run back before he went on. "When I agreed to accompany the team I never dreamed that we were going anywhere near where Galina had been sent. Do you realize how vast Siberia is? It is a whole continent. If it had not been for the accident of a young woman falling sick and needing an operation if she were to live, I would never have met her."

"So you *did* meet Galina, I knew it," she said triumphantly. "I was sure of it."

"I was with her for precisely two days, most of which were occupied in a race against time to get the wretched girl to a hospital in appalling conditions."

"You make it sound very plausible."

"It's not plausible as you put it, it's the plain truth." He moved away from her before he went on. "Galina has built her own life out there amongst these exiles and it's not been easy. I admire her for that. She is probably married by now."

"Married? Galina?" she sounded incredulous.

"Yes, a fellow exile, a very decent fellow from what little I saw of him and that, Nina, is the whole story. Satisfied?"

"I suppose I must be," she said grudgingly, but in her heart she knew it was true and the angry jealousy she had nursed all these months seemed suddenly childishly puerile. She looked across to where he was standing, the light from the window falling on his face showing up mercilessly the strain of the previous few months, and she longed to stretch out her hand to him, say "I'm sorry" and somehow didn't know how to put it into words.

Then the moment had gone and Simon said brusquely, "I should get up, my dear, you'll feel better if you do. Get out into the air, take the children for a drive. I am afraid I must get back to work."

As he moved to the door there was a knock and he opened it to see Marta outside with a huge bouquet of roses.

"Count Skorsky is here, doctor, asking to see the Princess."

"Show him into my consulting room. I'll see him myself."

He took the roses, shut the door and carried them to the bed.

"A peace-offering from your lover."

"Val is not my lover."

"Isn't he? I'm very glad to hear it."

But she knew that he was only teasing and felt an enormous relief. Not that she had not sometimes been tempted, if only in an angry defiance. Quite a number of the young wives she mixed with indulged in *affaires de coeur* never admitted openly but giggled over in private, but Nina had an innate kind of innocence and a dislike of the necessary lies and subterfuges. If she had slept with Valentin she would have flung it in his face, something Simon knew very well, and he had never doubted her loyalty.

Valentin was waiting in his consulting room and looked rather sheepish when he came in.

"Nina is not sick, is she?" he asked anxiously.

"No thanks to you if she isn't," replied Simon curtly. "What the devil induced you to escort my wife to an affair of that kind?"

"Dmitri is in the regiment and one simply doesn't turn down an invitation from the Grand Duke," said Valentin awkwardly.

"And you couldn't refuse Nina either, I suppose."

"She can be very persuasive."

"Indeed she can." Simon looked him up and down; the toy soldier soon to be turned into a real one. "It looks to me as if there isn't going to be much time for parties of that kind in the near future," he went on drily.

"Perhaps not. In actual fact mobilization orders have already come through but it is only a precautionary measure surely?"

"I wouldn't count on it."

"But the Tsar would never wish to commit Russia to war. We're far too unprepared." Valentin sounded deeply shocked.

"It's not what he would wish to do but what may be forced upon him. Nina asked me to thank you for the flowers and now if you will excuse me, I am just back from months away and I've mountains of work to catch up on."

"Yes, yes, of course, I mustn't keep you. I just wanted to make sure – you see when I looked for her last night and found that she had gone – I was worried. Dmitri said something but I couldn't be certain . . ."

"You might have known she would be quite safe with me."

"Yes, I did, but . . ."

Valentin bowed himself out still apologizing and Simon permitted himself a grim smile. What a fool the man was, and yet honest and decent for all that. He ought to be grateful that it was Valentin Nina had decided to fly a kite with and not someone less scrupulous.

Events moved with alarming speed over the next few days. While most of the well-heeled in Europe and Great Britain and Russia were still basking in that glorious summer, while the children built sandcastles, while their mothers indulged in summer flirtations with handsome young men and their fathers won and lost fortunes in the casinos of Monte Carlo and Baden Baden, in Paris or Yalta on the Black Sea, and even in Brighton and Blackpool, the polticians fought and argued, moving their countries step by step into war like the moves of some deadly chess game.

Austria, furious at the murder of their Grand Duke, demanded retaliation against Serbia and one by one the great powers became involved. Telegrams, threatening and conciliatory, flew backwards and forwards all over Europe but the result was inevitable.

On the afternoon of August 2nd the Tsar issued a formal proclamation of hostilities against Germany. It was another blazingly hot day and the square was packed with thousands of sweltering people shouting, singing, carrying icons, banners and flags. Within the Winter Palace stood the miraculous icon, the Vladimir Mother of God brought to Moscow in 1395 and said to have turned back the mighty Tamburlaine. The grey-haired General Kutuzov had knelt before it in prayer before taking command of the army against Napoleon. Now the Tsar took the same oath spoken by his ancestor Alexander I. "I solemnly swear that I shall never make a peace as long as a single enemy remains on Russian soil."

Standing on the red-draped balcony beside his wife he raised his hand to speak and the enormous crowd fell on their knees and spontaneously began to sing the national anthem.

It was the same through every city of Russia, crowds surging through the streets, laughing, weeping, singing, kissing one another, in an orgy of patriotism. The red flag of revolution was forgotten. Students from the universities rushed to enlist and every man in uniform was happily mobbed and cheered.

"It's been hovering over our heads all through this grilling summer," said Nigel over a cool drink in the English Club, "and now I don't know whether I'm relieved or frightened to death."

"It can't last surely," said Simon, "six months and it will be all over."

"Don't you believe it, old boy. Kaiser Wilhelm wants to be a world power and he'll not settle for anything else. He never thought Russia would dare to challenge him but now the gauntlet has been thrown down, he'll fight to the last man. I'm thankful I sent the children home to England in the spring though Lydia hated parting from them. What will you do, Simon, if Britain decides to come in?"

"Stay here of course. Doctors are needed in war. I can be of as much use here as in England, more probably. From what I can gather the army medical corps is in a shocking state, hopelessly unprepared."

Three days later on August 5th as Germany marched into neutral Belgium a telegram to Nigel's chief announced that England had entered the war. The Union Jack was hoisted to blow in the wind with the Tricolour of France and the Russian Imperial Banner. On that same evening the German Embassy was sacked by a violent mob, smashing windows, ripping down tapestries and pictures, hurling into the streets furniture, china, glass and the ambassador's collection of priceless antiques.

The wave of enthusiasm that swept through the country from Petersburg to the Black Sea penetrated to a certain mining camp in far distant Siberia.

It was extraordinary, thought Galina, that exiles who a few months earlier would willingly have hurled a bomb into the Winter Palace and blown it sky high and the Tsar with it, now thought only of marching out to fight and die for him and for Mother Russia.

"These Germans don't know how to fight, they only know how to make sausages," said Leon coming into the dispensary and bringing her the very latest news.

The longed-for amnesty had arrived at last. The geological team and the rest of their little group would be freed and drafted into the army.

"They will be simply exchanging one form of imprisonment for another and a much more dangerous one," said Galina drily, but none of them saw it like that, not even the practical clear-sighted Leon.

"You don't understand. We'll be fighting for a cause," he said, "for our country, for the very soil under our feet. That makes all the difference."

"That's a man's point of view, you all want to be heroes," but Leon only laughed.

"And what's wrong with that? If we can keep up that spirit, those fat Germans will turn tail and run like rabbits."

Lieutenant Rylof, overjoyed at being recalled to his old regiment, gave a party with his last bottles of vodka, cheap stuff but enough to send spirits soaring, and they forgot cold and hunger, loneliness and despair, while they joined in singing the chorus –

> "Long live the Tsar
> Mighty and powerful
> Let him reign for our glory – "

That quiet ineffective little man had suddenly become the living embodiment of Russia. In Moscow a million people had thronged the streets as the Imperial procession passed on its way to the Kremlin. In the flickering light of hundreds of candles, through clouds of incense, he and his wife prayed for victory before the jewelled iconostasis in the Cathedral of the Assumption where they had been married eighteen years before.

Leon threw down the newspaper impatiently. "That was two months ago and we're still waiting to hear when we are to leave." He looked across at Galina. "What will you do when we get back to Petersburg?"

"Volunteer for the nursing service."

"I'd like to try for that. I've not had much training except in a rough and ready fashion but a strong arm must be needed and I'd sooner try to save life than destroy it. Is there a chance do you think? Can your handsome doctor pull a few strings?"

"I don't know. It's possible."

She looked around the bare hut that had seen so many hours of bitter frustration. Outside, the first snow had fallen and the icy wind that they dreaded above all things moaned and howled through the trees blowing leaves and rubbish in great swirls along the track.

"It seems almost unbelievable that in a few weeks we shall be leaving all this behind us."

"It can't be too soon as far as I am concerned," said Leon. He had come to stand behind her. "I know what you're thinking."

"Do you?"

"You'll be seeing him again, isn't that true?" She didn't answer and he went on savagely. "And what damned good is that? He has his wife, his children, he's not going to leave them for you, is he? Is he?"

His fingers dug into her shoulders, then he swung her round pulling her into his arms kissing her roughly, lips, eyes, throat, and she did not move, letting him do as he wished until at last he thrust her angrily away from him.

"You don't feel a thing, do you? Christ Almighty, why is it that a dozen girls here would fight to share my bed if I so much as nodded and the one women I've ever wanted couldn't care less whether I live or die."

"That's not true, Leon," she protested. "I do care – very much."

"Oh I know, I know, about as much as you care for your blasted patients or for that sick old dog you persist in feeding!" and he strode out of the hut slamming the door with such force that the whole frail structure shook.

The first heady enthusiasm died down a little when they knew it might be weeks even months before they were to be moved back to the capital, and when they did finally set out the ice had begun to break up and there were further tedious delays. The whole of Russia seemed to be on the move. At the railway station the trains swarmed with soldiers on their way to the battlefront. Long lines of marching men grey with dirt and mud choked the streets and were packed into carriages, cattle trucks, anything that would move. Terrible news filtered through to them. The Germans had won a tremendous victory in East Prussia, the battle of Tannenberg it was being called, where thousands of Russians had died or been taken prisoner or lay dangerously wounded, leaving a gap which these trainloads of young men were destined to fill. It gave an added poignancy to the crowds on the platforms, the weeping wives and children, mothers bravely waving goodbye to sons they could never hope to see again, grey-bearded grandfathers sending them off with gallant words and despair in their hearts.

In face of this the return of a few exiles seemed a very small affair. There were frustrating waits, sometimes for days, sometimes for weeks. It was an evening in March before they came out of the station in Petersburg.

The newsboys were shouting about a great victory in Galicia. Leon snatched a paper and they poured over it in the dim light. It seemed that the Russians had captured the strongest fortress in Austria-Hungary and were pressing triumphantly forward. Though the city was partly blacked out for fear of Zeppelin raids, there were people in the icebound streets, laughing, hugging one another in relief, casualty lists forgotten for the moment. Some of the great palaces blazed with light. The theatres had reopened, Chaliapin was singing at the Opera House, Karsavina was dancing at the Maryinsky.

It was nine o'clock by the time they were climbing up the steep stairs on the island and Galina knocked at the studio door.

Luba came to open it and stared in astonishment before she flung her arms around her friend.

"It's you! It can't be and yet it is! How absolutely splendid. Conn," she shouted, "you'll never believe! Come and see who's here."

She pulled Galina in and then saw the man who stood back a little, cap in hand.

"Who is this with you?"

"He's a friend of mine and he's new to Petersburg. Can you give him a bed for the night?"

"Of course we can. Any friend of yours is a friend of ours." She held out her hand in her usual friendly fashion. "I'm Luba and this is Conn."

"Leon Pavlov," he gave her his little bow.

"Well, don't stand on ceremony, Leon. Bring in the baggage. Are you both starving? You must have had a terrible journey."

"Pretty bad but we're here at last and that's what is important."

Galina was laughing for sheer happiness. It was so marvellous to be back with the people she knew and loved, in this untidy familiar room with its smell of paint and turpentine, of burning wood, of cabbage soup and the spicy fish that Luba liked so much.

There was so much to talk about over supper and innumerable glasses of tea that by midnight they were still hard at it.

"I can't believe it even now," said Luba. "Are you really free?"

"Not entirely. We have to report to the police and be directed into whatever they suggest. I'm going to try for the nursing service and Leon is opting for medical orderly. Is there a chance do you think?'

"Why don't you ask Simon?"

"He must have his hands full just now."

"He has of course, all the doctors are working at full pressure. We've had to close down the clinic because the young man who has been helping us has joined the medical corps and gone with the troops and Simon doesn't have any spare time. Conn volunteered and they wouldn't have him because of his chest. Remember how he used to drive us mad with his hacking cough all winter?"

"Damned fools," growled Conn, "what's a cough between friends? I could fire a rifle with the best of them."

"Now he is hoping to be appointed military observer on one of the papers – you know a sort of official war artist drawing sketches of the battles and guns and men fighting and Generals looking important and doing nothing, all that lark."

Luba prattled on gaily but Galina guessed that she was hoping against hope that something would turn up to prevent it. She always used to say that Conn with his mind on his next picture could hardly be trusted to cross the street safely.

Most of their talk was about people and events of which Leon knew nothing but they did their best to make him feel one of them and after some friendly argument it was settled that he and Conn should sleep on a shake-down in the studio and Galina and Luba would share the small bedroom.

"I daresay you two girls will be hard at it most of the night," said Conn coming in with a pile of blankets and rugs, "but please to remember that Leon and I need our beauty sleep."

"Beauty sleep my foot, you old pussycat," said Luba affectionately. "Don't you listen to him, Leon. He'll probably have you up at dawn posing for him. There's not much going on in the art world just now and models are thin on the ground."

Alone together, the door shut between them and the two men, Luba sat on the bed and looked at Galina quizzically.

"Who is he? Quite the charmer, isn't he? And obviously regards you as the fairy princess on top of the Christmas tree."

"Don't be daft, Luba. He's just one of the exiles, a geologist if you want to know, and very clever in his way."

"Is he by any chance your lover?"

"No, he is not."

"Pity. I thought I sensed a romance."

"Well, you didn't."

"I see. Just good friends."

"That's right."

Luba got up and began to unbutton her blouse. "Have you ever thought of marrying him?" she asked casually.

"Yes. I have as a matter of fact."

Luba spun round. "Oh Galina, that's wonderful. Does Simon know?"

"Yes, he does."

"And he doesn't like it one little bit." Galina said nothing and Luba suddenly put her arms around her and gave her a hug. "Darling, you can't go on wasting yourself like this."

"I don't intend to. And now can we talk about something else please? Do you ever see Andrei?"

"Yes. Simon brings him sometimes, not so often lately because he's so busy and the boy is at school. Do you want to see him, Galina?"

"More than anything in the world but is it wise, Luba? It's four years and that's a long time for a child. He's probably forgotten me."

"I don't think he has, you know."

"It could disturb him, upset his whole life completely."

"He's a self-contained child," said Luba thoughtfully. "He doesn't give much away but I don't think you need be afraid."

"I don't know," said Galina, "I don't know. I've thought and thought about it but it's so strange. I feel as if I've come out of some dark place into the open air and I've got to grow used to it. It's quite a heady feeling."

Later when they were trying to settle down together in the narrow bed, Galina suddenly began to giggle.

"What's so funny?" grumbled Luba wriggling. "Your feet are like lumps of ice and you've got more than your share of the blanket."

"Sorry." Galina adjusted her feet and went on dreamily. "I just thought of something that happened a long time ago. Simon had been at Nina's birthday party, a very grand affair and I was madly jealous of all the beautiful women he would meet there and do you know what he did? He walked out because he was bored and came to me in my tiny room – do you remember it, Luba? I think the bed was even narrower than this one."

"And you didn't care a tinker's button."

"No, we didn't."

One thought led to another. Later Galina said, "Do you ever hear anything of Igor?"

"Not a word," said Luba drowsily, "and I hope I never will. Go to sleep, darling."

"I will. Goodnight."

But Galina could not sleep, not immediately, it was too new, too wonderful to be back in the real world. She felt tinglingly alive as if anything might happen. She had not thought of Igor for a very long time and now suddenly he had become vividly alive. She had an uneasy feeling that he was somewhere near, which was absurd. He would be safely out of reach in Switzerland with the other revolutionary leaders. Perhaps it was just being here in the familiar studio that had brought him to mind. She thrust it away from her.

The full impact of the war had not yet struck her but she felt ready to play her part in it. Of course she would see Simon but not yet. She wanted to enjoy the sensation of freedom first, the power to direct her own life. Afterwards who could tell? She cautiously stretched arms and legs so as not to disturb Luba and settled herself to sleep.

20

Simon came out of the operating theatre, thankful that it was the last for that day. All during the winter Red Cross trains had brought back wounded and dying men from the front, dirty, bloodstained and feverish, the treatment given at the field dressing stations often so hurried and botched that he despaired. Day after day he was treating ripped flesh and mangled bodies, at times the wards so crowded that beds ran out and the stretchers lined up along the corridors. With the coming of spring the flood eased a little and the relentless pressure was lifted. Everyone from the top surgeons to the women who scrubbed the floors gratefully took breath while they waited for the fresh onslaught.

He washed up, a nurse brought him a welcome cup of coffee and he had a few moments of leisure to read the letter that had reached him that morning, winging its way across a war-torn Europe. It was from his brother and headed "Somewhere in France". Robert had held a commission in the Guards before his marriage and being on the reserve he was one of the first to be recalled. Simon had not seen him for ten years but there had always been a strong affection between them.

"I was thinking of you this morning," he had scribbled in pencil, "there was a lull in the firing and I could hear larks singing high in the sky though I couldn't see them. Remember when we used to take the dogs and go shooting snipe on Wicken Fen and Jake's father fed us on 'sparrer pudden'? Lovely grub! Little birds with fat bacon and a thick suet crust. Just the thing for growing boys, he used to say. Couldn't I do with some of it now instead of bully beef and worm-riddled biscuit!"

It brought back vivid memories of those dew-wet mornings. Robert had survived the winter but for how long? Valentin had disappeared into the catastrophe of Tannenberg and there'd been no word from him for months. Niki was somewhere in Poland.

Simon knew how anxiously Nina scanned the casualty lists. She had thrown herself into the war effort with all the abandon of her tempestuous temperament. The Empress had set the example by turning the Catherine Palace at Tsarkoe Selo into a hospital and with other fashionable young wives Nina enrolled in the nursing service.

"I don't think I can ever be as brave as the Tsarina is," she confessed to Simon after the first few weeks, coming home in tears. "I had to run out of the operating theatre before I was sick and even helping at dressings turns my stomach."

"Don't be such a goose," he said comfortingly. "I've known men patients who look strong as an ox fall into a dead faint at a cut finger. There are plenty of other ways in which you can help, just as valuable as watching the surgeon at work."

He sighed as he put the letter back in his pocket. It had made him feel unbearably restless. He wanted to be out in the field with them, sharing in the dangers and hardships, not staying here in the ease and comfort of Petersburg.

He got up, slipping on his jacket. For the first time for what seemed like years he felt he could allow himself an hour or two of relaxation. He might even catch a few minutes with the children before they went to bed. He took up his hat, walked quickly along the corridor and collided with a very young nurse who had come racing up the stairs at such a speed she could not stop herself.

"Steady on," he said, "no need to break your neck surely."

"I'm sorry, doctor," she gasped breathlessly, "but I'm so glad to be able to stop you before you left. It's in casualty – a man who has just been brought in. The nurse on duty sent me to find you."

"Isn't Dr Ratin in charge this evening?"

"Yes, he is, but nurse was insistent that it must be you. The poor man looks terrible, there's so much blood and his leg – you can see the bone – " the childish face still bore a look of shock.

He could have ignored the plea and walked out of the hospital but Dr Ratin was young and comparatively inexperienced and this looked like an emergency.

"Go on down," he said abruptly, "I'll follow you," and he turned back to throw down his hat and reach for his white coat.

Down in the casualty ward Dr Ratin was dealing with the usual run of routine accidents. He looked up and waved his hand to the end of the room where a screen had been partly pulled forward.

The nurse bending over the stretcher turned round to face him and he saw it was Galina. Surprised stunned him for a moment.

"What the devil are you doing here?"

"Never mind about that now. Simon, you must look at this man."

At first it seemed impossible that anyone could have been so badly injured and still live. He was covered in blood, his clothes ripped and torn, his body badly bruised where he had been mercilessly kicked, one leg broken and twisted so that in places the bone showed white.

"Good God, what happened to him?"

"He was picked up some way from the Putilov steelworks. There has been trouble there apparently. A small group have been trying to incite the men to strike against making more armaments. It failed because the majority refused and turned on the rebels. There have been arrests but not the ringleader."

"And the police believe that this is their man?"

"They don't know about him yet. He was picked up at some distance from the works. He must have crawled there and he was brought in by our ambulance, a hit-and-run victim was what they thought." Galina had been wiping the blood and mud from the man's face. Now she stood back. "Look closer, Simon."

He bent down turning the battered face towards him so that the light fell upon it.

"Igor," he breathed, "of all people in the world, Igor Livinov."

344

"The ringleader of course, doing his level best to smash the war effort. Isn't it typical?"

She was gazing at him, her eyes wide, the man who had ruined her life and his and he lay there defeated, totally at their mercy.

"What do we do, Simon?" she went on. "The *Okhrana* have been hunting him for years and we are the only two who know who he is and what he has done."

For a few seconds there was silence between them but the instinct to save life was stronger in Simon than the desire for revenge.

"I'm a doctor, not a police informer," he said at last. "We treat his injuries first. After that we can think again."

Igor stirred a little. Drained of blood and sick almost to death yet intelligence still flickered in his eyes.

"Galina and her handsome doctor, that ought to be a laugh," the voice was the merest thread. "They've almost done for me – it's your turn now – am I going to die?"

"Not necessarily," said Simon coolly, "but you could lose a leg."

"No, no, not that." With a tremendous effort he raised his head a little and the voice cracked. "Not that, anything but that. I'll never live to be a cripple, never!"

The tiny burst of energy drained the last vestige of his strength and his head fell back on the pillow.

"Clean him up and get him ready," said Simon crisply. "There's no time to be lost."

Anyone else would have amputated and finished the job there and then, thought Galina as she assisted the other nurses through the two-hour operation while Simon conscientiously and patiently put together shattered bones and torn ligaments into some semblance of a whole once again. He had always maintained the view that even a leg that limped and caused pain was better than an artificial limb with its physical and mental handicaps.

"He's come through pretty well. He must have an iron constitution," he said drily when it was all over. "I thought with all that loss of blood, his heart might have given out."

There was time now to find out more about him. He had not been robbed. When they stripped the clothes from him, they had found money and a set of papers, excellently forged. Simon stared at them before they were taken away and

Vladimir Mirov, clerk in a small clothes factory, was duly entered into the hospital register.

After Igor had been carried to one of the wards, curtains pulled around his bed and a nurse instructed to keep constant watch, Simon telephoned Nina to say he might not get home that night as he had a difficult case, and then he and Galina were alone together.

"I should go," she said, "I'm off duty and Luba will be wondering what has become of me."

"You're not going anywhere until you've told me how you've got here from Siberia, what you're doing and above all why you left me in total ignorance so that I have to meet you by accident in this hospital."

"I've only been training for a week," she protested.

"Never mind. I take it very badly." He was speaking lightly but she knew there was anger and hurt. "We'll go somewhere and eat and you can tell me all about it."

"I don't think I could eat anything."

"Of course you can. My dear girl, if you're determined to take up this nursing business you must learn to eat where and how you can if you're going to survive. Now, don't argue. There is a little place near here, not very grand, but the food is still reasonably good and I use it sometimes when I can't get home. I'll leave word where I am in case of any emergency."

He overcame all her objections and within a very short time she found herself sitting opposite him in a small restaurant, dark and a little smoky, but smelling pleasantly of good homely food.

Why is it, she asked herself, as she sipped the wine he had ordered, that when we are together it is as if we had never been apart? What is this alchemy that binds us in a relationship that nothing seems able to break?

The food came and she began to tell him about the amnesty and the long frustrating journey from Siberia.

"And you're staying with Luba?"

"I did at first. Now I've taken a room in the studios, a lot of them are empty and Leon has rented one there too."

"He came back with you?"

"Yes."

He pushed at the food on his plate and then looked up. "Are you married yet?"

"No, not yet. He wants to be a medical orderly. He is

346

working temporarily on the hospital ambulances." She paused and then went on earnestly. "Igor is dangerous, Simon. He could do so much harm."

"Do you hate him so much?"

"It's not what he did to me. It's so much else. I met him in Kiev, only briefly, but he was linked with the Stolypin murder."

She found it difficult to explain her feeling about him, how in some queer way she had always known this would happen, that Igor would come back into their lives and with him would come danger for all of them.

Simon said thoughtfully, "I know how you feel. If I were to meet him alone on equal terms that would be one thing, but to hand a desperately sick man over to the *Okhrana*, that's something else. You know what they would do to him. They would question him unmercifully, use every means they could, and they have some damnably unpleasant ones, to find out who sent him here, before they hanged him as a traitor."

"He deserves it."

"For what he did to you perhaps but for the rest, I don't know. He is one of those who believe the only way to save Russia is by the violence of revolution. I don't agree with him but he has a right to his opinion."

"Oh don't be so fair-minded, don't make excuses for him," she said impatiently. "He would not treat you in that way if you were in *his* power."

"Perhaps not but that doesn't really alter it, does it? If you behave as badly as your enemy, then you have let him corrupt you. Isn't that true?"

"I suppose so. I can't always see things like that," she said doubtfully. "What if the *Okhrana* come to the hospital, demand his arrest?"

"In that case, except medically, it would be out of my hands. Why are we wasting time arguing about Igor?"

He called the waiter, ordered coffee and then smiled at her across the candle-lit table.

"Galina, you are a trained pharmacist. I could recommend you for work here in the city where people like you are badly needed. Why must you go out with the Red Cross unit?"

"I've been shut away from the world for so long. I want to be part of it again, Simon."

"It's not just to escape from me?"

"No, oh no, don't believe that. It's not like that at all." She sensed his hurt and put her hand on his. At even so slight a touch a current seemed to race between them and she withdrew it quickly. "I didn't think I would feel like that at first. I laughed at some of the other exiles, all those who had been waving the red flag suddenly willing to march out and die for the Tsar and Russia, but when we were travelling home, when I saw all those trainloads of soldiers, some of them only boys, Simon, I knew I must do what I could. I must share it with them in some way. Do you understand that?"

"Oh yes, I understand." It was still his Galina, the young girl with her starry-eyed dream of making the world a better place to live in who had stumbled into his apartment and into his heart ten years ago. "I understand very well. I feel it myself."

"It's different for you. You're doing such wonderful work here."

"I do what I can but is it enough? It's my war too, Galina. England even after all these years is still home. My brother is out there as well as Niki. Thousands of miles apart but on the same side."

"Will you go?"

"I don't know yet. If conditions worsen here, I may have to think of Nina and the children."

"Simon," she said hesitantly, "will you let me see Andrei? I know it is a long time and he has probably forgotten me but he *was* my baby once."

Despite her self-control her voice trembled and it touched him to the heart.

"He's not forgotten you. You can be very sure of that."

"It would be best if I didn't meet Nina."

"I'll bring him to you myself. He goes to visit Luba sometimes on Saturdays when there is no school. I'll come then."

They sat on in the quiet of the little restaurant until nearly midnight when he put her in a cab for her lodging and went back to the hospital to check on Igor's condition.

The next week was critical and made more so because a fresh influx of wounded had made the long painful train journey from the Carpathians. Even in their agony the men boasted of their comrades going forward gloriously, leaving the mountainsides behind them soaked in blood. But there were other stories too, lack of the right ammunition that made their rifles useless, food that never reached them so that men were going into fight day after day on a mouthful of black bread.

One afternoon that week the Tsarina came on one of her regular hospital visits, not the bejewelled figure they saw from a distance but wearing the plain grey of a nursing sister, and Galina saw how they called to her, holding out their bandaged hands, pitifully grateful when she knelt by the bed and prayed for them. She paused beside Igor laying a cool hand on his forehead.

"Still very feverish, poor fellow."

She picked up the cup of water beside the bed and held it to his lips. Galina saw his eyes flicker open and held her breath afraid that he might dash it away, but he didn't. He sipped a little and murmured thanks.

That was the day when Simon had to tell him that another operation would be necessary.

"What is it this time, doctor, the knife?"

"I hope not."

"You know I'd rather die than go on living only half a man."

"People often say that but very rarely mean it."

"Why are you taking so much trouble?" he asked curiously.

"I don't care to leave a job half done." Simon beckoned the nurse. "See that he is made ready. I'll operate this evening."

He had feared gangrene, that dreadful blood poisoning that was taking such a hideous toll of the wounded men, but Igor's flesh was healthy and after the second phase of repair work was completed, he began slowly to mend. And that was when the *Okhrana* came.

Galina saw the two men walking slowly down the ward with Simon and knew instantly who they were. Nondescript in dark suits with hooded eyes and undistinguished faces, yet there was something that stamped a man as secret police.

"So he is taking his revenge after all," whispered Igor, "typical, isn't it? Mend the broken body in time for the hangman to do his work."

"Don't speak like that," muttered Galina fiercely.

The two men were looking closely at the patients one by one. Checking them from the hospital list in their hands. They paused at the end of Igor's bed and and looked him over.

"Vladimir Mirov, clerk," one of them read. "Not a soldier then, doctor?"

"No, accident case, a truck ran over him, poor fellow," said Simon smoothly.

The two men looked at one another. "We could take him in for questioning."

"No, I could not permit it, not while he is in my charge," said Simon firmly. "He is too sick to be moved or subject to any undue pressure."

"Will he recover?"

"Perhaps, given time."

"Very well but keep him under observation."

The two men walked on with Simon and Igor let out a long breath.

"That was a near one."

"If it had been my choice I'd have let them take you," muttered Galina savagely.

"How like a woman! Run after them, Galina, denounce me. Go on, I dare you."

But she couldn't and he knew it. She longed to wipe the grin off his mocking face.

A week later when Simon was making his usual rounds he noticed that Igor's bed had another occupant and asked where the patient had gone.

"He has been discharged, doctor, didn't you know?" said the nurse on duty. "Yesterday it was, towards evening. Two men came for him."

"Who were they? Police?"

"Oh no, doctor, two rather rough looking fellows, I thought, but very well spoken and they had the Director's permission. One of them was a close relative and he said his sister would be happy to nurse poor Mirov back to health. Very grateful they were for all that had been done for him. We're so desperately short of beds, I was sure it had been all arranged."

"Yes of course, no doubt it had. Thank you, nurse."

He walked on to the next bed. So Igor had gone to ground with two of his fellow conspirators; he could not help feeling relieved though whether he had acted wisely, he could not be sure. That was hidden in a dark future that no one yet had glimpsed or believed possible.

He told Galina about it that evening when they met as they usually did at least once a day. Sometimes they came together merely to talk about the patients. But the warmth and simple happiness of being together was always there. Once or twice he took her to eat at the smoky little restaurant but only very rarely and he said nothing about it to Nina. She was occupied and happy these days, finding interest and satisfaction in the work she was doing. There was no point in upsetting her unnecessarily.

Spring had come at last and it seemed like a miracle to Galina after the long Siberian winter. Almost overnight the city was transformed, the ice vanishing, the river flowing free once again, the chestnuts budding and the flower sellers coming into the market with their crammed sweet-smelling baskets. She came back to her room with a great armful of willow, silvery buds beginning to break into golden puffballs.

She tried to persuade Leon to go with her and Luba to the Easter Mass but he shook his head.

"I'm not a religious man, never have been. Saw a bit too much of it as a boy, I suppose, watching my father's performances."

He and Conn walked with the two girls to St Isaac's Cathedral and saw them safely inside.

The throng of men, women and children all holding candles were packed tight into the body of the church in almost total darkness. Pinpoints of light gleamed here and there on a gilded tomb or the jewelled robes of a saint. The rich chanting of the psalms rose up to the roof with billowing clouds of incense. Slowly the procession came from behind the iconostasis, the vestments like a river of gold pouring towards the sepulchre with its empty shroud.

The priest turned to the congregation with the glad cry, "*Khristos voskrese!*" "Christ is risen!" And the congregation responded with a great joyous shout, "*Vo istinu voskrese!*" "He is risen indeed!"

The candles were lit one from the other till the Cathedral blazed with light. Husbands were embracing wives with the three ritual kisses and it was then that Galina saw Simon standing by one of the great pillars with Nina beside him and a tall slim boy very erect and very solemn at his first Midnight Mass. She saw Simon kiss his wife's cheek and then put his arm around the boy pulling him close.

It was Andrei! It had to be Andrei! She could not take her

eyes from him. He was *her* son, she wanted to take him in her arms, she wanted to share him with Simon and was shut out, cut off for ever from that simple family happiness. The boy turned and seemed to look straight at her and though she knew well enough that he could not possibly see her through the dazzle of the candles, it seemed that he rejected her and she could not bear it. She turned and began to push her way out through the packed church.

"Here, hold on," exclaimed Luba, "what's wrong?"

"It's the heat, the incense, it makes me feel faint."

She was saying anything, making any excuse, because she could not endure to stay, because they might see her. She would have to meet Nina and smile and reveal nothing. The pain, the feeling of injustice, were too sharp. They would be going home to the Easter feast with a few friends, Nigel and Lydia perhaps. Nina's cook would have prepared the *kulich*, the Easter bread topped with melted sugar, the delicious white cheese *pashka* filled with preserved fruits, there would be brightly coloured eggs for the children and gifts for everyone.

Outside the church people were laughing and happy, the agony of war and the gloom of the darkened city forgotten for an hour or two.

Luba caught up with her and took her arm.

"I'm sorry," said Galina, "I didn't mean to run out on you."

"I know. I saw them too."

"Why do I *care* so much?" said Galina fiercely.

"Why do we care about anyone?" The road was so crowded they were forced apart for a moment. "Conn is going, you know," went on Luba when they were together again.

"Oh Luba, no!"

"With the next trainload, going out west with sketchbook and pencils in his pack." She caught her breath in a half sob. "If only he weren't such a stupid donkey and half blind without his glasses. If they are broken, he'll probably walk into a gun instead of running like a lunatic away from it. It's all so crazy, isn't it? I wish I were a man, I could go out and get drunk."

"That wouldn't help much."

"It might. Why do we always want what we can't have? I thought I would be safe with Conn for ever and now he's going off to war and so pleased and proud about it that I could hit him. And you're mooning after Simon when Leon is only waiting for you to give a nod and he'd whisk you into his bed but you don't want him, do you?"

"No."

"I tell you, we're off our heads, both of us." In her anger and defiance of the trials that life sent her, there was something almost irresistible about Luba. "It's never been any good crying over it, has it? We've both learned that. Come on, we'll have our own Easter feast and be damned to the lot of 'em!"

And that's what they did sharing tea and savoury *zaguskies* and half a bottle of vodka with Leon and Conn and were very merry over it pushing heartache and anxiety to one side. They would come back all too soon.

At the end of that week, on the Friday evening Simon said, "I have a free morning tomorrow, I'll bring Andrei to see you."

She was suddenly seized with panic. She nearly said, "Perhaps it's wrong. Perhaps it won't work and we'd best leave things as they are," but she couldn't get the words out and now it was Saturday morning and he would be here at any minute. She looked at herself in the mirror a dozen times, which was stupid. Children didn't notice these things but she was thirty now. Would she seem very old to him? He was used to Nina, so young and beautiful still. She glanced around the bare room, its only ornament the jar of budding willow branches. Well, he must know her as she was, no fine clothes, no frills.

She was looking from the window when she saw the Mercedes pull up, Simon at the wheel. She saw Luba run out to greet them, kiss the boy and point upwards. She drew back nervously. She heard the footsteps on the stairs, the knock on the door, and then he was standing there, his hand on the big dog's collar, a little shy, a little uncertain, with his father close behind him.

"Mamma?" he asked tentatively and she trembled hardly daring to move or speak until with a great shout of "*Mamma!*" he raced across the room, her arms going around him holding him tightly against her.

"Andrei!" she was laughing and trying hard not to cry at the same time as she bent down to fondle the big dog, "and Ranji too!"

Simon had come in and was watching them but she could think only of the boy.

"So you've not forgotten me, Andrushka?"

"Oh *no* and neither has Ranji, just look at him!" The dog was pushing his head against her making little affectionate noises in his throat. "Papa has told me everything," went on Andrei, "all about Siberia and the sick lady and the wolves and how *brave* you were! And I've got heaps and heaps to tell you about Tanya and Paul and what we do at school and the ponies we ride at Dannskoye. Jake says my uncle who lives in England has *beautiful* horses and when Papa takes us there, I shall ride them."

The words were pouring out breathlessly, tumbling over one another. Then he paused looking up into her face.

"Papa says you're going to the war to help care for the soldiers like he does in the hospital. I wish I could go."

"Do you want to be a doctor, Andrei?"

"Oh yes. I'm going to be a surgeon like Papa."

"He fancies the idea of cutting people up, don't you, monster?" said Simon affectionately.

He wanted to know everything, hardly waiting for her replies to tell her more about himself until Leon came in with a tray loaded with coffee and piping hot *blinis*. He put it down on the table with a flourish.

"With Luba's compliments."

Andrei eyed the savoury pancakes. "Luba always makes them for me. May I have one?"

"Of course, but say hallo to Leon first. He is a friend of mine," said his mother.

"Were you in Siberia too?" asked Andrei politely.

"Yes. I was there too."

"Leon is a geologist. He digs into the earth and finds all sorts of wonderful things – gold and precious stones and even fossils. Do you know what they are?"

"Oh yes," he said, "they're animals and flies and things that have been dead for thousands and thousands of years and have turned to stone. Did you bring some of them back with you?"

"A few."

"May I see them?"

"Certainly."

"May I, Mamma?"

"Of course, darling, provided Leon doesn't mind showing them to you."

"It will be a pleasure."

Galina smiled at the boyish enthusiasm. "You'd better take the *blinis* with you."

So they went off together carrying the plateful of pancakes and Simon came to take the coffee Galina poured for him.

"Happy now?" he asked.

"Yes, I am. I was so afraid at first."

"We have had our problems but we got over them without too much damage."

"I'm grateful to Nina and to you. I shudder when I remember what could have happened to him out there."

Simon put down his cup. "Are you still determined to join this Red Cross unit?"

"Yes, of course, just as soon as I've finished my training and have received the badge."

He reached out and drew her towards him. It seemed that all through the years they had met only to part and now with the urgency of war, the ever-present fear that time which might never come again was rushing by, it had become unendurable.

"Would it be so impossible for you to stay here with me?"

In a moment, she thought, all her plans would be blown to the wind because her need of him was so great. She pulled away saying the first thing that came to mind.

"I came across something of yours the other day, a book that I took with me." She moved away to look through the few precious things she still kept with her and brought the little leather bound book.

"Do you remember? I could hardly read any English then and you used to translate them for me."

"Very badly I expect." He took the book from her with a wry smile. "Good Lord, John Donne. He used to be a favourite of mine. When you're young and very much in love, you enjoy reading about death and despair because you simply can't imagine it ever happening to you." He turned the pages. "Here's something I must have marked when nothing on earth would have persuaded me that we could ever be parted." He began to read –

"When my grave is broke up again
Some second guest to entertain . . .
And he that digs it, spies

355

A bracelet of bright hair about the bone,
Will he let us alone
And think that there a loving couple lies . . ."

He put the book down. "What a romantic idiot I must have been – a bracelet of bright hair," he took up a fallen strand of her hair and wound it around his wrist. "It has a great deal more point to it now, hasn't it? Would you cut it off for me?"

"Simon don't. You frighten me."

But she did not move away and he kissed her lips lightly; they were too absorbed in one another to notice the door opening.

"I thought I might find you here," said Nina. "I would never have known if Tanya had not given it away."

Galina took a quick step away but Simon did not move. He said coolly, "Did you want me for anything in particular?"

She came further into the room, her new spring costume in a deep violet trimmed with black braid was very smart and chic.

"How long have you been back from Siberia, Galina?"

"A few weeks."

"And is this where you and my husband spend the nights when he tells me he is working at the hospital?"

"Nina!" exclaimed Simon. "You will take that back?"

"Why should I? It's true, isn't it?"

"It most certainly is not. This is the first time I've been here. Surely Galina has a right to see something of her son."

"So that's the excuse, is it? That's how Tanya heard of it," she began to peel off her gloves with quick nervous gestures. "I don't believe you."

"You must," said Galina vehemently, "because it's true. I've seen him at the hospital because I'm working there before I go out with the Red Cross and that is absolutely all."

"And what about the cosy suppers at midnight and afterwards when you go back to the hospital? Do you spend all those hours by the bedside of dying patients? You must think me very naïve to believe that. I have heard quite a different story."

"Where from, for God's sake?"

"Never mind where."

"Marta, I suppose, nosing about and asking questions. I won't have her spying on me."

"Marta is loyal to me."

"She is nothing of the kind. Marta is a liar and cares only for herself and what she can wheedle out of you. It's high time you realized that." He took her arm. "Now come away with me, Nina. I'll drive you home. I'm not staying here listening to you insult Galina."

"*Can* she be insulted?" Her calm suddenly broke. "She wants to take you from me, it's what she has always wanted."

"You're wrong, Nina, believe me you're quite wrong," said Galina earnestly.

"You're just like Simon, so clever, both of you, always so reasonable, always so full of excuses, always putting *me* in the wrong, but not this time."

Her voice rose into a sob and carried away by a wave of hysterical jealousy she struck Galina across the cheek so hard that the ring she wore left a streak of blood behind it.

"Nina, stop that, stop it at once!"

Simon had gripped her wrist and swung her away. She stood there trembling while a small trickle of blood ran down Galina's face and it was at that moment that the door was flung open and Andrei came through with Leon carrying rock samples in his hands and full of excitement.

"Look, Mamma, just look at what Leon has given me," and then he stopped glancing at Nina in surprise. "I didn't know you were coming. Have you brought Tanya?"

"No, no, I haven't." She turned away from him.

It was Leon who sensed that something was very wrong. He put a hand on the boy's shoulder.

"I'll find you a box for those things, shall I? Then we'll take them down to the car."

"Don't go, Leon." Galina had taken out a handkerchief and dabbed at her cheek. "I'd like you to meet the Princess Nina, Simon's wife. Nina, may I present Leon Pavlov, my future husband?"

After one startled look at her, Leon played his part admirably.

"Charmed to make your acquaintance, Princess."

And Nina taken by surprise, the wind blown out of her sails, only half believing, replied almost automatically.

"I suppose I must congratulate you," and she held out her hand.

"Thank you." Leon bent his head and politely kissed the white fingers.

"I didn't know Mamma was going to marry *you*," said Andrei frowning.

"Neither did I till this morning. Isn't it exciting?" Leon gave the boy a smile. "Now, young man, what about taking those things downstairs?"

He shepherded the boy out of the room before he could ask any more awkward questions.

"Is it true?" said Nina when they had gone.

"Yes, quite true."

"Did Simon know?"

"Yes, I knew. I told you, Nina, when I came back from Siberia but you chose not to believe me." He was very cool and calm and Galina did not dare to look at him. She had acted on a crazy impulse and now was a little afraid of what she had done.

"Come, Nina," went on Simon. "Let's put an end to this sorry farce. I'll take you home. The boy can stay here with you, Galina. I'll send Jake to fetch him later."

"Thank you."

Galina watched them go, saw Nina pause at the door and look back as if to say "I'm sorry" and then go quickly followed by Simon. She had committed herself now, taken an irrevocable step, cut herself off from him once and and for all and felt no triumph, nothing but a devastating sense of loss as if a mainspring had suddenly snapped and there was no purpose, no meaning left in anything and the reckoning with Leon was still to come.

It haunted her at intervals all during the afternoon she spent with Andrei learning to know her son all over again, guessing at many things as he talked more freely, glad to see how happy and familiar he was with Luba and Conn.

When Jake came to collect him, he hugged her tightly, burying his face against her neck.

"I don't want you to go away again, Mamma, not now. Must you go?"

"It will only be for a little while then I'll be back."

"May I come and see you again?"

"If Papa says you can."

She came down to see him into the car. Jake touched his cap to her as the boy scrambled into the front seat beside him.

"Nice to see you looking so well, Miss."

"And you too, Jake. Look after the doctor for me."

"No fear of that, Miss."

She watched them drive away and then went slowly up the stairs to find Leon waiting for her.

He turned as she came in.

"Has he gone?"

"Yes."

"A bright boy. He should go far with the advantages his father can give him."

"Yes."

He stood with his back against the window looking unusually grave and formidable.

"I played my part in that miserable comedy this morning so now we must decide what we are going to do about it."

"I meant what I said," she replied nervously.

"Did you? I suppose I should feel honoured."

"You did ask me to marry you. Have you changed your mind?"

"That's hardly the point, is it? I have the strongest possible objection to being used as a pawn in the game you're playing."

"It's no game. Nina was accusing us of unspeakable things."

"And I was there, only too willing to provide the slap in the face."

"I'm ready to stand by what I said," she answered stung by the irony in his voice.

He paused staring at her. "You mean that? You really would marry me?"

"Yes."

"I'm not blind, Galina. I've seen you and this doctor of yours in the hospital – oh innocent enough I've no doubt – but people talk. No one could see you two together and not guess at what there is between you."

"It's all over, Leon."

"Oh no, it isn't and I'm not playing second fiddle to him or to anyone. It's all or nothing, Galina. I'm not marrying you as a stopgap and that's flat. Oh you can think up something to convince her ladyship. There's a war on. Time is short. I'm to be called away with the next draft, anything you like. They are screaming out for more recruits. It shouldn't be difficult."

"No, Leon, I can't let you do that. I couldn't bear to think I'd driven you into something you've never wanted."

"War's a bloody business, my dear, whatever we do and the sooner it's over the better. When I've marched off you'll be free of me. No obligation and afterwards who knows what's going to happen to any of us?"

"Leon, I've hurt you . . . I'm sorry."

"Why be sorry? Sometimes win, sometimes lose, that's the way it goes." He moved to the door and then stopped. "Only there are times when I wish to God I'd never set eyes on you!"

He went out, the door slammed behind him and she thought she had never felt so utterly alone in her whole life. She sat on while the light gradually faded, the courage and resilience that had so often saved her slowly draining away until there was nothing left but a dull kind of despair. When Luba looked in, the room was quite dark.

"Goodness, whatever are you sitting here for moping all by yourself? Leon stormed out a while ago with a face like thunder. What's biting him?"

"I offered to marry him and he won't have me."

"Like that, is it? He has a very odd way of showing it. I had the impression that he was going to bury his sorrows in the bottle. Come on, Galina, show more spirit, have supper with us. Everything always looks worse on an empty stomach. Leon will be back, sick and sorry I expect, but he'll get over it."

It was past midnight when she came back to her room a little cheered by Luba's determined efforts to distract her but still with the desolate sensation of being outside their happy relationship, with no one who was close to her, no brother or sister or lover, no one who belonged to her alone. Her son was wrapped up in his new family, Simon concerned with Nina and his children . . . it went round and round in her mind while she undressed and put on her dressing gown. She had sat down to unpin her hair when she heard the stumbling footsteps on the stairs and thought Luba had been right. Leon had come home drunk. She waited for him to pass her room and go on to the floor above but there was a long pause, then the door flew open and he was standing there, swaying a little, supporting himself with one hand against the wall. There was blood on his face and a great deal of it on one sleeve, his jacket had been ripped, his trousers and boots covered with mud and filth.

She sprang to her feet. "Leon, whatever have you been doing?"

"Fighting."

"I can see that but why?"

"I don't really know. This fellow said it would be a good thing if the Germans won, then the Tsar and the whole bloody lot of them could be thrown out and the slaughter would stop. Well, I couldn't let that pass so I let him have it." He grinned. "He looks a lot worse than I do."

"Were you both drunk?"

"Not so as you'd notice. Just came in to say I'm sorry. Didn't really mean all I said, you know. Marry you tomorrow if you really want it."

He turned to go and she stopped him.

"Leon, come here. You're bleeding. You can't go to bed like that. Let me look at it."

"I'm all right."

"No, you're not. It could be serious. Come and sit down."

The blood dripped to the floor as she got him to a chair. She stripped off his jacket and the bloodstained shirt. Someone must have been handy with a knife. There was a brutal slash down his arm that could have done with stitches. She pressed it close together as he winced with pain and then bound it very tightly. After that she dealt with the cuts and bruises on his face which were more superficial than serious.

"Are you in great pain?" she asked when it was done. "I can give you something for it."

"I will be all right. I'll survive."

He put his sound arm around her waist and drew her close to him.

"Thank you, Galina," he said huskily.

He leaned his dark head against her and her arms went around him almost as if he had been Andrei and suddenly it was two intensely lonely people finding comfort in each other.

After a few minutes he got to his feet, looked closely into her face and then kissed her. She did not move and a little fumblingly with one hand he began to undo the buttons of her dressing gown. He kissed her throat and then her breast. She knew what was coming and welcomed it, longing for the comfort of being loved, of knowing that for this night at least she was not alone and unwanted.

"A one-armed man is not much of a lover," he whispered

as he slipped the dressing gown off her shoulders. "I'll try not to bleed all over you."

He was gentle and he was strong and it was unexpectedly satisfying. Not as it had been with Simon, nothing could ever be like that, but there was warmth and tenderness and passion. Afterwards when she lay beside him careful to avoid any pressure on his wounded arm, she thought what a queer way to begin a new life, going into the horror and carnage of war with no knowledge of what was to happen or where it would ultimately lead them.

21

"And what have you been doing with yourself? That's a regular beauty you've got there," said Jake as Andrei came running to him through the school gate. "Walked into a door, did we?"

The boy had a plaster across his forehead from which blood was still oozing and the beginnings of a magnificent black eye.

"No, I was in a fight," he looked at Jake with a grin. "He's a lot worse than me. He's got two black eyes."

"That's the ticket. You remembered what I taught you, I hope?"

"Yes, I did."

"And what was this battle royal about, eh?"

"Oh . . . just things."

These two had been good friends for quite a time now and Jake guessed he wouldn't get much more out of the boy. He contented himself with saying, "Better let your Papa take a look at it this evening. Could be nasty."

Petrol had become desperately short this winter and the Mercedes had to be reserved for more important journeys but the unlit streets after dark were no longer safe for a well-dressed eleven-year-old boy so Jake was ordered to fetch him every evening from the gymnasium despite Andrei's protest that he was no longer a baby.

Petrograd, as the government had mysteriously decreed that Petersburg should now be called, had become a city of gloom by that January of 1916. It had been impossible to conceal from the ordinary population the disastrous news of the German counter-attack that had decimated the army through the previous spring and summer.

Anger and despair swept through the snow-bound cities of Russia at the ever-lengthening casualty lists. Theatres were closed, no opera, no ballet, no balls, no festive parties. The young men who had gone joyously into battle, who had laughingly suggested packing their dress uniforms for the victory ride down Berlin's Unter den Linden now lay dead on the mountains and plains of Hungary and Poland. The millions who had been sent to fill the gap left by the Tannenberg disaster were rotting in unknown graves or in vast prison camps or in the Red Cross trains that rolled slowly back filling every hospital to overflowing. Few ships were able to get through the German blockade of the Baltic ports so that food had become wickedly expensive and very scarce even for those who had money to buy. Food queues for even such simple necessities as bread and potatoes began at dawn. Fuel had to be strictly limited to the old, the sick and the very young, and everyone was finding it imperative to pile on every stitch of clothing against the bitter cold.

Even Christmas at Dannskoye had lost its charm. The snow mountain was not such fun without Valentin or Uncle Niki still lost somewhere on that vast battlefield. If Aunt Sonia put on a brave face, they all knew she wept in private, and the government in a reaction against everything German had forbidden even such a simple pleasure as a Christmas tree. It was Tanya who rebelled most fiercely against the gloom. She quarrelled with everyone until the twins, home from school, lost their temper and smacked her hard. Andrei flew to her defence, the boys' baby sister screamed and war broke out in the nursery, ending in punishment for everyone and dire consequences for Paul. The little boy joyously joining in the scrimmage was knocked down and his nose began to bleed and bleed so that no one, not even Papa, had been able to stop it for several hours. Simon in fact had spent his Christmas night sitting up with the boy in his arms to prevent any sudden movement that might start up the bleeding again.

It wasn't fair, thought Andrei, kicking angrily at the newly

363

fallen snow as they trudged home, that they should say such terrible things about his father when, as he knew very well, he had given up most of his private practice to spend his time with the wounded that came in a never-ending stream into the hospital.

He did not mean to tell anyone about his injury passing it off as nothing when he joined Tanya for supper and Missy wanted to know what on earth he had been doing with himself.

It was Jake who took it upon himself to mention it, so that later Simon came up to the little room where Andrei was struggling with his Latin homework.

"What's this I hear about you?" he said. "Been in the wars, have you? Better let me have a look at it."

"It's nothing, Papa, really it isn't."

"Let me be the judge of that. Come down to my consulting room."

He gently unpeeled the plaster and frowned at the deep split above the boy's eyebrow.

"This needs stitching. Why didn't they do it at school?"

"The nurse said it wasn't necessary."

"I beg to differ. If that's left as it is, it's going to leave a very ugly scar. You'd better sit down, Andrei, while I deal with it. I'll try not to hurt too much."

He sat very still determined not to make a sound while his father worked swiftly and efficiently with his needle before applying a light dressing and plaster.

"That's my brave boy," he said with a smile when it was all done. "That can come off in a day or two when I take out the stitches. Now tell me how you got it. I didn't think the gymnasium encouraged fighting among the boys."

"No, they don't, but some of them were saying horrible things about – about the British – that they were holding back deliberately, sparing their own soldiers and letting the Russians do all the fighting – and then – and then – "

"And then what? Come along, out with it."

He hesitated and then went on with a rush. "And then one of them called you a coward because you stayed safe in the city and left the fighting to others and that you treated German prisoners just the same as you did the Russians and it wasn't right because they were the enemy – and after that I hit him."

"And then you fought, I suppose."

"Yes, he got me down once but I pushed his face into the mud till he took it back."

"I see, and do *you* think I'm a coward?"

"Oh no! I told him that if he ever said it again, I'd *kill* him!"

The boy looked up at his father, his lips trembling, then suddenly he put his arms around him and buried his head against his chest.

"I hate this war, I hate it," he muttered incoherently, "I keep thinking of Mamma out there and Uncle Niki and . . ."

Simon held him very close. The boy had touched upon his own battle which he was finding it difficult to resolve. Presently he gently freed himself.

"You'd better get to bed now, Andrei, and if that's painful in the morning, I'll send Jake with a note saying you won't be at school for a day or two."

"No, Papa." Andrei raised his head resolutely. "That'll look as if I'm afraid and I'm not, I'm not!"

"Well, don't get in to too many battles on my account," he said drily, "I have quite enough wounded heroes to deal with as it is. Now be off with you. I'll come and say goodnight later."

He watched the boy go and then went back to the drawing room. Nina looked up as he came in.

"What's Andrei been up to? Tanya said he had hurt himself."

"He got involved in some schoolboy scrape. It's not serious."

He glanced across at her sitting as close to the stove as possible, a light shawl around her shoulders. Even they had to conserve fuel as much as possible. Surprisingly Nina who had never wanted for ânything in her whole life had put up with the shortages far better than he had expected. He waited for crises and they did not materialize. Perhaps it was because she now believed Galina was married and so no longer felt threatened or perhaps it was because she had felt a certain fulfilment in working for the war with the band of devoted young women closest to the Tsarina.

"She often speaks to me when we are going around the wards," she had told him over supper that evening. "Did you know the Tsarevich suffers the same attacks as Paul does? Of course she did not say exactly what it was but I knew and I could sympathize."

If she could find comfort in knowing that the heir to the throne was afflicted by the same sickness as her own son so much the better.

"I could wish she relied more on her doctors and less on that charlatan Rasputin," he had replied drily.

"But he does such wonders for him," went on Nina earnestly. "You know the boy suffered a terrible nosebleed just like Paul. The doctors could do nothing for him, they thought he would bleed to death until she sent for Rasputin. He came, looked down at him, touched his face and the bleeding stopped. The boy fell into a restful sleep and was quite recovered the next morning."

It was a pity that the rest of Russia did not realize that. Everywhere outside court circles scandalous stories circulated – Rasputin was the Empress's lover, he had ravished her two elder daughters, it was he and not the ineffectual Tsar who was ruling Russia through the Empress – and they were all the more readily believed because she was a German Princess, harbouring German spies perhaps – some of the tales grew wilder and wilder as the hatred of all things German turned to violence. Bakers' shops had their windows smashed, anyone speaking German or indeed any foreign tongue not understood by the mob was liable to be attacked in the streets. It had not touched Nina's household yet. Here in the wealthier parts of the city everything was still calm but it was impossible to avoid the feeling of tension, rather like living close to a volcano that could erupt at any moment.

Tonight was the first quiet evening for a long time and Simon sat with a book open on his knee but he was not reading. Instead his thoughts had strayed back to the last time he had seen Galina when she had announced her intention of marrying Leon. His instant reaction had been one of deep hurt that in all the time they had spent together she had not confided in him but when he looked for her at the hospital the following week she did not appear and it was only later that Luba told him what had happened.

"The chance came and they seized it, both of them. A Red Cross unit was being sent out immediately and there was one short due to sickness. Galina volunteered and they were only too glad to include her."

"I have been expecting an invitation to the wedding," he said drily.

Luba shot him a quick glance. "Oh they're not married. There wasn't time and in any case they could not travel together. It seems that the matron in charge of the nurses is an old diehard, guards them like a bunch of nuns against the evil ways of men, ravishers one and all to be kept at a safe distance unless they are wounded and incapable."

So she had gone without saying goodbye, without a single word, maybe it was for the best.

He shut his book with a snap and said brusquely, "How would you feel, Nina, if I were to leave you for a few months?"

"Leave? How do you mean?"

"The medical service has suffered severe losses as well as the troops and it's hardly work for the older doctors."

"So you're like all the others, you want to be in the thick of it."

"Yes, I suppose I do."

"Like Niki and Val . . ."

"And my brother."

"I'd forgotten that."

He got up walking restlessly about the room and then turned to face her.

"I've lived here so long, I never thought I should feel so strongly about England but I do."

Those schoolboy taunts still rankled. He'd not have any Englishman accused of cowardice.

"I shall miss you terribly. Must you go? Surely you do enough here."

"There are plenty to take my place at the hospital but out there at the front there is still desperate need."

"And Galina is out there, isn't she?"

"Perhaps that is part of it," he said honestly, "but I don't think so, not now."

She looked up at him. "You would still go, wouldn't you, even if I begged you to stay?"

"If I thought it was right to do so, then I would. I'm not running away from you, Nina."

He came to her then putting a hand on her shoulder.

She said, "Niki warned me once that in anything you felt really important I could never change your mind. He was right, wasn't he? I've learned that by now."

"It may never come. The decision is not entirely in my hands."

She leaned her cheek against his hand. "It will come because you want it to come and there's nothing I can do about it."

She was right and there were two things that hastened his decision.

The first was one evening at the beginning of March when he came home to see someone in the drawing room whom at first he took for a stranger and then with a sense of shock recognized as Valentin. It was not simply that he looked gaunt and spectre thin, wounds and sickness could do that; it was the haunted look in his eyes, the change from handsome confident Guards officer to this shaken man in ill-fitting field grey uniform who rose with a painful effort when he came into the room.

Then Simon had stretched out his hand in warm greeting. "Valentin, my dear fellow, this is tremendous. We'd heard nothing for so long we had feared the worst and here you are, alive and well."

"I'm one of the lucky ones."

"Val is only just out of hospital," said Nina quickly taking charge. "He shouldn't really have been discharged yet but they're so short of beds. The Skorsky house is shut up and I couldn't let him travel back to the country in the state he is so I've asked him to stay with us for a week or two. You don't mind, Simon, do you?"

"Of course I don't mind. We haven't as many creature comforts as we used to have but I'm pretty sure Nina and the servants, to say nothing of the children, will like nothing better than a wounded hero to care for."

"Not so much of the hero," murmured Valentin. "If you're sure I am not inconveniencing you. Nina was very insistent."

"I'm glad she was. Sit down, man, make yourself comfortable. Let me give you a drink. We still have some decent brandy, thank God."

It was a subdued evening. Valentin seemed unwilling to talk about his experiences and they did not press him. He ate very little and retired early, apologizing for being such poor company.

Nina looked after him with a worried frown. "He's so changed Simon, I can hardly believe it's the same Valentin.

You know his wound was very serious. The nurse told me. The lung was affected. I'm afraid he is still very sick."

A sickness of mind as well as of body, Simon thought. You can't go through hell and come out unscathed. He dealt with grievously wounded men all day long but somehow impersonally, it had to be like that. This was the first time it was someone well known to them and all the more distressing because of it.

"I'll go up to him presently. He may be glad of something to help him sleep."

It was much later after Nina had gone to bed and he had spent some time in his study putting away the books and folders of notes that he had collected in his work on haemophilia. No time to continue his investigations now. That might be something for the future perhaps when the war was over.

He was on his way to his own room when he heard a gasping cry that was instantly stifled but held such a note of agony that he stopped outside the guest room uncertain whether to intrude on another's pain and yet feeling that he might have it in his power to help. He paused a moment, then opened the door quietly and went in. The faint light from the lamp burning in front of the icon showed him Valentin sitting up in the bed, his head in his hands.

He said gently, "Anything I can do? Are you in pain?"

Valentin raised his head. "I'm all right. It's just that it gets me sometimes. It's difficult to breathe."

"I could give you something that would help you to sleep."

"No, no, not sleep," he said quickly. "It's worse, far worse to sleep."

"Nightmares?"

Valentin did not answer but Simon saw the long tremor that ran through his body, saw the sweat glisten on his face though the room was cold. He sat on the end of the bed.

"Tell me about them."

"You would laugh at me."

"I never laugh at anything patients tell me."

Valentin turned away his head. "I'm so ashamed. I never thought I was a coward, not until now. It sickens me to know how many of my friends are dead and yet I still go on living."

"You're not the first to feel like that."

"Does that make it any more bearable?" he said fiercely and then it was as if a dam burst, as if once started he couldn't stop. The words poured out tumbling over one another, two long years of glory and courage and indescribable horror.

"At first it felt wonderful. We were so sure of ourselves, so confident, so recklessly certain of victory that we hurled a cavalry charge full into the mouth of their guns. Can you imagine what that was like? A tangled mass of dying men and screaming horses. We lost two-thirds of our battalion on that first day and yet we still drove forward with our sabres, with our bare hands . . . oh God why am I telling all this to you? How can you possibly understand?"

"Go on," he said, "go on. That wasn't the worst of it, was it?"

"Oh Christ, no! We got through that, those of us who still lived, we pushed on into Hungary, into Poland, God forgive us but we actually believed we were winning!" He gave a choked laugh that was dangerously near a sob. "It was Easter and the men were singing in the trenches they had dug for themselves, singing the Easter hymn. 'Christ is risen' they said and kissed one another when they should have realized that He was dead in His tomb and would never rise again."

Not once in all the years Simon had known him had he ever heard Valentin so eloquent or so bitter. It was as if the shock and violence had somehow reached the depths that slept beneath the pleasant good-natured somewhat stupid young man whom Nina had so often despised.

"What fools we were, what utter blind fools, we might have known the Germans were only taking breath, gathering their strength to smash us once and for all. All this last year we retreated, every hard-won inch of blood-soaked ground yielded up while their artillery blasted trenches and blew to pieces every man in them and then we were running away, a million men, boys some of them, peasants like our own at Dannskoye come from the fields and the plough, scarcely knowing what it was that had hit them, dropping their rifles in terror, throwing them away, drowning in their own blood. We tried to rally them but you can't turn back the tide and we had nothing with which to fight, our ammunition, our guns, our food supplies, bogged down far behind the lines so that in the end I ran with them." He paused for a moment and then went on wearily, "That's what I can't get out of my mind that I ran with them while they died around me."

"And nearly died yourself," said Simon quietly, "don't forget that."

"You know what saved me? It was my old servant who'd been with me since a boy who couldn't read or write but had grown up with me. He dragged me to safety before a shell took off his head."

They were silent for a while, then Valentin went on more quietly. "God knows what made me tell *you* all this. I never thought you cared for me overmuch but I'm grateful. I couldn't have said anything of this to Nina." He looked up at Simon with a faint smile. "You must hear some damned queer stories in your work."

"Sometimes." Simon stood up. "If it helps in any way, then I'm glad to listen. Now I'm going to fetch you something that will give you a few hours of sleep."

Valentin stirred restlessly. "I sometimes think I shall never sleep again."

"Oh yes, you will. You've been bottling it up far too long. It will be easier now."

He brought the sleeping pills and watched him take them. Then he eased him back against the pillows that he had piled high behind him to help his breathing.

"That's better. Take it easy. Try to relax. Let Nina spoil you for a week or so as she does the children when they are sick."

Valentin looked at him curiously. "You don't mind?"

"No, I don't mind and it wouldn't be much good if I did. Nina has a will of her own, you know."

He went back to his own room but not to sleep. Valentin's outburst had brought vividly before his mind what he had already guessed at from the news that filtered through and from Nigel who had access to the reports sent back by General Knox, the British Military Attaché at army headquarters. It was a grim fact that the apparently invincible Russian army with its teeming millions lay in ruins. The glorious spirit of national unity that had swept throughout this vast country had disintegrated into suspicion, violent quarrels and bitter hatred. Revolt began to lift its head again. In Moscow a mob had gathered outside the Kremlin screaming insults at the Tsar, at the Empress, at the government with its inept handling of the war supplies.

The Grand Duke Nicholas had been relieved of his command after those months of agonizing retreat and the Tsar himself had taken over the command of the armed forces.

"God knows what will come out of that," Nigel had said. "The Grand Duke was a born leader, an aristocrat to his fingertips. Did you ever meet him? Six foot three and the presence with it but a brilliant soldier who understood strategy. His successor, General Alexeiev is a plodder but honest enough and hard-working, perhaps that's what is needed now. One thing, Simon, with the Tsar at headquarters, it does mean that Russia is not withdrawing from the fight. If they had and the whole weight of the German army fell on the West, God help Britain!"

It was deeply disturbing but there was worse to come.

The morning that the letter arrived the sun came out for the first time for weeks. The ice had begun to melt, the breeze had a faint smell of spring doubly welcome after the long hard winter. It came sealed in an embassy envelope and Nina looked at it doubtfully before sending Jake with it to the hospital.

It was brought to Simon just as he was preparing to go into the operating theatre. He put it to one side. Whatever it contained he could not let it disturb his concentration on the intricate piece of surgery in front of him so it was midday before he broke the seal. The letter enclosed was from Robert's wife. He guessed at its contents before he opened it.

His brother was dead. Robert who could have remained safely behind the lines at army headquarters had been stupidly and uselessly killed by a sniper. This had happened when he had insisted on going forward to the front on a mission of encouragement and support at a time when they were staggering under the continued German onslaught from the army newly released from the Russian pressure.

He stood staring out of the window seeing not the magnificent skyline of Petrograd but the rambling redbrick manor of Ravensley shrouded in early morning mist – he heard his brother calling the dogs, shouting to him to come riding with him or fishing for eels with the marshmen or tramping across the Fens, gun in hand – Robert who had laughed at him calling him "Old Sawbones" when he chose to study medicine, Robert angry with him but still supportive when he had left England after the death of the girl he had once loved.

He started at the knock on the door. A nurse put her head around to say, "Your next patient is ready for you, doctor."

"Very well, I'm coming."

There was no time to mourn, no time to weep for what had vanished. Somehow he had never envisaged death coming to Robert. He had always seemed indestructible.

Later in the day when he had a moment free he telephoned Nigel at the embassy.

"There's no doubt about it, I suppose."

"None at all, I'm afraid. I'm desperately sorry, Simon, so is Lydia. You realize what it means, don't you?"

"Yes."

"The estates, the title, will be yours. You'll have to go back to England."

"Yes, but not yet."

He had a simple savage desire to go out and kill, destroy the enemy that had brutally destroyed his brother, something he recognized as utterly futile. He couldn't do that but he could do the next best thing which was to be in the front line, sharing in its dangers, mending the broken bodies and sending them back to fight again. It hardened the half-formed decision into a firm resolution and before he left for home he went to see the Director of the hospital and told him what he intended.

Doctor Afim Afimovich Kirsky was an old man who had once in his youth known Simon's uncle, and both liked and respected his English colleague.

He said, "We shall miss you."

"I feel I could do more good nearer to the field of action."

"Perhaps. It's true that the service has suffered serious loss. I don't think there will be any difficulty about the medical corps recruiting you. They can do with more volunteers."

"Please count me among them."

By the time he returned home that evening the matter was already on its way to being settled.

Nina came out of the drawing room to meet him in the hall. "I was worried when the message came. Is it bad news?"

"The worst. My brother has been killed."

"Oh darling, I'm so sorry. I've always hoped so much we might meet. That he would come here or you'd take us all to England."

It was true. He had thought of it many times but always there had been something to intervene. Nina was pregnant or the children were sick or the pressure of work had made it impossible to leave. Now it was too late.

She had taken his arm. "How terrible for his wife, for his three little girls."

"Not so little now." The eldest must be seventeen, the baby almost as old as Andrei and now they had become his responsibility. The thought weighed heavily on him.

"There is one good thing, Simon. Sonia is here and she has had a letter from Niki. Isn't that wonderful? He was taken prisoner but it seems that he has escaped."

"He's not wounded or sick?"

"He doesn't say so."

So it was an evening of mingled grief and joy which they could share partly at least with the children.

"Where's Valentin?" he asked when they had sat down at last to eat.

"He insisted on leaving today," explained Nina, "though I don't think he is really fit. He said he is sure the man he left in charge of his estates is cheating him right and left and he wants to sort it out while he still has some weeks of sick leave."

Sonia, radiantly happy that Niki was not dead after all, was trying to persuade them to come to Dannskoye for Easter.

"Nina can go of course and take the children," he said, "it will do them all the good in the world, but I'm afraid I shall be gone by then."

"Gone? Where?"

They both turned to him so he had to explain and found it difficult to put into words the urgency that was driving him. In their eyes he was simply putting a great deal at risk for nothing, but he knew that if he stayed behind now he could not go on living with himself.

It took a few weeks to put his affairs in order and they all came to the railway station to see him off, Nina and the children and even Missy, with Jake at the wheel of the Mercedes.

"I wish you'd let me go with you, sir," he had said more than once.

"No. I'm relying on you to keep an eye on them all for me."

The compartment reserved for the medical team was in the front of the train. The rest of the coaches were packed with fresh troops, country boys for the most part, some of them laughing and joking, but many others bewildered and lost, weighed down by the packs on their backs. One of them, tall and thin, limping badly, stumbled and would have fallen if Simon had not held him on his feet. It was strange but in that split second he could have sworn that it was Igor's lean and bony face under the peaked cap. Then with a mumbled word of thanks he limped on and vanished into the carriage with his companions.

When the train drew out Simon stood at the window watching the small group diminish gradually, Andrei running a little, trying to keep pace with the engine, Tanya waving a handkerchief, Jake holding Paul high in the air so that he could see. He had not yet told them what the future would hold for them. Nina was so utterly and completely Russian. How would she fit into the life of an English village? For the matter of that how would he after all these years? Then he dropped into his seat and tried to put it out of his mind.

22

In the ramshackle little office at the end of the long farm buildings that had been converted into a temporary hospital Miss Macdonald looked at the young woman standing in front of her and felt annoyed that she could not even find fault with her appearance. Galina's Siberian experience of dealing with near impossible living conditions had stood her in good stead during the difficult months when they had been forced to shift back and back before the advancing German armies, sometimes bivouacking in tents, sometimes in ruined huts, sometimes lying on the bare ground because there was nowhere else suitable to snatch a night's sleep.

Miss Alexandra Macdonald's father had been a Minister in the Church of Scotland. She had grown up in a bleak manse in Fife and after forty years still believed firmly that one step outside the rigid principles instilled into her since babyhood would inevitably lead to hell-fire. She had served in the Red Cross in many fields of war, distrusted all that was not British and had taken an instant dislike to Galina. To start with she was the only Russian among her group of nurses, also she knew a great deal more about the drugs and medicines than she did herself and was not above saying so very forcibly if she thought it necessary; and what was worse she had a free and easy manner not only with the doctors but with the orderlies and stretcher bearers with whom they were obliged to work.

"I sent for you an hour ago," she said in her rasping sergeant-major voice.

"I'm sorry. I was assisting Dr Donovan with a dressing," replied Galina coolly.

Michael Donovan was a young Irish volunteer who had replaced a Russian doctor who had been seriously wounded and sent back home.

Miss Macdonald frowned. "I have received a message from the front line. There has been a series of heavy attacks and we can expect a great number of wounded in the next day or so. You and the other nurses will prepare those patients still in the hospital to be removed as soon as possible."

"But many of them are still very sick."

"These are our orders and it is up to me to make sure they are carried out."

"What transport will there be to carry them to the railway station?"

"There are the ambulance carts."

"You know what state the roads are in with the melting of the snow. Half the men will die long before they reach the railway. You should protest, Miss Macdonald, you should put in a demand for motor ambulances. The Germans have them and so should we."

"Nurse Panova," said the matron icily, "are you trying to teach me what I should do?"

"That's what is so wrong with us out here. No one ever raises their voice in protest. The men should refuse to fight unless they are granted better conditions."

"It's not for us to question. We are here to nurse the wounded and obey orders. I would have thought that with your *prison* experience," she went on cuttingly, "you would have learned the folly of rebellion."

Galina's eyes flashed. "I will always rebel against injustice." She turned to go and Miss Macdonald stopped her.

"There is one other thing. When I was going on duty last

night I saw you in close conversation with a young man when as you knew perfectly well nurses who are not on night watch are expected to be in their quarters by ten o'clock."

"Isn't that a stupid rule when we have so little leisure?"

"Please don't argue with me. I've spoken to you about this before. You are older than the others, you should set an example."

"He is not my lover, Miss Macdonald."

A hot flush ran across the older woman's face. "I should hope not indeed. If that were so I should take steps to have you dismissed immediately," and knew very well that she would not succeed. This objectionable young woman was approved of by the doctors and it was their opinion that carried the most weight.

"You may go," she said coldly, "and kindly see that the patients are prepared for evacuation as soon as possible."

Outside Galina paused for a moment annoyed with herself for losing her temper. The wind was cold but it blew fresh and clean, with a promise of new growth after the devastation of the winter. General Alexeiev had managed to stabilize the army along the Russian Polish border where they had been entrenched during the bitter winter, maintaining their position with stubborn resistance on Russian soil.

For some days now they had been aware of the roar of the guns after a brief lull on this part of the sector.

"Dear God," she found herself praying, "Dear God, don't let it be like last year."

She and Leon had arrived during the holocaust that Valentin had described so vividly to Simon. She wondered sometimes how they had lived through it, the endless stream of mangled bodies, the hideous wounds, the never-ending stench of sickness and death, the appalling shortages, not enough bandages, not enough drugs, chloroform running out, surgeons operating in despair, and the constant fear of bursting shells that tore men to pieces, that blew up ambulances, that destroyed field dressing stations so that in the end it became part of life and the terror turned into a fatalistic acceptance. You swabbed and bandaged and handed instruments for amputations, helped men to live and far more to die and at the same time somehow ate and slept and learned to survive.

In all these months she had seen little of Leon partly because there had been no time in the grim daily round, partly because he had been attached to another unit for a time. Last night had been the first few minutes they had spoken together for more than three months and she resented Miss Macdonald's insulting implication, her absurd restriction, just as they all did. Sandy Mac as they called her had become the bane of their young lives.

They were a good bunch, she thought, all English – Rita had worked with a famous brain surgeon in Moscow, Dora had been a children's nurse with an aristocratic family, the other three were volunteers freshly out from England – none of them with her burning indignation at the government in Petrograd, careless of the lives being senselessly thrown away, completely unaware of the growing restlessness, the feeling of being abandoned with no one caring whether they lived or died, a bitter resentful anger at the whole bloody business that could so easily grow into active revolt.

Someone slipped an arm through hers and a cheerful voice said in her ear, "What was Sandy Mac on about this time? Our shocking morals or our dirty aprons?"

Galina laughed. "Neither as it happens. She's had a directive. We are to clear all the patients out for a new intake."

"Crikey! The poor devils won't like that!"

"I know. I pointed out to her that she should at least put in a demand for better transport but it's like talking to a brick wall."

"Good for you. That icy look of hers as if I were something unpleasant just crawled out from under a stone makes me shiver right down to my boots. Come on, we'd better tell the others and get cracking on it."

Vicky was a cockney from the slums of London with a cheery sense of humour that reminded Galina of Luba. She got on well with all the girls. The fact that she had actually suffered at the hands of the dreaded *Okhrana* and been exiled to Siberia had given her a touch of mystery which deepened when someone accidentally saw that faded photograph of Andrei. A myth grew up that the boy's father must be a Prince or an Archduke at the very least and it gave her a kind of glamour. They knew about Leon too.

"Some people have all the luck," sighed Vicky. "I'd give my eye teeth for a fellow like that. Where'd you pick him up?"

"In Siberia."

"Lead me there!" she said dramatically. "If Sandy Mac goes on treating us like babies, I shall run screaming mad and bite somebody!"

But she worked harder than any of them and the men loved her even though they did not understand a word she said to them.

They carried out their orders, moved the men into the horse-drawn ambulances trying to make them as comfortable as possible and stood in the road to wave them goodbye. The next day the wagons came rolling in from the front and the hospital was temporarily full again.

Over the past year Leon had become the leader of the stretcher bearers, the hardworking team who brought in the wounded and cheerfully carried out many of the most unpleasant jobs. He had won a reputation for daredevilry, dodging through falling shrapnel to drag a wounded man to safety, sometimes finding a living body beneath a pile of corpses, going out on mercy missions when the moon was up, carrying a flask of water and the morphine Galina smuggled to him and taught him how to use though it was forbidden.

"I've got to do something," he said to her, "some of 'em – my God – I wouldn't leave an animal to die in that state!"

Once he brought back a small dog, a pathetic little creature that must have been abandoned by the refugees and had attached itself to one of the soldiers.

The girls fed it and petted it and called it Pepper. The daily round was so grim that it was a relief to laugh over its antics and vie with each other as to whose bed it should sleep on, until one day it disappeared. They hunted in every likely place but it was nowhere to be found and at last reluctantly they gave it up till the night Vicky burst into their quarters, her face scarlet and so filled with rage she could hardly speak.

"D'you know what happened to Pepper? That bitch Sandy Mac had him put down and why? Because we were making too much fuss of him, because she just can't endure anyone to be happy or to laugh or to take pleasure in anything, not even a harmless little dog!"

"How do you know?" asked Galina.

"One of the orderlies let it out. She told him to do it, painlessly of course, stick a needle into the poor little wretch and he's gone," she snapped her fingers, "just like that! I'd like to stick a needle into her *and* where it hurts most!"

*

At the beginning of June the weather turned very warm. Under a grilling sun conditions became very nearly intolerable. They fought a plague of flies that settled on everything, on the men's faces, on food, on infected wounds. It was an added torment. The bombardment grew closer, the number of wounded increased every day and the problem of shifting them on became more and more difficult. Another of the doctors fell sick and was sent home, leaving only Michael Donovan who was painstakingly efficient but grossly overworked. Urgent messages asked for a replacement but no help was forthcoming.

One day that month he was making his usual rounds with Galina in close attendance. For once the noise of the guns had grown fainter. The plague of flies had disappeared as mysteriously as they had come. A bee buzzed around them and the patients drowsed in the afternoon heat. Miss Macdonald had just come in. One of the men called feebly to her and she was bending over him when suddenly there was a whistling scream and the whole place seemed to explode. Dr Donovan flung Galina to the floor and fell on top of her. For a moment they could not move or speak, all breath blown out of them by the force of the explosion. They were surrounded by clouds of choking dust, with debris that fell around them, with screams of terror and pain. Gasping and winded they got shakily to their feet.

As the air gradually began to clear they could see that the shell had landed on one end of the building and had almost completely destroyed it. Other people had come running by now. Frantically they began to drag out the beds buried beneath the falling roof. Miss Macdonald had thrown herself protectively across the patient on the bed and was dead. The huge force of the explosion must have stopped her heart while the man half crushed beneath her, whimpering with fright, still lived. Three other beds and their occupants had been totally destroyed, others were bleeding from flying debris, shocked and distraught.

It took a great many hours trying to bring order out of chaos. The summer heat made it possible to carry some of the beds outside while they tried to assess the damage. Half the building had survived but would have to be shored up temporarily and some sort of awning erected.

Once during that terrible afternoon she found Vicky staring

down at where they had laid Miss Macdonald decently covered by a hospital blanket.

"I wished her dead and now she is," she whispered. "She gave her life to save that wretched man who's not half so sick as he pretends. Oh God, how bloody unfair life is! I thought I would be glad and I only want to cry."

To all of them it seemed as if the day would never end. Late in the evening Leon arrived with still another load of wounded and there was simply nowhere to put them while they were treated. They had to make up palliasses on the ground rigging up anything they could lay their hands on to make some kind of a shelter. Michael Donovan, driven almost to distraction by the calls made upon him relied on Galina more and more for advice and support. It was dawn before she could think of taking even a few minutes to rest. Vicky brought her a cup of boiling tea and she sipped it gratefully too tired even to speak. She gave the cup back and moved away, sick and dizzy with fatigue, leaning against a gate that swung crazily on its hinges. The chill morning air, the sky faintly tinged with pink, gave an illusion of peace away from the stench, the agony, the patient, weary acceptance of men tortured almost to death.

All this past year she had tried desperately hard to put Simon out of her thoughts, out of her life. She had made her decision and she was determined to stick by it. Now suddenly at this moment of stress her defences crumbled. She longed for him so violently with such an overpowering sense of need that it made her tremble. Why now, she thought despairingly, why now should she feel like this, gripped by this aching loneliness, and she did not realize how much these past months had taken out of her. Quite suddenly in reaction she began to cry, shaken by huge sobs that she fought against but could not control.

Someone came up behind her putting his arms around her. She knew it was Leon and couldn't bear it. She wanted only one man and he was far away and out of her reach. She shivered and pulled herself away.

"No, don't, please don't touch me."

"Galina," there was reproach in his voice. "I only want to help."

"I know." She turned to look at him, her face blotched with tears was white in the morning light. "I know you do

381

but it's no use, is it? Why go on pretending any longer? Let me go, Leon, let me go."

"Don't say that."

He caught at her hand swinging her towards him but she dragged herself free and ran away from him stumbling over the hard baked earth towards their sleeping quarters. Vicky was there but she brushed past her to fall face downwards on her bed.

Leon had followed her, was in the doorway but Vicky barred his way.

"Leave her, you idiot," she hissed at him. "Can't you see? She's had enough, she's done in, she doesn't want anyone just now."

She pushed him out and closed the door. She looked across at Galina, hesitated and then finished tying her apron strings. There was a time to speak and a time to keep her big mouth shut, she told herself, and went quietly out.

They struggled on through days of sticky heat and hot drenching rain that turned the dust to liquid mud until one day towards the end of the month. Galina, Rita and Dora were still asleep, having come off duty in the early hours of the morning when Vicky burst into their hut ruthlessly flinging the door wide open so that sun and wind came flooding in.

"Wake up, girls, wake up," she said, "time to be up and doing. He's here, all six feet of him, driving a motor ambulance if you please and with two orderlies and setting everyone by the ears."

They sat up, tousled, half asleep, furiously indignant.

"Who has come?"

"What's going on?"

"What on earth are you talking about?"

"Vicky, you beast, it's only seven. We've got another hour yet."

"No, you haven't, you've got exactly five minutes. He wants to see us all double quick."

"What for?"

"Who are you going on about?"

"Our new boss, a human dynamo if ever I saw one. He's already got them all running around him, even the patients have taken a new lease of life and Dr Donovan is like a little dog with a squib tied to his tail." She struck a dramatic attitude. "And do you know something, girls? He's British. Nearly took me breath away when he said, 'I know where you come from, Nurse. Stepney, isn't it? I've an aunt who runs a clinic there.' But I must say he speaks the lingo as well as any Russky."

Galina was sitting bolt upright, staring at her. It couldn't be, it wasn't possible. She was breathless suddenly.

"What is his name?"

"Lord knows. Haven't got round to that yet. Come on, girls, get dressed. Best bib and tucker. He wants to see everyone and he's got those lazy kitchen orderlies on the go, making tea and preparing breakfast."

They were scrambling out of bed by now, flinging on clothes, dipping faces in cold water, talking nineteen to the dozen, all except Galina. She was keyed up to a sort of expectancy, still sure that she was a fool and yet trembling with anticipation.

Simon was standing at one end of the half-ruined building, Dr Donovan beside him with the orderlies and Leon. The girls stood together, Galina half hidden behind them, her eyes noting every change, every new line in his face.

He spoke crisply telling them that he was sorry they had been neglected for so long, that a better place had been found for them, cleaner, better equipped, that he hoped they would be ready to leave by late afternoon, the worst cases travelling by the motor ambulance, the others necessarily by horse-drawn cart but he would do his best to make sure it moved as slowly as possible to save too much jolting.

"You've all been through hell but have come out on top," he went on, "from now on this is going to be the best run unit in this sector. And now to something even better. We've laid our hands on some decent food supplies, not caviare and salmon, I regret to say, but boiled eggs and fresh bread for everyone. Set to and eat and afterwards we'll get to work."

They laughed and they clapped at that. It was a long time since fresh eggs and white bread had appeared in their rations.

"Come on, girls," said Vicky, "what are we waiting for? let's tuck in while the going is good."

The girls sat on the grass cracking open their eggs and laughing with childish pleasure as they ate. Nobody noticed that Simon was standing in front of them until he spoke.

"May I join your picnic?"

They looked up only too ready to scramble to their feet and offer him all they had but he stopped them with a gesture.

It was Galina who held out the split crust on which she had put the hard-boiled egg.

"Have mine," she said.

"Thank you." There was surprise on his face and something else that made her heart turn over. Then he had taken it with a hint of a smile. "We've met before I believe."

"Yes, doctor, in Petrograd and elsewhere."

"Of course. I remember."

Their eyes met in a long look, then he had turned back to the others asking what part of England they came from and how they happened to be in Russia so that Galina could eat and study him at leisure until he gave them a cheerful wave and moved away.

Of course they besieged her with questions and she told them a little about her training in the hospital where he worked. It was only Vicky who was pretty sure there was far more behind it than she was willing to give away. After that there was no time for anything but all the necessary work of packing up the patients, putting their own baggage together and getting ready for evacuation.

Once during that afternoon Leon came up beside her, helping her pack the medical supplies in the large boxes for safe carriage. He had kept away from her since the day of the explosion.

"I suppose you're happy now," he muttered under his breath.

"I think we are all glad to have someone in charge who knows what he is doing."

"That's not what I meant."

"Leon, don't be angry."

"What do you expect? For a whole year I have lived in a dream and now you have destroyed it. You gave me a promise once. If it hadn't been for this damned war we would have been married by now."

"I know. I'm sorry I said what I did that night. It was just that it was the wrong moment. I'm willing to keep to our bargain."

"For God's sake, Galina, do you think that's what I want? He's only been here a few hours and already you can't keep your eyes from him."

"That's a detestable thing to say."

"Maybe but it's true all the same, isn't it?" He gripped her arms suddenly looking down into her eyes. "Tell me if I'm wrong, tell me honestly."

She knew she had hurt him deeply and yet for the life of her she could not deny it. She turned her head away.

"I thought so." He let his hands drop. "Why the hell do we fret so much? Another shell like the last and we could all be blasted into eternity, you and I and him."

"Leon, don't talk like that," but he ignored her, shouting to one of the other men to help him shoulder the heavy box.

She was to remember that moment months afterwards, long days through summer and autumn, hours of hard unremitting work but shot through with moments of pure happiness because she was seeing Simon daily, she was working with him in the close unity that had always existed between them and not even the disturbing news could entirely destroy it.

Stranded out in a kind of no man's land they were still aware that the resistance to the Germans was slowly disintegrating. Here and there along the two-hundred-mile front the Russians were making sporadic advances and even taking prisoners, but there were also worrying rumours of pockets of men who refused to fight, men who deserted, tramping the thousands of miles back to the fields they knew as home, men who turned on their officers when they tried to rally them and murdered them in cold blood. Once or twice Simon remembered that brief glimpse on the railway station and wondered if Igor and others like him were infiltrating among the ranks stirring up anger, spreading the poison of revolt.

Then one day in late October it was among them, a mind cracked suddenly and it became frighteningly real. That morning a soldier had come stumbling into the yard outside, his uniform filthy and ragged, his eyes wild, not visibly wounded, but thin and starving, his back bearing the marks of a recent flogging. When asked name and regiment he stared blankly but it was obvious that he had been savagely punished, probably for desertion. He was brought in, stripped and cared for. Simon tended the raw wounds of the lash but was more worried about the man's mental condition. After he had been given food and drink he seemed to calm down and lay quietly on the mattress put down for him.

It was late evening. The big ward was only dimly lit. Simon

was making a last round. Leon had come in because one of the beds needed to be shifted. Vicky was easing into the pillows a man whose shoulder had been badly shattered. Nobody was taking any particular notice of the unknown soldier when suddenly he had thrown back the blanket, he was on his feet, the shirt flapping around his bare legs, his eyes blazing.

"Look at him," he was screaming, "look at him, the British pig! He'll patch you up, he'll cure you and for what? Don't you know, you damned fools?" He glared round at the astonished faces. "To send you back into the furnace, to be crushed by the juggernaut, blasted by cannon fire, choked by your own blood! Kill him, kill him now and then get the hell out of here, go home before you die like all the rest!"

It had come so suddenly, no one quite believed in it. They thought it nightmare, feverish delirium, but Leon had glimpsed the pistol he whipped out from under the pillow. He saw him level it full at Simon and leaped between them. The man fired and he staggered falling to his knees. The soldier laughed crazily, waved the pistol around and fired again.

"Keep down, keep down, all of you!" yelled Simon and grabbed the nearest thing which happened to be one of the crutches used by the walking patients. He hurled it and it hit the soldier just below the shoulder, the pistol dropped from his hand and he buckled at the knees. Dr Donovan, who had heard the shots, came racing in followed by Galina. By that time Simon was grappling with the madman. He had got him down on the bed with some of the others holding on to his arms and legs. They lashed him to the mattress with lengths of strong bandage and suddenly he gave in, exhausted, the madness draining out of him, and Simon turned to Leon. He was still on his knees bent over clutching at his breast, his uniform stained with the blood that oozed through his fingers. Galina was kneeling beside him.

"Crikey!" whispered Vicky on a long breath. "I've never seen a man move so fast. If it hadn't been for him, you'd have copped it, doctor."

Simon was opening the tunic. He took the pad Galina handed to him and thrust it inside the shirt against the welling blood.

"How bad is he?" she breathed.

"Pretty bad. We'd better get him into the operating theatre. Careful now. Take him up gently. He's bleeding enough as it is."

Leon was a big man. It took more than two of them and they carried him with infinite care.

The bullet had gone in deep very nearly touching the heart and all through the long and delicate operation when Simon fought for Leon's life, the thought was in Galina's mind that he had done it for her, he had accepted the death meant for Simon.

Leon was well liked. The atmosphere in the ward was quiet and tense that night while she sat by the bed keeping watch till he should come out of the chloroform. Simon came and went constantly checking pulse and heart.

In the early hours of the morning Vicky was there with a cup of tea. "Why don't you rest on your bed for an hour? I'll take a turn, so will Rita and Dora."

Galina shook her head but sipped the tea gratefully.

"Did they tell you?" whispered Vicky. "That madman has escaped. Somehow got his hands free and bolted."

"They ought to have been more careful. He's dangerous."

"They're out searching now."

They found him later that morning hanging from a tree in a little copse half a mile away. He must have climbed high up into the branches, made a noose out of the twisted bandages used to fetter him and then jumped. They brought him in and Simon looked down at the white distorted face with all life jerked out of it, another casualty of war just as much as those who had lost arm or leg. He had already seen one mind near to cracking in Valentin. This one had gone over the edge.

For a week Leon was on the danger list and somehow to both Galina and Simon, without a word being said between them, it became almost a point of honour that he should not die.

Then there came a morning when he emerged out of the mists of pain and fever, when he stirred fretfully, tried to sit up and was gently pushed back against the pillows.

"Take it easy man," said Simon. "You're not running a race yet."

"God, I'm weaker than a blasted kitten," he mumbled. "How long is this going to last?"

"Quite a while yet, I'm afraid." Simon was checking his pulse. "Cheer up. It's getting stronger every day. It seems I owe you a debt of gratitude."

Leon managed a faint grin. "You flatter yourself, doctor. I

thought he was going to murder the lot of us." He closed his eyes, took a deep breath and then opened them again. "Where the hell did he find that pistol?"

"It seems it was a war trophy captured by the boy in the next bed from a German prisoner. He liked to show it around and our man must have spotted it. Well, he's paid for it now."

"How?"

"Hanged himself."

"Poor devil. It could have been any one of us, I suppose."

He slept for most of that day but next morning was awake early and begging Simon for news.

"Not too good, I'm afraid. We have our marching orders. We're to be disbanded, the lot of us, but not just yet. I'm not having you or any of the patients die on me. Within the next couple of weeks probably."

He was right. At the end of October the whole unit was broken up. The last of the wounded was packed into the ambulances. Leon insisted on walking out to it even though he had to stop every two seconds in order to breathe. Galina had brought blankets and her own pillow. She climbed in to put them at his back despite his protests.

"You'll do as you're told," she said firmly, and regardless of interested eyes bent over kissing him full on the mouth. For a moment his arm clutched her close against him, then he let her go, turning away his head, afraid in his weakness of revealing too much.

Vicky was to travel with them.

"Look after him for me," whispered Galina as the girl prepared to climb into the wagon.

"I sure will. You know you're off your head, duckie. He's a *nice* man, why let him go? He'd lay down and die if you so much as raised your hand."

"I know, he nearly did. Don't forget Luba's address, will you? If you're still in Petrograd when I get back, we'll meet up there."

Vicky gave her a quick hug, then she had clambered up and they were off, creaking slowly down the rutted road.

It was one of those still days that sometimes come in late autumn with a faint lingering warmth, a pause before the onslaught of winter sets in. There was a certain amount of clearing up to be done before they could leave early the following morning but afterwards Galina was free for the first time for more than a year, no duties to be performed, no sick men to be tended, free to think, to look to the future, perhaps simply to be alone, away from sickness and death, to breathe sweet cool air, to feel the wind blow through her hair.

Simon, putting together his few possessions in the tiny room that served as an office saw her through the window. She was walking quickly. She had discarded her nurse's uniform except for the thick heavy cloak and had shaken out her hair, tying it back with a ribbon. She looked like the young girl he had first known and not the mother of his eleven-year-old son. On impulse he shut the bag, pulled on his jacket, slammed the door shut behind him and walked after her. He caught her up as she reached the end of the encampment.

"Where are you going?"

"Nowhere in particular. Just walking."

"Do you mind if I walk with you?"

She shook her head and he fell into step beside her. The countryside was partly heath and very sparsely inhabited. The air had that autumn smell of rotting leaves and good wet earth with a faint tang of woodsmoke. The sky towards the west was apple green beginning to be tinged with pink as the sun slowly went down.

They walked in silence for a while side by side but not touching. It was odd, he thought, that though they had been working closely together for the past four months, they had only very rarely been alone. He had told her about Niki, about Valentin and the death of his brother but little else. He had scrupulously kept to the belief held by everyone that she and Leon were pledged to one another.

She paused where the path left the track and crossed a field leading towards a little wood.

"Can you smell them?" she said, "Mushrooms, I mean. When I was a child they grew all around Dannskoye and we used to go out and collect big baskets of them. The cook at the great house gave us a few kopecks for them. Sometimes Niki and Nina would come with us with their nurse."

He saw them in his mind's eye, the peasant child with bare feet and hair tawny in the sun, and the small princess with her muslin dress, her fair curls, her imperious manner, both of them become inextricably part of his own life.

In the wood it was soggy in places, moisture seeping up through the mounds of rotting leaves. He lifted her over the worst places and then they began to laugh and talk, to be at ease with one another as they had been at the beginning before Igor split them apart.

Beyond the wood the country changed. There were glimpses of scattered houses, wide distances apart, country *dachas* perhaps for city dwellers, surrounded by gardens and seemingly deserted for the most part, the owners caught up in the exigencies of the war.

Galina paused by a gate. A drive led towards a shuttered white house. Both the drive and the garden were overgrown. Late roses still bloomed raggedly here and there in tangled flower beds.

Galina looked up at him, her eyes full of light and laughter. "Shall we explore?"

"It may not be empty."

"Let's find out."

"Why not?"

It was scarcely the kind of adventure for a respectable doctor to indulge in but suddenly he felt free of all cares, all burdens, all anxieties. He laughed and took her hand. They started to run up the drive like two irresponsible children. A long thorny trailer from a climbing rose caught up in her long skirt and nearly tripped her up. He knelt to disentangle it.

The garden had once been lovely but now the flower beds were full of weeds, the grass of the lawn grown ragged and untidy. Round the back of the house there was a small paved courtyard where a few chickens clucked and pecked, scurrying away from them in a flurry of squawks. Their roosting house had been left open and three large brown eggs lay in the nesting box.

Daringly Galina pushed the door and it opened. She glanced over her shoulder and he followed her. The house was already filled with shadows. They followed a stone passage into a large kitchen with a wooden dresser along one wall. It was well furnished with copper pots and pans, with dishes, cups and plates, the table roughly laid as if for a meal that had never been eaten.

What had happened? Had the owner fled in fear of German invasion carrying fire and slaughter across the border or had he died somewhere out on that battlefield leaving the house inhabited only by ghosts?

Galina shivered, uncertain whether to stay or to run and it

was Simon who took the initiative. He took her hand in his and they went on through another passage and into a sitting room looking out on the garden and golden in the last glow of the sun. It was simply furnished with rugs on the wooden floor, comfortable chairs, a few scattered books and, unusual for Russia, a wide hearth where logs had once smouldered, leaving their pile of grey ash.

Here there were no ghosts but instead an atmosphere of peace, a retreat from the cares and harassment of daily life.

Simon said suddenly, "I could make a fire. We could stay for a while."

"Should we? It's a long way back."

"Not so far and the night is before us. We don't have to leave till tomorrow."

There was no oil in the lamp on the table but there were candles and as he lit them, the room sprang into welcoming light.

He took off his coat and began to roll up his shirt sleeves.

"I'll bring in the firewood. You forage for food."

"It's probably all eaten by rats or mice by now."

It had suddenly become a picnic, happy and carefree. He went to the courtyard while she took a candle and explored the kitchen cupboards. There was bread that had become green and mouldy, vegetables that had withered. It looked as if they had taken spare food with them or the store had already been rifled but she found an unopened tin of biscuits and tucked away on the bottom shelf a bottle of wine perhaps hidden by the servants for their secret pleasure. She waved it in the air as Simon came through, his arms filled with kindling.

"Look what I've found."

He paused to read the label. "Niersteiner from the Rhine. Wonderful! We'll drink to the damnation of Germany in their own vintage!"

With the fire beginning to blaze she brought in wine and glasses with the tin of biscuits but it was Simon who provided the finishing touch. He came in with the three brown eggs, a mixing bowl and one of the copper pans.

"What are you going to do?"

"Scramble them of course. Aren't you hungry? I am."

She stood, bottle in hand, a little doubtful. "Should we be doing this?"

"It's a war emergency. We'll leave money to pay for it."

She watched the firelight play across his face smoothing out the lines as he knelt by the hearth breaking the eggs into the bowl, whisking them with a fork and then pouring the mixture into the pan. It took her back to that attic room of hers, Simon rescuing her and feeding her with the eggs, the night of Nina's party when they had made love and it seemed impossible that anything could part them.

As it grew darker, the room became colder. Galina drew the curtains and when they had eaten they pulled the chairs close to the hearth, Simon refilled the glasses and they sat close together more at peace with one another than they had been for a long time.

He took out cigarettes and offered her one but she shook her head.

"Vicky used to puff away whenever she could get hold of them much to Sandy Mac's disgust but I've not taken to it yet."

He leaned forward to light the long brown Russian cigarette with a spill from the fire before he spoke.

"When I told you that Robert had been killed, did you realize what it meant?"

She looked at him doubtfully. "Only that the title will be yours now. You will be Lord Aylsham."

"Yes, but more than that, much more. Ravensley, the lands, the house in London, they will all come to me. Robert's wife and the three girls will be provided for but it's an inheritance, a responsibility that I can't shake off. I never wanted it, Galina. I never even thought of it. When I chose to study medicine, I knew I'd cut myself off but I didn't care. Robert was the one who wanted it. He loved the land with passion, never wanted to leave it. It's a damnable irony that he should be the one to go. Now it's mine, a burden handed on to me from God knows how many ancestors and I shall have to take it on."

"You mean you must leave Russia, make your home in England?"

"Yes. It will mean uprooting Nina and the children, that's going to be hard enough . . ."

He didn't finish the sentence but she realized the implication. He would be lost to her, in a different world, an alien world, the past here in Russia that bound them together destroyed for ever. The thought of it turned her dizzy. She closed her eyes against it but still heard what he was saying.

"Come with us, Galina."

He was leaning forward watching her face intently and a bitter unhappiness rose up within her.

"What as? Nina's companion, governess to your children or your mistress?"

"You know I didn't mean that. God knows what conditions are going to be like here in Russia or even in England but the war must end one day and I could provide for you."

She got up and walked away from him. "Whatever happens to Russia it is *my* country. I belong here. What would I be doing in England?"

"You could work at what you know best. You could study further if you wanted to. I could help you there."

"I've managed well enough alone so far."

"Oh my darling, are you still too proud to accept anything from me? After all these years do you still cherish that hedgehog pride of yours?"

The amusement in his voice maddened her. She turned on him fiercely. "It's not only that. You know the harm it could do. Don't pretend you don't. It could break up your marriage, damage your children. Besides I too have my duties, my responsibilities here in Russia."

"Are you thinking about Leon?"

"Yes. Have you forgotten already? He was nearly killed for your sake. Don't I owe him something for that?"

"He's the last person to exact it from you," he said drily. "I may be wrong but it has seemed to me that whatever there was between you has long since died."

"You're wrong," she said passionately, "absolutely and utterly wrong."

"I don't think I am and I'm going to prove it."

He was on his feet now and he crossed to her, swung her round and kissed her very deliberately, very thoroughly.

She wanted to yield, God knows how much, but she fought against it.

"That's unfair, Simon. Let me go."

"No."

He was holding her at arm's length but very firmly and she couldn't get away from him without an undignified struggle.

"Is that what you brought me here for? To kiss and make love?" she said with a calm she was far from feeling.

"I was under the impression that it was you who brought me." Then the laughter died out of his voice. "Galina, do you realize this may be the last time we can be alone together?"

"No, Simon, no. It's too late. We ought to go."

"It's not too late. We have the whole night before us. This is a moment out of time, out of my life, out of yours."

"That's madness, Simon.

"No, not madness, just a certainty that some kindly God brought us here, just that I love you and want you desperately."

"It's more than ten years ago, Simon," she said panic-stricken now, afraid of what it might do to them. "We've changed. We've grown older."

"Have we?" He dropped his arms and stood looking down at her. "If you can honestly look me in the face and tell me you no longer love me, that I've been living in some impossible fantasy, then I promise you we will go quietly out of here and shut the door on the past for ever."

She didn't answer and he put out a hand to tilt up her chin. In the flickering light of the candles he saw her eyes luminous with unshed tears and had his answer.

"You can't, can you, my darling, any more than I can. Do you remember what I said to you at Yakutsk? The fire bound us together and it still does."

He put his arm around her, drawing her with him towards the hearth where the embers still glowed and if she had feared what the years of parting, the stress of leading different lives, the shadow of Nina and Leon, might do to them, she was wrong. At the first touch of his hands, those strong capable surgeon's hands, her body shivered with remembered desire and delight. It was different yet it was the same, not the frenzied passion of youth but the tenderness and depth of maturity and shared experience.

They didn't think of the future but only of the timeless present and if it crossed her mind that she might bear a child, she accepted the thought with joy. She could never now take Andrei from him and another child would be part of him when he had gone.

Once when they woke out of drowsiness she murmured, "What will they be thinking back there at the camp?"

And he said, "Don't fret, my love. Who knows? The world may end tonight but nothing can take this from us."

It was very early and still dark when they knew they must go. They had not slept much. He kissed her eyes awake and they dressed quickly. The fire had died to grey ash and they shivered in the morning chill. When they were ready, everything put away and made tidy, they looked around the room that held so much of their shared fulfilment and Simon tore a leaf out of the notebook in his pocket.

"I'm going to leave a message. Who knows? Someone may see it one day." He thought for a moment and then wrote quickly. "Thank you for the peace of your home and the joy it has brought to us."

Then he folded some notes into it and put it on the table under the bottle.

It was a grey morning with the bite of winter in the wind. They walked quickly back to find everything in commotion, the whole place dismantled and baggage being loaded. Nobody remarked on their absence though the girls nudged one another and grinned when Galina collected her luggage from their quarters.

They were to travel separately, the girls in one van, the men in the other. There were hurried farewells before they climbed in and set off on their long journey to the railway station and then to Petrograd, not yet fully aware that the world they had known was slowly but surely falling into ruins.

Part Five

THE RAGING FIRE
1917–1918

23

This must surely be the worst February she had ever known, decided Lydia, shivering even in her fur-lined coat and thick boots, a bitter wind blowing huge flakes of snow into her face as she trudged down the Morskaya. Finding a cab these days was out of the question, but when Nigel had telephoned the news through to her early that morning she felt in duty bound to take it to Nina at once.

"I can't get through to her," he had explained, "the snow must have brought down the line but the poor girl has been worrying herself into the grave for weeks."

Outside the baker's shop a long queue of grey-faced women, huddled into shawls, were waiting for their daily ration of bread. At least she didn't have to do that yet, though her Russian servants were already surly and resentful of any demands made on them.

Nina was surprised to see her. They had never been intimate. Lydia and Nigel were Simon's friends rather than hers. She took her into the drawing room, apologizing because it was so cold.

"I tend to live in the nursery these days with the children. We manage to keep the stove going there. Shall I ask Cook to make us some tea? Coffee has become rather like diamond dust, I'm afraid."

"No, don't bother. Nigel asked me to bring you the news. Your telephone seems to be out of order. What isn't these days? We've heard from Simon."

Nina was gazing at her, eyes huge, hands clasped. "He's not . . . not . . .?"

Lydia put her warm hand on the icy fingers. "Don't look so frightened. He's safe. He has been very ill but he is better again. He hopes to be home within a week or two."

"Thank God, that's wonderful," she breathed and put out a groping hand to the table to steady herself.

"Are you all right?" exclaimed Lydia with concern. "You're white as a sheet and shaking. Sit down. Let me get you something."

"No, no, I'm all right, really I am. It's just that I've heard nothing since that brief note saying he was sick. I've been expecting the worst and now it's good news and I have to feel faint. Isn't it stupid?"

"It's reaction because you've not been looking after yourself properly, starving for the sake of the children, I expect. It's no good doing that, Nina, really it isn't. I'm very glad Simon is coming home. He'll look after you."

"It's kind of you to come all this way to tell me and through the snow too. I'm very grateful."

"I know how I would feel if I hadn't seen Nigel for nearly a year and hardly any news. You still look dreadfully pale. Are you sure I can't do something?"

"No, really. It's nothing. The children will be overjoyed. They ask me every day when Papa is coming home and it's not easy to make them understand."

"I'm so happy for you. I mustn't stay. I have a thousand things to do. The servants are becoming so unreliable, aren't they? Is your Miss Hutton still with you?"

"Yes. Missy is wonderful, so calm and sensible. I don't know what I would do without her."

"Good. There's something else I wanted to ask you," she went on as Nina went with her into the hall. "Do you ever hear anything of Galina?"

Nina's face stiffened. "In the first note I had from Simon back in July he wrote she was nursing in the same medical unit."

"Then she'll be coming back with him, I expect."

"More than likely."

"Do look after yourself," said Lydia. "It's all pretty ghastly, I know, but as Nigel says, 'Time and the hour run through the roughest day'. That's Shakespeare if you please! Honestly I could kill him sometimes!"

She waved cheerfully as she went down the steps.

Nina closed the door, leaned against it for a moment and then went slowly up the stairs to her bedroom. She stared at herself in the mirror and wondered what Lydia would have thought if she had known the real reason for that sudden dizzy spasm.

For the hundredth time she asked herself what had made her do it? What madness had possessed her that night? Was it anger or revenge or pity or a mixture of all three?

She sat on the bed shivering in the icy room and remembering. It had been just two months ago now at Dannskoye. It had been a very quiet Christmas and New Year, too many faces were missing, but a few old friends had joined them and the children had enjoyed being together. There were still the horses and the dogs, sleigh rides, the ice mountain and dancing at night to keep themselves warm. Valentin was there and stayed on for a few days when the other guests had left. He had never fully recovered from his wound and instead of being sent back to his regiment which he had passionately wanted, he had been assigned to a command in the Petrograd garrison with new untrained recruits and invalids like himself and he hated every single minute of it.

Perhaps it would never have happened if Paul had not been taken ill again. He was nearly seven now, a lively active child always rebelling against his frailty, always determined to do exactly as his sister and his cousins did. It was no one's fault that he had fallen against the iron rim of the toboggan and badly bruised his thigh but by evening the huge discoloured swelling had spread. He was in agony and Simon was not there. Somehow she resented that deeply. Surely his own son should have come first with him.

The next day the boy was a little better but still confined to bed and late in the evening she went to sit with him to let Marina go down to supper with Sonia's nanny and enjoy a few hours of rest. It was after two in the morning when the nurse came back and relieved her.

Even wrapped in her warm dressing gown Nina shivered when she came out of the nursery wing. She thought she might go down to the kitchens and make herself a hot drink. At one time the servants would have run at their bidding at any hour of the night or day but not any longer. There was a feeling of independence in the air, of rebellion especially among the younger ones. The old Princess complained bitterly and blamed Sonia for being too soft with them. A few beatings, a few harsh punishments were what they needed, she said, they would run fast enough then, but she was wrong. That time had gone. Even Nina had realized that. Meeting other young wives at the hairdresser's or at the café for cake and coffee, there were constant grumbles about servants' insolence and how maddening it was to have to do things for oneself.

Going down the stairs she saw a shadowy figure come out of the dining room and recognized Valentin. He came across the hall and looked up at her.

"What are you doing wandering around the house at this hour?" she whispered.

"I couldn't sleep. I came down to fetch my book. What about you?"

"I've been with Paul. I'm going to make myself a hot drink. Shall I bring you something? You could take one of the pills Simon gives me. It'll help you to sleep."

"If you're sure it's not too much trouble."

"No trouble at all. You go on. I'll bring it up to you."

She knew he still suffered a good deal of pain and felt sorry for him. When they were ready she took the two steaming cups of hot chocolate and went up to his room.

He was lying on top of the bed when she knocked and went in. He sat up as she put the cup on the table by the bed.

"I'll fetch you one of my pills."

"No, don't go, Nina, stay and drink yours with me."

At that moment he seemed almost like another child, like Paul asking for comfort against the terrors of the night.

"Just for a few minutes then."

She sat beside him on the bed holding the cup in both her hands.

He sipped the chocolate gratefully. "That tastes good. You know, Nina, it's the nights that are the worst. I have too much time to think. I wish to God I was still back in the front line."

"You sound like Simon. What's wrong with you men? You all want to be heroes. Wasn't it dreadful enough for you out there?"

"Yes, it was, appalling, but all the same you are there with a purpose. There is comradeship in being together. Here in the barracks there is only endless bickering, distrust of the government, anger against the Tsar." He got up, moving restlessly about the room. "Sometimes I wonder what is happening in this country of ours. If riots break out in the city, and there is danger of it with the food shortages, the men are more likely to join the rioters than help to put them down. It sickens me. I could knock their silly heads together."

Nina was staring up at him wide-eyed. "Are things really as bad as that?"

"I may be wrong. I hope to God I am."

She stood up. "I'll get that pill for you. You ought to try and sleep if you can."

He turned round to look at her. She saw his eyes glitter in the light of the lamp and was suddenly afraid. They seemed to be in another world, the only two still awake in this vast house.

"I must go," she said uncertainly but didn't move.

"No, Nina, no. Stay with me. I've never asked it before, I'll never ask it again."

"No, Valentin, no, I can't," but he had taken hold of her hand.

"Please, Nina, if you only knew how much I love you, how long I have ached for you, all my life it seems . . ."

"No, Valentin . . ."

But he had taken her in his arms. She was crushed against him, he was kissing her with a lingering despairing passion. She could have fought herself free. Even now she didn't know why she didn't except that somehow deep inside her was the memory of Simon's hurried note, the scorching knowledge that he was with Galina, Galina whom she had believed gone out of his life for ever. The bitterness welled up in her.

Valentin's hands were tangled in her hair, he was kissing her eyes, her mouth, her throat and she did not stop him. She thought of Simon and Galina working together, sleeping together, and jealousy rose up stiflingly, mingled with a deep pity for Valentin who loved her, Valentin to whom she meant everything. She let him lift her on to the bed. He was bending over her, unbuttoning her dressing gown, he was kissing her breasts, his hands moving over her body making her feel desired and beautiful. Simon might reject her but Valentin wanted her, needed her. In a wild mood of anger, defiance and thwarted love she put her arms around him and pulled him down to her.

What was the use of regretting it? It was done now. It was

over. She got up off the bed and began to walk up and down her bedroom. The one thing she had never thought of for a single moment was that she might become pregnant. It had been so long since the last time when she had crashed the car and suffered a miscarriage. Surely it could not have happened, not from that single night. Her cheeks burned as she remembered how she had let her wild mood carry her away, yield herself up to him so completely even though afterwards when she left him in the early morning, she knew without a doubt that it would not go any further. A secret love affair was not what she wanted. It could have been buried in the past, forgotten, if only . . . she stood still, bracing herself. She was not certain, not yet, she was probably worrying herself unnecessarily, but Simon would be home soon and he was a doctor, he would be the first to guess and then what would she do? Fling it defiantly in his face? She had lived with him for eleven years and still was not sure how he would react. He was kind, indulgent, but in some things he could be formidable and in the world in which she had grown up, it was the husband who always had the last word.

A knock at the door roused her from her gloomy thoughts. She opened it and Marta was there, Marta who was growing more insolent every day. She had a feeling that the girl's sharp eyes watched her every movement, knew more about her than anyone.

"What is it?" she said sharply.

"Luncheon is being served, Princess. Will you take it in the dining room or in the nursery?"

"I'll take it with the children. I have good news for them. The doctor will be home very soon."

"He'll find a great many changes, won't he, Princess?" Her eyes ran over Nina as if penetrating to the very heart of her. "In Petrograd I meant of course."

She bobbed her mockingly respectful curtsey before she moved away leaving Nina with a strong desire to slap the self-satisfied smirk off the girl's face.

Simon did not get back as soon as he had hoped. It was March before the train ground to a halt in the city. The months since leaving the front line had been chaotic. Barely adequate at the best of times the Russian railway system had all but collapsed under the weight of carrying six million men with food

402

and supplies as well as coal to the munition factories and provisions to the cities. During the coldest winter of the century boilers froze and burst, coal ran out, ice formed on the rails, enormous drifts of snow blocked the tracks and carriages sometimes stood motionless unable to move for as long as a week and more.

Outside a small town barely a hundred miles from the border Simon's train diverted to allow a troop train to go through, missed a signal in a blizzard and crashed at full speed into a freight train. The carriages crammed to bursting toppled over and rolled down the embankment. The resulting chaos, the mangled bodies of men, women and children, were something he thought he would remember as long as he lived. Working by the light of flares with hopelessly inadequate medical supplies, very few ambulances and only two doctors beside himself, it had been a gruelling few days and in those impossible conditions he had taken little heed of his own badly gashed hand until the pain became too intense to be ignored. With no real protection against infection the poison rapidly spread up his arm. During bouts of feverish agony he had been forced to instruct the young terrified doctor how to treat the condition. In the end it was his own strong constitution that pulled him through but he recovered very slowly in the little makeshift hospital. He was still suffering pain and discomfort not improved by being obliged to stand for nearly twelve hours in the crowded unheated train.

He alighted with a feeling of relief and fought his way through the swarming people to the barrier. Outside the streets were still thick with snow and the afternoon was beginning to draw in. There was not a cab to be seen so he took up his medical bag which was the only item of luggage he had clung to and walked out into the street and into the start of a revolution.

A crowd was surging up the Nevsky Prospect carrying red banners and chanting an incomprehensible jargon that resolved itself into "Down with the war! Down with the German woman! Down with the Tsar!"

Most of the shops had prudently closed their shutters. He drew back against one of them to let the ragged mob pass. Outside the Winter Palace they were confronted by a company of soldiers. The Cossacks halted but refused pointblank to fire into the rioters. Their Commander, young and inexperienced, yelled an order and the next moment had fallen from his horse, blood spouting, cut down by his own men. A cheer rose up from the crowd and they surged forward again trampling across his body, the soldiers marching with them. Appalled by the brutality there was nothing Simon could do but find his way home as best he could through back streets.

The door was bolted and barred. It was opened by Jake who took one look at him and then quickly let him through and shut it again.

"Thank God you're safe, sir. We've been expecting you for weeks. We've been hearing shooting all day so thought it best to keep off the streets. How is it out there?"

"Pretty bad. How long has this been going on?"

"For some time now."

Nina came from the drawing room scarcely able to believe that this tall haggard man with a two-day growth of beard could be her husband. Then she had run to him laughing and crying as she helped him off with his greatcoat.

The children had come racing down the stairs, throwing their arms around him, hugging him, the dogs were barking, he was kissing Missy's withered cheek, Marina was smiling all over her round peasant face, even Cook had come from the kitchen wiping the tears away with her apron. It was an enormous relief to strip off his stained uniform, bathe and dress and feel he was home at last whatever the immediate future might bring.

The next day or two were spent in taking stock of what had happened during his absence. Nigel gave him a brief run down on the political situation and told him about Rasputin's murder which had convulsed Petrograd in the New Year.

"It was Prince Yussoupov and his playboy friends who plotted it. Trust the Russians to turn it into melodrama," he went on cynically, "they invited him to one of their parties in the cellars of the Yussoupov Palace and fed him cakes and wine doctored with cyanide but the old devil refused to die. They chased him into the courtyard, two of them peppering him with bullets and he ended up in the Neva. When his body was fished out the Empress gave him a splendid funeral while the mob were dancing gleefully in the streets. It's a pity they didn't play out their little drama a couple of years ago then we would have been spared her listening to that damned charlatan as if he were the Lord God Almighty."

"Poor woman. She believed in him because of what he could do for that boy of hers."

"The mob don't realize that, Simon. To them she is a German Princess peddling Russian military secrets to the enemy. The riots began about a fortnight ago, peaceful enough to begin with, but they are growing uglier every day. The Tsar is away at army headquarters and doesn't seem to realize what's going on or how serious it is. The police are frankly terrified of reprisals and the soldiers are very unwilling to fire on the mobs."

"I saw something of that on the day I arrived. What is the government doing about it?"

Nigel shrugged his shoulders. "Nothing effective as far as any of us can see. The Imperial party is shaking in its shoes and the people's representatives in the *Duma* have a new leader – Alexander Kerensky, a lawyer, clever *and* eloquent, he has them all behind him in demanding the Tsar's abdication in favour of his son. There's going to be anarchy if something is not done about it fast. The best thing you can do, Simon, is to get out of it, go back to England while the going is good."

But that was easier said than done. To move a young family across war-torn Europe was no simple matter. He must first take passage in a British ship and that was a problem with the Baltic ports blockaded. Even if he moved them down to the Crimea, it was very doubtful if a cruiser could get through to the Black Sea. Nina was aghast when he discussed it with her only the day after he returned home.

"Leave now, abandon everything?" she said. "I couldn't do that, Simon, you can't expect it of me. This is our home." She looked around the drawing room with its fine furniture, the pictures they had collected, the cabinets filled with valuable treasures, some of them wedding gifts. They were part of her background, she could not imagine life without them. "Must we go and live in England? Can't you visit there, do all that is necessary and come back to us?"

He found it extremely difficult to make her understand that with the death of his brother, the duties and responsibilities of a great house with its lands, its farms, its many dependents had all fallen on him. Aylshams had never been absentee landlords.

Then there were other obligations. How could he leave Sonia and her children defenceless with Niki still so far away.

There was Galina. She had rejected him but she was never far from his thoughts. There were even some of his old patients. He had only been home for a few days and they were on the telephone asking for consultations, for advice, even when he pointed out that he was no longer in active practice. His colleagues at the hospital when he called there pressed him to return even if it was only temporarily. The street riots had resulted in innumerable casualties, many of them extremely serious.

Nigel's chief was inclined to believe that matters would soon right themselves and there was no need to panic but he was proved wrong. In the first week Simon was home events moved with a breathtaking rapidity.

On the morning of March 12th he went out earlier than usual, walking through a strangely silent city, the same wide streets, the same magnificent palaces, the same golden spires and domes rising out of the pearly morning mist, but no cars, no carriages, no traffic of any sort – an ominous hush over everything, the Neva still icebound and on the opposite bank the Imperial flag still fluttering from the Peter and Paul Fortress, yet when he returned that same evening, it was already all over.

The soldiers of the garrison had mutinied, ignoring their commanders and joining the disorderly mobs with their red flags of revolution marching through the city. The headquarters of the dreaded *Okhrana* was in flames, its members scattered in terror, the Law Courts were one gigantic furnace, shops had been looted, the palace of the Tsar's favourite ballerina had been broken into, its contents stolen or smashed, she was paying now for the hundreds of favours received. The Fortress for so long the most feared and hated prison in the whole of Russia had yielded up its guard and the prisoners streamed out from their cells bewildered, blinking in the strong light of day, some of them hurrying away before their luck changed, others joining the yelling triumphant mob. Frightened pedestrians hurried home through the noisy streets, everywhere could be heard the sound of gunfire, and army trucks rode around the city waving red banners and preventing the firemen putting out the flames because they enjoyed watching the palaces burn.

Some of the hospital staff deserted to join the cheering crowds while Simon with a handful of doctors and nurses worked grimly through the endless stream of victims brought in. Two hundred were already dead and many more seriously injured. One of them, an army officer, was carried in very late. He had been brutally attacked probably by his own men and he died while Simon was still examining his appalling wounds. It was Valentin, who had fought bravely guarding the Winter Palace with the last Imperial outpost to remain loyal.

Before he left that morning Simon had forbidden any member of the household to venture into the streets so that they were all eagerly waiting to hear his news when he returned at last. He played it down as much as he could and he did not tell Nina about Valentin until after they had eaten, the children were in bed, and they were sitting in the drawing room with a tray of the carefully hoarded coffee.

Nina was still finding it difficult to believe that the safe world which she had known for so long could suddenly erupt into such violence.

"It can't last, can it?" she asked anxiously. "As soon as the Tsar returns, it will all be over."

"I don't know, my dear. I think that this time he may have left it too long. I am afraid they may demand his abdication and he will have to yield."

"But what could we do without the Tsar? That sickly boy of his could never take his place."

"There is talk of his brother, the Grand Duke Michael, acting as regent or even taking the throne himself."

He had poured himself a small measure of brandy and was holding the glass in his two hands.

"I've some sad news for you, Nina. Valentin was brought into the hospital today."

"Val?" She had taken his coffee cup to refill it. "Is he sick again?"

"Worse than that. He was part of the guard defending the Winter Palace. He was very gravely wounded. He died before we could anything to help him."

"Val? Dead? Oh no, he can't be . . ."

The cup dropped from her hand. He was just too late to catch her before she fell knocking over a chair and grazing her forehead against the sharp edge of the onyx coffee table.

When she opened her eyes she was lying on the sofa and Simon was holding the handkerchief he had soaked in water against the bruised forehead.

"I'm sorry," she whispered. "It was just the shock. Poor Val!"

He fetched the brandy glass and held it to her lips. She shook her head but he was insistent.

"Take one or two sips. It will steady you."

"I'm all right, really I am." She struggled to sit up and he pushed her gently back.

"Take it easy now." He put the glass back on the table and stood looking down at her. "Are you pregnant?"

She turned away her head. "Yes."

"Was it Valentin?"

"Yes."

"How long has this been going on? All the time I've been away?"

His tone was harsher than he realized and she rounded on him with indignation.

"No. It was not like that at all."

"Then what was it?"

"It was only once," she went on falteringly, "just once at the New Year down at Dannskoye. He was so unhappy, so wretched and I was sorry for him."

"Sorry for him?" he said ironically, "Was that the only reason?"

His first reaction had been an instinctive one, anger against Valentin for seducing his wife, anger with her for not resisting him, quickly followed by something more familiar. The guilt he had always felt. Who was he to judge, with his love for another woman that had been for so long the canker at the core of their marriage?

He said more gently, "Do you want to tell me about it?"

"What is there to tell? It was one night. Paul had been very ill and I had been sitting up with him. Valentin could not sleep and I made him a hot drink . . ." She pushed herself up against the cushions suddenly flaring into anger. "I knew you and Galina were together out there ever since July. I couldn't get it out of my mind."

So much for honesty. He had told her, thinking if she found out by other means, then she would accuse him of deliberate deception.

"So to hit back at me you took Valentin as your lover?"

"What if I did?" she flung at him defiantly. "And if it made him happy for a few hours, I'm glad, do you hear, glad! For one night at least it made me feel alive, it warmed me through and through to know that someone valued what I could give him." Then she paused putting a hand against her stomach, suddenly looking young and frightened and helpless. "I never dreamed of this happening."

He did not say anything for a moment stooping to pick up the fallen cup and saucer and replacing them on the table.

"It's lucky it wasn't full."

"Simon," her voice was trembling in spite of herself. "Simon, what are you going to do?"

"Do? Nothing."

"Nothing?"

"What do you expect me to do? Valentin is dead. I can scarcely call him to account for sleeping with my wife, can I?"

"I thought . . . I don't know . . ." Other men would have flown into a rage but that had never been Simon's way. She watched his face before she went on huskily. "You mean . . .?"

"The child you are carrying is mine of course. What more natural? Husband returns after long absence, wife becomes pregnant. The timing may be a little difficult but you won't be the first young woman to bear a premature baby."

"But you haven't . . ."

He had been sleeping apart from her since he had come back, his recent illness, the fact that he was not yet fully recovered, providing an easy excuse.

"Well, no one knows about that except you and me and it is easily remedied."

She began to cry weakly. "If you know how worried I have been, how I've tormented myself . . ."

"What did you think I would do? Cast my unfaithful wife out into the snow with her bastard in her arms?" he said drily. "Surely you know me better than that."

She was looking up at him trying to brush away the tears. "You don't hate me? I couldn't bear it if you did."

"Silly child. Of course I don't hate you," he said wearily and realized how differently he would have felt if it had been Galina. He had never dared to question her about Leon. He did not want to know if they had been lovers, the pain would have been too sharp.

Then he was quietly practical. "You had better let me take a look at you tomorrow to make sure all is as it should be. We may have a very difficult few months ahead of us," and didn't know yet how prophetic his words were going to prove.

24

Petrograd had fallen. Everywhere in the city the mobs were triumphant and rival leaders were fighting for power. The Tsar was already being pressed to sign the papers of abdication when one morning Galina walked through the birch copse and looked across the gardens to the great house of Dannskoye. This year it seemed that the winter cold would never break. A blizzard had raged for the last two days but now the sky had cleared, the sun had come out and as far as the eye could see everything was covered with freshly fallen snow. In this clean icy air surrounded by this untouched purity, the agonies of war and revolution seemed very far away.

She had not realized how tired she was until she had come down to see her mother and had stayed on, letting the slow pace of country life calm her spirit and renew her strength. On the surface everything seemed as usual but when she helped out at the dispensary Niki had set up to serve the factory and the farm workers she had sensed an unrest, a burning anger, a bitter discontent. Many of the young men had gone from the village and never returned. Those who had come back, mostly deserters, were scarred in body and mind.

After an exhausting journey she had arrived in Petrograd just after Christmas and went to stay with Luba, helping her nurse Conn who had returned with a leg so shattered that he would never walk easily again.

"I knew it would happen. Nothing heroic about it. He lost his glasses and walked into an army truck," said Luba bravely trying to joke about it. "Thank God it's not his right arm. I don't know what he would do if he couldn't paint."

His sketches, brilliant, savage, provocative, were being used by the underground press as propaganda against the war but there was little money in it. Galina knew how hard Luba worked as a waitress in one of the working-class cafés while Conn eased his pain by turning some of his work into full scale paintings.

Vicky had not yet returned to England and was doing temporary nursing at the hospital and in her spare time caring for Leon who had developed a severe bronchial infection on that long freezing journey home.

Galina had not seen her mother since one brief visit when she returned from Siberia and it seemed at first as if nothing had changed. Vera was older of course, a sprinkle of grey in the dark hair, a few more lines on her fine-boned face. She wondered if lovers still came to the hut by night or whether the war had robbed her of them. Once she had been bitterly resentful, believing herself to be so different. Now she knew better. Sometimes helping with the never-ending chores in the bitter cold was like going back into childhood, an escape from reality.

Once as they were chopping wood for the stove, her mother said, "Your doctor brought the boy to see me. He's a good man and a good father. You know, Galina, you could have taken him from that silly little wife of his if that was what you wanted."

"I know and what would I have gained? A man with an uneasy conscience for the rest of our lives."

"Are you sure of that?"

"What did you do with Basil Makarov? Why didn't you tell him you were bearing his child?"

"That was different."

"Was it? I don't think so. I saw him, you know, in Kiev. He delivered his own grandson and didn't know it."

Her mother was frowning. "You never told me."

"Didn't I? Don't worry. I never breathed a word."

"What is he like now?" she asked curiously.

"Handsome still. A good doctor, rich, successful, with a fine house."

"He would never have achieved that with a peasant mistress hanging on to his coat tails."

"I wonder." She laughed suddenly. "We're fools, Mother, you and I. We don't know how to make the best of ourselves. We let our men escape us for a lot of stupid principles."

She was thinking about that now and wondering if Simon had gone back to England, yet, as she trudged through the snow. Sonia had sent a message by the stable boy asking her to come up to the house. She crossed the garden and went in by the back door running up the stairs to the room Niki had used for estate business.

411

Sonia was waiting for her. "I'm so glad you've come. I wanted to show you this." She held out a large sheet of paper. "It's from Yakov demanding that the factory hands should have their wages doubled immediately with a share of the profits. It's not the first time. They sent a petition before Christmas with one from the estate workers claiming a share of the lands as if they had a right to it. I dismissed them both as ridiculous but now they are uttering threats. You are closer to them than I am, Galina. I wanted to ask what you think. Do they mean what they say?"

She was staring down at the paper in her hand with its crude ill-formed writing, the scrawl of names at the end. "I believe they do mean it, every word," she said slowly. "I've been aware of something brewing, arguments, secret meetings. My mother heard that someone had come from Petrograd boasting that the military had mutinied against their officers, that the mobs had taken over and there were rich pickings for everyone. It greatly excited them."

"I can't possibly agree to these demands, it would be absurd," said Sonia, "we should have nothing left. I must try to hold things together for Niki's sake. How could I face him when he comes home if I let it all go?" She sank down in a chair by the desk. "It's so terribly unfair, Galina, when he has done so much for them, the dispensary, a school, help if they are sick, and this is the way they repay him."

"In a way I think that makes it worse. They don't want to feel grateful, they only want to hate. Give them something, Sonia, make some concession and perhaps it will calm them while we think of further action we can take."

"But that's showing weakness, that's giving in. Niki always used to say you must do the right thing, then stick by it, otherwise they would ask and ask till there was nothing left."

He was right too, but Niki was suffering for those landowners who kept their peasants at starvation level, for factories where the workers lived and died in filthy ratholes, conditions which someone like Sonia could never even imagine, and events were catching up with them in the country as they had done in Petrograd. The pressure began that very afternoon when the boys returned from school arriving from the station with their trunks in an ancient cab.

They were twelve now, tall, slim boys, and very excited as they came charging up the steps into the hall demanding money to pay the driver.

Sonia looked at them in astonishment. "What on earth are you doing here?"

"We've been sent home," they said together.

"In the middle of term? Why? What have you been up to?"

"The gymnasium has been taken over by the revolutionaries," said Boris, "they threatened to burn it down if the Headmaster didn't agree."

"So he gave in," went on Yuri taking up the tale. "He was terribly frightened, even we could see that, and then he sent us all home."

Sonia looked from one to the other of her handsome boys. "What is all this? Have you two got into some kind of a scrape?"

"No, Mamma, it's true, I swear it." Boris was very serious. "We drove through part of the city. There were fires burning and mobs cheering them on. Some soldiers tried to break through and they were struck down. It was horrible. Professor Bergman, he teaches us mathematics, was with us and he tried to stop us from looking. He kept on saying 'This is the end of our country,' over and over again. It isn't, is it, Mamma? It will be all right now we are here, won't it?"

Sonia exchanged a glance with Galina. "I hope it will. We shall have to wait and see. Don't tell your sister about the fires, it may frighten her. Now you'd better get unpacked. I expect you're hungry, you nearly always are."

Reassured they went bounding up the stairs. Revolution was good fun if it meant an unexpected holiday.

Sonia turned to Galina. "What does it mean?"

"I wish I knew," she said slowly, "but I think that Professor Bergman may be right and we may be seeing the end of our Russia."

Sonia urged her to stay on so she had supper with them and the next morning the boys were up with the lark and full of what they were going to do that day. As soon as they had eaten breakfast they galloped off to the stables to find out if the snow was soft enough for them to take the horses out and a few minutes later Boris was back, ashen-faced with shock.

"They're gone!" he burst out, "All of them."

"Gone? What do you mean?"

Sonia who was pouring tea for herself, put down the pot and stared at him.

"The horses, Mamma's, mine and Yuri's, and Papa's stallion,

the carriage horses, all of them, and – and the dogs are dead."
He swallowed convulsively. "They must have barked and the
brutes shot them."

Sonia had gone very pale. "Where's Yuri?"

"He stayed with Vassily. It must have been robbers. They
broke in and attacked the old man. We found him lying there
bleeding. Yuri thought he should stay there."

Galina was on her feet. "Is he badly hurt? We'd better go
and find out what we can do."

They bundled themselves into coats and shawls. Vassily lay
just inside one of the stalls with Yuri on his knees beside him.
He had put a folded horse blanket under his head. The old
man had been coachman and faithful servant for over fifty
years and slept in a little flat above the stables. He was conscious and groaning as Galina knelt beside him. He had been
struck on the back of the head. His white hair was thick with
blood and muck from the stable floor.

"Who was it, Vassily, do you know?"

"They had tied scarves over their faces but I'd take my
oath one of them was Yakov."

"Don't talk now. Let me treat your head. After that if you
feel strong enough you can try to tell us what happened."

Between them they got him up to the house. Fortunately his
injuries were less serious than Galina had feared at first. His
head would be sore and painful for some time but it was not fatal.

"It was very early this morning," he told them, "must have
been about four o'clock when the dogs woke me up. I went
down to quieten them. I thought it nothing – a stray animal,
even a cat, will start them off sometimes. Those ruffians were
there already leading out the horses. I shouted at them to
stop, then I heard the shots, one after the other. The dogs
yelped and were silent. I knew then that I must run to the
house, give the alarm, but I got no further than the gateway.
One of them must have hit me and I knew nothing more till
this boy was kneeling beside me."

Galina and Sonia looked at one another. This was the first
part of the threat – what form would the second take?

"It might be better to leave," said Galina, "pack up now
and take the children to Petrograd."

"I'm not running away," said Sonia stubbornly. "I'm not
giving up all we've fought for, all that Niki has worked at ever
since we were married, to brutes like that. Why should we?"

"They killed the General and Niki's father."

"That was a long time ago and it was not our people. Niki was always sure of that. They were assassins from outside. If we stand firm they will come to their senses."

Sonia was insistent that the work of the house should go on as usual but the servants were disturbed. They all knew what had happened and the boys working in the stables had all disappeared, terrified of being punished. It was a very uneasy atmosphere and during the morning Galina slipped out and found her way to the barn where Niki kept the car he had bought shortly before he went away. It was a Panhard, large and roomy. She wondered if she would be able to drive it should Vassily be still too sick. She had never driven anything but an old army truck for short distances at the front but she could make sure that it was in running order and filled with petrol.

In those heady early days when she had first gone to the meetings of the young idealists from the university burning with zeal for a better world for everyone, she had never worked it out to its logical conclusion, never dreamed that it could destroy those she knew and loved. Now she knew she was afraid for them and must protect them in spite of themselves.

Lunch was being served with all its usual care when she got back to the house even though nobody, not even the boys, had much appetite. Afterwards she went in search of Vassily.

"How do you feel?" she asked.

"None too bad. A fine headache but what of that? They'll not get rid of me so easily."

"I wanted to ask you about the car."

He looked up at her. "There's nothing wrong with it," he said with simple pride. "The Princess has never taken to it but I've always kept it ready for the young Master."

"If we had to leave suddenly, Vassily, could you drive us to Petrograd? Do you feel strong enough?"

"I can do it, Galina Panova. I'm not senile yet and if it would spite those rascals I'd drive it to the moon!"

The confrontation came sooner than anyone expected. Tea had been served in the drawing room, an English custom of which the old Princess approved and they were all there, even the boys with their two pet spaniels and Sonia's little daughter Elena in her pale blue velvet frock being teased by her big brothers and giggling over it.

It was a family party like any other until they came clumping into the pretty room, a dozen or so of them, Yakov at their head, thrusting aside the protesting servants, the dirty snow on their felt boots making muddy stains on the pale Chinese carpet.

For a few seconds they stared at one another, then the boys moved protectively towards their mother and Galina took the hand of the frightened little girl drawing her close beside her.

Yakov took a step forward. "We've come for your answer," he said, his voice overloud as if to overcome the years of ingrained respect.

Outraged the old Princess rose to her feet. "You'll take your hat off when addressing your betters," she said sharply.

He was bolder now. "Shut up, old woman, I'm not speaking to you."

"Sonia," she demanded, "do you permit this filthy peasant to insult me in my own house? If my husband were alive, he would not have dared to open his mouth."

"Please, mother-in-law," said Sonia, "please leave this to me." She raised her head proudly. "We received your petition, Yakov. I think you know as well as I do that what you ask is totally impossible. If Prince Nicolai were here with us, he would tell you the same. We made an agreement before he went away to the war and you have broken it. You have stolen our horses – do you want to steal our lands too?"

One of the other men, a big burly fellow, pushed Yakov roughly aside.

"We stole nothing," he shouted, "nothing. Don't you understand? Haven't you heard what is happening in Petrograd, everywhere in Russia? The horses are ours, the land is ours, it's all over. No Tsar any longer, no more rich, no more poor."

He thrust his coarse bearded face so close to her that involuntarily Sonia took a step backwards and one of the spaniels growled and sprang to her defence. The man aimed a violent kick, the dog yelped in pain and Boris launched himself at him.

"You beast! You leave my mother alone!"

The man hit out at the boy catching him so hard across the face that he was knocked off balance and fell to his knees, blood springing from his nose.

"Learn better manners, princeling, or it could be worse for you."

It was as if the violence, the sight of the blood, was a signal. The closed group broke up. The men moved around the room, kicking at the elegant gilded chairs, laying dirty hands on pale satin cushions, picking up the costly treasures that lay around them. One of them took up a valuable Chinese vase, held it high in the air and let it fall, laughing as it smashed. They began to pocket the fine jade ornaments, the jewelled snuff boxes, a Fabergé egg that had been one of Niki's Easter gifts, without an idea of their rarity or their value.

It was Yakov who brought them to order with a thundering command.

"Keep your greedy hands to yourselves, we are not thieves. We want only what is ours, to be shared amongst us. The documents of ownership, the house, the lands, the factory, that is what we want and what we intend to have."

"Never!" said Sonia trembling but strung to the height of pride and anger. "Never! My husband left them to me in trust for our sons!"

And suddenly Galina knew she must do something to bring this scene to an end. There was violence in the air, she could sense it, almost smell it, held in check so far but needing only a spark to set it alight and then anything could happen. She walked boldly forward. She took Yakov by the arm drawing him aside and the others gathered around staring at her, wolfish, threatening, stupid, dumb, but in a pack vicious as wild animals.

"Listen to me," she whispered, "you all know me, I grew up with you, I've suffered at their hands, three years starving in Siberia, two years at the war front, and what have I ever got out of it? Leave this to me. I know them. I'll make sure that the documents are handed over to you but I shall want my share. Don't you forget that. I'm not risking my neck for nothing."

It was touch and go but she had struck the right note, envy, hatred, that was something they could understand and they were not yet certain of their power. The revolution was still young and if it should be overturned they would have the documents in their hands as proof of their claim. She saw greed fighting with doubt then Yakov put a stop to their muttering with a raised hand. He glanced at the family drawn close together and then back at her.

"You'd better make sure of them, Galina Panova. Betray us

and you could go the same way as the rest. We'll be back and very soon, make no mistake about that."

She had won but it was only a temporary respite and there was very little time. The door had no sooner closed behind them than the old Princess turned on her.

"Traitress!" she spat at her. "I might have known. Don't listen to her, Sonia, she's hand in glove with them. She and her mother. They have always hated us. Don't let that scum deceive you!"

Galina ignored her. "Take all you can, Sonia, money, papers, your jewellery, everything of value and as many clothes as you can manage to pack. It can't be too much. There is not enough room but hurry, hurry. We haven't much time and they may be watching."

Even while she made her brave stand Sonia had realized the futility. With despair in her heart she urged them all to start packing at once. The next hour was hectic. It was so hard to decide what to take, so difficult to abandon beloved treasures. At one moment the old Princess was declaring she would never give in, that this was where she had lived and where she would die, and the next minute was refusing to go without all her fabulous furs, sable, fox and lynx. In the end Sonia took over ruthlessly throwing out everything but bare essentials. Elena's old nurse was weeping as she put the child's clothes together and tried to soothe her sobs because she could take only one of the collection of dolls that sat along the window seat in their splendour.

At last they were ready and were creeping down the servants' staircase, piling into the Panhard that Vassily had brought round to the other side of the house where it was not easily seen. The boys flatly refused to abandon their pet dogs so the two spaniels were pushed in at the last moment.

There were tearful farewells with some of the older servants who had seen the grand days when the old General was alive and had been looking forward to their return when the young Master came back from the war. What would happen to them now when there was no Tsar any longer and the Malinskys who had been part of their lives for so long had gone for ever?

Vassily, his fur hat perched on top of his bandaged head, took the wheel, Galina and Sonia beside him with Elena on Sonia's lap hugging her doll. The boys with their Grandmother were in the back, luggage heaped around them, the two dogs sitting on the top.

It was not snowing but the roads were icy and they had to take it slowly if they were not to skid with the overloaded car. They reached Petrograd by early evening, driving through strangely empty streets where fires still smouldered. They stopped outside the Malinsky house. It had been shut up during Niki's absence with only a few servants to keep it in order. Now the door stood wide open and a couple of soldiers, their uniforms dirty and unbuttoned, lounged on the steps, filthy with unswept snow and discarded cigarette stubs.

Sonia stared in disbelief. "What has happened? Where are the servants?"

"I'll find out," said Galina. "Better me than you. Drive on a little, Vassily, and then wait."

She climbed out and went up the steps. The soldiers stared at her but let her pass. In her plain long coat, a dark scarf tied over her hair, she was indistinguishable from a dozen others who had been in and out all day. The house had already been systematically looted, that was obvious; but she went boldly forward through the hall with its black and white marble floor and pushed open the door of what had once been the dining room. There were a number of men there but only one caught her eye. It was Igor seated at the far end of the magnificent mahogany table already dented and scarred by the bottles and used glasses, by slopped cups and half-eaten food.

She would have turned and fled out of the house but he had seen her. He muttered something to the man beside him and then got up limping heavily as he came towards her. He took her wrist in an icy grip and drew her towards the alcove by the window.

"What are you doing here, Galina Panova?"

"I thought this was the Malinsky house."

"It was once. Now it belongs to the people."

"And the people – they are you, is that it?"

"I and others, the new Soviet who will rule Russia. We fought for freedom, Galina, now it is here."

"Freedom to rob, to destroy, to murder?" she said fiercely. "Is that what was promised?"

"If necessary," he said calmly. "We will root them out, exterminate them, all those who battened on the poor, who

419

gorged while others starved. Who was it who said, 'The tree of freedom must be watered with blood'."

"Don't quote your stale old slogans to me. I want no part in it."

She had moved away but he caught hold of her and swung her round to him. "Remember one thing. He who is not with us is against us. Tell your English doctor that."

"He saved your life. Have you forgotten already?"

He gave her his twisted smile. "Maybe that was *his* mistake. He should have been more ruthless."

"What can you do to him?"

"When we hold supreme power there will be nothing we cannot do."

"You're not all-powerful yet."

"We will be, make no mistake about that and then you'll not escape me, Galina Panova, neither you nor the son that should have been mine."

Those brilliant eyes held hers for a moment, then he had walked away.

The cold passionless voice frightened her far more than if he had ranted and raved. She knew now who they were in this house. The combat section of the Social Revolutionaries who had become the Bolsheviki, whose leader, Vladimir Ilyich Ulyanov called Lenin hid himself in Switzerland while his henchmen did his work for him in Russia. They might not be in power yet but there was a cold implacability about Igor that chilled her through and through.

She ran back to the car and tried to explain to Sonia who stared at her in bewilderment. How was it possible to be happy and safe and secure one day and within a few hours be dispossessed of everything, without even a place where her children could lay their heads?

"Where can we go?" she said helplessly, for the first time beginning to break under the stress of the day.

"Uncle Simon will help us, won't he?" said Boris leaning over from the back seat.

"I'm sure he will if he can," said Galina, "but perhaps just for tonight it would be best for us to go somewhere where you're not known."

"Why should we? We've done nothing wrong," argued Yuri.

"I don't know, I just don't know." How to explain to the

boys that right and wrong seemed to have turned upside down in this topsy turvy world. "Sonia, I have some friends, not grand, only ordinary working folk, but good and kind. We could go there. It will be somewhere to rest and eat and Simon could come to you there. He'll know what to do for the best."

"If you're sure your friends won't mind," said Sonia wearily. "There are so many of us."

"That won't trouble Luba."

She directed Vassily through the city, over the bridge and into the artists' quarter. They stared up at the tall buildings with their huge windows surrounding the courtyard piled with dirty snow. There was a mouldering heap of rubbish in one corner over which cats were squabbling noisily. The boys were intrigued but the old Princess sat upright, rigid with disgust.

"You needn't think I'm stopping here," she said with contempt. "What does she think she is doing bringing us to this vile place where no doubt we shall be robbed of everything we possess?"

"Don't worry, Grandmother," said Yuri cheerfully. "Boris and I will fight off any thieves if they attack you."

"Personally I'd be glad of anywhere so long as it is warm," sighed Sonia wearily shifting the heavy weight of the drowsy Elena to another arm.

Galina had already run up the stairs and a few minutes later was back with Luba close behind her. She stood looking them over in her bright-coloured skirt and gypsy red scarf.

"Goodness, what a circus! Oh you poor dears, you must be frozen and hungry too, I shouldn't wonder. Well, there isn't much but you're very welcome to what there is."

Elena had woken up rubbing sleepy eyes and staring around her. Luba leaned into the car and lifted the child from Sonia's aching arms.

"You come with me, my poppet, and dolly too, that's the way. You can leave the car in the courtyard but bring all the bags. I wouldn't trust God himself, not these days."

They all trooped after her up the steep stairs, flight after flight, into the gaunt studio.

"Crikey!" exclaimed Vicky, "We've got a party!"

And in some strange way that is exactly what they did have. The room was warm but had little else to recommend it, the food was only *blini* stuffed with herring and bread with a morsel of cheese, but there were gallons of boiling tea and by the time Elena had been put to sleep in the tiny bedroom, they had all relaxed. The two boys, fascinated by Conn's war paintings were besieging him and Leon for stories. Vassily, overcome with shyness at sitting down to eat with his superiors, withdrew into a corner with his plate on his knee while Sonia with her innate courtesy talked English to Vicky and Russian to Luba with equal ease. The dogs, well fed with scraps, snored contentedly by the stove and only the old Princess sipping a cup of tea as if it were poison sat on a hard chair, disapproval in every line of her taut body, with Luba giving her now and again a half-rueful glance.

Galina stayed only for a bite of food and then went out again groping her way through badly lit streets. The lamp still burned outside the door but the house in the Morskaya was in darkness though it was not much after ten o'clock. She knocked and presently it was Jake who drew back the bolts and opened the door.

"I must see the doctor, it's urgent," she said in English.

He frowned. "He doesn't see patients at this hour of the night."

"I'm not a patient."

She moved so that the light fell on her face and he looked startled.

"Good God, it's you, Miss. I didn't recognize you. You'd better come in." He let her pass him and closed the door.

"Is he alone, Jake?"

"Yes. The mistress has gone to bed. The doctor is in his study." He showed her into the consulting room. "It is through there."

She crossed and knocked on the further door not waiting for an answer before she opened it.

He looked up from his desk and for the space of a heartbeat neither of them moved. It was always like that, instant recognition, almost as if something deep within them flowed together. He appeared as if he had been ill and her heart yearned towards him and he saw her pallor, the scarf fallen back, the bright hair dimmed, then the strain of the day washed over her, she swayed a little and immediately he was by her side.

"Galina, what is it? What has brought you here?"

"You may well ask."

For a second she leaned against him, then she had steadied herself.

"It's about Sonia."

"Sonia? Is she here? Is she sick?"

"No, it's not that." As quickly as she could she outlined the whole story.

"Poor girl. What hell it must have been for her. There have been similar happenings here in Petrograd but I never dreamed it would have spread into the country so quickly. I'd better come back with you. Perhaps I should bring them here, only it will upset Nina terribly and she has not been at all well."

"Seriously ill?"

"No, not seriously. She is pregnant and it's proving more troublesome than usual."

He said it without thinking, then saw the look on her face. She would think . . . he wished he could bite the words back but it was too late and he couldn't betray Nina, couldn't say it's not *my* child of course as if he were excusing himself.

And Galina said nothing. It was absurd to feel hurt. Nina was his wife, they had been parted for nearly a year, what was more natural? Yet in some perverse way it dimmed the memory of that magical night in the deserted house.

He said brusquely, "We had better go."

They went through the hall together. While he put his coat on, Marta came down the stairs.

Simon frowned. "If the Princess should ask, tell her that I've been called out and may not be back till very late."

"Yes, doctor, of course. Shall I say where you have gone?"

"No need. I'll tell her myself."

But her sharp eyes had recognized Galina as she opened the door. She watched how Simon took her arm and smiled to herself as she went slowly back up the stairs.

When they reached the studio Leon had already taken the two boys to his own room and made them comfortable on the floor with rugs and blankets. Luba and Sonia had done their best to persuade the Princess Malinskaya to lie down on the bed with her grand-daughter but she obstinately refused though fatigue had begun to tell and her face was the colour of old ivory.

When Simon came in holding out his arms to Sonia, she collapsed against him, her courage temporarily deserting her.

"I've failed Niki," she whispered, "I've failed him so miserably."

"You've done nothing of the sort."

"What will he think of me when he comes back? I've let everything go, all he has worked for."

"So long as he knows you and the children are safe he will only think how brave you've been. Now blow your nose and we'll settle down to decide on the next step."

Sonia choked and managed a smile before he went to the old Princess once so formidable and now shrunk to no more than a pitiful old woman.

He took her limp hand and kissed it. "This must have been a terrible trial for you."

She snatched it away. "Cowards, cowards, every one of them! I would never have given in to those ruffians, never!"

It was useless to argue with her. He turned back to Sonia.

"Do you still have the General's villa in the Crimea?"

"Oh yes. There is the housekeeper there with half a dozen servants to keep it in order."

"Then that's the solution. You must go there at once. A great number of people are running out of the city and going south but sometimes I'm told their baggage is searched. Have you brought any valuables with you?"

"All my jewellery. Such money as we had and as many clothes as we could carry."

"Hide the jewellery – on your person as far as you can and dress yourself and the children in your oldest clothes. Don't look conspicuous. You want to be as nondescript as possible."

It was decided at last that the safest way would be to drive the car to Moscow. It was a long journey but could be done if they drove night and day, Jake and Vassily sharing the driving. Once there they could take the train to Sevastopol.

"You should be safe there but if anything happens, Sonia, if you think you are in any danger, you must apply to the British Consul. I will ask Nigel to get through to him."

"There is Uncle Kolya," she said thoughtfully. "Do you remember him, Simon? He came to our wedding. He stayed with us all through that terrible time when the General and Niki's father were killed. He has lived in France for many years, on the Riviera. He would take us in if it were necessary."

"Write to him, Sonia, as soon as possible. In times like these anything can happen."

"What about Niki?" she said wretchedly. "What will he do

when he comes back to find everything lost? If I write, will he ever receive my letter?"

"Don't fret about Niki," he said, trying to comfort her. "I shall be here. I can't see myself uprooting Nina and the children for some months yet."

They talked far into the night and it was early morning by the time he reached home, woke Jake, told him what had happened and sent him off to Sonia with what money he had in the house to meet any contingency that might arise.

He was going quietly past the bedroom door when he thought he heard Nina call to him. He hesitated and then went in. The lamp was still burning and she was sitting up in the bed, flushed and feverish. In this cruelly biting winter she had caught a heavy cold and had insisted on carrying on as usual though he had ordered her to keep to her bed.

"What are you doing lying awake at this hour in the morning?" he said cheerfully. "It's only just past six."

"Where have you been?"

"Didn't Marta tell you? I was called out."

"Don't lie. You've been with her, haven't you? Marta said she saw Galina. How dare she come here so openly, so brazenly, asking for you? You despise me, I know you do, because of Valentin, so now you can feel free to do as you've always wanted, spend the night with your mistress . . ."

The words poured out in a burning flood, her voice hoarse with anger until she choked into a violent fit of coughing.

He waited until the spasm had eased before he said quietly, "If you really want to know, I also spent the night with Sonia, your mother, the twins, Luba, two dogs – shall I go on?"

She stared at him, still choked. "Sonia? I don't believe you."

"I'm afraid you must, my dear."

"But why, why? If Sonia is here in Petrograd, why didn't you tell me?"

"You haven't given me much chance, have you?" he went on drily and sketched briefly what had happened. She sat up abruptly.

"I must get up. I must go to her."

"You'll do nothing of the kind, unless you want to develop pneumonia. In any case they will have left by now. With any luck they will be at the villa by the end of the week. They should be safe there."

"Poor Sonia, how terrible for her. How can it happen like that, Simon, so quickly? What have they done?"

"It's not what they have done, it's what they are."

"I don't understand. Malinskys have always lived at Dannskoye. Grandfather used to tell Niki and me about the family far back in the old days when Petersburg was founded by Peter the Great."

"I know. It's hard to accept but it is something we are going to have to face." He sat on the edge of the bed and took her hand in his. "Nina, would you like to join Sonia there, go down to the Crimea, take Tanya and Paul with you?"

"Would you come with us?"

"Not immediately. There is still a great deal to be settled and I must think of Niki."

Her pregnancy was the worst possible thing to have happened with the ferment building up in Petrograd and the necessity of moving the whole household to England but it had to be faced. When the child was born and she was up again, then they would go. The thought oppressed him. Russia had been his home for twelve years and held a great deal that was very dear to him.

She turned her head restlessly on the pillow. "You want to be rid of me, that's the real reason you are saying this, isn't it?"

"Of course I don't want to be rid of you," he said wearily. "I simply thought you might be happier with Sonia and away from this biting cold."

"I don't want to leave you, Simon. I've never felt like this before. I'm afraid. I shall die if you're not with me."

She was sitting up in the bed, trembling, on the verge of tears and he took both her hands in a firm grip.

"Of course you're not going to die, what nonsense. I know you've not been feeling so well as usual but your condition is perfectly normal. You have a touch of influenza and you've not been taking care of yourself. From now on you are going to do exactly as I tell you, my girl, understand?" He kissed her cheek and got up. "Now I'm going to wash and shave and after that we'll have breakfast together and I'm going to make sure you eat something for once. All right?"

"All right," she said, "I'll try."

"Good."

He was treating her like a child but it still had power to comfort. Oh God, she thought, rebelling against the child that had invaded her body, why did this have to happen to me and why do I feel so afraid? And she could find no ready answer.

25

When the ice melted at last in that very belated spring and the trees were budding in the Mikhailovsky Gardens, Simon started negotiations to give up the lease of the house in the Morskaya.

Nina had made a very slow recovery not helped by the problems of running a household with acute food shortages. Eggs, milk and meat had all but disappeared even for those who could pay, and rebellion broke out among the servants who were demanding higher wages and refusing to stand in the long food queues. The laundress, two of the kitchen maids and all the outdoor staff deserted in a body, seduced by the slogans that mushroomed in the streets overnight promising a paradise that they very soon learned existed only in the minds of the writers. They joined the rapturous crowds who flocked to the Finland station to welcome Lenin, returning from exile in triumph and promising peace, land shares for everyone and all power to the People's Soviet.

The Tsar with his family were imprisoned at Tsarskoe Selo and controversy raged over what should be done with them. The Russian press, released from strict censorship, exploded into lurid tales of the royal family gorging on caviar and lobster, on roast goose and chickens, pork chops and fresh pineapple, while Petrograd starved; sensational rubbish but eagerly lapped up. A wave of hatred towards all foreigners swept through the city and even Simon whose years of brilliant work had earned him respect was now being shunned by those he had believed to be friends. He had always got on well with his Russian colleagues at the hospital but now he was aware of suspicion, mistrust, jealousy perhaps. It was painful and also deeply disturbing.

Occasionally during these weeks of early summer he called at the studio, taking Andrei with him so that he could spend a few hours with his mother; but he saw Galina very rarely. She had found work in a large pharmacy in the Nevsky Prospect where the chemist was only too glad to take on an experienced assistant when his own staff deserted him.

One night when she came home earlier than usual Simon was still there and she asked him when Nina's baby was due.

"In the autumn," he said guardedly.

"You shouldn't come here, Simon. It will upset her."

"Is it a crime to visit my friends?" he said drily.

"Nina doesn't think of it like that."

"My God, Galina, don't you care? Doesn't it matter to you that in a few months I shall be gone, there will be thousands of miles between us?"

"Oh I care, I care very much. There have even been moments these past weeks when I've been tempted to take Andrei from you. He is old enough to make his own choice. He would stay with me, you know, if I were to persuade him."

He looked at her aghast. "You wouldn't do that."

"Why shouldn't I? I am his mother and I have nothing. You have your wife, your children, but my life is empty. Go back to them, Simon, go back to them and forget about me."

She ran away from him then, up the stairs, shutting herself into her own room before he should guess how the thought of that parting haunted her daily and yet she could do nothing about it.

But she was right about Nina and he knew it. These visits, harmless though they were, irritated her profoundly. She took to questioning him the moment he came home so that sometimes he lost all patience and answered her more sharply than he intended.

In May the United States entered the war against Germany and pressure was brought on the Russian command to continue the vastly unpopular war. A new offensive was launched on the Galician front but it was half-hearted. The men rebelled against their officers and when the Germans brought up their reserves in a strong counter-attack, the defences crumbled, turning the Russian retreat into a rout.

There was still no news of Niki. Simon had written repeatedly and began to fear that he was lost somewhere on that distant battlefield until one night in late July. Hoping to please her he took Nina to the Maryinsky to see Karsavina dance in Delibes' *Sylvia*, a ballet of classical purity, both passionate and chaste, which he had always enjoyed, but the evening was not a success. Nina was distressed to see the theatre stripped of its golden eagles, the attendants in dirty grey jackets instead of sumptuous court liveries, an audience of workmen, students and soldiers in shabby uniforms while the royal box stood empty, its glory dimmed.

During the interval the orchestra played the Marseillaise which had replaced the national anthem and suddenly a young man in the uniform of a Guards officer stood up some few rows in front of them. He raised his hand, shouted 'Long live the Tsar' in a loud clear voice and bowed deeply to the Imperial Box. There was a startled silence, then they set upon him. He went down under a rain of blows.

Nina white as death clutched Simon's arm. "It's Niki," she whispered. "I'm sure it's Niki."

"It can't be, you must be mistaken. Niki would never do anything so foolish."

"Try and find out, Simon, please, please . . ."

The disturbance spread around them but she was so frantic that he took firm hold of her and battled his way through to the foyer. He left her there while he went back to see what had happened.

Attendants were milling around but it seemed the foolhardy young man had either fought himself free and escaped or had been taken prisoner.

He went back to Nina who was still very upset.

"It seems that whoever it was has disappeared."

"Let's go, Simon. I hate it here. It's not like it was."

It was still not dark by the time they were eating a light supper out on the terrace. It had been extremely hot during the day and they were glad of a breath of air. Jake appeared with a tray of coffee. He put it down and looked across at Simon.

"May I speak to you for a minute, sir?"

"Yes of course. What is it?"

"It's . . . it's about one of the horses, sir."

They still used the carriage when petrol was difficult to obtain.

Mystified Simon frowned. "Is it sick?"

"I'm not sure. Perhaps you'd come and take a look, sir."

"What's wrong with it?" asked Nina. She was lying on the chaise longue fatigued with the heat and still disturbed by the evening at the theatre.

"I'd better go and find out, my dear."

In the shadowy stables a man got up unsteadily, his uniform stained and torn, blood on his face, one arm hanging limply by his side.

"Niki!" exclaimed Simon. "Whatever happened to you?"

"I'm on the run and I couldn't think where else to go."

"So it *was* you in the theatre. Nina was right. You'd better come into the house."

"What about the servants? They mustn't see me."

"Most of them have left us. We'll go through the back door."

He was obviously in the last stages of exhaustion and he stumbled as Simon took his arm. They had reached the hall safely when they heard the sound of marching feet coming down the street. Niki stopped dead.

"I thought I'd given them the slip. I don't want you and Nina to suffer. I'd better give myself up."

"No, you don't. Go up the stairs, you can hide in the attic."

He pushed a reluctant Niki in front of him and they had reached the second floor when the thunderous knocking began. Missy opened the nursery door.

"What's all that noise? I'm just getting the children to bed." She peered at them through her glasses. "Good heavens, is that you, Niki? Whatever have you been doing to get yourself into that state?"

"Making a fool of myself as usual," he said with a wry grin.

"Are they after you?"

"Seems like it."

"Then we must do something about it, mustn't we? You go down, Simon, keep them off as long as you can. I know where he can hide."

In the hall Jake was delaying matters as much as possible by maintaining a stubborn ignorance of Russian. Then Simon had joined him, outwardly calm, inwardly filled with anxiety.

The men had pushed their way into the hall, half a dozen of them in sketchy uniforms and sporting red ribbons of revolution. Bosheviki more than likely. Simon was not sure.

"May I ask to what we owe this intrusion, gentlemen?" he asked in his most austere manner.

A babble of voices answered him. They were hunting a spy, a conspirator, a soldier plotting the escape of the Tsar who had refused to stop when commanded to do so.

"Have you seen anyone answering to that description?" he asked Jake.

"No, sir, certainly not here."

The ragged leader roughly pushed past them, flinging open doors. They tramped through the ground floor rooms ignoring Simon's indignant protests.

Nina came in from the garden looking alarmed. "What is it? What are those men doing here?"

"It seems they are hunting for a spy, my dear?"

"In *our* house?"

"Absurd, isn't it? I told them so but they won't listen."

The warning pressure of his hand told her to be careful.

By now they had started up the stairs with Simon at their heels. Apprehension grew inside him as they opened bedroom doors, one after the other, looking into cupboards and wardrobes and under beds until they had reached the second floor. One of them flung open the nursery door on a quiet domestic scene. Andrei and Tanya in their dressing gowns sat at the table, a chessboard between them. Paul was lying on the sofa covered with a rug in front of the toy cupboard while Missy in the armchair beside him was placidly knitting.

She looked up enquiringly as they glared belligerently around them.

"They are searching for a spy," said Simon apologetically.

"Indeed." She frowned at them over the top of her spectacles. "I'm afraid they won't find any spies here."

"I would ask you, gentlemen, not to cause too much disturbance in here as you can see my younger son is not at all well," said Simon.

"Sick, is he? I've heard tales like that before," said the leader whipping off the rug covering the boy. The nightgown was rucked up showing clearly the large horribly discoloured patch that spread from his thigh all down his leg.

The man took a step backward. "Christ! What's wrong with him?"

"It's a rare and dangerous blood disease," said Simon impressively as if he might be warning them of leprosy. He replaced the rug tucking it around the boy with great care. "Are you satisfied?"

They gave in reluctantly and trooped down again. In the hall Simon waited until he had seen them safely out of the house and then raced back up the stairs.

In the nursery the sofa had been pushed aside and the door to the toy cupboard stood open. How Niki had folded himself into the space below the shelves was a miracle but he came out grinning.

"It was Missy's idea but it worked, didn't it?"

The children crowded around him, excited and thrilled.

"Did I play my part well?" asked Paul.

"Better than any actor," said Simon. "Where did that colouring come from? It frightened me to death."

"Out of Andrei's paintbox," said Missy. "It was his idea."

"And I helped to put it on," added Tanya glowing with pride.

"Born conspirators, the lot of you, but now I think it's time we did something for poor Uncle Niki, don't you? He'll come and talk to you later."

Outside the door Niki leaned wearily against the wall. "Tell me the worst, Simon. I've been to Dannskoye and to the house here. I've seen what's been done to them. I've been nearly out of my mind. Where are Sonia and the children?"

"Didn't you receive any of my letters? They are at your grandfather's villa in the Crimea."

"Thank heaven." He swayed and would have fallen if Simon had not held him up.

"Come along with me, old man. You're done in. You need food and rest, then Nina and I will tell you the whole story."

There was a rapturous reunion between brother and sister.

"I knew it was you in the theatre. I told Simon but he wouldn't believe me."

"A good thing he didn't or he might have come under suspicion."

"Whatever made you do such a thing?"

"Crazy, wasn't it? But it had been hell, sheer hell out at the front, revolt, men deserting, I don't need to tell you what it was like, do I, Simon? I came back with two or three other fellows. We were sickened by all we saw and heard, that filthy rubbish being spread about the Tsar. God knows he may be weak, indecisive, dominated by his wife, but he's not a criminal. I'd seen what had been done at Dannskoye and the theatre seemed somewhere I could rest for a while, gather my thoughts, try to decide whether to come to you and suddenly it all exploded inside me. I had to make a gesture."

"A gesture that could have cost you your life," said Simon drily.

"I know but I suppose there always comes a moment when reason vanishes and a kind of madness takes over. It's rather like being very drunk." He grinned ruefully. "I'm stone-cold sober now."

They were sitting in Simon's little study. They still had to be very careful. The Cook and Marina were utterly reliable but Marta was still in the house and Simon had never trusted her.

He satisfied himself that Niki's hurts were mainly superficial, treated the cuts and bruises and found the pain of his injured arm was due more to a sprained wrist than to anything more serious. He strapped it up and after Niki had eaten they sat on far into the night discussing what was best to be done.

"You must go to Sonia in the Crimea," said Simon.

"Yes, that first of course but afterwards we shall see. I can't tell you how I felt to see Yakov, all of them, tramping through Dannskoye, destroying our home – it can't be allowed to go on. We must fight back."

"Darling Niki, don't throw away your life for a lost cause," whispered Nina.

"Is it lost? Are you so sure of that? I've been away so long from the city, the changes seem unbelievable. What do you think, Simon?"

"I don't know," he said slowly, "I could not prophesy, but whatever the outcome, Niki, don't indulge in any more heroic gestures. You have a wife, remember, and children. I'm certain of one thing. The old life is gone for ever and not only here in Russia. It will never return but what will come in its place only God knows."

Then they turned to more practical matters. He obviously could not travel with the papers he held at present. Prince Nicolai Malinsky, Captain in the Imperial Guard, would get him nowhere except possibly into prison or in front of a firing squad.

"Leave it to me," said Simon. "I have friends who may be able to help. In the meantime you can stay here, get your strength back."

It was Luba who came across with the best solution when he consulted her.

"He can travel with Conn's papers. You see, Simon, we both belonged to the Social Revolutionaries, we still do." She grinned at him. "You know, 'up the workers' and all that lark. It's a good safeguard."

Nina smiled reluctantly when she saw the spectacle Niki presented in his workman's blouse, bulky breeches and heavy boots, two days' growth of beard and grimy hands, a scarlet ribbon at his neck. Could anything be further from the elegant Prince Nicolai who had danced with her and Sonia at the winter balls? She was near to tears when he kissed her goodbye.

"Shall we ever meet again?"

"Of course we will," he said stoutly. "I shall come to visit you in England and make the acquaintance of my new nephew or is it to be a niece this time?"

"Whatever it is I shall call the baby after you," whispered Nina.

"Simon might have something to say about that."

He would not let her go with them to the station, the crowds were too great, and Simon saw him on to the train. He managed to crush into a long coach more like a cattle truck than anything else, with a small package of food which Cook in tears at the sight of the young master looking so unlike himself had plundered from her diminishing stock.

Niki's escape had all the elements of an exciting adventure story so far as the children were concerned and so it might have remained if the consequences had not been so serious.

It began about a week after he had gone when Nina came into her bedroom and saw Marta at the dressing table with the silver casket in which she kept the jewellery she was in the habit of wearing frequently.

She stood in the doorway and watched for a moment. The girl had a necklace in her hand, a lovely thing of rubies and diamonds set in fine gold that Simon had given her after Tanya was born. She was holding it around her throat, smiling at herself in the mirror, unbuttoning the neck of her blouse so that she could try the effect against her slim throat. Then as if satisfied she quickly closed the casket and slipped the jewels into her pocket.

Nina took a step into the room. "What are you doing in here, Marta?"

The girl looked round momentarily startled. "I brought up the fresh linen and saw that you had left your jewel casket on the dressing table," she said glibly. "I was about to put it away."

"Don't lie. I think you'd better give me what you put into your pocket just now."

"I don't know what you are talking about," blustered Marta.

"Oh yes, you do. Give it to me at once unless you want to be branded as a thief."

The colour rushed up into the girl's pale face. She snatched it from her pocket and flung it at Nina. It fell between them flashing red fire on the pink carpet.

"It won't be yours for much longer, none of them will," she said and turned the casket upside down so that everything fell to the floor in a tumbled heap of necklaces, bracelets, brooches and rings.

"How dare you speak to me like that?" said Nina in icy outrage. "You'll pick those things up and put them back at once."

"Pick them up yourself," retorted the girl insolently. "Haven't you realized it yet? It's different now. We are all free. There are no servants and no mistresses any longer."

"Stop talking this revolutionary rubbish and do as you're told."

"Rubbish, is it? I know more than you think. I know your brother was hiding here from the Bolsheviki. I know the doctor helped him to escape arrest," she went on tauntingly, "and I know those who would be only too pleased to hold it against him."

"You wouldn't dare . . ."

"Wouldn't I?"

"Who would listen to a slut like you?"

"And if I'm a slut then what are you? I know something about you, *Princess* Nina, something you wouldn't like your smart friends to know about. I know who fathered that baby in your belly. And it wasn't the doctor either. Does he know too and is that why he goes so often to his mistress?"

The biting words poured out of her in a flood of abuse and obscenity until Nina, provoked beyond all reason, slapped her across the face, first one side, then the other, so hard that Marta stumbled to her knees.

"Get out," she screamed at her, "leave this house at once. I never want to see you again."

The girl scrambled to her feet kicking aside the fallen jewellery, her eyes blazing with hate and spite.

"Oh I'm going. I never meant to stay. My father is a great man now at Dannskoye, not that Sonia with her high and mighty ways, not the old Princess ordering her servants to be flogged, treating them worse than the dogs in the stables. You'll find out soon, *Comrade* Nina, what it feels like to be forced to obey, to crawl and lick boots if you're not to starve, only it will be people like me who will be giving the orders."

"Go," said Nina, "get out of my sight or I'll call the police and have you arrested for a thief."

"What police?" jibed the girl. "It's you they will be arresting, my fine lady, for crimes against the Soviet, hoarding money and jewellery and food. Do you think I don't know what your Cook buys in the black market?"

She tore off her apron and threw it to the floor, then with her head held high went jauntily out of the room leaving Nina so shaken that it was several minutes before she could move. Then very slowly she got down on her knees picking up the fallen jewellery, pushing them anyhow into the casket, feeling that somehow the pretty articles she had delighted in had been contaminated by Marta's touch.

When Simon came in that evening tired after battling with lawyers all day over the house settlement she poured it all out to him and he listened in silence.

"Has she gone?"

"Yes. She bundled her things together and flounced out of the house. She can't really do anything against you, can she?"

"I doubt it," he said trying to quieten her anxiety but worried all the same. "Perhaps it would have been wiser not to have treated her quite so harshly."

"But she was insulting me, she said terrible things . . ."

"Well, it's done now and there's nothing we can do about it. I don't think we shall be able to replace her. How will you manage, my dear?"

"Somehow. I'm not helpless and I'm glad to see her go even if I have to scrub my own floors," she said vehemently.

"I don't think you will be reduced to that just yet," he said smiling.

"Don't joke about it. It makes my flesh crawl to think how she has spied on me."

"I must admit I never cared for her. If I'd had my way she would have been dismissed long ago."

"Simon, do you think those things of mine, especially those you gave me, should be put in your safe just in case Marta comes back?"

"Good idea. We'll do it at once."

The small wall safe was in Simon's study behind one of the bookcases. In it he kept the one or two ancestral pieces Nina had inherited, only suitable for wearing on state occasions, money for emergencies, some vital papers and the pistol he had taken with him to Siberia. It was a wise move since the robbing of wealthy houses was becoming more and more frequent and all over Russia people were hiding their treasures in attics or in walled-in cupboards or even in holes in the garden, some of the hoards never to be found again.

26

The days passed and it began to seem rather like a bad dream except that with so few servants they all now had their allotted household tasks, even the children who found it rather fun to make their own beds, to besiege Cook in her kitchen and fetch their own meals to spare Missy's poor legs.

It was at the end of that month that the power struggle between the Bolsheviki and the Provisional Government led by Alexander Kerensky reached a new crisis. The city was once again plunged into a series of riots. Half a million people erupted into the streets waving red banners, overflowing into every quarter of the capital.

Jake had gone out early that morning to join the queues foraging for food. Simon did not like leaving Nina alone when there was trouble brewing but one of his oldest patients on whom he had operated successfully some years before had fallen sick again and refused to submit himself to any other surgeon. It was a cry for help he found difficult to refuse. Reluctantly he left for the hospital, warning them to keep doors and windows locked and not to venture out. He had not reckoned on Marta.

Part of that vast mob surged along the Morskaya, Marta at their head wearing a military jacket, a red bandeau tied around her head, and enjoying herself immensely. Up the steps of the tall brown house she led a part of them hammering on the door. The small maidservant who opened to them fell back stiff with terror as they poured past her into the hall.

It was in many ways a largely joyous party out on a spree, some of them drunk already, all of them infected by the slogans they heard every day telling them the world was theirs and they could riot and rob among the rich at their pleasure. If they could tramp through the salons of the Winter Palace with its grand crystal chandeliers, its pillars of malachite and jasper, if they could lounge on the steps of the Admiralty smoking and spitting out sunflower seeds, what was to prevent them invading this rich foreigner's house?

They swarmed into the drawing room demanding money, jewellery, food. Nina was overwhelmed by them. They laughed at her protests, at her icy anger. They wandered into the dining room, the consulting room, pushing her in front of them, snatching at the pearl drops in her ears, at the gold watch pinned to her silk blouse. They met their match in the kitchen where Cook faced them with a butcher's cleaver in one hand and a saucepan in the other. They roared with laughter when one of them gave her a smacking kiss and she hit him over the head with the copper pan. They grabbed greedily at the pie she had just baked, stuffing great handfuls into their mouths and yelling because it was burning hot from the oven.

Led by Marta they swarmed up the stairs and into the bedrooms pocketing the gold and silver pots on the dressing table, trying on the rings, the pretty necklets, the brooches, screaming with laughter as they sprayed themselves and each other with the expensive perfume, leaving dirt and disorder behind them.

On the next landing the children were grouped together looking down fearfully through the banister rails and there Nina tried valiantly to make a stand.

"It's my children's nursery. They've done you no harm. Let them be."

They paused then. They'd had their fun, their pockets bulged, they might even have gone away if it hadn't been for Marta.

"Fools, can't you see?" she shouted at them. "That's where they'll have hidden their real valuables!"

That settled it. They began to surge up the last flight to be met on the landing by Missy, very stiff and upright, pistol in hand.

"I'll shoot the first man who comes a step nearer," she said in her impeccable Russian and hoped against hope that they couldn't see how her knees were shaking and that the gun in her hand was a very old one that had not been fired for years, unloaded and used by the children in their war games.

They were taken aback at the sight of the small defiant old woman so very like their own grandmothers, their *baboushkas*, who were capable of boxing their ears at any age, and they might have retreated if it had not been for Ranji. Getting on in years, his joints stiffening, he still had the high courage of his valiant breed. He advanced growling, teeth bared, back bristling, and one of them high flown with cheap vodka giggled as he cocked his gun and shot him.

Tanya screamed, Andrei fell on his knees cradling the dying dog in his arms and Paul, a small fury, launched himself against the enemy butting his head into his stomach, kicking out at him furiously. Quite suddenly the situation turned ugly.

"Fight me, would you, you little devil?" The man picked up the small boy lifting him high in the air. "You want to be taught a lesson, my lad."

Nina in an agony of fear for Paul clutched at his arm.

"Don't hurt him, please please don't hurt him, he's sick."

"Sick, is he? Can't see much sign of it. Here you go then!"

He flung the boy away from him. Paul crashed into his mother knocking her over so that she fell heavily backwards against the stairs as her arms went around him. There was a momentary silence and abruptly their mood changed. The impetus was broken. They'd had their fun and were bored with it. They began to clatter noisily down the stairs, laughing, squabbling, dragging a reluctant Marta with them into the hall and out of the house, leaving a trail of destruction behind them.

The door slammed. In the sudden silence their victims

began to pull themselves together, to count the cost and assess the damage.

"We've escaped with our lives, that's one thing to be thankful for," said Missy on a long breath.

Nina dragged herself up by the stair rail still holding on to Paul. Missy gave the pistol to Tanya and went down to her.

"Are you hurt, my dear?"

"I don't think so, only terribly bruised. It was Paul I was worried about."

"I'm all right, Mamma," said the boy bravely. "Bumped my head, that's all."

"What about Ranji?"

"I think he's dying," said Andrei valiantly trying to keep back the tears. The dog had been his loyal and loved companion for as long as he could remember.

"Carry him into the nursery," ordered Missy, "and ask Marina to see if anything can be done for him. Jake should be back soon, he will know what's best. Now we'd better go and find out how much havoc these wretches have left behind them."

Nina followed her slowly down the stairs, stiff and aching, but buoyed up by pride that would not allow her to give in to such a band of ruffians.

Cook came out of the kitchen followed by their one surviving kitchen maid. Frightened out of her wits the girl had taken refuge in the coal cellar.

They surveyed the drawing room, the fallen chairs, the filth on the carpet, the smashed ornaments. The silver candelabra had vanished with a great many other costly trifles.

The dining room, the consulting room, had been similarly ravaged, the decanters, the bottles of wine all gone, glasses smashed and ground into the carpet under a careless heel, Simon's valuable equipment damaged and phials of drugs unstoppered and turned upside down.

There was nothing to be done but set to work with brooms and buckets and they were still hard at it when Jake came back with his baskets of provisions, horrified at what he saw and deeply regretting that he had not been there.

"Shall I go to the hospital? Shall I fetch the doctor?" he asked Nina.

"No." Nina was firm. "We can't interrupt him when he is at work. It will be soon enough to tell him when he comes home."

She was holding on to the back of a chair. Her back was breaking but pride forbade her to give in while the others were still at work.

Jake exchanged a glance with Missy and then turned to her. "You go and lie down, Madam," he said gently. "I'll see to all this. Don't you worry now. We'll get it all shipshape before the master comes back."

She crawled up the stairs sick and dizzy not only with pain but with a desolate feeling that this house, their own private place, had been violated and she would never feel safe in it again.

She took her dress off and lay down on the bed in her dressing gown but the dragging pain became worse. She felt as if she were being torn apart and when later Missy came with a tray of food she could eat nothing, only sip a little of the hot tea.

"How is Paul?" she asked anxiously.

"He has a nasty bump on the head but Marina has put a cold compress on it. Don't worry, Nina. She watches him very carefully. They're all in tears over poor Ranji. Jake is promising them a hero's funeral, anything to distract them. It's you I am anxious about."

"It will pass, I expect. I must have hurt my back more than I thought when I fell against the stairs."

But it didn't pass and by evening she was sweating badly, racked by long shudders of pain and Missy called Marina down to her. The old nurse had seen both Nina and Niki come into the world and knew a great deal about pregnancy and babies.

"I don't like it," she whispered to Missy outside the door. "She is bleeding and I don't know how to stop it."

"I'm sending Jake to fetch the doctor," said Missy decisively. "He must come. At a time like this I wouldn't trust anyone else."

But Jake came back with disquieting news. "They wouldn't let me see him. He has been arrested."

"Arrested?" exclaimed Missy. "Why? For what reason?" It seemed like the last straw.

"They wouldn't say, only that he was being detained for questioning."

They stared at him aghast. It couldn't be true. They felt as if the bottom had fallen out of their world.

Tanya shaken by this last dreadful blow looked anxiously at Andrei.

"What's going to happen? Do you think Mamma is going to die?" she whispered.

"No, of course she isn't. Don't say such things, Tanya."

But he had been deeply shocked by the glimpse he had of Nina when he had carried in a tray for Missy. Supposing Papa was sent to prison? Supposing he did not come home for weeks and weeks? His thoughts flew to his mother. She knew all about nursing. Hadn't she cared for the wounded all that long time? She would know what to do until his father was freed.

No one noticed when he buttoned his coat, took his cap and escaped out of the house by the back door. The city was quieter now, though here and there fires burned and small squads of soldiers were moving purposefully through the streets. Once half a dozen of them burst out of a house dragging their victim with them. He stumbled and they kicked him to his feet. Andrei flattened himself against a wall till they had disappeared, then hurried on his way across the bridge and began to run towards the studios.

Galina was late home from the pharmacy. The doors had been firmly shut during the early part of the day but opened later for the victims of minor injuries, cuts, bruises, fainting fits, children trampled underfoot. It was dusk by the time she reached the studios and ran up the stairs. She opened the door and paused. There had been the faintest rustle of movement and she knew instantly that someone was there, hiding in the shadows. The studios were old fashioned, many of the rooms had neither gas nor electricity. She conquered her alarm, struck a match, lit the lamp on the table and looked around her.

"I know there is someone here. You had better come out and show yourself before I call for help."

A curtain was fastened across one corner behind which she hung her clothes. A man stepped out, dirty, dishevelled, a dark bruise on one lean cheek but she knew him at once. It was Igor!

"You!" she exclaimed. "You dare to come here! What can you possibly want from me?"

"Nothing," he said, "nothing more than a few hours' shelter."

"Why? For God's sake, why?"

She knew as everyone did that day that the Bolsheviki had suffered defeat in the struggle for power. The Provisional Government had been clever enough to seize their opportunity, had labelled them peace-lovers shamelessly betraying their country to the Germans. All that day the leaders had been mercilessly hunted down.

"They had me on the run," he went on with his wry thin-lipped smile. "I had to find refuge somewhere."

"Why me? What is to prevent me going out into the streets, telling them where you are. There are still soldiers everywhere."

"Will you?"

"Why shouldn't I? Tell me why."

He shrugged his shoulders. "It's your choice."

She knew he was using her, quite certain that she could no more stand by while he was dragged brutally from her room than Simon had been able to betray him when he was at their mercy in the hospital and it enraged her.

"So you lost your battle after all?" she said derisively. "What has become of your mighty Soviet, the will of the people?"

"This means nothing, a mere stumble on our path to victory."

There was a force, a frightening strength of purpose about him even in defeat. His eyes were fixed on her and she had a queer sensation of being caught in a trap from which there was no escape. The knocking on the door startled them both.

"Who is it?" he whispered.

"I'll find out."

He slid silently back behind the curtain as she went to the door.

"Andrei," she said in surprise. "Whatever are you doing here and so late? Is something wrong?"

"It's Tanya's mother."

To the boy Nina had always been Tanya's mother, never anything closer and even at this moment it pleased her.

"What's wrong with her?"

He poured out the story of that appalling day and she guessed at the outrage, the terror, in the voice that he tried to keep steady.

443

"Where is your father?"

"He went to the hospital to see a patient who is very sick. Jake went to fetch him and they told him Papa had been arrested."

"Arrested? It's not possible. Why?"

"I don't know. Oh Mamma, please please do come. Tanya is so frightened and so is Paul."

If it had been anyone else she would have gone at once but this was different. This was Simon's wife, she was bearing the child which once in a crazy moment she had hoped might have been hers and yet ... why had Simon been arrested? Why? She sighed. There was no help for it. She had to go, do what she could if only for his sake.

"Very well," she said at last. "There are one or two things I'd better bring with me. Wait for me downstairs, Andrei."

When she turned back into the room Igor was there again watching her.

"Was that your son?"

"Yes. Did you hear what he said? You must be very proud of yourselves, terrifying women and children, shooting a harmless dog, arresting an innocent man."

He shrugged his shoulders. "It's the luck of the game."

"A game I want no part in, now or ever. I'm going now. When I come back, please don't be here."

She had gathered a few necessities together and moved towards the door when he came silently behind her putting his hands on her shoulders and turning her to face him.

"Till we meet again, Galina Panova," he whispered and his mouth touched hers briefly.

An icy shudder ran through her. It was absurd to feel so threatened but the chill had always been there. He dropped his hands and she ran away from him down the stairs to where Andrei waited for her.

They walked quickly through the darkening streets, not speaking much, and entered the house by the back door. Missy got up when she went into the bedroom and she saw the surprise on her face.

"Andrei came to fetch me," she said briefly. "How is she?"

"She's in so much pain. I'm afraid for her."

"Perhaps I can do something to ease that."

Nina looked up at her as she moved to the bed, eyes hazed with pain, the fair hair damp with sweat. She frowned trying to concentrate.

"Is it Galina?"

"Yes."

She hesitated and then took the hand that lay limply on the coverlet holding it in a firm clasp and for a few moments it was as if the years had fled away. They were young girls again exchanging secrets, full of hope, unaware of sorrow, unbruised by life. Then Nina stirred fretfully.

"Why doesn't Simon come?"

So they had not told her about the arrest. "He will be here soon. I'm going to try and make you more comfortable."

She was not a trained midwife but she had learned a great deal during the years in Siberia where they had been forced to fend for themselves without benefit of doctor or any other assistance and where she had seen similar cases.

"Help me, Missy," she said. "I think she would be better if she were to lie flat in the bed."

They eased her down and put a pillow under her legs and if she was able to do little medically, she brought with her a feeling of calm, a relaxation of stretched nerves because someone capable was in charge. Missy went upstairs to see the children into bed. Galina moved quietly about the room setting things to rights and in a queer way Nina seemed to draw comfort from her being there, suspicion, jealousy, forgotten for the time being.

An hour passed and then two more, it was past midnight before Simon came. She heard the voices in the hall when Jake let him in, then he was running up the stairs and into the room and with him came relief and reassurance.

He looked surprised to see Galina but went straight to the bed and if she had ever had any doubts of Nina's utter dependence on him, they vanished now for ever. He had taken both her hands in his and she was clinging to him as if he were a rock from which she drew strength and courage.

"My poor girl," he was saying, "what a wicked day you must have had."

"It seemed such a little thing, I thought it would pass, but now . . ." Her breath caught in a sob.

"It's all right. I'm here and everything is going to be fine. I'm going to take a look at you now, find out what damage you've done to yourself."

He looked across to Galina and she came to him at once, personal feelings set aside. She watched him as his hands moved gently, probingly over Nina's body, noting where she

445

felt most pain and she guessed by his face that he was not altogether happy about it.

"What you need more than anything is to relax the tensed nerves and sleep," he said when he replaced the blankets. "I'm going to give you something that will help you to do just that."

"I'm afraid those brutes wrecked your medicine cabinet," she whispered anxiously.

"So Jake told me. I hope to God they have left me something."

"I brought one or two things with me," said Galina. "I always keep them. I suppose I shouldn't but some of my neighbours have come to rely on me."

"Playing the physician, are you?" he said with a faint smile. "I must look to my laurels. Let me see what you have."

When he brought it to Nina she clutched at the hand that held the glass.

"You won't leave me."

"I shall be here, my dear."

He took the damp towel Galina handed to him and wiped the sweat from her face. She was calmer already, simply from the comfort of his presence. After a while when she grew drowsy he got up and beckoned to Galina.

"How serious is it?" she asked.

"I don't know yet. We can only wait. Babies are tough little creatures. A fall, even a bad one, does not always cause too much damage. How do you come to be here?"

"Andrei fetched me. I think the children were scared. What happened at the hospital?"

"God, what a frightful day it has been!" He passed a hand over his face. "It began when the Director told me my services were no longer required and I could no longer be allowed to work in the hospital. I was the foreigner and definitely *persona non grata*. I've felt it coming for some time but I suppose you always hope the worst won't happen."

"What about your patient?"

"That was the point. His life was hanging by a thread and for some reason the poor man had made up his mind that it had to be me and no one else – people can be like that sometimes when they are very sick – so what was I to do? I insisted on carrying out the operation. A good number of the staff are loyal to me and we carried it through. I did what I could but

446

afterwards the whole thing blew up in my face. I had acted without permission and to make matters even more suspect from their point of view it seems my patient is of German origin, as if it matters whether a sick man is German, Russian or Hottentot! There was a lot about spies but in the end I think even the Director began to see the absurdity of it and I was allowed to leave. It's the finish of course. I can never go back."

He had been making light of it but she knew how much it must mean to him.

"I'm sorry, Simon."

"And then to come home to this – this mindless brutality. What kind of a country is this turning into?"

She thought of Igor lurking in her room, of those who had fled and those who had already been murdered.

"Perhaps now the Bolsheviki have been defeated, we can look forward to a little more stability."

"I doubt it. Anyone can start a revolution but when it's in full spate, nothing in the world can turn it back. Have you heard what is happening to the Tsar? He and his family are being sent to Siberia. Ironic, isn't it? Justice, they call it but I wonder if he ever realized what was being done in his name." He glanced towards the bed. "I think Nina will sleep for a little now. I'd better eat something, I suppose. I've had nothing all day. Come and eat with me."

"I've already supped with Missy."

"Then drink a glass of wine if they have left us anything."

"Better not. Now you're here, Simon, I think I should go."

"I'd rather you stayed, at least for another day. It's not going to be easy for me to obtain the services of a trained nurse, not now. Marina is very willing but I don't altogether trust her remedies and Missy is goodness itself but she is getting on in years."

"Nina may resent me, Simon."

"I don't think she will. Is it asking too much?"

She didn't answer at once. He had always asked too much and she had always given it.

"I do work, you know, at the Nevsky Pharmacy."

"Couldn't you send word just for a day or two?"

"I suppose I could."

"I'd be enormously grateful.

Downstairs he opened the bottle of wine he had brought up

from the cellar, a German wine, dry, sharp and refreshing. He smiled as he filled her glass and she knew he was thinking of the night in the empty house though he said nothing.

The dining room had a ravaged look even though it had been cleaned up. This was where he had lived with Nina all these years, where she had scarcely set foot until this night and yet while he ate and they talked quite impersonally for a little, she lost the feeling that she had no right to be there and was happy even though she was aware of its impermanence and its dangers.

Just when they believed the worst had been averted and Nina seemed to be making a good recovery, she suddenly went into labour and Valentin's daughter was born late on the following evening. It lasted for longer than it should have done and was made excruciatingly painful by the injury to her back but the baby though she was small was perfectly formed and extremely strong and vigorous. She began life scarlet in the face and screaming furiously, yet when everything had been done and Simon took her from Galina, wrapped in the white lacy shawl, she stopped yelling, the puckered little face with the large brown eyes staring up at him as he went to the bed where Nina lay white and very exhausted.

"We have a daughter, my dear."

Her eyes flickered open, then she turned her head away in utter rejection.

"Do you remember what you promised Niki? Shall we call her Nicola?"

"Call her anything you like," she whispered and refused even to look at the baby.

It did sometimes happen that a woman who had suffered a painful delivery would temporarily reject her child. Nina, unlike most young women of her class had yielded to Simon's insistence and had breast fed her two babies for the first few months instead of employing a wet nurse and at this time of extreme difficulty and acute shortage of food, particularly milk, it was even more essential. At first she absolutely refused. Galina marvelled at Simon's patience, gentleness and tact through the next two days but there did come a moment at last when he put the baby into her arms, when the tiny hands pummelled against her, the little mouth sought for her breast and she suddenly clutched Nicola to her and began to cry soundlessly and he sighed with relief.

448

Galina yielded to his persuasion and stayed for a few days longer and wondered at herself for being such a fool. Surely it was the most ridiculous and painful situation imaginable for a woman to watch the man she loved nurse his wife through the painful trauma of bearing his child. There were moments when she couldn't bear it, when she hated him for expecting it from her, when she wanted to walk out of the house and never see him or Nina again, and strangely there were other times when they were simply doctor and nurse caring for a fractious patient so that once or twice during those difficult few days they could sit together for an hour or so in the evening talking quietly and could find in it a kind of content.

What they did not guess at was Nina's reaction. It did not strike them though perhaps it should have done, how she lay watching every tiny gesture, listening to every casual word, misinterpreting them, reading into them far more than was there. Although she was physically much recovered, she lay and brooded, letting suspicion gnaw at her, rejecting the first gratitude she had felt for Galina until one day it came to a head.

She was up by then, partly dressed and lying on a sofa in her room. Simon who had been out came up to her as he usually did, asking how she felt. The children had come down to say goodnight and were standing around the cradle looking at their new sister. Baby Nicola had a little knot of dark hair and deep brown eyes very different from Tanya's pale gold curls.

"She's not like any of us," she objected. "I think she's a changeling."

"Don't say such stupid things," said her mother sharply.

"But she is different, isn't she, Papa? Who does she look like?"

"What about me?" said Simon. "I tell you one thing, my poppet, she's a good deal prettier than you were at her age."

"What a perfectly horrid thing to say," said his daughter indignantly. "You used to say I was the nicest baby you had ever seen."

He tweaked her nose. "Ah but then I'd not seen Nicola."

"I think she looks like me," said Paul who had taken a great fancy to the baby and would hang over the cot letting the tiny hand close round his finger.

"Be off to bed, the lot of you," said Simon, "I'm going

down to supper and your Mamma needs her rest. Where is Galina?"

"She's been teaching us a new game."

"Oh and what was that?"

They clung to him as they went out telling him what they had been doing during the afternoon. Nina heard the young voices happily topping one another, as they trooped down the stairs. She felt isolated, rejected, filled with an angry self-pity. Galina had stolen Simon and now she was stealing her children while she was shut away with the baby she had not wanted and was finding so difficult to love. No doubt she and Simon would be supping together, pleased with themselves, while she was cut off from them. She thought she had conquered her feelings about Galina but now they sprang into new life. It was like an abscess growing and growing inside her until suddenly it burst and she could not endure it a moment longer.

She was still feeling very shaky but she got up, her dressing gown trailing after her as she went slowly down the stairs. The dining room was empty and so was the drawing room. Where were they then? She walked through the consulting room. Some of the smashed medical equipment was still there. He had not felt it worth while to replace it when they would be leaving Russia so soon. The door to his study was open and she stood for a moment looking at them. Galina had asked to see some of his work on haemophilia. She was seated at his desk, notebooks open before her. His arm was along the back of her chair, his head close to hers as he leaned forward pointing something out and explaining. The air of familiarity, the way she looked up at him asking some question, the warmth in his voice when he answered, filled Nina with a wild furious jealousy. This was part of him she had never known or understood, something in which she had never shared. She took a step inside the room.

"So this is where you are."

Simon straightened up. "Good heavens, whatever are you doing down here, Nina? Is anything wrong?"

"Oh no, nothing wrong, nothing at all, except that you seem to prefer Galina's company to mine."

He frowned. "I was showing her some of my medical work, that's all."

"So that's the excuse, is it?"

"Excuse for what? What are you talking about? Oh come along, my dear, you shouldn't be standing there like that. It's not good for you. I'll take you back to bed."

"No," she said stubbornly, "No. I'm staying here."

Galina stood up shutting the notebooks. "Nina's right. It must be getting late. Time for bed for all of us, I expect."

"Oh yes, time for bed and which bed is it to be? You've robbed me of my children, now you're robbing me of my husband too, I suppose."

"Nina, for God's sake," he said impatiently. "You're talking absolute nonsense. What has come over you?"

"I've woken up to what's been going on, that's all. It's so easy, so convenient, isn't it? I'm shut away upstairs and you two are alone together. Have you told her all about your faithless wife? About the poor little bastard upstairs in her cot? Have you? But then I forget she knows all about bastards, doesn't she? She has made sure she has planted hers here, a nasty little spy who tells her everything." She knew she was being foolish but she could not stop the words pouring out of her in a hot poisonous stream. "I'll not have her here a moment longer."

Galina said quietly, "Don't worry, Nina, I'm going. I'm leaving this house at once. You won't be troubled by me any longer."

"No, you're not," said Simon, "not like that. I'll not permit it."

"You must. It's best, Simon. I should never have come."

"Go, go now," said Nina violently. "Go, take your bastard with you and never come back."

"Stop it, stop it at once," said Simon. "Have you taken leave of your senses?"

"Don't upset yourself on my account, Simon. I'm going now." Galina came round the desk and paused as she passed Nina. "I wonder if you've ever stopped to realize how very fortunate you are," she said with a quiet dignity. Then she had gone.

Outside she paused, taking a deep breath, too shaken to notice the shadowy figure that slipped through into the hall in front of her. After a moment she pulled herself together and went upstairs to fetch the few articles she had brought with her. The sooner she left the better.

Simon looked at his wife and then turned away. "I hope you are satisfied."

Now it was all over Nina was trembling, sick and frightened at what she had done.

"I am the mistress of this house. I have the right to say what I did."

"Oh yes, every right to insult someone who came to help you when you most needed it."

"I never asked her to come or to stay."

"No, I did that for your sake. You might at least have shown courtesy if you couldn't be grateful."

The rage had died and she was suddenly so weary she could scarcely stand. She looked at her husband's stony face and could find no comfort.

"Simon, I'm sorry," she faltered.

"So you ought to be."

He had begun to gather up the books and papers replacing them in his desk and on the shelves for once too tired, too sick at heart to respond to the pleading note in her voice.

"I wish you didn't despise me so much."

"Nina please. We've been all over this so many times, can't we put it behind us once and for all, forget it? Now be sensible for heaven's sake. Do you want to make yourself ill? Go back to bed."

"Will you come?"

"Presently."

A wave of intense depression washed over her. He had never been like this before, so cold, so unfeeling. She had lost him now, lost him for ever, and it was her own fault. Why did this have to happen to her? Why? It was so unjust.

She trailed slowly out of the room and up the stairs, shaken by a black despair. Everything seemed to crowd in on her, all the unhappy events of the recent months. The loss of Dannskoye and all the richness of her family life, Niki gone, Sonia gone, very soon she would be gone herself, living in an alien country among strangers who would resent her, with a man whose love – no, perhaps not love because she had never really had that, she thought drearily – but whose tenderness, whose affection and strength to which she had clung would now be lost to her. She stood looking around her feeling totally alone with no one who cared whether she lived or died.

A sudden feverish idea took possession of her. She took off her dressing gown and opened the wardrobe searching frantically through the clothes. At random she pulled out a fur coat, a silvery mink which once had been her pride and delight. Now she scarcely looked at it, huddling herself into it with a desperate haste. She tied a scarf over her hair and stood looking down at the cradle, the baby who would never know her real father, who would one day be as lost as she was. On a sudden impulse she took up the sleeping Nicola wrapped her in a large shawl and stole quietly down the stairs, through the silent house and out of the front door.

Although it was only August, the night was cool. A chill little wind bit into her making her shiver. She hurried down the Morskaya bent on making her way to a lonely spot beyond the canal where she had sometimes walked with the children on summer afternoons. Restaurants were still open and there were people hurrying to and fro looking for entertainment, but out of the fashionable quarter the streets were empty except for a few night vagrants who stared at her curiously.

When she reached the canal and crossed the bridge the river flowed dark and mysterious. To slip into its depths, to be lost in it with all her fears and uncertainties, had seemed a wonderful solution but now the dank smell, the leaves and debris lapping at the water's edge filled her with disgust. A tramp lying on one of the stone benches looked up as she came nearer, muttering something and catching hold of the hem of her coat. She jerked it away moving to the far end of the seat sinking down as her legs gave way under her. Perhaps in a few minutes when she could breathe again she would regain her courage. The baby woke up and began to cry. She hushed her holding her close against her breast and rocking her to and fro.

After a while the tramp seeing no hope of getting anything out of this lost and desolate figure in her luxurious furs slowly struggled to his feet picking up his bundle. She saw him leave with relief. Now there would be nobody to witness what she did, no one to guess at what had happened to her until the river police – if there were any left in this beleaguered city – plucked her sodden body out of the water and with her the baby that should never have been born.

It was about half an hour later when Simon knew he could not leave things as they were. He must find Nina, comfort her somehow, make her realize how wrong she had been. He blamed himself severely. He should have realized this might happen, but lately there had been so much weighing on his mind that he found it almost impossible to deal with her wayward moods as calmly as he had done once.

He went upstairs to make his peace with her and she was not in the bedroom. With a touch of alarm he saw that the cot was empty and ran up the stairs to question Missy and Marina but they had seen and heard nothing. He was coming down again when he met Andrei and frowned at him.

"What are you doing up at this time? Why aren't you in bed?"

"Papa, are you looking for Tanya's mother? I saw her. She went out."

"Went out? When?"

"About half an hour ago. She didn't see me. She was carrying the baby."

"Why didn't you tell me?"

The boy looked away. "I thought she might be going after my mother."

He seized Andrei by the shoulder. "Why? Why should you think that?"

"I heard you talking. I didn't mean to – really I didn't – I came down to fetch some books I'd left – you were all in the study and I heard her tell my mother to leave the house – and take me with her . . ."

The boy looked desperately upset but he couldn't deal with that now, it must wait.

"We'll talk about it later, Andrei, but just now I must find Nina. She is not well, do you understand? She might do something foolish. Have you any idea where she might have gone?"

The boy shook his head before he said doubtfully, "There is a place where we used to walk with her sometimes. It's down by the river on the other side of the canal bridge. Tanya and I liked to watch the boats from there."

"Listen, Andrei, don't say a word about this to anyone, do you hear? Not to Tanya or Missy or Marina, not a word."

He nodded. "I won't."

"Good. Now get to bed. We'll talk in the morning."

He watched the boy go slowly up the stairs. Another problem with which he would have to cope but Nina must come first. He knew only too well how impulsive she could be. He should have realized her state of mind. Supposing he was already too late – supposing she had already drowned them both – fear lent him speed. Hatless, coatless, he hurried along the streets past the Winter Palace and down to the riverbank. Beyond the bridge a shuffling figure with a ragged bundle on his back came up the stone steps. He grabbed hold of him.

"Have you seen a young woman with a baby in her arms?"

The man nodded sullenly. "She's there all right, wrapped in furs like a princess but not a thing out of her. Turn your back, I reckon, and she'll be in that river quicker than you can blink."

But Simon had gone already throwing him a handful of coins and running down the steps. He saw her then. She was standing close to the parapet which only reached her knees staring down at the water as it slapped at the stone. One touch, one unwary word, and she could be over and lost in its depths. He slowed down, came up behind her, sliding his arms around her waist, speaking to her gently as he drew her back against him.

She shuddered deeply, then he felt the tenseness go out of her. She was limp in his arms. He drew her back to the seat holding them both close against him.

"Why, Nina, why must you frighten me like this?"

"I was going to jump," she whispered, "I meant to do it, I really did, and then I hadn't the courage."

"Thank God for it."

Now it was over she was shaking with reaction.

He said anxiously, "We must get you home. Do you feel strong enough to walk or shall I go and look for a cab?"

"No, don't leave me, don't ever leave me."

One hand clutched at him in panic. His arm tightened around her.

"Come then, we'll go together."

He got her back to the house and then into bed, helping her to undress, wrapping her in a warm blanket. Amazingly the baby cocooned in her shawl seemed none the worse when he tucked her into the cradle. He went down to the kitchen coming back with a cup of hot milk and sat by Nina while she drank it and obediently swallowed the pills he gave her.

"Never do that to me again," he said when he took the cup from her. "Never, promise me."

"Did it matter to you so much?" Her eyes, huge in the face that had grown thinner during these past weeks, were fixed on him. "I thought it was the best way to set you free."

Free! My God, did she know what she was saying? The thought of it appalled him. How could he live believing he had driven her to destroy herself and her child.

He touched her hair gently, leaning forward to kiss her cheek. "Try to sleep. In a few hours Nicola will be demanding her breakfast."

She was exhausted and feverish the next morning, all the strength drained out of her, but the crisis had passed. It began to seem like a bad dream, a nightmare from which she had come back to sanity. He kept her in bed for a few days and told no one of the escapade that could so easily have ended in tragedy and in the meantime he had other problems to face.

There was Andrei looking at him with troubled eyes. He was nearly twelve now, old enough to understand what he had previously simply accepted as children do. It was not easy to explain and when Simon came to an end the boy asked a question he found difficult to answer.

"When we do go to England, Papa, will my mother go with us?"

"I don't know, Andrei. It must be her decision."

"But if she stays in Petrograd, she will be alone, won't she?" And when his father didn't answer immediately, he suddenly stood up, flushed and resolute. "You will have Tanya and Paul and Nicola but she will have nobody. I think I should stay with her."

Somehow he had never expected it and momentarily it took his breath away.

"Did she ask you to do that?"

"No, never."

"Is that what you want?"

"I don't know, I don't know." The boy caught his breath. "I never really thought of how it would be. Oh why does it have to happen like this?"

"Listen, son," said Simon slowly feeling his way. "I think your mother would like you to do what you've always wanted, study medicine, and then one day you can come back to Russia."

"Could I? Could I do that?"

"Why not? And nothing is certain yet. Perhaps before we do leave we can persuade her to go with us."

But that hope was shattered later that same day when he went to the studios. He had to see Galina. He couldn't leave things as they were. He had to explain about Nina.

"She's gone, I'm afraid," said Luba. "She came back late last night and went off this morning."

"Where? Where has she gone?"

"I don't know. She said she'd not made up her mind. When she settled somewhere she would let us know."

"But she can't just go like that without a word to me."

"I'm afraid she can, Simon. She didn't say very much but I think something had hurt her badly."

"I know, I know. That's why I'm here. Has she gone alone?"

"So far as I know," said Luba drily. "Leon is still here. She did say she thought it best for you and for Nina."

Perhaps it was. Perhaps she was right but that abrupt parting took him back to the shattering moment twelve years ago now when he had come back from England to find her vanished out of his life.

It seemed that it had always been like that. They were thrown together by circumstances and then parted, only this time it was final and he must accept it as she had done. At least the boy would be spared an agonizing decision. She had made it for both of them.

27

On a morning in November Nina was walking up the Nevsky Prospect with a basket of provisions for which she had been queueing since early morning. She turned sharply into the Morskaya and then stopped abruptly. An army truck filled with Red Guards was stopping all cars and ordering their passengers out on to the pavements. It was something that happened every day but this time there was strong resistance. Argument became noisy. Another truck drew up and the soldiers fired indiscriminately into the air. These street riots were dangerous and anyone with any sense took cover. Nina flattened herself against the wall. More shots were fired and a young woman screamed, dropping the bundle she was carrying. Nina turned to run and was stopped by one of the armed guards grabbing her roughly by the shoulder.

"You! Where do you think you're going?"

She drew herself up haughtily. "I'm going home if you must know."

"What are you carrying in that basket?"

"Food of course. What do you think I'm carrying – a machine gun?"

"It could be."

It was never wise to argue. The soldier eyed her up and down. It was one of those grey November days when the damp bitter wind penetrated to the very bone and she was wearing one of the most luxurious of her fur coats.

"Papers," he demanded, holding out a dirty hand.

She scrambled quickly through her handbag. It was very foolish to take even the shortest walk without identification papers as you could be challenged half a dozen times in as many minutes. The papers were not there. She remembered suddenly she had taken them out for some reason and not replaced them.

"I've left them at home. It is not far, only a few steps. I will fetch them."

"I've heard that tale before. You'll come along with me."

"But I've done nothing," she protested indignantly.

"That remains to be seen, doesn't it?"

She was forced roughly into the army truck along with a man who held a handkerchief against a bleeding cheek and a flashily dressed young woman who screamed abuse at the guard until he threatened her with the butt of his rifle. They were driven rapidly through the streets to the Smolny Convent, once a high-class school for aristocratic pupils and now the headquarters of the Bolsheviki.

They were marched up the steps and into a large room with nothing left of its former splendour but the high ceiling and the gilded cornices. There were other people there looking lost or bewildered or angry. They stared curiously at her sable coat, the silk scarf over her hair, the bulging basket of food. This was how it had been ever since the Bolsheviki had seized power, invading the city, occupying stations, bridges, banks, the post office, the telegraph, all the public buildings almost without a struggle. No safety anywhere, fear and uncertainty stalking the streets even though theatres and restaurants were still open for the few who still had money to buy luxuries.

Simon had carefully explained to her how the Provisional Government under attack from the right, fearing the counter-revolution, had unwisely called on the help of the Bolsheviki, releasing the leaders from prison, inviting the exiles to return. It was what they had been waiting for. They had seized their opportunity ruthlessly. She did not understand completely how it could come about so quickly, she only knew that now she longed to leave, longed to find somewhere where you did not have to think twice before you spoke, where you did not step over dead and dying bodies in the streets, where they did not smash your front windows because your husband had gone out into the road to tend the miserable victims lying in their blood. Once he had even been arrested for it and it had needed Nigel's intervention to rescue him.

"You shouldn't do it, Simon," she had said pleadingly.

"I'm a doctor, I must give what help I can no matter who they are," was the stubborn reply.

There was nowhere to sit that wasn't filthy and she walked up and down the room fuming at this maddening imprisonment and trying not to feel afraid. They should have left Russia by now but in the last few months everything that could conceivably go wrong had done so. There had been the infection she had developed that came and went intermittently despite all Simon's care, weakening her so greatly that he dare not risk her life on such an exhausting journey and that was not the only hindrance. He was suddenly advised by Nigel that since he had not officially adopted Andrei, the boy was still a citizen of the new Soviet and would very likely be refused a pass to leave the country. It could not be rushed through at the last moment. They must simply take the risk.

One hour passed and then another. Some of the people were called to the inner room and did not return. Nina became more and more impatient. She had never been able to reconcile herself to casual insolence where before she had always known instant respect. She stormed up to the Red Guard at the door demanding to know how soon she would be free to go.

"You'll wait your turn with the rest," he said thrusting her back so roughly that she stumbled and fell against the wall. Infuriated she tried to push past him. He grabbed at her and she resisted angrily till a voice from the inner room interrupted them.

"What the devil is going on out there? Let the woman through."

The guard gave her a violent push. She landed on her knees, struggled to her feet and found herself facing the man seated behind the desk, a man she knew, whose lean bony face was regarding her with some amusement. It was Igor.

She was speechless, then terrified. From the first moment she had seen him hiding in the stables of the Malinsky house till that last time when she had believed him responsible for the murder of her father and her grandfather she had been haunted by him. During the years of marriage it had faded but now suddenly it leaped into life.

He leaned back in his chair still with that faint smile.

"Well, well, who'd have believed it? The Princess Nina Malinsky in person and what crime have you committed?"

"I'm no longer the Princess Nina, I'm the wife of Dr Aylsham, Lord Aylsham as it happens, and he is British. There is nothing you can do against me."

"Isn't there? I'm afraid that is a very dangerous assumption. Have you papers to prove it?"

"Of course I have."

"Hand them over."

He was mocking her, she knew that, amusing himself at her expense and it maddened her.

"Send one of your guards with me and he can see them for himself."

"And why should I waste my time and his? Answer me that, Princess. We don't run at your bidding now. We command and you obey."

She stood proudly erect. She was not going to plead with him. She would die first. He looked at her consideringly while the men around him watched and wondered. Comrade Livinov could be a law unto himself and they had learned to fear the lash of his tongue and his difficult temper.

He got up and came over to her. She saw how he limped though he tried hard to conceal it. He took her by the shoulders and shook her impatiently.

"Don't show your contempt so openly, you little fool," he said in a harsh whisper, "not if you want to live, and tell that precious English doctor of yours to go now, do you understand, *now* or it could be too late for him and for your children." Then he clicked his fingers for one of the guards. "I know this woman. She can go." He gave her a piercing look. "But take care. Next time you may not be so lucky."

She was so relieved that she ran out of the building and down the street before she remembered that she had left her basket behind. Useless to return. Those others would have fallen on it by now, more than likely fighting over its contents.

She arrived at the house to find everyone alarmed because she had been gone for so long and she poured the whole story out to Simon.

"Why did he let me go so easily, why? What does it mean? Are they plotting something against us?"

"We're not so important, my dear," but all the same he took the warning seriously. Could this be Igor's way of repaying the moment in the hospital when he had saved him from the *Okhrana*?

Two days later everything was finally arranged. They could take very little with them, one small bag with essentials for each of them and that was all. Nina wept over so many treasures that must be left behind and Simon deeply regretted his library as he packed the notebooks that contained the years of research. The train left at midnight but they must be at the station hours beforehand if they were to have any hope of getting on it, let alone obtaining a seat even in the first class.

On that last evening Nigel and Lydia came to say goodbye. They gathered in the dining room, the children with them, eating a brief meal together. Simon had brought up a couple of bottles of champagne.

"What's left in the cellar is yours, Nigel. Make sure you collect it before the rabble get their dirty hands on it."

He filled their glasses and they rose to their feet. It was Nina who gave them the toast.

"Goodbye to the old Russia, our Russia," she said. She met Simon's eyes and he knew what was in her mind. It was goodbye to Galina and the ache was still there though God knows in these last weeks he had tried hard enough to stifle it.

She drained her glass and with a dramatic gesture flung it to the floor. They followed her, one by one, even down to Paul drinking his half glass.

"Shouldn't there be one for Nicola, Papa?" he asked seriously.

"Why not?" Simon poured a little in another glass and gravely the boy sipped it and then threw it to the floor.

After that there were tearful farewells. Simon had tried hard to persuade Missy to go with them but she had refused.

"What would you be doing with an old woman like me?" she said. "I would only hamper you. I shall be safe enough in my little flat. I still have my British passport you know."

He had provided for Marina and Cook as well as he could. They would go back to Dannskoye. In the village among the peasants they should be safe enough. There were hugs and kisses for the children before they climbed into the Mercedes. Baby Nicola was tucked into a carrying basket. Jake would drive them to the station and then take the car to Luba and Conn. They might be able to sell it before the Bolsheviki commandeered it as they had done so many cars already through the city.

The platform teemed with people, soldiers, peasants, well dressed groups like themselves, children, dogs, piles of motley baggage, everyone bent on only one thing, to escape out of Petrograd as soon as they could.

They stood together, Tanya and Paul close to Nina, Andrei with his father, prepared to do battle when the train came in.

It was a sorry end to his years in Russia and Simon felt it deeply. During the last few months he had fought against it but it had to come and he was more fortunate than others. He knew where he was going and what awaited him, so why this feeling of rejection, this uneasy certainty that fate had still some trick that he had not guarded against and which could strike unexpectedly.

He made a strenuous effort to put it out of his mind. He must think of Nina and the children and nothing else.

Andrei moved closer to him. "Do you think she will come to say goodbye?" he whispered.

No need to ask of whom he was thinking. He shook his head. He was not even sure that he wanted it, not now. She had made the decision final. There was no going back on it and he must learn to live with it.

On the morning of that same day Galina was walking briskly across the river from Vassilievsky Island. She paused on the bridge to look across the Neva to the Peter and Paul Fortress empty now of its miserable prisoners and flying the red flag of liberty. The first snow had fallen during the night and brilliantly coloured spires and domes and cupolas showed up in gilded barbaric splendour against the dazzling white. For a brief instant Petrograd became again the city she had known and loved all her life. She walked on past the Admiralty and the Winter Palace looking strangely drab without the handsome uniforms of the guards, the double-headed eagles, the coming and going of sleighs and carriages. Instead army trucks pounded up the Nevsky Prospect. People had begun to come out from their houses and cellars, looking about them fearfully. Perhaps at last the worst of the revolution was over, perhaps they could begin their everyday lives again.

A feeling of intense rejection, of isolation, washed over her. What part had she to play in any of this? Everywhere there were printed notices promising a kind of workers' paradise with groups of men and women staring at them, those who could read mouthing the words for those who could not.

After that wretched night with Nina's accusations still echoing in her ears, she had fled from the city. She had deliberately cut the knot that bound her to Simon and it still bled. The last couple of months she had spent with her mother but there was no peace to be found at Dannskoye. The great house stood empty and desolate, its magnificent rooms despoiled, everything of value stolen or smashed. The first wild joy of plundering all they had envied for so long had ended in quarrels and bitter argument. The factory stood idle, its markets lost while the workers squabbled among themselves. Yakov who might have controlled them had gone to Petrograd. Clever and ambitious he would no doubt rise high in the party, he and Marta together.

There had been work for Galina to do, plenty of it. When that first burst of independence was over, there were still cows to be milked, timber to be cut, chickens to be fed. Sickness struck and she took it upon herself to deal out medicines and deal with the usual accidents since the clinic set up by Niki had been recklessly abandoned, but the atmosphere sickened her. Somehow she must find a new directive, something to fill her life. She was thirty-one. Surely there was still time to study, maybe to achieve that long cherished ambition to qualify as a doctor in this new Russia. Simon could have given her that opportunity and she had rejected it partly out of that pride of hers, partly because Nina stood between them and always would and to fight against it was impossible as they had proved over and over again.

Leon came to see her one day looking awkward and half ashamed.

"Vicky and I are going to be married. I wanted to tell you before," he said abruptly. "God knows what she sees in me but that is what she wants."

"I'm glad," she said and meant it. She had always felt guilty because she could not give him what he wanted from her.

He had been staring out of the window, then he turned to her. "It was you I wanted, Galina, I still do, but I knew right back in Siberia when that doctor of yours came to us. It was no good, was it, though I went on hoping."

"I'm sorry, Leon, I never meant it to be like this."

"Supposing I were to say come with me now – would you say yes?"

She smiled. "Don't ever tell Vicky that you made that offer."

"She and I will do well enough, I suppose. We are going to my father's village in the Caucasus. It is so far from anywhere it will give us time to find out what we truly want from each other. I'm not sorry about the Tsar, I think he deserves most of what has happened to him. I don't care much about the rich, they've had it good for far too long, but I find it hard to swallow what is being done to ordinary folk like you and me in the name of liberty. Perhaps given time I can get back to the work I've always wanted to do. Whoever rules Russia will need to exploit her resources and when that time comes, if it ever does, I shall come into my own."

"I hope so with all my heart."

"And you – what will you do?"

"God knows. Live and work – what else is there? People still get sick, they still need to be doctored."

He looked at her for a moment. "Why are you like you are?" he said suddenly. "Why don't you reach out and grab what you want like everyone else?"

Before she guessed at what he was going to do he had pulled her into his arms kissing her long and deeply.

"That's for goodbye," he said huskily and went quickly out of the hut and along the path with his long stride and she looked after him wondering why she had been fool enough to let him go. One word and she could have kept him by her side, a good man with qualities that she admired and perhaps it was for that very reason that she could not cheat him of what he deserved.

*

464

She had returned to Petrograd the night before, had found her little room still unoccupied and had dumped her bag there before finding the doorkeeper who looked after the studios. She had not yet spoken to Luba, wanting to make some kind of a decision about her future before she did. She was standing on the corner of the Nevsky Prospect thinking that she might apply to the pharmacy where she had worked before when an army truck with half a dozen soldiers in it swept past her and then pulled up. Someone called her name. She looked up and saw Igor standing up gesturing to her to join him. She shook her head but he said a word and two of the guards leaped out, took her by the arm and forcibly lifted her into the truck beside him. Immediately the driver shot forward again.

"What do you think you are doing?" she said furiously. "Are you arresting me?"

"No, not arresting, sharing it with you, the most wonderful moment in my life."

He was standing up and he pulled her closely against him, his arm around her waist. She had never seen him like this. He was transfigured, exultant, his eyes ablaze under the peaked cap, his face alight with pride and joy.

"Haven't you realized it yet? Where have you been these last few days? It's victory at last. We've won through. Now nothing can stop us." He swung his arm around in a wide gesture. "Mine, all mine, Petrograd is mine, Russia is mine!"

He's mad, she thought, he's drunk, not with vodka but with success, with the fulfilment of years and years of waiting, of being hunted, of scheming, lying and murdering to reach this moment and she felt a kind of horrified admiration and at the same time a mounting fear. In this kind of crazy mood what would he do, what would he demand from her?

"Oh don't imagine there aren't a thousand things still to be done. Petrograd is only one small part of Russia but the floodgates are open, I'm on my way and you're coming with me."

His arm tightened and the brilliant eyes held hers for a moment.

"We're going to the *Duma*. You are going to see and hear for yourself."

She made one attempt to escape but the soldiers were close behind them and he kept her beside him all that long afternoon while she listened to speech after speech. The meeting roared on, leader after leader explaining, arguing, soldier after soldier, workman after workman, standing up to speak his mind and his heart while from time to time the vast audience shouted and yelled and applauded, until a messenger came racing up the hall carrying a telegram.

It was grabbed and read aloud, some of the words staying in her mind long afterwards.

"This is a moment to go down in history. The counter-revolution is smashed. There is no return to the past. Before us are struggles, obstacles, sacrifices, but the road is clear and victory is certain."

There was more and the cheers rocked the hall. They were tossing caps in the air, embracing one another. Igor reached out for her. His mouth clamped down on hers and she shuddered. His arms around her were like iron, she felt stifled, trapped. It was evening before she was released, when at last Igor turned to her, his face still alight with passion and joy. In that moment she thought she saw him clearly for the first time. All his life he had denied himself every simple pleasure, obeying that stern command that a revolutionary has no right to love, no right to any personal joys, but now the time had come and he could pause even if only momentarily to claim his reward; and she knew with a terrible fear that in that austere twisted mind of his she had always been the desired, the prize of his success and nothing was going to stop him, he would pursue her with the same relentless determination.

He held her by the shoulders staring down into her face. "I will come to you," he said, "when the meeting is over and you will be there, you must be there. Don't think you can escape now. I shall hunt you out. I shall find you wherever you hide. You were mine from the beginning, Galina Panova, and you'll be mine again."

He was being called to the platform with the others. He let her go and she ran out of the building knowing that time was short and she had to get away from him, but where and how? Maybe it was absurd but she had a feeling that wherever she went he would be there, that over the years this had always been her fate, her destiny.

She raced back to the studios. In her room she began to repack her bag, the clothes slipping through nervous fingers. She could go back to Dannskoye but that was useless. It would be the first place he would look for her. She had very little

466

money, certainly not sufficient for a long train journey. She ran down the stairs to speak to Luba but she and Conn were out and there was no reply to her frantic knocking. She went back upstairs closing her bag. She couldn't think, her mind seemed blank. It was already dark. She lit a candle in its heavy brass candlestick and counted the money in her purse. She looked at the one thing of value she had clung to all these years, the ring that Simon had put on her finger. The sapphire glinted with cold blue fire in the light of the candle. She couldn't part with it, she couldn't, and in any case it was too late to try and sell it even if she could bring herself to do so. Perhaps if she could hide somewhere in a different part of the city just for tonight, by the morning she might be able to think again.

She was about to blow out the candle when she knew she was too late. There was the sound of a truck pulling up outside. She heard the halting step on the stairs and backed against the wall. The door opened and Igor was there, still aflame, his cap at a jaunty angle. He took her in with one sweeping glance.

"Running away, were you? Why? Surely you're not afraid of me. We know one another too well, don't we?"

She couldn't move. She stood there as if paralysed, her mind running back to that other time when he had come to her, when remorselessly he had claimed her as his own. He took the bag out of her hand and put it aside tossing his cap after it. The reddish hair caught the flickering candlelight. In desperation her hand closed around the heavy brass holder. He was smiling as he came towards her and at the same moment she picked it up swinging it at him with all her strength. It hit him on the side of the head. He grunted, swayed and crumpled to the floor. For one second she looked down at him horrified, then she grabbed the bag and raced down the stairs and out into the courtyard. A large car was being carefully manoeuvred into it. She stepped aside to let it pass and saw that the driver was Jake. It seemed like salvation. She didn't stop to wonder why he was there but waited trembling as he got out and closed the door.

He started as he saw her standing under the light of the lamp at the gateway.

"Miss Panova, isn't it?"

"Yes. Why have you left the car here?"

"The doctor has given it to Luba and Conn. Didn't you know? Haven't they told you? We're leaving the city tonight. I'm on my way to the station now."

"Jake, I have to get away. I must leave Petrograd and I have very little money," she said hurriedly. At any moment Igor would recover, he would come limping down those stairs in search of her.

"That's easy," he said. "Come with me. The doctor will help you. It's what he would wish."

To go to him now – it was something she had sworn never to do but the situation was desperate.

"I'm afraid we must hurry," he said, "there's not a great deal of time."

She looked back once as he took her arm, but all was still quiet. Pray God she had not killed him!

He had taken her bag from her and was hurrying her along the street. By the bridge they were lucky enough to pick up a cab. The snow had turned to mud and slush, the fresh beauty of the morning already vanished.

"When does the train leave?" she whispered.

"At midnight but it will be in long before that."

When they reached the station Jake was proved right. The train was already standing at the platform and the fight to get on it had begun. Jake put his arm firmly through hers and battled his way through the crowds.

Simon had engaged a first class compartment but such distinctions had already lost their force and it looked as if they were not going to be able to keep it to themselves. He had installed Nina and the baby. He lifted Tanya and Paul in while he and Andrei waited on the platform for Jake. It was the boy who saw them first.

"It's Mamma," he shouted, "she's here after all." He rushed to meet her, putting his arms around her, hugging her. "Papa said you wouldn't come but I knew you would."

It was the sight of Simon that broke her down. She had meant to be calm and sensible, meant to explain that she had not gone back on her decision, she was not travelling with them, all she wanted was his help to get away from Petrograd but when she saw him her resolution collapsed. His arms went around her and she was clinging to him.

"What is it?" he asked. "What has happened?"

"It's Igor. He came to the studios – I don't know what he

468

wants from me, I don't know, Simon, but I had to escape, I couldn't stay . . ." the words were pouring out in a muddled stream quite unlike herself. "Oh Simon, I didn't know what to do – I hit him – suppose I've killed him . . ."

"Very unlikely," he said comfortingly, "a man doesn't die so easily." She was shaking so much he held her more firmly against him. "It's all right. He can't touch you now. You're with us. You're safe."

He was urging her towards the train but she drew back. "No, no, I can't. I'll find somewhere else."

"Don't argue. You'll never find another place in this crowd and if they come round demanding papers and ticket, then what will you do?"

The train had already begun to snort and shake. There was a long drawn out whistle, a loud clanking, the slamming of doors. Simon pushed her in and followed with Andrei and Jake. At the last moment as the train began slowly to draw out four others crowded in after them. Simon would have protested but Galina stopped him. Any kind of argument, any demand of privilege, could only provoke trouble.

Nina had seen Galina come and how Simon's arms had gone around her. Had he lied to her all this time? Had he arranged this so that at the last moment she could raise no objection? She shut her eyes against it and knew that she was misjudging him. She heard the disjointed explanation – Igor again, a dark shadow threatening her, threatening all of them, somehow embodying in himself all the fear and uncertainty and fanaticism of the last few months.

The train slowly began to gather speed and they sorted themselves out. Simon had come to sit beside Nina, Tanya and Paul were opposite, Andrei with Galina pressed up against the intruders, young men, mere boys in their workmen's clothes, sporting their red ribbons, probably on their way to one of the munition factories.

They were rattling along now at quite a good speed. However long and frightening the journey, they were on their way to freedom or so they hoped.

28

It was strange during the night and the following day how despite everything Nina and Galina drew close together. Maybe it was because Nina had never before travelled a long distance without nurse and servants. Simon was attentive and thoughtful but in these sometimes quite appalling circumstances another woman was an infinite comfort. For the first few hours there was a kind of armed truce between them. They spoke very little. Forced to share the compartment with their unwelcome companions they could not turn the seats into couchettes but were obliged to rest how they could crushed against one another, cramped and uncomfortable. The children dozed and woke fretfully at intervals. Fighting their way to the lavatory was an ordeal. Galina took them one by one down the corridor climbing over drunken soldiers, over piled luggage, running the gauntlet of curses, abuse or what was worse coarse jokes, obscenities and men who tried to make a quick grab at them. Tanya, tall and slim for her age, her fair hair hanging in curls around her pretty pointed face, was a particular target. She bore it bravely, holding up her head proudly, every inch a princess, unconsciously inviting the jibing, half-admiring comment till back in the carriage she clung to her father in a wild burst of tears.

One of the most difficult moments came in the early morning when the baby woke and began to cry. Nina was still feeding her which was the only possible thing to do when they could not obtain milk and had no means of preparing it, but how was she to perform this simple task with four young men sprawling across half of their compartment.

Simon said, "Jake will help me rig up one of the travelling rugs. We'll shelter you from them."

She shook her head despairingly. The very thought of putting the baby to her breast with those loutish peasants only a few feet away from her was more than she could endure.

The baby wailed incessantly. She took her from the basket

and rocked her to and fro but the hungry Nicola would not be appeased and it was Galina who came to the rescue. She had already spoken to the young men. One of them had once travelled east to a labour camp. They were only youngsters, nineteen or twenty, hiding their awe of the tall distinguished foreigner by a show of bravado.

"The little one must be fed," she whispered, "think of your own mothers, of your baby brothers and sisters."

They might sport their red ribbons and boast of their new found liberty but they had not yet lost a natural decency. They looked at one another and nodded sheepishly, then filed out into the corridor so that the baby could be fed in peace.

"How did you manage it?" said Simon gratefully.

"I met plenty like them in Siberia. Behind all that bullying manner, they're just like the peasants at home."

A kind of rough cameraderie grew up between them. One of the youngsters had a crude bloodstained bandage tied round one hand. Simon's instinct to heal rose to the surface. He offered to treat it.

He had brought a small emergency kit with him. Half afraid the boy held out his hand. He unwound the filthy rag, cleansed the ugly gash as best he could, put on an antiseptic and re-bandaged it. At one of the stations the young man fought his way on the platform and came back with a mug of tea, watery but hot, offering it shyly to Nina.

They parted from them somewhere near Tula. They shook hands all round and were sorry to see them go. They were replaced by three Red Guards who forced their way in and spread themselves across the seats. They smoked incessantly, spitting sunflower seeds on the floor. The heat in the compartment with the smoke and the sour reek of sweat and unwashed bodies became unbearable. Simon wrenched a window open. The air poured in cold and refreshing but they had hardly taken a few breaths of it before one of the guards blaspheming crossed the carriage and slammed it shut again.

The interminable hours passed very slowly. Galina tried to organize simple games for the children but none of them had ever endured such conditions and they kept asking how long it would be before they arrived. At one point they were all ordered off the train and stood on the platform, the icy wind blowing about them, a thin snow falling, for an hour or more while a search went through the whole length of the train.

"What are they looking for?" whispered Andrei.

"There is some talk of foreign spies," said his father, worried for Nina, worried for all of them.

Their papers were scrutinized. They frowned over Galina and one of them seeing the prison stamp said roughly, "You should be marching with us, Comrade, not working for these British pigs!"

There were times when it seemed impossible that they would ever reach their destination but towards evening on the third day the train slowly drew in to Kiev and they heaved a sigh of relief. More than half their journey was over.

Once again everyone was ordered off the train. This time Simon managed to gather his little flock into one of the waiting rooms where at least they were out of the bitter wind. Outside the passengers had been lined up and a systematic search begun. They waited in nervous anticipation with a Red Guard standing sentinel on the door. Now and again they heard a gunshot and looked at one another in fear. The children sat huddled together on the hard bench shivering with cold. At last Simon could stand it no longer.

"This is ridiculous," he exclaimed. "I'm going to find out what's going on."

He reached the door and was thrust roughly back by a group of guards coming in, their rifles at the ready.

"What is the meaning of this delay? Why are we being kept here?" he demanded furiously.

"All in good time, Comrade, all in good time," said one of them, his peaked cap and the red star on his shabby uniform proclaiming him the leader.

Once again their papers were examined with painstaking care while Simon fumed but dared not make any protest.

One by one their cases were opened and searched. Dirty hands were plunged into Nina's carefully packed clothes in a hunt for guns, valuables, anything they believed incriminating. They missed the family heirlooms simply because after an earlier search Galina suggested they should be transferred to her bag. She had found the Siberian stamp on her passport gave her protection and hers had been the only item of luggage left untouched.

It was Simon's medical notes that unfortunately provided the damning evidence. They pulled out the loose leaf notebooks and stared at the closely written pages.

"What language is this?"

"German," he admitted reluctantly. "It is a medical treatise."

"Medical, eh?" The man stared at him insolently. "How do we know that? We've been informed that spies for the Germans are everywhere."

"I'm British and like you Britain is fighting the Germans. Why should I be spying for them?" said Simon in exasperation. "If you can't read, I suggest you find someone who can. He will tell you what these papers are."

It was a mistake to lose his temper. The man thrust his dirty unshaven face close to him prodding him with the butt of his rifle.

"You'll treat me with respect, Englishman, or we'll take you out there and give you the only punishment traitors deserve."

Galina said quickly, "If I may speak, Comrade Comissar, Dr Aylsham is well known in Kiev. There are medical colleagues of his at the hospital. They could tell you what this writing means."

The leader stared at her. "Why are you doing this for these people?" he said suspiciously. "A good Soviet citizen doesn't help traitors."

"He's no traitor, Comrade, and also it is my job I am anxious about." She lowered her voice. "There are good things to be had from families such as these nowadays. I don't want to lose them."

It was a long shot but it worked. She had appealed to something they all understood. Get what you could out of the rich while the going was good because who knew when it might stop.

"There is one more thing, Comrade," she went on impressively. "If he is what he says he is and anything happens to him, the Bolsheviki in Petrograd won't like to stir up trouble with the British."

"We've no truck with Petrograd here. In Kiev we have our own Soviet, we're not in Lenin's pocket," said the man aggressively, but all the same no one was too secure these days. "Who are these doctors?" he went on grudgingly.

Galina took a chance. If he had moved away or was dead then their luck was out.

"Dr Basil Makarov, Director of the State Hospital," she

473

said boldly. "If you would telephone him or if you would allow me to do so . . ."

At last he permitted her to go to the Station Master's office while they all waited, Simon fretting because there was so little he could do, and in the meantime those passengers who had been found satisfactory were being allowed back on to the train.

Galina was a very long time and they watched the engine draw slowly out of the station with sinking hearts. Were they all destined to die in this cold filthy room with its foul smell, its littered floor and stained walls?

Presently when all hope had almost died Galina came back. "I've spoken with Dr Makarov. He will be coming himself. He should be here in ten minutes," she said without looking at Simon in case they should suspect some kind of collusion between them.

It had taken her some time to locate him but when she had his response had been warm and immediate. Perhaps now the worst was over.

It seemed the longest ten minutes any of them had lived through. Then a big car pulled up outside and Dr Makarov came striding into the room looking bulky and impressive in his fur-collared greatcoat bringing with him the weight of power and authority.

He frowned down at the leader. "Don't I know you, Mikhail Petrovich? Didn't I deliver your wife's last baby? You should go easy, my good man. Six little ones is more than enough in these times," he said reducing him to size and they saw the angry colour spread up from his neck. "What the devil is going on?" went on the doctor not giving him time to protest. "What do you mean by locking up my dear friend and colleague in this fashion?" He advanced on Simon embracing him. "And this is no doubt your lovely lady." He bowed to Nina kissing the hand she tentatively held out to him. "Now what is all this nonsense about being a German spy?"

"If you would examine these papers, doctor. Surely any person carrying papers written in German must be suspect."

Dr Makarov took out his eyeglasses and ran his eye through the closely written pages.

"A medical treatise on haemophilia," he said impressively, "with illuminating comments by our friend here and if you don't know what that is," he went on fixing the peasant sol-

474

diers with a stern eye, "it is a rare and extremely dangerous blood disease. German spy indeed! You might well be destroying a valuable addition to medical knowledge."

His opinion carried a good deal of weight but Mikhail Petrovich believed he had made a valuable capture and was unwilling to give up too quickly the importance it gave him.

"There will have to be further interrogation," he said stubbornly.

Dr Makarov shot a quick glance at the children, shivering and white-faced, at Nina and the baby in her basket and came up with a suggestion.

"You know me, Mikhail Petrovich, everyone in Kiev knows me," he said, "supposing I relieve you of their charge. I will take them with me and hold them in custody for you to examine at your leisure in the morning."

"We are extremely grateful but we cannot trespass on your hospitality to that extent," said Simon unwilling to put their saviour into any danger on their account.

"Nonsense, my dear fellow, my wife and daughters are in the country just now. I should enjoy an hour or two in your company."

He was one of those men who always seem to have the power of carrying all before them. He himself took the baby's basket.

"Let me relieve you of your burden, dear lady," he said to Nina. "My car is outside."

The children got wearily to their feet. Tanya's fur hood had fallen back. Her hair shone pale gold in the dim light. She looked enchantingly pretty. One of the guards grinned at her.

"What about a little kiss, Princess, eh?"

He pulled her towards him bringing his face close to hers. She gave a little cry as she shrank away and Simon's frayed temper suddenly snapped.

"Take your dirty hands off her!" he exclaimed swinging the soldier away so roughly that he stumbled backwards. His reaction was swift and savage as he cocked his rifle.

"Damned British swine!"

"Simon!" screamed Nina and threw herself at the man to stop him. The gun exploded and she received the charge full in the breast.

For an instant the shock held them rigid, then Simon was beside her, his arms round her as she collapsed against him.

Dr Makarov came hurrying back. "What has happened?"

He gave the basket to Galina and went quickly to where Simon had lowered Nina gently to the floor. Her fur coat had fallen open showing the stain spreading on her grey dress.

"Mother of God, how bad is she?"

"I don't know . . ." Simon was unfastening the high neck of her gown.

Nina's eyes were fixed on him. "I thought . . . thought . . . he was going . . . to kill you . . ." she breathed and choked on a rush of blood.

"I know, I know, my darling . . ." He had taken the handkerchief from his pocket and was pressing it against the welling blood.

"We can do nothing here," whispered Dr Makarov. "Carry her to the car. I live only a few minutes away." He got to his feet turning on the peasant soldiers with bitter scalding words. "Is this what your revolution leads to, shooting an innocent woman in front of her children?"

"It was her own fault. If she had not thrown herself at him . . ." but the sudden violence had temporarily disturbed them.

"Out of my way, you fellows." Dr Makarov helped Simon to lift her and then led the way out of the station, the children trailing after, Andrei with his arm around Tanya and holding Paul by the hand, too stricken and upset to cry or even to speak.

Outside Jake helped Simon to get into the back of the big car cradling Nina in his arms while Tanya and Paul crouched on the floor at his feet. Galina and Jake were in the front with Andrei as Dr Makarov drove away.

The doctor's house was large and comfortable and his housekeeper, a decent elderly body, gave them a warm welcome. She watched Simon carry Nina in and sent one of the maids upstairs with them to prepare a room

"Is she sick?" she asked Galina.

"She was shot by one of the guards."

"Dear God, what wicked days we live in!" she exclaimed. "And those poor mites of children looking near frozen to death. You come along with me, my dears," and she took them into the huge well-furnished kitchen smelling deliciously of newly baked bread. "Nowadays it's the warmest place in the house," she told Galina. "The dining room is cold as the North Pole."

She bustled around getting them seated at the table.

"Let's put some good hot soup inside you, then you'll begin to feel better."

They had scarcely yet realized what had happened, only that their safe world had fallen apart. Nina had been hurt and their father must be with her. They dare not look beyond that.

At first they could only stare at the bowls she put in front of them but then the comforting warm smell of the hot broth became too tempting. Andrei put in a tentative spoon and the other two followed.

"Now let me see to the little one," said the housekeeper turning to Galina. "You sit down, my dear, take some of the soup. It's good and nourishing though I say it myself. Give the baby to me."

"I'm afraid she's not yet weaned."

"Now don't you worry. I'm accustomed to babies, the doctor doing the work he does. I'll find a bottle and some warm milk. Revolution or not babies still come into the world and have to be tended and fed."

The warmth and the food were making the children drowsy. She made them as comfortable as she could with pillows and rugs.

"Let them sleep for a little, poor lambs, they've still a long way to go."

It was the first moment Galina had to herself. It had been so unexpected, so totally unbelievable. Events had piled up so quickly it was only now that the real shock of what had happened overwhelmed her. There had been moments, of course there had, she was only human, moments when the thought had come – supposing Nina was no longer there. Now she shrank from it in horror. She must think only of practical things. It had upset all her plans. She had meant to leave them at Kiev, go her own way as she had decided months ago but even if Nina were only wounded, it was going to take time for her to recover. They would have to stay in the city which was already in the hands of the Bolsheviki, and if not, if that trigger-happy guard had killed her, what then? She couldn't think, she dared not think.

"Thank you for the soup. It was delicious," she said and put down her spoon as the door opened and Dr Makarov looked in.

"Everything going well, Ilona?" he asked and the house-keeper nodded.

She was nursing the baby on her ample lap. "I'm watching over them, doctor. Poor loves, they need their rest."

"Keep up the good work," he said and beckoned to Galina.

She followed him into what was obviously his work room, walls lined with books, untidy heaps of pamphlets, with the scent of old leather and good cigars.

"Fuel is so wretchedly short, we have half the rooms shut up when my wife is away," he explained. "Come and sit down, my dear."

He closed the door and stretched his hands to the big stove. She saw how grave he looked and feared the worst.

"How is she?"

"There was nothing we could do. She died on the way here though he wouldn't accept it at first. Never saw a man so distressed. I've left him with her. He blames himself severely of course but who could have possibly foretold such an unfortunate accident?"

"Would the guard have fired?"

"Oh yes. That kind of incident has happened all too frequently. She died in saving him. It's that which has hit him so hard."

They were silent for a little, then he turned to look at her.

"I know you, don't I? We've met somewhere before."

"It was a long time ago, nearly twelve years. Do you remember a young woman, a friend of Ivan Zubov, whose baby you delivered?"

"That's it," he exclaimed, "the young woman he befriended and who afterwards became his assistant in the pharmacy." He paused. "The boy – is he one of those children with you?"

"Yes, the elder of the two boys."

She thought he must have guessed then that Simon was the father but be did not pursue it. Instead he said, "I heard later that Zubov died in Siberia, a sad waste of an excellent brain."

"I know. I was with him when he died."

"So you were exiled along with him." He looked at her curiously. "Then our friend upstairs did not succeed in gaining your release. I remember well how passionate he was about it when he asked my help."

"It all happened a very long time ago."

478

"And yet I find you travelling with them?"

"Purely by accident. I intended to break my journey here in Kiev."

"I see. And now what will you do?"

"I don't know."

She looked up at him, this big kindly man who was her father. How different her life might have been if he had acknowledged her, taken her to live with him as Simon had taken Andrei. It seemed to her then in that quiet room in the middle of the night with only one small lamp burning that it was important they should know something of each other.

She said, "Dr Makarov, may I ask you a personal question?"

He looked surprised. "Certainly. I can't promise I will answer."

"Do you recall in your student days taking a course at Petersburg?"

"Yes, I did do that."

"And in your lodgings there was a very pretty young maid who washed and ironed your shirts for you?"

"Now you're taking me back to my ill-spent youth," he said with a smile. "It so happens that it's one of my happiest memories. What was her name now – Vera, I believe. We had a very pleasant summer together as I recollect. That was in my salad days long before I was married."

"Vera had a daughter."

"Mine? But she never told me."

"She thought it might hamper your career."

"I believed she thought of it as I did, a delightful summer idyll."

"Oh she did, but she also loved you very much."

"How do you know this?"

"I am that daughter."

"You? Why didn't you tell me before?"

"You might have thought I was asking something from you. She never wanted that and neither did I."

"Why are you telling me now?"

"I don't know. I shall probably never see you again but Andrei *is* your grandson and he intends to be a doctor too."

"Oh my God, my grandson, and I have only daughters!" He shook his head as if unable to take it in. "And this Englishman is his father?"

"Yes."

"And he deserted you, left you to bear his child alone here in Kiev?"

"No. Like you, he didn't know."

"And you still love him?"

"Yes – absurd, isn't it, when he has been married to Nina for twelve years."

"What will you do now?"

"Who knows?"

They both heard the step on the stairs and Dr Makarov went to the door.

"We are in here, my friend."

She thought Simon looked years older when he came in but he was very quiet, very composed.

"Where are the children?"

"They've had some food and they're sleeping," said Galina. "Do you want me to tell them?"

"No, I'll tell them myself later. Don't wake them now." He passed a hand wearily over his face. "There's so much to be done and just now I'm finding it difficult to think."

"Come and sit down," said Basil Makarov, "take it quietly." He poured a measure of brandy and brought it to Simon putting the glass into his hand. "Now listen to me. There is something very important that must be discussed and settled now. I don't trust Mikhail Petrovich or indeed any of the Bolsheviki who have usurped power in the city. I'm tolerated at the moment because I'm useful, they can't do without a doctor when their children are born or fall sick, but although we've won the first round, they won't be satisfied with that. When they get their teeth in, these cursed Bolsheviki are persistent and they are particularly strong here in Kiev. We must get you away from here as soon as possible."

Simon swallowed half the brandy at one gulp and then put down the glass.

"And what do I do about my wife?"

"My dear friend," went on Makarov gently. "I know how this must distress you but the fact is that she is dead. There is nothing you can do for her but there are her children. They may attempt to justify what they have done by proving some accusation against you and if they do, what do you think will happen to that pretty girl of yours or those two boys? I appreciate how painful this must be for you but leave your wife with

480

me. I will make sure she is buried with decency and honour and I will drive you with your family at dawn to a wayside station some miles out of Kiev. I happen to know that the train always halts there to take on water. It comes through from Moscow about seven in the morning. You can board it safely there with no officials hovering around and asking questions. That will carry you through to the Crimea."

"I can't allow you to put yourself into danger for us."

"I'll get around that somehow. I'll make a great noise about that serving man of yours stealing my car and driving you out of the city. There will be a devil of a fuss but I have a strong feeling there will be relief too. Shooting the wife of a distinguished Englishman in cold blood won't sound too good. Britain is still one of our allies and your embassy could raise hell for them."

"I know you're right but I can't bring myself to face it squarely. The children I can manage well enough but the baby – she is hardly more than three months."

It was the first time that Galina had ever seen Simon look helpless and her heart went out to him.

"I'll take care of her, Simon," she said quickly.

He looked at her for the first time since he had come into the room.

"You will come with us?"

"Of course. To the Crimea at least."

"I'm grateful."

"Now we must make preparations," went on Dr Makarov briskly. "There's no time to be lost. I will ask my housekeeper to pack some food for you to take with you. We will try and contrive milk for the baby. With any luck the journey will not take more than twelve to fourteen hours but you must be prepared. It will be crowded and there may be a great number of delays."

It was still dark when they piled into the big car and were driven out of the city. Simon had told the children and taken them to say goodbye to their mother. Tanya was crying soundlessly, the tears running down her face as she clung tightly to her father's hand. Paul was very white and very quiet, a child who felt things deeply but rarely showed it. Galina had Andrei's hand in hers. In that huge old-fashioned bed Nina seemed very slight and young as if the years had

481

rolled back to that far off summer day at Dannskoye when radiant with joy she had fallen in love with Simon for the first time. A sob caught in her throat and she swallowed it down. Then it was time to go. They filed silently down the stairs to the waiting car.

When they reached the wayside halt there were a few people already waiting there, peasants who had been driven out of their village, their bundles at their feet. One young woman far gone in pregnancy kept looking fearfully around her but there were no officials, no Red Guards, only the empty fields wet with slushy snow. Dr Makarov dared not stay, it would attract too much attention. He embraced them all in turn. When he came to Andrei he looked into the boy's face for a long moment before he hugged him. He took Galina's hand.

"Perhaps one day if any of us survive this, you'll send him to me so that we can get to know one another."

Then he got back into the car and they waved to him as he drove away.

They still had an hour to wait in the cold grey morning before the train came in and they saw to their dismay that it was packed with men travelling on top of the wagons and even clinging to the steps. There was no question of first class. Simon with one of the peasants forced open the door of the long third class coach and they pushed their way into a compartment meant to hold thirty and now crammed with more than twice that number. There were no proper seats only shelves one above the other, all of them occupied. After a little Simon managed to hoist Tanya and Paul up on to one of them; Galina holding the baby in her basket was perched on a few inches of the bottom shelf while Simon, Jake and Andrei stood close beside her. The important thing was to keep together at all costs. There were no windows to open and the ventilators had all been tight shut so that the heat and the sour smell of smoke, sweat and dirt became very nearly intolerable. There was nothing to be done but grit one's teeth and live through it as best one could.

It was midday when the train ground to a halt. The doors were opened and a flood of welcome cold air poured in but with it came the Red Guards forcing their way brutally along the corridor.

"What is it? What's going on?" whispered Galina to her neighbour, a little man who sat shivering beside her clutching at the bundle on his bony knees.

"Guns," he muttered.

"Guns? What do you mean?"

"Haven't you heard? Anyone carrying firearms is liable to be taken off and shot."

"Oh God, no! Surely they couldn't do that."

But she knew they could and only that morning before they set out she had seen Simon take the pistol from his luggage and drop it into his pocket. Nina's death was too recent to let him go unarmed. She looked up at him. He had his back against the shuttered ventilator seemingly oblivious of the commotion going on throughout the train.

She said urgently, "Simon, give me the gun."

"What?" he looked at her uncomprehending.

"Your pistol – quickly. They are searching the train."

He woke then to the danger. He took it from his pocket and slipped it to her. The little man beside her watched in horror as she dropped it into the baby's basket burying it under the blanket. She was only just in time. The guards had reached their compartment and were bullying the passengers one after the other demanding that pockets should be turned out. In the midst of protest, argument and struggle there was a sudden distraction. Someone in the corridor was being dragged off the train. There was a great deal of shouting, a piercing scream, then the sound of a shot. In the sudden silence she shuddered. The narrowness of their escape made her feel sick.

The day wore on. They opened the packets of food but the stifling heat and the foul smell had destroyed any appetite. They passed some biscuits up to Tanya and Paul but they only nibbled at them.

"I've terrible pins and needles," complained Tanya. "How long must we stay here, Papa?"

"I don't know, my pet, you must try and be very brave."

It was during the afternoon that they heard the first scream. It was followed by another and then another, half stifled as if someone were trying hard to smother them. A ripple of sound came back along the corridor. Galina caught a few words and saw that Simon had heard them too.

"That girl at the station," she whispered.

"Yes, I'd better try and do something."

He began to edge his way through the compartment and Andrei at a nod from his mother went with him. He pushed and fought through the closely packed corridor.

"Let me pass. I'm a doctor. I may be able to help."

He reached her eventually. Even in these frightful conditions there was still a certain decency. They had spread a piece of sacking on the floor and then drawn back to let the women through to her. They parted when they saw Simon and he knelt beside her. He saw at once with thankfulness that it was not going to be difficult. She was a sturdy peasant girl who in ordinary circumstances would have borne her child with ease and probably gone back to work in the fields the next day. But these were not ordinary circumstances.

He took his handkerchief and gently wiped the sweat from her face.

"Don't be afraid, my dear. It's going to be all right."

She stared up in wonder, a cultured gentleman who spoke to her in elegant Russian. She managed a smile before the next rending pain convulsed her round plain face.

He worked as expeditiously as he could. The place must be swarming with germs but there was little he could do about that. One of the women had somehow managed to procure a small bowl of water. She took the baby from him, washing it as best she could with the handkerchief he gave her but there was nothing but an old piece of rag to wrap it in.

Andrei had been hovering outside the circle, a little frightened, half afraid to watch but determined to stay the course. Simon beckoned to him.

"Go back to your mother. Ask her to find something, a towel, a petticoat, anything that we can use for the child."

Their cases had been piled up on the highest shelf. Tanya opened the one on top, pulled out something white and passed it down to him. He fought his way back and put it into his father's hands.

For a moment Simon could not move or speak. It was one of Nina's lawn nightdresses, exquisitely tucked and trimmed with fine lace. Her suitcase must have inadvertently been packed with their own. He put it to his face. It still smelled faintly of her favourite perfume. Then he wrapped it around the baby and put the child into the young mother's arms. She touched the gown wonderingly. She had never seen anything so fine in all her hard life.

"It's so beautiful," she murmured.

"It belonged to my wife."

"Thank her for me."

"She is dead."

It was absurd but at that moment he came near to breaking down for the first time. He touched the baby's small round head and then got up quickly.

Back in their compartment Galina said, "Was it all right?"

"Yes. She has a boy God help her."

She saw his face and asked no more questions but the incident had a consequence they had never expected. The journey as Dr Makarov had warned them took far longer than it should have done. By early morning on the following day they had still not reached their destination but the pressure had lessened just a little. A few passengers had got out, they could breathe more easily but it was then that Nicola who had long finished the last of the milk began to cry with hunger and there was absolutely nothing they could do about it. The train was rattling along at a good speed and did not stop, not that there would have been much chance of obtaining any milk at a station even if it had.

She wailed and wailed. Galina was despairingly rocking her in her arms when there came an interruption.

"Let me take her," said a timid voice.

She looked up to see the peasant girl, her own baby in the crook of her arm. She must have battled her way through the corridor looking for them.

"May I please?" she said appealingly to Simon. "I have enough for two."

He smiled touched by the gesture and shifted so that she could sit beside Galina. She took the baby and put her to her overflowing breast.

They arrived at last in the early evening and it was as if they had gone back to earlier happier days. No one at the station seemed to have heard of revolution or of Red Guards. Everything appeared the same as it had always been, even to the carriage with the two elderly horses and the ancient coachman waiting to drive them to the villa.

It was cold and it had been raining but the air was sweet and smelled of flowers and the setting sun flooding the sky with pink and gold seemed indescribably beautiful as they toiled up the long winding road.

That first night the relief was so tremendous that no one could think beyond the pleasures of hot baths, clean clothes, well-cooked food and a comfortable bed. The housekeeper and the two maids had known Tanya and Paul since they were babies. They exclaimed over how they had grown and were shocked and deeply distressed to hear of Nina's death. They were full of how Sonia with Niki and the children had been taken off by a French ship and by now should have reached France.

There was only one disturbing incident. Simon himself saw the children into bed. Just now they clung to him as the one stable factor in their shifting lives, something Galina understood very well and left him with them.

In the room Tanya was to share with Paul she sat cross-legged on the bed in her nightgown and watched her father as he bent over her brother.

"Is *she* going to stay here with us?" she asked suddenly.

Simon straightened up. "And who do you mean by 'she'?" he said frowning down at his daughter.

She wriggled under his stern gaze. "Oh you know who I mean. Andrei's Mamma."

"Don't speak of her like that, Tanya."

She stood up on the bed putting her arms around his neck, pressing her cheek against his.

"We don't want her here with us now that Mamma's gone, do we, Papa? We only want you."

"You may think yourself very grown up but what about Paul and Nicola? If Galina consents to stay with us we should be grateful to her so don't let me hear you speak like that again." He gave her a light slap on her bottom. "Now into bed with you."

Neither of them had noticed Galina in the doorway. She had been making sure that the baby was settled down in her own room. She heard the sharp dislike in Tanya's young voice and slipped away quickly not willing to hear any more.

A fire of crackling wood had been lighted against the chill of the night and she was sitting by it when Simon came in. He crossed to her looking down at the blaze and adding a few more pieces of the aromatic olive wood before he spoke.

"I've just been putting Paul to bed. Did you know the boy has a bruise all down one side reaching his thigh. He must have been in agony in that cramped position yet he never complained. We must watch him carefully." He began to walk restlessly up and down the room. "I may have to go into

Yalta and possibly on to Sevastopol. I have to see the British Consul and the Transport Officer. We should not delay too long. I must find out what British ships are likely to come through and whether there is any chance of them picking us up. We shall not be the only people waiting for some kind of transport at least as far as Constantinople."

"Simon, do you really want me to stay on here with you?"

He paused to look down at her. "I'm afraid I rather took it for granted for the time being at any rate. When I know more about the situation we may have to move down to Yalta or even to Sevastopol so as to be quickly available, but for the time being the children desperately need the rest and quiet to be found here, though God knows how long it will last. I cannot be here very much. I need someone I can rely on."

"Very well. I will do what I can."

"You look dead tired. Get some rest. Would you like me to give you something?"

"No. I shall be all right."

"Goodnight then."

"Goodnight." He paused on his way to the door and looked back. "Thank you for all you've done for us."

She sat on for a while after he had gone, feeling desperately tired yet knowing she would not sleep easily. How extraordinary that for more than twelve years when they had been separated by distance and by their own wish they had still been close in spirit and now when all obvious barriers were removed an enormous gulf seemed to have opened between them which she did not know how to bridge. Simon was withdrawn into himself. The instant recognition, the flow of feeling between them so that sometimes they seemed to be aware of each other's thoughts before they spoke had totally vanished. She felt as if something enormously valuable had suddenly been taken from her leaving her bereft.

She sighed as she got to her feet. She had better look in on Paul and the baby would be waking early. It was not going to be easy with Tanya's active dislike but then nothing that Simon had asked from her had ever been easy.

She went slowly up the stairs. The baby was sleeping peacefully. The servants had found the old wooden cradle and placed it in her bedroom. Tough little Nicola had survived the rigours of the journey better than any of them. With her soft dark hair and deep brown eyes she was not like the other two children and yet her conception must have marked Simon's return after the months of war. For a moment she felt the old pang of regret that she seemed to stand between them, then she banished it from her mind. There were far more important things to worry about than foolish personal regrets.

29

"I shall dress exactly as I choose," said Tanya defiantly. "You're not my mother. I don't have to obey your orders."

"I'm not ordering you to do anything," said Galina trying hard to keep her temper, "I simply think it would be advisable not to appear conspicuous in any way, that's all."

"I suppose you think I should look dull and dowdy like you and Andrei. Well, I'm not going to dress like a servant even if you do. I'm the Princess Tanya and I don't care who knows it."

"Have you forgotten that the Red Guards murdered your mother?"

"It's hateful of you to remind me of that and there aren't any Red Guards here. The Bolsheviki will never break through into the Crimea. There's an army to drive them back."

"I only hope you're right."

"Besides Papa is someone very important. The British Vice-Consul positively crawled when he visited us that time and he likes me to look pretty when he comes home."

And it was true. At only twelve Tanya knew how to make herself attractive. She looked very dashing that morning in her white piqué dress with its blue sailor collar and Galina sighed. There had been a great many arguments of a similar kind during the past three months and she knew only too well that they sprang from Tanya's jealous love for her father though God knows she had not given her the slightest cause. She was never anything other than governess or nurse whenever Simon was with them.

After weeks of bleak winds and driving rain spring had come

with startling suddenness. The cherry trees were breaking into drifts of snowy blossom. The sun warmed them through and through and Paul, up again after a miserable few weeks of pain and discomfort, had been left in the garden with Andrei while Tanya and Galina each carrying a basket walked the two miles to the market.

Food though not so scarce as in Petrograd was still not so abundant as it had been and they were extremely glad of the fresh butter, the creamy cheese and green vegetables brought in by the peasants from the surrounding hillsides. Usually they enjoyed these little excursions, sometimes returning with a chicken or even a plump duckling, and keeping it for when Simon returned so that they could turn it into something like a feast. But though everything on the surface seemed so quiet and peaceful, there were many undercurrents. There was, as Tanya said, an army who called themselves the Anti-Bolshevik Volunteers composed largely of army officers, cadets, university students and schoolboys. She doubted if they would stand much chance against the Bolsheviki if and when the time came.

On this blowy March day of bright sunshine there was a change in the usual friendly atmosphere of the market. They were aware of it at once. Men stood about talking with grave faces. Strangers moved purposefully from group to group. One of them stared hard at them. They had taken with them the little dog belonging to the villa. He had been ill with a cough during the winter and Galina had made him a coat from a scrap of red velvet. A knot of peasant women nudged one another and pointed.

"Look!" they said jeeringly, "Look at them! They even dress their pet dog like a prince!"

There was envy and spite in the voices. Tanya tossed her head angrily but drew closer to Galina. She took the girl's hand in hers.

"Something has happened. I don't like it. We had better not stay too long."

For once Tanya did not argue. They hurried over their purchases.

The woman packing up eggs said sourly, "Best make the most of this lot. There won't be many more."

"Why?" Galina tried to smile. "Have the hens stopped laying?"

The woman shot her a glance. "Better to say nothing. It doesn't do these days. Get home and stay home, I say, especially the little Princess with her fancy ways."

They looked at one another, then filled their baskets as quickly as they could and set out for the villa.

They did not learn the truth of it until a few days later when Simon returned very late one night.

"The trains have all been taken over for the army," he explained. "I was lucky to get away."

"The Bolsheviki have made a breakthrough," he said privately to Galina so as not to alarm the children until it was necessary. "Sevastopol is already a shambles. They're ravaging the town, opening the gaols, freeing the convicts, using them to terrorize the people. That pitiful Volunteer army can't hold out. They are fighting to escape already before they are cut down."

"I knew that something appalling had happened. It was in the air when Tanya and I were at the market. You could sense the suspicion, the uncertainty. What are we going to do, Simon?"

"At the moment we're still reasonably safe here. I managed to contact the Vice-Consul again. He assures me that a British ship is due in mid-March. We must keep ourselves as quiet as possible till I have more information of date, time and place. We will probably have to move down to Yalta or even Sevastopol."

He gave the children a guarded account of what had happened and told them to stay within the gardens of the villa.

"I'd rather you didn't go outside at all."

"But those beastly Bolsheviki are not here," objected Tanya, "and the country people *like* us."

"They may seem to do so but there are revolutionaries everywhere and a great many people are in sympathy with them. Don't trust anyone, not even the servants. Do you understand? Andrei, I rely on you to keep them in order when I can't be here."

"Yes, Papa, I'll try."

Tanya shot him a defiant glance but catching her father's eyes said meekly, "Yes, Papa, of course."

Paul said, "Are we *all* going to England, Papa? Galina as well?"

"Naturally we are all going. Anyone left behind could be in the gravest danger."

The days passed slowly while they waited for news of the British ship. Simon went back to Sevastopol with the intention of booking rooms at the Hotel Kist which overlooked the harbour since they would have to move down there as soon as definite news came through.

They had one scare while he was away. Two men arrived one day wearing some kind of a uniform with the customary red ribbon but Galina did not believe them to be Bolsheviki, more likely the hangers-on of any revolution out to grab what they could. They demanded to see their papers, staring at them so hard that she was practically sure they couldn't read and then tramped through the villa turning out cupboards and drawers. She guessed that it was money and jewellery they were looking for but everything of value had been carefully concealed and they found very little. They stormed down the stairs kicking the little dog out of their way.

Tanya looking far older than her twelve years faced up to them furiously.

"My father is British. You have no right to come here and treat us like this."

"Mind your manners when you talk to us," said one of them insolently and he slapped her cheek hard. "Damned British traitors!"

They stamped out of the villa angry that they had not found more to fill their pockets.

"How dare they do that to me! How dare they!" sobbed Tanya, one hand to her flaming face.

"Think yourself lucky that they did not do something worse," said Galina, but she put her arm around the girl's shaking shoulders. She was too young to be brought up against such callous mindless brutality.

Simon came back with the heartening news that an English ship should be in Sevastopol Bay during the next fortnight and the sooner they made the move down to the coast the better. While he had been away Baby Nicola had developed a rash and Galina was worried in case she had developed measles or chickenpox at this crucial time.

She did not want to frighten the children so she waited until they were in bed before taking him up to the bedroom.

"She was very restless and feverish this morning. I've been anxious about her," she said.

He examined the baby closely. "I don't think it is anything infectious. It looks far more as if she has eaten something that has disagreed with her. Fruit juice perhaps, something of that kind."

"It's possible. I'll ask the servants. They spoil her, you know, and I can't always be watching them."

"I don't think you need worry."

She sighed with relief. "Thank goodness. I had a terrible vision of us all being put into quarantine and the ship sailing off without you or the children."

He stood looking down at the baby, a curious expression on his face which she could not read. Nicola was seven months old now, small but remarkably sturdy, already developing a strong will of her own. Her eyes watched him and one baby hand clung tenaciously to his finger.

"Poor Nicola," he said, "no father and now no mother."

"No father?"

"I thought you might have guessed already. She's not mine."

"You mean . . .?"

"Oh Nina was never unfaithful to me, you must not think that. She was unhappy and lonely and tormented by the thought that we were together and so far away from her. Jealousy and compassion took advantage of her and played a cruel trick. Poor Valentin! If she gave him a few hours of happiness before he died a horrible death who am I to grudge it to him?"

"So when you came home that March she was pregnant."

"Yes, and terrified of telling me, poor child."

The surge of happiness was so great it nearly overwhelmed her but she made no move towards him, knowing that she must not. He was still locked into the shock and guilt of Nina's death.

"I've never told anyone," he went on, "but that night she drove you from the house she took the baby and went down to the river. God knows what would have happened if I had not reached her in time. Nicola is as much my child as the others. I owe that to Nina at least."

Tanya who had been sent to bed early with Paul and deeply resented it had heard them come up the stairs together. She crept to the door and opened it a crack. She saw them go together into Galina's bedroom. She was too young and innocent to know exactly what it was she suspected, only that Galina in some way was close to her adored father and usurped the position held by her mother. Her bare feet made no sound as she slipped along the landing and saw them standing together beside the baby's cradle. She could not hear exactly what they were saying but she did see her father turn to Galina and heard the urgency in his voice.

"I learned something in Sevastopol which you ought to know. In all the confusion there was one name being spoken of constantly, one who was obviously high in authority . . ."

"Igor Livinov," she breathed.

"Yes. I'm afraid so."

"Oh my God, no!"

She felt as if an icy hand had clutched at her heart squeezing it, restricting her breath. She believed she had escaped and here it was again, the threat and the terror.

"Don't let it upset you." He went on. "He can have no idea that you are here. We shall be gone long before there is any danger of him finding out. Tomorrow I must try and arrange some transport to take us to Sevastopol. The trains are impossible and dangerous too. There are Red Guards everywhere."

When he said goodnight and came out to go to his own room Tanya had gone.

She lay on her bed, her mind seething with what she had seen and heard. Without understanding how or why, she had sensed that something deep and real lay between her father and this interloper who was Andrei's mother and who had stolen her way into their lives. She did not know how she was going to use it but she stored away in her mind the information she had grasped.

It was not easy to obtain any kind of transport. The breakthrough of the Bolsheviki had brought panic and confusion. Trains were out of the question and there were no cars of any sort to be hired. The best Simon could procure was a wagon with two horses whose owner was willing to drive them to Yalta for a scandalous price. From there they might have to find further transport. The cart had no springs and they had not gone far before every bone ached, while the going was so slow that it was evening before they reached the town and found some kind of accommodation for the tired children. Yalta was in a state of intense excitement. Vehicles of every description were pouring into it, carts, cabs, handcarts, horses ready to drop with exhaustion, perambulators, wheelbarrows, anything that would move.

When they were fed and settled down for the night Galina walked down as far as the bay, that beautiful wide sweep of sea where years ago in the honeymoon of their love, Simon had taught her to swim in those few marvellous months of happiness. The moon had risen turning the sea into a sheet of silver, but it was horribly strewn with wreckage, with corpses floating in on the tideless currents, their arms waving in a ghastly lifelike appeal. She shuddered. Was it because Yalta had been the playground of the rich and the privileged that the reprisal had been so savage? The past was destroyed and the dream with it. She shut her eyes against it and hurried back to the small uncomfortable room she shared with the children.

The next morning very early Simon persuaded the driver of the wagon to take them the remaining miles to Sevastopol and by evening they were settled in the Hotel Kist, crammed to the doors so that one room was all that could be allotted to them and they must consider themselves fortunate to have even that much accommodation.

The following day Simon went at once to the Transport Office to find out when the ship could be expected. It was due in a week's time in the early evening and would only be able to pick up British subjects, said the hard-worked official who had been besieged every day for weeks with people frantic to escape out of Russia.

"You must be there, all of you, waiting on the shore for the boat which will come in from the cruiser. It's the best I can do for you, Dr Aylsham – Lord Aylsham, I suppose I should say."

"Oh for heaven's sake, what do titles matter? Only get us on that ship, that's all I ask."

"Believe me, sir, we are doing the best we can but with the Crimea in this state we'd need a fleet to take off everyone!"

On the day they were to leave they were all keyed up to the highest pitch of excitement. Confined to the one room Galina let the children sit at the window looking out across Suva Bay.

"Watch and you might even see the ship," she told them.

The hard-pressed hotel could only supply sketchy meals and a limited service so at midday she went down to the kitchens to see whether she could fetch something for them herself even if it was no more than tea and bread with some cheese and fruit.

When she had gone Tanya got up, slipping on the plain dark coat Galina had persuaded her to wear. Andrei stopped her as she went to the door.

"Where are you going?"

"Nowhere. It's just that this room is so stifling. I can't breathe. I want to walk out in the air for a little while."

"You mustn't go, Tanya. It's dangerous. You know what Papa told us."

"I'm not going into the town. Only down by the harbour. There are not so many people there."

"No, Tanya."

He took hold of her arm but she wrenched herself away.

"You can't stop me. I can look after myself. You must stay here with Paul and Nicola."

He hesitated, torn between the two, and she took advantage of it by running from the room and down the stairs, not sure what she was going to do but with that secret knowledge still in her mind. Commissar Livinov wanted Galina for some reason so why shouldn't she let him know where she was?

She very soon discovered that Red Army headquarters were not easy to find and the crowded streets terrified her. Soldiers, refugees with vehicles of every kind swarmed in the road and on to the pavements. She was pushed, jostled, stared at until afraid she began to run. She tripped on a rough piece of paving and picked herself up panting. An army truck held up by the traffic stopped beside her. A man beside the driver looked at her keenly, then snapped his fingers and gave an order. Two soldiers leaped off the truck before it moved on.

By then Tanya had realized that she had been very foolish. Scared she turned back quite unaware that she was being followed. She climbed the stairs to their room to find Galina not only extremely worried but justifiably angry.

"How *can* you be so stupid?" she said. "Do you want to put your father, all of us, into danger?"

"I only went out for a breath of air but it's too crowded so I came back. Where *is* Papa?"

"He will be here soon. Now sit down, Tanya, and eat something. There will be nothing more till we leave and it's still a long time till nine o'clock tonight."

It was about two hours later when the Red Guards burst in on them and it was easy to see after the first few minutes that they had come with only one purpose.

The leader glanced perfunctorily at the children's papers when Galina showed them and asked where Simon was. Then he raised his hand. Two of the soldiers stepped forward and took hold of Galina and Andrei.

"You two will come with us."

"Why? What have we done?"

"Your papers are not in order. You are Soviet citizens. You are not permitted to leave Russia."

"But I am not leaving. It is the British doctor and his children who are leaving and they are free to go surely."

"We are not concerned with them just now but only with you and your son. You will come with us at once."

There was nothing she could do. She turned to Jake speaking in English which she knew they did not understand.

"Look after them till the doctor returns. You must tell him not to worry about us. He must think only of himself and the children."

"I'll tell him."

Tanya suddenly rushed to Andrei putting her arms around him facing up to them squarely.

"He's my brother. You can't take him away."

He put her aside. "It's all right, Tanya, I must go with my mother."

"No, no, you mustn't. It's not fair."

One of the guards took hold of her and lifted her roughly away. Then Andrei and Galina were pushed in front of them out of the room.

Tanya watched them go. She had wanted this to happen, she had even tried to make it happen, but now that it had she was terrified and upset.

"Why have they taken them away?" she asked Jake. "What will they do to them?"

He had seen Galina's face when she had escaped from the studio and thought he knew the reason but he only shook his head.

"Don't ask me, Miss, but I tell you one thing. Your Papa is going to raise hell about it when he comes back."

He was right. Simon was appalled. It was something he had not anticipated and now at the last moment with the rendezvous with the British ship only a few hours away there was so little time. His mind raced through all kinds of possible solutions. There was only one desperate measure that he could think of. Whether it would work, whether the British Vice-Consul, a man of the strictest conventional principles as well as being grossly overworked, would do what he asked at such short notice was doubtful in the extreme, but it was the only expedient he could think of and it must be tried.

He gave explicit instructions to Jake. "If I'm not back before eight-thirty you must take the children down to the shore and meet the boat when it comes in. Get them aboard that ship whatever happens and if we don't come, then sail without us. Understand? If humanly possible we will be there."

"Yes, sir, I understand." He paused and then added quietly, "What chance is there, sir?"

"I don't know, Jake, a very slim one, but if God is with me we might just win through."

The children did not want him to leave them. Without Galina or Andrei they felt suddenly bereft. They clung to him. He hugged them in turn and then took Tanya's hand.

"Go with Jake, do what he tells you and take care of Paul and Nicola for me."

"Don't go away from us, Papa, please don't leave us. Can't we go with you?"

"No, my pet. Do as I say. I'll be there. I promise I'll be there before you board the ship."

They saw him go and then under Jake's orders began to pack the few possessions they had brought with them. There was Nicola to be fed and made ready and as the day darkened they sat by the window waiting while lights began to flicker through the town and towards Suva Bay. But their father did not come back.

Galina and Andrei had been herded into an army truck and driven rapidly to the Bolsheviki headquarters which appeared to be in some kind of a hall used for public meetings. They were marched up the steps, shut into a small room and the door was securely locked. It had happened so swiftly that she had only now begun to gather her thoughts. It was Igor, of course, somehow he must have found out where she was and this was his way of taking his revenge. She thought back to their last meeting, the light on his face when he had approached her, her dread of him, the way she had hit him, the fact that she had escaped. He would never forgive her for that bitter rejection, never, and now he had the power. It had always riled him that Andrei was Simon's son and not his. He could imprison them, send them to a labour camp, banish them to Siberia, kill them, as easily as in the days of the Tsar. What difference was there after all? Where was their boasted freedom if it meant hunting down the innocent, destroying their liberty because they would not conform?

Andrei asked, "Why have they brought us here? What have we done?" and she found it hard to explain, to make him understand that though his father was British, he was not all-powerful, and they were still Russian citizens, part of this new Soviet which could now command their lives.

What would Simon do? She knew he would not let it rest, he would try his utmost to rescue her from Igor's clutches and in doing so might well endanger himself. Oh God, why had she let him persuade her to come with them? She should have gone away long ago as soon as they reached the Crimea. He could have found someone else to take charge of the children. There were young British women here, refugees, who would have been only too glad to take advantage of such a position.

One hour passed and still another, the room grew dark and there was no light except that which came in through the window from an outside street lamp. She groped for her watch. It was nearly eight o'clock, only another hour before the British ship would be sending their boat ashore.

The opening of the door, the sudden dazzle of light, nearly blinded them. Then they were led away down a long corridor and into another room where Igor sat at the desk, half a dozen Red Guards lined up behind him. Simon was there with another man, half a head shorter, dressed very formally, and looking as if he wished passionately that the floor would open and swallow him up. The British Vice-Consul dragged there forcibly by Simon was shaking in his shoes. He had a very healthy respect for Bolsheviki officials.

Igor looked up as she came in. His peaked cap had been pushed up a little as if he felt the warmth of the room and she saw clearly a jagged scar that ran down the side of his forehead to his ear. He was staring straight at her, the brilliant eyes paralysing her, forcing his will upon her.

"Galina Panova," he said harshly, "I wish to ask you a question."

She took firm hold of herself. She must not give way to the fear that he had always inspired in her.

"What is it?"

"Can you stand there and in the name of the God you believe in swear to me that you are married to this man?"

Simon was watching her tense but silent. It was the last thing she had expected. Bewildered she parried the question.

"I understood that the Bolsheviki denied the very fact of God."

He thumped the desk angrily with his fist. "Don't dare to split hairs with me."

He looked from her to Simon and then back again before he went on, his voice abrasive with a smouldering anger.

"I have been informed that you and this man, this British doctor, were married a week ago in the village church at Alushka. Is this true?"

The Vice-Consul took a deep breath and said in a loud voice, "Are you doubting my word, sir?"

"I was not speaking to you," snapped Igor. He rose to his feet and crossed to Galina taking her by the shoulders, his fingers digging into her, looking into her face. "It is you I am asking. Is this true?"

She trembled but she stood firm. "Yes," she said, "yes, it is true."

"His wife dead scarcely two months and you could not wait to fall into his bed," he said with a scalding contempt.

"Yes," she replied bravely, "if that's how you think of it?"

"How else should I think?" he dropped his hands. "Why did you not say this when my guards arrested you?"

"He had not yet told his children. I did not wish to distress them."

"Ashamed, were you, ashamed of this indecent haste? The habits of the bourgeois British fill me with disgust."

"You forget," said Simon, his voice calm and steady, "I was absent collecting from our office here the necessary passports for my wife, Lady Aylsham, and for my son Andrei which were in the course of preparation."

"Your illegitimate son," said Igor raspingly.

"My acknowledged son," he said firmly, "as this gentleman will assure you."

The Vice-Consul only too well aware of the demand made by the desperate man beside him and also uncomfortably certain that he had acted totally illegally, was still not going to allow any jumped-up revolutionary ignore the rights of British subjects, particularly one who had lately succeeded to an ancient title.

He said formally, "I am afraid I must point out to you, Commissar Livinov, that in these circumstances you have absolutely no right to detain Lord Aylsham, his wife, or any member of his family and if you do so, I shall feel obliged to put in a very strong complaint not only to our embassy in Petrograd but also to the British government in London."

It was a very brave thing to do and Simon shot him a grateful glance. There was a momentary silence, no one moved. They waited holding their breath. The decision could go either way and there was nothing they could do about it. They were totally in his power and Igor had always been unpredictable. Then suddenly he strode back behind his desk.

"Get out!" he said, his voice vibrant with an angry bitterness. "Get out, all of you, now! Now, do you hear, out of the Crimea, out of Russia!"

They did not wait, they dare not. He could still change his mind. Simon seized Galina by the hand and with the Vice-Consul followed by Andrei they fairly sprinted down the corridor and out into the street. Simon clasped the hand of his fellow countryman.

"Thank you," he exclaimed, "thank you a thousand times. I could have done nothing without you."

"Lord knows what my chief will do to me for twisting the law," he said ruefully. "He's due back any day now."

"Put the blame on me. I swear I'll see you don't suffer for it."

"You'd better hurry. It's late and the Navy won't wait, you know. They are fighting a war." He clasped Galina's hand and suddenly kissed it. "God go with you, with all of you."

It was nine o'clock and the clocks were striking. No time to go back to the hotel. They ran all three of them down the winding streets slipping on damp cobbles and losing their way in the older part of the city but at last they were there. They saw the dark bay, the few boats drawn up, far out on the Black Sea the distant shape of the British ship and no one, no one at all, waiting on the shore.

"They've gone," breathed Galina, "they've gone without us."

Had they lied their way to freedom only to see it disappear? They strained their eyes through the darkness and it was Andrei who suddenly clutched at his father's arm.

"Look! They're there, they've not gone far yet. Couldn't we shout and wave?"

It seemed impossible that they should be seen and the fear was still there. Igor could still send the Red Guards after them. It had happened before to others. They kept looking fearfully over their shoulders while they waited. Then miraculously they saw the boat turn. It crept slowly back. They waded out to meet it. The Naval Lieutenant in charge seized hold of Galina and helped her in.

Tanya choked back a sob. "We thought you weren't coming, Papa."

"I promised, didn't I? Don't cry, pet. We're here and we're on our way."

Swayed up the side of the ship, they were welcomed with wonderful calmness by the Captain and a British crew who seemed to take everything in their stride including a baby angrily demanding her supper.

"We're a little short of accommodation, Ma'am," apologized the naval rating ordered to look after their comfort. "Can't give you and the doctor a cabin to yourselves, I'm afraid."

"Don't worry about that. I will do very well with the children."

"Lively as a cricket now, ain't she?" he said leaning over the basket where Nicola was sucking contentedly at her thumb. "Pretty as a picture too. Yours, Ma'am?"

"No, I'm afraid not."

"Anything you're needing, Ma'am, just you say the word."

"Thank you. You're very kind."

"All part of the service, Ma'am."

"Funny set-up," he confessed later on to his mate when they were off duty and enjoying a comfortable gossip. "His wife knocked off by them Bolshies a couple of months ago and now he's married to this one."

"If they are married," murmured his friend darkly.

"You don't mean . . .?" he looked suitably shocked.

"Use your loaf, man. He had to get her out somehow, didn't he? Wouldn't care to leave a dog in the hands of that lot!"

Galina having made sure that the children were settled down went up on deck. It was very dark. The Black Sea that could whip up into sudden and frightening storms was very calm as the ship glided through it. Simon was leaning over the rail looking back to the shore where a few stars of light outlined the town and somewhere a fire was blazing. The flames leaping up into the night seemed to hold all the rage and fury they had left behind them. She moved to the rail beside him.

"Everything all right?" he asked.

"Yes. They're so tired they fell asleep almost at once."

They were silent for a while before she said, "Simon, why did you do it?"

"It was the only thing I could think of. I had a devil of a job persuading that poor man to risk his reputation for me." He turned his head to look at her. "For a frightful moment I thought that hedgehog pride of yours was going to make you deny it."

"You left me no choice, did you?"

"We'll have to make it real, you know, or my name will be mud. The British government doesn't care for false passports extorted by force. Shall I ask the Captain to marry us tomorrow?"

"It can wait."

"For what?"

"Till you are sure that is what you want."

He paused before he said, "I've known that for a good number of years now, but after Nina's death I lost my way." He was staring into the thick darkness. "If only I had kept my temper it would never have happened. I keep thinking of that over and over again. That time when she thought to drown herself, she said, 'I believed it was the best way to set you free'. Was that in her mind? I don't know. It has haunted me ever since."

She thought that to confess it was like drawing out a poisoned arrow. Now the blood could flow free and cleansing.

The lights began to fade as the ship drew further away and the land disappeared.

Presently she said, "It never seemed possible that one day I would leave Russia. Once many years ago Nina said if your brother died, you would be Lord Aylsham and what would I do then?" I never dreamed that such a thing could ever happen."

"Neither did I but then we didn't bargain on a war, did we, or a revolution? It's something we must face together."

He put his hand lightly on hers and quite suddenly and with a shiver of joy she knew it had come back, that indescribable force that had held them in its grip ever since that night in Dannskoye when they had leaped across the magic fire. Like 'gold to airy thinness beat' the love between them had proved indestructible.

She made no move towards him, only let her hand lie within his and presently felt his fingers close over it.